S0-ASB-553

Wild Ecstasy

Wild Rapture

Wild Embrace

Wild Ecstasy

Wild Rapture

Wild Embrace

Rhapsody

Garden City, New York

This edition was especially created in 2003 for Rhapsody® by arrangement with New American Library, a division of Penguin Group (USA).

Published by Rhapsody®, 401 Franklin Avenue, Garden City, New York 11530.

ISBN: 0-7394-3926-X

Printed in the United States of America

Contents

Introduction

When I was asked to choose the three books I've written that I find special, the first three volumes of my Indian series came to mind. The *Wild* series was established to spread knowledge about our country's first people—the Native Americans—not only in this country but worldwide. The series gave me the unique opportunity to help achieve my goal of writing about every major Indian tribe in America.

My editor gave me the chance to choose the tribe for the first book of this series, *Wild Ecstasy*. As I did with my first Indian romance that I wrote back in the 1980s, I chose to write about the Chippewa Indians. Why? I wanted to write about a nonwarring, peaceful tribe. I didn't want to write about bloody wars and deaths, but to mainly focus instead on the customs of the tribe, as well as the romance between my hero and heroine. For the most part, the Chippewa have been neglected by historians, perhaps because they fought no bloody battles against the western-driving pioneers who overwhelmed them in the nineteenth century. Yet, historically, the Chippewa were one of the most important nations north of Mexico. Their expansive northern woods of Minnesota contained valuable resources, which caused them to play an important role in regional enterprises. The Chippewa remain on their native lands today, still a proud people, and continue to make their living from fishing, farming, lumbering, and mining, as they have done for centuries. I found my study of the Chippewa a most rewarding and heartwarming experience, a pleasure to write about them again and again.

The first in my *Wild* series was *Wild Ecstasy*, about the beautiful, flame-haired Mariah Temple, daughter of a tyrannical father who despised all Indians and had given them every reason to hate him. Echohawk is the handsome, daring Chippewa brave sworn to avenge the wrongs done to his father and his people. But when Mariah and Echohawk meet, something wonderful happens; suddenly their bloodlines do not seem to matter, and their differences are swept away. The two are inseparable until a fiercely guarded secret is revealed and the shattering truth tears them apart. A future together would seem impossible, yet nothing can diminish the smoldering heat of their desire—the pure intensity of their passion that propels them over all barriers, and lifts them to a love that defies all odds.

My special feelings toward the characters in *Wild Ecstasy* helped me write the second book, its sequel—*Wild Rapture*. It's about Mariah and Echohawk's son, Night Hawk, and Briana Collins, the woman with whom he falls in love. Fresh from Paris's finest art academy, exquisitely lovely Briana Collins comes home to paint the beautiful wilderness of her native Minnesota. Her ambitious uncle wants her to be a pretty ornament for his political career. But the future Chippewa chief—proud, fierce Night Hawk—wants far more for Briana the moment he casts his dark eyes on her. He cannot resist her, despite the warnings of his tribe. And Briana meets his open desire with her own fervent longing, defying her uncle's threats. Theirs is a passion that sets the frontier aflame, staking their undying love against all the forces of hate.

Enjoying my research about the various Indian tribes, I decided to break away from the Chippewa to write about a different tribe in my third book. I studied and searched through the Indian section in my personal library (I own a vast number of Indian reference books . . . I love reading and studying them!), and I discovered the Suquamish tribe of the Pacific Northwest. Their lives were vastly different from the Chippewa and so much fun to write about. They hunted whales, not deer and bison. They lived in longhouses, not tepees or wigwams. What a discovery it was when I found this interesting, nonwarring tribe to write about. Therefore the third book was born—*Wild Embrace*. Exquisite, flame-haired Elizabeth Easton thought Seattle a raw, rough frontier harbor after her elegant upbringing in San Francisco. But she discovers what the real wilderness is when the noble Indian brave Strong Heart forces her to go with him to his village. Here, deep in the breathtaking forests of the Pacific Northwest, Strong Heart is free from intolerant injustice. Here Elizabeth is free of the smothering control of her ambitious businessman father. Here both of them are free of all pride and prejudice that kept them apart in the white world—as this superbly handsome, strong and sensitive man becomes her guide on passion's path to unfettered joy . . . and she stands beside him to defy all that seek to end a love that will not be denied.

I hope you all read and enjoy my collection, and if you want more, there are many other of my Indian romances to choose from, for there are now sixty-one different titles that I have written, and I plan to continue writing them until the well runs dry on ideas for any more . . . which I hope will not be for a long, long time.

Always,
Cassie

Wild Ecstasy

For Audrey LaFehr,
a special editor . . .
a joy to work with.

My face in thine eyes, thine in mine appears,
And true plain hearts do in the faces rest,
Where can we find two better hemispheres
Without sharp north, without declining west?
Whatever dies, was not mix'd equally;
If our two loves be one, or thou and I
Love so alike that none can slacken, none can die.

—John Donne

1

> The day is done, and the darkness
> Falls from the wings of night,
> As a feather is wafted downward
> From an eagle in his flight.
>
> —Longfellow

The Minnesota Wilderness August 1824

The evening shadows were long. The sky was awash with a crimson blush as the sun faded on the horizon, a mellow sighing of turtle doves breaking the cool, deep silence.

Riding in a canter ahead of a slow procession of many travois being dragged behind horses and dogs, Echohawk saw a frightened buck on the run, the white rosette of its rump seeming to hang for the smallest fraction of time at the top of each frantic bound, like a succession of sunbursts against the darkening forest.

Then Echohawk gazed down at the river at his one side, admiring the reflection of the green foliage of the maple, birch, and aspen trees that lined the riverbank, disturbed only by silver-scaled fish that now and then came to the surface with a sudden flip that started circles of ripples.

A deep, throaty cough, one that was filled with pain, drew Echohawk from his silent reverie. Echohawk jerked his head around, and rage filled his dark, fathomless eyes as he gazed down at his father, Chief Gray Elk, who lay on a travois behind Blaze, Echohawk's prized rust-colored stallion. Echohawk's father's pride had been stripped from him, as well as his health, by a vile white man the whites of whose eyes were *o-zah-wah,* yellow, the color of a coward's.

Echohawk's gaze moved beyond his father to the many other travois. Some transported bundles of blankets, parfleches of dried meat, and those who were too elderly to ride or walk.

Others carried the wounded from a recent raid on their village, a village they had chosen to leave behind—a place of sadness and many deaths.

Even to let himself conjure up memories of the man he now called Yellow Eyes sent spirals of hate throughout Echohawk. Because of him and his Sioux friends, led by the renegade White Wolf, many proud Chippewa had died, Echohawk's wife and unborn child among them, his father among the wounded. Because of Yellow Eyes and White Wolf, the Chippewa had been uprooted and a new place of peace and prosperity was now being sought.

Echohawk's eyes narrowed when he recalled another raid on his father's people twelve winters ago, when Echohawk had been a young brave of eighteen winters. His people had suffered many losses at the hand of those vile white men that day. And then, as now, the conflict had caused his band of people to move elsewhere, never wanting to stay where there had been so many deaths . . . so much blood spilled.

But Echohawk was proud to know that his chieftain father had wounded the white leader *that* day. Surely the man even now hobbled around on only one leg!

Echohawk tightened his reins and brought his horse to a halt. He turned to his people and thrust a fist into the air. "*Ee-shqueen*! Stay!" he shouted, the responsibilities of his father's people his own until his father was able to perform in the capacity of chief again. "We shall rest for a while, then resume our journey!"

Echohawk sat for a moment longer in his saddle, observing his people. He could see relief in their eyes over being allowed to rest, and realized only now how hard he had been driving them to get them to their planned destination.

But the fate of his people lay in *his* hands, and he realized the importance of getting them settled in a village soon, and into a daily routine. When the snows began coloring the ground and trees in cloaks of white, many deaths would come to those who were not prepared.

Dismounting, his brief breechclout lifting in the breeze, his moccasined feet making scarcely a sound on the crushed leaves beneath them, Echohawk went to his father and knelt down beside him, resting himself on his haunches. "How are you, *gee-bah-bah,* Father?" he asked, gently rearranging the bear pelts around his father's slight form. His heart ached with knowing how it used to be before the vicious raid. His father had been muscled and strong. Vital. All of this had been robbed from him at the hands of Yellow Eyes and White Wolf, and someday, somehow, the evil man would pay. . . .

"*Nay-mi-no-mun-gi,* I am fine," Chief Gray Elk said, his voice weak. With squinting eyes he looked past Echohawk at the loveliness of the surroundings, feeling serenity deep in the core of his being.

He turned his gaze back to Echohawk, a smile fluttering on his thin bluish lips. "Soon we shall be there, my son," he said, wheezing with each word. "Do you not see it? Do you not feel it? This is a place of peace. A place of plenty. Surely we are near Chief Silver Wing's village. Surely we are also near Colonel Snelling's great fort, where Indians come and go in peace. Ah, my son, they say there is much good trading at Fort Snelling. We have been wrong not to move our people closer before now." He coughed and paled. "It is best that we are here, my son. It is best."

"*Ay-uh,* yes, and we will soon be making camp," Echohawk said, nodding. "Our scouts have brought us to the Rum River. It is the same river that flows past Chief Silver Wing's village. It is this same river that flows into the great Mississippi River that flows past Fort Snelling." He nodded again. "*Ah-uh,* soon we will be there, *gee-bah-bah.*"

Gray Elk slipped a hand from beneath the pelts and clasped onto one of Echohawk's, in his eyes a gleam of hope. "My son, Chief Silver Wing and I have been friends since our youth, when, side by side, we fought the Sioux for territorial rights," he said, sucking in a wild gulp of air, then continuing to speak. "It will be good to see him again."

Gray Elk's grip tightened on Echohawk's hand. "When Chief Silver Wing last came to me and we shared in a smoke and talk, he spoke of the abundance of wild rice plants that bend heavy with rice in the countless lakes and marshes near his village, and skies that are alive with waterfowl," he continued softly. "Soon we share all of this with Chief Silver Wing and his people. Soon you will participate in the hunt again while our women gather the rice. Once more our people will be happy, Echohawk."

"We shall ride together on the hunt, *gee-bah-bah,*" Echohawk encouraged, wanting so badly for this to be so. If his father died, his heart would be empty. He had lost his mother during an intensely cold winter fifteen winters ago, and his wife and unborn child only recently. Surely the Great Spirit would not take his father from him also!

"You will get well," Echohawk quickly added. "You *will* ride your horse again."

But Echohawk doubted his own words. His father was a leader who had ruled his people with kindly wisdom, and was struggling to stay alive long enough to see that his people could begin a life anew close to two old friends, one Indian and one white. They planned to make camp within a half-day's ride from Chief Silver Wing, also Chippewa, and a half-day's ride from Fort Snelling, where Colonel Josiah Snelling was in charge—a friend to all Indians.

Echohawk, a wise and learned man at his age of thirty winters, knew that his father had another reason for having chosen to make camp close to Chief Silver Wing's village. Gray Elk hoped that perhaps Echohawk might find a wife among Chief Silver Wing's people to replace the one that he was mourning.

But Echohawk did not see how anyone, ever, could take his wife's place in his heart, nor the child that Fawn had been carrying within her womb at the time of her death. Because of her death, Echohawk had thought strongly of taking his own life, his grief was so intense, but had known that his father and his people needed him too much for such a cowardly act—and also because a suicide had no chance to enter into paradise.

"It *is* wise, my son, to move more closely to people that can be relied upon," Gray Elk said, as though sensing his son's doubts. "And trading will be profitable with the white people who frequent Fort Snelling. Echohawk, you can trade in beaver. As you have seen on our journey here, buffalo and deer abound in this region, and Silver Wing spoke of muskrat and marten that were as plentiful as mice."

"*Ay-uh,* it will be good hunting and trading, Father," Echohawk said, remembrances of his last hunt flooding him. Had it only been thirty sunsets ago when he had brought home a fat venison for his wife to cook? Had it only been thirty sunsets ago when he had watched her lovingly as she had sat across from him eating and laughing softly at his tales of the hunt? His gut ached with loneliness and despair, even now hearing the ring of her laughter and seeing the peace and love in her dark, beautiful eyes.

Gray Elk slipped his hand from Echohawk's and patted his cheek gently. "Echohawk, it is soon the smoky time, when leaves put on their war paint and the war drums of the wind become louder," he said, a quavering smile touching his lips. "It is time to place sadnesses from your heart and choose a woman to warm your bed. And must I remind you, my son, that you are the only son of your father and must sire a son yourself. My grandson, your son, will be the future defender of our people, whose lives will depend upon his courage and skills. If the child is a girl, she will be the future mother of a noble race."

Gray Elk patted Echohawk's cheek again, then lowered his trembling hand and slipped it beneath the warmth of the bear pelts. "For our people, place sadnesses of your loss from your mind and heart," he softly encouraged. "That is the way it should be. It is for you to ensure the future of our band of Chippewa. Only you, my son. My time is soon over."

Weary from the lengthy dialogue, Gray Elk exhaled a heavy sigh, then closed his eyes. "*Gee-kee-bing-gwah-shee,*" he said, barely audible. "My son, I am getting sleepy. I . . . must . . . sleep."

Guilt spread through Echohawk like wildfire. His father, a man of fifty-seven winters, was recovering much too slowly from a bullet wound in his chest. It had been hard to listen to his father pour his heart and soul out to him without being torn with anger and guilt, Echohawk having failed at defending his people the day of the raid. The raiders had come too suddenly upon his people while so many of them were away from the village, burning off the pine needles from the ground to ensure against forest fires later. Echohawk had been among those setting and controlling the fires. By the time word had reached him of the massacre, the raiders had had a head start on him and his braves, and during the chase had slipped away like ghosts in the night.

Echohawk had returned to his injured wife just as she had spoken her last words to him. She had revealed to Echohawk that a white man with the eyes of a coward and the renegade Sioux White Wolf had led the attack. It was the man with the eyes of a coward that had fired the bullets that had felled both Fawn and Chief Gray Elk.

Echohawk brushed a kiss across his father's brow, then rose to his full height, tears streaming down his cheeks. He doubled his hands to his sides in tight fists and looked up at the darkening heavens, vowing revenge.

But first he had his father's wishes to fulfill. *Then* he would find the man with the eyes and heart of a coward. Also, one day he would come face-to-face with White Wolf. The renegade Sioux would *not* die an easy death.

"Vengeance will be mine!" he said beneath his breath, then turned his gaze back to his father when he awakened long enough to speak a few more words.

Dutiful son that he was, Echohawk knelt down again beside his father. He leaned his ear close to his father's lips, for his words were now no more than a whisper.

"May the Great Spirit watch over you, my son," Gray Elk said, very aware of the despair and hurtful anger in the depths of his son's dark eyes. "He will guide you in which way is best for our people once I am gone. Remember this, Echohawk. Hungering for vengeance is like a festering sore inside one's heart. It will never heal.

"Peace, on the other hand, can give you comfort. Even as I lie here, a victim of hate and greed, I am at peace, for it was not I who initiated the raid which ended in many deaths and sorrows. Those that did are condemned forever to walk paths of darkness, their souls never to find peace. Practice restraint as taught to you as a child, and live in peace, my son. It is best for the future of our people."

Echohawk flinched when his father again grasped his hand. "Echohawk, if you should die before you father a son, the future chief of our people, what then of our people?" he said, his voice filled with desperation. "Find a woman who will be the 'flower of your wigwam.' Have a son soon. At a very early age see that he assumes the task of preserving and transmitting the legends of his ancestors and his race."

Echohawk was at a loss for words, not knowing how to cope with his father's soft, tormented pleadings for a grandson. Echohawk did not see how he could ever desire another woman. His very soul even now cried out for Fawn, his beloved. He could still feel her softness within his arms. He could still hear how she so sweetly spoke his name. None other could be as sweet! As wonderful! How could he make such a promise that he felt he could not keep?

Yet he knew that what his father had said was true. The future of their people did depend on a succession of sons, and to have sons, one must have a wife.

But one's heart must be ready for a wife! Echohawk despaired to himself.

"Go to *nee-ban,* sleep, Father," Echohawk urged as he once again slipped his father's hand beneath the warmth of the pelts. "*Wah-bungh* tomorrow. We shall discuss wives and grandsons tomorrow."

Gray Elk gazed up at Echohawk, the slowly rising moon casting enough light on his son to enable him to see him and his handsomeness, and be assured that here was a man who would not go wifeless for long. How could any woman resist such a tall and vigorous, good-looking man with sparkling dark eyes? How could any woman not notice Echohawk's hair that was as thick and long, and as black as the raven's wing, and his hard and proud mouth? And how could any woman not want to bear Echohawk a son, knowing that his offspring would have the same muscular strength, the same easy grace, and the same power of endurance as his father?

Echohawk arched an eyebrow when he saw a strange sort

of peace pass over his father's face as he closed his eyes, his features smoothing out as if he had just entered into a pleasant fantasy. As troubled as Echohawk was, he wished that he could join his father in the same sort of magical place, where all sadnesses are left behind.

But he realized all too well that many responsibilities awaited him.

Rising to his full height, he did not turn to look at his people. He quickly mounted his horse and began riding away in a slow canter, his father's travois dragging behind him, knowing that soon everyone would follow.

Ay-uh, so much depended on him.

His people's very existence.

2

> One morning, very early, before the sun was up,
> I rose and found the shining dew on every
> buttercup. . . .
>
> —STEVENSON

One Year Later,—August 1825

The bedroom was flooded with sunlight, revealing a room of inexpensive tastes, and a father and daughter in conflict. Mariah Temple stood defiantly before her father, her jaw tight with anger. She clenched and unclenched her hands at her sides, finding it hard to continue obeying a father who, since Mariah's mother's death twelve long years ago, had become unreasonable in his demands.

"Papa, you can't force me to cut my hair," Mariah said, her voice flat with determination. "You can't expect me to go that far to please you." She glanced down at the way she was dressed and shuddered, then gazed angrily up at her father again. "I've worn these damnable shapeless breeches and scratchy shirts because I had no choice after you burned all of my dresses. You even burned Mother's so I couldn't sneak into one of them." Her lips curved into a sullen pout. "Papa, I can hardly even recall how it felt to *wear* a dress."

Her fingers went protectively to her hair. She drew its long red tresses back from her shoulders and cupped as much of it as possible within her hands. "I shan't *ever* forget how it feels to have long hair, because I won't ever agree to cutting it," she snapped, taking a step back from her father as he moved toward her, dragging his lame leg behind him.

"Are you finished?" Victor Temple said in an impatient growl. "My, but you do go on sometimes, just like your mother used to. Not only do you have her looks, but also her temperament."

His gaze swept over Mariah. Each time, it was a new shock to him to see a daughter so startlingly pretty, with eyes so dark and velvet brown on a flawless face, and abundant hair that gleamed and rippled with such life it seemed more vivid than the brightest red. Her short straight nose was that of an appealing and mischievous young woman. Her lips were rosy and soft, and there was nothing weak about her pretty chin.

She is so small and vulnerable, Victor thought to himself with a quick rush of tenderness. And so proud and bullheadedly stubborn!

"If I am like my mother, so be it," Mariah said, lifting her chin proudly. She had been six when her mother had died, the mystery of it always troubling her. Her father had not let Mariah see her mother on her deathbed, nor had he explained how or why her mother had died at such a young age.

But it was the remembrances of her mother the six years that she had shared with her that still filled Mariah's heart with such love whenever she let herself get caught up in missing her. No mother could have been as sweet—as understanding.

She peered intensely up at her father, recalling how he had been before his wife's death. In appearance he had changed, now weathered with age at fifty-five. He was a round-shouldered man with a leathery face and brush of chin whiskers, and with a lame leg that made his movements jerky and sometimes uncontrolled.

Those many years ago, before his leg affliction, he had been handsomely neat, always clean-shaven, and had always stood proudly tall and square-shouldered. Although Mariah had thought him to be a decent sort of man at that time, it was the years since that had colored her image of him.

And it had not only been the death of his wife that seemed to have changed him, she mulled to herself. The change had happened shortly after the burial, when he had left to have council with some of the Indian chiefs in the area, having brought his wife and daughter to the Minnesota wilderness to establish a trading post long before Fort Snelling had been a part of the setting.

At that time, as now, it was not unusual for her short-tempered father to get into conflicts with the neighboring Indians to establish his territorial rights if they would not meet with him and speak peacefully of sharing the abundance of wildlife in the area.

This one time in particular, when her father had been gone for several days, he had returned from a skirmish with some Indians, wounded. He had almost lost his leg as a result of that battle, hardening his heart into someone Mariah did not even enjoy calling "father." He had become a bitter, unpleasant man, one whom most called sinister. Mariah herself was very aware of the crooked dealings and raids that her father participated in with the devious, evil Tanner McCloud.

Just the thought of Tanner McCloud made shivers run up and down Mariah's spine. He was a man of no scruples, who surely did not know the meaning of honesty. And with the whites of his eyes yellowed by some strange, unknown disease, he was also a man who was anything but pleasant to look at. When he gazed at Mariah with those yellow eyes, she always felt as though he was undressing her. For sure, Mariah wearing men's attire had not fooled him. He knew what lay beneath the bulky oversize jackets worn over her cotton shirts, and breeches twice the size of what she should be wearing, held up by a rope tied at her waist—a girl having developed into a woman at her ripe age of eighteen.

"And so you want to be like your mother, eh?" Victor said, brandishing the scissors in the air as he talked, as though they were a weapon. "Do you want to be dead at age twenty-three?" He slipped the scissors into his rear pants pocket and grabbed Mariah by the arm. "Daughter, that ain't going to happen if I have anything to say about it. I've protected you just fine these past years. I don't intend to stop now."

Mariah paled. "Papa, please don't," she begged, trying to jerk free of his grasp. "My hair is all that is left that is pretty about me. At least at night, when I remove my dreadful mannish clothes, I can look in the mirror and see that I *am* a woman. Papa, do you want me to forget? Do you? Don't you ever want to see me married to a fine gentleman? Don't you even want grandchildren?"

"And where do you expect to find what you call a 'fine gentleman' way out here in this wilderness?" he scoffed, grasping her arm more tightly. "Those I have met are anything but what I would want for a son-in-law. Most are filthy, with only one thing on their minds when they see the flash of a woman's skirt. Their one concern is getting that skirt lifted and pokin' her until they get their hunger for sex filled for that moment."

Mariah gasped and her face became flushed with embarrassment, her father having never before spoken of sex in her presence.

But even this did not stop her argument. "While gathering supplies at Fort Snelling, I saw many men who were surely gentlemen," she said, daring him with a haughty gaze. "The soldiers are all so very polite. And . . . some are *quite* handsome."

She cast her eyes downward. "But of course, none have ever approached me," she murmured. "They think they are walking past a young lad when they pass by me in the courtyard of the fort."

She looked back up at him with an anxiousness in her eyes. "Papa, I've always fooled them before by wearing my hair coiled beneath my hat," she said in a rush of words. "Please? Please let me continue hiding my hair instead of cutting it."

"That only works if the hat stays in place," Victor said, going to the window, peering down below at the pack mules being unloaded. He could see many prime pelts among those being carried into his trading post, and did not want to take much more time with this chore at hand. He wanted to make sure those who assisted him at his post did not cheat him while his back was turned.

He wheeled around and faced Mariah again. "The day you tripped over a bale of hay at the fort? Your hair came rushing out from beneath your hat like streamers of sunshine. And who had to be there, to be witness to the truth of your identity? That damned Colonel Snelling and his wife, Abigail. Since then they haven't let me alone, chiding me for forcing you to wear breeches and shirts. Why, Abigail even forced one of her dresses on me one day and flat told me to let you wear it. Of course I burned it as soon as I got it home."

Again he turned and stared out the window, anger filling him at the thought of Josiah Snelling and of their relationship long before they had met again while Fort Snelling was being built. Victor had assumed that Josiah Snelling was in his past when he brought his family to the Minnesota wilderness.

But after all those years they were forced to endure one another's company again, for Victor was not about to move his successful trading post to rid himself of the colonel again. He had even had to place all thoughts of vengeance against Colonel Snelling from his mind, finding the supplies at Fort Snelling too valuable not to go to the fort and buy them when necessary.

Mariah often accompanied him, only because he had seen her worth in assisting him choose the proper kitchen supplies.

Otherwise she would have been kept at the trading post, away from the wondering eyes of Colonel Snelling. Should the colonel have ever looked close enough, he might have seen too much that was familiar about her.

Victor turned abruptly and went back to Mariah. He grabbed her by the wrist and turned her so that her back was to him. He yanked the scissors from his pocket and lifted them to her hair. "Now, let's not hear any more argument about this haircut," he snarled. "It'll be done in a flash."

Tears began streaming from Mariah's eyes when she felt the first yank on her head as the scissors began to slice through her thick hair. "Oh, Papa, why? Why?" she demanded, sobbing. "I'll never understand! Never!"

"First, Mariah, there's that damnable Tanner McCloud. I've got to put his ideas of wantin' you from his mind once and for all. I've got to make you as unpleasant to look at as possible. Cuttin' your hair seems to be the only way. That damn Tanner. He's been askin' me every day for permission to marry you. *Now* he won't bother me with such nonsense."

"You don't have to cut off my hair because of him," Mariah wailed, feeling ill at her stomach when she saw her first lock of hair fall at her feet. "You know that I'd never let that man get near me. Papa, I have a mind and will of my own. And I can shoot a firearm same as you. You taught me well enough. If that man came near me, I'd not hesitate shooting him."

"It's not only him," Victor said, continuing to snip away at her hair. "Your mother's prettiness got her in trouble with men more than once. I'm here to make sure that don't happen to you."

A sob lodged in Mariah's throat when another thick hunk of hair fell at her feet. She closed her eyes, knowing that she would end up being the ugliest woman in the world!

"What do you mean by that?" she finally said, slowly opening her eyes again, forcing them away from the hair piling up on the floor. "What sort of trouble did my mother get into with men?"

Victor momentarily drew his scissors away from Mariah's hair. He stepped around in front of her. He looked down at her with narrowing gray eyes. "You forget I ever said that," he flatly ordered. "That was a slip of the tongue. Just remember that when you're as pretty as a picture, men are drawn to you like bees to honey." He stepped behind her again and resumed his cutting. "That's what I meant about your mother. She had men fallin' at her heels from all walks of life. It'd be the same with you, if I'd allow it. But I ain't. So don't give me no more mouth about it."

Mariah stood numbly quiet until her father was finished with the dreaded chore. When she heard him place the scissors on her nightstand beside her bed, she stared blankly down at the hair on the floor, and became choked up all over again with the need to cry.

But there were no more tears. What seemed to have taken their place was a building resentment toward her father, which she feared was nearing hate.

Kneeling, she began to scoop up her precious strands of hair, its softness like the down of bird feathers against the flesh of her hands. She stiffened inside when her father's shadow fell over her.

"There is something else I have to say to you," Victor said, drawing Mariah's eyes quickly up. He placed a hand at her elbow and helped her up to stand before him.

"Oh, no, Papa," she cried. "Whatever more could you want with me? Haven't you already done enough?"

"What I have done, for the most part in your behalf, is to guarantee your survival here in the Minnesota wilderness in case something happens to me," Victor said, gripping Mariah's shoulders with his hands. "I have taught you enough of the Sioux and Chippewa tongues for common purposes, and taught you the trick of the Indian trade to perfection. I have taught you how to shoot all firearms, and how to ride a horse better than most men. Today . . . today . . ."

Clutching her loose strands of hair to her bosom, Mariah looked fearlessly up at her father, yet wary of what else he had planned for her. Even he seemed hesitant to tell her.

"Today? What about today?" she asked, almost afraid to hear the answer.

"I plan to teach you further ways of survival," Victor said, dropping his hands away from her. He went to the window and stared into the shadowy depths of the forest that stretched out far beyond the land that had been cleared for his trading post.

An instant dread grabbed Mariah at the pit of her stomach. "What do you mean?" she said in a low gasp.

Victor turned on a heel and stared at her. He reached a hand to his pants leg and ran his fingers over his leg, feeling nothing, only numbness. "An Injun took too many important things from my life. Because of him, I am half-crippled and . . ."

He stopped in mid-sentence, then went and stood over Mariah. "A year ago, Chief Gray Elk settled within only a half-day's ride from Fort Snelling. His village is only an hour's ride from our trading post. And by damn, that's way too close for my liking."

He paused, then added, "You've questioned me many times this past year about why I've not gone to Fort Snelling as often for supplies, and why I've forbidden you to go at all. I've avoided your questions before, because I had not yet decided what to do about Gray Elk. But now that I've made my plans, there's no reason not to tell you. It's because Echohawk, Gray

Elk's son, is at Fort Snelling so often. Even the Injuns do most of their trading at the riverbank, instead of inside the walls of the fort, which, for the most part, is reserved only for civilized people. I did not want to chance coming face-to-face with Echohawk. I thought he just might recognize me. He saw everything the day I was wounded. I'm sure he hates me no less now." He paused and an evil glint rose in his gray eyes. "It seems that Echohawk is in my way now as much as his chieftain father ever was. He's got to die also, Mariah. And anyone else at the village who gets in the way of the gunfire!"

He cupped her chin in his hand. "And you're going to ride with me," he said flatly. "If nothing else, that'll make a man outta you."

Mariah was rendered almost speechless by what her father was saying. And that he had chosen to make her a part of such a vicious plan made her heart grow cold. "You can't be serious," she finally said, inching away from him. "Papa, what you are planning to do is wrong. It's out-and-out murder. And never would I be a part of such an act. I hold no grudges against the Indians. In fact, I admire them. They are an innocent, proud people. How can you want to just go and kill them? Nothing any one Indian has done to you can warrant you going and slaughtering a whole village of Indians."

She slipped the hair from her arms, onto her bed, then placed her hands on her hips in defiance. "And were the truth known, I imagine you were the one who shot off that first gunfire against Gray Elk and his people all those years ago. You deserved what you got. It could have been worse, you know. Your scalp could be hanging in Chief Gray Elk's wigwam even now."

Victor took a quick, clumsy step forward, his face red with rage. He raised his hand and brought its backside against Mariah's face, causing her head to go sideways in a jerk. "I will have no more of your insolence," he shouted. "You are going with me. That's final."

Her cheek stinging from the blow, her eyes filled with tears of anger, Mariah placed the coolness of her palm against her face. "Never," she hissed.

"Then I will have no choice but to lock you in the storm cellar for several days for punishment," Victor said, bending to speak into her face.

Paling, Mariah wavered. "You wouldn't do that to me," she gasped. "You . . . just . . . wouldn't."

"I have no choice," Victor said, picking up his cane from Mariah's bed. He leaned his weight against it as he walked toward the door. "Come on, now. We may as well get the punishment on its way."

Mariah stood her ground. "No," she murmured, fearing the rats that frequented the cellar, which were sometimes as big as cats. "That won't be necessary. I'll do as you say."

But she vowed to herself that this was the last time he would force anything on her. At her first opportunity she was going to escape his wrath. Tonight, after they returned from the venture she dreaded with all of her heart and soul, she would flee from her father's trading post and go to the protective custody of Colonel Snelling at the fort. From there she would chart her future.

"How will you explain your attack on Chief Gray Elk and his people to Colonel Snelling?" she blurted. "Don't you know how hard he is trying to keep peace among the Indians and settlers?"

"He ain't trying hard enough," Victor said, smiling crookedly. "All I'll have to tell him is that some of Gray Elk's murderin' redskins came to my trading post and stole from me and came close to killing you in the process. I'll just say I was defendin' you from such an assault."

"And you expect him to believe that?" Mariah said, her voice rising in pitch, daring another face slap. But her father had not even heard her. He was staring intensely out the window. Mariah was hearing the arrival of many horses outside, and went to look out the window also. When she saw the lead rider, she froze inside and turned quick eyes to her father.

"And so the cheating, vile Tanner McCloud is going to assist you in this raid?" she accused. "That's why he's come with so many men?"

"Dammit, no," Victor said, kneading his brow. "We've

enough men of our own workin' for me here at the post without bein' bothered by anyone else." His face became flushed again with anger. "That sonofabitch. He's come again to speak in your behalf. He told me the last time he was here that he was goin' to bring a great bride price." He wheeled angrily around and began working his way toward the door, his cane, as it came in contact with the wooden floor, sounding ominous. "You see? He's lived in the wilderness so long he thinks he's bargaining for an Injun squaw! Well, I'm goin' to set him straight once and for all. In fact, I'll tell him that I don't want to see his lousy yellow eyes around here again. He's pestered me one time too many."

Mariah didn't have time to say anything else. With the aid of the cane, her father moved quickly, and was soon gone from the room, slamming the door behind him.

Mariah stifled a sob behind a hand as she gazed with a deep longing down at her hair on the bed.

Then she went to a drawer in her nightstand and pulled out a mirror. Her fingers trembled as she lifted it. When she saw her reflection, and how her hair now lay flat and lifeless against her head, only just past her ears, she turned her eyes away and threw the mirror across the room.

As it shattered into dozens of pieces, it was not enough to silence the loud shouting going on below her in the main store of her father's trading post. Never had she heard her father so mad.

Never had Tanner McCloud cursed so loudly, so violently.

And then it was all quiet. She went to the window again and watched Tanner and his men ride away in a cloud of dust, her father standing outside with his rifle aimed at Tanner's back. She wished she could go back to bed and then get up again to find that everything was as it had been those many years ago when she had had a mother to confide in.

Never had she felt as alone as now.

3

> We should often be ashamed of our very best actions, if the world only saw the motives which caused them.
>
> —La Rochefoucauld

A vicious storm had delayed the attack on the Chippewa, leaving the rivers and creeks rumbling with swollen, rushing water, their banks being eaten away with the churnings.

But it had not delayed the ambush indefinitely. Soon the sun had replaced the dark clouds in the sky. And as though living a nightmare, Mariah rode her mouse-gray mustang into the Indian village beside her father, her face smeared with ash, the same as the others under her father's command—a disguise against possible recognition.

She witnessed the carnage as her father and his men swarmed through the Indian village in a senseless frenzy, spraying the Chippewa with volleys of gunfire and tossing torches, which soon had the bark dwellings wrapped in sheets of flames, the smoke and fire belching out with a sound like thunder.

The crash of Indian pottery split the air like a shriek. Pistols flamed and bullets spattered, the reports from the guns deafening. Horses reared and plunged, trampling fallen Indian women who tried to flee from their outdoor cooking fires, into the protection of the forest.

A few of the aged were saved at the expense of the younger women who so very bravely interposed their slim bodies between the elderly and the firing weapons. Old men and young boys alike were running around, frantically snatching up whatever weapons they could find, but too soon falling among the bloodied figures strewn across the ground.

The village was a chaos of screaming confusion and the pall

of smoke. The air was thick with the acrid stench of black powder, of burning hides, and of blood.

"Be sure not to leave anything of value!" Victor shouted to his men. "And get some of that corn yonder for roasting!"

Mariah, having not fired a shot, thanked God she had at least been spared that. She hung back and looked pityingly at the women and wailing children who huddled in the center of a circle of braves. The men fought valiantly, keeping the foe off by firing into the attackers.

Then her heart sank as several of her father's men began charging and firing point-blank into those braves. The Indians soon became a ring of bodies, those surviving reaching for the attackers to pull them from their horses. The horses reared, hooves flailing, trying to get away.

Outraged by the horror of it, Mariah had a strong urge to switch sides and fight alongside those Indians, who were dying like wolves, fighting to the last gasp without noise or complaint.

Instead she pulled at her horse's reins and swung her around, desperate to get away from the massacre. She didn't get far. Too soon she found herself face-to-face with an Indian brave standing in her horse's way, who if he had chosen to, could have killed her instantly.

But she was still dressed in the clothes of a boy, the jacket loose over her shirt, her breeches large and slouchy, hiding beneath them the curves that she could now boast at the age of eighteen.

And the ploy seemed to have worked well. The Indian must have taken her for an innocent lad forced into battle, for the handsome brave did not raise his firearm against her, nor did he grab for his knife, which was so handy in a sheath at his waist.

For what seemed an eternity, but was in truth only a few moments, Mariah and Echohawk stared at each other, long enough for Mariah to be struck by his extraordinary presence. A young man of obvious physical power, he wore no shirt, his copper body reflecting the sun like fire. His legs were sheathed in fringed leggings that were so tight she could see their muscled contours. He was tall, with raven-black hair framing his noble shoulders. His eyes were the darkest of all midnights, large and flashing. He had high cheekbones and a mouth that was hard and proud.

As quickly as he had appeared, the brave was gone, leaving Mariah shaken by how intensely he had affected her. Shivers ran up and down her spine as she realized that soon he could lie dead among the already fallen braves.

Desperately she looked around for her father, wanting to go to him and beg him to give up this senseless assault.

When she finally caught sight of him on his horse, still wreaking havoc in the village, she grew weak all over, gasping when she saw a brave take aim at her father with his rifle.

"No!" she screamed, knowing that her father was not aware of being targeted. It didn't take much thought to know what she must do. In an instant she had her rifle removed from its gun boot at the side of her horse. She aimed, pulled the trigger, and winced when she saw the bullet graze the Indian's shoulder, causing him to drop his weapon.

Feeling eyes on her as she thrust the rifle back inside its boot, she turned and found the handsome brave staring at her again, apparently having witnessed her action. She knew that he must be regretting having let her pass when he had had the perfect opportunity to kill her.

Her insides grew cold and a scream froze on her lips when her father was suddenly there behind the brave, the butt of his rifle cracking across his skull. She watched, horrified, as the handsome brave stumbled forward, dropped his rifle, fell to his knees, then crumpled to the ground, unconscious. She felt the prick of tears as she gazed at the blood seeping from his head wound, knowing that it could soon snuff the life from him.

Victor eased his horse up next to Mariah's. "It looks as though Echohawk won't be causing me any more problems," he said, staring triumphantly at the fallen brave.

Mariah looked over at her father, then down at the handsome brave, her face ashen. "That's . . . Echohawk?" she said, her voice quaking. Then her jaw tightened and she glared at her father. "And what of his father? Did you also brutalize him?"

"More than that," Victor bragged. "He's now entering what the Injuns call the Land of the Hereafter. And none too soon, I'd say. He lived way longer than what was civil for the likes of him."

Mariah stared disbelievingly at her father a moment longer, hardly able to bear this cold, heartless side of him that made her not want to admit that he was any kin to her at all, much less her father.

She gazed with contempt around her, seeing the men under her father's command heavy-laden with plunder. She wheeled her horse around and rode away, wanting to distance herself from it all. As soon as she could, she would slip away from her father and go to Fort Snelling, and not only for her own welfare. She would plead with Colonel Snelling to come to the aid of the Chippewa. If there were survivors when this was over, they were going to need someone with compassion to help them through the winter.

That man with compassion had to be Colonel Snelling! He was there to help everyone, both red- and white-skinned. And no matter what harm befell her father when she revealed his role in the massacre, she knew that she must.

As she saw it, it was time that her father was stopped. His ruthlessness must not be allowed to go on.

For now, she had no choice but to return to her father's trading post, along with the others. But when night came, she would flee the life that she had grown to abhor.

She flinched when her father rode up beside her, his men following on their sweating steeds. Even though some of them were wounded, and some were tied across their horses, dead, loud laughter and shouts of victory filled the air, the Indian village having been left in a heap of smoking ruins.

She would never forget the sight of the fallen braves being wept over by women and children. And how could she forget that among those fallen Chippewa was the tall and handsome brave with the sparkling dark eyes? In that brief moment of eye contact, there had been something about him that had stirred strange longings within Mariah—longings that she did not even recognize or understand.

Thinking of the valiant brave lying there, even now possibly dying, sent her heart into a tailspin of regret. Should he die, she would never forgive herself for this damnable raid—a raid that she had participated in, for she *had* shot one of the braves herself. She gave silent thanks to the heavens that she had inflicted only a flesh wound.

Still, guilt soared through her, making the journey back to her father's trading post even more unbearable. And once there, she was forced to sit with the men, outside by a roaring fire, part of a victory celebration. As she sat stiffly on a blanket, watching the sky darkening overhead, she bided her time while wine and whiskey flowed like fountains on into the night.

When she saw that her father was perhaps too drunk to notice, she slipped away from the celebration and went to the barn, readying her horse for travel. Watching over her shoulder, she led her mouse-gray mustang away from the barn by foot and onto the open prairie.

Feeling safe enough, she quickly mounted her steed and rode away into the shadows of night, in search of the beaten paths that would lead her through the forest to Fort Snelling.

* * *

Echohawk awakened to wails of mourning on all sides of him, the women of the dead braves clawing at their own faces and arms with their fingernails, producing deep, bleeding gashes. Dazed by the blow to his head, he slowly pushed himself up from the ground. When he was standing, he swayed from a light-headedness that nearly felled him again.

But he had to go to the aid of his people, their cries reaching into his heart with a tearing sadness. He staggered ahead, events blurring in his mind.

He blinked, trying to focus on things around him. But no matter how hard he tried to see, all that was there was a strange sort of dark haze.

The throbbing pain of his head led his hand to the lump, and he soon felt the break in the skin and the blood that had caked dry.

"A head injury," he whispered to himself, fear cutting through his confusion. Now he recalled the very instant that the white man had cracked the butt of his rifle over his head—recalled, even, that had he not been engrossed in looking at the young lad who had wounded one of his braves, the older white man would never have been able to sneak up on him.

Now both the lad and the white man were the target of his hate, as both were responsible for so much.

He blinked and rubbed his eyes again, his heart sinking when realization came that the white man had not succeeded in killing him, but instead had taken his vision from him! All that he could make out was shadow and light!

Knowing what was expected of him at this time of sorrow for his band of Chippewa, no matter his condition, he collected himself.

His father.

His people.

They needed him!

As hands began clutching at him, and voices reached him with utter despair, begging him to help, Echohawk felt his way through the ravaged village, soon discovering the true depths of the massacre. Everywhere there were bodies to be stepped over and around.

For a moment his brain burned, the world seeming to have been annihilated. So many innocent women, children, and braves were dead and now entering the Land of the Hereafter.

But he was relieved that many of his people's most valued braves had not been at the village to be slain or maimed. These braves were far away, on a hunting expedition. Upon their return, they would find much sorrow, and then they would aid Echohawk in his thirst for vengeance.

"Father," he whispered to himself, having not yet found his way to his father's large dwelling that sat back from the others on a slight rise. He welcomed strong hands on his arms as two braves came and steadied him between them after seeing his legs begin buckling beneath him, his weakness worsening with each step.

The braves identified themselves when they realized that Echohawk could not actually see them.

"It is I, Yellow Wolf," one of them said. "Of the St. Croix band of Chippewa."

"And it is I, Helping Bear, also of the St. Croix band," the other said. "We were passing by in a canoe, on our way to Fort Snelling, when we saw smoke. We followed it to the scene of this massacre. We have come to offer assistance. We will continue on our own journey later."

"I know you both well. It is good of you to come to my people's aid," Echohawk said thickly. "My eyesight. It has been robbed from me."

"If you wish, we will be your eyes," Yellow Wolf said solemnly.

"For now, *ay-uh*, yes," Echohawk said, nodding. "But only for the moment. It is important that I learn to fend for myself."

He paused, then said, "*Gee-bah-bah*. Take me to my father." His heart was anxious to see his chieftain father, yet wary that he might not have survived the attack. The white man who had led the attack had seemed determined to wipe out this band of Chippewa, and surely that included their chief.

Helping Bear and Yellow Wolf exchanged troubled glances, then looked solemnly at Echohawk. "Chief Gray Elk . . ." Helping Bear said, his voice drawn. "He is dead, Echohawk."

Knowing that his worst fear had proved true, a sudden, stabbing despair filled Echohawk. It fully engulfed him when Helping Bear and Yellow Wolf helped him down beside his father and he was able to touch the coldness of his flesh.

Drawing on the restraint that his father had taught him from the moment he could understand right from wrong, Echohawk stilled the cries of remorse that so badly wanted to escape from deep within him.

Kneeling beside his father, he embraced him. Ah, how blessed he had felt when his father's health had returned after having established their new village along the Rum River, only a half-day's ride from his father's longtime friend Silver Wing.

But, Echohawk despaired to himself, he had not been

blessed a second time. Gray Elk had not been given another chance.

His palate parched from rage, Echohawk felt as though he was suffocating. In a husky low voice he vowed to his father that he would be the kind of chief Gray Elk would expect him to be. He vowed that he would be a strong and loyal leader of his people.

But to himself, alone, Echohawk was wondering how he could follow the road of peace that his father had always taught him. His blood was boiling with anger and humiliation; he could feel it flowing in his veins like molten lava.

Vengeance!

His heart—his very soul—cried out for vengeance.

Echohawk clung to his father and mourned silently for a moment longer, then found himself surrounded by more survivors of the massacre, who had fled into the darker depths of the forest during the attack.

Yellow Wolf and Helping Bear helped Echohawk to his feet. Although he could not see his people, he turned to them and faced them, to give them the confidence they needed in their new leader. They looked to him now for their future. For leadership. For survival. He was their chief, and he knew that for now he must place them and their welfare even before his desire to have revenge.

Helping Bear leaned closer to Echohawk and whispered, "Echohawk, perhaps it is best that you cannot see. Some who stand before you are wounded. Some are carrying their dead children. It is a sight that is most unbearable."

Echohawk's heart ached, and he could not help but feel the helplessness of this situation, especially now that he could not see well enough to be the leader that his people needed at this time. So much depended on him.

"One by one, come to me, my people," Echohawk said, reaching his hands out toward them. "Let me embrace each of you. Then I shall tell you what we must do to survive."

Although his knees were growing weaker by the minute, and his head was throbbing incessantly, Echohawk began embracing his people, himself drawing much comfort from them.

When this was done, he stood before them all, tall and unbending like a tree, his eyes unfocused yet bold and fathomless as he spoke to them. "My people, for the moment my eyesight has been weakened by the blow to the head that I received during the white man's attack," he said, forcing his voice to sound strong, and most important of all, calm. "But do not fret. We shall endure! We will go to Chief Silver Wing's village and ask for assistance until the wounds of your hearts and flesh are healed, and until my vision clears, to ensure you a chief that can work at full capacity."

He held his chin high and squared his back. "Busy yourselves at making many travois," he instructed. "Go and find the dogs and horses that were scattered during the raid. The dead and most seriously injured will travel by travois."

Soon this was done and the slow journey began to Chief Silver Wing's village. To prove his worth to his people, Echohawk had chosen to travel on foot, only occasionally accepting Yellow Wolf's and Helping Bear's assistance as they walked beside him.

As Echohawk took each step, his weakness worsening, his hate for the raiders deepened inside his heart. Hate was etched inside his heart for all mankind, it seemed. How could he forget that white man who, those many winters ago, raided, killed, and maimed so many of his father's people? How could he forget the cowardly "Yellow Eyes," who had recently taken so much from Echohawk and his people?

And now there was another white man whose heart was as evil and black, and whose face troubled Echohawk. Although smeared with ash, he had seen something familiar in his features, yet he could not put his finger on just what.

His thoughts went to a white man that stood out from all of the rest, a man who was everyone's friend. If not for the kindness of Colonel Snelling, and of the honest traders that Echohawk had become acquainted with at Fort Snelling, he would believe that all people with the white skin were bad.

But he knew that this was not so. It was just a few that he vowed to kill. In time vengeance *would* be his. One by one the evil men would die. Even if Echohawk had to learn how to fight without his eyesight!

Echohawk's troubled thoughts went to the youngest of the raiders today. There had been something different about the young lad. Strange, how through the smeared ash he had seen such feminine features.

And there had been some hidden mystery in those dark eyes.

An intense bitterness seized Echohawk, and he vowed that this lad, also, must die. No one involved in the raids on his people would be spared his vengeance.

No one!

The sound of the horses' hooves behind him made another cause for sadness enter Echohawk's heart. His beloved horse, Blaze, had been among the missing horses today, and he felt that a man without a horse was only half a man.

This, also, gave him reason to hate—to plan a terrible vengeance.

4

> Think that the day lost whose low descending
> sun views from thy hand no noble action done.
>
> —Bobart

As Mariah drove her mustang endlessly onward, feeling as wild as the breeze that blew, she tilted her face toward the flaming glory of the sunrise. She inhaled a quavering breath, so glad that she was finally free of her tyrant father.

Wearily she lowered her eyes, momentarily closing them. Oh, how they burned from lack of sleep! Her head would nod, and then just as quickly she would become alert again as to why she had not taken the time to sleep in her flight from her father. She must get to Fort Snelling. The colonel would send assistance to the Chippewa as soon as he was aware of their needs.

Oh, God, she lamented to herself, she felt as responsible as her father for the Indians' desolation, yet she reminded herself that she had been forced to ride with him and his men.

Knowing that, however, did not lessen her guilt. Perhaps it would lessen once she was able to get assistance for the Indians.

"But is it too late for Echohawk?" she despaired aloud. The instant his chieftain father had died, he had become chief of his people. His people needed him, for if he died, they would have lost two chiefs in one attack.

To think of that possibility, and to know that she had been a part of it, though an unwilling participant, made Mariah thrust her heels into her horse's flanks, urging him faster, into a harder gallop across the land.

Then her spine stiffened as she became aware of the stench that was troubling her nostrils, and soon she caught sight of a black pall of smoke that lay heavily in the air through the break in the trees a short distance away. Clearly she was not far from the ravaged Indian village.

She yanked her reins, causing the mustang to come to a sudden shuddering halt. She studied the low-hanging clouds of smoke, seeing in her mind's eye what was hiding behind it, the scene of the Indian village having been etched onto her consciousness like a leaf fossilized in stone. She knew that she should make a wide swing around it, to avoid the survivors seeing her and possibly killing her.

But some unseen force made her snap her reins and nudge her steed with her knees, sending her mustang into a slow trot, until she was through the smoke and near enough to the village to see that it was deserted.

Her mustang slowly loped into the village, and she was torn by what to do. Even if she did arrive at Fort Snelling as planned, how could the colonel help the Indians if he didn't know where they were?

"He'll know where to look for them," she whispered to herself.

She urged her horse into a hard gallop away from the burned-out village, knowing that she must get to the fort in haste. The Indians must be found quickly and offered assistance in their time of need and sorrow! And she was anxious to see if Echohawk was among the survivors.

She gazed heavenward. "Oh, God, please let him be alive," she prayed softly. "Please. . . ."

She rode hard across straight stretches of meadows, then was forced to wind her way through forest land, still fighting the urge to sleep, hunger now joining her miseries, gnawing at the pit of her stomach.

She came to a creek that had to be crossed before going onward. She dismounted and studied the rushing waters, a rude reminder of the storm that had delayed the attack of the Chippewa village. The water in the creek had not yet receded, even now tearing savagely at the banks, leaving them torn and furrowed in its wake.

Mariah caught sight of a black snake as it glittered and slid into a rift in a cottonwood tree near her, reminding her that water moccasins were prominent in this area, should she try to cross the creek, and fail.

Casting fear aside, she looked farther upstream, seeing that it wandered willfully to the right and left, with many a turn.

Then she spied an irregular line of large stepping-stones that the water was rushing across. That seemed to be her only hope of crossing the creek today, or perhaps even tomorrow, unless she traveled farther upstream to see if it was shallower somewhere else.

"I don't have time for that," she murmured to herself. "The *Indians* don't have that much time for me to waste. . . ."

Wary of her decision, yet knowing that she didn't have much choice, Mariah rode onward until she reached the stones. Gripping hard to the horse's reins, placing her knees solidly against the sides of her mustang, she urged her horse onto the rocks, its hooves unsteady as the rush of the water slapped against them.

Wide-eyed, scarcely breathing, Mariah watched as her horse seemed to brave the savagery of the water well enough, sighing when the opposite shore was almost reached.

But just as she was urging her mustang to solid ground, its hooves slipped. Mariah was thrown forward to the ground as the horse toppled back into the creek, swiftly carried away in the current. When Mariah landed on the ground, her head hit with a thud, momentarily stunning her.

When she regained her full faculties, her eyes became wild as she looked desperately around her. Her heart sank when she recalled her mustang being taken downstream. She hoped it would climb ashore where the current slowed.

But now she would have to travel the rest of the way to Fort Snelling on foot!

"How can I?" she sighed woefully, placing her hand to the small of her back. It seemed that every bone in her body ached from the damnable fall.

A more terrifying thought seized her. "My rifle!" she gasped aloud. "It was on my horse!"

Weaponless, and without a horse, she knew that she was at the mercy of anything and anyone that happened along. She had no choice but to get to her feet and start her long journey to Fort Snelling. Delaying even a moment longer could cost her her life!

"But I'm so tired," she whispered lethargically. "I'm . . . so . . . hungry." She stretched out on the ground, hugging herself to ward off the chill. "I'll sleep for just a little while, *then* go on my way. . . ."

Her eyes closed. Sleep came to her quickly . . . a *deep* sleep.

* * *

Exhausted from the journey, and weak from his injury, Echohawk staggered toward Chief Silver Wing's circle village of skin lodges that were fitted among birch trees, the leaves of the white birch trembling in the breeze. A few children at play on a slight rising of ground were the first to perceive Echohawk and his people. A cry of "Strangers arriving!" sounded the alarm, and mounted braves soon rode out of the village and stopped close to Echohawk, recognizing him.

Yellow Wolf held Echohawk alert as Wise Owl, one of Chief Silver Wing's most valued braves, dismounted beside him.

"Echohawk, what has happened to you and your people?" Wise Owl said, recalling the last time he had been with Echohawk. They had shared in the hunt. They had later shared cooked venison over an outdoor fire before going their separate ways to their own villages. Theirs had become a special friendship.

Echohawk recognized the voice of his friend. "Wise Owl," he breathed out, his voice barely audible. "My father, Gray Elk, lies dead on a travois behind me. Our people were attacked by white men. Our village . . . It was . . . destroyed."

With a weak and limp hand Echohawk gestured toward his people, who stood devotedly behind him. "These are but a few of the survivors," he said sadly. "Others are on the hunt and will soon discover the carnage left at our village."

He paused, inhaling a quavering breath, then resumed speaking. "We have come to ask Chief Silver Wing for assistance. He was a valued friend of my father's." He swallowed hard. "And since I have become acquainted with him this past year, he is also a trusted friend of mine."

"It is with much sorrow that I hear of your misfortunes," Wise Owl said, taking Echohawk by the arm. "Come. You will ride with me. I will take you to Chief Silver Wing. He will be saddened also by the news you are bringing him. He held Chief Gray Elk in the highest regard."

Echohawk shrugged himself away from Wise Owl's gentle grip. "I enter your village on foot with my people," he said, lifting his chin proudly, even though sieges of light-headedness were throwing him off balance. He was not sure how much longer he could stay alert, much less continue walking.

But he must, he thought stubbornly.

For his people, he must!

"As you wish," Wise Owl said, giving Helping Bear a troubled glance as Echohawk grabbed for Helping Bear to keep himself from tumbling to the ground.

After Wise Owl saw that Echohawk was going to be all right, with Yellow Wolf moving quickly to his other side to offer assistance, he mounted his horse again and rode ahead, escorting Echohawk and his people on toward the village.

As Echohawk entered the village, he felt the presence of many on all sides of him. He did not have to see to know that these were Chief Silver Wing's people coming to gaze and to ask questions about those who were arriving so downtrodden.

But if he *could* see, he knew that he would recognize many of these faces, having joined them in feasting and celebrating on various occasions this past year, his father so proudly sitting at Chief Silver Wing's right side.

But that was in the past, those good times of camaraderie with his beloved father. Now all that he had were memories—wondrous, precious memories.

It was hard for him to accept what his education had taught him—that death is but a change for the better, and that it is more than anything unworthy and womanish to shun it.

Oh, but if only his father had been able to shun death this time, as he had in the past.

When Chief Silver Wing's large domed conical lodge of

bark and reed mats was reached, Helping Bear and Yellow Wolf stepped away from Echohawk. "We will return now to our journey to Fort Snelling," Helping Bear said, placing a friendly hand on Echohawk's shoulder. "*Nee-gee,* friend, let hope fill your heart, not despair."

Yellow Wolf took Helping Bear's place before Echohawk as Helping Bear stepped aside. He embraced Echohawk, then stepped back from him. "May the Great Spirit bless you with sight again soon, my brother," he said, his voice choked with emotion.

"In time I *will* see again," Echohawk said firmly. "Pity then those who have gone against my people."

There were more fond embraces and words of thanks, and then Wise Owl escorted Echohawk, alone, inside Chief Silver Wing's dwelling.

Chief Silver Wing was sitting at the fire in the center of the room, carving a pipe stem. On Echohawk's entrance, he looked up, startled. "*Nee-gee,* friend, what has happened?" he said, stunned to see Echohawk's wound, and also his eyes, which seemed to be blank.

Wise Owl guided Echohawk over to Chief Silver Wing. Echohawk looked down at the chief, seeing only shadows of what he knew was a man of fifty-seven winters, a man of dignity and reserve, with graying hair and lined face.

"It was the *chee-mo-ko-man,* white men," he said between gritted teeth. "They came and burned and killed. My father. He was one of those who is now entering the Land of the Hereafter."

Chief Silver Wing shook his head with grave sorrow, then waved his wife over to Echohawk.

Nee-kah knew what he asked of her even though he had not voiced it aloud. She cast a glance of recognition on Echohawk and spread a robe for him to sit on. Wise Owl led him down onto the robe, and Nee-kah then removed Echohawk's moccasins and gave him another pair for present use.

She then went and stood obediently behind her husband, feeling Echohawk's pain as she gazed sadly down at him. He was a man much younger than her husband, and had she not already been wedded to Chief Silver Wing, she would have offered herself to Echohawk to be his wife. She had never seen such a handsome Chippewa as he.

As for her husband, she had been chosen by him, a much younger person than he, to bear him children that his other wives had failed to. She placed a hand on her abdomen, smiling, knowing that even now that child he wanted was growing within her womb.

She prayed that it would be a son. That would please her husband twofold!

"It is with a sorrowful heart that I have heard of the misfortune of your people and of your father's passing," Chief Silver Wing said. "My village is now your village. Your people will live as one with my people until you see fit to leave."

"That is kind," Echohawk said, nodding. Then he spoke with more anguish. "Chief Silver Wing, my father is dead! My eyes are dry and I want something to make the tears come in them!"

"In time, my son, tears will come to you," Chief Silver Wing said solemnly. "Then all of your sadness will be washed from your heart." He leaned closer, studying Echohawk's eyes. He waved a hand before them, seeing only a slight sense of reflex on Echohawk's part. "You do not see. Why is that?"

"That is something I am living with," Echohawk said in a grumble. "When I was wounded, my eyesight was impaired."

Chief Silver Wing gazed at the head wound, then turned and looked up at his wife. "*Mah-szhon,* go. Take Echohawk to the wigwam that was yours before our marriage," he said softly. "You will see to his comforts. Tend to his wound. Give him food. Until he is better, my wife, he is yours. Do you understand?"

Nee-kah's dark eyes widened as she glanced over at Echohawk, then down at her husband. "*Ay-uh,* I understand," she murmured. "I will do this for you, my husband."

Chief Silver Wing turned his attention back to Echohawk. "I lend you my wife for a while," he said, smiling. "She is my fourth wife, but can cook better than all other three put together." He took Nee-kah's hand and urged her to a kneeling position beside him. "And, Echohawk, finally I have a wife who is capable of bearing me a child. She is four months pregnant. She makes me proud. So very proud."

Such talk of wives and children catapulted Echohawk's thoughts back to the time when he was so proud to boast of his wife being with child. It tore at his heart, this absence of a wife—and of a child that would never be.

"That is good," he said, rising slowly to his feet. "And may the Great Spirit bless you more than once with children." He recalled Nee-kah in his mind's eye, and her innocent loveliness, and smiled as he felt her presence at his side as she stepped up next to him. "And your beautiful wife will bear you beautiful children.' "

Nee-kah cast her eyes downward, her face burning with a blush.

And then she took Echohawk's hand. "*Mah-bee-szhon*, come. I will now take you to your dwelling," she said, her voice lilting. "You must mend quickly, for your people need you. I will help in that mending."

Wise Owl stepped aside as Nee-kah led Echohawk outside and slowly to his assigned wigwam.

Once inside, she helped him down onto a sleeping platform and covered him with a bear pelt and blankets, and soon had a roaring fire blazing in the firepit in the center of the dwelling.

"I must leave now to go and get supplies for your stay here," Nee-kah said, looking tenderly down at Echohawk. "I shall return soon."

Echohawk nodded, then closed his eyes, sighing deeply.

He opened his eyes again in a flash as he felt another presence in the room. He bolted to a sitting position, trying to see who was there. He damned the white man who had taken his sight from him when he could not make out anything but the shadow of a man kneeling beside him.

"It is I," Silver Wing said, kneeling down close to Echohawk's sleeping platform. "I have brought you many things." He placed a rifle in Echohawk's hand. "This is for you. Keep it with you at all times. If white men destroyed your village, ours might be next."

"*Mee-gway-chee-wahn-dum,* thank you," Echohawk said, lifting the rifle, liking the feel of it in his hands.

"Also I have brought you a bow and arrows, should you prefer that weapon over the firearm," Silver Wing said, placing the bow and arrows at Echohawk's side on the sleeping platform.

"You are more than kind," Echohawk said, laying the rifle aside. He reached out for Silver Wing, searching, then clasping his hand on his shoulder. "My father was right to want to rekindle your friendship and live close to you. You are a special man, a man of heart."

"You would be as generous had it been I who came to you sightless and fatherless," Chief Silver Wing said solemnly. He paused, then added, "I also offer you land for burial of your people's loved ones."

Echohawk almost choked on a sob, so moved was he by Chief Silver Wing's continuing generosities. "My people," he said. "Those who have survived. Are they all being seen to? I do not want to be favored over them. I am now their chief. My oath as chief binds my life first to the lives of my people."

"Each has been taken in by a separate family," Chief Silver Wing assured. "None will want for anything. And this will be so until you choose to leave our village."

Echohawk reached out and hugged Chief Silver Wing tightly, for a moment feeling as though he was in his father's presence.

Then, embarrassed, he drew away.

A kind, firm hand on his shoulder made Echohawk warm clear through. "My heart is grateful," he said. Then he scowled as he once again remembered the massacre. "I will avenge my people. I will begin hard practicing with weapons soon, to perfect what sight that I have left. They who are responsible for my people's misfortunes will die!"

Chief Silver Wing gazed down at Echohawk, saddened by and wary of the bitterness in his voice and heart. He knew that no good could come from it. The white people had become the law in these parts. If Echohawk killed for revenge, then so would more Chippewa be slain because of it.

It was Silver Wing's sincere desire to help curb Echohawk's anger and to find a more peaceful solution to what had happened again to the red men of the forest. For their survival, that was the only way. Too quickly the white people were outnumbering the red man in the Minnesota wilderness.

"I have brought you something else," Silver Wing said, placing a pipe and otter-skin tobacco pouch on Echohawk's lap. "When you smoke from this pipe, think peaceful thoughts."

Echohawk's mind was no longer on what Silver Wing was saying or was offering. He was feeling hot, and then cold. Yet he did not complain out loud, although he knew that he was being weakened even more now by a fever.

"I shall return later to see how you are faring," Silver Wing said, rising. "Nee-kah will be here shortly. She will bathe your wound. She will feed you broth. Tomorrow will be a brighter day for you, Echohawk. You will see that I am right."

After Chief Silver Wing left the wigwam, Echohawk laid the pipe and tobacco pouch aside and eased back down onto the thick layer of pelts. His thoughts were becoming fuzzy. His scalp seemed on fire.

"*Gee-bah-bah,* Father," he whispered, reaching a hand out toward the fire, thinking that he saw his father's image in the dancing flames. "Father, do you hear me? Do you see me? Your *nin-gwis,* son, oh, how he misses you!"

He moved to his side and closed his eyes, his body racked with hard chills as his temperature began to rise.

He found himself drifting somewhere between midnight thoughts and the flaming glory of a Chippewa sunrise. . . .

* * *

Fully clothed, reeking of dried perspiration and alcohol, Victor Temple tossed fitfully in his bed, his drunken slumber broken by dreams of horror. In the nightmare, he and Mariah were nude and chained together, forced to stand upon a scaffold, while Indians looked at them with hate in their eyes, ready to shoot arrows into their flesh.

Victor awakened with a start, a cold, clammy sweat on his brow, his hands drenched with perspiration, and his eyes fixed.

Shaking himself out of the dream, he jumped from the bed and poured himself a glass of whiskey, drinking it in fast gulps.

Then, recalling Mariah's part in the dream and in the Indian massacre that he had commanded, he rushed to her room to see if she was all right. When he discovered that she was not there, alarm filled him.

"She's been abducted!" he cried aloud. "While I slept, my daughter was abducted!"

His thoughts became scrambled as he wondered who could have done it. "Tanner?" he whispered, then shook his head, thinking that Tanner wouldn't be that foolish.

"Injuns?" he said, panic rising inside him.

He ran down the steps to the lower floor, then from the house, frantically waving his hands. "My daughter's gone!" he shouted, drawing men from their bunks. "Saddle up! We've got to find her!"

5

> More firm and sure the hand of courage strikes,
> When it obeys the watchful eye of caution.
>
> —THOMSON

Autumn's warming rays filtering down through the stands of hemlock and spruce were welcome as Mariah awakened from a night of bone-chilling temperatures. She wiped her eyes with the back of her hand as she slowly rose to a sitting position beside the creek, trying to organize, think logically, slowly recalling what had happened. She had braved the raging waters of the swollen creek, but had lost the battle, it seemed. She had been thrown from her horse, her beloved mustang having then been carried away in the current. She had been momentarily stunned, and then had discovered that she had been too tired to travel onward by foot. She had not meant to, but she had slept all night!

Her parched lips drew her eyes to the creek, its waters having receded. Crawling to the embankment, she cupped her hands and lowered them into the water for a drink, then winced when she caught her reflection in the shine of the water. She hardly recognized herself! Her face was covered with mud, also her hair was tangled with its muck and mire.

She glanced down at her clothes, seeing that they were no better off. They were stiff with dried mud.

The crunching of leaves behind Mariah made her turn her head in a jerk to see what had made the sound, again feeling her helplessness since she had no rifle for protection.

But she was soon relieved and rose slowly to her feet when she found only an Indian maiden standing there gazing down at her, instead of a fierce brave. And wasn't the Indian maiden lovely with her eyes of a deep, deep brown, her braided waist-length hair even darker than her eyes?

Mariah's gaze traveled over the maiden, seeing that she was attired in a long-sleeved buckskin dress, tightly drawn over her stomach, revealing that she might be with child. She also wore a lovely blue tunic beaded in a leaf-and-flower design, and knee-high moccasins.

Mariah did not even feel threatened when she realized that the maiden's one hand was on a sheathed knife at her waist, her other hand clutching a basket filled with what appeared to be an assortment of wild herbs, apparently picked from the forest bed. There was too much kindness in the gentle features of the maiden's face for her to use the knife against Mariah—a person quite visibly without weapons.

"I am *nee-gee,* a friend," Mariah said softly, so glad that her father had taught her enough of the Chippewa language to get by.

She then tried to reach the beautiful maiden in her own tongue, knowing that most Indians in this region knew the English language well enough, since they traded with the white people at Fort Snelling. "I am a friend in need of help. Can you offer me assistance? I no longer have a way to travel to Fort Snelling, my destination. My horse lost its footing and threw me, then was swept away in the swift current."

Still the maiden did not speak, seeming to be taking her time to come to a decision about Mariah, about whether she spoke the truth or lied.

Then Mariah became wary herself. "Are you Chippewa or Sioux?" she asked, her voice revealing her wariness. She feared the Sioux. They had not made peace with the white people as readily as had the Chippewa.

To Mariah's relief, the maiden finally spoke.

"Nee-kah is Chippewa." Her eyes roved over Mariah, then locked eyes with her. "Your name?"

Mariah stiffened, afraid to reveal her name to Nee-kah, unsure of whether or not the news had spread of her father's attack on Echohawk's village, and her part in it.

Nee-kah's eyebrows lifted, finding it strange that this white lad who had been so talkative before now chose to be quiet.

But she could not delay returning to her village any longer by playing word games with the lad. She had left only long enough to find the herbs necessary for Echohawk's healing. He had become fevered and now awaited her return.

Through the night she had become concerned about this temperature that had risen so quickly, seeming to rob him of his senses. She was frightened over this, for the white man's attack had not only taken away most of his eyesight but also could perhaps eventually cost him his life.

"*Man-bee-szhon,* come," Nee-kah said. "White boy, you will go with me to my village. Chief Silver Wing will decide what then will become of you."

Mariah fell into step beside Nee-kah, through woods mixed with meadow, the pine forest crowding up to the shore of the land. She was relieved that the maiden had not demanded a name, yet feared being taken to a powerful Chippewa chief, especially since she had been part of a Chippewa massacre only yesterday.

And she did not know if she should correct Nee-kah's mistaking her for a boy and tell her that she was a young woman, like herself.

She quickly decided that revealing too many truths at this time could be dangerous.

Especially claiming the name "Temple" in these parts now could possibly be her death decree.

She set her jaw angrily when she thought of her father. He had not taken into consideration the outcome of his decision to slay many Chippewa yesterday, when there were other villages of Chippewa in the area who could avenge their fallen comrades!

Her father had not considered the danger in which he had placed his daughter, which proved to her that his caring for her came second to his lusty need of vengeance against a Chippewa that had rendered him a half-cripple all of those years ago.

Dizzy from hunger and the trauma of the fall, and fearing

the outcome of her appearance in the Chippewa village, Mariah stumbled and fell.

Nee-kah stopped quickly and set her basket on the ground. She knelt down beside Mariah. *"Ah-neen-ay-szhee-way-bee-zee-en?"* she said, gently touching Mariah's arm.

Then, assuming that the white person who looked at her with a keen puzzlement in her eyes surely did not understand her Chippewa language all that well, she decided to speak in the English tongue that she had learned quickly enough from her chieftain husband.

"What is wrong with you?" Nee-kah asked. "Are you ill?"

Mariah blinked nervously at Nee-kah and smiled weakly. "I'm fine," she murmured. "Or I will be, once I get some food in me."

"You will be given food after you have council with my husband," Nee-kah said, placing a hand to Mariah's elbow, helping her up from the ground. She smiled at Mariah. "And do not despair. My husband, Chief Silver Wing, is a fair, kind man. He will not treat you harshly. You are but a mere lad. And you carry no weapon with which to harm my people. *Ay-uh,* yes, you will be treated kindly by my chieftain husband."

"You are Chief Silver Wing's wife?" Mariah said, her eyes widening in surprise. "I know of him. He is much . . ."

"Much older?" Nee-kah said, laughing softly as she gave Mariah another sweet smile. "*Ay-uh,* yes, my husband is older. I was chosen because of my youth to be his wife so that I might bear him a child." She placed her hand on her abdomen. "This I do for him gladly. I have not had a blood course for four moons! I am with child."

Mariah was stunned, even embarrassed by Nee-kah's innocent openness. She had always imagined the Indian women to be bashful and quiet, living only in the shadow of, and for, their husbands.

But Nee-kah seemed filled with a love of life led by a free spirit. Mariah liked her instantly.

"How nice," Mariah finally said, yet offered no further conversation. Her attention was drawn to the village that was now within sight through a break in the trees a short distance away.

The birchbark wigwams were ranged in a great horseshoe shape in a wide bend of a tree-fringed creek, the dwellings all facing the east, offering the traditional welcome to the spirit of the rising sun. The first thin smoke of the morning cook fires rose in the cool air, drifting to the southeast.

Mariah was now aware that all along, while asleep on the ground beside the creek, she had not been very far from the Indian village. From the very beginning she had taken wrong paths on her journey to Fort Snelling!

But of course she should have expected no more from herself. Always before when she had traveled to Fort Snelling, she had been with her father, and not especially attentive to which particular paths he was taking to get there.

"We are there," Nee-kah said, her chin held high as she led Mariah into the village. She smiled at the women who were moving to and fro, some carrying firewood, others water. And she understood why they stared questioningly at the stranger at her side. The young lad was in desperate need of a bath. Though he was covered with mud, it was quite clear that the lad with her was white, and at this moment in time any white people were cause for alarm in their village.

Yet surely they saw this young lad as she did—harmless, and as someone who would perhaps be frightened of *them*.

The smoke from the fires outside the wigwams and the food cooking over them gave a pleasant scent to the morning air, making Mariah's stomach growl unmercifully from hunger. She gaped openly at the great sheets of buffalo backs roasting over the fires, dripping their fat into the blaze, the dripping, burning grease sputtering.

It had been too long between meals. At the time of her escape from her father, food had been the last thing on her mind. Though a part of survival, food had taken second place to getting away from the evil clutches of her father and seeking help at Fort Snelling.

Mariah walked as close to Nee-kah as possible, aware of the many eyes on her as she was taken through the village of wigwams. She tried not to look at the Chippewa women and children soon clustering around her. She kept her focus straight ahead, on a wigwam that was larger than the others, most surely Chief Silver Wing's. While shopping at Fort Snelling, she had heard much talk about Chief Silver Wing, and most prominent of this gossip was that he was a kind Chippewa leader. She had even gotten glimpses of him at times throughout the years. He had been a muscled, tall, and noble-visaged man with kind eyes.

But if he was aware of the attack on his Chippewa neighbor, she wondered warily to herself, what then of his kindness toward people with white skin now, no matter that she was only one person, taken as a defenseless lad, at that?

A scowling brave stepped suddenly in Mariah and Nee-kah's path, his eyes two points of fire, his arms folded tightly across his bare copper chest.

Fear grabbed Mariah at the pit of her stomach when the brave glared down at her, his jaw tight.

Then she sighed with relief when he gave Nee-kah the same sour look, making Mariah realize that not all of his anger was directed at herself—but instead, obviously, at Nee-kah.

"And so you succeeded at eluding me again, did you, Nee-kah?" Wise Owl said, his voice a low grumble.

"Nee-kah is not a frail thing who cannot fend for herself," Nee-kah said stubbornly.

"You again defy your husband, your chief, by going into the forest without me, your appointed guard?" Wise Owl said, his eyes shifting to Mariah. "And should this white lad have been an adult, with adult weapons. What then, Nee-kah?"

"Nee-kah knows not to approach large white men who sport weapons," she snapped. "This boy? I saw that he was no threat. I offered him assistance." She firmed her chin and looked defiantly up at Wise Owl. "Perhaps I should have killed him, Wise Owl, with my knife? And left him as food for bears?"

"You may wish you had," Wise Owl said, his eyes roving over Mariah. "This lad has family. His father could be near with firearms. Perhaps you have opened ways for an attack on our people." He grabbed Mariah by a wrist. "Come. You will tell my chief why you are close to our village."

Mariah paled as Nee-kah grabbed her wrist away from Wise Owl.

"He is mine," Nee-kah hissed. "I will take him to my husband. Not you!"

"One day you will trust white people too much," Wise Owl said, then turned and strode away.

"Come with me," Nee-kah said, leading Mariah on to the larger wigwam. "And do not let Wise Owl's harsh words frighten you. His heart is in the right place. He is one of my husband's most devoted braves."

Stepping up to the larger wigwam, Mariah glanced over at Nee-kah, trying to get reassurances again from her that she would be treated fairly, but Nee-kah was no longer paying heed to her fears. She was raising the moose-skin entrance flap, and soon stepped aside for Mariah to enter.

Swallowing back her fear, Mariah went inside the conical dwelling, immediately seeing Chief Silver Wing. He was sitting beside the firepit, attaching colorful feathers on the bowl of his pipe. She was quickly in awe of this man, as she had been before. He wore only a breechclout, revealing to her a man of over six feet, surely packing two hundred pounds of brawn on his massive frame. The only things about him that came close to revealing his age were the wrinkles grooved into his wise face and some threads of gray woven through his shoulder-length raven-black hair. A bear-claw armlet on his right arm proved him to be a man of distinction.

"My husband?" Nee-kah said, setting her basket of herbs aside. She went and sank onto her knees beside Chief Silver Wing. "I have brough you a young lad whose horse threw him and left him stranded not far from our village. I have offered him assistance. Was I wrong to?"

Chief Silver Wing gazed up at Mariah, his keen and piercing eyes roving slowly over her. "And why were you so close to my village?" he finally asked, his kind face solemn.

"I was on my way to Fort Snelling," Mariah said, fearing having to tell him more than she wanted to.

"You, alone, were going to Fort Snelling?" Chief Silver Wing asked, his jaw tightening. "It is not a normal thing for a boy your age to be riding alone." He set his pipe aside and folded his arms across his chest. "Where are those who were riding with you? Are they also near my village? Do they come to do us harm?"

"I was riding alone," Mariah said, fear gripping her insides when she realized that he saw her as an enemy. "There was no one riding with me when my horse threw me."

Chief Silver Wing looked over at Nee-kah. "My wife, why is it that you brought the white lad to me, instead of Wise Owl?" he asked, his eyes accusing. "Did you again turn your back on my orders? Did you go into the forest alone?"

"I do not like to search for medicinal herbs with a brave always there, spoiling my concentration," Nee-kah said softly. "And I did not travel that far, my husband."

"What am I to do with you, my young wife?" Chief Silver Wing said, a gentle smile tugging at his lips.

Then he became solemn again. "This time your escapade caused you no mishap. But what of the next?"

The scolding sent Nee-kah's gaze to the floor, humbled by her husband's words and by his sincere love for her.

Then she looked quickly up as Chief Silver Wing rose to his feet, clapping his hands. Two braves soon came into the wigwam and took their places on each side of Mariah.

"Take him away!" Chief Silver Wing said in a snarl. "He will be our prisoner until we see if what he says is true. If we discover that he was riding alone, then we will release him, lend him a horse, and let him go on his way. If we find others close by, then we will know that he has lied, and he will suffer for such a lie!"

"I am not lying," Mariah cried, wincing when the braves grabbed her wrists painfully and began dragging her away. "Please listen to me! Please!"

She looked frantically at Nee-kah. "Nee-kah!" she begged. "Tell your husband that I am not your enemy! Tell him again, Nee-kah, that I do not even carry a weapon!"

"Young lad with the shrill voice of a woman, your words are wasted on my wife," Chief Silver Wing said, drawing Nee-kah next to him possessively. "She, too, knows the dangers of the white people's words, which are so often said with forked tongues!"

Forcing herself not to cry, wanting to look brave in the eyes of this stubborn Indian chief, Mariah quit struggling and was allowed to walk peacefully between the two braves to a small wigwam set back from the others.

When she was taken inside and shoved to the floor, she expected to be tied and gagged, and was relieved when they did neither. They soon left her alone in the small cold dwelling, the fire in the firepit having burned down to only smoldering ashes.

She wanted to busy herself, to try to bide time until the chief decided to believe her, now wishing that she had been brave enough to tell him the full truth. That might have been better for her, if she could have convinced him that she had had only the Chippewa people's welfare at heart all along.

Moving to her knees, crawling to the firepit, she gathered up some loose twigs scattered on the floor beside the firepit and laid them on the glowing embers. Leaning low over them, she began to blow on them, sighing with relief when her efforts stirred up some sparks that soon turned into flames burning along the twigs.

And when a pleasant fire was burning, she looked more closely at the wigwam. It was neat and clean. Cedar boughs were spread on the floor, with mats spread over them for comfort. On a sleeping platform at one end of the dwelling were more mats and coverings, rolled up into bundles. Toboggans and snowshoes hung on the walls.

She crawled across the soft mat floor and took one of the bundles from the platform. Unrolling the furs, she spread them on the floor beside the fire, then sat down close to the warmth and tried to see something positive in that the chief had not ordered his men to kill her or to tie and gag her. She could not tell whether or not he had heard of the massacre in the neighboring village, or if he was cautious every time any strangers came near, without reason.

"Whatever," she whispered to herself, "I am an Indian captive!"

Just as she was trying to think of a way to escape, a noise

at the entrance flap made a quick fear grab at her heart. She sighed and smiled when Nee-kah came into the wigwam, all sweetness and smiles.

"I have brought you nourishment," Nee-kah said, handing Mariah a makuk, a dish made of thick bark, filled with rabbit stew. She then filled another makuk with a cold drink made of raspberries and water, and placed this on a mat before Mariah.

"Did your husband give you permission?" Mariah asked, eyeing the stew hungrily, its rich smell causing her stomach to growl.

"I do not have to ask his permission for every move I make," Nee-kah said, shrugging. She sat down beside Mariah. "And I did promise you food, did I not? *Wee-si-nin.* Eat."

Mariah's eyes lit up, most definitely seeing a friend in this beautiful mother-to-be. She had been given no spoon or fork, so she began to eat ravenously with her fingers, realizing that Nee-kah was studying her even more closely in the light of the fire.

"Beneath that mud I believe I would find a face that is too pretty to be a boy's," Nee-kah said, moving a hand to flick some of the dried mud from Mariah's chin.

Mariah almost choked on her food. If Nee-kah did discover that she was a woman, then Nee-kah would wonder why Mariah had not been truthful about this, and perhaps see that Mariah could have lied about other things as well.

"Nee-kah!"

A voice outside the wigwam was Mariah's reprieve, for Nee-kah scrambled quickly to her feet, just in time for Chief Silver Wing to come into the wigwam and find her there.

"You are here instead of seeing to our most valued guest?" Chief Silver Wing said, his voice sharp.

"I went to him," Nee-kah quietly explained. "He was asleep. Nee-kah did not want to disturb his sleep. Rest is valuable also. When he awakens, then I shall force more medicinal liquid between his lips."

"And so, while waiting, you spend time with the white lad?" Chief Silver Wing said, his brows meeting together as he frowned. He gestured with a hand for Nee-kah to go to him.

"My wife, you trust too easily. Come. We leave the boy to the food you were so generous to bring to him."

Nee-kah smiled weakly over her shoulder at Mariah as her husband led her to the entrance flap, then left with him, leaving Mariah alone, fearing that the new friendship she had thought to have found had just ended.

"I must find a way to escape," she whispered, her heart pounding at the thought of trying. She gazed at the closed entrance flap, having seen a guard standing just outside as Nee-kah and her husband had left. "If I could slip past the guard and steal a horse and resume my journey to Fort Snelling, then later I could explain everything to Nee-kah and let her know that her trust had not been misplaced."

Yes, that was what she would do. Later tonight, when the villagers were asleep, hopefully the guard would also drift off long enough for her to flee past him.

She began stuffing the most solid pieces of the stew into her mouth, not wanting to get stranded again somewhere without a full stomach.

* * *

Nee-kah slipped back inside Echohawk's wigwam and took her place at his side.

Echohawk stirred awake momentarily. He gazed through his blind haze up at Nee-kah, his limbs too weak to rise from his sleeping platform.

"Lie still," Nee-kah said, running a cool, gentle hand across his fevered brow. "Nee-kah will make you feel better."

Her thoughts returned to the young lad in the wigwam not far from this one in which Echohawk lay so ill. She looked questioningly down at Echohawk, then shrugged, having decided it was best not to reveal to him, at least yet, that a white boy was in the village, fearing it would upset him.

Yet, would he even be aware of what she was saying? she wondered. He had become mindless with the fever.

She moved away from Echohawk and stood in the shadows as a Mide priest entered and began performing his healing rituals over Echohawk.

6

All's to be fear'd, where all is to be lost.

—BYRON

Mariah placed another log on the fire, then peered up at the smoke hole. A full night had passed. The sky was just beginning to lighten, which meant that escape would be virtually impossible should she wait much longer. Soon the sun would rise, and with it the Chippewa people, bustling around, doing their morning chores.

Having slept erratically through the night, checking on the guard outside her door each time she had awakened, she was still bone-tired.

She glanced toward the entrance flap, frustrated over having not once found the guard asleep through the night.

Her chance to escape had become an impossible task!

Yawning, stretching her arms over her head, Mariah decided that she would try just one more time. If the guard was still awake, then she would have another full day to wait.

The mud on her face even tighter this morning, since she had not been given a basin of water to wash herself, Mariah rose quietly to her knees and crawled to the entrance flap. With trembling fingers and an anxious heart she lifted the flap, and her heart frolicked within her chest when she discovered that, finally, the guard had fallen asleep!

And not only had he fallen asleep. While he was asleep, his fingers had loosened around the rifle and he had dropped his weapon!

Her pulse racing, her eyes searching wildly around for any signs of anyone stirring in the village, she was filled with exhilaration.

Finally!

She would be able to leave this horrid place!

She would steal a horse and hurry on to Fort Snelling. The colonel would be a godsend to those Chippewa who had lost not only a good number of their people but also their means of survival—their village!

Mariah wondered just how far Echohawk and his people had traveled by now, and if Colonel Snelling would ever be able to find them, to offer assistance.

Determination firming her jaw, Mariah crawled stealthily from the wigwam, her eyes never leaving the sleeping brave. She smiled to herself when his snores reverberating into the air gave proof that it was safe not only to slip past the brave but also to take his rifle for good measure.

Her heart pounded as she inched her hand toward the rifle. When her fingers were securely around its barrel, she brought it slowly toward her.

Then, clutching it hard, she crawled on around to the back of the wigwam and out of the viewing range of the brave, should he awaken.

Mariah moved slowly to her feet and leaned her back against the wigwam, taking time to get her breath, trying to get her heartbeats slowed. She was afraid that if she got caught escaping, she would be shot on the spot, without further questions.

Especially now that she had a firearm in her possession.

Getting her bearings before going any farther, Mariah scanned the land for a good route of escape. Her eyes stopped when she found the Indians' horses at the edge of the forest, grazing inside a fence. She studied them closely and chose which one would be the easiest to steal. Several of them were still saddled, apparently ready for riding should an emergency strike the village.

Again she looked slowly around her. When she still saw no one, she took a deep quavering breath, then sprang away from the building and began running toward the horses. Once there, she scooted beneath the fence.

Going to her chosen steed, a palomino pony, she ran her

hand down its withers in an effort to make an instant friend. When it turned to her and nuzzled her hand with its snout, its eyes dark and warm as it gazed up at her, she knew that she had won her first victory today.

Smiling, she took the pony's reins and led it to the gate. After getting it outside, she felt that it was best to lead it away from the village on foot. That would make less noise.

After peering back at the village again to see if anyone had come out of a dwelling since she had started out for the horses, and seeing that she was still safe, she hurried the pony onward until she found the river. She had decided to follow it to its outlet at the Mississippi River, which then would take her on to Fort Snelling.

Just as she reached the sand beach at the river mouth and felt that it was safe to mount the palomino pony and ride away, she stiffened inside. Up ahead, through the thickness of the trees, she could hear voices and soft laughter.

"Who could that be?" she whispered to herself, an eyebrow forking. It was early. She had thought that everyone was still asleep in the village.

She tethered the pony to a low-hanging limb, and with her rifle poised for firing, tiptoed on through the forest and stopped suddenly. She stared disbelievingly at two young Indian lovers on a blanket beside the river, nude. Her face turned crimson at having caught the young brave and maiden in the midst of a passionate tryst, their bodies tangling while making love, their mouths hungrily kissing.

Embarrassed, feeling quite the intruder on such a private moment, Mariah started to turn and leave, realizing that these two lovers were so intense in their lovemaking they wouldn't be aware of a horse riding through the forest close to their love nest.

But then something else caught her eye, stopping her further escape. Her heart began to pound as she watched a water moccasin slithering across the water in a determined fashion, heading straight for the embankment where the two were making love. One of these young people would soon be the target of this snake! It was obvious that it had spied them and was going straight for them!

"What do I do?" Mariah worried to herself, knowing that should she intervene and kill the snake, her escape to Fort Snelling would be stopped. One blast from the rifle and the whole Indian village would be drawn from their sleep. Her escape would soon be discovered, for they would follow the sound of the gunfire and find her.

Beads of nervous perspiration pearled up on her brow as she watched the snake getting closer and closer to the shore, the young lovers still too involved in their passion to know that something evil was moving their way.

"I must!" Mariah whispered agonizingly to herself. Having learned well the art of shooting a firearm from her father, who had taught her most of the skills of young men, she lifted the rifle, aimed, and just as the snake began slithering from the water, pulled the trigger. A perfect aim, she hit the snake broadside, spattering its body back into the water in scaly pools of blood.

Mariah gazed at the young couple, who had bolted to their feet. They were watching the snake as its severed body floated away, then looked over to Mariah, their eyes wide with wonder.

The young maiden was the first to realize the dilemma that she was in as she glanced down at her nudity, then up at her lover.

In a rush, the young woman had pulled on her dress, the young brave his breechclout, as their eyes never left Mariah.

Mariah started to leave without explaining, explanations not necessary since they had seen the slain snake, but she was stopped when suddenly Wise Owl and several braves were there, in her path.

In what seemed a flash of lightning, Wise Owl had taken the rifle from Mariah, while another brave had her wrists twisted behind her.

"*Gah-wen,* no! Do not harm him," the young brave said, stepping forth. "He killed a water moccasin that was only moments away from biting me or Wild Flower."

Mariah bit her lower lip to keep herself from crying out as the brave's hand did not lessen its grip on her wrist. It seemed that Wise Owl and his companions had not heard what the young brave said. They apparently did not think that her having saved the two young lovers was a redeeming act at all. And because of their stubbornness, she was going to lose all of her freedoms again, and perhaps her life.

Yet Mariah could not feel that she had made a wrong decision. She was proud of her act of selflessness, and would do it again if given the choice between her own freedom and the lives of these two beautiful young people.

Wild Flower stepped to the young brave's side, her eyes downcast as he slipped an arm possessively around her waist. The blush to her cheeks was proof of her embarrassment.

"Wild Flower, you leave your bed before your mother and father and come and meet Brown Bear by the river? You were so caught up in each other you did not see the snake approaching you? What were you doing, daughter? Better it not be that you went further than holding hands!" Wise Owl grumbled, stepping up to his daughter, lifting her chin with a forefinger, so that her eyes were forced to meet the anger in his. "My daughter, you shame yourself by such actions. Go. Return to our dwelling. Do not leave again until you have my permission!"

Sobbing, Wild Flower turned with a jerk away from her father, and without casting her lover a glance, ran toward the village.

Wise Owl stepped up to Brown Bear. "It would be simple to banish you from our tribe for what you have done this morning," he said blandly. "But you have proved more than once that you are a young brave with much promise. And so shall you also be a good husband. You will marry my daughter. Soon."

"This I do with much pride," Brown Bear said, lifting his chin boldly. Then he glanced over at Mariah. "And what of the young lad? In my eyes, he is a hero, and should be treated as such."

Wise Owl went to Mariah and stood over her, glaring

down. "Release your hold on this lad," he ordered his brave. Then he stood there a moment longer, as though contemplating her fate.

Mariah went almost limp with relief when he suddenly smiled at her and clasped a friendly, gentle hand on her shoulder.

"I will forget that you did this act of bravery in the midst of escaping from our village of Chippewa," Wise Owl said. "It would have been easy for you to have gone on your way, with only selfish thoughts of self. Instead, your thoughts and deeds were for someone else. My daughter and her future husband! And because of this I shall encourage Chief Silver Wing to give you your freedom." He nodded. "But you will not leave our village before I offer you clean clothes, a bath, and much food."

Mariah's heart thrilled at the thought of having become an instant friend of this powerful Chippewa brave. It seemed that he had much influence with Chief Silver Wing.

Yes, she would soon be free. Then she would ride with haste to Fort Snelling.

She regretted with all of her heart that she had been sidetracked so long. The wounded, ailing Indians from Echohawk's village had needed assistance immediately. Some had perhaps even died because of her inability to get help sooner than this.

But she knew that she could not act too hastily in wanting to leave these Indians. Again they might get suspicious of her. And she was not free to confide in them about why she was so desperately eager to get to Fort Snelling. They must never know her part in the massacre. Too soon their trust of her would be cast into the wind.

"Brown Bear, take the white boy back to the wigwam that he escaped from," Wise Owl said. "I will talk to Chief Silver Wing. He will also see the lad as someone who is a friend, not a foe." Wise Owl moved to Mariah and gazed down at her. "Soon you will be free to go wherever you choose to go. If you need an escort, even that will be arranged."

"Thank you for everything," Mariah said, her voice low, trying to sound boyish. "I appreciate everything that you are doing for me." Seeing so much kindness in these Indians made her guilt twofold for having been forced to be a part of the raid against others of their same race. Oh, but if they should ever discover this truth, how quickly their attitude about her would change! As quickly as she had become their friend, she would again be their enemy.

"Come," Brown Bear said, nodding to Mariah. "I am indebted to you. How can I ever repay you?"

"It's not necessary," Mariah said, falling into step next to him. "That I am being looked to as a friend is all that is important to me." She smiled at him. "And I was glad to be able to save you and your beautiful friend from that horrid snake. Water moccasins are deadly. Your death would have been instant."

"*Ay-uh,* yes, instant," Brown Bear said, his smile fading. Then he looked quickly over at Mariah, his eyes dancing. "I shall give you my most prized bow. My grandfather made it for me. While you carry it into the hunt, my grandfather's spirit will be with you, always."

Mariah smiled weakly over at him. "Truly, you don't need to give me anything," she murmured. "Especially not something that has so much meaning to you. All I want is to be able to go on my way. Soon."

"As Wise Owl said, first you must accept clean clothes, a bath, and food," Brown Bear said, guiding her on into the village and toward the wigwam in which she had been imprisoned. "This is expected of you, white boy. You must accept our gifts graciously, or look to my people as though you see our ways as beneath you."

Mariah swallowed hard, not wanting to do anything to upset the Indians now that she had gained a foot-hold with them. "I appreciate all of your people's kindnesses," she said, glad to see Nee-kah waiting for her at the doorway of the small wigwam.

"I heard of your heroism," Nee-kah said, rushing toward Mariah. She took Mariah's hand and led her into the small dwelling. "I have been assigned many duties these past several days," she giggled. "You are now one of them."

Mariah looked down at a basin of water, then over at a

clean fringed outfit of breeches and shirt, and then at the food awaiting her beside the fire. It was a feast. There were fish, broth, rice with maple sugar, and dried berries.

"First I bathe you," Nee-kah said, her hands eager on Mariah's heavy jacket, already removing it.

Mariah panicked, knowing that if she did not stop Nee-kah, her secret would soon be revealed. And she did not see that as wise. She now had the Indians' trust. Should they see her deceit, then what?

"I can undress and bathe myself," Mariah said, gently easing Nee-kah away from her. "You can go on to your other duties. Your husband seemed angry at you last night for having neglected someone who was in need of your care. Perhaps that is where you should be, even now. We don't want your husband getting mad at you again."

"My husband sent me here," Nee-kah said, shrugging. "And as for Echohawk, I have seen to his head wound and fever already today. I have even bathed him with herb water to help get his temperature down. And even after all of this, all he does is sleep." She slipped Mariah's shirt over her shoulders. "Now, just stand still. I think it is time that mud is washed off your face so that I can see the true features of my friend." Mariah was in a stunned state from having heard Nee-kah mention Echohawk's name, and that he was here, only a few dwellings away.

Of course, she thought, her pulse racing. Why hadn't she thought of it earlier? Echohawk *would* bring his ailing people to a neighboring tribe of Chippewa, for assistance.

"This Echohawk you mentioned," Mariah dared to say, trying to hold on to her shirttail so that Nee-kah couldn't lift it over her head. "Is he . . . going to die?"

"Echohawk is a courageous fighter," Nee-kah said, jerking and yanking on Mariah's shirt, trying to get its tail end away from her. "He will live. But it will take time. His body is racked with fever." She stopped and sighed heavily as she placed her hands on her hips, staring frustratedly at Mariah. "Will you quit fighting against my undressing you? I have seen boys without clothes before. Seeing you will be no different."

Mariah laughed softly, seeing a trace of humor in the moment, yet fearing the end result. She panicked again when Nee-kah forgot the struggle with the shirt, yanking Mariah's breeches down, to rest around her ankles. The only thing left to hide the fact that she wasn't a boy were her bland cotton undergarments. And Nee-kah had already placed her hands at the waistband, beginning slowly to lower them.

Mariah backed away from Nee-kah. "You don't want to do that," she said shrilly.

"I have never before in my life seen such a bashful boy," Nee-kah fussed, again placing her hands on her hips.

"Then Echohawk is going to be all right?" Mariah said, changing the subject in an effort to postpone her having to undress, besides wanting to know more about Echohawk.

"Not entirely," Nee-kah said, taking a slow step toward Mariah. "He was partially blinded by a man's rifle that was used to knock him unconscious. But in time I think Echohawk will be victorious over even that. He will see again. The Great Spirit will make it so."

Mariah paled, in her mind's eye recalling Echohawk's beautiful large eyes. "Blind?" she gasped. She placed a hand to her mouth, stifling a sob behind it. "I'm so sorry. So very sorry."

"As we all are," Nee-kah said solemnly. "But he will see again. I do not doubt that for a moment. He is a fighter. He will win this battle. For his people, he must."

"Why is he here instead of his own village?" Mariah asked, still inching away from Nee-kah, and knowing too well the answer to her own question. She just needed more time to figure out how she could refuse to undress any further.

"People with skin of your coloring came and ravaged Echohawk's village," Nee-kah said, taking a firm grip on Mariah's shirttail. "He brought his people to my husband's village. They are all being seen to."

In a flash Nee-kah had Mariah's shirt over her head, and what Nee-kah discovered beneath it sent her head reeling with surprise.

"A boy with breasts of a woman?" she gasped, then fled from the wigwam screaming.

Mariah grabbed up her clothes and held them against her to hide behind, knowing that she didn't have enough time to get back into them.

And she was right.

Too soon Nee-kah had returned, Chief Silver Wing at her side.

7

> All our actions take their hues from the complexion of the heart,
> As landscapes their variety from light.
>
> —BACON

Mariah could not help but tremble as Chief Silver Wing stood before her, for a moment a quiet question in his eyes.

Then she paled and her heart lurched when he grabbed her clothes from her arms, his gaze settling on her well-formed breasts.

Finally he spoke. "Nee-kah came to me with a tale that the young lad who is being celebrated a hero in our village has the body of a woman," he said, his eyes showing the puzzlement he felt as he looked slowly up at Mariah. "What she said is true, yet I, the wise chief that I am, know that cannot be so."

He stepped closer and ran his fingers through Mariah's hair. "Yet, still, your hair, the color of the sun's flames, is short, the same as a boy's," he puzzled further. "It is very strange that you, a woman, should choose to dress and behave as a boy. The Chippewa women would be shamed should their hair be clipped, unless, of course, it is done while mourning the loss of a loved one. And they would not wear men's breeches and shirts to hide the wonders of their bodies. Why would you? Tell me. I am here to listen. Tell me, even if your deceit is for the Chippewa only!"

Feeling cornered, Mariah realized that she had no choice but to answer him.

Yet for now she would tell him only half-truths.

"It is not of my doing that my hair is cut and that I am wearing the clothes of a boy," she blurted out, her pulse racing. "I am a woman forced by an evil father to dress and behave like a boy! I have fled my father's wrath. I was on my way to

Fort Snelling, to seek help there, and to live my life as a woman."

Without taking his eyes off Mariah, Chief Silver Wing spoke to Nee-kah. "Go. Get one of your dresses and a pair of moccasins," he said softly. "Bring them here. *Wee-weeb,* quickly, my wife. Quickly. This woman has suffered enough humiliations because of an evil father."

Nee-kah rushed away. Mariah breathed much more easily. Then she stiffened again when he resumed questioning her.

"Am I wrong to believe you?" he said, thrusting her clothes back into her arms for her to hide behind. "Or is that innocence I see in your eyes enough, to know that what you say is true?"

"I am telling the truth," Mariah said, fearing that, as astute as he was, he would see beyond that which she had already said, and would demand to know more.

"Why did you not reveal this to us sooner?" Chief Silver Wing asked calmly. "And how did you know the skills of a rifle so well that you killed the water moccasin with one gunfire?"

"Not only did my father force me to dress as a boy, he also forced me to behave like one," Mariah said, glad to see Nee-kah there again, hoping that she would somehow draw the conversation away from the direction it was taking. "I was taught well the art of firearms. Also, the art of speaking some of your Chippewa language. My father told me that all of this was for my survival."

"In part, he was right," Chief Silver Wing said, taking the buckskin dress and moccasins as Nee-kah handed them to him. He leaned toward Mariah. "Take these. Wear them. You are now a woman. And you are a pretty woman, except for your hair. It looks like it is just growing out from a scalping."

"My father even forced this disgrace of cutting my hair upon me," she said, taking the garments, relishing their softness against her flesh.

"This father you speak of with anger," Chief Silver Wing said, kneading his chin thoughtfully. "Would I know him? Is he among those who trade often at Fort Snelling?"

A sudden fear gripped Mariah's insides. "My father has been to Fort Snelling," she murmured. "But not often. It has been a while now since he has been there. Others go for our supplies."

"Then I would not know him," Chief Silver Wing said, shrugging. His eyebrows forked. "You have yet to tell us your name."

"Mariah," Mariah said, yet not offering her last name. There was a chance that Echohawk had recognized her father and had known his name. Never could she breathe the name "Temple" across her lips while in the presence of the Chippewa.

"Mariah," Chief Silver Wing said, his eyes smiling down at her. "That name—it has to do with the wind, does it not?"

"Yes, Mariah is the wind," she said, smiling back at him, relieved that he did not ask her last name.

"*No-din,*" Nee-kah offered softly as she stepped to Mariah's side. "*No-din* means 'wind' in the Chippewa language. Would you mind if we called you No-din?"

"Please do," Mariah said, sighing. "That is so lovely."

"After you eat and rest, you will be accompanied by many braves safely to Fort Snelling," Chief Silver Wing said, placing a hand to her bare shoulder. "You will always be remembered by my people. You saved two of our most prized possessions. Our youth is our future."

Mariah was not hearing everything that he was saying. What had stuck in her mind was that she would soon be escorted to Fort Snelling. Earlier, that was what she would have wanted. But now that she knew that Echohawk was in this village recovering from his head wound, she did not want to leave.

Somehow she wanted to be able to see him. If she could, she even wanted to find a way to make everything up to him.

"Does it matter how long I stay in your village?" Mariah asked guardedly, not wanting to arouse their suspicions about her reason for asking.

Echohawk!

"But you were trying to escape our village only a short while ago," Chief Silver Wing said, his eyes narrowing. "And you now wish to stay? Be a part of us?"

"I only now realize how weak I am from my recent adventures," Mariah quickly explained, the white lie slipping easily across her lips. "It could take me days to get my strength back. Would you mind if I stayed until . . . until . . . I have?"

She paused, then smiled up at him. "And until only a short while ago I wasn't welcomed in your village as a friend," she murmured. "You considered me an . . . enemy. I saw no choice but to try to escape."

Chief Silver Wing's eyes lit up and he nodded. "*Ay-uh,* yes, that is so," he said. Then he touched Mariah's mud-caked cheek. "*Nee-gee,* friend, it is time for my wife to make you pretty."

With that, he turned and left, leaving Mariah and Nee-kah alone, quiet in their exchanged admiring glances.

And then Nee-kah giggled and rushed to Mariah, taking the buckskin dress and her other clothes from her arms. "First you must be bathed," she said, tossing the clothes aside. "And then your hair will be washed and combed, your cheeks will be reddened with the juice of bloodroot, and then you will eat heartily! Your weakness will soon be gone. You will be shown everything of my village. My people see you as someone very special." She stifled another giggle behind her hand. "They are going to be very surprised to see your transformation from a mere boy to a beautiful lady."

"You don't know how anxious I am myself to be able to wear a dress," Mariah said, gazing down at the buckskin garment, beautifully decorated with colorful beads.

She gazed also at the moccasins. They were puckered around the front, Chippewa-style, intricately designed with beads and dyed porcupine quills.

Mariah fell to her knees beside the basin of water, bent over it, and splashed some onto her face. When Nee-kah offered her a cloth and a scented bar of soap, Mariah looked up at her questioningly. "The soap," she said. "It is perfumed." She looked then at a comb that Nee-kah had removed from a birch-bark case. "And you even have a comb. I would have never guessed that you would have such luxuries as these."

Nee-kah knelt beside Mariah, proudly clasping the comb. "*Ay-uh,* Nee-kah has both perfumed soap and a comb," she said, her eyes dancing. "My chieftain husband acquired these for me at Fort Snelling after he heard that I was carrying his child." She glanced down at her comb, then back at Mariah. "I consider both things my most cherished possessions."

"And you are sharing them with me?" Mariah said, touched by Nee-kah's continued generosity and show of friendship.

"Friends share many things," Nee-kah said, laying aside her comb. "Now let this friend scrub the rest of the mud from your face and wash your hair." She frowned as she gazed at Mariah's short-cropped hair. "You father should be ashamed for forcing you to wear your hair in such a fashion. It would please Nee-kah so much to be able to braid your hair and wrap it in long rolls of otter fur, to make you even prettier for my people to see."

"It will take many months for my hair to grow long enough for braiding," Mariah sighed, then bent lower over the basin as Nee-kah busied her fingers smoothing the soap across Mariah's hair, then washing it vigorously. "I know that I will grow impatient while waiting, for I was so proud of my long hair. While Father was cutting it, it was as though a part of my heart was being torn away."

"If you wish, I will help you pass the time required for your hair to grow," Nee-kah said anxiously. "It is wonderful that you proved to be a woman! We can do so much together!" She paused and leaned her face down close to Mariah's. "And we can talk about so many things. I love to talk. Do you? How many words do you know in the Chippewa language? I can teach you so many more!"

Mariah laughed softly, finding Nee-kah so refreshing, and such a joy to be around. Mariah had been denied any female relationships since her mother's death. Her father had been determined to turn her totally into a man.

"I know some Chippewa words," Mariah said, wrapping a towel around her hair, rubbing it briskly. "It would be so nice to be taught more." Her eyes wavered as she wondered just how long she could delay leaving.

She placed the towel aside and quickly washed the rest of

herself, then was glad to finally be able to put on the dress. She ran her hands down the full length of the buckskin garment, having never felt anything as soft, as comforting, to a body that had become so used to coarse fabrics.

Nee-kah stepped away from Mariah and gazed with parted lips at her. "You are most *mee-kah-wah-diz-ee,* which means 'beautiful,' " she said, sighing. "The mud had hidden your better qualities beneath it. But not so much that I was unable to know that you were too pretty to be a boy."

Mariah smiled at Nee-kah, enjoying feeling feminine again. She had ached to wear a dress for so long, and to have someone compliment her, instead of having those sidelong glances from men who were surely thinking that she was one of those "strange" boys that preferred boys over girls.

Nee-kah went to Mariah with a buckskin pouch. "Hold this," she said, thrusting the pouch into Mariah's hand. "It contains a mixture of herbs and bark that I will rub into your hair. It will give your hair luster, strength, and life. Hopefully, it will even encourage it to grow much faster." She began rubbing the mixture into Mariah's hair. "The Chippewa wear their hair long not only because it is more beautiful that way but also because we believe our strength is in our hair. So shall it be for you one day, once your hair has grown to its desired length."

Mariah was half-hearing what Nee-kah was saying, her thoughts having strayed back to Echohawk. She had to see him. And she wanted to spend some time with him. It was her plan to get permission to assist Echohawk however she could, to make up for his misfortunes caused by her father, and even herself.

And because he was partially blind, not able to see her and make out her true identity, she would be able to get away with her scheme.

"Nee-kah," Mariah began, ready to test Nee-kah's true strength of friendship, "you have spoken of Echohawk. You said that he was not well. And you also said that you have been assigned to look after him."

"*Ay-uh,* yes, that is so," Nee-kah said, stepping away from Mariah, nodding approvingly when she saw the shine of her hair. She then took the pouch from Mariah and handed her another one, then proceeded with dipping her fingers into this mixture, soon reddening Mariah's cheeks with the juice of a bloodroot plant.

"I know of Echohawk," Mariah dared to say. "I have heard of his courage. Of his bravery. It would please me so to be able to do something to help him in this time of his sorrow." She gazed into Nee-kah's eyes as Nee-kah stepped back and smiled, again pleased at how she had made Mariah even more beautiful than before.

"Nee-kah, you know that you can trust me, don't you?" Mariah continued, her voice sounding more guarded than what she would have preferred.

"*Ay-uh,* you have proved that you are a trustworthy person. My people look to you as a hero—or should I now say heroine?" Nee-kah said, taking the pouch from Mariah, setting it aside. "And why do you ask?"

"Let me relieve you of some of your duties to Echohawk. Let me go to him and offer him *my* services," Mariah said in a rush of words, watching for Nee-kah's reaction. "This is something I could do to repay your people's kindnesses to me while I am regaining my strength before leaving for Fort Snelling."

Nee-kah was quiet for a moment as she gazed studiously into Mariah's eyes. "You need not do anything else for my people," she murmured. "You have already done enough. Because of your bravery and concern for human life, did you not save two of our beloved young ones?"

"But I want to do this, Nee-kah," Mariah said, taking Nee-kah's hands, squeezing them affectionately. "Please allow it. You could show me which herbs to use in doctoring Echohawk's fever. And while I am with him, you could rest awhile, you and your unborn child. Please, Nee-kah? It would make me feel important to be able to assist you in such a way."

Nee-kah pondered over the decision a moment longer, then smiled at Mariah. "All right," she murmured. "I see no harm in it. You are a most sincerely sweet and caring person for wanting to do this. You are not what I would have thought white people would be like. You are filled with much love and compassion."

Mariah's heart began thudding wildly. "Then you are saying that I can go to Echohawk?" she said, trying to hide the anxiousness in her voice. "That I can sit with him and offer him assistance?"

"When he discovers it is you offering this assistance, he will be honored," Nee-kah said, discounting for the moment the hate that he was feeling for the white people who had recently caused him so much heartache. Mariah was different. He would soon see that also, once his fever was cured and his senses were returned to normal.

Nee-kah placed a blanket around Mariah's shoulders, its background like new-laid snow, interwoven with symbols in the scarlet and russet and gold of autumn leaves, and the blue of summer skies. "Nodin, wear this, a gift from Nee-kah, to keep you warm on these cooler nights of autumn," she said softly.

Mariah thrilled inside at the thought of having found such a friend, and also loving the way Nee-kah had called her Nodin, her newly appointed Chippewa name. She stroked the blanket, feeling its utter softness, then eased into Nee-kah's embrace. "Thank you," she murmured. "I love it. Oh, how I love it."

Nee-kah walked Mariah through the village until they came to the small dwelling that once had been hers before she married Chief Silver Wing. In it now lay an ailing chief—the beloved Echohawk.

Mariah stiffened when she heard some sort of chanting coming from inside the wigwam. She looked quickly over to Nee-kah, questioning her with her eyes.

"That is a Mide priest, one of our people's shamans of the grand medicine society, the Mide-wi-win, that you are hearing," Nee-kah said matter-of-factly. "He comes now and then to work his cures over Echohawk. Come. Let us go inside. You can watch."

Mariah's knees were weak at the thought of seeing Echohawk again, having never forgotten their eye contact during the surprise ambush. Should he recognize her, so much would be lost to her.

Shakily she followed Nee-kah into the wigwam.

8

In what distant deeps or skies
Burnt the fire of thine eyes?

—Blake

Upon entering Echohawk's wigwam, Mariah scarcely breathed. The room was dim, the fire's glow and the faint light drifting down from the smoke hole in the ceiling giving off only enough light for her to see a man standing over Echohawk, who lay on a sleeping platform in the deep shadows along one wall, furs spread over him, up to his chin.

From this distance Mariah could not see Echohawk's face, but seeing how still he lay proved that her father had inflicted upon him a terrible injury.

Guilt spread through her like wildfire when she thought of that very instant she had seen her father bring the butt of his rifle across Echohawk's skull. She ached inside to know how this injury had affected him.

He was partially blind—and he just might die!

Oh, but she wished from the bottom of her heart that she would be given a chance to make things up to him.

To see him full of life again.

To see the sparkle of his fathomless dark eyes. . . .

"Come," Nee-kah whispered, drawing Mariah from her troubled thoughts. Nee-kah tugged on her hand. "Let us sit down. We do not want to disturb the Mide priest's healing ritual."

Mariah smiled weakly and nodded. She followed Nee-kah's lead and sat down on a soft mat in the far shadows, away from the Mide priest. She straightened her back and folded her legs beneath her as she leaned forward, wanting to see Echohawk's face, yet still faint to her because of the damnable darkness of the wigwam.

She could not relax. The Mide priest's appearance was frightening. Two dark lines were painted upward from his eyes, signifying he could foretell the future. The lines from his ears meant that he knew what was happening far away. He wore a white buckskin *auzeum,* breechclout, embroidered with porcupine quills and decorated with silver and copper ornaments. His arms and hands had two lines painted on them, to show that his touch was lethal. The *megis* at his throat, the white seashell from the ocean, indicated great power.

Folding her hands on her lap, Mariah watched attentively as the priest sat down beside Echohawk's platform. When he picked up his drum and began to sing a high-pitched chant, his rawhide-covered drum thumping out the beat as he sang, the thump-thump of the drum unnerved Mariah even more.

To her, it seemed to carry with it the sound of doom.

As though Nee-kah had read Mariah's thoughts, she leaned over and whispered into Mariah's ear. "The deep throb of the water drum the Mide priest is playing represents the heartbeat of the creator, the Great Spirit," she explained. She lifted her nose into the air and sniffed. "And, No-din, do you smell the sweetness? Cedar boughs are burning in the lodge to purify the air."

Again Mariah smiled weakly, too soon realizing the complexities of the Chippewa's beliefs. She wondered if it was wise at all to try to fit into the culture, even if only for a while, in an attempt to make up to Echohawk and his people the wrongs she and her father had done them. Her efforts might be looked on as too foreign—as trivial, and wrong.

Yet she must not let anything dissuade her. She must do it for Echohawk.

Nee-kah leaned even more closely to Mariah. "Do you see the eagle feather in the Mide priest's beaver hat?" she whispered. "This is worn as a badge of his profession. Do you see the pouch at his belt? In the pouch are sacred items used in his magic practices . . . the claw of a bear, the rattle of a snake, a bird's wing, the tooth of an elk, and bits of tobacco. Now, watch further the exhibition of his Mide magic."

The priest bent over Echohawk and placed a sacred white shell on the furs which covered him, and began to shake his medicine rattle over him, and sang:

You will recover,
You will walk and see again.
It is I who say it;
My powers are great.
Through our white shell
I will enable you to
Walk and see again.

The Mide priest droned song upon song. Mariah swallowed hard as she continued to watch, becoming fearful that perhaps what she saw as witchcraft hocus-pocus might do Echohawk more harm than good. What Echohawk needed was real medicine, not strange songs sung over him and strange shells placed atop him.

She wanted to get up and speak her piece about how she felt, yet she knew to do so would be to condemn herself in the eyes of not only her friend, Nee-kah, but also the whole village. She was here because of their tolerance. She did not have the right to interfere in their beliefs, no matter how strange they seemed to her.

She stretched her neck to see what the priest was now about to do. He had gotten a cloth bundle from behind him and was unwrapping it. Her eyes widened as he took out a tail feather from an eagle, yet she saw that something still remained covered in the cloth.

Exhaling a nervous breath, she made herself relax as she continued to observe the curing ritual.

The Mide priest took the feather in his right hand and smoothed out its edges with his left. Settling himself on his haunches beside Echohawk, he leaned forward and wedged the feather in an upright position in the furs that were spread over

Echohawk. After placing the feather there, he picked up his drum again and began another song.

Mariah got caught up in the melancholia of this song, finding it beautiful—even mystical. She closed her eyes and let herself get carried away, as though on soft downy clouds above the earth. She experienced many things while in this semitrance state. She could hear so many things—the sighing of the wind as it blows through the tall pines; the soothing sound of waves lapping against the stones on the beach; and the fading noise of an animal crashing its way through the brush.

The song suddenly rose to a high vibrato, wrenching Mariah out of her reverie. Her eyes blinked nervously and her heart pounded, wondering about this moment of strangeness that she had just experienced. It made her fear the priest even more. He did seem to have powers that she had only moments ago scoffed at.

She flinched with alarm when the last drumbeat sounded and the feather jumped from atop Echohawk and fluttered to the floor as though it had a life of its own.

Confessing to herself that she was spellbound by the priest's performance, Mariah watched almost anxiously as he unwrapped the remainder of the cloth bundle.

Now he held two wooden figures in his hand. One apparently represented a male, the other a female. They were carved out of white ash and had movable heads and arms, and were attached to the bodies in a manner not discernible to her.

The medicine man then smoothed out a square of white cloth on the mat-covered floor and laid the figures on their backs on one half of the cloth, and carefully folded the other half over them so that they were completely covered.

Once again taking up his drum, he sang another song. It consisted of many repetitions of the sound "ho-ho" in a rather deep and guttural tone. As he sang, he closed his eyes and seemed unaware of anything around him. Sweat formed on his brow.

Craning her neck to take a better look, Mariah was startled to see movement under the cloth. The heads seemed to be turning back and forth, and the arms were moving up and down.

She did not know if they were actually moving or if she was the victim of some sort of illusion.

Nee-kah leaned over and took her hand. "Do not fear this that you see," she reassured softly. "The spirits have given the Mide the powers to do these feats of magic. But he is exhausted now. He will go to his medicine lodge and rest."

Mariah watched almost breathlessly as he picked up his paraphernalia and was gone, leaving the wigwam strangely quiet.

"Let us now go to Echohawk," Nee-kah said, yanking on Mariah's hand.

Mariah needed no further encouragement. She was anxious to see how Echohawk had fared during the performance that had mystified, even frightened her. Never had she seen anything like it, and deep within her heart she hoped never to see it again. It seemed to defy all teachings of the Bible that she had absorbed on those long winter nights before her mother had died. She could even now hear the soft, sweet voice of her mother as she had read the verses, explaining the meaning of those that seemed too difficult for a child of four and five.

Her heart thumping wildly, Mariah went with Nee-kah to Echohawk's side. She had expected him to be asleep, for he had lain so quietly while the medicine man performed over him.

But his eyes were open. His gaze seemed to be burning into her flesh as she knelt beside him, Nee-kah no longer there, instead at the far shadows, picking up some buckskin pouches from the floor.

Mariah breathed anxiously, afraid that at any moment Echohawk would speak accusing, angry words at her. For it did seem as though he was looking not only at her face but also deep into her soul, where her secrets were hidden—secrets that would condemn her in his eyes.

"Nee-kah?" Echohawk said, his voice revealing his weakness. "You have come again to sit at my side? Did you witness, also, the beauty in the Mide's performance today?"

Realizing that Echohawk did not know her, Mariah sighed with relief, and her heart jumped with a sudden joy, knowing that her plan would be easily carried out under these conditions.

Yet again she was plagued by remorse, seeing firsthand how her father's blow to Echohawk's head had affected him. She wondered if he would ever see again.

And his face was so pale. He was so ravaged by fever.

She reached a hand to Echohawk's brow and touched it soothingly. "No, I am not Nee-kah," she said softly, seeing a quick, wary puzzlement cross his face.

"It is No-din," Nee-kah quickly interjected as she came to kneel beside Mariah. "She has come to assist me. She will sit at your side and look after you while I give myself and my unborn child much-needed rest."

Echohawk squinted his eyes, so badly wanting to see this sweet-voiced woman at Nee-kah's side, yet still unable to make out anything but movement and shadow.

He again cursed the white man for having impaired his sight.

"I do not know a No-din," Echohawk said, finding it hard to stay awake, the fever having sapped all of his energy. But at least for the moment he had regained a portion of his senses and could talk as someone not crazed. He had surely worried Nee-kah as he had rambled on in his delerium, saying what, he did not even know himself!

Mariah stiffened and drew her hand from his brow, looking cautiously over at Nee-kah, wondering how she would explain to Echohawk just how she happened to be there, offering her services, when, in truth, she was not of Chippewa descent at all.

"She is not of our band of Chippewa, or yours," Nee-kah explained softly, sinking a cloth into a basin of water, handing it to Mariah. She nodded silently toward Echohawk, Mariah soon catching the meaning. She took the cloth and smoothed it gently across Echohawk's hot brow.

"Then from which band is she?" Echohawk said, sighing as he enjoyed the cool cloth on his brow. "Why is she giving of herself to make me more comfortable?"

"She is not Chippewa at all," Nee-kah said, her voice thin,

unsure of his reaction when he discovered that Mariah was white.

But he seemed to be drifting off even as he had spoken, so that even if she took the time to tell him the full truth of Mariah, and how she happened to be there, he would not recall it the next time he awakened.

"Do not worry yourself over who she is," Nee-kah murmured, leaning close to Echohawk's ear as his eyes fluttered closed. "Just accept her kindness, Echohawk. She is special, Echohawk. And soon, when you are better, you will see for yourself just how special she is."

Mariah bit her lower lip, wishing that Nee-kah wouldn't make over her so much, when, if the truth were known to this sweet Chippewa maiden, Mariah would be hated.

Perhaps even put to death!

"He is asleep again," Nee-kah whispered. "He no longer feels the cool softness of the cloth. Let me take this time while he sleeps to show you the medicines used to make him better."

Mariah sat down beside Nee-kah and listened, yet her heart was elsewhere. This close to Echohawk, so that she had been witness again to his handsome face, many things had stirred within Mariah that had felt deliciously strange.

As before, it had been an instant attraction, one that unnerved her.

And it was futile, this attraction to a man who would one day loathe the sight of her. Once he regained his sight and could see who this No-din really was . . . Oh, but how *would* he react?

Chills rode Mariah's spine as she envisioned that moment of eye contact, when truths were revealed. She could almost feel his powerful hands on her throat, squeezing the life from inside her!

"No-din?" Nee-kah said, looking questioningly at Mariah. She placed a hand to her brow. "Your brow is cold with perspiration. Do you regret being here? Would you rather leave? Although I do not wish to I would tell my husband that you would prefer going on to Fort Snelling. Would that make you more comfortable, No-din?"

A quick panic seized Mariah. She couldn't leave Echohawk now, no matter what the outcome would be in the end.

Hopefully, after he saw her devotion to him, he might be able to forget the ugly past—including her part in the ambush.

"No, I do not wish to go on to Fort Snelling," she said in a rush of words. "But please be patient with me, Nee-kah. All of this is new to me. I've never been in an Indian village before, much less participated in its daily functions. I will be all right. I promise you." She glanced over her shoulder at Echohawk, a warmth swirling through her so wonderful when her gaze rested on his face, she knew that she would chance anything to be with him.

"Then so be it," Nee-kah said, nodding. "Now, let me continue teaching you our ways of doctoring our ill, other than that which is done by our medicine men." She gestured with a hand over an assortment of herbs and roots that she had spread on the floor for Mariah to see. "These are collected from the forest. There are black root, bur-vine root, wild cherry, and dogwood, all dried and ready to use. And also you can make some boneset tea. You boil down walnut bark till it is pitchy. . . ."

Mariah listened eagerly, intrigued anew by the Chippewa beliefs.

* * *

Victor Temple drew his reins tight, urging his black stallion to stop. Groaning, he rubbed his lame leg. "Where is that damn Tanner McCloud?" he growled, looking over at his men, who had followed his lead and stopped. "He seems to have dropped off the face of the earth!"

"I'd begin lookin' for Mariah elsewhere," Bart, one of his most devoted trappers, said. "Dammit, Victor, we've been everywhere lookin' for Tanner, when you're not even sure he's the one who abducted her."

Another trapper edged close to Temple. "Did you ever think that it's just possible that she left on her own?" he said, nervously twisting and untwisting the end of his thick mustache. "That was a foolish thing to do, Victor—makin' her become a part of the Injun ambush. She can't be havin' much respect for any of us after that, especially you, her pa."

Victor raised a hand and slapped the trapper across the face, causing an instant hush throughout the cluster of men. "I didn't ask for your opinion," he shouted. "So don't give it to me!"

"Victor, what say we go to Fort Snelling?" Bart suggested, having ignored Victor's angry outburst against the other trapper. "Let's just take a look-see. She might be there."

Victor turned glaring eyes to Bart. "Are you sayin' you also think she ran away on her own?" he said, his teeth clenched.

"I ain't sayin' nothin' 'cept we can't rule out anything," Bart said, his dark eyes daring Victor to lash out at him, ready to fight back. "If you want your daughter back, I'd say we'd best think of every angle. Wouldn't you agree, Victor?"

Victor's gaze dropped to the ground. He shook his head wearily, then nodded. "Yup, I guess so," he said, looking back up at Bart. Then he doubled a fist into the air. "Let's ride, boys! And if she ain't there, we'll be goin' from Indian village to Indian village to find her."

Another hush accompanied this order, everyone fearing even the sight of Indians now, after having wreaked havoc on one of their villages—leaving one Indian chief dead, the other one wounded, perhaps dead by now.

Victor flicked his reins and nudged the sides of his horse with his knees, sending it into a hard gallop across the straight stretch of meadow, his insides an upheaval of dread and fear.

9

> Act well at the moment, and you have performed a good action to all eternity.
>
> —Lovater

Several Days Later

Fresh from a bath and a hair washing, Mariah felt lovely today. She was attired in a buckskin dress studded with beads resplendent in colors significant of the green earth and the blue sky, and a tunic with the most costly adornments of the milk teeth of the elk fastened in a row on front.

She had a spring in her step as she hurried toward Echohawk's wigwam. Nee-kah had just told her that when she last saw Echohawk, he had been more alert—had even attempted standing.

This change surprised Mariah. For days now she had sat with him while he slept most of the time. And when he was awake, they had not shared in conversation. Seemingly troubled, he had stayed aloof, staring blankly into the flames of the fire, yet occasionally accepting her gentle hand on his brow, as though her being there had been enough.

He hardly said a word to her, which she thought was fortunate for herself, since she was not ready to share in conversation with him. She knew that in time she would be faced with his questions, fearing that he would immediately discover who she was. She wanted this special time with him to develop a bond between them that he might find hard to break, no matter the color of her skin or her identity.

He had questioned her only that first time about who she was, after the Mide priest's performance. But it seemed that his memory of that moment had deserted him. It was as though he still thought that Nee-kah was with him most times.

Casting aside fears that today might be the day of discovery, Mariah lifted the entrance flap to his wigwam partway. But just before entering, she stopped and inhaled a nervous breath.

Courage.

She needed much courage to get past what could be awkward moments with Echohawk. His health had apparently improved.

Then what of his eyesight?

Wanting to get the wonder behind her, she stepped inside, stopped instantly, her heart lurching when she found herself looking into the barrel of a rifle.

Her eyes remained locked on the rifle, her knees feeling rubbery, thinking that she had not only been discovered, but was perhaps breathing her last breaths of life.

Surely Echohawk was not going to shoot her!

"Nee-kah?" Echohawk said, lowering the rifle to his side, swaying in his weakness as he settled back down onto his fur-covered platform. "I did not mean to frighten you with the rifle. When I discovered that my legs would hold me, I wanted to test the strength of my hands by holding a rifle. Soon I will be using the firearm in daily practice. I do not want to forget how!"

Her pulse racing, Mariah went weak with relief that he had meant no harm, and still did not realize who she was. She stepped further into the wigwam and moved to her knees beside Echohawk's platform.

"No, it is not Nee-kah," she murmured, gazing into his dark eyes, realizing that they were still partially sightless, for as his eyes locked on her, she could tell that he was not truly seeing her. There was the same blank stare, the frustration evident in his slight frown.

"Then who is there?" Echohawk said, resting his rifle on his lap. "I have felt your presence before. Your name. What is your name?"

"Her name is No-din," Nee-kah said, suddenly entering the

wigwam. She came and knelt beside Mariah. "Echohawk, do you not recall the one other time I spoke her name to you? Are you not aware that she, too, sat at your bedside and bathed your feverish brow? She fed you and gave you herbal medicines?"

"I now recall another time, but until this moment it faded from my consciousness when my fever worsened," Echohawk said glumly. "From then on, time and everything else have been a blur. Nee-kah, only *your* name came to mind when I felt a presence at my side."

He reached a hand out to Mariah and began roaming his fingers slowly over her face, causing a melting sensation to spread at the pit of her stomach. "Until only moments ago I did not realize that her presence was different from yours," he said. "There is something unusual about her, yet I do not know what."

"Her skin coloring, her language, and her way of speaking are different," Nee-kah said guardedly.

Echohawk drew his hand away, recoiling now at the thought of having touched a woman whose skin matched that of those he hated so much. "She is white?" he growled, circling a hand around his rifle again, clutching hard to it. "Why is she here? Who is she?"

The moment of warmth that had filled Mariah at the mere touch of his hand on her face changed to something cold and fearful knotting inside her abdomen. She eyed the rifle warily, then looked slowly up at Echohawk again, recoiling when she saw the intense hate in his eyes and the set of his jaw.

"She is a friend," Nee-kah said, herself eyeing the rifle. "A special friend."

"I have only one true friend whose skin is white," Echohawk grumbled. "That is Colonel Josiah Snelling. Others I do not trust. I have reason for this mistrust. I am here today, partially blinded, because of evil people with white skins and black hearts! Now that my mind is cleared of its feverish haze and I can think clearly, I live for the time when I can torture and murder the man with the limp and the young boy who rode at his side!"

Mariah shivered and paled at his words, having never thought that his hate for her and her father could be this strong. Her first instincts were to flee, but deep down inside, where her desires were formed, she knew that she felt too much for Echohawk to leave him. Now she must work twice as hard to make him trust—even love—her before he realized that she was in truth the lad he sought to kill!

She would volunteer her services to him in all manner of endeavor.

She would be his eyes!

"Echohawk," Nee-kah said, placing a gentle hand to his cheek. "Do not upset yourself so with such talk of vengeance. Your father was a man of peace. My father shares in such efforts. Please try to forget those who have wronged you. Live for the future. Your people's future. They have suffered too much already. Regain your strength, Echohawk. Use your wisdom and strength to better your people, not cause them more suffering by going into warring against the whites."

"Not all whites," Echohawk said, his voice a sneer. "Only those who have caused this heartache for my people. I soon will begin practicing with my weapons, to learn to fire accurately, even with my affliction. I will soon avenge my people!"

"A few white people's lives are not worth what it could bring your people," Nee-kah warned. "Please, Echohawk, forget your need to avenge your people, when all they want now is to rebuild their village and begin their lives anew."

Mariah had sat stiffly quiet, listening to the debate between Nee-kah and Echohawk, fearing offering her own thoughts on the subject, then finally spoke up. "Echohawk, I am sorry for any wrong that has been brought to your people because of people of my skin coloring," she said, reaching her hand to touch one of his, recalling so blissfully those few times that she had held on to his hand while he had slept. Even then she had known that she loved him.

Yes, she marveled to herself:

She loved him!

With all of her heart and soul!

Echohawk jerked his hand away from hers as though it

were a hot coal. Again he clutched onto his rifle, glaring at Mariah, still seeing her as only shadows and light. "You have not said why you are here," he said flatly. His gaze went to Nee-kah. "And why did you allow it, Nee-kah? She does not belong! Why would you think that she did?"

"She belongs in our village now, as much as you or I," Nee-kah defended. "She is a woman of much courage. She, alone, saved Wild Flower and Brown Bear. In the eyes of our people she is a heroine. It was I who brought her to our village. I found her alone, weakened after being thrown from her horse. And she has asked to stay until she is stronger, and also has offered to help care for you. I saw no harm in it. And she has been dutifully at your side since."

Echohawk's mind was swirling with questions, finding it unacceptable that Nee-kah, or even her husband, would have so carelessly allowed a white woman into his wigwam, no matter if she was being called some sort of heroine.

Yet he was recalling the sweetness of Mariah's voice and the gentleness of her hands, all the while thinking they were Nee-kah's. He had not wanted to feel anything at the time, knowing that Nee-kah was married to Chief Silver Wing, but a bond had been formed, and now he knew that it was the white woman that he had begun to have special feelings for.

He turned his head away, distraught over this discovery.

"Echohawk," Mariah said softly, "I want to do more for you now that you are stronger. Please allow it. I feel so ashamed of how your people have been treated by my people. I want to compensate, in some little way, for the harm that has befallen you. I would even like to stay at your side at all times and become your eyes until you can see. I could accompany you when you start practicing with your weapons. I could be your eyes, telling you when your aim was right or wrong. I could help you hone your skills by doing this."

Deep down inside herself, Mariah was torn with loyalties. If she did help Echohawk hone his skills with his weapons, she had to expect that he would use those skills against her father.

Yet she understood why Echohawk wanted to kill him—was *driven* to.

And she felt that she owed Echohawk so much. He had lost almost everything because of her father.

Echohawk turned his eyes quickly back to her, squinting, so badly wanting to see her. When he had touched her face, he had felt its fine, delicate features, knowing that she was surely even more beautiful than Nee-kah.

"Echohawk needs no more of your assistance," he said, his voice drawn. "Especially when I practice firing my weapons. That is a man's work. Not a woman's. Especially not a *white* woman's! Leave. That is what would make me happy. Go. Return to your home."

He squared his shoulders and leaned closer to Mariah. "Your home," he said, arching an eyebrow. "Where do you make your home?"

Mariah's insides tightened, fear grabbing at her heart. "I have no home," she said quickly, in a sense telling the truth.

"Why is that?" Echohawk asked, again reaching a hand to her face, roaming his fingers over it. Then his hand went to her hair, gasping when he discovered its length. "Your hair! What has happened to your hair? Did you cut it while in mourning for a loved one?"

Mariah's heart was pounding, feeling trapped. If he would put two and two together, recalling the length of the hair of the lad that had partaken in the ambush, then he could conclude that the lad, in truth, was she!

Yet she had no choice but to tell him as much of the truth as she dared to.

"If you must know, I fled an evil father who forced many unfortunate things upon me," she said. "He even cut my beautiful hair. That is why I have no home. I was fleeing his wrath. I was on my way to Fort Snelling to seek help. But I was stopped when my horse lost its footing in the creek and threw me. I was then at the mercy of whoever found me." She smiled over at Nee-kah. "I was fortunate that it was Nee-kah, the sweet, kind person that she is."

Echohawk peered sightlessly over at Nee-kah. "At a time when our people had just suffered so much at the hands of white people, you dared bring one into your village?" he said, his voice sharp. "And your chieftain husband? Did he approve?"

"*Gah-ween,* no, not entirely," Nee-kah said weakly. "No-din was taken prisoner. She escaped. And while escaping, she discovered Brown Bear and Wild Flower at the river. They . . . they did not notice a water moccasin ready to bite. No-din, knowing that she would be forfeiting her escape by killing the snake, shot it. This is why all of our people see her as trustworthy. This is why she is being celebrated as a heroine. So must you, Echohawk, accept this as true. Mariah is very much a part of our village now."

"Mariah?" Echohawk said, frowning over at Mariah, yet still not seeing her. "Your name is Mariah? You have called yourself No-din."

"That is my Chippewa name," Mariah said, gulping hard when she saw an instant look of horror on Echohawk's face.

"You have even been given a Chippewa name?" he gasped. His jaw tightened and he shook his head back and forth. "This I do not understand. Never shall I understand."

"Echohawk, I wish you no harm," Mariah pleaded. "I only wish to help right some of the wrongs done you. Please allow it."

"*Gah-ween-wee-kah,* never," he hissed. He gestured with a wave of a hand toward the entrance flap. "*Nah-quszly,* leave. *Ah-szhee-gawh,* now! I am soon to be taken to the resting place of my father and those of my people who are buried with him. I do not wish to have a white woman accompany me where she is not wanted."

Stifling a sob behind her hand, Mariah rose and ran to the entrance flap, rushing outside. Blinded with tears, she went to her wigwam and threw herself on a pallet of furs close beside her firepit.

The fire was warm on her flesh, but her heart was cold and aching. She saw no chance at all of getting close to Echohawk, yet she was not going to give up this easily! She would stay at the village indefinitely. She would find a way to make him realize that she was a friend—even more than that. She had felt a bonding between them, that which could develop into something more, now especially since he had admitted to having felt a difference in hers and Nee-kah's presences when they had taken turns sitting with him.

"I know he doesn't hate me," she cried to herself. "He just wants to so badly, he won't allow himself to give me a chance!"

When she heard hoofbeats passing by just outside of her wigwam, Mariah went listlessly to the entrance flap, lifted it, and peered out. She wiped tears from her eyes as she watched Echohawk riding by, flanked on each side by two braves, who were keeping a close eye on him, lest he should start to fall from the horse in his weakness.

A deep sadness engulfed her as she went back to the fire and sat down beside it. She felt helpless—totally helpless.

Drained of all energy and hope, she stretched out beside the fire and fell into a restless sleep, then was drawn quickly awake when she heard a voice that was familiar to her speaking close by outside. She paled and her insides tightened when she realized who was there, in the very same village as she! And thank God Echohawk had gone to his father's burial grounds! For the man he hated with all his might was there, bold as an eagle, mixing with the Chippewa, after having just slain so many!

She went to the entrance flap and scooted it aside only slightly, spying her father still on his stallion, yet most of his identity hidden in the shadows of a large-brimmed hat pulled low over his brow. He wore a large buckskin cape, hiding his lame leg beneath it.

Yes, Mariah thought bitterly, he was very well disguised.

She watched breathlessly as Chief Silver Wing went to her father and stared coldly up at him.

"I do not know you," the chief said, his voice far from friendly. "Why do you come to my village?" He looked cautiously from side to side, at Victor's two companions, realizing that there were others hidden in the forest, for his braves had come with such a warning. The three white men had entered the village only because Chief Silver Wing allowed it, his braves' weapons drawn on them at all times.

"I come in peace. I am searching for my daughter," Victor said, keeping his voice low and unthreatening. "She disappeared several days ago. Is there a chance that you might have seen her?"

Mariah's heart raced, praying that the chief would recall why she had fled her father. And she prayed that the chief would recall how she had been welcomed into the village, almost as one of them, since her act of bravery.

"This daughter," Chief Silver Wing said, his voice steady. "What is her name?"

"Mariah," Victor said softly. "She goes by the name Mariah."

Chief Silver Wing's jaw tightened as he recalled how Nodin had spoke so unfavorably of such a father, and how she had fled his wrath. "*Gah-ween,* no, I do not know of such a person named Mariah," he said, the lie coming easy across his lips. "Now leave, white man. You have no cause to be here."

Victor glared down at the chief for a moment, then wheeled his horse around and rode briskly away.

Mariah went limp with relief. When Nee-kah came into the wigwam and lunged into Mariah's arms, she clung to her friend, feeling blessed for having found someone so compassionate, when in truth, it could have been so different. These Chippewa could have burned her on a stake, or could have gladly handed her over to her father, to rid themselves of her.

Instead, they were protecting her as though she were truly one of them.

She clung to Nee-kah, hoping that Echohawk would eventually feel the same about her.

10

An able man shows his spirit by gentle words
and resolute actions; he is neither hot nor timid.
—Chesterfield

Several Days Later

The day was pleasantly warm, even though the trees had changed to marvelous shades of gold, russet, and crimson. To bide time until she could find out where Echohawk had gone for target practice, Mariah was with Nee-kah and several other Indian women on a root-digging expedition, helping to collect roots to dry for the upcoming winter's use.

As she trod through the forest, Nee-kah at her side, Mariah became lost in thought. She had decided never to give up on her promise that she would find a way to make wrongs right for Echohawk. Sitting vigil at his side while he had been recovering had not been enough, it seemed. Once he had recovered enough to be alone, to do things as he liked, and at his own pace, he did not allow her near him.

Yet Mariah did not take that too personally. He had not allowed anyone to be with him in his time of awkwardness while trying to learn again how to survive in everyday ritual and to aim accurately at a target with impaired eyes. True, he had refused to let her become his eyes, but he had also refused trusted braves who had offered their services.

"No-din, we Chippewa are constantly aware of the need of conservation," Nee-kah said, quickly wrenching Mariah from her thoughts. "When we gather roots, some plants are left for seed. Earth is mother, who furnishes the food, and we Chippewa are considerate not to leave her scarred." She paused and brushed away a string of cobweb as it floated just in front of her face, one of the aggravations of autumn. "A few berries are always left on bushes for birds and squirrels and other animals," she further explained. "We never forget that the animals are the future food for our people."

"That is such a lovely way of explaining it," Mariah said, shifting her basket from one hand to the other. "I am discovering that the Chippewa are quite artistic, not only in designs I have seen on their clothes and dwellings but also in expressing their thoughts."

Nee-kah's lips parted to talk some more, but she giggled when one of the young boys accompanying their mothers on the outing sneaked up behind her and hit the underside of the basket she was carrying, dumping the roots she had gathered, then went to Mariah and did the same.

"Why, he's a little scalawag, isn't he?" Mariah said, giggling as she looked down at her spilled roots, then at the lad as he scampered away, soon spilling another woman's basket.

Nee-kah turned to Mariah, eyeing her questioningly. "Scalawag?" she said, an eyebrow forked. "I know many words of your language, but never have I heard that strange-sounding word before."

Mariah knelt to the ground and began scooping up roots, placing them back in her basket. "It has the same meaning as 'rascal,' which suggests mischievousness. I would say that little brave is one of the most mischievous boys I have ever seen." She glanced over at the boy, whose mother had just caught up with him, scolding him. "A scalawag," she murmured, laughing softly. "But cute."

She helped Nee-kah gather her spilled roots, then her smile faded and she rose slowly back to her feet, stunned to see how the small brave was being reprimanded. His mother had placed him in a basket cradle, tied him into it, then stuck the point of the frame into the ground.

"The poor child," Mariah gasped, paling.

"He will not dump any more baskets," Nee-kah said, shrugging. "We can now finish gathering our roots beneath the trees without further annoyances from the . . ." She gazed over at Mariah, screwing her face up into a curious look. "What was the word, No-din, that you used to describe his behavior?"

Mariah gazed a moment longer at the child, who was crying fitfully, then over to Nee-kah, knowing that this was just another custom that she would learn to accept. "Scalawag," she said, pronouncing the word slowly.

Nee-kah placed her hand on her abdomen. "I must be sure that my son or daughter is not a scalawag," she said, giggling.

"I'm sure mine will be," Mariah said, laughing softly. "I would play with and torment a child with my own mischievous ways. The poor child would not be able ever to have a solemn moment."

Mariah's laughter faded, her thoughts catapulted back to Echohawk. Loving him so much, and missing him terribly, she allowed herself to wonder how it might be to have his children, should she ever be given the chance. His handsomeness would surely transfer into any child borne of him.

A son.

Ah, a son with a copper skin and eyes of midnight would be such a wonder, such a joy, to experience!

And a daughter. How beautiful a daughter by him would be!

She glanced over at Nee-kah, seeing her utter loveliness. It would be wonderful to have a daughter that looked exactly like her and had the same generous, sweet personality. . . .

She was brought back to reality when out of nowhere a lone buffalo wandered into the area, way too close to the child. The boy's eyes caught sight of it, elevating his crying to something piercing, fright evident in the child's huge dark eyes.

"*Gah-ween,* no!" the mother screamed, dropping her basket to the ground, rushing toward her son as the buffalo began wandering even closer to the screaming child.

Mariah watched with horror, stifling a scream when the buffalo bent low over the boy, eye to eye, nose to nose.

The boy's mother kept running, waving her arms and screaming at the bull. Then she stopped and gasped, horrified as the bull suddenly thrust out its massive tongue and licked the boy's face.

Mariah leapt up and ran toward the boy, then stopped, dismayed when the buffalo sauntered away, soon out of sight.

Her shoulders relaxed and she inhaled a nervous breath when the mother released the child from his prison, holding him in her arms, hugging him tightly.

"Nee-kah has never seen such a sight," Nee-kah said, stepping up to Mariah's side. "I thought the boy would be killed. The Great Spirit must have touched the buffalo's heart, making him love the Chippewa, instead of hate. The Great Spirit will now also look over the buffalo and allow no arrows or bullets to pierce its flesh."

The sound of gunfire carrying on the wind made Mariah's heart skip a beat. She glanced quickly in the direction of the sound, hearing another gunshot, and realized that, unaware, she had found the place where Echohawk had chosen to do his target practicing.

"*Mah-szhon,* go to him," Nee-kah said, placing a gentle hand on Mariah's arm. "I know that it has been hard not to."

"Would you really mind?" Mariah said anxiously, looking down at her basket of roots, then back up at Nee-kah. "Have I gathered enough roots? I want to play a beneficial role in your village. I do not want to just take, and not give."

"You have given of yourself in many ways," Nee-kah said, smiling softly at Mariah. "It is my people who still owe you so much."

Mariah's eyes wavered and she looked away from Nee-kah, guilt awash throughout her again as she recalled the bloody massacre and her part in it. She feared the day that Nee-kah and her people would discover the truth. They would then regret all of the praise they had bestowed upon her.

But this was now. Echohawk was near. And even though he had forbidden her to accompany him, she could not stay away now that she was so close.

Nee-kah took Mariah's basket. "Go," she said, nodding toward the repeated gunfire. "If you do not feel comfortable letting him realize you are there, at least watch Echohawk and see how he fares today with his practicing." She frowned, sadness heavy in her eyes. "I so fear for him if he cannot find any accuracy with his weapons. He has always been a proud man. And he has the need to regain that pride."

"If only he would allow me to help him," Mariah said, frustrated. "I would so enjoy being the one who helped him regain some of his confidence, even if he can't see clearly enough to shoot as well as he did before . . . before . . . the attack."

"He would not even allow any braves to accompany him today," Nee-kah said, sighing heavily. "This, too, is a part of that pride. He wants to prove that he can fend for himself, totally."

"Then I shall just go and watch," Mariah said, although she wanted far more than that. She hungered to hear him ask her to stand at his side—be his eyes. It would be a fair exchange, she thought to herself, for he had her heart!

"Go with care," Nee-kah said, leaning a kiss to Mariah's cheek.

"*Mee-gway-chee-wahn-dum,* thank you," Mariah said, then began running softly in the direction where she had heard the gunfire, which had now ceased, troubling her. She feared that she had dallied too long and that he had ceased with his practicing, already moving back toward the village.

Breathlessly she continued onward, then stopped with a start. Up ahead, through a clearing in the trees, she caught her first sight of Echohawk. The reason she had not heard any more gunfire was that he was now practicing with a bow and arrows.

She crept closer and hid behind a tree only a few yards away, watching with an anxious heart as he shot one arrow after another at the remains of a weathered buffalo skull positioned in the fork of a tree.

She ached for him when he missed the skull altogether each time he shot at it, but was proud of him when this did not dissuade him from trying again. A determined man, he kept notching his arrows onto the string of his bow, continuously shooting.

Mariah moved closer, her moccasins silent on the thick grass, until she stood within only footsteps of Echohawk. She was afraid that with his weakened eyes, his sense of hearing might be better and that he might realize that she was there.

But so intent was he on practicing, he still did not know that she was there.

Mariah stood her ground and continued to admire Echohawk more and more by the minute for his determination and endurance.

Ah, but wasn't he handsome! she marveled to herself, as though this were the first time she had set eyes on him. He wore a breechclout and moccasins, revealing all his muscles and the sleekness of his copper chest and broad shoulders. Held by a beaded headband, his raven-black hair framed his face and was worn loosely to his shoulders, occasionally lifting from his shoulders to flutter in the gentle breeze. His jaw and sculptured lips were tight. His midnight-black eyes were mystically beautiful, which made Mariah even more regretful over his sight having been impaired.

Realizing that she was getting too caught up in the wonders of this man, Mariah wrenched her eyes away from him, swallowing hard. She knew that if she allowed herself the feelings of a woman, which had for so long been denied her by her ruthless father, she could love this handsome Chippewa with all her heart.

Being swept up too much in feelings that were all but forbidden to her, Mariah turned to leave, but was stunned at what she found approaching, its narrow gray eyes on Echohawk.

A wolf!

And she could see by the slaver of its jaws that it was not just any wolf.

This animal was rabid!

She glanced from the wolf to Echohawk, then back at the wolf, realizing that Echohawk was not aware of the wolf's presence, no more than he had been of her scrutiny. And even if Echohawk had been aware of the wolf stalking him, he surely would not be able to see well enough to kill it before it leapt on him!

Without further thought, knowing what she must do, Mariah made a mad dash for Echohawk's rifle, lunged for it, and aimed it at the wolf, shooting it between the eyes just as it was getting ready to make its final approach on Echohawk. She watched wild-eyed as the impact of the bullet caused the wolf's body to lurch wildly in the air, then fall dead to the ground.

Startled by the rifle fire, Echohawk whirled around, and when he saw the hazy shadow of Mariah standing there, he dropped his bow and arrow to the ground and lunged for her, tackling her by the ankles. As she fell to the ground, the rifle fell out of her hands, and she soon found herself pinned to the ground, Echohawk atop her.

"Your aim was bad," he growled, leaning his face down into hers. "Why did you fire upon me? What enemy of mine are you?"

"I am not your enemy, Echohawk!" Mariah cried, her heart pounding, her wrists paining her where he so unmercifully gripped them. "It is I, No-din, Echohawk. I . . . I . . . was not shooting at you. I shot and killed a wolf that was stalking you. It was rabid, Echohawk! Rabid!"

"No-din?" Echohawk gasped, releasing her wrists. "You fired the weapon? You say that you fired upon a wolf?"

"*Ay-uh,* yes," Mariah said, her voice drawn. "I came to . . . to watch you practice. You did not know that I was here." She paused, her pulse racing at the nearness of him. That she was with him at all made her heart hammer almost out of control. Never had his lips been so close! She could even feel the heat of his breath upon her face, warming her insides into something deliciously magical.

"Nor did you know that the wolf was there," she quickly added. "Had I not been here, Echohawk, you would even now be the victim of the wolf's rabid bites."

Echohawk could not find the words to explain his feelings at this moment. He was torn between anger at her for not honoring his wish to be alone in his disgrace, not being able to fire a weapon at a target accurately, and gratefulness that she had cared enough to defend him, even though, had she missed the wolf, it could have turned on her and torn her to shreds.

And he was stunned at her ability to kill the wolf in the face of danger. He was used to men rescuing women—not women rescuing men. Although his wife had been a woman of gentleness and sweetness, he had always admired a woman who possessed grit. A woman of fire!

No matter, perhaps, if her skin was white. . . .

"No-din, I am forever in your debt," Echohawk said softly, yet not venturing to rise away from her. His heart was pounding as though someone was within his chest beating a drum. This woman with the sweet voice, and gentle, caring heart, and skin that was as soft as all snows in the winter, had been slowly capturing his heart as she had sat at his bedside. And the feeling was no less now that she was here, her body captured beneath his, at his mercy.

He became annoyed and frustrated, so wanting to see the face of this woman, and knowing that he could not.

Would he ever be able to? he agonized to himself.

Was he blinded for life?

Yet wasn't it best that he couldn't see her face?

He reminded himself that No-din was white, born into this world of those who were the Chippewa's natural enemies.

"You owe me nothing, Echohawk, for what I have just done for you," she murmured, guilt plaguing her again, for if he only knew the truth, he would see that it was she who was forever in *his* debt. Oh, but she did owe him so much!

"No-din," Echohawk said, sliding away from her and helping her to her feet. "Woman of the wind. Such a beautiful name." He reached a hand to her face, sending waves of desire crashing through Mariah. His fingers moved gently over her features. "You feel as though you are as beautiful as your name. Your features are delicate. Your lips are as soft as a rose petal . . ."

Echohawk could not deny to himself that he was intoxicated by Mariah. She had proved that she was indeed a friend, perhaps even more. He drew her into his arms and with trembling lips kissed her heatedly.

Mariah was taken off-guard by the suddenness of the kiss, momentarily stealing her breath away. But having wanted this for so long, and soon overcome by a sweet, unbearable desire, she twined her arms around his neck and returned the kiss with a passion that she had never known was locked inside her.

And when his hand crept between them and moved down to curve over her breast through her buckskin dress, she was shocked at the intensity of her feelings. It was as though something was melting at the pit of her stomach—such a wonderful, blissful melting that was spreading . . . spreading . . .

And then he was gone from her arms, his back to her, leaving Mariah shaken and staring at him.

"Let us return to my wigwam," Echohawk said thickly. "There we will share a night of talk and pleasure." He turned and faced her, reaching out to cup her chin in the palm of his hand. "Until today I have been cold to you. No matter that you had sat vigil at my side, I still saw you as no better than an enemy. But today that has all changed. You will see. We shall share much that I have been denying myself as well as you."

Mariah started to reply, but her words were stolen from her when he kissed her again, making the world spin around, frightening and thrilling her in the same breath and heartbeat. She so badly wanted to be free to love him, but she did not see how that ever could be possible. Not while the threat of unspoken truths lay heavy on her heart.

Echohawk reluctantly released her, a desire gnawing at him that he had denied himself since his wife's burial. Perhaps it was time to place the past in the past, yet something kept nagging at him not to be hasty in this thing that he was feeling for a woman—a white woman who, in truth, should be his enemy.

"No-din, for now you can be my eyes if you wish," Echohawk said, on his knees, trying to find his weapons. "Please help me gather my rifle, bow, and as many arrows as you can find."

Mariah was glad to be able to busy her hands and mind, yet could hardly take her eyes off this man—the man she would never be able to forget, much less deny herself loving.

She began gathering up arrows, feeling his presence behind her before she felt his hand on her wrist. Her body turned to liquid as he drew her up next to him again.

She moved into his embrace and snuggled next to him, glad

that this time he was just wanting to hold her. She knew that if he kissed her again, while she was still recovering from the last kiss, she would be lost to him.

"You feel right in my arms," Echohawk said, stroking her back. "And how do I feel in yours, No-din?"

"Wonderful," Mariah sighed, closing her eyes, relishing the rapture she was feeling. "Oh, so wonderful."

"Then you do care?" Echohawk whispered, turning her face up to his. "You sat by my bed, tending to me, because you truly cared?"

"*Ay-uh,* because I truly cared," Mariah said softly, his eyes, though sightless, mesmerizing her.

"And why is this?" Echohawk asked, puzzling over it. "Why would you?"

"The moment I first saw you I knew that I must do whatever I could to make you get well again," she said.

"Then am I, a Chippewa brave, the first?" he asked. "How can that be? When I touch the features of your face, my fingers tell me that you are beautiful."

"I have never thought of myself as beautiful," Mariah murmured, casting her eyes downward, knowing that her father had tried to make her feel anything but pretty.

"Not only do my fingers tell me that you are," Echohawk said, again moving his fingers over her face, memorizing her every feature, "but also my heart."

Delicious shivers of desire enveloped Mariah, her body screaming for something further, yet not quite understanding what. She was breathlessly glad when he moved away from her.

"Gather up the weapons," he said huskily. "We can share more talk when we return to my wigwam."

Mariah smiled weakly at him, wondering where else their feelings would take them tonight. She was anxious to experience more of these sensations that had been awakened today, to fulfill this need that seemed to be torching her insides into a heated inferno.

11

So sweet the blush of bashfulness,
Even pity scarce can wish it less.

—BYRON

Feeling almost bashful now in Echohawk's presence, her lips still tasting his kiss, Mariah munched away at an apple, while Echohawk sat beside her eating cranberries sweetened with maple sugar.

Since their arrival at his wigwam, there had been a strained silence between them. Mariah's nervousness stemmed from having never experienced feelings of desire before.

Echohawk sucked the tart juices from the cranberries as he swirled them around inside his mouth, his thoughts troubled. He had never wanted to have feelings for a white woman, had even thought it might be impossible, until now.

No-din! He could not get her off his mind. She had proved her loyalty to him in more ways than one.

And she had responded to his kiss as one does who is in love.

Yet he kept reminding himself that *ay-uh,* yes, she *was* white. He did not see how it could be wise to reveal to her his true feelings for her.

"Tell me something about your family," Mariah blurted out, surprised herself by the suddenness of her decision to break the silence between them.

And to ask about his family, when she already knew the fate of his father!

How could she?

But she did not know about a wife.

A mother.

Perhaps even children?

Echohawk turned to face Mariah, again regretting not being able to see her face—a face that he knew must be beautiful and alluring. He so badly wanted to run his fingers along her delicate features again, but thought better of it, remembering how touching her had affected him.

Until he could resolve within his heart and consciousness this fear of allowing himself to love a white woman, he must keep his feelings to himself.

"My family?" he said, scooting his birchbark dish aside. He stared into the fire, frustrated anew when he was able to make out only the color and shadows of the dancing flames. "I am the last. There was only one son born to my *gee-bah-bah* and *gee-mah-mah*. And there were no daughters."

"I, too, was an only child," Mariah said, dropping her apple core into the fire. "Throughout my childhood I was very lonely. There were no neighboring children for me to play with. My mother spent time with me until . . . until she died. But after that I was so very much alone."

"You had your father," Echohawk said, turning his eyes to her. "You seem to have spent much time with him. You shot the firearm today with the skills of a man."

"Yes, my father made sure I knew how to shoot weapons so that I could always defend myself in the Minnesota wilderness," Mariah said, realizing that she was sounding bitter, and unable not to. Whenever she thought of her father and how little love he had given her through the years, she could not help but be filled with a strange, painful longing. "He also taught me how to ride a horse. But that was the only sort of companionship I ever had with him. Other than that, I had to fend for myself."

"And that is why you fled from him?" Echohawk asked, forking an eyebrow. "Because you were *nah-szhee-kay-wee-zee*, lonely? Because you needed more than what he had given you?"

Mariah's eyes wavered as she looked slowly over at him. She swallowed hard, afraid that this conversation was leading to too much that was dangerous to reveal. "Yes," she murmured. "I had hoped to begin a new life. I had hoped that

Colonel Snelling and his wife, Abigail, might help me in deciding how this could be done."

Echohawk wanted to tell Mariah that she did not need to ask Colonel Snelling and his wife for guidance. What she needed was a man—a man who would treat her like a princess.

And *he* was that man!

But still he could not find within himself the courage to tell her anything of the kind, especially since he still had so much to sort out within his own mind and life.

"And when will you travel on to Fort Snelling?" he said instead.

Mariah tensed at this question she did not have an answer to. In truth, she never wanted to go to Fort Snelling at all. She wanted to find a way to resolve all her differences with Echohawk and stay with him. Forever! She had found in him everything that she could ever desire in a man.

"I have asked Chief Silver Wing if I can stay awhile longer in his village," she said softly. "And since I have no one expecting me at Fort Snelling, I would like to stay even longer than first anticipated. Nee-kah has become a special friend, something that I have never had. And . . . and . . ."

"And in me you see a special friendship also?" Echohawk said, having to force himself not to reach out to touch her.

"*Ay-uh,* yes," she murmured, having to force herself not to reach out and touch him. She even had to fight back the urge to scoot over next to him, to snuggle. Within his arms she had found such a wonderful, blissful peace. They were so strong, so comforting. This was something quite new to her, since her father had never afforded her a single hug.

"You speak the Chippewa word 'yes' quite excellently," Echohawk said, chuckling. "Nee-kah has told me that you are an astute student."

"My father taught me many words of your people. I have enjoyed being taught more of your language and also your customs," Mariah said, picking up a stick, idly stirring the cold ashes at the sides of the fire. She glanced over at him. "Echohawk, I truly love everything about your people."

Echohawk's heart soared with this knowledge. If things

could work out between them, she had already taken her first steps to becoming Chippewa!

And she had done this willingly.

"That is good," he said, trying to hold back any excitement that he feared might be there, evident in his voice.

"Echohawk, you did not tell me much about your family," Mariah said, her voice filled with caution, yet needing to know about his love life.

"There is no more to tell," he said, his jaw tightening. "There is no wife. There are no children. My mother died many winters ago after wasting away with some strange coughing disease. My father and I—we were quite alone in the world, except for the love and devotion of our people."

Mariah smiled sweetly over at him, her heart filled with delight to know that, indeed, there was no wife, yet finding the fact hard to understand, since he was so handsome, so virile.

But perhaps he had chosen to center his life around his people. And if so, would he truly ever find room for her inside his heart?

His kiss had revealed that he wanted her, yet since they had returned to his wigwam he had not made any more overtures toward her. There seemed to be something there, stopping him, just as there were her own doubts there, plaguing her and keeping her from boldly going to him.

Echohawk rose to his full height and went to the back of the wigwam, searching inside a buckskin bag. He circled his fingers around the flute that he had asked Nee-kah to lend him, then went back and sat down beside Mariah.

"I shall play some tunes for you in a way to repay you for your continued kindnesses to me," he said, positioning his fingers on two of the three holes of the flute.

"How lovely," Mariah said, drawing her legs up before her, circling her arms around them. As he played on the flute, she became mesmerized by the sweetness of the tunes. They were soft and lilting, reminding her of the birds in the trees outside her upstairs bedroom window that she had heard at daybreak in the early spring every year. She had lain there marveling at the sweet melodies, the same as she now marveled at the sounds that Echohawk was creating with the flute.

She sighed as she watched him, wondering how her father could have ever wanted to see him dead. Here was a man who was gentle and tenderhearted. Here was a man who stirred her into feelings that made her heart soar . . .

A commotion outside the wigwam drew Mariah's eyes to the entrance flap, then back to Echohawk as he laid the flute aside and rose to see what was causing the interference.

Mariah rose quickly to her feet and followed him from the wigwam, her eyes widening when she discovered a beautiful horse that had apparently wandered into the village, now standing there as though it belonged.

Echohawk walked over to the horse, his heart pounding, and began running his hands over its withers. He then offered the palm of his hand to the horse for nuzzling.

When the horse did as Echohawk bade, lovingly nuzzling his hand, neighing gently, Echohawk's lips lifted into a quavering, thankful smile. "It *is* Ish-sko-day, Blaze, my horse," he said, placing an arm around the horse's neck, hugging it. "He is not dead and he has found his way back to me. No-din, do you see? Blaze has searched until he found me!"

"I would say that is a miracle," Mariah said, smiling at the man and horse. "I didn't know that animals could be this devoted."

She watched the reunion of "friends," silently recalling how the horses had become so frightened by the gunfire during the raid on Echohawk's people. She could see even now, in her mind's eye, how they had feverishly broken through their protective fence and scattered in all directions. That his horse had found him again, under these circumstances, *could* be no less than a miracle.

"A man is nothing without a devoted horse," Echohawk said, now smoothing his hand across Blaze's rust-colored mane. "Now that I have mine back again, the burdens of that fateful day are lessened inside my heart."

Mariah stepped up next to Echohawk and ran her hands over Blaze's left flank, the fleshy part of the side between the ribs and the hip. She had never seen such an elegant horse. And he was so very, very muscled!

And strangely enough, the horse still wore a saddle—a cushion of leather stuffed with buffalo hair and ornamented with porcupine quills.

A rope around the underjaw seemed to be there to take the place of a bit.

"He is a magnificent horse, Echohawk," she murmured. "No wonder you are proud. I'm so glad that he found you."

"Blaze is of the wild breed of Mexican horses," he explained. "Long ago, during a raid on the Sioux to reclaim things stolen from my people, I stole this horse. The Sioux had stolen it themselves from some other tribe on lands far from the Minnesota wilderness."

"I would love to ride the horse," Mariah said, thrilling at the thought. "Perhaps one day soon . . . ?"

"Ay-uh," Echohawk said, taking Blaze's rope, leading him to the corral. "And it will be an interesting experience for you. I do not even need reins while on Blaze. He requires no guidance. He knows my every mood. He is even so accustomed to my silent commands that he could lead me into battle without any prompting from me. His skills are honed to such a degree that I can depend on him at all times, for anything."

"That he has found his way to you today is proof of that, it seems," Mariah said, opening the gate to the corral and stepping aside as Echohawk led Blaze in with the other grazing horses. She gazed warmly up at Echohawk, wishing that this closeness to him would never end. She could not deny that she felt as though she were becoming entwined within a golden web of magic, and she would not—*could* not—give this up. She would have to find a way to make him understand and forgive her role in the attack against his people.

Yet, while doing so, she had to find a way to protect her father. Although she had grown to loathe him, she did not want to see him harmed.

She did not want to see him die!

Yes, she concluded to herself, she had to find a way to

resolve all of these differences, first in her heart, then with Echohawk.

She helped Echohawk feed and water Blaze, and then went back to Echohawk's wigwam with him, going only as far as the entrance flap. When he didn't invite her inside, Mariah felt awkward and a little embarrassed that she had actually wanted him to.

"I guess I'd best go," she said softly. "I don't want to wear out my welcome."

Her breath escaped her in a slight gasp when he placed a hand at the nape of her neck and drew her close to him. Scarcely breathing, she gazed with a building passion into his dark eyes. His lips so close, his hands so gentle—her insides tingled and her heart cried out to be kissed.

Disappointing her, he then turned away from her, his brow furrowed with a frown. "It is time to retire for the evening," he said smoothly. "Tomorrow there will be more shooting practice, but this time for live prey. I must rest for this outing."

Mariah placed a hand on his arm. "May I go with you this time?" she asked, her voice a soft pleading. "As I said before, Echohawk, I am quite skilled with firearms. I would enjoy the hunt. Please allow it?"

Echohawk turned back to her, his eyes squinting as once again he tried to see her features, dying a slow death inside when again he could not. "It is not a usual thing, a woman hunting with a man, but *ay-uh,* you can join me," he said, nodding. "It is good—these times with you."

"I am so glad you feel that way," Mariah said, her knees weakening as he ran his fingers along the curve of her chin and over her cheeks. "I so enjoy being with you also, Echohawk."

He drew away from her, his jaw tight. "You go now," he said softly. "You rest also. It has been a long day, has it not?"

"It has been a glorious day," Mariah said, daring to lean up and brush a quick kiss across his lips. Not giving him time to respond, she turned and ran from him toward her own wigwam, almost overwhelmed by her erratic heartbeats.

She looked to the darkened sky. "Lord, I love him," she cried to herself. "What am I to do? I love him!"

* * *

Putting his full weight on his cane, Victor Temple limped slowly up the stairs to the second story of his house, defeat slouching his shoulders even more than usual.

Weary from the long ride, during which he had not found Mariah, he felt empty, clean through to the core. Until now, when he was forced to believe that he might never see her again, he had not realized just how much he loved her.

And recalling how brusquely he had treated her at times, he did not expect her to have even an inkling of how he truly felt about her. The purpose first and foremost on his mind had been to protect her from becoming like her mother.

But now he felt that he had been wrong. He should have put more trust in her.

Yet hadn't he trusted his wife? When he had discovered her infidelities, all of his trust in mankind had been stolen away, it seemed.

Stopping at the head of the staircase, he turned solemn eyes to Mariah's bedroom. Tears filled his eyes, in regret at what he had forced on her before leaving for the Indian attack. He had given her just cause to hate him, that was for sure!

Limping to her bedroom, his fingers clasped hard to the handle of the cane, he stepped just inside the room and saw her long strands of hair lying across the foot of the bed in the dimming light of evening.

A sob grabbed at his chest as he went to the bed and picked up some of her hair and held it to his cheek. "Soft," he whispered. "So thick and soft. Why did I cut it? Why?"

Sitting down on the edge of the bed, he gathered up the rest of her hair and held it to his chest and slowly rocked back and forth, immersed in thoughts of the daughter that he had loved, perhaps too much. If he had not loved her so much, he would have been more generous with her. He would have given her more freedom.

"And now I will never be given the chance to make it up

to her," he said, almost choking on another sob. "I'm sorry, Mariah. So damn sorry."

He stretched out on the bed and closed his eyes. "Mariah, Mariah . . ." he whispered until he fell asleep.

12

Thou waitest late, and com'st alone,
When woods are bare and birds are flown—
—BRYANT

The day was brilliant with sunlight, the air sporting only a slight chilling breeze. It was a fun and carefree day for Mariah as she stood beside Echohawk in a meadow spotted with autumn wildflowers, amazed at his quickly improving skills with a rifle, though he was still half-blinded.

She watched breathlessly as he reloaded his rifle, then aimed and shot at the blue-winged teal, the most delicious of feathered creation, as the flock flew past. When one fluttered to the ground lifeless, the others changed directions in unison, yet did not immediately fly away from the danger of more gunfire. They continued to soar overhead, seemingly oblivious of the continuing threat.

Echohawk went to the fallen bird and picked it up by its legs and carried it to his horse, securing it with a rope behind the saddle. "As you see, though my eyesight has been impaired by the white man's blow to my head, I shall master again my weapons," he said as Mariah stepped up beside him. He gazed into the sky, seeing only smears where there were birds—the teals still enjoying sweeping high, then low across the wide stretches of the meadow.

"I am so proud for you," Mariah said, smiling at him, trying not to think about the man responsible for his dilemma.

Her father!

She knew that she would never wholly relax until somehow she settled things with Echohawk about her true identity.

"You see how the birds fly high, then low?" Echohawk said, resting the barrel of his rifle in the crook of his left arm.

"It is best not to fire upon the blue-winged teal if they are flying high in the autumn of the year, for they are fattened on the wild rice of the river and would burst open upon falling."

"I went on hunts with my father often, but mostly for animals, not birds," Mariah said, feeling sad when she gazed at the beautiful thing hanging lifeless on Blaze. "It seems such a pity to kill something so . . . so . . . beautiful."

"When you live solely off the land and animals, as the Chippewa have for generation after generation, you close your eyes to the beauty of those birds and animals that you kill," Echohawk said softly. "You look at them as food for your people, for their survival."

He frowned down at Mariah. "Until the white people came to our land, there was not such a struggle each day to find food," he said, his words edged with bitterness. "Each day there are fewer animals, for the white trappers have used steel teeth in which to trap the innocent animals, and not only a few daily. They trap many each day. Soon, even, some of the animals that roam the lands today will become extinct. Then what of the red man?"

Mariah's lips parted, and she blanched, knowing exactly what he was referring to. Her father and his men moved through the forest daily, taking from it what they could, not stopping to think about the harm in killing in numbers.

They wanted the pelts, at any cost.

"Let us travel onward," Echohawk said, offering Mariah a hand. "There is some place I would like to take you."

Mariah sighed shakily as she let him help her into the saddle, then relished the solid strength of his arm as he placed it around her waist and settled into the saddle behind her.

Echohawk took the reins and wheeled his steed around, soon galloping across the sun-drenched meadow. They rode for some time; then he drew rein at the foot of a butte.

"We must go the rest of the way on foot," Echohawk said, dismounting, then assisting Mariah from the saddle. "Up there," he said, pointing at the high butte overhead. "What I want to share with you is on the butte, a place of peace, where land and sky become as one."

"What is it you wish to show me?" Mariah asked, falling into step beside him as they started walking up a narrow path.

Echohawk did not respond. He moved determinedly upward. A strange sort of haunting in his eyes caused Mariah to become apprehensive. What had he so adamantly chosen to show her?

She quickly reminded herself that she had thus far placed much trust in him, as well as the rest of the Chippewa, and hoped that such trust was warranted.

Yet now, with their adventurous day marred by his indifferent, cold attitude, she was not sure if she had trusted too quickly!

What if he had discovered who she was and planned to shove her off the butte as payment for her treachery. It would be so simple for him to lead her into a trap!

But her worries were cast into the wind, so it seemed, when they reached the top of the butte. Where the land leveled off, her breath was stolen away when she saw the site of many graves lying side by side.

"My fallen people's resting places," Echohawk said, looking glumly down at the mounds of earth.

He walked to a grave marked with a cedar post and knelt beside it, placing a hand on the mound of earth. "This is my father's," he said, his voice breaking.

"If only it were I lying there instead of my beloved father!" Echohawk said, his voice filled with anguish. "My heart cries out for him both night and day. Never were a son and father so close! So devoted!"

As Mariah watched Echohawk despairing so deeply over the loss of his father, she covered her mouth with a hand, stifling a sob behind it, regret and guilt fusing within her. She wanted to shout to Echohawk that she was sorry for his distress. She had never had such a shared love with a father, and now that she knew such things could exist, she ached inside for having participated in destroying that special bonding.

Echohawk turned to Mariah and offered her a hand. "Come," he said. "Kneel beside me. Let my father feel your presence at my side. Because of you, his son is still alive."

His words, his trust in her, made Mariah's heart feel as though it were tearing in shreds. But she had to put on a good front, for even though he could not see the pained expression on her face, he would be able to hear it in her voice. This was not the time to reveal truths to him. Not while he was at his father's grave, where only peaceful thoughts should be shared.

But the fact that he was presenting her as someone special—as someone who had saved him—made her feel ashamed. His father was dead because of *her* father. What a travesty she was acting out! What a sham!

Having no choice but to do as he asked, no matter how torn she was inside over being there in the presence of so many that had died because of her dreadful father, Mariah knelt beside Echohawk, her eyes wavering, her heart pounding.

"I cannot see, but on my father's grave marker should be emblazoned his ranks and achievements," he said, reaching to run his fingers across the engraved letterings. "Also there should be three black emblems posted there, representing the three scalps that he had taken from evil white men."

He doubled his hand into a fist and his jaw tightened angrily. "Soon I will present my father with, not one more scalp, but four. The scalp of the evil white man who led the recent raid, that of the young lad who rode with the raiding party, the renegade Sioux White Wolf's scalp, and that of the man with yellow eyes who also took much from me, even my heart! Someday, somehow, these scalps will sway in the wind from my father's grave post!"

Mariah grabbed at her stomach, suddenly ill, Echohawk's warnings reaching clean to her soul, for although he did not know it, her scalp was one of those he sought!

"Please take me back to your village," she said, stumbling quickly to her feet. She grabbed at Echohawk as he rose quickly beside her. "I . . . I . . . feel ill, Echohawk. I . . . need to lie down."

Echohawk placed his hands to her shoulders and steadied her. "Speaking of scalps was unpleasant to you, and unwise of me for being so thoughtless," he said gently. "I am sorry, Nodin. It was not my intention to upset you."

"Echohawk, it's not so much that," Mariah said, sighing deeply. "I . . . I just never thought *you* could be capable of . . . of scalping. That is a savage act. You are anything but savage!"

"Killing innocent Chippewa is savage!" he defended hotly.

He spun away from her and began working his way down the side of the hill. When Mariah saw his feet slip, endangering him, she ran to him and placed her hand at his elbow, which he just as quickly wrenched away from her.

"I did not mean to use the word 'savage,' " she tried to explain. "And I did not use it to describe you, Echohawk. Only the act of scalping."

"Many white people have referred to the Indians as savages," Echohawk grumbled, walking steadily downward. "They should look in mirrors more often! They then would see who is the true savage!"

Not to be dissuaded, and not wanting him to stay angry at her, Mariah grabbed his hand and would not give up her hold when he tried to jerk it free. She forced him to stop and turn to her. "I'm sorry, Echohawk," she murmured. "Please forgive me? I would never do anything to hurt you, nor your feelings. I . . . I think too much of you *and* your people. Have I not proved this to you by staying instead of going on to Fort Snelling?"

"I have wondered about this decision of yours," Echohawk said, his voice wary. "But of course you know that. I have voiced this aloud to you more than once."

"Then why question it again?" she murmured, her pulse racing as she moved closer to him. "Echohawk, we have found something special between us. Please, let's not do anything to jeopardize it."

Echohawk reached his free hand out to her, placing it on her cheek. "*Ay-uh,* there is something special between us," he said hoarsely. "But before it grows any stronger, there is much I must resolve inside my heart. Also, yourself. Do you not have much troubling you, that you have not spoken aloud to me? I have felt it in the hesitation of your voice at times."

Mariah's face paled at the thought that he might be astute

enough to catch her moods, which she had tried to keep hidden from him.

"But of course I have been torn about many things of late," she murmured. "I am eighteen and I have just left home. Would you not feel somewhat unsettled were it you having made such a decision about family? I have separated myself from all of my life as I have known it. I have found a different way of life with your people—and am dismayed that I am able to accept it so easily, even enjoy it. So do you see why you felt my moods? Echohawk, I have not learned how to master them. Perhaps I never shall."

"Nor have I, mine," he said, in his mind's eye recalling so many things of his past that were gone from him forever. A wife. An unborn child. A mother. And now a father. "I, too, have things to resolve within my mind and heart. And I plan to resolve some of them today."

He stepped closer to Mariah and framed her face between his hands, drawing her lips to his. "You are so much what I desire in a woman," he whispered against her lips. "This is a part of what I must find answers to today. I will return you to my village and then I shall leave again, to go and commune, alone, with the Great Spirit. He will guide me. He knows everything about everything. He rules over all."

His mouth covered Mariah's lips with a gentle kiss that left her weak. She drew a ragged breath when he drew away from her, her eyes filled with a soft wonder.

* * *

Mariah sat in Nee-kah's wigwam, trying to be an alert student as Nee-kah explained about the storage of food, but her mind kept wandering to Echohawk. He had been gone into the depths of the forest for several hours. The sky had just darkened into night, wolves baying at the full moon an eerie sound in the distance.

"No-din, the meat from the deer should be sliced up thin and hung up to dry in the sun," Nee-kah said, quite aware that Mariah's mind was elsewhere. Her thoughts were clearly with

Echohawk, who had left the village to commune with the Great Spirit. And from past experiences Nee-kah knew that Echohawk could be gone for days. As troubled as he was, he would not return until he had answers that would guide him into right decisions about his future, about his people, and about No-din.

"No-din, you break up the bones of the buffalo and boil them to get the grease out," she explained softly, trying to reclaim Mariah's attention. "You take the large intestine and stuff it with a long piece of meat, raw. This whole thing is then boiled and eaten . . . No-din!" Nee-kah said, moving to her knees in front of Mariah, blocking her view of the fire that she had been so intensely staring at. "Our teachings are over for the night. Let us join our people outside by the fire. They are singing. Do you not hear them? They are singing in an effort to lift the spirits of those who have recently lost so much." She took Mariah by the hand. "Come, No-din. Let us join them. You need some uplifting yourself."

Mariah jumped with a start, having been shaken from her reverie by Nee-kah's determination. "What did you say?" she said, her voice lilting, her eyes wide.

"Let us join those outside by the fire," Nee-kah urged, yanking on Mariah's hand as she rose to her feet. "We will sing. We will be happy!"

Mariah forced a smile and went outside with Nee-kah and sat down beside the fire with the rest of the people. Yet she could not help but glance toward the forest, wondering when Echohawk would be back, and what decisions he might have reached. She prayed to herself that the Great Spirit did not give him too many answers—those that could condemn her in his eyes.

* * *

In a place of serenity, where the stars and moon reached down through the umbrella of trees overhead, Echohawk placed tobacco on a rock as a tribute to the Great Spirit, begging the Great Spirit for guidance.

"O Great Spirit, what am I to do?" Echohawk said in a

troubled whisper, lifting his eyes to the heavens, yet seeing with his impaired eyesight only the blur of the moon smeared across the sky in strange, quivering whites. "Am I selfish for thinking of a woman now, at a time when my thoughts should only be on my people's sorrows? I cannot get her off my mind! She is there. Day and night. I have not wanted a woman as much since my beloved wife departed from this earth."

He swallowed hard, then continued voicing his concerns in agonizing whispers. "I do not want to love a white woman!" he despaired. "In my mind and heart I despise the white race for the cruelty inflicted on my people. Yet No-din is separate from those evil ones! She is not responsible for any of my hurts. Yet somehow I cannot erase from my mind that she is an enemy because her skin is the color of those who are!"

Not getting any signs from the heavens which could give him answers and direction, he spoke awhile longer, telling his sorrows to the rock and stars, then stretched out on the ground, fatigued.

"*Wah-bungh,* tomorrow," he whispered to himself. "I shall receive answers tomorrow. I shall stay and wait for those answers!"

A noise behind him drew him to his feet. He whirled around, wary. "Who is there?" he asked guardedly.

"It is I, Proud Thunder," one of his most valiant braves said. "Echohawk, it is with a sad heart that upon our return from the hunt we braves found our ravaged village. We have searched for you and our people. We have finally found you. Tell us, Echohawk. What of your father, my chief? Echohawk, the Great Spirit has led us to you. We are all here to listen."

Echohawk reached a hand out and found Proud Thunder's shoulder and clasped his hand to it. "*Ay-uh,* the Great Spirit led you to me tonight," he said softly, marveling over this miracle and feeling guilty that his thoughts only moments ago had been only on No-din!

Not of his people. His braves.

So often of late his thoughts strayed, and always to No-din!

"Proud Thunder," he said firmly, "let me tell you the extent of our people's sorrows."

13

My lips pressed themselves involuntarily to hers—a long, long kiss, burning intense—concentrating emotion, heart, soul, all the rays of life's light, into a single focus.

—Bulwer-Lytton

The wind pushed dark clouds across the autumn sky—a deer paused on a ridge close by. The river was like a clear mirror, the surface only slightly ruffled by the waves made by many canoes slicing through the water, all crewed by women.

Mariah was only half-aware of moving the paddle in and out of the water, Nee-kah sitting beside her in the canoe, doing the same, a woman kneeling at the stern, both paddling and steering the vessel. Mariah's thoughts were not on the chore at hand—the *manomin,* wild rice, that she would soon be helping the Chippewa women to harvest.

Mariah had spent a sleepless night, *still* worrying about Echohawk. And when she had discovered that he had not returned home at all through the night, her worries had increased twofold. She would never forget how defenseless he had been against the rabid wolf that she killed before it got close enough to attack him. Last night the wolves were howling in the distance incessantly. What if they had sniffed out Echohawk while he was absorbed in his meditating?

"Is it not beautiful here in the river, with the autumn foliage reflecting like bursts of sunshine in the water?" Nee-kah said, smiling over at Mariah. "Are you not glad that you came with me? Has it helped get your mind off Echohawk?"

Mariah smiled weakly at Nee-kah, pausing momentarily in her paddling. "It is beautiful here," she murmured. "But, no, it has not gotten my mind off Echohawk. I doubt if anything would." She then added quickly, "I do appreciate you asking me. You are ever so kind, always, to me. I'm not sure if I deserve such a friendship as yours."

"Your friendship is cherished by me, No-din," Nee-kah said, reaching over to place a hand on Mariah's shoulder. "Mine to you is enduring, *ah-pah-nay,* forever."

Mariah's eyes wavered and she looked away from Nee-kah, worrying again about Nee-kah's, reaction when she would one day discover exactly who this "friend" was.

Then she looked slowly back over at Nee-kah. "Mine, also, to you is as enduring," she said, wishing their promises to each other could be true, as everlasting as they both wished.

But too soon so many things could change—especially such friendships.

Her paddle dipped smoothly into the water as they continued traveling upstream between tree-lined banks. The canoes were made with a birchbark box in the middle and used only for the wild-rice harvests, the flails lying in the bottom of the box.

A blue-gray kingfisher that lived along the river, nesting in the banks, swept from a high bank to Mariah's right and hovered above the river. Then he dived into the water, appearing a moment later with a fish struggling in his long black bill.

And then the wild rice came into view, the canoes moving steadily toward it.

"*Ee-nah-bin,* look!" Nee-kah said, her eyes beaming. "Have you ever seen such a sight, No-din? See how the wild rice grows so abundantly in the shallow waters of the river? The plants are so heavy with rice this year! And they are the tallest I have ever seen. They must stand twelve feet above the water."

"Rice is an important food of the Chippewa?" Mariah asked as they finally reached the rice, and along with the other canoes, began poling their vessel among the plants.

"*Ay-uh,* it is a staple food of the Chippewa," Nee-kah said. "It is eaten in a great variety of soups and broths, as a vegetable with fish or meat, boiled on its own, or mixed with maple sugar, or parched. It is a most delicious and versatile food."

Mariah was amazed at how simply the rice was harvested.

The stalks of rice had been tied in bundles during the previous moon. The women had only to bend the rice-laden stalks inboard with their hooked flails, the curved ricing sticks pulling down the stalks so that the heads of the plants hung over the birchbark box in the center of the rice canoe. With a flat flail, Mariah followed Nee-kah's lead and beat the heads until the long needlelike grains spilled into the box.

Mariah was glad to have something productive to do, which, for the moment, did lighten the burden of her worries about Echohawk. She became absorbed in the process of the harvest, now paddling their rice-heavy canoe toward shore.

Once there, the women transferred the rice from their canoes with wooden buckets, then poured the rice into a deerskin-lined hole in the ground, six inches deep and two feet across. The rice was then flailed with curved sticks to loosen the husks. Winnowing was then done by pouring it from a bark tray in a breeze.

The rice was then placed on mats to dry in the sun. After drying for three days, it would be put into a large kettle to parch so that the tough hulls would split open. The women would then take turns tending the fire and stirring the grain so that it would parch evenly.

And again they rowed back to the stalks of rice, and the process was repeated. Even though there was a lot of work involved in collecting and preparing the rice, Mariah was enjoying her day, and for the moment was able to place Echohawk from her mind if not her heart.

* * *

In another part of the forest, Mariah was the center of Echohawk's thoughts. He had directed Proud Thunder and his other braves to Chief Silver Wing's village to rejoin their relatives. A blessed thing, Echohawk had thought upon seeing Proud Thunder, that the Great Spirit would send him in his time of meditation.

During his long vigil in the forest the previous night, he had recalled many things, yet resolved nothing within his troubled heart and mind. He was haunted by his father's words spoken to him over and over again this past year—that it was time for him to take a wife so that a son might be born to him to help ensure the future of his people.

Deep inside himself, where his desires were formed, he knew that he had chosen a woman for a wife—No-din. She was the only woman who stirred his passion since the passing of his lovely wife.

"But why must she be white!" he whispered remorsefully through his clenched teeth, his hands circled into tight fists at his sides.

Then he rose slowly from his prostrate position and took a small buckskin pouch from the waist of his fringed breeches. Again he sprinkled tobacco from it onto a rock, an offering to the Great Spirit. He moved to a kneeling position and raised his eyes to the heavens, his heart pounding. The sighing of pines came to him as the rustle of eagle wings, to help carry his cries to loftier heights. The whispering winds told his tale to the clouds. He then uttered the cry of his soul to the Great Spirit.

"Great Spirit, you who guide my every thought and action, hear my pleas!" he cried. "My heart is heavy! Give me strength and courage to guide my people in this, their time of sorrow. Give me a sign that will free me of my bitterness and allow me to love the white woman without resentment." He bowed his head humbly. "O Great Spirit, I thank you for sending Proud Thunder and my braves to me, but I have waited all night long for another sign. Is there not to be one? Must I return to my dwelling without your blessing? Do I not deserve such a blessing? Am I wrong to ask for so many things?"

A close-by noise, coming from the direction of the river, drew Echohawk's head up. His pulse raced and hope rose within him that the Great Spirit had heard, and had finally sent him a vision.

Suddenly, through the haze of his impaired eyesight, he could see movement ahead. Trembling, he was awe-struck by what was now within the sphere of his vision. He watched breathlessly as his eyes suddenly cleared to see a snow-white doe followed by a fawn of the same color.

Surely it was a vision, for he could not believe that this was truly happening. One moment he was alone, and the next moment he was in the presence of a mystical phenomenon. The creatures were there so suddenly, it seemed that they had come out of the water!

Echohawk slowly pushed himself up to a standing position and stood rooted to the ground, never taking his eyes off the beautiful animals. And he, who had never feared the face of man, was trembling like an aspen with terror!

The animals, seemingly unaware of Echohawk's presence, advanced slowly toward him, and passed so near that he might have touched them with his hand. But transfixed by wonder, he did not attempt it.

Slowly he turned and watched them as they ascended the bank, soon losing sight of them.

When he recovered from the shock, he stretched out his arms after them. "Do not leave me!" he cried. "Come back. Let me see you again!"

Having regained the use of his limbs, he rushed up the bank, but did not see them.

Humbled by the experience, he fell to his knees and smiled as he looked to the heavens. "O Great Spirit, thank you!" he cried, appreciating the meaning of what he had just witnessed. The white doe was No-din and the fawn must represent their future child. He was suddenly feeling great rushes of happiness throughout him. He was free to love—to love No-din!

And freed, also, was he of the other burdens of his heart. He knew now that he had the power—the courage—required of him to guide his people.

And he also knew that in time his eyesight would be restored. Had not the Great Spirit allowed him his eyesight long enough to witness the vision? In due time, when the Great Spirit deemed it necessary, his eyesight would return—to be his forever!

An anxiousness suddenly seized him. "No-din," he whispered, his heart soaring. "I must go to No-din. There is so much to say to her that I was not free to say before."

His chin held high, feeling blessed and guided by the Great

Spirit's power, Echohawk began running in the direction of the village. "No-din will be mine!" he shouted, so that everything would share in his happiness.

He shouted to the wind . . .

the sky . . .

the trees . . .

the forest animals!

* * *

Her arms and back aching from her long day of rice harvesting, Mariah slipped a clean buckskin dress over her head. It fell below her calves, belted at the waist with a beaded thong, a fringe at each end. She pulled on fringed knee-high moccasins resplendent with colorful beads. Her skin smelled clean, like the river, after her bath. Her hair was dripping and fragrant from Nee-kah's precious soap.

After getting dressed, she began running the comb that Nee-kah had lent her through her hair, wincing when again she was reminded of its dreaded length.

Laying the comb aside and picking up a mirror, Mariah began practicing with bloodroot juice, dabbing it onto her cheeks to redden them. She needed to do something to keep her worries about Echohawk from worsening. It was now midday, and still he had not returned. She did not want to envision him lying injured or dead in the midst of the forest. She would not allow herself to conjure up any more fears. He was a man of the forest. He was in tune with all nature, and he knew how to survive within it.

A noise at the entrance flap drew Mariah's eyes away from her reflection in the mirror. An anxious blush, even more red than the juice of the bloodroot that she had dotted onto her cheeks, rose from her neck upward when she found Echohawk standing in the doorway smiling down at her.

"You have returned," Mariah said, moving shakily to her feet. She so badly wanted to go to him and lunge into his arms. She wanted to cling to him and never let him go again. Never had she been as relieved as now. He was alive! He was well!

And he was smiling at her as though all of the burdens that had been troubling him had been lifted!

"*Mah-bee-szhon,* come," Echohawk said, going to her to take her hands. "Come with me to my lodge. There I will say many things to you. There you will have decisions to make and answers to give."

Caught up in an ecstasy that just being with him evoked, and speechless, Mariah nodded and went with him to his wigwam. There she found the air scented sweetly with the perfume of sweet grasses that burned in the embers of his lodge fire. There she found many beautiful pelts strewn around the fire. There she found platters piled high with all sorts of delicacies.

There she found herself being held within Echohawk's arms as he led her down beside the fire, seeing a blissful peace within his eyes and in the soft smile that he gave her.

"We shall eat, and then, No-din, there is so much I wish to say to you," Echohawk said, releasing her from his embrace.

They sat down side by side and ate in silence. Mariah's heart raced excitedly, so happy that Echohawk had reached some sort of peace with his Great Spirit, and within himself. She only wished that she could come to the same sort of peace within her own self!

Her God seemed to be taking longer to answer her prayers than Echohawk's.

After they had eaten their fill, Echohawk lifted Mariah onto his lap, facing him, his hands holding her there at her waist. "No-din, the Great Spirit gave me a vision while in the forest," he said eagerly. "This vision gave me hope—and courage. No-din, I have come away from that vision with a happy heart, one that I wish to share with you for a lifetime."

Mariah's pulse raced and her head was reeling with the wonder of the moment, anxious to hear what else he had to say, yet also fearing it. Because of who she truly was, she had many things to fear in Echohawk's presence.

"No-din, woman of the wind, be the 'flower of my wigwam,' " he said softly.

Mariah was taken aback, not having expected this. She was stunned speechless. Marriage? That was what he meant?

She knew that marriage to him was an impossible dream. She had lied to him about her true identity.

For so many reasons she could not accept a proposal that her very soul cried out for!

"No-din, I love you," Echohawk said, easing her down onto the pelts, moving over her. "My heart has been so lonely. No-din, fill it and my life with your sweetness!"

Before she could refuse Echohawk's proposal, Mariah felt the press of his lips against hers, so warm and soft, yet demanding, for a moment frightening her.

She welcomed the lethargic feeling of floating and swooning, glad to forget everything but Echohawk and the way he made her realize that she was very much a woman.

How fiercely Echohawk wanted Mariah, yet he fought against going too quickly with her. She was inexperienced, hardly more than a girl in her innocence. It was easy to tell that she had not yet been with a man intimately, and he wanted the experience to be something that she looked back on with pleasure. He wanted her to desire such a union as badly as he. Their future would be filled with such moments, for he would not take no for an answer when he again asked her to marry him!

As he continued to kiss her, he slowly snaked his hand up inside her dress and cupped her at the juncture of her thighs, where he could feel the pulsing at the center of her passion. As he began to caress her there, he felt her body tremble, her gasp of alarm against his lips.

But he did not pull his hand away. He continued to gently stroke her, smiling to himself when he felt her relaxing, and now emitting soft sighs against his lips.

Mariah was becoming weak, her senses dazzled by his skills of awakening her to passion. His hand was where no other man's hands had been before, and his other hand—it was lifting her dress slowly up away from her.

She knew that she should stop this madness that had begun between them.

But she was too full of strange, wondrous desire to turn her back on whatever else lay ahead these next wondrous moments with the man that she loved with all of her heart.

Echohawk leaned slightly away from Mariah in order that he could remove her dress. Then, once it was tossed aside and his hands were smoothing over her body, feeling her slim, graceful loveliness with his fingers, excitement leapt inside him. His hands moved to her breasts and cupped them, his lips lowering to a nipple, nipping it with his teeth.

Mariah's heart raced, her breathing almost out of control. She was acutely aware of Echohawk's body as he now knelt beside her and discarded all his clothes. Mariah's face heated with a blush as she gazed down at his manhood, the first time she'd ever seen this part of a man's anatomy.

Something strange happened at the pit of her stomach, as though someone had set a fire within her, when he began to move his hand in slow strokes over his hardness. It was such a seductive sight, and Mariah realized by the way his jaw tightened and the muscles of his legs corded that what he was doing must be intensely pleasurable.

Boldly, as though he silently beckoned her to, Mariah crept to her knees and replaced his hand with hers, her heart leaping when she felt the heat of his velvety shaft, and how it seemed to jump with a life of its own as she began moving her hand on him.

She watched his expression as his eyes closed and his teeth gritted together, wondering how anything could feel that wonderful, to cause such a reaction.

Suddenly Echohawk placed his hands to her shoulders. "*Mee-eewh,* enough," he said huskily. "It is time to share our pleasure. It is time to fit our bodies together as one."

Little stabs of warmth ran through Mariah and she felt a strange new sensation rise in her as his hands slid down her back, cupping her buttocks. Slowly Echohawk laid her down on the soft pelts, then moved over her.

Trembling, she let him part her thighs and caress the damp valley, unleashing waves of weakness in her lower limbs. She was acutely aware of his pulsating hardness, now pressed against her thigh.

And when he parted her legs with a knee and she felt the

first burning touch of his hardness at the center of her passion, she melted into him.

As he slowly entered her, coaxing sweetness from her, Echohawk kissed her again, his mouth forcing her lips apart, his tongue hungrily surging between her teeth.

She felt herself surrendering to him, thrilling to every nuance of his lovemaking. She did not even cry out with the shock of his first plunge inside her. A sharp pain only momentarily robbed her senses of pleasure, before she once again abandoned herself to a wild ecstasy.

Sculpturing himself to her moist body, Echohawk anchored Mariah fiercely still as he pressed endlessly deeper inside her. She knew that the passion he offered her would overshadow any pain that she had felt.

His hands moved down her body and cupped her buttocks, relishing their softness, then urged her hips into his, glad when she strained toward him on her own. Their naked bodies sucked at each other, flesh against flesh in a gentle rhythm.

A surge of ecstasy welled within Mariah, filling her, spilling over and drenching her with a sweet warmth. She twined her arms around Echohawk's neck and clung to him as she felt a great shudder in his loins and then experienced an incredible splash of bliss, crying out at her fulfillment as his body subsided exhaustedly into hers.

Stunned by the intensity of the feelings that had overwhelmed her, like white heat traveling through her veins, she lay within Echohawk's arms, breathing raggedly. She was afraid that if either of them moved, she would discover that all of this had been of her imagination, caused by her longing to be free to love this handsome Chippewa.

But when he stirred and slid away from her, yet only as far as to lie at her side, one of his hands still on one of her breasts as though it belonged there, she realized that, yes, all of this had been real enough.

"My *ee-quay*, woman," Echohawk said, his voice deep and husky. He drew Mariah next to him, her breasts pressed into his hard chest. He ran his fingers along her delicate facial features. "I cannot see you clearly with my eyes, but you are quite real in my arms and in my heart, and that is enough. Stay with me. Warm my bed every night until we are old and gray. Say that you will gladly be my wife."

Mariah was glad that he could not see her at this moment. He would see the tears of regret in her eyes—regret for loving him so much and knowing that he should despise her!

Echohawk saw her hesitation in agreeing to be his wife. He was troubled by this, yet thought that perhaps she was carrying some pain in her heart at leaving her people forever. He would no longer press her for answers. He smiled to himself, knowing there was truly no need. Yet he would give her time to go and release her own sorrows within the peaceful confines of the forest and then reveal to her that she had already become his wife, through their own private ceremony tonight.

They lay within each other's arms, for the moment blissfully content. For Mariah it had been proved tonight that no matter to what lengths her father had gone to turn her into a man, she was every inch a woman. And she owed it all to Echohawk. He had brought out the true woman in her.

And, oh, how she adored him!

14

> Sweet were his kisses on my balmy lips. As are the breezes breath'd among the groves of ripening spices in the height of day.
>
> —Behn

Feeling herself to be part of a magical dream when she awoke in Echohawk's arms at daybreak, Mariah now rode beside him away from his village. She liked the feel of the horse beneath her again. There was something about being on a horse, the feeling of freedom that it evoked, as though for that time, at least, she was the master of her own destiny.

Her gaze went to Echohawk, who rode tall in his saddle, the fringes of his buckskin shirt and breeches lifting gently in the breeze. He had said that their plans for today were special, but had yet to tell her exactly what these plans were.

But she had noticed that he had taken a much different weapon with him today. A spear. It seemed their hunt today would be for much larger prey than birds.

She turned her eyes away from Echohawk, just enjoying the moment, knowing that he would tell her in good time what their destination was. It was just enough for her that she was with him today, and at his very own request. He had told her that he trusted her and her skills with a horse and a gun, even though he was still amazed and puzzled by her prowess.

His confidence in her made her proud. Without knowing it, her father had taught her skills that had saved the very Indian he had wanted dead!

Mariah smiled to herself, feeling anything but manly today. In her mind's eye she replayed last night's love scene, thrilling inside as though she were experiencing it again at this very moment.

And the dress she wore today was so utterly feminine—

fashioned from snow-white doeskin, designed intricately with many-colored beads, and fitting her snugly, like a glove. She knew that Echohawk would be quite taken by her appearance if he could see clearly.

She glanced at him again, saddened by his impaired eyesight.

Not wanting to get into feelings again that could ruin this special time with Echohawk, though, she wrenched her eyes away from him and blocked out sad thoughts by observing the wonders of this land that lay on all sides of her. The sunrise mist was hanging above the river and somber hills. Small cottonwood trees of sleepy sparrows swayed in the morning wind. Two pheasants stood in a forest of sunflowers. And broad, jagged leaves of wild grape vines rustled in the wind.

Mariah's lips parted with a gasp when not so far in the distance she saw what looked like hundreds of antelope and buffalo grazing amidst patches of red, brown, and gold wildflowers called *gaillardias,* or Indian blankets.

She was not at all surprised when Echohawk reached a hand toward her as he drew his horse to a shuddering halt.

"Do my eyes see correctly?" he said, squinting as he peered ahead. "Is that not many buffalo grazing in that valley?"

"Buffalo *and* antelope," Mariah said, still marveling at the sight. "Echohawk, I have never seen so many!"

"That is good," Echohawk said, smiling confidently. He motioned with a hand. "*Mah-bee-szhon,* come. We shall settle ourselves close by until one strays from the others. Then I will show you the worth of my spear!"

"It is the buffalo you are hunting today?" Mariah said, paling. "Now I understand why you didn't tell me earlier. You were afraid that I would try to talk you out of coming."

"And was I right to think that?" Echohawk said, his lips tugging into a smile. "Would you have tried to convince me not to come?"

"You know that I would have," Mariah said, sighing heavily. "And it is not too late to turn back. Echohawk, I have never killed a buffalo before. And what if your eyes aren't as accurate as when hunting birds? When missed, birds do not attack. Buffalo do! Certainly I am not the right person to back you up, should you miss."

"But the size of the prey counts for something valuable," Echohawk tried to convince her. "Do you not recall my accuracy at shooting the blue-winged teal? It was small, Mariah, and we carried one home for a hearty meal, did we not? The buffalo is a large beast, making a wide target. When I aim, I will not miss. I am very practiced, so much so that even if I closed my eyes, I would still find the animal with my spear. I have brought home many buffalo for my people in my lifetime. They find many uses of the buffalo, not only for food but also for household utensils."

"But, Echohawk, still—"

Echohawk interrupted. "Now, follow me. We shall position ourselves down by the river. When a buffalo strays and comes to the river for a drink of water, we shall be there, ready."

Knowing that it was no use to try to argue further with him, Mariah followed his lead and led her horse to a narrow steep-sided ravine and dismounted. She and Echohawk secured their horses behind a boulder and thick stands of forsythia bushes, then hurried away from them and crouched down in the ravine, scarcely visible.

In the ravine, the river only footsteps away behind her, Mariah thought the air seemed colder, sending chills across her flesh. She hugged herself, her teeth chattering, then was warmed clear through when Echohawk placed his arm around her and drew her next to him. In his other hand he held the spear.

"*Wi-yee-bah,* soon," he whispered. "We will have company soon. There is always a curious one that strays from the others. If not for a drink of water, just to see if the grass is greener. The mild weather has kept the buffalo close by, and made hunting easier."

"How will you know it is near if we cannot see it?" Mariah worried aloud. "I . . . I do not feel at all comfortable about this, Echohawk."

"No-din, have faith in your man," Echohawk said, placing a finger beneath her chin, drawing her face around. He squinted in concentration, again so wishing that he could see her features! In his mind's eye he had already seen her—but that was not enough.

Mariah searched his face, then looked intensely into his dark eyes, seeing their blankness as he peered down at her. "I'm sorry," she murmured. "I don't mean to make you feel less a man by my complaining. Forgive me, Echohawk."

His mouth covering her lips in a passionately hot kiss was his response. His kiss was all-consuming, setting fires within her that threatened to rob her of her senses. She was relieved when he drew away from her, her heart having almost gone out of control with its erratic beatings.

"No more talk now," he said, smoothing a hand across her cheek. "We must be quiet or the buffalo will go elsewhere."

Mariah nodded and knelt beside him, quietly admiring Echohawk, both for his determination to prove his worth even with half his eyesight, and because he was so magnificent to look at, especially now, as he moved not a muscle, only the wind lifting a lock of his hair, then laying it back along his neck. His jaw was tight with determination, his eyes two points of fire.

Oh, how she loved him . . . how she admired him!

Echohawk scarcely breathed, taut with the excitement of the hunt. He felt as though he were the lord of the universe. For him the universe was this landscape today, the vast Minnesota wilderness. For him there was no possibility of existence elsewhere.

Suddenly there was a blowing—a rumble of breath deeper than the wind.

Wide-eyed, her heart racing, Mariah looked quickly over at Echohawk, then looked up when overhead some of the hard clay of the bank broke off and some clods rolled down, scarcely missing hers and Echohawk's heads.

"It is here," Echohawk said in a whisper that resembled a hiss. "Do not move, No-din. Just watch."

Then there appeared on the skyline just to the left of where Mariah and Echohawk crouched, watching . . . waiting, the massive head of a long-horned buffalo, then the hump, then the whole beast, huge and black against the sky, standing to a height of seven feet at the hump, with horns that extended six feet across the shaggy crown. For a moment it was poised there; then it lumbered obliquely down the bank to the river.

Still Echohawk and Mariah did not move, though the huge beast was now only a few steps upwind. There was no sign of what was about to happen.

The buffalo meandered.

Mariah and Echohawk were frozen in anticipation.

Then, as Mariah watched in awe, the scene exploded.

In one and the same instant Echohawk sprang to his feet and bolted forward, his arm cocked, the spear held high.

The huge animal lunged in panic, bellowing. Its whole weight was thrown violently into the bank, its hooves churning and chipping earth into the air. Its eyes were wide, wild, and white.

Its awful frenzy caused it to become mired and helpless in its fear.

Echohawk hurled the spear with his whole strength, and the point was driven into the deep, vital flesh of the buffalo. The animal, in its agony, staggered, crashed down, and was dead.

Mariah was stunned silent by the performance, her eyes glued to the animal. Then her awe of Echohawk was so intense, she moved her gaze to him and her insides quavered with a giddy warmth as he stood over the animal, his chest swelled with pride.

Scrambling to her feet, Mariah went to Echohawk and lunged into his arms. "You did it," she murmured. "Oh, Echohawk, you did it!"

Then she leaned away from him. "I knew that you could," she said, smiling sheepishly up at him.

Echohawk chuckled, knowing that her pretense was too obvious, but understanding why. He drew her close and gave her a soft kiss. "Before taking the largest portion of the beast back to my people, we shall have a private feast ourselves," he said. "But we must wait until the other buffalo wander onward."

Mariah gazed down at the buffalo, then back up at Echohawk. "My, but he is huge," she murmured.

"A beast his size feeds many mouths on a cold winter's day in our village," he said reverently. "But these animals are dwindling in number because of the arrival of the white man. It is impossible to understand how they can kill without reason."

Mariah sighed heavily, again reminded of her father's slaughters. Then she forced such thoughts aside. She was no longer a part of that life. She gazed up at Echohawk, wishing that she had half his courage. If she did, she would confess so many things to him.

* * *

Mariah sat comfortably on thick pelts beneath the lean-to that Echohawk had fashioned from a blanket, having attached it to the side of a cliff that he and Mariah had found close to the ravine. He had collected a dozen large stones and laid them across the spot chosen for a fire. The fire had been quickly kindled, and over it cooked a steak cut from the yet-warm flank of the animal he had slain. While the steak was cooking, Echohawk cuddled Mariah close to his side and sang to her.

Enraptured, warmed not only by the campfire but also by Echohawk's strong arms around her, Mariah listened as he sang of the bluebells and wild heliotrope; of clematis, called "ghost's lariat"; of the horned lark, called "little black breast"; and of the chinook winds that he called "good old man." It was a time of wondrous peace and love, undisturbed by thoughts that could destroy the moment.

And when his last song had faded into the wind, Echohawk eased Mariah downward, her back pressing into the soft pelts spread beneath her. "My woman, let us stay here forever," Echohawk said huskily, smoothing Mariah's dress down from her shoulders, freeing her breasts. "Let us pretend there are no worries, no sorrows, no tomorrows filled with bitternesses. There is only us, only today. . . ."

Mariah sucked in a breath of wild ecstasy and closed her eyes when he leaned over her and covered the nipple of one of her breasts with his mouth. He teased its taut peak, his hands roaming her body.

Her head spinning, she was hardly aware of how they became fully unclothed, or that the day was dimming, a heavy chill slicing the air. All she knew was that Echohawk had moved his body over hers, molding himself perfectly to the curved hollow of her hips.

She stifled a sob against his muscled shoulder as he pressed gently into her, then began moving within her in a steady rhythm. She lifted her hips to him, taking him even more deeply, and rocked and swayed with him.

She locked her arms around his neck and drew his mouth to her lips. She trembled with passion as he kissed her long and hard, his hands at her breasts, softly kneading them.

Caught in passion's embrace, she felt her entire body responding to his loving her, all of her senses yearning for the promise he offered.

Gasps echoed like thunder throughout her when again his lips moved to her breast, sucking on her nipple until it throbbed. She thrust her pelvis toward him, now only half-aware of making whimpering sounds, and then a surge of ecstasy raged and washed over her, and she again reached the ultimate experience a man and a woman can share.

Echohawk had been holding his own pleasure back, wanting it to linger until he was near the bursting point. He smiled to himself when he sensed her intense pleasure, glad that again he had been able to pull her into that realm of sheer bliss.

Breathing hard, his loins on fire, Echohawk withdrew from inside Mariah and moved into another position that she was not familiar with, yet she knew that she had much to learn—and Echohawk seemed to be the most masterful teacher!

Echohawk stretched out on his back and very gently moved Mariah so that her face was only a heartbeat away from his throbbing hardness. Placing his hands on each side of her face, he urged her lips to him.

Mariah recoiled at the thought of what he seemed to want her to do, yet, loving him so much, and wanting to please, she thrust her tongue out and briefly touched his satin hardness. When she heard his groan of pleasure and watched his expression become passion consumed, she resumed with what she knew had to be perhaps the keenest pleasure of all.

She loved him in that fashion, the strange ritual even firing her own desires again. When he placed his hands at her waist and lifted her atop him in a sitting position, so that his hardness was soon inside her, again she was introduced to a new way of loving him.

Riding him, moving with him as he drove himself up into her, she held her head back and closed her eyes, feeling a strange soft melting energy warming her insides. The air became heavy with the inevitability of release, each stroke within her promising more.

And then they both seemed unable to hold the energy back any longer, and in unison trembled and shook against the other.

When the bliss slowly ebbed away, Mariah crept from atop Echohawk and snuggled next to him, feeling so wonderfully at peace, deliciously in tune with the man she loved.

When her fears of his discovering who she was began edging back inside her consciousness, she quickly cast them aside.

For now she must forget the doom that awaited her when she revealed all truths to the man she loved. For now there was a pure and beautiful understanding between them.

She glanced over at the meat cooking over the fire, ravenous, yet not wanting to give up whatever time she had with Echohawk to eat. Food meant absolutely nothing to her in his presence.

Echohawk was all that she desired.

Only him.

15

> We both can speak of one love,
> Which time can never change.
>
> —Jefferys

Sunrise splashed a golden sheen through the smokehole overhead. After a breakfast of pemmican cakes made of meat, dried and pounded to a pulp, and wild honey, Mariah was filled with joy as she left the wigwam with Echohawk to again accompany him to target practice. Just as they reached their tethered horses, a familiar voice behind them drew them around.

"There is something I would like to show you," Chief Silver Wing said, a mischievous sparkle in his dark eyes. He beckoned with a hand. "Come with me to my dwelling."

Having grown comfortable even with this noble, powerful chief, Mariah walked in a casual gait beside Echohawk as they went with Chief Silver Wing to his wigwam.

"*Nah-mah-dah-bee-yen,* sit," Silver Wing said, gesturing toward mats that lay thickly cushioned beside the lodge fire. Snug in a finely dressed buffalo robe that befitted his high position, he sat down opposite them, reaching for something inside a small buckskin pouch that hung from the waistband of his fringed breeches. "I may have something of interest for you, Echohawk."

Mariah eased down onto a mat beside Echohawk. Then her whole world as she had come to know it these last wonderful days was threatened as she saw what Chief Silver Wing took from the pouch. She paled and stifled a gasp as she looked warily at a goldframed pair of eyeglasses that he was handing toward Echohawk.

Eyeglasses! she fretted to herself.

Her whole body became enveloped in cold shivers as she

guardedly watched Echohawk take the eyeglasses, seemingly puzzled by them as his fingers familiarized themselves with their shape and with the glass that lay within the frames.

"What is this?" he asked, still fingering the object. "It feels like what I have seen white people wear. I believe they are called eyeglasses?"

"*Ay-uh,* I offer you eyeglasses that I took from a white pony soldier many, many snows ago while defending my village against their attack, long before the time of our mutual friend Colonel Snelling," Chief Silver Wing said, nodding. "I have heard that eyeglasses are supposed to better one's vision. You have a problem with your eyesight. Perhaps they will benefit you somehow—make you see. Wear them. See if there is magic in them."

Mariah felt light-headed in her fear as Echohawk continued feeling the glasses, his fingers smoothing slowly over the lenses.

This was the moment she had dreaded most.

His discovery of who she truly was!

If the eyeglasses should work for Echohawk, he would soon see to whom he had given his heart and his total trust.

With that thought, an ill feeling swept through Mariah. One moment she had been so happy her heart had sung, and the next, her whole world was tumbling around her.

Mariah's heart pounded and she held her breath as she watched Echohawk slowly slip the eyeglasses onto the bridge of his nose.

Echohawk squinted as he looked through the lenses; then the blood pumped maddeningly through his veins in his excitement over discovering that, *ay-uh,* he *could* see! The eyeglasses *were* made of some sort of white-man magic! He could make out everything distinctly!

A slow smile tugged at his lips as he turned to Mariah, having so badly wanted to see the woman of his heart.

But what he discovered made everything within him turn cold. The person he was seeing—the woman he had poured out his feelings to—had a face familiar to him before his eyesight had been impaired.

Then his gaze moved jerkily to her hair, seeing its length.

His gaze went to her dress as he now recalled that on that dreadful day of many deaths she had not been dressed as a woman, but as a lad!

Ay-uh, that had been the difference the day of the attack. She had been disguised as a boy, to fool him and his people. It had been the dark ash spread on her face to strengthen her disguise that day that had kept him from seeing the truth!

Mariah went limp with fear, having seen within his eyes the horror of recognizing who she truly was. She was frozen to the spot, afraid to move, then flinched when he suddenly leaned close to the lodge fire and gathered up a handful of ashes.

A scream froze in her throat when he turned suddenly to her, roughly spreading the ash all over her face. She wanted to die when he let out a ear-splitting wail when he fell back away from her and gazed at her knowingly.

"It was you!" he cried, rising shakily to his feet. "Without the ash on your face, I . . . I . . . was not sure. But now I am! You are not at all who you pretend! You betrayed me! You betrayed all Chippewa! You are an enemy!"

"What is this?" Chief Silver Wing asked, dismayed at Echohawk's performance. "Why did you color her face with ash? Why do you call her an enemy? She has proved her loyalty to our people! She cannot be an enemy!"

Mariah finally found the courage to scramble to her feet. She reached a hand out to Echohawk, tears streaming from her eyes. "Please listen," she cried. "Oh, Echohawk, that day . . . it was not of my doing!"

But she could not find it within herself to go further with her confession. She could not openly blame her father. Thus far, Echohawk did not know his identity. She would not be the one to point an accusing finger at him. If she did, she would never be able to live with herself.

So she stopped short of what she knew had to be said to make Echohawk believe her. She could not involve her father, even though he did not warrant such protection from her. But to convince Echohawk that she had been forced to join the raid, a full explanation was needed.

"Echohawk, I love you," she murmured, still reaching a

hand out to him. "I love your people. And Nee-kah! I feel toward her as though she were my sister—a sister that I never had! Please don't turn me away! Please . . . ?"

Her words did not seem to reach him at all. He stood solemnly still, coldly staring at her, his arms folded across his chest. She took a shaky step away from him; the hatred in his eyes appalled her very soul.

Sobbing, her heart breaking, having lost everything now because of her evil, marauding father, Mariah turned and fled from the lodge.

Blinded with tears, she ignored Nee-kah as she cried out for her to stop. She ignored the Chippewa people as they stopped and stared at her in her frenzied flight toward her horse. She was only vaguely aware of mounting the horse and grabbing the reins, for everything within her seemed dead and empty.

She had lost Echohawk!

Not only that, she had lost her very reason for living.

Wheeling the horse around, Mariah sank her heels into his flanks and sharply snapped the reins. Tears splashed into the wind as she rode through the village, dogs yapping at her heels, children shouting at her in dismay.

She was glad when she reached the outskirts of the village, able then to send her steed into a hard gallop across the flower-dotted meadow. She was no longer numb inside. With the realization of what had truly been lost to her came the hurt. She could hardly bear these feelings ravaging her insides, racking her body with torture. Everything within her now ached, especially her heart.

When she heard a horse fast approaching from behind, she did not take the time to glance over her shoulder to see who it was. She feared many things. Now that her true identity had been revealed, Echohawk could have sent a brave to stop her escape. Soon she could be tied to a stake in the center of the village, a victim of their vengeance—of intense hatred.

But she would not save herself if it meant seeing her father take her place at the stake—or at the end of a hangman's noose—for his crimes against the Chippewa. He deserved punishment, certainly, but she would not be the one to cause it.

Never!

Terror leapt through her when out of the corner of her eye she discovered the horse pulling alongside of her. Her eyes widened and she screamed when an arm reached out and grabbed her, dragging her onto the other horse. She was held firmly on the lap of her pursuer as he drew his reins tautly, stopping his horse.

Her pulse racing, weak with fear, Mariah turned and gazed frantically up at the man whose muscled arm held her prisoner. Her heart bled when she saw that it was Echohawk, the hate in his eyes no less as he looked down at her through the eyeglasses.

She swallowed hard, then tried to squirm free of her bondage, surprised when he let go of her and she tumbled away from him and the horse to the ground. Dazed, she lay there for a moment; then, when a shadow fell over her, her eyes turned slowly upward, and she recoiled against the ground when she found Echohawk staring flatly down at her, his arms folded stiffly across his chest.

"Echohawk, I didn't mean you any harm," she cried. "I did not purposely betray you. What I did, caring for you and learning your ways, was done from the goodness of my heart. The day of the raid, I—"

Her words were stolen from her when he leaned over and grabbed her by the arms and jerked her to her feet. Echohawk now seemed to be a giant as he towered over her in his anger. When he began shaking her, her senses seemed to scramble, yet she heard what he shouted at her, understanding well the word he spoke in his Chippewa tongue.

"*Gay-gay-nah-wi-shkee,* liar," Echohawk gritted out between clenched teeth, his eyes two points of fire as he continued shaking her. "Liar! You . . . are . . . a . . . liar!"

He released her so suddenly she again fell to the ground.

Devastated by his accusation and tormented by his final good-bye, she watched him mount Blaze and ride away, tears flowing fiercely from her eyes.

And when he was gone from her eyesight, she buried her face in her hands, her crying having turned to low sobs.

She had lost everything.

Everything!

And all because of a father who did not deserve such loyalty as she had afforded him, she thought bitterly to herself.

Slowly regaining her feet, Fort Snelling again her destination, she went to her horse and pulled herself into the saddle. As she urged him to a gallop, a sudden pain gripped her insides. There would be no more moments in Echohawk's arms, ever again.

* * *

The day had been grueling, Mariah having stopped only to get an occasional drink and to wash from her face the dreaded ash that had condemned her in Echohawk's eyes.

It was now growing dusk and she thankfully saw Fort Snelling in the distance, relieved to finally be there after her long and arduous ride.

The fort, an outpost of western civilization in a vast wilderness, was the northernmost fort in the Mississippi Valley, having been established to prevent the British from carrying on the fur trade in America, as well as to keep peace between the Sioux and Chippewa Indians.

Mariah had studied Fort Snelling's history extensively in newspaper articles and from fliers and brochures that were passed around to the settlements to entice everyone to go to Fort Snelling for supplies. She knew that the fort was manned by up to two dozen officers, most of whom were graduates of West Point—and as many as three hundred enlisted men.

A four-story commissary carved into the perpendicular riverbank stored four years of provisions and supplies.

The fort's strategic position and stone construction made it virtually impregnable. It had never been attacked by Indians, Colonel Snelling being a friend to them, one and all. Fort Snelling, built to Snelling's personal specifications, was *the* finest fort in the American West.

As Mariah drew closer, she admired the fort once again, as she had in the past. Walled and turreted, it might just have been a castle on the Rhine! There was a small settlement along the river, protected by the fort set on the cliff above it. Even now, although it was nearly dark, merchants crowded in to supply the fort and the needs of the heavy flow of river travelers. The air was humming with the sound of saws and hammers. On the outskirts of the cleared ground men and women were returning in their carts from the forest, where they had been cutting wood.

Mariah caught sight of several canoes traveling the river, manned by copper Indian braves, passing silently on their way to the fort. Waves of melancholia swept through her, she missed Echohawk so much. She then looked toward the banks of the river, where many braves were unloading the hides they had brought along to trade.

Not wanting to be swallowed by grief again over her loss of Echohawk, Mariah sent her horse into a faster gallop, soon entering the wide gate that led into the courtyard of the fort. Colonel Snelling had served as both architect and construction superintendent during the building of the fort. Mariah gazed around her, familiarizing herself with the setting again. The buildings and a diamond-shaped parade ground were enclosed within the twelve-foot stone wall. A round tower had been erected to command the western approach to the post from the prairies. Cannon had been placed on platforms atop the roof, and muskets could be fired from loopholes placed stragetically in the lower walls.

The hexagonal tower had five of its six sides extending beyond the wall. A powder magazine and guardhouse flanked the round towers, and wooden pickets bristled atop the wall adjacent to the round tower.

In one sweep of her eyes she saw well houses, sutler's store, two barracks, several shops, and many other buildings. Then she became aware of something else—many eyes following her as she rode on toward Colonel Snelling's house, set at the east end of the parade ground.

Mariah held her chin high, ignoring the gaping soldiers on all sides of her, eyeing her, surely confused by her Indian attire.

As she had previously done, she silently admired the colonel's house, thinking that he lived like a country squire in a house whose every inch resembled a European manor house. The square cut-stone house, Georgian in spirit, but with a flamboyant Flemish gable, was known to be a jewel of the frontier.

When she drew rein in front of the house, she had to reach deeply within herself for the courage to go and knock on the door, begging assistance from those who clearly disliked her father for one reason or another. Although they had treated her with much kindness in the past, she feared that when faced with her request for assistance, they would surely see her as a nuisance in their lives.

But they were her only hope, now that she had lost Echohawk's trust and love.

Dispirited, she slowly dismounted her horse.

16

Tell me not in mournful numbers,
Life is but an empty dream!
—LONGFELLOW

Mariah's knees trembled as she stood at the massive front door of the Snelling residence, awaiting a response after having knocked. A new fear suddenly grabbed her. What if Colonel Snelling had found out about her father's raid, and her part in it? What if her father was even now imprisoned at the fort?

She would be walking right into a trap!

Not understanding why she hadn't thought of this possibility before, Mariah turned and began to leave, thinking that she would have to pick up the pieces of her life elsewhere, but stopped dead in her tracks when the door opened and a voice as soft as a summer breeze spoke behind her.

"Yes? What can I do for you?" Abigail Snelling said, stepping out onto the narrow porch.

Her heart pounding, Mariah turned slowly around and faced Abigail, her eyes wavering, fearing a quick tongue-lashing once Mrs. Snelling recognized her.

She squared her shoulders and straightened her back, awaiting Abigail's reaction to seeing her there, herself admiring the colonel's wife, as she had so often in the past.

A woman with the reputation of performing grandly as the commandant's lady, Abigail was beautiful, with raven-haired tresses that nearly reached the ground. She was slender, with an oval face and dancing green eyes with thick lashes shadowing them. She was surely the most lovely of all the women today at the fort, in her highly gathered pale blue velveteen dress with lace at the high collar and at the cuffs of its long sleeves.

Mariah knew firsthand that Abigail was full of compassion, for not long ago, upon discovering that Mariah was a girl instead of a boy, dressed in boy's garb because of a paranoid father, she had scolded Mariah's father almost unmercifully.

"Mariah?" Abigail gasped, paling as she took in Mariah's cropped hair. Her hands crept slowly to it, her lips parted in horror. "Your beautiful hair! Lord, Mariah, did your father . . . ?"

Mariah sighed heavily, relieved that her hair appeared to be the only cause for Abigail's alarm—not that Mariah was a fugitive at her door, asking for asylum!

"Yes, my father cut my hair," she said softly. "I begged him not to. But . . . but . . . he wouldn't listen." Her bottom lip stiffened angrily. "Mrs. Snelling, nothing anyone said or did could dissuade my father from wanting to turn me into a man! My being a woman threatened him, somehow." She lowered her eyes. "He . . . he even burned all of mine and mother's dresses. All that was left of my wardrobe were the horrid men's breeches and shirts."

Abigail smoothed her fingers over Mariah's hair, tsk-tsking, then placed a gentle hand to Mariah's cheek as she roved her eyes over her attire. "You are not wearing men's clothing today," she murmured, then gazed into Mariah's sad eyes. "Mariah, you are wearing a buckskin dress—one quite beautifully decorated with beads. Did your father approve of the dress? Perhaps he got it in a trade with the Chippewa?"

Then Abigail placed a hand to her mouth, gasping behind it, her eyes wide with remembrance. "Mariah, I am just now recalling a visit from your father!" she cried. "Seeing your hair cropped short momentarily stole my memory from me."

"My father was here?" Mariah asked, panic filling her. "When? What did he say?"

"Mariah, he was here at Fort Snelling searching for you," Abigail said, cocking an eyebrow quizzically. "He did not give any details as to why. After he found out that no one had seen you at the fort, he rode away without any further explanation."

Tears filled Mariah's eyes; she understood her father's desperation to find her, since he had ruled her life for so long. Upon discovering her gone, he had lost control. Victor Temple was not a man who ever let anyone dictate to him about anything. His alarm was surely not caused by having possibly lost her, but because she had openly defied him by leaving!

Down deep inside himself, he had to know that she had not been abducted . . . that she had left on her own initiative.

"Oh, my dear, you are about to cry," Abigail said softly, placing an arm around Mariah's waist. "Do come inside my home. Let me get you a lemonade to make you feel better. And then we will talk this out."

"Thank you," Mariah said, wiping a tear from her cheek as she was whisked into the parlor.

"I shall return shortly," Abigail said, guiding Mariah to an upholstered chair that sat before a roaring fire in the massive stone fireplace. "Sit yourself down, dear. You do look in need of my special refreshment."

For a moment, while awaiting Abigail's return, Mariah was catapulted into another world as she gazed with awe around her at the handsomely furnished sitting parlor. The room, furnished in the best European traditions, bespoke the Snellings' polished tastes. Lemon-colored satin draperies hung at the windows, a thick Brussels carpet covered the floor, and cherrywood tables with marble tops were positioned around the room. A tall clock ticked away time close by; a Latin dictionary stood open on a stand beside a massive oak desk.

Something quite grand grabbed Mariah's full attention.

A piano, she marveled to herself as her eyes locked on the ebony-wood upright that sat against the far wall, a candelabrum, its half-dozen candles burning, gracing its top.

She had only seen pictures of pianos in books, and heard them described by her mother, but never had they seemed as beautiful as the one in the Snelling parlor.

She was tempted to go to it and run her fingers across the keys, but thought better of it when Abigail entered the room carrying a tray which held a pitcher of lemonade and two glasses.

"You *will* feel much better after drinking my lemonade," Abigail said, setting the tray on a table beside Mariah. She enthusiastically poured two glasses of lemonade, handing one to

Mariah. She then sat down opposite Mariah, sipping from her own glass.

Although she was hungrier than she was thirsty, both Mariah's tongue and her lips seemed parched from the grueling ride.

And she had never tasted lemonade before!

As the sweet liquid rolled down her throat, her eyes widened. Never in her life had she experienced anything to compare with this delicious drink!

She drank it in fast gulps, then blushed with embarrassment as she took the glass from her lips and noticed Abigail watching her with a soft smile.

"Let me pour you another," Abigail said, her eyes dancing. She gazed over at her box of imported chocolates, then picked it up and handed it toward Mariah. "And please have a chocolate."

Mariah's lips parted in another slight gasp as she peered into the box of cream-filled chocolates. She had never seen any such delicacy, much less eaten one.

Her fingers trembled as she reached for the one closest to her. "Why, thank you," she said, plucking the chocolate from the others.

When she placed it between her lips, her taste buds danced wildly, the chocolate even more wonderfully delicious than the lemonade! She chewed it slowly, savoring the taste as long as possible.

"And now more lemonade?" Abigail asked, setting aside the chocolates and again lifting the pitcher.

"Yes, please," Mariah said, smiling bashfully at Abigail. "It is a most delicious refreshment."

Not wanting to make a complete fool of herself, Mariah sipped the second glass for a moment, then set it aside. She wanted to get the preliminaries behind her. Rarely had she asked for anything from anyone. Most times she had been forced to just take what had been handed her, which, in truth, had been the bare essentials of everyday life.

"Now, tell me, Mariah, why are you here?" Abigail said, reaching over to pat Mariah's arm. "I will do anything I can to help you."

Apprehensive, not wanting to reveal any truths to Abigail that might jeopardize her father's welfare, Mariah paused for a moment, then looked wide-eyed at her hostess. "You know how forceful and determined my father is," she blurted out. "Mrs. Snelling, I . . ."

Abigail reached a hand to Mariah's cheek, within her eyes a deep compassion. "Please call me Abigail," she murmured. "Being called Mrs. Snelling makes me feel like a stodgy old maid." She laughed softly. "And, my dear, you know that I am anything but an old maid. I have seven beautiful children."

Mariah laughed nervously, yet felt wonderfully breezy inside to know that Abigail Snelling would do anything to make a troubled person more comfortable in her presence.

"That is very sweet of you," Mariah said softly. "I would love to call you by your first name."

Abigail sat back more comfortably in her chair. "Now, continue with your story," she said, relaxing her hands on her lap. "I am a very good listener." She leaned forward and smiled at Mariah. "And I have instructed my servants to keep the children out of the parlor. I feel you do not need their noise while confiding in me."

Mariah smiled back at her, amazed at the woman's consideration. She then sighed deeply and scooted back in the chair, feeling strangely at home. "I just could not stay with my father any longer," she said, gazing into the fire, for an instant reflecting on the shared moments beside the fires in Echohawk's wigwam.

"You made this decision after your father cut your hair?" Abigail said, wrenching Mariah's thoughts back to the present.

Mariah looked quickly over at Abigail, troubled that she could get lost in thoughts of Echohawk so easily, when, in truth, she knew that she had to forget him.

"Yes, I left after father cut my hair," Mariah said in a half-truth. She could never tell Abigail that what had really made her flee her father's wrath was the attack on the innocent Chippewa. At that point she had lost all respect for her father.

"Where did you go?" Abigail asked, her gaze settling on the buckskin dress. She looked back into Mariah's eyes again.

"Just before your father left the fort, after discovering you weren't here, he said something about going to check the Indian villages for you." She paused, then added, "Mariah, have you been with a band of Chippewa? Is that where you got the dress?"

"Yes, I've been with the Chippewa," Mariah said, lowering her eyes, troubled as to how much more she could reveal to Abigail. Not only was telling too much dangerous, it would also be painful to talk about Echohawk, Chief Silver Wing, and Nee-kah's kindnesses to her.

At this very moment, back at their village, she was looked on as a traitor!

"How did you happen to be there?" Abigail persisted softly. "You . . . you weren't forced, were you? The Chippewa in these parts are known for their civility."

"And what is said about them is true," Mariah said, tears burning at the corners of her eyes as, in her mind's eye, she reenacted that fateful day when so many Chippewa had died.

She blinked nervously to erase the painful thoughts, then continued to explain.

"Upon my flight from my father, my horse threw me," she said. "Nee-kah, the wife of Chief Silver Wing, found me. She took me to their village, where I was treated graciously."

A sudden thought seized Mariah, making her heart skip a beat. Echohawk could come to Fort Snelling and inform Colonel Snelling of her role in the raid. Abigail could soon lose all belief in her!

Even by now Echohawk could have put two and two together and realized that it was her father who had led the raid. Even now he could be at her father's trading post. Her father could even now be dead!

"Mariah?" Abigail said, reaching to take one of Mariah's hands in hers. "Dear, you have suddenly grown so pale. Is there something more you wish to tell me? I am here to listen. Pour it all out to me. You will feel much better for it."

"There is nothing more," Mariah said softly. "I left the Chippewa village to come to you to see if you might assist me in some way, to help me decide what I must do with the rest of my life."

She swallowed hard, knowing that she would have to live from day to day, praying that Echohawk would not hate her so much that he would come for her and demand that she be handed over to him to be taken back to his people and punished for being a traitor.

Her only hope was that Echohawk would search deeply within his heart and realize that she could never have done anything purposely against his people. Time was her ally, it seemed, for if Echohawk would weigh it all inside his heart, he would know that she was sincere in all of her thoughts and deeds.

"Perhaps I could work here at Fort Snelling in some capacity," Mariah suddenly stated. "I can ride a horse and handle firearms as well as any man . . ."

Abigail gasped with horror at Mariah's suggestion. "My dear, I want to hear no more talk of you mingling with the men, behaving as one of them," she scolded. "You cannot be serious in wanting to continue living the life your father forced upon you—a life that you have rightly fled from."

She rose from her chair and took Mariah's hands and drew her up before her. She gently embraced Mariah, then held her at arm's length. "My dear, it would delight me to help you," she murmured. "But in a much different way than you have suggested. You have suffered enough since your mother's death. I demand that you stay with me and Josiah. It would delight us both to have you in our home."

She reached to Mariah's cheeks and smiled into her eyes. "I will take you to my wardrobe and let you choose the laciest dress that you can find," she said softly. "Now, do you understand that you are to forget that foolishness about shooting firearms and riding horses? There are better things to do with one's time!"

Mariah gasped and her eyes widened. "You would do that for me? You would take me in? You . . . you would even give me dresses to wear?" she said, her cheeks coloring with an anxious blush. "I can't expect you to be that generous, Abigail. How would I ever repay you?"

"My dear, I must confess I am guilty of being a trifle selfish in my offerings to you," Abigail said, smiling mischievously at Mariah. "You see, I am always searching for excuses to give parties or hold a grand ball. The fort is a most boring place for married women of breeding! My dear, your entrance into our lives is the perfect reason to give a ball. It will be in your honor. I will show you off to all of the other women at the fort!"

Mariah was stunned at first by this confession, then recognized that Abigail was teasing, and she laughed softly along with her. "But, Abigail, I shall shock all of the women with the length of my hair," she teased back, finding this sudden lighthearted mood so refreshing.

Then again she was catapulted back to the real world when she thought of her father. "My father," she said warily. "He will find out. He will come for me."

"Don't fret, dear," Abigail said, firming her chin. "My Josiah will handle him."

"Did I hear my name being spoken in a conversation between two lovely ladies?" Colonel Snelling said, making a grand entrance into the parlor.

Mariah turned with a start, then smiled at Colonel Snelling as he walked stoutly into the room, resplendent in his blue uniform. He was a red-haired man, slightly balding, and she had never considered him handsome, but he had a smile that could melt one's heart.

Yet she knew his reputation of being a tough-minded disciplinarian with the men under his command. A veteran of the War of 1812, he was a practical man who valued highly his soldiers' capacity for work, but neglected the drills and smart appearances usually associated with army life. The rank and file of his garrison were kept busy maintaining or constructing buildings and roads.

Colonel Snelling promptly recognized Mariah, and his steps faltered; his smile faded when he caught sight of her hair. He went and stood tall over her, running his long lean fingers through her hair.

"And whom do we blame for this?" he grumbled, his brow furrowed with a deep frown. "But of course, I need not ask. It was your father. He went this far to make you take on the appearance of a man. Damn him. He ought to be horsewhipped!"

"Darling, Mariah has left home," Abigail said, going to Josiah's side, locking an arm through his. "I have asked her to stay with us. Of course I knew that you would approve."

Josiah smiled again, and placed a hand to Mariah's cheek. "Our home is yours for as long as you like," he said softly.

So grateful was she, tears pooled in Mariah's eyes. Yet she did not know how long even this happiness would last.

Always there were truths that would condemn her!

Always!

"Thank you so much," she murmured. "Thank you both."

Josiah slipped a silver snuffbox from his inner jacket pocket and opened it. Pinching out a quantity of the brown powder, he dusted it onto the back of his left wrist and drew it up with two quick sniffs.

"Let Abigail take you to the guest room," he said, slipping the snuffbox back into his pocket. "We'll talk more at length later."

Abigail took Mariah by the hand and ushered her from the room, down a corridor, up a short flight of stairs, down another corridor, and into a room that took her breath away at first sight. She stepped delicately across the threshold, eyeing the great Tudor oak four-poster bed hung with crewelwork curtains; bamboo-backed chairs that had surely come from China; and hand-painted Chinese wallpaper which lent a gay touch to the room. The lone window was draped with a sheer lacy curtain, drawing Mariah to it, to touch its softness.

"It is all so beautiful," she said, sighing deeply, yet her thoughts were quickly drawn elsewhere when she looked through the window upon a half-moon shining in the sky, encircled by a great hazy ring. She could not help but wonder if Echohawk was looking at the same moon, perhaps thinking of her.

She looked away from the moon, and then at the sky, which

was unsullied by a single cloud. She gazed at the stars, wishing upon them that Echohawk could find it in his heart to recall their moments together. The sincerity of her feelings for him, if he would only let himself believe it, would prove that she was not capable of anything but love for him and for his people.

She felt an arm circle her waist and was drawn back to the present. "My dear, in time you will forget all the ugliness of your past," Abigail assured her. "I will see to it, Mariah. I promise."

Sobbing, Mariah turned to Abigail and eased into her embrace, allowing herself to pretend, at least at that moment, that it was her mother who was comforting her.

17

Who is the happy warrior?
Who is he that every man in arms should wish to be?

—Wordsworth

Two Weeks Later

The air was crisp and cool. The autumn leaves had fluttered from the trees to the ground, making a bed of color beneath them. Kneeling beside his father's grave, Echohawk bowed his face into his hands. *"Gee-bah-bah,"* he whispered mournfully. "It has now been fourteen Chippewa sunrises and still I have not been able to place No-din from my mind. How can I continue to love a woman who is my enemy? How?"

Except for the wind whispering in the soft breeze of late afternoon, there was a keen silence.

And then the silence was broken by a sound behind Echohawk. He turned with a start and found himself looking up at Chief Silver Wing.

"My son, I have come to urge you to join the other braves around the council fire in my lodge," Chief Silver Wing said, placing a solid hand on Echohawk's shoulder. "We have much to discuss and you have an integral role in the discussions. Place all sadnesses from your heart and mingle with your people again. You cannot forget that you are now the leader of your band of Chippewa. They await your guidance. Come. Show them that you are now ready to be their leader again."

Echohawk moved slowly to his feet and faced Chief Silver Wing with a humility never known to him before. In the elder chief's presence, more and more, Echohawk felt as though he were once again with his father. This chief's heart and thoughts were so much in tune with his father's, it seemed—even including his paternal love of Echohawk.

"It is *because* of my people that I come to commune with my father," Echohawk finally said. "In life he guided me. Even though he is dead, I still await a vision that he might send to me from the Land of the Hereafter."

He swallowed hard, then clasped a hand onto Chief Silver Wing's shoulder. "But I now see that it was not necessary to escape here each day, when it was you I could share my thoughts and sorrows with," he said humbly. "And my *gee-bah-bah* would want that."

"*Ay-uh,* my son, he would want that," Chief Silver Wing said thickly. He stepped closer to Echohawk, then quickly embraced him. "Soon you will see the good in life again, if you will just allow it to happen. The woman. You will soon forget the woman."

Echohawk relished the embrace, closing his eyes, pretending it was his father, then stiffened at the mention of "the woman," knowing to whom Chief Silver Wing was referring.

No-din.

She was on everyone's mind, it seemed.

He eased from the elder chief's embrace and peered at him through the eyeglasses, finding that each day his eyes were improving, if only slightly. "You have asked me more than once why I called her an enemy," he said, his voice drawn. "Until now I could not tell you. The anger within my heart was too intense to allow me to discuss her."

"But now?" Chief Silver Wing said, folding his arms casually across his chest. "You wish to speak of her now?"

"*Ay-uh,* perhaps it is best," Echohawk said, turning to view the darkening meadow below him, aching inside when he recalled having ridden across that meadow beside No-din, a happiness so keen within him he had feared it would not be everlasting.

And he had been right.

Nothing seemed everlasting for the Chippewa.

Nothing!

"Then I will listen," Chief Silver Wing said, taking a noble stance beside Echohawk.

"I trusted No-din," Echohawk gritted out through clenched teeth. "I even gave her my total love!" He turned to Chief Silver Wing. "Though she is not aware of it, I took her as my wife after she shared a feast with me and then my bed. And all along, this woman that I poured out my heart and soul to was guilty of having been a part of the raid that took my father from me!"

Chief Silver Wing's eyes wavered. "She was a part of the raid?" he gasped.

"You saw how I spread ash on her face?" Echohawk said, his voice softening. "It was to see if her face then matched that of the young lad who rode with those who ravaged our village."

"And it did?" Chief Silver Wing said, his voice showing the strain of the discovery. He kneaded his chin and looked down at the meadow, nodding. "It makes sense now—the way she was dressed when she arrived at our village. And the short hair . . ."

"The way she was dressed when she arrived?" Echohawk said, turning questioning eyes to the chief. "How was she dressed?"

"No one told you?" Chief Silver Wing asked, dropping his hands to his sides.

"I am sure that no one saw the need," Echohawk said, his eyes narrowing. "Tell me. How was she dressed?"

"In clothes worn by white men," Chief Silver Wing said solemnly, now recalling Nee-kah's dismay when she discovered that No-din was a girl, not a boy. For a moment he could see the humor in it again and chuckled low. "When Nee-kah saw her undressed and saw her breasts, it gave her quite a fright. She thought it was a boy with breasts."

Then his brow furrowed into a deep frown. "You say she was among those who raided your village?" he grumbled.

"Ay-uh," Echohawk grumbled back.

"Let us talk more before returning to the council meeting," Chief Silver Wing said, needing to sort out within his mind the reasoning behind all of No-din's actions. He had seen her as something special—a woman with pride and spirit—but never a woman of deceit!

"Come with me to lower ground," Chief Silver Wing encouraged him. "Let me get my pipe from my horse. We will share a smoke while we discuss the 'Woman of the Wind.' "

Echohawk nodded and left the butte with Chief Silver Wing. When they reached their grazing horses, Echohawk took a blanket from his saddlebag and spread it on the ground, then watched Chief Silver Wing's slow, dignified gait as he went to his horse and removed his long-stemmed pipe from a buckskin bag. It was evident to Echohawk that Silver Wing had planned this meeting of minds between just the two of them, for he had brought not only a pipe but also a pouch of tobacco and a case fashioned from stone that carried within its confines a heated coal with which to light the pipe.

When Chief Silver Wing returned, they sat down in a cross-legged fashion on the blanket. Echohawk sat stiffly, his hands resting on his knees, watching the elder chief prepare the pipe for smoking. In the red stone bowl he sprinkled tobacco from its pouch—a mixture of tobacco and the dried and pulverized inner bark of the red willow, known to the Indians as *kinikinik,* which was like incense, pleasing to the spirits, a vehicle of prayer. The peace pipe was the tribe's "secret to Happiness," its "good heart maker."

Echohawk silently admired the chief's pipe. Its stem was three feet long, ornamented with eagle feathers, porcupine quills, and human hair that had been dyed red, which had been taken from the scalp of the enemy of the Chippewa—the Sioux.

Echohawk's thoughts would stay away from Mariah for only a short time, and then, as now, his mind would drift back to her and he would be torn with remorse and anger all over again for having loved a woman who proved to be his enemy. He did not see how talking about her to the elder chief was going to change any of his feelings. For fourteen Chippewa sunrises he had awakened with thoughts of her, torn between loving and hating her. How could it be any different today, tomorrow, and many moons to come?

No-din had stolen his heart, and almost his sanity!

Chief Silver Wing could see how Echohawk drifted between being troubled and being angry, then back again to being troubled. He plucked a twig from the ground and leaned it against the hot coal, soon setting it aflame.

Straightening his back, he placed the flame to his tobacco and puffed eagerly on the stem until the smell of burning tobacco filled the evening air with a pleasant sweetness.

He puffed from the pipe for many more breaths, staring at the night shadows thickening in the forest beyond, then pointed the stem north, east, south, and west, and finally toward the sky and the earth, and blew smoke in these six directions.

Silver Wing then passed the pipe on to Echohawk, and he in turn puffed, then pointed it in the same six directions Chief Silver Wing had, before passing it back to the elder chief.

Silver Wing rested the bowl of his pipe on his knee and remained silent a moment longer, not giving way to something so undignified as a smile, but breathing easily.

He then turned to Echohawk, his eyes reflecting his kindness, his warmth for the young chief. "Echohawk, this woman who to the Chippewa is called No-din should not be looked upon with hate or anger," he said softly. "Remember always that she is the victim of a cruel father. But she is a courageous woman. She fled the life forced on her by a father whose heart is dark. I welcomed her in our village with open arms because I saw much gentleness in her eyes, a reflection of her inner being." He paused and frowned, contemplating his next words. "Yet you say that she rode with those who ravaged your village. There has to be an explanation which will reveal that her role in the raid was an innocent one."

"Would you call her innocent if you knew that she fired upon one of my braves?" Echohawk said, seeing it in his mind's eye as though it were happening now.

Chief Silver Wing leaned forward and placed a hand on Echohawk's knee. "Sometimes a gun is fired against another because the life of the one who fires the weapon is threatened," he said reassuringly. He wanted so badly to find the truth behind No-din's actions, not only to make peace within his own heart about this woman who had become a heroine in his people's eyes but also to soothe Echohawk. He wanted to end Echohawk's torment.

Echohawk gazed into the forest, which was now cloaked in darkness, again reliving that day that would forever haunt him. He recalled the hate he had felt for the young lad who had fired upon his brave, yet he now also recalled that his brave had taken aim on a white man—the man that No-din had defended by shooting the brave.

"That was her father!" Echohawk said, his voice shallow.

He turned quick, wide eyes to Chief Silver Wing. "It had to be her father!" he said anxiously. "She shot the brave to . . . to save her father!"

"So you do see, Echohawk," Chief Silver Wing said, nodding. "She is a woman of much courage and loyalty. Although she held much resentment against her father, she could not let him die. She shot your brave only because her father's life was in jeopardy."

Echohawk was alert to Chief Silver Wing's words, himself beginning to see why No-din had been with the raiders. "Her father forced many things upon No-din," he hissed. "He cut her hair. He made her wear men's clothes."

He again looked quickly at Silver Wing. "She was also forced to ride with her father to witness the spilling of Chippewa blood."

Silver Wing nodded, his eyes locked with Echohawk's. "*Ay-uh,*" he said softly. "That is how I also see it."

"And she fled from her father soon after," Echohawk said, his heart thundering within his chest at the thought of being freed of all resentments toward No-din.

"It seems so," Silver Wing said, again nodding. "And so you see, Echohawk, you have been wrong to condemn No-din within your heart. *Her* heart has always been in the right place. With *us*."

"*Ay-uh,*" Echohawk said, nodding slowly. "I am seeing it all very clearly now." His eyes widened as another thought grabbed him. "Her father! *He* is the one responsible for my people's sorrow. Do you know him, Silver Wing? Do you know where he makes his residence?"

A warning shot through Silver Wing, who realized that Echohawk was still plotting vengeance whenever he thought about the day of the raid. Silver Wing also felt a deep, burning resentment toward certain white men, yet he had his people's welfare to consider. Once an open war broke out between the Chippewa and *any* white man, no matter that the white man might deserve to die, in the end it would be the red man who would suffer.

"I know of him, and where he resides," Silver Wing said solemnly. "But I think it best if you do not know. Think peaceful thoughts, my son. Too much Chippewa blood has already been spilled on Mother Earth. Do not let your life be guided by hate and the need of revenge. Put your people first, your hunger for vengeance last."

"The *ee-szhee-nee-kah-so-win,* name," Echohawk said flatly. "The location of his dwelling."

"I will give you what you ask only because I feel honor-bound to share it with you," Silver Wing said, reaching a hand to Echohawk's shoulder, clasping his fingers gently to it. "His name is Victor Temple. He runs a trading post not far from Fort Snelling. I have never dealt with him because he is a *wah-yah-szhim,* a cheat and a liar. If you insist, I will instruct one of my braves to point out his residence to you. But before I do, promise me that you will only look, not attack."

"I can promise nothing," Echohawk said, his voice hard.

Silver Wing's eyes filled with sadness. "You will be shown the location," he said, sighing heavily.

"That is good," Echohawk said, nodding.

"No-din," Silver Wing said. "Have you thought of her? Will you kill her father—a man she defended with such courage?"

"I cannot say," Echohawk said.

"Will you seek her out?" Silver Wing further questioned. "Will you ask her to return with you to our village as your wife?"

"I cannot say," Echohawk repeated.

"She will be at Fort Snelling," Silver Wing offered. "That was her destination before her horse threw her, leaving her helpless in the forest. I am sure that is where she went when fleeing from your anger and accusations."

"Fort Snelling . . ." Echohawk said contemplatively. "Fort Snelling."

"*Ay-uh,*" Silver Wing said. "And the mention of Fort Snelling brings me back to why the braves wait in council for us even now, Echohawk."

"The great powwow at Fort Snelling is soon," Echohawk said, nodding. "The yearly powwow between the neighboring tribes, even the Sioux. I have heard of this powwow that Colonel Snelling has every year at his fort, hoping to draw the Chippewa and Sioux into a lasting friendship." He laughed sarcastically. "How can that ever be? The snakelike Sioux will be the enemy of the Chippewa *ah-pah-nay,* forever! I shall carry within my heart much hate for that renegade Sioux White Wolf! Always!"

"I dislike White Wolf no less than you, and I do not expect he will be among the peace seekers at Fort Snelling," Chief Silver Wing said solemnly. "It is for Colonel Snelling that I urge you to go to the powwow. He makes an attempt to bring peace among the Chippewa and Sioux, whereas no other white man before him even cared. In fact, I'm sure they were glad to see us kill each other off."

Echohawk turned his eyes to Silver Wing. "You are going?" he questioned.

"*Gah-ween,* no," Chief Silver Wing said, shaking his head slowly back and forth. "I think it is wise to let others who are younger go and experience this time of camaraderie and bring back the news of it to their chief."

Echohawk rose quickly to his feet, his eyes and heart alive again. "I will go," he said, smiling at Silver Wing as he rose before him. "I am eager to go to the fort. My chosen braves and I will proudly ride with the representatives of your band of Chippewa. We will listen to words of peace with open hearts and minds."

"That is good," Chief Silver Wing said, wrapping Echohawk within his arms, giving him a warm hug. "And remember, my son, keep peaceful thoughts about those who have wronged you. Somehow they will pay for their evil ways. But for now, your thoughts must remain pure to ensure the safety and future of both your people and mine."

Echohawk could not help but be attentive to Chief Silver Wing's warnings. Like Echohawk's beloved father, Silver Wing was a man of wisdom. Echohawk wanted so badly to respect his wishes, yet hate was eating away at his heart for this man who he now knew beyond a shadow of a doubt was No-din's father.

"Still I can make no promises to you," Echohawk said, easing from Chief Silver Wing's embrace. "But hear me when I say this to you. I respect you and your reasons for asking me to have a peaceful heart. In you I see my father. With you I feel as though I am *with* my father. I hope somehow to repay you one day for your kindnesses to me."

Chief Silver Wing placed a hand to Echohawk's shoulder. "Echohawk, from this day forth, you *are* my son, in every respect," he said sincerely. "Now, let us go and sit together in council with our respective braves. It is best that they share these good feelings between two chiefs."

"*Ay-uh,*" Echohawk said, warmed through and through by Silver Wing's gifts of love and guidance.

18

> Beauty is truth, truth beauty—that is all
> Ye know on earth, and all ye need to know.
>
> —KEATS

A Few Weeks Later

The aroma of smoke awakened Victor Temple with a start. He bolted from his bed when he heard men shouting outside, and quickly saw the reflection of fire on the ceiling of his bedroom.

"Damn!" he gasped, scurrying into his breeches.

Shirtless, he left his room, but just as he stepped out into the corridor, he cried out with pain as something came down hard on his head. Blacking out from the blow, he crumpled to the floor, unaware of rough hands picking him up, carrying him down the stairs, and outside, tying him to a horse.

When he finally came to, his head throbbing with pain, he squinted into the darkness, soon realizing that he had been shackled to a wall, nude.

"Lord have mercy," he cried, the room darker than a moonless night. He winced and tried to pull his feet up from the floor when he heard rats scurrying around, squeaking, but his legs were tied too securely to the wall for him to move his feet.

"Help!" he shouted. "Someone, please help me!"

He became quiet, listening. Fear gripped his insides and sweat pearled up on his brow when he still heard no sounds but the rats.

"Who are you? *Where* are you?" he cried. "Why have you done this to me?"

But still no response.

It was as though he was in a deep dark tunnel, alone except for—

A rat's sharp teeth sank into the flesh of one of his bare feet. He let out a bloodcurdling scream, then fainted. . . .

* * *

Excitement welled up inside Mariah as she stood before the mirror. She stared in amazement at her reflection, thinking that by some miracle Abigail had fussed enough with her hair to make it actually look pretty with all of its waves and curls.

Mariah gazed down at the satin gown Abigail had let her choose for the ball. It had transformed her into someone that even she thought might be called beautiful! Pale green, it was trimmed in delicate white lace, its bodice low, revealing a cleavage that made her blush. So captivated was she by the vision in the mirror, she didn't hear soft footsteps coming up behind her.

"My dear, you are absolutely ravishing," Abigail said, stepping to Mariah's side, a picture of loveliness herself in her off-the-shoulder black velveteen dress, her hair coiled at the top of her head with long, lustrous ringlets hanging down at the back. The top curves of her breasts were just barely exposed, and above them lay a sparkling diamond necklace.

Abigail clasped her hands before her. "Mariah, you are going to turn every man's head at the ball tonight," she said, sighing dreamily. "And my but aren't you going to be busy dancing the night away! I will have to assign Josiah to stand guard, just to fight the men off you."

Mariah paled and turned quickly to Abigail. "Abigail, I don't know what I was thinking of, getting so dressed up for the ball, or why I was so excited to attend it," she said, her eyes wide. "I don't know the first thing about dancing! I . . . I will make an absolute fool of myself should I even attempt to!"

"There will be many anxious to teach you," Abigail said, gently patting Mariah on the cheek. She glanced toward the window, hearing a commotion outside in the courtyard. Some Indians had already started arriving for the powwow.

She glanced again at Mariah, having succeeded thus far this evening in getting her mind off the gathering of the Indians. In time, Mariah had felt more comfortable in taking Abigail into her confidence, and had spoken of her love for Echohawk, yet had not given her reason for having left him. But it was quite evident to Abigail that Mariah still loved him. It was always in her eyes and voice when even the mention of the Chippewa came into the conversation at the dinner table.

Mariah grew tense, having noticed Abigail's sudden apprehension. Mariah herself was acutely aware of the noise coming from the Indian camps in and around the walls of Fort Snelling. She had been told of the powwow that Colonel Snelling had planned to create a peaceful union between two warring factions of Indians.

Last night she had been unable to sleep while listening to the low thumping of the drums, and the songs and chants of the Indians. She had watched all day for signs of Echohawk—yet had not seen him. She had to wonder if he would eventually come. And if so, would she see him? Would she speak to him?

Unable to stay away, and having only a faint evening light left to study the gathering Indians, Mariah brushed past Abigail and went to the window and slowly eased the sheer curtain aside. Her gaze roamed slowly around below her, watching for a tall, handsome Indian who would be set apart from all of the others by an incongruous pair of spectacles.

Those damn eyeglasses! she fussed to herself. If not for them, she would still be a part of Echohawk's life!

But she knew that it was foolish to blame eyeglasses, for even without them, he in time would have discovered her deceit.

"He could be among those encamped outside the walls of the fort," Abigail said, moving to Mariah's side, slipping an arm around her tiny waist. She gazed down at those who were inside the fort, sitting and smoking around a great outdoor fire. Some were Chippewa. Some were Sioux. She hoped with all her heart that they would feast and fraternize in perfect accord.

"I know," Mariah said softly. "And I am foolish for even caring." She caught herself, having come close to telling Abigail truths that would condemn not only herself in the commandant's wife's eyes but also her father.

"Yes, it is a bit foolish, my dear," Abigail said, brushing her fingers across Mariah's brow, smoothing some red curls into place that had fallen from the rest. "His culture and yours differ so much. You were wise to leave when you did and not allow your feelings to grow stronger. Although it has been done, it is unwise for a white woman to marry into a family of Indians. The life is hard, Mariah. So very hard."

"I am sure it is," Mariah said, sighing. Then her heart fluttered wildly in her chest when she caught sight of many more Indians approaching the courtyard, Echohawk in the lead.

"He's here," she whispered just loud enough for Abigail to hear. She clasped her hands tightly together before her. "Echohawk has come." Then her eyes wavered. She was not sure if he even knew she was at Fort Snelling. Of course he had come only for the powwow. By now she would be completely banished from his mind and heart!

"How odd," Abigail said, gasping. She moved away from Mariah and leaned closer to the window. "Mariah, Echohawk is wearing eyeglasses. I have never seen an Indian wear eyeglasses. And where would he have gotten them? Had he traded for them at the fort, everyone would have been talking about it, for an Indian, no matter how handsome he is, looks rather odd in eyeglasses."

Guilt spread through Mariah like wildfire, since she knew all of the answers yet was unable to tell Abigail.

Her father!

He alone was responsible for Echohawk's injured eyesight!

"Yes, it does seem odd," Mariah said, her voice drawn, taking her eyes off Echohawk just long enough to see others in the courtyard stopping to stare at him.

Then she turned her attention back to him, thinking that nothing could diminish his handsomeness. Everything within her seemed to melt as she watched him ride further into the courtyard, so proud and tall in his saddle. He wore fringed white doeskin breeches and a shirt embellished with colorful beads and porcupine quills, his raven-dark hair held back with a colorfully beaded headband.

There was just enough light left to see his chiseled bronze face with its bold nose and strong chin and night-black eyes behind the absurdly out-of-place eyeglasses.

Tears burned at the corners of Mariah's eyes as she envisioned him nude, seeing even now in her mind's eye the expanse of sleekly muscled chest, the wide shoulders tapering to narrow hips, and the hard, flat stomach.

She could even now feel his hands on her face, framing her lips before kissing her.

She could even now feel his hard strong arms pressing her willing body against his. . . .

"Mariah?" Abigail said, interrupting Mariah's thoughts. "Dear? Let us go down to the ballroom. The string quartet is even now starting the waltzes."

Abigail placed a hand to Mariah's elbow as Mariah looked gloomily at her. "Come, dear," she persisted. "We must give you a reason to erase that frown from your lovely face. It will be better for you to mingle with other people and get your mind off Echohawk."

"Yes, I'm sure you are right," Mariah said, swallowing hard. She wanted to take a last glance at Echohawk, but she turned away from the window.

"We will have such a wonderful time tonight," Abigail said, sweeping Mariah from the room and hurriedly down the corridor and then the narrow staircase.

Mariah's heart pounded as they moved down another corridor, the sound of music and laughter drawing closer. She sucked in a nervous breath, then went into the ballroom at Abigail's side. She stopped and took a quick step back, struck almost numb with fear when she saw the throng of people. Some were milling about, sipping either punch or wine from long-stemmed glasses, while others were whirling across the polished parquet, crinolines and silken ruffles billowing, the string quartet on a platform at the far end of the room.

Abigail laughed softly and took Mariah's hand, leading her into the room. Mariah's heart fluttered and her face became flushed with a building excitement, and she was glad for the moment to be able to put Echohawk at least partly from her mind. She allowed Abigail to usher her around the room, introducing her to the other guests.

Soon Mariah found herself spinning around the room with one handsome gentleman after another, her dress billowing prettily about her, the ruffle of her petticoat seeming to foam around her delicate ankles.

She excused herself each time she stepped clumsily on the feet of the men, trying to hide her embarrassment behind winning smiles.

But too soon her merriment became strained, and even more awkward, when Tanner McCloud was suddenly there, his strange yellow eyes gleaming into hers. She did not have time to protest when he grabbed her roughly by the hand and took her among the dancers and began whirling her around the room, all the while smiling in his leering way.

Everything about him made her uncomfortable. She saw him as a repulsive, vile old man. And he always seemed to have the stench of death on him after working with dead animals all day, removing their pelts.

"Tanner McCloud, this one dance is all you will get from me," she said icily. She glared up at him. "Must I remind you that my father sent you away when you brought the bride price to pay for me?"

"That was then," Tanner said, chuckling. "This is now."

"Nothing has changed," Mariah fumed. "Nothing!"

"I'd say everything has changed," Tanner said, leaning down into her face, the stench of alcohol on his breath causing Mariah to turn her face away, gagging. "It's apparent you've run away from your pa. As I see it, because you ain't with him and his bossin' ways any longer, you can make your own decisions." His yellow eyes gleamed into hers. "It's all up to you, Mariah. Marry me. I'll give you the world."

"Marry you?" Mariah said, staring disbelievingly up at him. Then she threw her head back and laughed. "Not if you were the last man on earth!"

Then she grew sober and looked up at him with narrowing

eyes, trying to jerk herself free when the string quartet stopped playing and all of the dancers paused between songs.

"Let me go," she said, her voice a low hiss. She tried to jerk herself free again, but to no avail. Tanner continued to stand there, his hold on her wrist solid, his lips twisted into an ugly smile.

"I'd let her go if I were you," a man said suddenly behind Mariah.

She turned her head with a start, finding herself looking at a young man with ruddy yet handsome features and hair the same color as hers—as red as autumn sunsets. He was taller than Tanner, and when he bowed civilly and cut in to rescue her, she smiled up into dark and dancing friendly eyes.

"Thank you, sir," she said as Tanner released his hold on her and quickly lost himself in the crowd, moving away from her and the stranger.

Abigail came in a rustle of petticoats to Mariah's side. "My son, William Joseph, is your hero for tonight," she said, laughing softly as she placed a gentle hand to her son's cheek, patting it. "And, son, this is the young lady I told you about. This is Mariah Temple."

Mariah blushed and her hand went to her hair when she found William Joseph gazing bemusedly at it, then sighed with relief when his attention moved from her hair, to smile warmly down at her again.

"And she is everything that you said she would be," William Joseph said, lifting Mariah's hand to his lips, kissing it. "Lovely. Enchantingly lovely."

Mariah lowered her eyes, blushing; then, before she could say a word to William Joseph, he had whisked her into the midst of the whirling dancers and begun guiding her masterfully around the floor.

"Mother told me about your father," he said frowning. "I think it was very courageous of you to leave home on your own to seek a new way of life without Victor. You have come to the right people for assistance. My mother and father are most kindhearted. They will do right by you."

"I am ever so grateful," Mariah murmured, gasping with

embarrassment when she half-stumbled over one of William Joseph's feet as they made another wide turn on the dance floor.

"Pardon me," she said, laughing softly as she looked up at him, so glad that she did not find mockery in his eyes. "I . . . I have never danced before tonight. It is such an awkward thing to do!"

"You dance like an angel," William Joseph said, firming his grip on her waist. He leaned his face closer to hers. "And may I say, my dear Mariah, you *look* like an angel."

Not used to a man flirting with her, and wanting never to become enamored of a man again, she changed the direction of their conversation.

"Tell me about yourself, William Joseph," she said, smiling up at him. "Your mother said that you are a restless soul, seeking adventure wherever you can find it. If I were a man, I would want to live the same sort of life."

"My wild life has taken me too often from my family," William Joseph said, glancing over at Abigail, who was busy chatting with several women as she stood at the refreshment table dipping punch into cups and glasses. "But of course my father is too busy to notice, and my mother has other children to take her mind off a wandering son."

"Tell me about your adventures," Mariah said, her heart crying out for Echohawk. Above the string quartet's music she could hear the singing and the thumping of the drums outside, where the Indians had gathered.

Oh, how she wanted to be there!

She wanted to be by Echohawk's side, sharing the powwow with him.

She forced herself to be attentive to William Joseph's tales about his adventures with the different Indian tribes while serving as an interpreter.

But when William Joseph spoke sadly of his marriage to a lovely Indian maiden, and how circumstances had torn them apart, that was all it took to break Mariah's composure.

Sobbing suddenly, she broke away from William Joseph and fled from the ballroom, out onto the terrace, then down several steps which led to a small flower garden behind the stately mansion.

She buried her face in her hands and cried a moment; then, when she heard anxious footsteps approaching, she dried her eyes with the backs of her hands and squared her shoulders, just as William Joseph appeared, his eyes troubled.

"Why did you run away?" he asked, peering down at her through the darkness. "Was it something I said?"

"It was my clumsiness," Mariah said, forcing the lie across her lips. "I . . . I just couldn't stay there and continue making a fool of myself while all of the other women were dancing so smoothly. I am sure you understand."

"The air is damp," William Joseph said, reaching a hand toward her. "Come back inside with me. I promise I won't ask you to dance. I will get you some refreshment."

Finding it impossible to return to the ballroom when her heart ached for Echohawk, Mariah shook her head. "No," she murmured. "Please go back without me. I . . . I need a breath of fresh air."

William Joseph removed his green velveteen coat and slipped it around her shoulders. "At least wear this so that you won't get a chill," he said softly. "Stay awhile, then come back inside. I will serve you punch and cake."

"That would be delightful," Mariah said, snuggling into the coat. "I shall return shortly."

William Joseph smiled warmly down at her, then began to walk away. As Mariah turned longingly toward the powwow grounds, she pulled up with a start and almost fainted when Echohawk was suddenly there blocking her path.

She composed herself and looked up at him, and thrilled through and through when she could tell by the way he looked at her that he still cared for her, regardless of what she'd done.

"You knew that I was here?" she said, her voice trembling with emotion.

"Ay-uh," Echohawk said, his gaze taking in the gentleman's coat on her shoulders. He had watched William Joseph place it there, and jealousy plagued him. "I know this and much more."

"What else?" Mariah dared to ask, her heart pounding.

"Your reason for having been among those who raided my village," Echohawk said stiffly. "It was one more thing your evil father forced upon you. Chief Silver Wing told me your father's name and where he resides. He also told me that your father not only abuses his daughter but also is a liar and a cheat!"

Realizing that the secret was out—who her father was, and where he lived, and his part in the raid—Mariah paled. Although she no longer loved or respected her father, she did not want him to be killed.

And she did not want the man that she loved to be responsible for his death.

But she also knew that she had no control whatsoever over her father's destiny, nor over Echohawk's role in it.

"No-din," Echohawk said, taking her hands in his, "I forgive you your part in the raid. I forgive you everything! I want you back. My heart has been lonely without you. Return with me to my dwelling. Be the 'flower of my wigwam' again! You filled my heart with love and happiness. It can be that way again, if you will allow it."

Hearing the sadness and pain in Echohawk's voice, and feeling so deeply for him, and feeling free to show her emotions to him, Mariah moved into his arms and hugged him tightly. "Echohawk, I'm so sorry about so many things," she cried. "Oh, Echohawk, I love you so much. Let me show you how happy we can be!"

Echohawk's heart thundered wildly. "You will be mine again?" he asked, placing a finger to her chin, tilting her eyes up to his.

"Ay-uh," she murmured. She smoothed her fingers over the lenses of his eyeglasses. "How is your eyesight? Has it improved at all?"

"Somewhat," he said, then very intently brushed William Joseph's coat from her shoulders.

But as he leaned down to kiss her, footsteps approaching made him draw away from her and move quickly into the bushes to hide.

Mariah reached a hand out to him, to tell him that it was not necessary to hide from anyone. She was going to shout their love to the world! She was proud of him—proud to be his woman!

William Joseph rushed to Mariah and placed gentle hands on her bare shoulders. "Mariah, I've got some bad news to tell you," he said, his voice drawn.

"What?" Mariah asked, a sudden fear grabbing at her insides. "What is it, William Joseph?"

"Your father's trading post has been burned and your father is missing," he said in a rush of words.

Mariah stared up at William Joseph, stunned numb by the news. Then her gaze went to the bushes where Echohawk hid, her eyes locking with his before he turned and ran soundlessly from her, hidden from William Joseph by the black cloak of night.

Echohawk, she whispered to herself. *Oh, God, no. Surely not Echohawk. . . .*

But she would never forget how he had vowed revenge against those responsible for his people's sorrow.

All he had lacked was a name.

19

The good are better made by ill,
As odors crush'd are sweeter still.

—ROGERS

"Mariah?" William Joseph said, clasping his fingers more tightly to her shoulders.

Her name being spoken wrenched Mariah out of her sad reverie, her grief over having perhaps lost with one blow both her father *and* the man that she loved. If Echohawk was responsible for this latest tragedy in her life, then what they had said only moments ago to one another meant nothing at all.

"I must go and see for myself what happened at my father's trading post," Mariah said, wrenching herself free from William Joseph.

She gathered the skirt of her gown into her arms as she rushed away from him, determined not to think about Echohawk's likely role in what had happened. Her father had to be her prime interest now.

She had to find out if he was alive—or dead!

"Perhaps I might find tracks that could lead me to him," she said over her shoulder as William Joseph came after her. "I won't let myself believe that he . . . that he is dead. I just won't."

"You can't do that, Mariah," William Joseph fused. "I'll go. I'll take care of things."

"William Joseph, he is my father and I insist that I ride with you to see if there is anything that can be done to find him," Mariah said, taking the steps up to the veranda two at a time.

"It won't be safe," William Joseph said, hurrying ahead of her, opening the door for her.

She breezed into the ballroom, past gawking partygoers, and into the corridor, very aware now that Abigail had joined William Joseph, one on each side of her. "Abigail, tell your son that I am capable of riding with him to search for my father," she said, giving William Joseph an annoyed glance. "I can ride a horse as well as you, William Joseph. And I can also handle a firearm just as well."

"But, Mariah," Abigail fussed, walking on into Mariah's bedroom with her as William Joseph paused and waited in the corridor, "you are so beautiful tonight in that gown. You can't seriously want to . . . to play the role of a man again. Let William Joseph take care of things. I assure you he is a most capable man. He can do anything he sets his mind to."

Mariah turned and gave Abigail a stern stare. "So can I, Abigail," she said flatly. "And so shall I tonight!"

"Oh, Mariah," Abigail said, nervously clasping and unclasping her hands. "Please don't do this."

Mariah was already out of her dress, petticoats, and fancy slippers. She went to the chifferobe, grabbed her buckskin dress from a hook, and hurried into it. Again her thoughts returned to Echohawk, the dress a reminder of the many hours spent with him.

She did not want to believe that Echohawk could come to her, professing his love for her, even forgiving her for her role in the raid, right after having taken vengeance against her very own father.

She could not see how he could be gentle and caring one moment, a vicious savage the next.

Even though Echohawk had many reasons to hate her father, she just couldn't envision him burning and killing at the very same moment he was planning to come to her to ask her to be his woman.

No.

It did not make sense.

But she had to be sure.

The buckskin dress turning her back into the woman that Echohawk had fallen in love with, Mariah slipped hurriedly into knee-high moccasins, ignoring heavy footsteps that entered the room.

"What is this that William Joseph told me?" Colonel Snelling said in a threatening growl.

Mariah turned with a start. Her eyes widened and her back stiffened when she saw the anger in Josiah's eyes. "I must go to my father's trading post and see for myself what has happened," she murmured, feeling dwarfed as the colonel towered over her, a sternness in his flashing dark eyes that she had never seen before.

"I have assigned a unit of men to ride to the trading post," Josiah said, his hand clasped to a saber at his side. "William Joseph will lead them. You will only be in their way, Mariah." His gaze raked over her, seeing her change of clothes; then he glared at her again. "Change back into your gown. Return with Abigail to the ball. Let men do men's work."

Firming her chin, insulted that Josiah would think that she could dismiss the welfare of her father so frivolously from her mind, Mariah placed her hands on her hips and glared up at him.

"I do not need reminders that I am not a man," she said stubbornly. "And caring about what has happened to my father does not make me any less a lady. I am going to accompany your men, Colonel Snelling. If you still say that you will not allow it, I shall ride alone."

Josiah kneaded his chin, slowly shaking his head back and forth, then placed his hand on her shoulder. "I can't have you riding anywhere alone beyond the walls of the fort," he said glumly. "Not while those who are going around killing and burning are running loose close by. I'll tell William Joseph that you are riding with him and his men." He leaned closer to Mariah's face. "But I'll also tell him to keep an eye on you. I don't care if you can ride and shoot like a man, I am not going to let anyone hurt you!"

Tears welled up in Mariah's eyes and she felt ashamed for having been so harsh with this man who was only looking out for her welfare. She crept into his arms, so wishing that her own father could have been as compassionate—as caring.

When his strong arms swung around her waist, holding her to him, she relished the moment, pretending he was her father—wishing it were so.

And then, realizing that time was passing quickly and that her father's life might be ebbing away as the clock ticked away each second, she eased from Josiah's arms and walked toward the door. When she found William Joseph outside waiting, having changed into buckskin riding attire, she walked proudly with him outside and mounted her horse beside his.

When Colonel Snelling and Abigail came to look at her, she was touched deeply when Josiah handed her a rifle.

"Ride with care," he said as she took the rifle.

"Please be careful," Abigail said, blowing Mariah a kiss as Mariah nodded and wheeled her horse around, riding beside William Joseph at the head of the group of soldiers.

"Please be careful!" Abigail said again, waving frantically at Mariah and William Joseph until they rode on through the opened gate that led out into the forest.

Abigail sobbed and turned to her husband. "I wish they had waited until morning," she said, shivering as she looked into the dark depths of the forest, hearing the howl of a wolf and the hoot of an owl somewhere in the distance. "The killers could be just waiting outside the fort walls. It would be so easy . . . to . . . to ambush our loved ones."

"Now, now," Josiah comforted her, placing an arm around his wife's waist. "Let's not let our imagination run away with us."

"So many tragedies have happened of late, Josiah," Abigail said sullenly. "The attack on Echohawk's village. And now on Mariah's father's trading post. Her father is missing. What can happen next, Josiah? As long as those who are responsible are running around loose, how can I not be afraid for our son and for Mariah?"

"We must have faith in God that we will find those responsible soon," Colonel Snelling said, sighing heavily. "Until then, darling, you must keep your faith."

Abigail nodded, but found it hard at this moment to feel secure about anything.

* * *

Riding his horse hard through the night, Echohawk desperately needed to get back to Chief Silver Wing's village. Those white men who might point an accusing finger at Echohawk for the tragedy that had befallen No-din's father tonight would come searching for him, and once they were at Chief Silver Wing's village, might decide to punish all of the Indians there for good measure.

He could not allow that to happen. He had to warn Chief Silver Wing. He and his people, and Echohawk's must disband and take their village elsewhere.

Having won and lost Mariah again almost in the same breath tonight made a bitterness soar through him. It did not seem that he was meant ever to have a peaceful heart. If not one thing, it was another! And that his losses included Mariah over and over again made it almost too hard for him to bear.

It was up to him to clear his name before ever approaching No-din again. Even if she was with him, she would not be safe. If tragedy befell the Chippewa again, and if she were with him, performing in the capacity of wife, transformed, herself, into Chippewa, she could be counted among the dead. . . .

The reflection of orange in the sky from outdoor fires made Echohawk realize that he was almost at Chief Silver Wing's village. His heart ached over having to tell the noble chief that he would no longer be safe in the village that he had established many moons ago—a village where corn grew in abundance and where wild rice was always there in the autumn, thriving, just for the Chippewa, it seemed.

When he advised Chief Silver Wing that he, Echohawk, had brought possible doom to Silver Wing's people, he did not want to think of the emotions the chief would be feeling. To survive an attack, they must move elsewhere, or stand and fight a fight that was not theirs and risk losing a whole generation of Chippewa children.

Had it not been for his own troubles, he despaired, Chief

Silver Wing's people would continue to be safe—would continue to be content.

Echohawk rode into the village, his chin held high, yet his heart aching with an utter sadness and remorse for what lay ahead of him. After he helped uproot Chief Silver Wing's village, and also his own people, and saw them to safety, Echohawk and several braves would disband and travel alone, to search for the *real* culprits.

* * *

Lightning, a strange phenomenon for the month of November, was flashing in the sky overhead, illuminating everything around Mariah for seconds at a time, making her discoveries worse, even eerie, at what was left of her father's trading post—and what had been her childhood home.

Torn with how she should feel, Mariah stood beside the charred remains, recalling so many things, both happy and sad. Her happiest times had been when her mother had still been alive.

Her mother had been everything to her.

But since her mother's death Mariah had found it a hard struggle to live in the company of a father whose heart had seemingly turned to stone.

Except for her memories of her mother, there was no sorrow at viewing what was left of the trading post.

"There are no signs of your father anywhere," William Joseph said, stepping gingerly to Mariah's side. "And there are no clear tracks leading anywhere. Whoever abducted your father was clever. They erased all tracks leading to and from the trading post."

"Then you are certain that my father is not . . . is not among those ashes?" Mariah said, gesturing toward the smoking rubble.

"One of his men who survived the fire told of seeing your father being dragged toward a horse," William Joseph said somberly.

Mariah turned quickly to him. "If there was a man alive to

tell that, surely he saw who was to blame for everything else that happened here tonight," she said, looking anxiously up into his dark eyes. "Or someone else. Surely there were others to ask."

"They were apparently all slain while running from their bunkhouse," William Joseph said, gesturing toward that burned-out structure. "Only one lived long enough to talk to those who discovered the massacre."

"And? What else did he say?" Mariah asked, her voice rising in pitch. But she felt close to being able to know the truth about Echohawk.

Whether he was innocent or guilty.

"Before he had a chance to say who did it, he died," William Joseph said, sighing heavily. "And so now we must return to Father and ask his advice. I'd say a search party must be formed. And soon."

Disappointed that she had not been able to get a clear answer about Echohawk, Mariah nodded weakly, then walked limply to her horse and swung herself into the saddle.

Disconsolately she rode beside William Joseph back in the direction of the fort. Although she was concerned over her father's welfare, her thoughts kept wandering to Echohawk. Just prior to William Joseph's appearance in the garden to tell her the disturbing news about her father, she had made promises to Echohawk—promises that now meant nothing, it seemed. Echohawk had fled from her like a man guilty of a fiendish crime, and she had immediately accused him within her heart, as though she had no faith in him whatsoever.

How can one base a future on such weaknesses as that? she wondered sadly to herself.

The fact that she could think Echohawk guilty of the vicious deed lay heavy on her heart.

Dispirited, she rode with the others, yet felt no better even when they reached the fort and were once again in the company of Colonel Snelling, reporting their findings. Soon they would depart again and search for not only her father but also those responsible for his abduction or death.

* * *

The rain was splashing hard against the study window as Colonel Snelling paced his study, his hands clasped behind him. William Joseph and Mariah stood quietly by, watching him. Just as he turned and faced them again, they were interrupted.

"What is it?" Josiah said in a snarl, gazing without affection at Tanner McCloud as he stepped into the room, soaked to the skin, sending off an aroma similar to wet dog's fur. "I hope you have good reason for entering my study without first being announced."

Tanner swallowed hard and shifted his feet nervously on the carpet as he came to a sudden stop beside Mariah. "I heard about Mariah's father," he said, glancing guardedly at her, then back at Josiah. "I think I may have some valuable information you should be interested in hearing."

"It had better be valuable enough to warrant you being here in my office, when I can hardly stand to look at you, much less be in the same room as your stench," Josiah said, his eyes filled with warning. He went to Tanner and leaned into his face. "When you had the gall to mix with my acquaintances at the ball tonight without a formal invitation, I had a good notion to shoot you on the spot. If not for my beloved wife's prohibition on blood spilling in her home, I'd have done it. Now, say your piece and get the hell out of here."

Tanner gasped and took a step back from Josiah. "I've heard rumors that an Injun wearing eyeglasses was seen leading a raiding party tonight close to Victor Temple's trading post," he said in a rush of words. "The ones who saw this were just passing through or I'd have brought them here to tell you what they saw, eye to eye."

Mariah had stood by listening to Tanner's tale, then blanched and felt suddenly dizzy when he was through. She reached for the back of a chair and steadied herself, finding it hard to think clearly, much less speak in Echohawk's behalf.

And how could she? Hadn't she already been doubting Echohawk, even before Tanner had brought the news to Colonel Snelling? The knowing made her feel desperately ill to her stomach.

"An Indian wearing eyeglasses?" William Joseph said, kneading his chin. His eyes widened. "Why, Echohawk was wearing eyeglasses tonight. Everyone saw him. It was such a strange sight on an Indian brave that surely no one missed it."

"Perhaps you saw Echohawk wearing eyeglasses tonight, but that doesn't mean that he is the guilty party," Colonel Snelling said in Echohawk's defense. "I have never known Echohawk to be anything but wise and reasonable. I won't believe that he is guilty of this crime tonight."

"Now, just how many Injuns do you see wearin' eyeglasses?" Tanner scoffed, his lips twisting into a smug smile. "None, I tell you. None. Only Echohawk, Josiah. Only Echohawk! I say he's guilty as sin!" He turned to Mariah. "He's the one, Mariah. He's got your pa hid away somewhere. Don't let Colonel Snelling tell you otherwise."

"How can anyone ever believe anything you say?" Mariah said, finally finding her ability to speak. "My father despised you, Tanner. I know you didn't care beans about him. So why would you even care what's happened to him?"

"I don't want to see anyone at the mercy of Injuns," Tanner quickly explained. "I wouldn't wish that on my worst enemy."

"And you are so sure it was Echohawk?" Mariah said, her voice trembling.

"Positively certain," Tanner said, squaring his shoulders.

"Well, I'm not," Colonel Snelling said, slouching down in his chair behind his desk. He looked up at William Joseph. "Go out to the powwow and find Echohawk. Bring him back inside so that he can have his say in the matter. Echohawk must be given a chance to convince me that he *is* the son of his father—a man of peace."

"I don't believe that Echohawk will be found at the powwow," Mariah said, firming her chin defiantly at their surprised expressions. "He'll be at Chief Silver Wing's village. I assure you of that. He is innocent. And thank you for letting him prove it to you."

"Mariah, how is it that you know where Echohawk has

gone?" William Joseph asked, looking down at her with concern in his eyes.

"It's . . . it's not important now," Mariah said, giving him a set stare, "but if he's left the powwow, he will have returned to his people."

"It's a waste of time," Tanner said, shrugging. "He won't be there either. He'll be runnin' scared."

Mariah turned and glared at Tanner, suddenly feeling strangely suspicious of how adamant he was to get everyone to believe that Echohawk was the guilty party, when, in truth, Tanner had as much reason as Echohawk to kill her father.

The vile man was capable of all sorts of evil deeds!

All along, she hadn't wanted to believe that Echohawk was guilty, and she didn't now that Tanner had pointed an accusing finger at him. She especially wanted to prove Tanner wrong, not only for her own and Echohawk's sakes but also to possibly turn the accusing finger back at Tanner.

"I don't think I need any more advice, Tanner," Colonel Snelling said, rising from his chair. He went to Tanner and took him by the elbow and ushered him to the door. "Now, go and find someone else to pester, will you?"

William Joseph chuckled; then his smile faded when he gazed down at Mariah, seeing so much seething hate for Tanner McCloud in the depths of her eyes. "Mariah?" he said, gently taking her hand. "Are you all right?"

"Yes, I'm fine," Mariah said, then swung away from him. "William Joseph, we're wasting time standing here talking. Let's go to Chief Silver Wing's village. Let's prove Tanner wrong!"

William Joseph fell into step beside her, Colonel Snelling giving them a salute as they walked past him.

* * *

The rain had stopped. Daylight was just breaking along the horizon, and birds were chattering in the trees overhead when the search party arrived at Chief Silver Wing's village—what was left of it.

An eerie feeling gripped Mariah at the pit of her stomach and she grew numb as she looked slowly around her. There were now only the remains of wigwams where they had once stood stately beside the river. Stripped clean of their rush mats and bark coverings, they gave the appearance of skeletons standing across the land.

William Joseph edged his horse close to Mariah's. "Seems that Tanner may have been right about Echohawk," he said, his voice drawn. "I hate it like hell, Mariah. Like hell."

"I still don't believe it," Mariah murmured. "There has to be an explanation. There just has to be."

A soldier rode up next to them. "All signs of departure have been erased from the land," he said. "We'll have one hell of a time trackin' them."

"We'll do our best," William Joseph said, resting his hand on a holstered pistol at his right hip.

Mariah's eyes lowered; then she nudged her horse with her knees and rode along with William Joseph. She dreaded finding the answers—which would surely condemn Echohawk. Not only had he fled the fort upon the discovery of what had happened to her father, but apparently he had also encouraged Chief Silver Wing to pull up roots and run.

"We need to rest before moving on," William Joseph said, dismounting. "Let's make camp for a while. We'll sleep, then leave again around noon."

Mariah did not like this decision of William Joseph's—to make camp where the Indian village had just been vacated. It did not seem right, as though they were trespassing on hallowed ground.

But having no heart to argue, she dismounted and helped make camp while some of the men went in search of food.

After they had eaten and she was finally alone snug in her bedroll, she found that sleep would not come for her. Although it had been a full day and night since she had slept, her mind kept wandering to Echohawk, and where he might be.

Loving him so much, she felt guilty for being a part of the search for him, but if it would lead her to her father, and if it would clear her beloved's name . . .

Mariah tossed and turned in her bedroll for a while longer, then decided that no matter how hard she tried, she wasn't going to be able to go to sleep.

She rose on an elbow and looked into the distance, recalling the burial grounds where Echohawk's father lay. Something compelled her to slip out of the bedroll, draw a blanket snugly around her shoulders, and sneak from camp. She led her horse a short distance from the campsite, then mounted it and rode away. She was not sure why, but she had to go to the burial grounds.

20

Kiss the tears from her eyes, you'll find the rose
the sweeter for the dew.

—Webster

Fog pressed in on Mariah as she rode beside the river, the early-morning sun peering through in shadowy orange sprays. She turned her horse in another direction and rode briskly across a wide stretch of meadow, the dew on the knee-high grass sparkling like tiny diamonds.

Mariah's heart began to race when she saw ahead the butte to which she had gone with Echohawk not long ago to visit his father's gravesite.

As the day grew brighter with sunlight and she came closer to the butte, something else made her almost go limp with joy.

Blaze!

Blaze at the foot of the butte!

Her gaze darted upward, now able to make out a man standing at the edge of the butte, watching her approach.

"Echohawk!" Mariah marveled, not understanding how she had been drawn there, yet clearly for this purpose!

She took one long lingering look, seeing that today he was dressed in only a brief breechclout, the wind fluttering it against his muscled thighs. She swallowed hard, lost in desire, admiring his stance of a noble leader.

And his leadership was being threatened.

She looked to the heavens and silently mouthed a prayer: *Oh, God, let me help him. Please prove to me that I have been wrong to doubt him! Please let him be innocent!*

A soft breeze brushed against her face, a caress, and she shivered, believing that somehow she had just been given an answer from the Almighty.

And at that moment she suddenly felt a gentle peace wash over her.

Smiling, sending a silent thank-you to the heavens, she nudged her heels more deeply into the flanks of her horse and rode hurriedly on, soon losing sight of Echohawk as she drew rein beside Blaze in the shadows of the butte.

Her pulse racing, she quickly dismounted. As she turned to climb the steep terrain, she found that it was not necessary.

Echohawk was there.

He had come to her. . . .

"No-din," he said, momentarily standing before her, his eyes heavy with doubt.

But when she moved into his arms and hugged him, all doubts were erased and he embraced her long and hard.

"Echohawk," Mariah said, clinging, her cheek against his powerful bare chest. "Oh, Echohawk, I've been so worried about you. Thank God you are all right."

Echohawk embraced her for a moment longer, then eased her away from him, holding her at arm's length. "You came," he said thickly. "All night long I summoned you here. It was with the Great Spirit's blessing that you came."

"It was you?" Mariah said, gasping softly. "You are the reason that I felt compelled to come to the place of your father's burial?"

"That is so," Echohawk said, nodding.

"But what if I were followed?" Mariah asked, taking a quick glance over her shoulder, having not once thought of that possibility while forging onward through the night.

"I did not beckon anyone else," Echohawk said dryly. "Only you. So no one followed. When William Joseph awakens and finds you gone, only then will you be missed."

"They will come looking for me," Mariah worried, looking quickly up at Echohawk.

"But they will not find you," he said, smiling smugly. "You are going with me and my braves to learn the truth. William Joseph and his men will be looking elsewhere."

"How did you know that I was with William Joseph?" Mariah asked, her eyes wide.

"My scouts watch. They see many things," Echohawk said, dropping his hands from Mariah. "Come. We must go. My men wait in the forest."

"Where are you taking me?" Mariah asked, not hesitating to mount her horse as Echohawk helped her into the saddle.

"Where you will see my innocence," Echohawk said, going to Blaze, quickly mounting. "And then, my *ee-quay,* woman, we will prove to Colonel Snelling that he has been right to put faith in me."

"You are being accused of burning my father's trading post and of his abduction," Mariah said, easing her horse closer to Echohawk's.

"And did you also accuse me of such crimes?" he asked, examining her through his eyeglasses. His eyesight was improving more quickly each day, yet not enough to cast aside the white man's magic.

Mariah lowered her eyes so that he would not see the guilt in their depths. Then, knowing that she must, she looked slowly back up at him and locked her eyes with his. "I could not help but doubt you," she murmured. "You had spoken of vengeance more than once to me. And when you fled after hearing William Joseph tell me of my father's tragedy, what was I to believe? You could have stood your ground and defended yourself. But you fled, Echohawk! You ran away. And not only you, but Chief Silver Wing's entire village."

"And do you think that had I stayed and professed my innocence I would have been exonerated by the white man's law?" he said in a growl. "No, No-din. It would have not been that way. Not even Colonel Snelling has the power to keep the white men from hanging an Indian who in their eyes is guilty. Once white people are enticed to kill an Indian, no one can stop it."

"You think someone purposely spread the word that you did this to my father?" Mariah asked, thinking of Tanner McCloud and how he had so adamantly spoken against Echohawk to Colonel Snelling.

"Ay-uh," Echohawk said, frowning at Mariah. "One man alone has done this. My scouts probed and found out who. It

is the man I call Yellow Eyes. It is he who has caused much sadness in my life. It is because of him that my people's number has been reduced, my beloved Fawn among those who were killed during the massacre led by Yellow Eyes and his renegade Sioux companions led by White Wolf. It is time for Yellow Eyes and White Wolf to die!"

"Yellow Eyes?" Mariah said, her heart skipping a beat. She was picturing Tanner McCloud's eyes, having always wondered why the whites were so yellow. Echohawk must be referring to Tanner!

"Ay-uh," Echohawk grumbled. "Finally I have found him. It is good to know that the evil white man with the eyes of a coward is near. I am going to make him pay for his deeds."

"This man you call Yellow Eyes," Mariah said guardedly. "Do you know his true name? Could it be Tanner McCloud?"

"*Ay-uh,* that is what he is called by the white men," Echohawk said.

Anger suddenly raged through Mariah. Her eyes narrowed. "Then I was right," she said, circling her hands into tight fists. "He is the one who did this to my father."

Then she looked anxiously over at Echohawk. "You said that you would take me with you to find Tanner," she said, grabbing up her reins. "What of my father? Once we get to Tanner's hideout, we will surely find my father there. Echohawk, now that you know my father's role in the most recent raid against your people, is it in your plans to kill him?"

"And what would you have me do?" Echohawk asked, his jaw tight.

Mariah swallowed hard, not knowing how she could answer him, not wanting to be forced to choose between the man she loved with all of her heart and her father, whom she despised. It would be far too easy for her to make the choice. Oh, but how torn she felt at this moment!

"So you see?" Echohawk said, leaning a gentle hand to her cheek. "The answers are not always so easy to sort out within one's heart."

With that he grabbed his reins, wheeled his horse around, and rode away.

Mariah stared after him for a moment, then rode in pursuit, soon pulling up beside him. "Where are we going?" she asked, the warmth of the autumn sun welcome on her face. "Where is my father?"

"Nothing is known about your father," Echohawk returned, glancing at her. "Yellow Eyes is the only one I truly seek at this time. And my scouts discovered that he hides from the world across the river from the Falls of St. Anthony. This is my destination."

Soon they met and joined with several other braves, and rode on together through the forest. Mariah had heard of the beautiful Falls of St. Anthony but had not seen them.

She had also heard of the river's treacherous waters at the foot of the falls, which she would soon be crossing.

* * *

It was late afternoon when they arrived at the Falls of St. Anthony. Mariah was stunned by the grandeur of the falls, the river there no more than half a mile wide, breaking into sheets of foam and rushing to the pitch over a steeply inclined plane.

The falls themselves, she noticed, were not high—the rock face broken and irregular. Huge slabs of rock lay scattered below, in wild disorder. Some stood on their edges, leaning against the ledge from which they had broken. Some lay piled upon each other in the water, in random confusion.

A long, narrow island divided the falls nearly in the middle. The eastern fall was not perpendicular, but broken into three distinct leaps, below which the twisting and swirling eddies threatened destruction to any living thing that entered them.

On the western side, in the boiling rapids below, a few rods from the fall, lay an island—rising steeply from the waters and covered with forest trees. Tanner McCloud was on this island, somewhere deep within the forest.

And, perhaps, her father. . . .

They made camp, planning to attack Tanner McCloud's encampment early the next morning. Hungry and bone-tired, Mariah welcomed this pause, and now, having eaten a delicious meal of cooked rabbit, she sat with Echohawk in a cozy lean-to beside the simmering logs of the campfire. Echohawk's braves had fanned out from the camp to stragetic spots, keeping watch for any sudden intruders in the night.

It was nearing dusk, the air filled with a damp chill. Echohawk placed a blanket around Mariah's shoulders and drew her next to him. He gazed down at her without his eyeglasses, seeing her clearly and wonderfully as his. Nothing would separate them again.

He knew that he would have to think through this question of her father, should he be found at Tanner McCloud's hideout. No-din came first. If that meant having to let her father go, to keep from causing her further pain and guilt, then that was how it must be.

And perhaps because No-din was with Echohawk and his people, her father would not cause any more problems for the Chippewa. He would surely think twice before doing anything that would endanger his daughter.

"The falls are lovely yet frightening," Mariah murmured, snuggling closer to Echohawk. "This wild and picturesque beauty is surely unequaled."

"Many spirits abide here," Echohawk said, looking into the distance as the tremulous laughter of a loon came wafting over the water. "Do you hear the loon? The great northern diver is restless tonight. He does not like sharing his habitat with strangers."

"I have been told that ghosts haunt this spot," Mariah said, trembling. "There have been many deaths in the crashing waters of the falls. I . . . I even fear having to cross them myself."

Even now she could hear the crashing of large tree trunks as they drifted over the falls, plunging down into the chasms of the rocks, tumbling then into the foaming and roaring rapids, never to be seen again.

"*Ay-uh*, there have been many deaths here," Echohawk said solemnly. "The Chippewa tell of a warrior who, in the darkness of night, was deceived by the false beacons lighted by the ancestors of his enemies and paddled his canoe into the rapids. He never came out alive. And that is only one tale. There are many more."

"How awful," Mariah said, gazing around her when the loon's cries seemed closer.

"There was a song written about this warrior's death in the rapids," Echohawk said, turning to her. "Shall I sing it for you?"

"Please do," Mariah said, smiling at him.

" 'The Great Spirit calls,' " he sang softly. " 'I hear his voice in the warring waters. Soon, soon, shall they close over my head, and my song shall be heard no more. . . .' "

Echohawk took Mariah's waist in his hands and eased her onto her back on a thick pallet of furs. "My heart has been so lonely without you," he whispered. "Stay with me forever, Nodin. Forever."

Mariah twined her arms around his neck, oblivious of the night's chill, aware only of Echohawk's mouth closing over hers in a fierce kiss, and of the warmth of his hand easing beneath her dress. She raised her hips, making it easier for him to remove her undergarment. After that was tossed aside and Echohawk closed his hand over her throbbing center, she sucked in a wild breath of ecstasy. When he thrust a finger within her, and his tongue began probing between her lips, the pleasure was so intensely beautiful, the world seemed to be melting away beneath her.

Moving over her with his body, his breechclout now cast aside, Echohawk smoothed her dress up past her hips and moved gently into her, then pressed endlessly deeper as she raised her hips and strained to meet him.

Mariah sucked at his lips and tongue, her hands traveling over his muscled back and then around to where she could get occasional touches of his satin shaft as he moved generously in and out of her.

She closed her eyes, a spinning heat seizing her, rising and flooding her whole body, pushing at the boundaries of her senses. That she was with Echohawk again, sharing the wonder of his embrace, was all that mattered. Their bodies and souls fused, becoming one entity.

When he moved slightly away from her, she reached out for him and drew him back. Placing her hands at the nape of his neck, she brought his lips to hers and kissed him passionately, as once again he entered her. Her gasps of pleasure became soft whimpers as she felt the pleasure mounting, then sweeping through her as his body reached a matching passion, finally subsiding exhaustedly into hers.

They lay there for a long while, Mariah gently stroking his back. "I'm sorry for having doubted you," she whispered. "You do forgive me, don't you?"

"It is easy to doubt the red man," Echohawk said, turning on his side toward her, tracing the outline of her face with his forefinger. "I am not sure that will ever change."

"It must," Mariah said, moving into his embrace, hugging him to her. "It's not fair."

"Not much in life is fair," Echohawk said. He eased away from her and drew on his breechclout and eyeglasses.

Mariah pulled her dress over her head, slipped her undergarment on, and placed a blanket around her shoulders as she moved closer to the fire. She began to speak more apologies to Echohawk, but something else drew her attention. Wide-eyed, her heart skipping several beats, she saw a loon in the fading light of evening, surely the one that they had been hearing. It was caught in the rapids.

Horrified, Mariah watched the bird as it struggled with fate for a while, but finding escape impossible, it faced downward and went under, screaming hideously, soon lost in the foaming, roaring rapids below.

"How awful!" Mariah cried, paling.

Echohawk moved to her side and sat down, his face solemn. "The red man is like the loon," he said somberly. "We struggle with fate, but to no avail. Like the river to the loon, the white man is the victor, always."

An intense chill encompassed Mariah, his words like ice water splashing through her consciousness.

"And yet you love me?" she murmured. "A woman whose skin is white?"

Echohawk turned her to face him. He lifted her onto his

lap and cradled her close. "My woman, you too were a victim of a man with white skin, a man whose heart was black," he murmured. "It is I, a red man, who will make the wrongs right for you."

Mariah's eyes filled with tears. She moved her mouth to his lips and kissed him softly, sweetly. "*Mee-gway-chee-wahn-dum,* thank you, my love," she whispered against his lips. "Thank you."

21

'Tis not the richest plant that holds the sweetest fragrance.

—Dawes

The shore was low and wet where Echohawk's braves dragged several macinac boats into the water. They had brought them there ahead of Echohawk's arrival, for the purpose of crossing this treacherous river. Mariah hugged a blanket around her arms. The chill of morning was more biting each day as autumn turned into winter.

Seeing these larger boats, instead of canoes, gave Mariah more confidence in their ability to make it across the wide river. They were large and strongly built, flat-bottomed, and pointed at both ends to ascend and descend dangerous rapids.

Mariah stifled a scream and took several shaky steps backward when out of the corner of her eye she saw a huge king snake basking on an exposed part of the riverbank. It lay in the warmth of the morning sun, its entire length ringed with narrow bands of brilliant red, black, and light yellow.

"Do not fear the snake," Echohawk said, moving to Mariah's side. "It has been slowed down by the coldness of the night. By the time it is warmed clear through, we will be on the other side of the river."

"Thank goodness for that," Mariah said, laughing nervously.

"*Mah-bee-szhon,* come," Echohawk said, placing a hand to Mariah's elbow. "The boats are loaded into the water. They are ready for travel."

The pit of Mariah's stomach felt somewhat woozy, and her throat was dry at the thought of attempting such a dangerous expedition with Echohawk and his braves. Yet, so much good could come as a result of the river crossing.

She needed to find her father, and to clear Echohawk's name.

These things alone made her step determined as she walked with Echohawk toward the boats.

The water lapping at her moccasined feet, Mariah stood in awe of Echohawk all over again when he broke into a sad, lamenting song, gazing with arms outstretched to the heavens. She listened to the words, knowing that they were meant for Echohawk's Great Spirit.

" 'Master of Life!' " Echohawk sang. " 'Look down on my braves, who have suffered wrong at the hand of the white man, and are now about to avenge it.

" 'Master of Life! Let our enterprise prosper. Let us not be seen by the enemy, and defend us from evil spirits.

" 'Master of Fate! Return us safely to our people.' "

When the song was over, Echohawk stood quietly and with great dignity in the midst of his men. Then, as he motioned to them with the gesture of a hand, his braves dispersed to their respective boats, while Echohawk helped Mariah into the one that he would command.

Once on board, sitting among many soft pelts, Echohawk and several other braves manning the oars, Mariah clung to the sides and shivered as the damp river wind dashed against her face.

Her eyes kept alert, watching the fevered changes in the water's currents. When the water slammed against the sides of the boat, it shuddered dangerously. The pit of her stomach stirred strangely when the boat would dip low, then quickly rise again as the white water tossed it about.

But, she noticed, not a sound could be heard over the roar of the falls as the boat moved steadily toward the opposite bank. As the oars dipped rhythmically in and out, it was with a silent cadence that they flowed soundlessly through the water.

Mariah inhaled a shaky breath, so relieved that the opposite shore had finally been reached. Her nose and cheeks were so cold they felt as though they might snap in two at a mere touch.

Echohawk and his men beached their boats, then Echohawk came and helped her from the boat, carrying her to land that was not damp with mud.

Once higher grasses were reached, Echohawk placed Mariah to her feet. A brave came to them. He gave Echohawk a rifle, then placed a rifle in Mariah's hand.

Echohawk smiled down at Mariah, gave her a light kiss, then nodded for her to follow him to where they soon found a faint footpath that led into the forest.

The pines were tall and straight and clean-trunked . . . worthy pillars of the forest temple. There was a light undergrowth of saplings, and many fallen tree trunks, upturned roots, and a tangle of dead branches. Quiet reigned, and sunlight flickered down through the treetops, dappling the cool greens in light and shadow.

They continued following the path for a time, then stopped sharply when through a break in the trees a short distance away they caught sight of two sentries asleep beneath a tree. Echohawk gave a signal to his braves to go on ahead and do what was necessary while he stayed behind with Mariah.

Mariah's eyes were wide as she witnessed the silent approach of the braves, creeping as silently as the padded footsteps of the panther. They grabbed the men and had them gagged and tied to the tree without even a small outcry.

Echohawk nodded for her to follow again as he began moving through the forest, the path more distinct now.

Soon voices could be heard up ahead. Mariah's eyebrows quirked when she realized that she was hearing a noisy, gleeful group of children at play.

And when she and Echohawk came close enough to see them, she watched as the children played with their dogs. She could tell that the dogs were more than likely beasts of burden and instruments of torture, for their fur was hopelessly matted, and where there was no fur, there were signs of deep lacerations across their backs. And most limped as they tried to romp with the children.

Echohawk gripped Mariah by an arm and held her close to his side as he peered at the children through a cover of bushes, and then at the women who were bent upon their tasks close to several run-down log cabins that stood in a circle of the clearing. Some were carrying great loads of wood into the camp on their backs. Some were washing clothes in a wooden tub.

But it was not so much the labor of the women or the play of the children that caught Echohawk's eye. It was that the women were a mixture—both white and Indian. The children were either half-breeds or white. This confirmed his belief that Yellow Eyes consorted with the Sioux. The proof was there for him to see.

"What of the children and women?" Mariah whispered, leaning closer to Echohawk.

He inhaled a deep breath, then set his jaw as he nodded toward the braves awaiting his commands.

Mariah watched as one by one the women and children were seized. Some of the braves took them to the boats to guard them until they could be taken to a place of safety once the confrontation with Tanner and his men was over.

Echohawk and his braves raised the war whoop and poured a shower of bullets and arrows into the cabins. The true fight began as men scurried from their cabins, some only half-dressed, surprise etched on their bearded faces.

But to Echohawk's confusion, none of these men were Sioux!

Every last one was white-skinned!

The battle raged for only a short time, the ambush having been successful. All of the men were slain. Even Tanner McCloud lay on the ground with a mortal wound.

Echohawk and Mariah went to Tanner. Mariah glared down at him as Echohawk began grilling him.

"Yellow Eyes, where are the renegade Sioux who so often accompany you on your raids?" he asked, his eyes filled with fire. "Where is White Wolf?"

Mariah knelt beside Tanner. She did not pity him the wound in his abdomen, blood pouring from it. "Where is my father?" she demanded, then paled when she saw him clutch feverishly at his chest, emitting a loud scream of pain. If he died before she discovered where her father was, she might never find him! Her eyes swept around her. The cabins seemed deserted now. Her father was surely not there.

A thought came to her which made her feel ill. If her father was not here, then he was probably dead.

Reaching a hand to Tanner's shirt collar, grasping it frantically, Mariah leaned closer to his face. "My father!" she cried. "Where is he? I know you are the one who burned his trading post. You are the one who abducted him. Where did you take him? *Where?*!"

Tanner's breathing was shallow, yet he managed a sly smile as he gazed up at Echohawk, then glared at Mariah. "You are accusing the wrong man, Mariah," he said, wheezing. "I'm not responsible for what happened to your father."

Mariah's lips parted in a gasp and her hand dropped away from Tanner. She paled when Tanner looked slowly over at Echohawk and raised a shaky finger and pointed it at him.

"He . . . did . . . it," he whispered. "Echohawk did it. Dammit, Mariah, why don't you believe me?"

Rage lit Echohawk's eyes. He grabbed Tanner by the throat and yanked his head up from the ground. "You lie!" he hissed. "Even taking your last breath, you lie, white coward. Do you know that you cannot enter paradise with a lie on your lips?"

Tanner tried to laugh, but gurgled instead. "The Sioux? White Wolf?" he said, his voice only a thread now. "Not long ago they were defeated in a skirmish with other Sioux." His eyesight was getting hazy, but his mind was still clear. He knew that White Wolf and his renegade companions were at Fort Snelling, mingling with the other Indians at the powwow. Tanner knew that once they heard of his demise, they would retaliate, to avenge their friend's death. Tanner naturally wanted this to come as a total surprise to Echohawk.

"How can I believe that this is true when you have lied so easily about No-din's father?" Echohawk said in a snarl. "Surely honor in death is not as important to the white man as it is to the Chippewa!"

"No-din?" Tanner said, coughing up blood. "Who is this No-din you speak of?"

Mariah leaned down into his face. "*I* am No-din," she said, proud of her Chippewa name.

Tanner looked from Mariah to Echohawk. "You are with the Chippewa, dressed in Chippewa garb," he said, blood now curling from his nose. "And you now have a Chippewa name?" He grabbed at his chest and groaned, yet his eyes were still locked with Mariah's. "You choose a savage over me?"

"You are the savage," Mariah said flatly. "And you have always turned my stomach, Tanner. As for Echohawk, I adore him. I proudly warm his bed at night!"

Panic seized Mariah when she saw the wildness in Tanner's eyes and heard the shortness of his breath. She realized now how foolish it had been to speak of anything to him but her father. She still did not know where he was, and she was absolutely positive that Tanner did.

She leaned closer to his ear when his eyes closed. "Please," she begged, "tell me where I can find my father. Before you die, Tanner, please do one decent thing. For me, Tanner? Please?"

When Tanner's eyes opened and looked up at her, a strange sort of peacefulness in their depths, she felt hope rise within her, thinking that somehow she had reached a corner of his heart that hadn't hardened.

But with a shock she discovered that she was wrong. The reason for the restfulness in his eyes was that he was dead!

"*No!*" she screamed. She grabbed his shoulders and began shaking him. "You can't die! Not before you tell me where my father is!"

A gentle hand on her shoulder drew Mariah's head around. Through her tears she saw Echohawk. "He's dead," she cried. "And he didn't tell me where Father is! Echohawk, now what will I do? I shall never be at peace until I know of his welfare!"

"Perhaps it is best," Echohawk said quietly. "Yellow Eyes had no compassion. How your father died may not be a pleasant thing to know."

Mariah rose slowly to her feet, wiping tears from her face with the back of a hand. "Echohawk, it is the same for the white people as it is the red man when a beloved person has died," she said, choking back a sob. "The loved one is given a proper burial." She lowered her eyes. "Although I did not approve of my father's ways, it is only appropriate that I, his only child, see him laid to rest."

She gazed quickly up at Echohawk again. "He would want to be buried beside my mother," she murmured. "So that they can rest in peace together."

"We shall try to find him," Echohawk reassured, drawing her against him, giving her a warm hug. He looked around him at his braves, who were awaiting his orders. "Search the cabins, remove what is valuable, then burn them."

Mariah eased from Echohawk's arms and watched guardedly as the braves went from cabin to cabin. When one came out of Tanner's cabin carrying five raven-black scalps, war whoops filled the air as they went and stood beside Tanner's body, waving the scalps over him.

"Those are scalps of my people," Echohawk said angrily. "I know this to be true, for Yellow Eyes would not take from his friends, the Sioux."

Some cabins were already burning, with one left to enter. The door was bolt-locked and had to be forced open by several braves crashing their shoulders against it. A ray of hope sparked inside Mariah's heart when she heard the braves shouting that they had found another white man.

"Could it be . . . ?" Mariah said, looking questioningly up at Echohawk.

"We shall see," he answered, taking her by the elbow, walking her to the cabin.

Mariah approached to step inside, but jumped with a start when a rat scampered past her, desperate to get outside.

Collecting herself, Mariah went into the cabin, and grew instantly numb when through the dim light of the room she viewed her father shackled to the wall, nude and emaciated, his eye sockets like two holes in his face, one foot partially gnawed away.

"Papa!" she gasped, fighting back a strong urge to faint.

"Release him!" Echohawk ordered his braves. "Take him outside!"

Her knees trembling and weak, Mariah could not help but

cover her nose with a hand to ward off the stench as her father was carried past her.

Pale and nauseated, Mariah ran after him and knelt beside him as he was placed on the ground.

Echohawk came quickly to Mariah's side and placed a blanket over her father's body, up to his chin.

"Papa," Mariah cried, reaching out to touch him, but drawing her hand back as though she had been shot when he began wheezing and trembling violently with a chill.

"Mariah? How can it be? How . . . can . . . you be . . . here?" Victor Temple said, turning his weakened bloodshot eyes up to her, making out only a hazy shadow. "Thank God. You . . . are . . . all right. God, Mariah, I looked high and low for you. Where have you been? I . . . I thought you were dead."

"I was with Echohawk and his people for a while, and then I went and stayed with Colonel and Mrs. Snelling," she said, trying to keep her composure even as she saw that her father was near death. She could tell by the rattles in his chest. And she could tell by looking that he had not eaten for days. "I am here now because Echohawk brought me. Papa, I—"

"Echohawk?" Victor said, interrupting Mariah. He squinted as he tried to make out Echohawk beside Mariah. He slowly rolled his head back and forth. "No, Mariah. Not Echohawk. You can't be consorting with Indians. And especially not Echohawk. His father . . . he and your mother . . ."

"His father and my mother . . . ?" Mariah said, leaning closer to his face. "What about them, Papa?"

Victor turned his head away from her, not knowing how to tell her the truths that would hurt her. He would talk of something else. He licked his parched lips, and felt the warmth of tears flooding from his eyes and across his cheeks. "Damn that Tanner," he said, only barely audible. "He abducted me. He hated me. But with reason. I . . . I . . . I've cheated Tanner on a regular basis, and because I refused him your hand in marriage, he did this to me, Mariah."

Wonderfully happy to know that Echohawk had just had his name totally cleared of any crime, Mariah flashed him a warm smile. Her father continued to ramble on, as though seeking a way to repent for all the wrongs done to her. She listened attentively, growing more numb by the minute.

"Before I die I've many things I've got to tell you. And now," Victor said, looking pleadingly up at her. "I've protected you from so many things in your lifetime—among them the truth that could have hurt and confused you as a child. But it is only fair to you that you know everything. You are now an adult and can stand up against such knowledge better than you could have as a child."

He paused and coughed, blood spewing from between his lips.

Mariah winced and bit her lower lip, still caring too much for her father not to feel remorse for him as he lay dying before her eyes.

"Long ago, Mariah," Victor continued, knowing that he could not delay telling her any longer. "When me and Colonel Snelling were stationed with General Hull's army in Detroit, your mother had an affair with Colonel Snelling. Mariah, you are the offspring of that affair, but even I didn't know of this deception until your mother confessed the truth on her deathbed."

He coughed again and stopped to take a long shaky breath, then continued, oblivious of Mariah's bloodless complexion and wide eyes, her hands at her cheeks, stunned speechless by this revelation.

"Mariah," Victor said, lifting a bony hand to her cheek, patting it, "I knew of your mother's affair with Josiah Snelling, but I had not been aware that you were his. She was very clever in her deceptions! She had more than one affair while married to me. She had an affair with Chief Gray Elk. She killed herself over that Indian who put his people's welfare before hers, a white woman."

Echohawk grew stiff and his jaw went slack, to hear such a thing about his beloved father. Even while a dutiful father to Echohawk, Gray Elk had been in love with a white woman!

He turned his eyes away, ashamed, yet now understanding why Mariah's father had hated Chief Gray Elk with such a vengeance—and why he had long ago come to the village of Chippewa and killed and maimed so many.

He looked down at the dying white man, knowing that if it had been he whose wife had wronged him with another man, he would have hated as much. He would have become as hard-hearted.

Ay-uh, it was easy now to see the reasoning behind this man who had pretended to be Mariah's father for her sake.

In truth, he was a man of good heart!

Mariah was finding it hard to comprehend what was being said to her, yet knew that it must be the truth. It would make no sense at all for her father to lie to her now.

Yes, she concluded sadly, it was all true. Her dear sweet mother had been guilty of many infidelities. It was hard to accept—harder still to know that this was not her true father who lay at her feet dying.

But she did understand so much now—why Victor Temple had grown to hate all women and why he had forced Mariah to dress and behave like a man. She understood why he had become a cold and embittered man.

And the fact that he was not her true father? How could he have loved her at all, except that he had already raised her as his for six full years before knowing the truth. By then, in his heart, she *was* his daughter.

Mariah now saw many more pieces fall into place. Her father's coolness toward Colonel and Mrs. Snelling. And the way he tried to keep her from becoming their friend, when she accompanied her father to the fort for supplies. And the true reason for Victor Temple attacking Chief Gray Elk again after all those years. It was not so much for his lame leg as because of a grudge that he had carried with him over a woman!

Mariah stared down at the man she had always called Papa and watched him reach out to her, pleas for forgiveness on his parched lips. Knowing what he had been forced to endure because of his faithless wife, and now understanding this man whose heart had turned bitter, yet still had done his best to raise a child that was not his, Mariah leaned over and hugged him, her tears wetting his clammy cheeks.

"Papa," she sobbed. "I'm so sorry about everything. If I had only known. I would have made life much simpler for you. I . . . I would have been nothing but good to you."

"Mariah," he whispered harshly, coughing. "My dear sweet Mariah!"

She winced when his body tightened, then went limp, and his breathing ceased.

"No," she whispered, still clinging. "Please, Papa, let me make it all up to you!"

"Mariah, he is gone," Echohawk said gently, placing a hand on her arm, drawing her reluctantly to her feet. He drew her into his embrace. "We were both wrong about him. Deep within his heart, there was much good."

"I know," Mariah murmured. Yet as much as she pitied Victor, she could not help but be relieved to know who her true father was.

Colonel Snelling was a man of honor.

Colonel Snelling was a man of morals.

He was a father who could be revered, trusted, and relied upon.

This man at Mariah's feet had long ago lost all of those virtues.

Filled with sadness and regret, Mariah turned to Echohawk. "We must travel to Fort Snelling soon to clear your name," she said. "And I want to face my father with the truth. Surely he will be as happy as I to know this. There has been a bond between us from the very beginning. Now I know why. Somehow we surely sensed our blood ties."

"It may be best to keep this truth hidden within your heart," Echohawk suggested.

"I doubt that I can," Mariah said, thinking of William Joseph, and that he was her half-brother. How grand to know that she actually had a brother. And Colonel Snelling had fathered seven children by Abigail! That meant that Mariah had seven brothers and sisters, if even only half kin to her.

"Let us leave this sorrowful place," Echohawk said softly.

Mariah glanced back down at Victor Temple. "After I see to his burial," she murmured. "It can't be as I had at first wanted it. He would not want to be buried beside my mother's grave, after all."

A deep sadness came into her eyes as she thought about her mother and how she had always worshiped her in her memories.

She did not know how she should feel now.

22

A merry heart goes all the day,
A sad tires in a mile.

—Shakespeare

The sound of singing and throbbing drums marked a victory celebration at Chief Silver Wing's newly established village—a village bordering a serene lake, very pretty with its encircling of majestic pine and maple trees.

Mariah was taking comfort in Echohawk's arms as she sat beside him before a roaring fire in the dance lodge, venison steaks simmering and dripping tantalizing juices into the flames.

As the drumbeats quickened, Mariah tried to enjoy the merriment. But she was unable to shake her sadness over Victor Temple's death and his last confessions. She snuggled closer to Echohawk and concentrated her thoughts on the celebration. Several men and women in colorful attire formed an immense circle inside which sat seven drummers around a huge drum. As the drummers beat a continuous rhythm, lusty voices shouted and wailed the songs which belonged to each dance. The sound was a strange mixture of a raucous coyote chorus and the minor music of a storm-brewing wind.

A young girl dressed in white doeskin stepped away from the others, shaking a *she-she-qua,* rattle, and started a rhythmic chant that seemed to be all timing and no tune. Soon other young girls joined in her chant and began to dance.

"Is it not a beautiful performance by the young Chippewa maidens?" Echohawk said, taking Mariah's hand, clasping it. "They would welcome you if you wish to join them."

Recalling her clumsiness at Abigail's ball, Mariah gazed over at Echohawk, smiling. "I don't believe I would be welcome for long," she said. "I am not a skilled dancer, Echohawk, I seem to have four feet instead of two when I try to dance."

He laughed heartily, then turned and nodded a hello to Nee-kah as she came and sat down beside Mariah. "And how are you faring, Nee-kah?" he asked, eyeing her abdomen, which was developing rapidly with child. His eyes softened with affection as he reached around Mariah and placed a gentle hand on Nee-kah. "Soon you will have a child to join the dancing and singing. Of course the child will be a son."

"*Ay-uh,* a son," Nee-kah said, in her heart praying that it would be so. For her husband she must bear a son! And for herself—for she did not want to be cast away so that he could take another wife who might have more luck at birthing sons than she.

Echohawk's gaze returned to Mariah. "No-din and I will have many sons and daughters," he said, his eyes twinkling into Mariah's. "Is not that so, No-din?"

Mariah's face reddened with a blush; then she looked at Nee-kah. "*Ay-uh,* many," she murmured. "Just like Josiah and Abigail Snelling. It is not fair to a child to be raised without brothers and sisters." She smiled radiantly at Echohawk. "For so long I was without brothers and sisters. But now I have many!"

The sound of horses arriving outside the dance lodge caused all merriment to cease. Everything became so quiet, only harsh, frightened breaths could be heard.

A brave, one who had been guarding the approach of the village, entered the lodge and went to stand before Chief Silver Wing, who sat opposite the fire from Echohawk.

Chief Silver Wing rose slowly to his feet, frowning. He tried to hide the alarm in his eyes that had sprung there upon hearing so many horses, when he knew that almost all the braves were in the dance lodge attending the celebration. Only a few had been outside in strategic places to keep watch for intruders.

"What is it?" Chief Silver Wing grunted as Echohawk came to his side, as stern and as quiet as the elder chief. "Whom have you escorted into the village of Chippewa?"

"William Joseph Snelling and soldiers from Fort Snelling,"

the brave said, his gaze moving from Chief Silver Wing to Chief Echohawk. "He comes in peace. He wishes council with the two chiefs of this village. Do I escort him to the council house? Should I say that you will be there soon to smoke the pipe of peace with him?"

Mariah's heart was thundering wildly, torn over how to feel. She was anxious to see William Joseph, now knowing that he was her blood kin. Yet she was apprehensive of him being here, for Chief Silver Wing had moved his village far from Fort Snelling and all white people because he felt safer in isolation.

Also, she feared for Echohawk. Although his innocence had been proved, they had not yet gone to Fort Snelling to clear his name.

"Tell him we will share a smoke with him," Chief Silver Wing said after getting a nod of consent from Echohawk. "Take him there. We will soon follow."

As quickly as the people had gathered for the celebration, they were gone, leaving the dance lodge eerily quiet.

Mariah went to Echohawk and placed a hand on his arm. "Take me with you," she said. "Let me sit in council with you. Echohawk, I may be needed to convince William Joseph of your innocence. Neither my father nor Tanner McCloud is alive to explain it. Let me sit beside you to speak for you, if necessary."

Nee-kah went to Chief Silver Wing and clung to his hand. "I, too, wish to sit in council," she said softly. "My chieftain husband, I am saddened greatly that the white pony soldiers have found our village again."

Chief Silver Wing and Echohawk exchanged troubled glances, then nodded. Mariah warmed clear through when Echohawk placed a blanket around her shoulders. Chief Silver Wing placed a blanket around Nee-kah's, and together they left the lodge and stepped out into the frosty night air.

Mariah shivered as the cold pressed against her face. The first snows were near. Every morning and evening now the little streams which led away from the rivers were puckered with ice.

Tonight the moon was high in a velvety clear sky, and the stars shone so brightly, it was as though hundreds of thousands of candles were burning in the heavens.

In the distance the silence was broken by a lone coyote howling at the shadow of the moon. A shiver not related to the cold fled down Mariah's spine as she caught sight of several soldiers standing beside their horses close to the large council house.

Her gaze swept over them. William Joseph was among them. When their eyes locked, Mariah's pulse raced, for now that she knew that he was her brother, she could see so many resemblances in their features!

But her attention was quickly drawn from her brother. With Echohawk she entered the council house, where a fire was already burning brightly. Solemnly, and with a humble heart, Mariah went with Echohawk and sat down beside him on a platform cushioned with many animal pelts, while Chief Silver Wing and Nee-kah sat down beside them on the same platform.

A young lad entered, carrying a large pipe with many colorful feathers attached at its bowl. He took the pipe to Chief Silver Wing, which he accepted and rested on his lap, while the young lad knelt on his haunches on the floor beside him.

"Tell William Joseph that he can now enter," Chief Silver Wing said, nodding at a brave, who quickly responded to the command and soon returned with William Joseph at his side.

Remaining seated, Chief Silver Wing gestured with a hand to William Joseph. "*Nah-mah-dah-bee-yen,* sit," he said without expression. "Let us share in a smoke. Then tell us why you have come with many pony soldiers to my village."

As William Joseph settled down on a rush mat beside the fire, his gaze stopped at Mariah. He looked at her quizzically. It looked as though she belonged beside Chief Echohawk, but why?

The young lad rose and brought a flaming twig to Chief Silver Wing and placed the flame to the tobacco. Chief Silver Wing drew on the stem, the sweet aroma of tobacco soon rising into the air.

Chief Silver Wing then straightened his back, waved the lad away, and puffed on the pipe for a moment, passing it then to Echohawk, who also smoked from it and in turn handed it to William Joseph.

After all three had shared in the ritual, Chief Silver Wing rested the bowl of the pipe on his knee. "Now, William Joseph, tell us why you are here," he said, his expression guarded. "It was not my intent that any pony soldiers ever ride into my new village. I meant to lead my people to a place of peace. Your presence threatens this peace."

William Joseph's gaze moved from chief to chief, then momentarily locked on Mariah again, still confused by her presence here. But of course she was here on her own initiative. Neither Echohawk nor Silver Wing abducted white women! His mind was swirling with questions, yet he straightened his back as once again he focused his full attention on the chiefs.

"For several days I have been in pursuit of Chief Echohawk," William Joseph said. "One of my trusted scouts came to me with the news of this location. I had hoped to find Chief Echohawk with you."

"And what do you want with Echohawk?" Chief Silver Wing asked, his shoulders stiffening.

"Answers to questions about the disappearance of Victor Temple," William Joseph said, his gaze once more moving to Mariah. "And also the disappearance of Mariah from my camp. I see that she is safe. That is good."

"And what questions do you have concerning me?" Echohawk interjected, seeing William Joseph's intenseness as he stared at Mariah, yet no longer jealous of such attention. William Joseph did not know they were related, but it was enough that Mariah knew.

"We at Fort Snelling received word that an Indian identified by his eyeglasses was involved in raids close to Victor Temple's trading post," William Joseph said, clearing his throat nervously as he felt everyone's eyes heatedly looking at him, even Mariah's. "Of course I had to follow such leads and question Echohawk. That is why I am here. To get answers and take them back to my father, who has sent me on this mission."

"And does your father see me as guilty of such crimes?" Echohawk said, his voice a low growl. "He has always known me to be a peace-loving man. Would gossip mean more to him than how he has always perceived me?"

"My father did not believe the gossip," William Joseph said, placing his hands on his knees, leaning forward. "That is why he has sent me to ask you to return to Fort Snelling. All he needs from you is your word that you had no part in what happened to Victor Temple." He glanced over at Mariah. "I need no further explanation myself. Mariah wouldn't be sitting at your side if you had had anything to do with her father's disappearance."

William Joseph paused, then added, "Mariah, I don't understand. Why are you with Echohawk? You sit at his side as though you are his—"

"Wife?" Mariah said, interrupting. She lifted her chin proudly. "William Joseph, I am not his wife yet. But I will be soon. I plan to make my future with Echohawk."

"But you went to Mother and Father, asking for their assistance," William Joseph said, his confusion and dismay apparent.

"That was only because I did not think Echohawk wanted me," she said in defense. She slipped a hand over one of Echohawk's. "But I was wrong. He wants me very much."

Mariah wanted to reach out to William Joseph and tell him that he was her brother, but she did not think this was the appropriate time. It would be best, she thought to herself, first to tell William Joseph's father—and then the rest of the family.

She suddenly realized that the truth might be hard for all concerned to accept, except for herself. She, of course, was jubilant with the knowledge.

"And how is it that you *are* with Echohawk?" William Joseph asked.

"Because I could not sleep that morning in your camp, I took a ride," she softly explained. "And I came across Echohawk at that time. I went with him then to—"

"She accompanied me and my braves to find out the truth," Echohawk said, taking over. "The truth about her father's disappearance—and many more things. Tonight when you arrived my people and Chief Silver Wing's people were celebrating a victory over the truths that were uncovered."

"Truths?" William Joseph asked, arching an eyebrow. "What do you mean?"

"Yellow Eyes," Echohawk said blandly. "The truth about Yellow Eyes."

William Joseph leaned forward. "Who is this Yellow Eyes?" he asked, looking from Echohawk, to Mariah.

"That is Echohawk's nickname for Tanner McCloud," Mariah quickly explained.

"Tanner McCloud?" William Joseph said, again arching an eyebrow. "What about him? What does he have to do with any of this?"

"Tanner McCloud is the one who spread the lie about Echohawk," Mariah said before Echohawk could speak for himself. "Tanner was the one who burned my father's trading post. He's the one who abducted my father." She swallowed hard, then added, "He's the one responsible for my father's death."

"Your father is dead?" William Joseph said in a low gasp.

"After abducting my father, Tanner locked him up in a cabin without food and water," Mariah said, lowering her eyes, the thought of her father's dying breaths almost too painful to bear. "He died because of this mistreatment."

"And Tanner?" William Joseph dared to ask. "What of him?"

"He is no longer among the living," Echohawk said without hesitation. "And that is good. For years he has abused my people *and* yours. He was a worthless cheat and liar. He was greedy. His spirit hovers now, somewhere between darkness and light, never to be at peace."

William Joseph wiped a hand across his face, shaking his head slowly back and forth, then peered at Echohawk with a warm smile. "I'm glad that your name has been cleared," he said softly. He gazed with compassion at Mariah. "But I'm sorry about your father."

Mariah's lips parted, and she came close to telling William Joseph that he wasn't her father—that *his* father and hers were one and the same.

William Joseph rose to his feet. "I will return to Fort Snelling and tell my father everything," he said, smiling down at everyone. "And when you have the time, Echohawk, *and* Silver Wing, come and speak peace with my father. It will look better in the white community for those who will still carry doubts about your innocence in their hearts."

Mariah rose along with Echohawk and Silver Wing and Nee-kah and went to William Joseph. One by one William Joseph embraced them, and when he came to Mariah, she looked adoringly into his eyes, seeing a reflection of herself in their depths. She was so very happy that he was her kin!

"Thank you for everything," she whispered, clinging to him as he pulled her into a hearty hug. "Tell Abigail and your father that I appreciate what they did for me, and that I'm sorry if I gave them one moment of concern. I should have sent word to them that I was all right."

"That you are is all that is important," William Joseph said, easing her from him and holding her at arm's length. He winked down at her. "Whenever you like, Mariah, I'll give you a few dancing lessons."

Mariah covered her mouth, stifling a giggle. "I have dancing lessons to learn here," she finally said. "And the Indian dances are even more complicated than those I encountered at the fort."

"No-din is an apt student," Nee-kah said, smiling at Mariah. "She will learn everything of the Chippewa culture very quickly."

"No-din?" William Joseph said, stroking his chin as his eyes smiled at Mariah.

"She is 'Woman of the Wind' to the Chippewa," Echohawk said, placing a possessive arm around her waist, drawing her close to him. "No-din. Woman of the Wind."

As they all stepped from the council house, the first snowfall of winter was upon them. Mariah looked up at the snow as it fell from the sky, the flakes so big it was as though petals from wild plum trees were settling on her upturned face.

She looked at the wigwams, the snow on them making them look like huddled ghosts on the open plain.

"Come soon to Fort Snelling," William Joseph said, swinging himself up into his saddle. He gave a vigorous wave, then barked the command that sent the soldiers away in a hard gallop.

Chief Silver Wing turned to Echohawk. "It is good that that is behind us," he said, heaving a long sigh. "Now, Echohawk, before the snows become heavier and more frequent, you must concentrate on establishing for yourself a new village. If you so desire, build it side by side with mine. We will be as one, yet led by separate chiefs."

Echohawk contemplated this suggestion for a moment, then placed a gentle hand on Chief Silver Wing's shoulder. "Thank you," he said, smiling broadly. "My people will accept your offer with a glad heart!"

"That is good," Chief Silver Wing said, clasping Echohawk's arm in brotherhood and good faith.

"I am cold," Nee-kah said, clinging to the blanket around her shoudlers.

"The woman with child must be seen to," Chief Silver Wing said. He whisked Nee-kah to his side and walked her away to their wigwam.

Echohawk and Mariah went to their own wigwam and embraced with a long, sweet kiss.

"Lie down beside the fire and cover yourself with the warm buffalo robes," Echohawk said softly.

Perfectly content, Mariah did as he suggested, then watched as he busied himself heating several smooth round stones in the fire.

After these were thoroughly heated, Echohawk wrapped the rocks in strips of warm blankets, then knelt beside Mariah and placed them at her feet. "You will be warmed clear through soon," he said, crawling beneath the piles of heavy robes beside her. He embraced her and drew her against him. "When will you say that you are ready to be my wife? How much longer do I have to wait for you to voice this aloud to me, the man who loves you?"

"Do you doubt at all that I will be your wife?" Mariah asked, smoothing her hand along the sculptured lines of his face. "I am here, am I not?"

"*Ay-uh,* and I will never let you go," Echohawk said, brushing a kiss across her lips.

"Echohawk, before we speak vows of marriage, I first want to make things right in my life," she murmured. "I want to reveal myself to my true father."

"I understand," Echohawk said, nodding. "As soon as the new wigwams are built and my people have a sense of belonging again, we will travel to Fort Snelling. We will both meet with Colonel Snelling, but for separate reasons."

"Ay-uh," Mariah sighed. "And then, my love, I will go through whatever ceremony is required to be your wife."

Echohawk smiled to himself, knowing that she would be greatly surprised when he told her that a private ceremony had already been conducted that had made them man and wife.

When the time was right, *ay-uh,* he would tell her!

He looked through the smoke hole overhead and to the sky. It was no longer snowing, the clouds having drifted away. Tonight the stars seemed to be the eyes of the gods, shining down at him and his beloved . . .

23

Of all the tyrants the world affords,
Our own affections are the fiercest lords.
—Earl of Sterling

Several Weeks Later

The wind swept across the snow-silent slopes. Mariah and Echohawk's horses loped along the crusty white trail, obscured by a blizzard of spinning snowflakes. Even though Mariah was wearing a snug bearskin coat, its hood framing her face, and winter moccasins lined with rabbit fur, she still trembled, her teeth chattering, as the bitter chill of the early evening stung her cheeks and nose. When she and Echohawk had set out for Fort Snelling earlier in the day, the sun had been brilliant overhead, and the snow that had fallen the previous day had begun to melt from the limbs of the trees.

And then an unexpected snowstorm had blown in over the land. In the forest that fringed the river, powdery snow smoked into the wind from the limbs of the great cottonwoods, and grass spiked upward through the icy crusts that stretched across the meadows.

Mariah and Echohawk had been too far from their village to turn back. They had decided that it was best to travel on to Fort Snelling, since they had postponed the trip already too many times. Their newfound love, free of all doubts and suspicions, absorbed them completely. And the unusually harsh weather had made it hard to gather the appropriate materials for the new village's wigwams.

But in time, when the dwellings were finally built, Echohawk's people were able to settle in for the winter. Chief Silver

Wing's generosity extended even to helping supply Echohawk's people with enough staples to get them through the winter.

And now Echohawk felt free to leave his village and people to take care of his affairs at Fort Snelling—to talk peace with Colonel Snelling and to see that his name was completely cleared.

Mariah glanced over at Echohawk, seeing how wonderfully handsome he was, even though mostly covered by a bearskin coat which matched hers. He rode tall in the saddle, as though he were an extension of his prized Blaze.

And he no longer had to wear the eyeglasses, although he still found them useful for hunting and target shooting. Mariah didn't mind them at all, in fact she secretly loved the quirky addition to his rugged features.

But she knew that *he* detested the eyeglasses and was awaiting the day he could cast them aside entirely, for he felt that they took away from his nobility—his prowess as a great hunter and invincible leader.

Her mittened hands clutching onto the reins, her eyes now directed straight ahead, she tried to ignore how, the wind continued to hurl stinging pellets of snow at her. Her thoughts turned to her own reason for going to Fort Snelling, besides traveling with the man she loved for moral support. She was finally going to come face-to-face with her true father. She was determined that he know she was his daughter. And, surely he would be as happy about it as she. He had always treated her as though she were someone special.

But perhaps that was because he had always felt sorry for her, never having approved of the way she had been forced to live with Victor Temple—as though she were a boy, instead of a girl with a girl's desires and dreams.

She wanted more than pity.

She wanted the love of a true father.

Her thoughts went to Abigail. What would she think of this revelation? It was not Mariah's wish to hurt her feelings, yet Abigail did not seem the sort whose feelings could be injured all that easily. She was a strong breed of woman who had experienced many misfortunes in life while accompanying a husband whose ambitions took him in the way of opportunity and temptations. But of course Mariah would tell Josiah privately and let it be his decision whether or not to break it to his wife.

And then there was William Joseph. Mariah was proud to be able to call him her brother. He was such a dear sweet man, kindhearted through and through. She had even felt a strange sort of bonding with him upon their first acquaintance.

Now she knew why.

And she had to wonder how *he* would feel!

Evening shadows were beginning to lie long and dark on the snow as Fort Snelling came into view through the break in the trees ahead. Mariah was barraged by assorted emotions as she anticipated the moments ahead with her true father. She had waited a lifetime, it seemed, to tell him her secret.

She looked guardedly at Echohawk. He had not offered much conversation this entire journey, and she understood why. Even though William Joseph had assured them that Echohawk's name would be cleared, she and Echohawk knew that it was hard for the white community to cast aside suspicions where an Indian was concerned. So many could still insist that Echohawk was guilty in spite of the evidence to the contrary. It was those people that she feared.

Echohawk turned to Mariah. He reached out to her, smoothing the cold flesh of his fingers across her cheeks, rosy with color from the freezing air. "Your face is too cold," he grumbled. "This journey would have been best delayed again."

"No, I don't believe so," Mariah said, extending a mittened hand, covering his. "I am fine. Just a little bit chilled, but fine. But what of you? You don't have as much on as I."

When they had first set out on the journey, she worried about him withstanding the cold, for he said that a chief did not wear hand coverings, nor did he hide beneath a hood. His peripheral vision must not be impeded by anything worn around his face, having to be alert for any unsuspecting traveler on the trail, and his hands must not be encumbered, having to be free to use a weapon quickly should the need arise.

"Since childhood I have learned to endure many things," Echohawk said, frowning. "among them the cold months of winter. It is the Chippewa brave who must learn early how to withstand the cold, for it is the brave who must see that food is on the table. The hunt does not end just because the snows come."

As the wide-open gate of the fort was upon them, Mariah and Echohawk became silent as they rode into the courtyard.

Mariah sighed with relief when she found the courtyard all but deserted, seeing only a few straggling soldiers trudging through the snow, their heads bent to the wind. Only a few looked up and stared at Mariah and Echohawk.

Other than that, only the sentries posted at each side of the gate had taken full notice of them.

But the sentries, knowing Echohawk so well, had waved him and Mariah on without questioning them.

Mariah's attention was now on the house that sat at the far end of the courtyard. Her heart began to pound at the prospect of knocking on the door, her father perhaps the one to open it. Even though the Snelling household was well staffed, she had noticed in the short time that she had lived there that if Josiah was at home and not busy with his ledgers in the study, he would go to the door instead of the butler.

Riding onward in a slow lope, Mariah looked over at Echohawk. "Soon, Echohawk, things will be cleared up and we can return to a peaceful life with your people," she said, anxious for that also. Through all of the difficulties these past weeks, they had not yet taken the time for the marriage ceremony. Mariah did not like to feel as though she were living in sin by not being married. She only hoped that as the good Lord looked down from his place in the heavens, he would have seen her recent difficulties and understood.

"I owe so much to Chief Silver Wing," Echohawk said. "It was with a sad heart that he did not accompany us on this journey of peace. But I saw his reasoning as wise. Our villages should never be left without a chief. Our people need the reassurance a chief's presence affords them."

"I believe that he again was thinking of your welfare by deciding not to accompany us," Mariah said softly. "He wanted this moment to be yours alone. It is your vindication sought here, Echohawk. Not so much Silver Wing's."

Echohawk nodded. "*Ay-uh,* that is so," he said, then grew silent as the shadow of the great Snelling mansion loomed over them.

Together Echohawk and Mariah dismounted and secured their reins to a hitching rail. With an anxious step and heart, Mariah walked beside Echohawk up the stairs to the porch, inhaling a nervous breath before knocking.

She waited with wide eyes for the door to open. When it did, she took a step back, not recognizing the man who answered it. While living with the Snellings, she had become acquainted with all of their servants, and this man's face was not familiar to her.

There was something unnerving about the man, a cold aloofness to his stance that made a chill ride Mariah's spine. He was tall and thin, his clothes black except for a stiff white collar that framed a long, narrow face with tight, drawn features—and eyes that appeared empty in their opaque grayness.

"Yes?" the man said, looking suspiciously from Mariah to Echohawk. "What can I do for you?"

"We have come to meet with Colonel Snelling," Mariah said, firming her chin. "Please tell him that Mariah and Echohawk are here."

"That would be impossible," the man said stiffly. "Colonel Snelling no longer resides here. So if you will excuse me, I must see to my other duties."

Mariah was stunned speechless by the man's words. She stared up at him for a moment, her lips parted, then placed a hand to the door, stopping him from closing it. "You must be mistaken," she said, her voice quavering. "This is Colonel and Mrs. Snelling's house. They must be here."

"Mariah? Echohawk?"

Mariah and Echohawk turned around in unison when the familiar voice spoke behind them.

"William Joseph!" Mariah said, rushing down the steps, grabbing one of his gloved hands. "Your parents. Where are they?" She gave the servant a quick glance over her shoulder, then turned questioning eyes back to William Joseph. "Tell me that he is wrong. They aren't gone, are they?" Her gaze lowered, and she swallowed hard, then looked up at William Joseph again, panic rising within her. "They have to be here. Tell me they are!"

Echohawk came to Mariah's side. He swept an arm around her waist and drew her next to him. "We have come to have council with your father," he said. "If he is no longer living in this house, take us to his new residence. We have traveled a long way, through much cold weather, to speak peace with your father. We wish to do it now, William Joseph."

"My father has been transferred to Jefferson Barracks in Saint Louis," William Joseph said, looking apologetically from Mariah to Echohawk. "I've neglected getting a message to you. I now see that I should have, but the weather has been bad. I was waiting for it to break, and this happened so suddenly."

Mariah paled. "Your father has been transferred?" she gasped, her hopes of ever being able to reveal her special secret to her true father waning. "Why? When?"

"He received his orders from Washington only last week," William Joseph said solemnly. "My parents departed for Saint Louis on a riverboat as quickly as they could get things settled here."

"But what about Echohawk?" Mariah blurted, for the moment forgetting her own reasons for having come to Fort Snelling. "Your father was to assure him that his name has been cleared. Now what is Echohawk to expect? Will the white community still condemn him? Will he never be able to ride free of worry, in danger of someone ready to shoot him in the back for . . . for crimes he didn't commit?"

"I assure you both that Echohawk's name has been cleared," William Joseph said, placing a hand of friendship on Echohawk's shoulder. "Before my father left, he sent out a decree wide and far, stating your innocence. You have nothing to fear, Echohawk. Nothing."

Echohawk smiled warmly at William Joseph. "That is good," he said. "When you see your father again, thank him for me."

"I will not be seeing him soon," William Joseph said his eyes wavering as he glanced down at Mariah. "I'm returning to Boston. I am through with my adventuresome days of being an interpreter. I am going to pursue a career in politics in Boston."

Mariah's heart skipped a beat with this news, now realizing that she was going to lose William Joseph from her life almost as quickly as she had discovered that he was her brother.

It wasn't fair.

None of it!

A part of her wanted to cry out to William Joseph that she was his sister, yet another part warned her that this was not the best thing to do, since she might never be able to tell her father the truth.

This saddened her—this silence that she felt compelled to maintain.

"No-din, we must return to the village," Echohawk said, turning to her. "The weather. It could worsen. It is best that I get you home, warm between blankets beside our fire."

William Joseph gave Echohawk and Mariah an anxious look, then said, "You are surely tired from your travels. Why not stay the night in my cabin, then leave tomorrow? You will travel much more safely if you are rested."

Mariah was bone weary, and her disappointment seemed to have worsened her fatigue. And she felt strangely empty, having so looked forward to seeing her true father, and now he was gone.

Echohawk considered William Joseph's offer for a moment. He looked at Mariah, knowing of her disappointment and sadness, and feeling that was enough to cope with tonight without forcing her to ride the entire night in the freezing cold.

He turned grateful eyes to William Joseph. "*Mee-gway-chee-wahn-dum,* thank you. Your offer is accepted," he said. "Your warm fire will be welcomed tonight."

"You can leave your horses here," William Joseph said, stepping between Echohawk and Mariah. "I'll send my groom to take good care of them." He placed an arm around each of their waists and led them on across the snow-covered courtyard. "And you can have my cabin all to yourselves. This is my last night at Fort Snelling. I've a few things to settle with some of the men." He chuckled when he saw Mariah's anxious look, knowing she'd misinterpreted what he had said. "A poker game, Mariah. I plan to get into a hot game of poker tonight."

Mariah laughed loosely, sighing with relief. She gladly walked with Echohawk and her brother to William Joseph's cabin. Once inside, she went to the fireplace and let the warmth soak into her flesh, then removed her coat and gloves. Echohawk followed her lead, removing his.

"You two make yourselves at home," William Joseph said, his gaze sweeping around the sparsely furnished room, where he had stayed only since his parents' departure for Saint Louis. "It's not much, but there is plenty of food. Eat what you like. I'll see you two in the morning."

William Joseph turned to leave, but stopped, having just remembered something. He went to a cabinet and opened a drawer, taking a small buckskin pouch from inside it. He took it to Mariah and placed it in her hand.

"My father left this with me to give to you when I next saw you," he murmured, closing her fingers around the pouch. "He said that he'd owed your father a debt for some time—something about gambling while they were stationed with General Hull's army in Detroit a long time ago. Somehow they both forgot about the debt. Father just happened to remember it the other day. He said that since your father is no longer alive to collect on it, then it should be yours."

Mariah's lips parted in a surprising gasp. From the heaviness of the pouch, she knew there must be considerable money there. "Why, I don't know what to say," she said, her face coloring with an excited blush. She had never had anything she could call her own. The money she had spent at Fort Snelling had always always been her father's, used only for supplies.

Oh, how often she had eyed the lacy bonnets in the mercantile!

And the satin ribbons!

Now she could buy what she chose, yet it felt strange to be taking money that was not really hers.

"Thank you, but I can't accept this," she murmured. "Please, William Joseph, take it back. It was my father's. Not mine."

"Mariah, it is now rightfully yours," William Joseph said, moving toward the door. "And you deserve it. From what Mother and Father told me, you were hardly more than a slave to your father." He smiled at her over his shoulder. "Take this as fair payment."

Mariah stared at the pouch, then looked up at William Joseph. "Yes, I shall," she said, smiling.

As William Joseph placed his hand on the door latch, she rushed to him and flung herself into his arms. "Thank you," she murmured. "I shall miss you."

"We shall never truly be apart," William Joseph said, relishing having her in his arms, at least just this once. "You will always be in my thoughts."

He gave her one last hug, then swung away from her and left, Mariah feeling strangely empty in his absence. But she understood why. She had only recently discovered that she had a brother, and she'd expected to develop a close relationship.

It tore at her heart, thinking of this loss.

Seeing Mariah's sadness, Echohawk drew her into his embrace. He ran his fingers through her hair, comforting her. "I am sorry about your father," he said softly. "That you did not see him is unfortunate. And I am sorry about your brother—that you did not feel free to tell him that you are blood kin."

Mariah sniffled, fighting back tears. "I wish there was a way . . ." she whispered, clinging to Echohawk. "Being able to see my true father and telling him my discovery meant so much to me."

Her eyes widened and she leapt from Echohawk's embrace, the pouch of coins still heavy in her hand. "Echohawk, there *is* a way!" she said in a rush of words. "I am sure that I have enough money to take us to Saint Louis by riverboat! And there would surely be enough for our lodging once we arrive there. What a wonderful idea! We can go to Saint Louis and surprise my father with the news!"

Echohawk's jaw tightened and his eyes narrowed. "It is not

a thing a Chippewa does—ride in a white man's great wheeled vessel, the 'walk in the water.' It is a strange canoe, even larger than the voyageurs' big transport canoes," he said uneasily. "The Chippewa's place is with his people. Not on a giant canoe among whites."

"Echohawk, this is something new for me also," Mariah pleaded. "Let us share this new experience together."

When he did not answer her, she knew that she had no choice but to defy him, for she had made up her mind to go to Saint Louis. She would never be totally content until she came face-to-face with her true father.

"Echohawk," she quickly added, "I *must* go to Saint Louis. *Please* understand. And if you do not go with me, I will be forced to travel alone."

Echohawk's eyes blazed with fire. "You would do this even if I forbid it?" he said, his voice drawn.

" 'Forbid' is a strong word," Mariah said, taking a step back from him. "My father forbade me so much. Am I now to expect such behavior from the man I love? I cannot live like that, Echohawk. My judgment—my decisions—must be considered important or I . . . I cannot live with you."

Stunned by Mariah's stubbornness, Echohawk stared at her for a moment, then went and jerked a blanket from the bed and placed in on the floor close to the fireplace. Stretching out on it, he ignored Mariah as she gaped at him in disbelief. It was not a time to speak further words. He had much to sort out within his heart.

Seeing that Echohawk was settled in for the night, his back to her, Mariah stifled a sob of agony, then went to the bed and threw herself across it. Silent tears flowed from her eyes. She had never thought that her need to see her father would come to this. Echohawk was actually making her choose between him and her father, a father she had only recently discovered.

24

> Laugh if my cheek too is misty and drips—
> Wetness is tender—laugh on my lips.
>
> —Eastman

The pit of her stomach feeling hollow, seeming always to lose more than she gained, Mariah wiped a fresh flow of tears from her cheeks, yet did not allow herself to cry out loud. She did not want Echohawk to know that he had hurt her so deeply.

Yet he had, and she was not sure if she could ever forgive him.

His mood—his anger—had stung her heart, her total being!

So caught up was she in her hurtful feelings that Mariah did not hear Echohawk's approach to the bed. When he was suddenly there, stretched out behind her, his body pressing into hers from behind, her breath was momentarily stolen away.

Then she closed her eyes in ecstasy as he turned her around to face him, his mouth soon covering her lips in a tender, loving kiss. She was fighting her feelings, appalled that she could so quickly forgive him his anger. Even that he had made demands of her seemed to be dimming in her consciousness.

She loved him so much, so very, very much. . . .

Echohawk drew his mouth from her lips. His hands framed her face gently. "No-din, I was wrong," he said, drawing her eyes flutteringly open. "I should never have made demands on you. While with me, my woman, I want you to feel free to make your own decisions. I understand how it was for you while living with the man you thought was your father. I never again want to be compared to that tyrant. If you have the need to seek out your true father, I will not object. It is not my right to. Although you have promised yourself to me, that does not mean that you have handed over to me your freedom. Perhaps that is so between many men and women. But with us it will not be so. I love you too much to stifle you."

"But moments ago you . . . you behaved so differently," Mariah murmured, unable to completely relax with Echohawk's change in moods. She wanted to, oh, how she wanted to! "Echohawk, you made demands on me. Are you saying that you will no longer do this? Ever? Once I speak wedding vows with you, it is to be *ah-pah-nay,* forever. I want to live with you with a peaceful heart."

"My woman," Echohawk said, brushing a soft kiss across her lips. "Did you not listen well to what I said? I have seen the wrong in my demands. Never will I do this again. While with me, you will have the freedoms you desire, to make you feel a complete woman. No-din, your pride is as important to me as my own. Never will I give you cause to ride with lowered, humble eyes. While riding at my side on your steed, always you will have a lifted chin and proud, bright eyes!"

Tears filled Mariah's eyes again, but this time they were of pure joy. She crept into Echohawk's arms. "My darling, handsome Chippewa chief," she said, her heart soaring. "Oh, how I adore you."

They kissed. They embraced feverishly. And then Echohawk drew his lips away only a fraction. "One thing," he said thickly. "You cannot go alone to Saint Louis on the white man's large canoe. My people are at peace and safe with Chief Silver Wing. I will send him a message that my return will be delayed. *Our* return will be delayed. Together, you and I, we will go in search of Colonel Snelling. You will have that opportunity to speak words of love to your true father."

"You would do that for me?" Mariah said, breathless at the thought of traveling on the riverboat, the thrill now doubled at the thought of being with Echohawk on such an adventure.

"For you, anything," Echohawk said, smoothing his hands through her hair. "My woman, you have been without a happy heart for too long. It is my duty to see that your heart has cause to sing all the days of the rest of your life."

"Only moments ago I was filled with such despair," Mariah said, gazing into his fathomless dark eyes. "But now? I feel as though I am floating. And all because of you, Echohawk. You are so understanding. So kind."

"And I am sorry for having caused you despair," Echohawk said, gazing lovingly at her. "You have forgiven me my moment of stubbornness?"

"Ay-uh," Mariah said, smiling softly up at him. "How could I not forgive, when you are giving me the world? And how could I not, when I love you so much? You are my life, Echohawk. When I thought that I had lost you because of a misunderstanding, I could hardly bear it. I . . . I felt completely hollow. Thank you for giving me back my reason for living, darling."

She frowned as a sudden thought came to her. "You say that you will send word to Chief Silver Wing about your decision to travel with me to Saint Louis," she said. "Darling, whom would you trust to do this? You do not want the location of your village known to anyone but the Chippewa."

"It is no longer a secret," Echohawk said, his voice strained. "Do you forget the pony soldiers who accompanied William Joseph there?"

"How could I have forgotten?" Mariah said, paling slightly at the thought.

"I will question William Joseph about those who rode with him," Echohawk said, his fingers busy working Mariah's dress over her shoulders. "I will ask him to assign his most trusted scout to go to my people—to speak with Silver Wing. He will do this for us, No-din. William Joseph is a man who cares, not only for his own welfare but also for yours—and mine—for everyone who deserves his kindnesses."

"Yes, he is a most special man," Mariah said, again filled with sadness over not being able to share her secret with William Joseph. "My brother is a very, very special man."

"Enough talk," Echohawk said, smoothing Mariah's dress on down her body, revealing her silken pink flesh to his feasting eyes. "We are alone. We are in love. Let us *make* love."

Mariah sucked in a wild breath of ecstasy as he moved his lips to one of her taut nipples, taking it in his mouth, his tongue swirling slowly around it. Her heart pounding, she busied her fingers disrobing him.

When he was also nude, she ran her fingers down the smoothness of his copper skin, stopping one of her hands where his velvety shaft lay against her thigh, hard and heavy. As though having done this thousands of times before, in truth having only recently learned such skills, Mariah curled her fingers around his hardness and began moving her hand on him. When he threw his head back in a throaty groan, she knew that she was giving him pleasure—the same as he then gave her as his hands cupped her breasts, kneading them.

And then he urged her hand away from him and moved over her with his body. Gently nudging her knees apart, he pressed himself into her and began his rhythmic strokes.

Her body quivered with the wondrous rapture his movements created inside her. She locked her legs around his hips and rode him, her hips moving with him. She closed her eyes and moaned against his lips as he kissed her, the feelings awash throughout her a mixture of agony and bliss.

When he paused in his loving her, drawing his body away from her, she beckoned for him with outstretched arms, her heart on fire with need.

Echohawk smiled down at her as he moved to kneel beside her, his lips moving close to her again. Her blood quickened when his lips burned a trail down her neck, teasingly brushing them against her breast in only a slight touch, and lower still, across her abdomen.

When he moved his body again, this time positioning himself between her outstretched legs, she felt as though she was soaring above herself when he began loving her gently with his mouth and tongue where she so unmercifully throbbed.

She felt uneasy about this way of loving, yet she abandoned herself to the torrent of feelings that overwhelmed her, her excitement rising with this different, exquisite fashion of loving.

When Echohawk began to bring her to that ultimate of sensations, she gripped his shoulders lightly and urged him up and over her again.

His eyes dark and knowing, Echohawk twined his fingers

through her hair and brought her lips to his. He kissed her long and hard, darting his tongue into her mouth, causing new sensations to awaken within her.

When he entered her again with his pulsating hardness, she shuddered and lifted her hips to meet his every thrust. His mouth moved from her lips, brushing the glossy skin of her breasts. Her head rolled and she bit her lower lip to stifle a cry of sweet agony when he began sucking her nipple. His mouth was hot and demanding on her breast. His movements within her were becoming more intense. She opened herself more widely to him, absorbing each of his bold thrusts.

And then she could feel his body stiffen and could hear his breath coming in short raspy sounds. He paused loving her for a moment, stopping to gaze at her with hot passion in his eyes. Then he brought his mouth to her lips with a savage kiss as once again he plunged into her, over and over again.

The euphoric moment they had been seeking suddenly claimed them. Their bodies jolted and quaked into each other, their moans of pleasure mingling as their lips met in an even more heated kiss.

Then at last they lay clinging, sweat glistening on their bodies like small pearls shining beneath the sunshine. Mariah ran her fingers through Echohawk's thick hair and kissed his wet brow. "Will we truly have a lifetime of such moments as these together?" she whispered, her body still slightly trembling from the intensity of the lovemaking. "It is like a dream, Echohawk—being able to share such wondrous bliss with you."

A sob rose from deep within her and she hugged him tightly. "I adore you so," she whispered. "Please always, always love me as much as you do now."

"Our lives are now intertwined, as one entity," Echohawk whispered back, softly kneading her buttocks with his hands. "Your heartbeat is mine. Mine is yours. Our souls are the same. *Ah-pah-nay*, forever, No-din. Until the Great Spirit decides to take us from this earth." He leaned away from her, smiling. "Even then we will be together. We shall walk hand in hand, always, in the Land of the Hereafter."

"How wonderful it is," Mariah said, smoothing her forefinger across his full sculptured lips. "That you are mine forever is a miracle."

He rolled away from her and rose from the bed. Drawing a blanket around his shoulders, he went to the table and eyed the fruit that lay on a platter. He glanced over his shoulder at Mariah.

"Making love makes you hungry, does it not?" he asked, laughing softly as he heard her stomach growling even from this distance. He picked up an apple and took it to Mariah. "We shall share the fruit, like we have shared our bodies."

He placed the apple to her lips. Leaning up on an elbow, Mariah smiled at him with dancing eyes as she sank her teeth into the apple, taking from it a large hunk. She began to chew, and watched as Echohawk took a bite, chewing also as he gazed at her with his deep black eyes.

Mariah rose suddenly to a sitting position and ran the fingers of a hand over his brow. "Darling, I'm so glad you can see more clearly now," she said, looking into the depths of his dark eyes.

Echohawk sat down on the bed beside her and looked around the room, having to squint to be able to see the objects in the far, shadowed corners. "*Ay-uh,* I can see perfectly," he said, "but when I look into the distance, there is still a slight blur."

Mariah hopped from the bed, excitement filling her. "That means, Echohawk, that you will surely be able to see one hundred percent soon!" she cried, clasping her hands together before her. "Isn't that wonderful?"

Seeing her standing there, silkenly, exquisitely nude—the fullness of her breasts, her slimness, the supple broadening into the hips with their central muff of hair, and her long, smooth thighs—made his hunger increase, but not for food. He wanted his No-din again. This was evident in how his manhood had risen into a tight hardness again, the ache the kind that only being with No-din could quell.

Mariah saw the sudden passion filling his eyes, and as he tossed the apple and the bear pelt aside, she felt the heat of desire flood her through and through when she saw his readiness for her.

With a feverish need, she went to him and quivered with ecstasy as he gathered her into his arms and led her back down onto the bed. The sensations were searing within her as his fingers and lips moved purposely slowly over her body, teasingly stroking her flesh.

Her hands sought and found his pulsing hardness and caressed him, making him shiver and groan with the ecstasy. When he leaned away from her and brushed her hand aside, she molded her body up against his as he knelt over her and filled her with his length. She absorbed the bold thrusts with rhythmic upward movements of her hips, his mouth crushing her lips with a fiery kiss, drugging her.

Their bodies strained together hungrily, and then once again their passion was sought and found.

Afterward Mariah nestled close to Echohawk, breathing hard, her loneliness banished forever. When he leaned away from her and looked down at her with adoring love in his eyes, she pulled his head down and kissed him.

She melted into him when once again he entered her with his revived hardness. She shuddered and gripped his buttocks lightly. Her mouth clung to his in a long, blistering kiss. The delicious pleasure filled her again, and her body rocked and swayed in her passion.

She moaned throatily as once again she found that wondrous ecstasy within her lover's arms. . . .

"How can it be?" she whispered against Echohawk's perspiration-dampened face afterward. "We have made love three times so quickly. My darling, not long ago I did not even know the *ways* of making love!"

"In time I shall show you many ways of taking and giving pleasure," Echohawk said, smoothing dampened strands of hair back from her brow. "Nee-kah was right when she said that you were an astute student. My woman, you have learned already many ways of loving."

"Only because it was you teaching me," Mariah said. She sucked in a wild breath as he lowered his head to her nipple and circled it with his tongue, then trailed his lips wetly downward, stopping at the juncture of her thighs. As he thrust his tongue against that part of her that still throbbed from his lovemaking, she closed her eyes and let herself enjoy it all over again.

This man, she marveled to herself. *Ah, this delicious, heavenly, wonderful man.*

Because of Echohawk, she had been transformed into a woman, and felt blessed that it had not been too late for her.

25

A girl with eager eyes . . . waits me there . . .
Oh heart . . . ! . . .

—BROWNING

Several Days Later

For the first several days the riverboat had moved calmly through the waters of the Mississippi. But on the seventh day, the day planned for the arrival to Saint Louis, snow had begun to fall, the wind blowing with tremendous violence.

Mariah and Echohawk were in their cabin waiting out the storm, uneasy as they could feel the boat pitching to and fro in the water. They could hear her the pounding of the waves, beating like thunder against the sides of the boat. The splash of the great paddle wheel seemed puny as it struggled through the fevered water. Oh, how the noise grated against Mariah's nerves!

"Perhaps we shouldn't have boarded this . . . this monstrosity," Mariah said, gladly accepting Echohawk's arms around her. "At first I thought the boat was beautiful with its lacy latticework trim and fancy spindles, but now I feel as though it is nothing more than a toy." She clung more strongly to him. "I'm afraid, Echohawk. What if the boat suddenly gets swallowed whole by the angry river?"

"Without people manning the paddles, I do not see how the boat is maneuvered anywhere," Echohawk grumbled. "It is not at all like the canoes of my people."

Mariah clung a moment longer, then eased out of his embrace when she became aware of a lessening of the howling winds and the steadying position of the boat as it moved more smoothly through the water.

She went to the small window and gazed outside through the muck and mire of the glass. She felt much relieved when she saw that the snow was no longer whirling about, so obscuring the atmosphere that objects could not be distinguished at a distance of one hundred yards. It had been one of those tremendous storms called *poudries,* in which neither the Indians nor white people normally dared to stir abroad and when even the wolves flew to the woods for shelter.

"It's finally stopped snowing," she sighed heavily. She turned and gazed eagerly at Echohawk. "We haven't left the cabin much since we've been aboard. I would like to now, before arriving at Saint Louis. Would you go with me, Echohawk, to take one last look?"

"If you can stand the cold," he said, going to her, taking her hands. "No-din, living with the Chippewa, you will *have* to learn to accept the cold temperatures of winter better than you did living the life of a white woman. There are always duties for both men and women outside the wigwam. After the lakes are frozen, it is required that all men and women be strong enough to ward off such temperatures, to be able to get wood for warmth and water for drinking. The winter months require more stamina than the summer months."

"And I won't disappoint you," Mariah said, smiling. She eyed the door, then looked up at him again. "Let's go. Let's explore."

She had not encouraged much exploring after boarding the boat. She could not help but see an uneasiness creep into Echohawk's eyes, even though only moments ago he was trying to convince her of so many things. Earlier, as they had boarded the boat, and the few times they had mingled with the others, she had seen how the other travelers gaped openly at him, then had looked at her with disgust when they recognized that she was with him, a woman whose skin was white.

She understood quite well that to most people it was a forbidden thing—the union of an Indian man and a white woman. She herself had feared ugly comments while traveling the full week to Saint Louis. But she had prepared herself for any and all snide remarks. She would defend her right to be with Echohawk to the end, if necessary.

She would defend Echohawk with her life, if need be!

Echohawk helped Mariah into her bearskin coat and then slipped into his own. Together they stepped out onto the deck. The temperature was not much below the freezing point, but the wind pierced their garments like a knife. The snow had finally stopped, and Mariah went to the rail and peered over the side, seeing that the riverboat was following close to the banks, partially sheltering it from the blast of the wind.

At times during the journey the boat had struggled, grating upon snags, and hanging for two or three hours at a time on sandbars. The weather had now cleared, showing distinctly the broad and turbulent river with its eddies, sandbars, ragged islands, and forest-covered shores.

Mariah had read in her studies that the Mississippi River was constantly changing its course, wearing away its banks on one side while it formed new ones on the other. At present the river was low, and it was almost frightful to see dead and broken trees firmly embedded in the sand, all pointing upstream, ready to impale any riverboat that at high water should pass over them.

Shivering, Mariah looked up at Echohawk. "I've seen enough," she said, laughing softly. "Let us return to our cabin. I plan to place much more wood in the small stove. I am ready to be toasty warm again."

Echohawk swept an arm around Mariah and led her across the deck past several cabins before reaching their own, the passengers consisting of traders, gamblers, soldiers and their wives from Fort Snelling, and Oregon emigrants and "mountain men."

Just as they reached their cabin, Mariah and Echohawk were stopped when suddenly a man in a black cape blocked their way as he quickly exited the cabin on their left side. Mariah stiffened when his dark eyes shone with mockery as he glanced from her to Echohawk. He looked like the villains that she had read about in books, his mustache as black as the hair that was partially exposed at the edges of the top hat he was clutching with one hand, a cigar between the fingers of his other.

"What do we have here?" the man said in a snarl, his eyes still roaming over Mariah and then Echohawk. "I've seen you once or twice these past several days. A white woman and an Injun. Now, ain't that an interesting combination?"

Echohawk's eyes lit with fire, yet he willed himself not to show the anger he was feeling. "Step aside, white man," he said, his voice smooth and even. "No-din is cold."

The man's dark eyes widened and his mustache quivered as he smiled wryly down at Mariah. "No-din?" he said mockingly. "It wasn't enough that you chose a damn savage as a travelin' companion, but you let the Injun give you the name of a squaw?" He reached a hand out for Mariah. "Come on. Let me show you the real world."

Before Echohawk could stop him, the man had jerked Mariah into a cabin filled with laughing, raucous men sitting around a table, cards scattered across the top, along with many coins, and bottles of whiskey.

Frightened, not only for her own safety, but also for Echohawk's should he do anything to antagonize these men, Mariah did not attempt jerking herself free. She scarcely breathed when Echohawk moved stealthily into the room, illuminated by one lantern, smoke hanging low over the table like billows of fog.

"Men, look what I've brought you. A little plaything," the man said, shoving Mariah further into the room, close to the table. "We have us a little squaw here." He jerked Mariah's coat off, revealing her buckskin dress. "She ain't only travelin' with an Injun, she has an Injun name and she's dressed like one."

The men cocked their eyes up at the man and gave him annoyed stares. "Blackie, goddammit," one of the gamblers said exasperatedly, "what do you think you're doin'? Let her go. Do you hear? We don't want no trouble. We just want to sit here peaceful-like, playin' poker. The last thing we need is Injun trouble."

"It's only one Injun," Blackie said, turning glaring eyes at Echohawk. He took a step toward Echohawk and stared up at the eyeglasses. "And I can't figure this one out. He's wearin' spectacles." He laughed throatily as he grabbed the eyeglasses from Echohawk's nose and dropped them to the floor, crushing them with the heel of his boot. "Now. Should you decide to defend your little whore, I can fight you fair and square, since you don't have spectacles on to hide behind."

Goaded beyond human endurance, Echohawk could not hold back his rage any longer. He reached a hand out to Blackie and locked it behind his neck, forcing him quickly to the floor, on his stomach. Echohawk straddled him, and leaned his mouth close to his ear. "Hear me now, white man," he warned, his voice a low hiss. "You push me too far and you will regret it."

"All right, all right," Blackie said, his eyes wild, one cheek pressed hard against the floor. "I apologize. Just let me up. I won't bother you no more."

Believing him, Echohawk let his hold on the man grow slack. And just as Echohawk started to rise away from Blackie, Echohawk found himself at the disadvantage and on the floor. A knife was quickly drawn from a sheath at Blackie's waist and held close to Echohawk's throat.

"Now who is threatening who?" Blackie said, laughing boisterously.

Her heart pounding, and seeing that the other men were not going to intervene, even though they apparently did not approve of Blackie's tactics, Mariah knew that she must be the one to make the next move. Eyeing a whiskey bottle on the poker table, she inched her hand toward it. She was surprised that the men allowed even this, for when she picked the bottle up by its slender neck, they did not shout out a warning to Blackie.

Her knees weak with fear that she might cause Blackie to plunge the knife into Echohawk's flesh, she crept closer to the man, then stopped and said his name—sweetly and seductively.

"Blackie? Why bother with him when you can have me?" Mariah said tauntingly.

Seemingly stunned by her flirting, Blackie forgot his concentration and eased the knife aside as he turned to look up at Mariah. She grabbed this opportunity to bring the whiskey bottle down on his head, the knife in his hand no longer a threat to Echohawk.

Glass shattered and Blackie's body lurched from the blow, his eyes wild as they locked with Mariah's, and then he tumbled over sideways onto the floor, unconscious, the knife at his side.

One of the gamblers scrambled to his feet. Mariah was expecting to be assaulted for what she had done, but instead found kind arms propelling her away from the unconscious man, allowing Echohawk to rise from the floor.

"We apologize, ma'am," the gambler said, his blue eyes soft and kind as he gazed down at Mariah from his six-foot-four height. "Blackie ain't nothin' but a troublemaker. And rest assured we'll keep him away from you and your friend until you are safely off the boat."

"That is kind of you," Mariah said. "Thank you ever so much."

Echohawk came to her, brushing his hair back from his eyes. He grabbed up Mariah's coat, took her by the hand, and whisked her out of the cabin, embarrassed that it was she, a woman, who had defended him, the man, again!

Yet by doing so she had demonstrated her intense love for him, and that made his heart swell with pride.

"Your eyeglasses," Mariah said, going into their cabin beside Echohawk, closing the door behind them. "Echohawk, that evil man broke your eyeglasses. Now what are you doing to do?"

"I will do well without the white man's magic," Echohawk grumbled. "I can see nearly as well as I did before."

Relieved to be back in the privacy of their cabin, Mariah held her hands over the stove and rubbed them together, warming them. "You don't have to be inconvenienced for long," she said, glancing at him over her shoulder. "While we are in Saint Louis we can use some of my money to fit you with new eyeglasses."

"The man did me a favor," Echohawk said, tossing his coat aside. "I am glad the eyeglasses are gone."

When someone knocked on the door, Mariah turned with a start and her face paled, wondering if Blackie had come to finish what he had started. She stifled a gasp behind her hand when Echohawk went to his belongings and grabbed a rifle in his large hand.

He turned to Mariah. "You step out of the way," he whispered harshly. "I don't want you taking a bullet that was meant for me."

"Oh, Echohawk, I hope we're wrong," Mariah said, moving around to stand beside the bunk. "I hope that man doesn't ever wake up!"

"You hit him hard enough," Echohawk said, moving stealthily toward the door when someone continued to knock. "But it always seems that an evil man's head is harder than that of one born with kindness in his heart."

Aiming the rifle with his right hand, Echohawk moved his left slowly to the door latch. He opened the door quickly and found himself aiming the barrel of his firearm directly into the eyes of the riverboat captain, whose color drained instantly from his face.

"Please . . . ?" Captain Johns muttered, his eyes frozen wide. "I've only come to apologize for the inconvenience you encountered at the hands of . . . of that damnable gambler Blackie. I've forbidden him on my ship in the past. So shall I now, in the future!"

Echohawk turned the barrel of the rifle away from the captain, holding the firearm at his side. "Your apologies are accepted," he said, feeling Mariah's presence at his side as she came quickly to him.

"Also, I have come to tell you that Saint Louis is within range should you wish to view it," Captain Johns said, lifting his hat, wiping beads of perspiration from his pale brow.

"Let's go and watch as the boat is moored, can we, Echohawk?" Mariah said, looking anxiously up at him.

Echohawk inhaled a nervous breath, then stood the rifle against the wall and stepped outside with Mariah and the captain.

Mariah's breath was taken away when she saw the size of the city set back from the waterfront. The buildings were quite impressive, some even four stories high! And the roads! They were filled with many horses and buggies and fancy carriages!

But what she was most anxious to see was Jefferson Barracks. Even though she wanted to go into some of the fancier shops to see the ribbons and laces, and perhaps even purchase herself a fancy bonnet and dress before presenting herself to her father, it was Colonel Snelling himself who was most prominent on her mind now.

"Sir, where might I find Jefferson Barracks?" she blurted as Captain Johns moved beside her at the rail.

"Ma'am, Jefferson Barracks is up the river a ways," he said, pointing beyond Saint Louis proper. "You can hire a carriage to take you there."

Mariah beamed up at Echohawk as he gazed down at her. "Echohawk, I shall see my father soon!" she said, thrilling to the thought. "Can you imagine? We are finally here and I . . . I will be able to see my father."

"Your father?" Captain Johns asked, forking an eyebrow. "Does he make his residence at Jefferson Barracks?"

"Yes," Mariah said, clasping her hands excitedly together before her.

"What is his name?" the captain asked, smiling. "Perhaps I know him."

Mariah's smile faded, not feeling comfortable about revealing her father's name before he knew himself that he *was* her father.

But somehow it just came out.

"Colonel Josiah Snelling," she blurted. "He's my father."

She frowned and cocked her head when she saw a sudden sour look come across the captain's face. He turned and walked away without another word.

"Why did he behave so strangely?" she asked, looking confusedly at Echohawk. "Perhaps he doesn't like my father."

"Do not let one man's attitude take away your excitement today," Echohawk said, placing an arm around her waist. "It is *your* day. Yours and your father's."

Mariah inhaled a shaky breath, Echohawk's comforting words already causing her to forget the strange behavior of the riverboat captain. She was looking dreamily into the distance, ready to count out the moments until she could embrace her true father, until she could proudly present herself as his daughter.

26

> She is most fair, and thereunto,
> Her life doth rightly harmonize.
>
> —LOWELL

After leaving the riverboat, Echohawk held on to Mariah's elbow as they climbed the steep incline that would take them into the major part of the frontier town of Saint Louis. In 1825 it was a mere village on the western bank of the great Mississippi, on the edge of a vast unexplored land.

The sun warmed the snow, melting it, making their footing more sure as they finally reached the cobblestone street that reached out on both sides along the river. The town extended in both directions on either side, clusters of stone houses standing on the western bluffs.

Mariah was absorbing everything as she and Echohawk crossed the thoroughfare and stepped up onto a wooden sidewalk, soon mingling with an assortment of passersby—white-, red-, and black-skinned alike.

A scattering of teams and saddled horses were hitched to the wayside posts. And mingled amidst the buildings were picturesque whitewashed houses which stood close to the street behind high picket fences. Most of them were built of logs set upright on the ground, but some were puncheon walls and shingle roofs, with piazzas running all four sides. All were clean and white, surrounded by fruit trees, long gardens stretching behind them.

In one sweep of the eye Mariah saw several saloons, a millinery shop, two hotels, and various merchant shops. Her nose took her to stand at the window of a bake shop, emanating from it a rich aroma of cinnamon, apples, molasses, yeast, and the smoke of hickory and oak.

She looked anxiously up at Echohawk, who was tense and quiet beside her. Although she had never been to such a large town herself, she knew that it had to be an even stranger experience for Echohawk. She had seen how he had looked so warily at the men who sported large firearms at their hips, those men having stared just as warily back at him as he held his rifle tightly within one of his powerful hands.

She saw how Echohawk looked with wondering eyes at the dark-skinned men and women hustling by, apparently having never seen black people before. She had tried to explain that most were more than likely slaves, perhaps in town gathering up supplies for their masters, but he could not fathom the idea of one man owning another.

She saw how Echohawk flinched as he walked in the shadows of the taller buildings, having never seen anything as high, except for the walls at Fort Snelling and the high bluffs in the Minnesota wilderness.

"Echohawk, I have enough coins not only for lodging and a new dress and bonnet but also for a sweet bread," Mariah said, trying to draw him into conversation. He had been so subdued, so quiet, since their arrival in Saint Louis. She wanted him to relax and enjoy it, the same as she. Before the end of the day she would even have cause to celebrate. She was going to claim her birthright!

"Sweet bread?" Echohawk said, forking an eyebrow. "What is a sweet bread?"

Mariah took his hand and began leading him toward the door of the bake shop. "It is something quite wonderful and delicious," she said, giggling. "Come on. Share with me."

Echohawk was hesitant, then went inside with her, his nostrils flaring with the pleasant aromas wafting through the air. He watched silently as Mariah transacted the business of acquiring what she called sweet bread. He saw her shake several coins from her buckskin pouch and hand them to the proprietor, dressed in white, then watched as she smiled broadly as she was handed something in a small sack.

"It smells and looks delicious," Mariah said, leaving the bake shop with Echohawk. "After we settle down in a hotel, we shall have ourselves a private feast. I have had a sweet bread only once, and that was at the Snellings' residence. The icing! It just melts in one's mouth!"

They walked on, once again in silence, taking in everything. Men in colorful frock coats, narrow trousers, and high boots, and women in their silken finery, fur capes, and fancy bonnets brushed past them, ignoring them as though they weren't there. A boy was sweeping out a stableyard. A man strolled by, slouched, his aged shoulders seeming heavy beneath his ragged coat, a basket on his arm, apparently carrying his eggs and butter to the market for selling. An occasional pig rambled by, scavenging. They were lean, lanky creatures and had noses long and slender enough to drink out of a jug. A few pigeons also strutted along the thoroughfare, scattering in all directions when threatened by an approaching, thundering carriage.

But something else drew Mariah's keen attention, making her wonder how she could have forgotten this special season of the year.

Christmas!

With all of the recent traumatic experiences, she had forgotten about Christmas!

They were now walking in the part of the frontier town that displayed only the finest of boutiques and art galleries, where the shopping was enhanced by a town-wide effort at seasonal decorating. Beribboned greens wreathed and outlined the shops and buildings. Trees with shining ornaments graced each window.

The powerful perfume of the pine boughs reminded Mariah of the Christmases that she had shared with her mother before she had passed away. Without the aid of her father, Mariah and her mother had gone into the forest and had chosen the largest tree they could drag back to the house. They decorated it together, giggling and singing.

Once done, its boughs were heavy with myriad precious things. Amid many tapered candles had been hung intricate paper cutouts, cookies, pieces of taffy, tiny toys, gilded ornaments, strings of popcorn and cranberries, ribbon bows, and dried flowers.

At the tree's peak had floated a delicate angel. . . .

Tears burned at the corners of Mariah's eyes, her vision of her mother clouded with the truths she now knew about her. She glanced over at Echohawk, knowing now that her mother had been immoral not only once, but many times. And Mariah was the result of one such affair!

Deep within her heart, Mariah knew that she could never forgive her mother for these infidelities.

This, again, reminded her of her mission today. Her true father! She did not want to delay seeing him much longer. She must hurry and buy herself a beautiful dress and bonnet. She then must find a hotel that would accept her and Echohawk as guests in the same room.

Mariah smiled up at Echohawk as they stopped in front of a shop that displayed velveteen dresses and matching bonnets. "Do you understand my need to dress differently today?" she asked softly. "I so want to look as pretty as I can for my father. And, Echohawk, I have wanted a velveteen dress and bonnet for so long! Just this once, darling. Then I shall never again wear anything but buckskin."

She paused, then added, "And I want to buy a gift for Neekah . . . something that she will treasure."

Echohawk placed a gentle hand to her cheek. "Today is your day," he said softly. "You do what you must."

Mariah hugged him, then grabbed his hand and led him into the shop with her.

When the woman in charge caught sight of Echohawk, she inhaled a quick startled breath and paled. She covered the diamond necklace that lay against the velvet of her dress, her thin lips pursing angrily as she glared at Mariah.

"I wish to see your most lovely velveteen dress," Mariah said, ignoring the frustrated sales clerk, whose beady eyes annoyed more than angered her. "The color I prefer is pale green."

"There are no dresses here for you," the woman said, her narrow face pinched into a deep frown. "Now, be on your way."

Echohawk took a bold step toward the woman. He towered

over her and his eyes narrowed. "My wife sees many dresses," he said, his voice drawn. "One of them will be hers." He nodded to Mariah. "Find the one you wish to buy. Choose a bonnet. I have no doubt the lady here will take your gold in payment."

The lady took a step back from Echohawk, fear in the depths of her eyes. "Yes, my dear," she said thinly. "I will be . . . be happy to help you choose, if you wish."

"No, that's not necessary," Mariah said, hurriedly finding her size, the correct color, and then the bonnet that she felt was the loveliest of the many, with lace in abundance on it. She chose her special gift for Neekah, Echohawk's warm smile showing his approval, then quickly paid the clerk and waited for her purchases to be wrapped. She was glad to leave the shop, having hated putting Echohawk in such an awkward position.

Prejudices, it seemed, ran rampant everywhere, even in this frontier town of Saint Louis. She was saddened that it was hard for anyone to believe that there was such a thing as a peaceful Indian.

She dreaded the next chore, feared entering the hotel with Echohawk, and what the desk clerk's attitude might be when she paid for only one room—and only one bed.

But of course the clerk would not know that they were not married, so that did not concern her as much as what his attitude might be over an Indian staying in his hotel.

Again there were difficulties to be faced—and conquered!

Under any other circumstances Mariah would have been thrilled at the prospect of staying a full night in a fancy hotel room. Many times she had passed her lonely nights reading books that her father had acquired for her at various trading posts. She had read of the hotels where plush carpets covered the hardwood floors and satin draperies hung at the windows. She could not even conjure up thoughts of how soft the beds must be in such elegant rooms.

She silently said a prayer of thanks to Josiah Snelling for having remembered owing her father a gambling debt. She was taking much delight in spending the money!

The shadow of a four-story hotel fell across Mariah and Echohawk as they stepped up to the door. She looked at Echohawk, his arms filled with her purchases, his rifle resting in the crook of his left arm.

Then she walked on into the hotel, her chin held proudly high. Without hesitation, ignoring the murmurs and glances as people broke away on both sides, making room for her and Echohawk, Mariah went to the desk clerk and shook many coins from her buckskin pouch.

"I would like whatever room my money can pay for," she said, looking square into the desk clerk's nervous eyes.

His eyes shifting to Echohawk, the clerk reached for a key behind him and grabbed one without seeing even which one he had chosen, then slapped it down on the desk. "And how will you be signing the register?" he asked, running a thin finger around the stiff white collar of his shirt.

"Mariah Temple," Mariah said matter-of-factly. She took up the pen and scratched her name on the register, then grabbed up the key and held it out for Echohawk to see.

"And how about . . . about the Indian?" the clerk asked, now running his fingers nervously through his thinning gray hair.

"He is to share my room, of course," Mariah said over her shoulder, prancing toward the steep staircase.

She again ignored those curious eyes in the lobby as Echohawk walked beside her to the stairs. But when he stopped and gazed slowly around, at the grandeur of the lobby, and then up the staircase, his eyes filled with wonder, Mariah understood.

"It's as new and as awesome to me," Mariah said, leaning close to Echohawk so that only he heard her. "I've never seen anything as grand. Nor have I ever been on the fourth floor of a building. My, but we shall see perhaps clean down the river to Jefferson Barracks!"

They went up the stairs, stopping at each landing take a look from the window at the end of the corridor, then proceeded until they reached the fourth floor and found their room. When they stepped inside, Mariah's heart leapt with delight. It was as she had always dreamed a hotel room would be—grand and spacious.

She rushed into the room and jumped onto the bed, sinking deeply into the feather mattress. Her eyes took in the satin draperies . . . the plush cream-colored carpet . . . the heavy oak furniture.

Then she went to the window and grew solemn, anxious. From this vantage point she *could* see Jefferson Barracks on the edge of the river in the distance. It was not as grand as Fort Snelling, but that did not matter. It housed her father!

Echohawk laid the packages aside, and also his rifle. He walked lithely across the soft carpet, comparing it to thick beds of moss in the forest. Very gingerly he bent low over the bed and pressed his fingers into the mattress, jumping back, startled, when it gave way to his touch.

And then he crept over to stand beside Mariah, his heart thundering wildly when he took a look from the window and saw how high he was off the ground, and how the river looked like a large snake winding along the ground not far from the hotel.

Mariah leaned into his embrace. "Isn't it beautiful?" she marveled; then her smile waned when she looked into his eyes. His expression had taken on a wistful, somber quality that did not match her giddy joy.

He peered into the distance, at the forest that stretched out far onto the horizon on the opposite side of the river. He could see many tepees, and wondered which Indians made residence so close to this frontier town of Saint Louis. It would be good to smoke with them, yet this was not the time for powwows between two factions of Indians. The powwow today was to be between Mariah and her father.

He drew her around and framed her face between his hands. "Let us wait no longer to go to your father," he said earnestly. "Your heart is anxious. I can see it in the pulsebeat at the hollow of your throat."

"*Ay-uh,* I am very anxious," Mariah murmured, her face beaming with anticipation.

Echohawk lowered his mouth to her lips and kissed her

gently, then went and stared curiously at an upholstered chair. He eased himself into it, and watched comfortably as his woman changed clothes and became transformed into a vision of loveliness.

* * *

Mariah and Echohawk arrived by carriage at Jefferson Barracks. Once inside the massive stone walls, Mariah saw a neat row of buildings. She noticed that Jefferson Barracks was a hubbub of activity, soldiers and civilians coming and going, mingling in the courtyard on foot, and on the roads, on horseback and in carriages.

Mariah's gaze stopped at the stone headquarters building as the carriage stopped before it. Soldiers soon appeared at the carriage, one on each side.

As the door was opened beside her, Mariah quickly explained why she and Echohawk were there, and the hesitation of the soldiers seemed to be because Echohawk was with her.

Mariah and Echohawk were not invited from the carriage. One of the soldiers went inside the building, and soon a stout man dressed neatly in a blue uniform, with brass buttons picking up the shine of the sun, came to Mariah and reached a hand out to her, helping her from the carriage.

"Young lady, what is this about you having come to see Colonel Snelling?" the soldier asked, casting troubled glances at Echohawk as he kept his seat in the shadows of the carriage.

"I have made a long journey to see the colonel," Mariah said, her voice edged with irritation. "He is the commandant here. Please take me and my companion to him."

Again the stout man gave Echohawk a questioning stare, then focused his attention on Mariah again. "My dear, your travels were in vain," he said blandly. "Colonel Snelling is no longer here." He cleared his throat nervously and kneaded his chin as one of his thick gray eyebrows arched.

Then he spoke further without hesitation. "You see, Colonel Snelling has been ordered to Washington," he said, clasping his hands together behind him. "He is being charged with mishandling government funds. The gossip is that Colonel Snelling has been plagued with a peculiar ailment for many years and has become addicted to opium, the standard treatment for the disease. The treatment is expensive. Snelling used some of the government's money to purchase it."

Having admired Colonel Snelling for as far back as she could remember, Mariah was stunned speechless by the news. Her stomach suddenly felt hollow. She had now been disillusioned by two fathers!

Without saying another word to the stout man, who was perhaps her father's replacement at Jefferson Barracks, Mariah climbed back inside the carriage and ordered the driver to return her and Echohawk to the hotel.

"Echohawk, how could he have done this to me?" Mariah said, staring blankly into space. "How?"

"He did not do it to you," Echohawk said, taking her hand, squeezing it reassuringly. "He did it to himself. His loss is greater than yours. He will never know the wonders of a love such as yours."

"No, he shan't ever know me," Mariah said, stifling a sob of regret. "For my search is over. My secret is best left unspoken."

She turned tear-filled eyes to Echohawk. "Take me home, darling," she murmured. "I . . . I feel so foolish to have even asked you to bring me on such a . . . such a fruitless mission."

She flung herself into his arms, her bonnet slipping from her head. "Take me home to your people so that I may become your wife soon," she softly pleaded. "*You* are my life. I will forget my foolish notion of ever calling Colonel Snelling father to his face."

"The boat we will travel on back to our people does not depart until morning," Echohawk said, gazing down into her eyes. "Forget your disappointments. Being together is all that matters."

"I *have* looked forward to staying in the hotel room this one night," Mariah said, struggling to be grateful for what she did have in life. She had never truly had Josiah Snelling to call her father, so it should not be so hard to accept that she could not call him father even now.

Yes, she stubbornly decided. She *could* accept the loss, for it was a loss that she had lived with all of her life.

Mariah cuddled close to Echohawk, and when they arrived at the hotel, dusk had fallen. When they went inside the hotel lobby, the only candles that were lit were those on the branches of a ceiling-high Christmas tree. A fire crackled in the large stone fireplace at the far end of the room, casting a romantic glow around the room.

"Come and join in the merriment," a kind voice said to Mariah and Echohawk from among those sitting around the fireplace and tree. "It is a time dearer than any other part of the year, a time to open hearts to one and all alike. Tomorrow is Christmas!"

Mariah questioned Echohawk with her eyes, and when he nodded yes to her, she went with him and sat down on the floor beside the tree, removing their coats, placing them on the floor beside them. They were each given a stout mug filled with a sweet convivial brew of hot hard cider made of crabapples and spices.

A tall lean man stood among those enjoying this peaceful moment, and raised his potion in a spirited toast. "*Waes hael,*" he cheered in an Anglo-Saxon tongue. "Be thou hale!"

They all put their mugs to their lips and drank, Mariah slipping a hand over to Echohawk, taking hold of his hand, needing it for reassurance. She could not quit thinking about Colonel Snelling. He had been disgraced! He had always been a proud, kind man. Now his reputation was a ruin of what it had once been.

Echohawk set his mug aside and placed a finger to Mariah's chin. "You still worry about Josiah?" he said softly.

"*Ay-uh,*" she whispered back. "How can I stop? I had so counted on today—seeing him again."

"My people lost an ally when he left the land of lakes," Echohawk said solemnly. "But always remember the good that he did. Keep that thought, and you will not be as disappointed in the man you now know is your father."

Mariah gazed raptly up at him, always in awe of how wise he was. He seemed to be able to reason things out so that one could see what was unpleasant in a different light. And he was right about her father. She should not condemn him for his faults, because his kindnesses outweighed his faults ten to one.

"Thank you for reminding me," she murmured.

Then her eyes were drawn quickly away from Echohawk, when across Echohawk's shoulder, behind him, in the dark shadows of the room, stood someone she would never forget. Blackie! The gambler from the riverboat!

She turned her eyes back to Echohawk and yanked on his hand, urging him up from the floor. She did not want him to see the gambler. She wanted their night in the hotel to be one of sheer pleasure. Even though she would wonder the night through what Blackie had on his mind, at least Echohawk would not be bothered with the threat.

"You are ready to leave?" Echohawk asked, leaning down to retrieve their coats.

"I am bone-weary," Mariah said, making sure that Echohawk did not turn and make eye contact with Blackie, glad that Blackie was standing in the darker shadows of the room.

"Then you will have your rest," Echohawk said, ushering her up the stairs to their room.

Once inside, the door closed and bolt-locked, both of them soon forgot that anyone had spoken of being weary. They quickly undressed and found incomparable pleasure in lying on the feather bed, making long, enduring love filled with promises.

27

Contentment, rosy, dimpled maid,
Thou brightest daughter of the sky.
—Lady Manners

Several Days Later: New Year's Eve

On the return trip to Fort Snelling, Mariah stood beside Echohawk on the main deck of the riverboat, keeping watch on the clouds building overhead. The weather had become threatening again; the sun, low in the west, was gradually effaced in a gloom of thickening clouds. A rough wind had just risen, and there was a spitting of snow from the sky.

"We should be arriving at Fort Snelling soon," Mariah said, watching the activity of the river, fearing it. It was always tearing away at the banks, an aggressive, implacable monster, it seemed.

Yet she knew that there were some positive benefits in the raw energy of the river. As the water washed off land on one side, a sandbar would start opposite, and soon willows would begin to grow, at length building up so that it could be cleared and cultivated. The stream progressed by many loops, so that the valley was full of abandoned channels.

Captain Johns stepped up to the rail. "Since we will be arriving at Fort Snelling before midnight, our crew are celebrating the new year now," he said, puffing on a fat cigar. "Join us in my cabin. Share a glass of wine with us." He nervously cleared his throat. "I regret what happened on the other voyage. Let me make up for your inconvenience." He paused, clasping his hands behind him as he gazed intensely into Echohawk's dark eyes. "I understand about prejudices. My grandmother was a full-blooded Cherokee. My mother had many of her mother's features. She was shunned by many because of that." He eased his hand onto Echohawk's shoulder. "Chief Echohawk, it is my sincere pleasure to have met you."

"I welcome you as my friend," Echohawk said, placing a fist over his heart. "My heart welcomes you."

Mariah was moved almost to tears by what she was witnessing, Echohawk so noble, so handsome as he accepted the captain's friendship. She almost melted into Echohawk as he swung away from the captain and placed an arm around her waist, ushering her to the captain's master cabin.

Shedding her coat, Mariah smiled at each crew member as they passed by her, introducing themselves to her and then to Echohawk, creating a relaxed atmosphere that turned into a time of laughter and camaraderie. Mariah accepted a tall-stemmed glass of wine and looked over at Echohawk as he refused the one offered to him.

"I do not put firewater in my body," he said, folding his arms across his chest. He gazed down at Mariah and started to tell her that it was not wise for her to drink the firewater either, that he had seen it discolor too many red men's logic.

But he quickly reconsidered. He had promised Mariah freedom of choice. The firewater was no different from anything else. He did not want to interfere with his woman's free spirit.

Captain Johns placed an arm around Echohawk's shoulder. "It is a wise man who refuses to put alcohol into his system," he said, nodding away one for himself when it was offered. "For a spell I depended on alcohol too much to get me through the day. But after a tragedy aboard my riverboat, for which I was responsible, I have never touched another drop of whiskey, nor any sort of alcohol. Normally my crew doesn't drink while on the job either. But this is New Year's Eve. I did not think a glass or two of wine could do them harm."

"What sort of tragedy?" Mariah asked, setting her half-empty glass aside on a table.

"It didn't occur on this boat," Captain Johns said, stepping away from Echohawk, taking a long stare from the small window. "It was another one, in fact the first riverboat I ever commanded." He turned slowly and looked at Mariah and

Echohawk. "It was a beautiful boat, but it burned quickly, and along with it several . . . several passengers."

Mariah paled and placed a hand at her throat. "How horrible," she gasped.

Captain Johns looked down at his cigar, and just as quickly mashed it out in an ashtray, a sudden involuntary shiver visibly gripping him. "It was a mixture of whiskey and cigars that did it," he said, his voice strained. "I drank too much and fell asleep with the cigar in my hand. The fire and smoke awakened me, but I was too drunk to save anyone but myself."

He looked admiringly at his crew. "Most of these men you see here today were part of the crew on that fateful journey. They are responsible for saving those that were saved. If not for them . . ."

He shook his head, swallowed hard, then looked again at Mariah and Echohawk with wavering eyes. "It took many years of building up my courage to invest in another riverboat," he said thickly. "But when I finally did, most of my crew came back to me. And here we are today, one big happy family."

"It is good that you have resumed life again as you knew it before your tragedy," Echohawk said, placing a gentle hand on Captain Johns's shoulder. "You are a man to be admired. Not every man would have the courage that you have shown." His eyes darkened with remembrances of his own recent tragedies. He looked at Mariah. She accounted for so much of his own regained confidence. If not for her . . .

A loud commotion surfacing from the adjoining cabin made a startled silence grip the room.

"It seems as though someone's New Year's celebration has gotten out of hand," Captain Johns said, rushing from the cabin, his crew following him.

Echohawk and Mariah were left alone, but for only a moment. Soon Blackie slunk into the room, a drawn pistol in his right hand, a sinister smile on his lips. "I'm pretty good at sneakin' on a boat and causin' distractions, wouldn't you say?" he said, smirking. "I chided one of the suckers into accusin' one of the gamblers of cheatin'. In no time flat a fistfight broke out, and I slipped past them without no one noticin'. I hid in the shadows until after the captain and his men left you alone. Now, Injun, I'm at the advantage, wouldn't you say?"

Mariah's pulse raced. She had forgotten about Blackie when he hadn't made any attempts to bother Echohawk at the hotel. Now she understood why. His plans were for later, while in the middle of the river, away from lawmen.

Fearing for Echohawk, she gave him a quick glance. With a firearm aimed at him, he was powerless.

Then she looked toward the window. The storm had worsened, causing the waves to thrash wildly at the boat's hull. She had to grab for a chair for support when the boat lurched sideways, and at the same time she saw that the advantage was now Echohawk's, for Blackie had lost his balance, his feet sliding from beneath him as the boat quickly righted itself again.

In a blur, it seemed to Mariah, Echohawk was on Blackie, knocking his firearm from his hand and wrestling him to the floor, straddling him. Mariah scrambled to grab the pistol, then stood back and watched wide-eyed as Echohawk suddenly jerked Blackie to his feet and yanked his arm behind him, forcing him to the door.

"Open the door, No-din," Echohawk said, looking at Mariah over his shoulder. "There is only one solution I can think of to rid ourselves of this man, without killing him."

Mariah rushed to the door and opened it. "What are you planning to do?" she said, following Echohawk as he forced Blackie ahead of him.

The wind was wild and cold, the snow stinging her cheeks as Mariah followed the two men to the rail. Still clutching the pistol, she sucked in a shallow breath when she realized what Echohawk's intentions were for the gambler. She cringed when Blackie began shouting for help as he looked over the side of the boat into the swirling muddy water.

"You can't do this to me!" Blackie cried, struggling to get free as Echohawk began lifting him over the rail. "No! Don't! I'll freeze to death!"

Echohawk looked at Mariah. "Aim the firearm at the gambler!" he shouted, then looked with an amused smile down at Blackie. "If you prefer a bullet to the water, she can very easily pull the trigger." He paused, laughing beneath his breath when he saw the wild pleading in the gambler's eyes. "What is it to be, white man? A bullet? Or the muddy, cold Mississippi?"

"Neither!" Blackie cried. "I beg of you. Let me go. I won't bother you again. Ever!"

Echohawk held him even lower over the rail for a while longer, then brought him back to the deck and let him go, the suddenness of his release causing Blackie to tumble to the floor, cowering. "I think the boat's captain can think of a place to put you until we reach Fort Snelling," Echohawk said, wiping his hands on his buckskin breeches, as though to remove the stench of the gambler from his flesh. "There you will be seen to by the white pony soldiers. They will not like to hear that you threatened Chief Echohawk and his woman's life—not once, but twice. They are friends of No-din and the Chippewa. They will see to your punishment. I believe you would prefer their choice of punishment over that of the Chippewa!"

"Yes, yes, I would," Blackie said, nodding anxiously as he scooted back from Echohawk on the deck.

A loud round of applause broke out. Mariah looked quickly around, having been so absorbed in Echohawk's performance that she had not seen Captain Johns and his crew arrive, also to observe.

"Well done!" Johns said, coming to lock an arm around Echohawk's shoulders.

He gave his crew a stern look. "Take that scoundrel Blackie below!" he ordered. "Secure him well!"

Then he turned back to Echohawk. "Now, if it had been up to me, I'd have tossed the sonofabitch overboard. I'd have loved seeing him choke on the muddy river water," he said, laughing heartily. "But since you are an honorable man, of course you have spared him the humiliation."

"This time, *ay-uh,*" Echohawk grumbled, taking the pistol from Mariah's hand, quickly ushering her away, toward their cabin. "But next time? *Gah-ween,* no. My patience is running thin for this man whose heart is bad toward me and my woman."

"I must see to my duties," Captain Johns said, since they

were nearing land, the fort's walls now in sight. His brow knit into a worried frown. "I hope the blizzard doesn't impede our landing."

Mariah looked over her shoulder at the snow tumbling from the sky in a sheet of white, then was glad to reach the warmth of her cabin. Once inside, she stepped close to the small stove, trembling.

"We are near to Fort Snelling," Echohawk said, placing a blanket around Mariah's shoulders. "Soon we will be with our people again."

"We are lucky to be anywhere," Mariah said, sighing deeply. "This journey was fraught with danger and disappointment."

"But we survived it all, didn't we?" Echohawk said, smiling down at her, his finger at her chin, tipping her face up to his. "My woman, my No-din, you worry too much."

Echohawk was worrying, wondering if the riverboat could get to shore during the ravaging storm that was upon them. "I will be back soon," he reassured Mariah, slipping into his coat. "I wish to see if it is too hazardous to take the white man's large canoe to shore."

Mariah smiled weakly at him, and after he left, turned her eyes back to the window, seeing the ever-swirling snow floating past. She was not fearing the landing of the riverboat as much as the journey back to Echohawk's village. This weather was not favorable to traveling on horseback!

Echohawk hurried across the top deck to the rail, and held on as the boat slowly pushed its way up into the willows skirting the bank close to Fort Snelling, the gangplank succeeding in reaching out to the shore.

His gaze went further, into the far stretches of the forest. He knew the dangers of traveling during such a storm, but he had had enough of the white man's world! Nothing would delay his travels back to his people! Nothing!

* * *

Eight moons heavy with child, Nee-kah panted hard as she trudged through the snow from the river, carrying a jug of water. Chief Silver Wing had warned her against not only traipsing out alone in the dangerous weather but also carrying their water. He had told her to assign another, younger woman to do the chores.

And she had, for a while, but boredom had set in.

And she had felt useless watching someone else do what she had always been able to do for herself and her husband.

A thick hooded fur cloak secured around her shoulders, Nee-kah blinked snow from her heavy lashes as it began to fall more furiously from the sky. Her snowshoes were awkward as the snow deepened, and a quick panic rose inside her when she could no longer see the village through the raging snowstorm.

But she kept trudging onward, holding faithfully to the jug of water, stopping in shock only when someone stepped out of the snowy shadows directly in her path.

Nee-kah stifled a scream behind her mittened hand, knowing that the Indian standing threateningly before her, his knife drawn from his sheath, was not a Chippewa. All Chippewa were friends! Not snakes who threatened helpless pregnant women! It could only be a Sioux!

She dropped the jug of water and felt her knees weaken when several other Indians, attired in thick fur coats, stepped into view, their dark eyes narrowing as they gazed down at her.

"Nee-kah?" White Wolf said in very simple Chippewa language. "Wife of Chief Silver Wing? And friend of Echohawk and his white woman who is called No-din?"

"I could lie and say that I am someone else," Nee-kah said, stubbornly lifting her chin. "But I am too proud to behave in such a weak, cowardly manner. I declare to you that, *ay-uh,* I am Nee-kah. And now that you know, what are your plans for me?"

She was grabbed suddenly from behind and half-dragged to a waiting horse. She did not fight back as she was placed into the saddle, for she feared for her child more than for herself. Finally her husband had found a wife to bear him children . . .

and now this wife was being stolen from him—perhaps never to be seen again!

She still held her head high, but could not stop the flow of tears that sprang from her eyes. She had let her husband down by disobeying him.

Now he might lose not only his wife but also his unborn child!

She looked to the heavens and prayed to the Great Spirit not to let this happen, and promised never to be so bullheadedly, stubbornly willful again.

Then her gaze was drawn to her abductors and her eyes narrowed when she heard the lead Indian being addressed by a name. White Wolf. It was the renegade Sioux who was guilty of this cowardly act today!

It would be with much rage and hate that Chief Silver Wing would avenge what White Wolf did today!

* * *

The council meeting over, Chief Silver Wing leaned into the wind and blowing snow and hurried to his wigwam. Once inside, and after shedding his fur wrap, he looked around the room for Nee-kah, a sudden foreboding lurking at the pit of his stomach.

She was not there.

And the weather was too bitter for her to have gone out into it.

His gaze went to the water jugs that sat at the side of the wigwam, and mentally he counted them. One was missing.

"She has gone to the river!" he said, his teeth clenched. "She still persists in believing she is capable of fending for herself, even . . . even in this blizzard!"

Throwing his fur cloak around his shoulders, he went from the wigwam shouting orders to his braves. He told several to go and search for Nee-kah down by the river. He told others to go in all directions close to the village, checking to see if she had lost her way in the blinding snow.

He mounted his horse and rode ahead of those on their way

to the river, his heart pounding out the fear of not finding her before she froze to death.

He did not get far. He saw the water jug lying partially hidden in the snow. Quickly dismounting, he fell to one knee and grabbed up the jug; then his heart sank when he looked in all directions and could not find any footprints.

Fresh snowfall had covered them.

He looked to the heavens and let out a loud wail of despair, then bowed his head in a silent meditation with the Great Spirit.

When he arose back to his full height, he found himself circled by his braves on horseback.

"She is nowhere near," one said, this pronouncement agreed on by the others.

"Then we must search until we find her," Chief Silver Wing said, his jaw tight with determination.

"The blizzard . . . ?" Wise Owl said, gazing up into the swirling snow.

"We will ride until we cannot see to ride any farther." Chief Silver Wing wheeled his horse around, urging it through the thick, heavy snow. Doubts of ever finding his woman were pressing in on his heart, yet he could not believe that she could have gotten far, unless . . .

His eyes narrowed with hate. "Unless she was abducted!" he cried aloud, alarming the men who rode beside him.

"The Sioux!" he whispered to himself. "If they came on my land and took my woman, they will pay!"

He shook the snow from his shoulder-length hair and snapped his reins, regretting that he could not go faster on his steed.

Time.

Time was his enemy in this weather of life-threatening temperatures.

His Nee-kah.

She could even now be lying beneath a covering of snow.

Or, he thought bitterly, she could be lying beneath her enemy!

28

Oh! Who would inhabit
This bleak world alone?

—Moore

The sky was lightening along the horizon. The storm clouds had diffused into something tranquil—into white puffs of clouds floating gently across the sky. Mariah's fingers were cold and stiff as she clung to the horse's reins. Her cheeks felt tight from the stinging cold wind.

The ride on horseback from Fort Snelling through the snow and cold, frosty air had been hard, but she had weathered it all and could only grieve to herself that her main complaint was that of being sleepy. Even food did not sound all that good to her. In fact, the thought of it made her feel ill to her stomach. Her main desire now was to stretch out on her pallet of furs beside the fire in Echohawk's wigwam.

Her eyes were burning with the need of sleep.

She was finding it hard to keep her eyes open . . .

The aroma of smoke wafting through the air caused Mariah's eyes to widen and her heart to sing.

Finally!

Finally, after almost a full night of riding through the snow, and fighting occasional drifts piled high against the trees, they were near their village.

"No-din, soon you can be warmed by a fire," Echohawk said, giving her a worried look. "I fear my decision to ride directly to our village was wrong. The night has been long and cold." He smiled at her. "Yet you did not complain once. My woman, tonight, as so many times before, you proved to me that you can withstand anything. You are a woman of grit—of strength. I am proud of you, No-din. Very proud."

"Echohawk, you have given me so much strength, by just loving me," Mariah murmured. "I never want to disappoint you. I want you to be proud of me always."

Echohawk did not have the chance to reply. Two of his braves were suddenly there on horseback, approaching them, rifles clutched in their hands, their faces painted with red streaks—the color of warring.

Echohawk jerked his horse to a shuddering halt and awaited their arrival. He eyed them warily as they stopped before him. "What has happened?" he asked. "You do not greet me with a friendly hello. You wear war paint. Why is that, Proud Thunder?"

Mariah drew her horse to a stop beside Echohawk's, shivering at the sight of the braves, who seemed hell-bent on vengeance.

"Nee-kah!" Proud Thunder said, his eyes narrowing with rage. He thrust his rifle into the air. "She is gone. It is believed to have been the Sioux who are responsible for her abduction. We help Chief Silver Wing search for her. We cannot find her, nor the Sioux camp."

Echohawk's face paled. So Yellow Eyes had lied! White Wolf, the renegade Sioux who was responsible for so many of Echohawk's sadnesses, was alive, and again creating havoc.

But this time White Wolf was taking his vengeance out on Echohawk's friend Chief Silver Wing. Could White Wolf have done this thing against Chief Silver Wing only because it would draw Echohawk into a confrontation with them?

The terrible news about Nee-kah made Mariah feel faint, and then her shock registered even more sharply when she remembered Nee-kah's delicate condition.

The baby!

It was due in only a month.

The trauma that Nee-kah was going through, if she were still alive, could cause her to deliver early.

"And where is Chief Silver Wing?" Echohawk said, his voice drawn.

"He and many braves are still searching," Proud Thunder said, gazing into the distance, through the snow-laden trees of the forest. Then he looked at Echohawk, an apology in his eyes. "Brown Fox and I searched the whole night through. We returned hesitantly, but we feel that further searching is in vain." He paused, then added, "And we fear the villages being left so unprotected." He looked guardly at Mariah, then back at Echohawk. "We can never forget raids of the white people. We cannot relax our guard, ever."

Echohawk nodded. "This is so," he said, reaching a heavy hand to Proud Thunder's shoulder. "But I must go and find Silver Wing. Together we will search a while longer for Nee-kah, and if she cannot be found, I must encourage the elder chief to return to his village. He is no longer a young man with the endurance of a bear. But of course I will be delicate in saying so."

Echohawk then reached his hand to Mariah and placed it gently to her cheek. "No-din, go ahead to the village," he said. "Brown Fox will take you. You get your rest. When you awaken, hopefully I will be there at your side to give you good news that not only is Chief Silver Wing back in his village, but also Nee-kah."

"I so badly want to go with you," Mariah said, sighing deeply. "I love Nee-kah as though she were my own sister."

"You have been in the cold long enough," Echohawk said firmly. "It is time for you to be warmed and to get some rest."

Mariah felt dispirited about having to agree with him, but she *did* know that she could not go another mile on the horse. She was exhausted. And she would only delay Echohawk's search.

"*Ay-uh,* you are right," she said, again sighing deeply. "I would only get in the way." She turned and smiled at Brown Fox. "You do not need to travel with me to the village. Go on with Echohawk. He needs you more than I."

Echohawk edged his horse closer to Mariah's. He placed a finger to her chin and brought her eyes back around, to meet and hold with his. "There has been one abduction, there is not to be another," he growled. He nodded at Brown Fox. "Go. See to my woman. Stand guard outside her wigwam. Watch over her for me, for she is my life, Brown Fox."

Mariah was touched deeply by how Echohawk so openly spoke of his feelings for her to his braves. She would have thought that a powerful Indian chief would not want to express such feelings to his braves—perchance looking weak in their eyes.

Over and over again Echohawk proved his intense love for her, she marveled to herself, and she suspected very strongly today that she just might have a way to repay him. She had missed her monthly weeps. She was feeling nauseated. Just perhaps . . . she was with child! What a gift to give her husband!

"*Mah-bee-szhon,* come," Brown Fox said, nodding to Mariah. "Do not fear. I will see to your safety."

Mariah's eyes wavered as she gave Echohawk one last look, hoping it would not be the last time she was allowed to. She wanted to believe that he would return to her. Their lives would soon be tranquil. They would wed, and together they would watch her body grow with child.

Sinking her heels into the flanks of her horse, she rode away from Echohawk, a feeling of foreboding hanging over her, as though she were engulfed within a dark cloud. She swallowed back a fast-growing lump in her throat, knowing that this was not the time to lose faith and waver in her courage.

Echohawk gave Mariah a lingering look, concerned for her as she rode away, her shoulders slumped. It seemed the burdens he kept placing on her shoulders were many.

And now?

What of sweet Nee-kah?

Would there ever be cause to celebrate a lasting peace among the Chippewa tribes?

Always there was cause for delay in the laughter and smiles!

He had begun to think that it never would change.

If not—he had drawn his No-din into a life of continued miseries.

Wheeling his horse around, he rode off beside Proud Thunder. They rode and searched with their eyes for what seemed hours; then suddenly before them were many horsemen riding toward them across a vast snow-covered meadow.

"Silver Wing!" Echohawk said beneath his breath, recognizing the elder chief from the others by the slight slouch of his shoulders—a chief who had once ridden so tall and straight in the saddle, now bent with age and years of disappointment and sadness.

He urged his horse into a strong gallop, then came to a halt beside Silver Wing's steed.

"I have heard!" Echohawk said, placing a hand on Silver Wing's shoulder. "I am saddened."

Silver Wing's eyes lowered and he shook his head slowly back and forth. "It is with much regret that I have to return to my village without my Nee-kah," he said glumly. "But we have searched, it seems, to the ends of the earth, and she is nowhere to be found. I fear she is dead, somewhere in the snow, the snow her grave."

"Chief Silver Wing, you are weary from the search," Echohawk said, his voice thin. "Return to your village. I shall search awhile longer. When you go to your bed alone tonight, you will then know that everything has been done to find Nee-kah."

"She is *gee-mah-gah,* gone," Silver Wing said, lifting weeping eyes to the heaven. "My wife! My unborn child! They are gone! Why, Great Spirit, why? What have I done to deserve such sadness as this?"

"Silver Wing? My husband?"

Echohawk and Silver Wing gave each other a sudden quizzical look.

"Did you hear a voice?" Echohawk said, his eyes wide as he stared over at Silver Wing.

"Did you hear the voice also?" Silver Wing said, his jaw tightening, having thought that wanting it to be so, so badly, he had imagined hearing Nee-kah's voice calling his name.

Suddenly in view, only a few yards ahead, where they now could distinguish the small figure of a woman from the brightness of the snow, Echohawk and Silver Wing saw Nee-kah stumbling through the snow, one hand clutching a blanket around her shoulders, her other hand outstretched toward them.

"My husband, it is I, Nee-kah!" she cried, suddenly clutching her hand to her abdomen, sharp pains gripping her there. "Silver Wing, come to me. Silver Wing!"

Silver Wing sank his moccasined heels into the flanks of his horse and rode off in a hard gallop toward Nee-kah, and when he reached her, dismounted in one leap. He grabbed her into his arms and hugged her tightly.

"My wife. My sweet Nee-kah. You are safe!" he whispered, his heart pounding with joy. He held her away from him and looked her up and down. "And are you all right? The baby?"

"Nee-kah is fine," she said, then grabbed at her abdomen when the pains assaulted her again. She did not want to tell him that she was concerned about the child—that perhaps she was going to have the child early. She knew her husband well enough to know that he would want to go and settle things with the Sioux himself, instead of sending warriors to battle them for him. She would have to pretend that she and the child were fine.

Later, she decided. Much later she would tell him of her concerns.

Perhaps by then he would already be a father!

Silver Wing clasped his fingers to Nee-kah's shoulders. "I looked everywhere," he said softly. "How is it that I did not find you?"

"The Sioux camp is not far," Nee-kah said, giving Echohawk a soft smile as he rode up and dismounted. "Beyond the meadow, just inside the forest, there is a cave. The horses and the Sioux are well hidden there. I . . . I escaped when they slept. Being heavy with child, they did not think I would chance escape." She laughed softly. "But they do not know Nee-kah, do they?"

"You are a different sort of woman, that is true," Silver Wing said, his shoulders relaxing in a heavy sigh.

"Nee-kah is so sorry to cause you such worry," she said, moving into Silver Wing's arms. "I did not listen to you. I went to the river for water. Because of that, because of my stubbornness, I was abducted."

"That you are here now, safe, is all that is important," Silver Wing said, easing her out of his arms. "You go now. Rest beside a warm fire until my return. We go and take many scalps today!"

"The Sioux who is responsible for Nee-kah's abduction is called White Wolf," she murmured.

Echohawk and Silver Wing exchanged knowing glances, fire quickly lighting their eyes.

Then Silver Wing looked down at Nee-kah. "Your abduction will be avenged," he growled. "White Wolf's scalp will decorate my scalp pole tonight!"

Nee-kah bit her lower lip with worry, then let Proud Thunder help her onto another brave's horse, and smiled weakly at Silver Wing as she clung to the brave as he rode gently away.

Echohawk and Silver Wing nodded, then swung themselves into their saddles and rode hard across the meadow. They entered the forest, but were stopped when a volley of arrows came at them seemingly from out of nowhere. The bowstrings twanged a death song, arrows humming like angry hornets at the Chippewa.

Suddenly many Sioux braves appeared on horseback, riding toward the Chippewa, White Wolf in the lead. Guns bellowed. Gunfire filled the air. More arrows screamed from their bows.

Echohawk threw back his head and uttered a war whoop almost in unison with Silver Wing's throaty cry. Kicking his horse into a run, Echohawk soon lost sight of Silver Wing as the Sioux and Chippewa mingled, all whooping and charging. They met in a head-on clash, clubs striking deadly blows, horses floundering and slamming onto their sides in the snow when they received the bullets meant for their riders.

The air soon thick with black powder smoke, Echohawk fought hard for his life, unable to look around him, to see how anyone else fared.

But soon the firing ceased and all that could be heard were the groans of the wounded.

Echohawk sat stiffly in his saddle as his gaze moved around him, seeing the death that lay strewn around him, the blood like roses in the snow.

And then his heart plummeted with despair when he spied a familiar face among the fallen. He quickly dismounted and ran to Chief Silver Wing, easing his head up from the snow onto his lap.

"Take the scalps of our enemy to our people," Silver Wing said between deep, quavering breaths. He grabbed at his chest, where his fur cloak had been ripped open from the explosion of a bullet, blood freezing in shreds along the matted fur.

"There is no time for scalps," Echohawk said, his voice drawn. "That time will be spent in taking you to your people. To your wife. Your Mide priest will perform magic over you. Your wounds will soon be healed!"

"Gah-ween," Chief Silver Wing said, blood now trickling in a stream from the corner of his mouth. "The Mide's magic will not be strong enough for this elder chief this time. The wound is a mortal one." He struggled to get up. "Take me to Nee-kah. I will not let myself take that last breath until I can hold her in my arms again."

"If only it were I lying there wounded," Echohawk said, his voice filled with regret.

"You are young. You have a lifetime ahead of you. I have had a full, rich life." Silver Wing paused, closed his eyes for a moment while taking some quick breaths, then looked up into Echohawk's eyes again. "And soon, Echohawk, a child will be born to Nee-kah. *My* child. And . . ." He managed a peaceful smile. "And it *will* be a son, Echohawk. I know that to be so."

"Ay-uh," Echohawk said, filled with remorse. It was as though he was holding his father in his arms, watching *his* life ebb away, all over again. In so short a time, two men of his heart had been robbed of him! What in life *was* fair?

He looked slowly around him, seeing that not one Sioux had lived through the fight, and his heart swelled with pride. Never again would this band of renegade Sioux be able to take loved ones from him!

His heart skipped a beat, a thought springing to his consciousness, making him groan with a frustrated anger. In the confusion and concern over Silver Wing's welfare, he had forgotten about White Wolf!

"He is not among the dead!" he whispered between gritted teeth. "He escaped. Even now I do not get my full vengeance!"

Turning his attention back to Silver Wing, Echohawk placed his arm gently beneath him and lifted him from the snow and carried him to his horse. Tears filled his eyes when he saw how Silver Wing found that last ounce of strength to hold himself upright in the saddle. He would enter his village one last time as the great proud chief of his people. They would see him as the noble man that he was.

Echohawk eased onto the horse behind Chief Silver Wing and placed an arm around him and held him in place before him. Leaving behind enough braves to tend to the wounded, the others followed humbly behind their two chiefs.

29

There is nothing held so dear as love, if only it be hard to win.

—INGELOW

Mariah was cozy warm beside the fire, many pelts drawn up to her chin, but yet she could not sleep. She was feeling guilty for being safe and warm while Nee-kah was out there somewhere, perhaps dying in the snow, or at the hands of unmerciful abductors.

And Echohawk and Silver Wing!

Both were riding into the face of danger, perhaps instant death, should they find Nee-kah's captors.

Unable to bear just lying there, so troubled by her fears for those she loved, Mariah smoothed the blankets and pelts aside and moved to her knees before the fire, wishing that she were with Echohawk, riding as boldly as his braves at his side.

Then she placed a hand to her abdomen, knowing that now, as never before, it was best to behave responsibly. If she *were* with child, she had to protect it at all cost. And she tended to think of the child as a boy—Echohawk's son, the future leader of his people.

Her thoughts were catapulted back to the present when she heard the sound of an arriving horse outside, sounding as though it were nearer to Silver Wing's wigwam then Echohawk's. She grew tense when she heard people shouting Nee-kah's name.

"Nee-kah?" Mariah said, rising quickly to her feet. "Have they found her? Has Echohawk returned safely?"

Having not taken off her dress before lying down, Mariah scrambled into her knee-high moccasins and snatched up her fur cloak, then rushed toward the entrance flap. Once she was outside, she fled over the short distance dividing Echohawk's and Silver Wing's villages, and was soon torn with feelings. She was joyous over seeing Nee-kah just being helped from a horse by a brave, yet troubled over not seeing Echohawk with her.

So many worries flashed through her consciousness.

Had only one brave and Nee-kah survived an attack on the Sioux?

Was Echohawk even now lying in the snow, dead?

A sob lodged in her throat. Afraid to hear the answers, yet knowing that she must, Mariah tore from the wigwam and ran through the ankle-deep snow until she reached Nee-kah, who was being helped to her wigwam.

"Nee-kah, oh, thank God, Nee-kah," Mariah said, clutching Nee-kah into her arms, giving her a fierce hug. "I was so worried about you."

"I am fine," Nee-kah said, smiling up at Mariah as she stepped away from her. "I am like you. Strong-willed and able to fend quite well for myself."

"Echohawk?" Mariah asked, her pulse racing. "Where is Echohawk? Where is Silver Wing?"

Nee-kah's eyes wavered. "When I last saw them, they were well," she said, then grabbed at her abdomen when another pain assaulted her. "But they now will be fighting the Sioux," she breathed out between clenched teeth, her eyes closed. "I so fear for our Chippewa braves!"

Mariah was quickly alarmed when she recognized the pain that Nee-kah was in, and how sweat was pearling on her lovely copper brow, even though the temperature was way below freezing.

Though her every heartbeat belonged to Echohawk, Mariah was thrown into worries about her friend, knowing that even though Nee-kah had another full month before the time of her child's delivery, it had been as Mariah had earlier feared: the trauma forced upon Nee-kah could cause an early labor.

"Let me help you into your dwelling," Mariah said, taking Nee-kah by an arm, slowly walking her to the entrance flap. "I can tell you're in pain. Nee-kah, it's the baby, isn't it?"

"Ay-uh," Nee-kah said, brushing the entrance flap aside,

gingerly stepping inside, every footstep seemingly causing the pains to increase in intensity. "It is the baby." She turned wild eyes to Mariah. "It is too early, No-din. Do you know any white-people secrets that can make the pains of childbirthing stop? I . . . I fear birthing my child early. If anything should happen to the child . . ."

Mariah helped Nee-kah to her sleeping platform beside the fire. She was aware of much commotion behind her, and out of the corners of her eyes saw many women coming into the wigwam, each carrying assorted items to be used during the birthing procedure.

She turned her full attention back to Nee-kah when Nee-kah grabbed at her stomach again and screamed, her color paling. "Let's get your cloak off, and then your dress," Mariah said, trying to keep herself calm, though her heart was pounding with fear. She had never even seen a small baby before, much less helped bring one into the world.

But of course she saw that she was not needed at all. Nee-kah was soon surrounded by many women looking down at her adoringly. They had come to help. They had all the knowledge necessary to help Nee-kah deliver the baby.

After Mariah had Nee-kah undressed and a blanket drawn over her up to her armpits, she stepped aside and watched as the women began their ritual of assisting Nee-kah as her labor pains came more frequently, now scarcely seconds apart.

"Silver Wing," Nee-kah cried, her eyes wild as one of the women slipped her hand up the birthing canal, trying to help the baby move through it. "My husband! Oh, Silver Wing! If you were only here!"

Nee-kah turned frightened eyes to the circle of women. "No-din!" she said, her voice quavering. "Where . . . is No-din?"

Two of the women stepped aside and made a space for Mariah at Nee-kah's side. Mariah smoothed her hand over Nee-kah's side. Mariah smoothed her hand over Nee-kah's perspiration-laced brow. "What can I do?" she murmured. "I . . . I feel so helpless."

"Just hold my hand," Nee-kah said, circling her fingers

around Mariah's hand. "Just . . . hold . . . my hand, sweet friend."

"I wish I could do more," Mariah said, holding tightly to Nee-kah's hand as Nee-kah squeezed her fingers into Mariah's, once again crying out with pain as she bore down.

"Surely it won't be long," Mariah said, yet greatly fearing the early birth. "And, Nee-kah, just you wait and see. Your child will be healthy, like its mother and father."

"It . . . is . . . coming!" Nee-kah cried, grunting as she bore down again, harder . . . harder. . . .

And soon the child was lying in the hands of one of the Chippewa maidens, proving its lungs were of adequate capacity with wails that reached far from the wigwam to the outside, into the early-morning air.

"It is a son!" Mariah said as the child was held high for all to see. She leaned down into Nee-kah's face, Nee-kah having momentarily fainted from the trauma of the delivery. "Nee-kah," she whispered, brushing a kiss across Nee-kah's cheek. "You and Chief Silver Wing have a son!"

Mariah's joy was short-lived when Nee-kah did not awaken abruptly, but still lay in what seemed some sort of comatose state.

Her fingers trembling, Mariah placed them at the vein of Nee-kah's neck. Tears of relief flooded her eyes when she felt a very steady pulsebeat there. Nee-kah's eyes fluttered open and she looked around her, still stunned and confused.

When her gaze fell on the small bundle being held by one of the Chippewa women, her son now wrapped in a blanket, Nee-kah swallowed back a choking sob and held her arms out to the child.

"Let me see my baby," she murmured, her voice weak.

Knowing the bond that had formed between Mariah and Nee-kah, the woman laid the child within Mariah's arms, then nodded toward Nee-kah.

Mariah felt a strange sort of melting at the pit of her stomach when she peered down at the tiny copper face, dark eyes shaded by thick black lashes blinking back at her. "So lovely," she whispered, then laid the child in Nee-kah's arms. "Nee-kah, your son. He is so very, *very* lovely. And healthy. You have nothing to fear. He will grow up to be a great man."

Nee-kah looked through tears at her son, then with one hand unfolded the blanket from around him. She gasped with delight. She smiled up at Mariah, then looked slowly around her at those who had ministered to her in her time of need.

"My son will be called Strong Branch until he has his special vision," she said proudly. She looked adoringly back down at her child again, sighing. "Is he not a long, slim baby, as straight as a northern pine?"

"He is wonderful," Mariah said, very gently touching the baby's tiny arm, then smoothing her fingers over his even tinier fingers. "And soon he will have a friend to play with. As soon as I—"

"You are with child?" Nee-kah asked, wonder in her eyes and voice.

"Perhaps," Mariah said, blushing bashfully. "I hope so."

Their moment of joyous beginnings was drawn abruptly to a halt at the sound of many horses stopping outside the wigwam. All eyes were locked on the entrance flap when it suddenly was drawn back and Echohawk came in, carrying Silver Wing.

Mariah rose quickly to her feet, her knees weakening when she caught sight of the blood on Silver Wing's clothes and the paleness of his face. And she also recognized the sound of death, for she would never forget hearing the death rattles only moments before her mother had died, and also Victor Temple's.

An instant dizziness gripped Nee-kah when she caught sight of her beloved husband as Echohawk carried Silver Wing toward her.

"No!" Nee-kah cried, fighting to stay alert as the trauma of seeing her wounded husband sent her heart into a tailspin of despair. She clung to her baby and tried to rise to a sitting position, but her weakness would not allow it. "My husband!" she cried, reaching a hand out to Silver Wing. "No! Tell me you are not injured badly!"

"Nee-kah?" Silver Wing said, his voice barely audible.

Echohawk took Silver Wing to Nee-kah and placed him

beside her on the sleeping platform, then stepped back and stood beside Mariah, circling a comforting arm around her waist.

"My wife, I have come back to you to say a final good-bye," Silver Wing said, his failing eyesight not having even seen the child, nor that Nee-kah was on the sleeping platform. "Take my hand. Let me feel the softness of your skin one last time."

Fighting back tears, Nee-kah turned to him as best she could, but it was not her hand that she placed in her husband's hand.

It was the small hand of their son.

When Silver Wing became aware of the size of the hand, reaching his other hand to cover it, to feel the tiny fingers, tears began flooding his eyes. "The child," he said, his voice breaking. "You . . . had . . . our child . . ."

"Ay-uh," Nee-kah murmured, leaning to kiss her husband's cold cheek. "And, my darling, it is a son. I have already named him. He is to be called Strong Branch. Can you not see? He is as straight as a northern pine!"

Silver Wing's hand roamed over his son, a look of bliss entering his eyes as he felt all of his son's features and his tiny body. When he found that part of him which told him that, *ay-uh,* he was a son, a deep rush of emotion filled him. "A son," he said, smiling through tears at Nee-kah. "*Ay-uh,* a son. Strong Branch? That is a good name. It fits him well."

Silver Wing felt a tightening in his lungs. "Take our son," he said, fighting back the urge to cough. "And remember that I will always be with you, Nee-kah, even though I soon will enter the Land of the Hereafter."

Nee-kah took Strong Branch back into her arms and wrapped him securely in the blanket, feeling as though a part of her was tearing away when Silver Wing turned his head from her and began coughing hard, blood now spewing from his mouth.

She sought deeply within herself for the courage to live through the next moments of her life, knowing that she would be saying a final good-bye to her dear, wonderful husband.

Oh, it was hard!

When he took his last breath, a part of her would be forever gone!

But she had to fight for the courage to want to live. She would live for their child. For Silver Wing, she must see that their son was raised to be a great leader, in his father's footsteps.

Silver Wing turned to his people, who had come into the wigwam. "Elders of my village, come and stand around me and hear my farewell words—listen to my last ruling as chief," he said, his voice almost failing him. When they were positioned, somber and sad as they gazed down upon him, he continued:

"My infant son shall rule upon my death," Silver Wing said. "I took a young wife for the bearing of a son who would be chief. Strong Branch *is* to be chief. But until he is of age, you who are the elders of this village must see that both villages, Echohawk's and ours, work together as one under the leadership of Chief Echohawk. If Echohawk will agree, he will become Strong Branch's father, to teach him everything about life."

Satisfied, Silver Wing closed his eyes and coughed again, exhausted from the long speech.

Echohawk was touched almost speechless. He knelt beside Silver Wing and took one of his hands into his, squeezing it affectionately, yet cringing when he felt its cold limpness. "I am here to do whatever you ask of me," he said, his voice drawn. "You so humble me, Silver Wing."

"Take my child," Silver Wing said, wheezing, now unable even to open his eyes. "Hold him to your heart. Acquaint yourself with him. From today forth, Echohawk, he walks in *your* shadow, not mine. Your children will become his brothers and sisters. They will be as one family within their hearts and souls." He coughed, and exhaled a quavering breath. "The same as it has been for you and me."

Echohawk swept the baby up into his arms. He unfolded the blanket and looked down at the tiny face, quickly taken by the child, as though he were his own.

He held the child up high, for all to see, chanting, then relinquished the child back to his father, laying him across his chest so that Silver Wing could be with his son until his last breath.

Silver Wing reached out a hand. "Echohawk, lean close," he said, his voice growing weaker.

Echohawk bent to one knee beside Silver Wing. "I am here," he said softly.

"Echohawk, for so long I have labored diligently for peace between the red man and white," Silver Wing managed to say between bouts of wheezing. "Repeatedly . . . I have averted bloodshed by taking hot-blooded braves out of a projected raid." He paused, inhaled a shaky breath, then added, "Echohawk, argue against war of retaliation. Renew pleas for peace."

"But what of White Wolf?" Echohawk questioned, deep inside his heart wanting to seek out the renegade and kill him slowly. "He still lives. *You* die!"

"The Chippewa have a high sense of honor to defend," Silver Wing said, his breathing becoming more shallow. "Forget White Wolf. He flees even now the wrath of the Chippewa, like a dog whose tail is tucked between his legs." He closed his eyes and sighed. "Echohawk, I have . . . spoken . . . my mind. Heed what I have said. . . ."

Nee-kah managed to scoot over close to Silver Wing. Sobbing, she clung to him, then stifled a scream behind a hand when she realized he had taken his last breath.

Mariah clutched Echohawk's arm and looked away from Silver Wing, overtaken by grief. Echohawk leaned down and took the child from Silver Wing, and after Nee-kah composed herself, gently placed the child back into her arms.

Echohawk took Mariah's hand and urged her down on her knees beside Silver Wing. Echohawk began to chant quietly, while Mariah listened. Recognizing the torment in her husband's voice, she knew of only one thing that could fill his heart with gladness again. That she was with child, *their* child. . . .

30

She was swayed in her suppleness to and fro
By each gust of passion.

—DESPREZ

Several Days Later

Her cloak around her shoulders, Mariah went to the entrance flap and smoothed it aside, anxious to go and visit with Nee-kah and Strong Branch while Echohawk was hunting, not only to see her best friend and her godson but also to try to lift Nee-kah's spirits since the death of her husband. Nee-kah knew of Mariah's anxiousness to become Echohawk's wife. But she did not know that Mariah was most definitely with child. Mariah was going to share two secrets with her best friend today.

Everything wonderful would happen tonight, Mariah marveled to herself, feeling giddy. She would finally be Echohawk's wife, and she was going to reveal to him that their lives were going to be blessed with a child.

Just as she stepped out into the snow, Mariah found a large buckskin bag lying close to the entrance flap, bulging with something inside it.

She lifted an eyebrow as she looked questioningly down at the bag, wondering why it was there, and what was in it.

"Take it inside," Echohawk said, suddenly there on his horse. He swung himself out of his saddle and went to Mariah. "This is yours. Take it inside and see what the women of the village have given you."

Mariah's lips parted in a surprised gasp. "But why?" she then said, looking with wonder up at Echohawk.

A young brave came and got Echohawk's horse and led him away to the others inside the fence at the far end of the village.

Echohawk lifted the heavy bag and placed his free hand on Mariah's elbow, ushering her back inside the wigwam as she lifted the flap for their entrance.

"Remove your cloak," Echohawk said, setting the bundle on the mat flooring. "Sit by the fire and see what gifts the women of our village have given you."

Mariah slipped her cloak off, still marveling over the surprise. After Echohawk had his cloak off, she went and sat beside him close to the buckskin bag. Her fingers trembled as she opened the bag, sucking in a breath of delight when she caught sight of the lovely beaded necklaces, moccasins, and dresses.

"I still don't understand," she murmured, taking the items from the bag one by one, loving them all.

"These are yours today because I have given the women permission now to give you wedding gifts," Echohawk said, lifting one of the beaded necklaces, running his fingers admiringly over its intricate design.

Mariah's heart thrilled not only over the loveliness of her gifts and the generosity of the women but also over knowing that finally the time had arrived for their marriage ceremony.

Until now so many things had gotten in the way.

Mariah laid aside the blanket with beautifully colorful designs sewn on it and lunged into Echohawk's arms, causing him to drop the necklace he had been admiring. "Darling," she whispered, brushing his lips with a kiss, "I am so happy. We soon will be married! I had begun to . . . to feel like a loose woman, perhaps my mother's true daughter. I don't want to be like her, Echohawk. Please tell me that I'm not."

Echohawk held her away from him and looked intensely into her eyes. "Your heart belongs to only one man, now and forevermore," he said, his voice low. "I am not like the man you thought was your father for so long. I am a man of compassion. A man whose love is infinitely deep for you. I am a man who wishes to share your deepest thoughts. Your deepest longings. I will never give you cause to look elsewhere for these things that your mother did not get from her husband."

"As I will never give you cause to go seek from another woman what you wish from me," Mariah said, reaching a hand to his face, running her fingers over his handsome features. "I will be here for you, Echohawk. Always."

Echohawk framed her face between his hands and drew her lisp to his mouth. He kissed her softly, then slipped his hands down and cupped her breasts through her soft buckskin dress.

Surges of ecstasy began washing through Mariah, flooding her whole body, the spinning sensations delicious as Echohawk eased her down to the mats, quickly undressing her.

His clothes removed, he rose over her. She lifted her hips as she felt his satin hardness seeking entrance inside her. And when he filled her, pressing endlessly deeper, she gave herself over to the wild ecstasy.

Echohawk's lips slid down, across her neck, and locked on one of her breasts, flicking a tongue across the nipple. Mariah closed her eyes, and when soft whimpers filled the wigwam, she knew they were her own.

His senses dazzled by the fire licking at his loins, his hot pulse racing, Echohawk savored the sweet taste of Mariah's flesh. He moved his body rhythmically within her, the fires of his passion burning brightly.

Again his mouth closed hard upon hers, his hands clasping her buttocks, molding her sweet, slender body against his. How fiercely he always wanted her! While with her, loving her, he was frantic with the need to have more of her.

And how he loved the way she clung and rocked with him, her hips responding in a rhythmic movement all their own.

His fingers moved from her buttocks, up to her hair, and twined through the red tresses, then moved downward again, making a slow, sensuous descent along her spine until again his fingers were locked against her buttocks, squeezing her flesh gently as he felt the heat nearly exploding within himself.

Mariah's body turned to liquid as she was carried deeper and deeper into that sweet delicious state. A tremor went through her as Echohawk bent his head to her lips and gave her a gentle, lingering kiss.

And then, just as she was feeling the euphoria spreading within her, and felt his body stiffen and pause as he buried a groan between her breasts, she knew that they were close to that moment of exquisite bliss.

Their bodies shook and quaked together, exploding in spasms of desire.

Breathing hard, they clung together. Mariah gasped in rapture when Echohawk's lips brushed her throat and reverently breathed her name.

And again he kissed her. One hungry kiss blended into another, and again he buried himself deeply inside her and their bodies tangled.

Mariah felt the drugged passion mounting again. She moaned throatily as once again the incredible sweetness swept through her, but this time leaving her limp and satiated in his arms.

Echohawk lingered awhile longer atop her, then rolled away, lying beside her. The flood of emotions that he always felt while with her, which were doubled after sharing in passionate lovemaking, was there, his whole body strangely at peace with the universe.

He closed his eyes for a moment, relishing the feeling, one which no one could take from him and his No-din.

This love they shared, it was a wondrous thing! No more did he think of the past—of his losses. His No-din swept away all of his regrets, doubts, and unhappiness.

With her, everything was possible.

Mariah moved into Echohawk's embrace, loving the feel of his powerful body pressed against hers. She sighed, so perfectly content. She had never felt so desired. So at peace.

Then she eased away from him, looking into his eyes as he opened them, smiling at her. "The wedding gifts are truly a surprise," she said, giggling.

"They are gifts from the heart," Echohawk said, brushing a loose lock of hair back from her eyes. "As is mine that I now give to you."

Her eyes wide, Mariah moved to her knees beside him. "A gift?" she said, clasping her hands on her bare lap. "You also have a wedding gift for No-din?"

Echohawk leaned on an elbow and reached a hand to her

cheek. "No-din, for so long you have not mentioned marriage to Echohawk," he said seriously. "I did not mention it to you. Always there were interferences. But today, No-din, I speak of it to you. I now tell you that we have been married since our first sexual night together. It is the Chippewa custom that all that has to be done to seal the bonds of the hearts in marriage is for the woman to accept food offered her by the man she wishes to marry, and also the holding of hands while speaking words of love together."

Mariah was stunned speechless, torn by mixed feelings. She was glad that she had been married to him all along, let free of her guilt for having given herself to him so brazenly, yet puzzled by his not having told her.

"We are man and wife?" she finally said in a soft murmur. "For so long, we have been man and wife?"

"Ay-uh," Echohawk said, moving to a sitting position beside her. He placed his hands to her waist and lifted her onto his lap.

Mariah held back from twining her arms about his neck, feeling hurt for his not having been open with her. Being married was sacred! Not something to be kept a secret from the one you loved.

"Why?" she blurted. "Why did you wait so long to tell me?"

"At first I did not look on it as a marriage," he said, his eyes wavering as he saw her hurt expression. "As you will recall, I was wrestling with many feelings within my heart. I had experienced many losses. I did not want to allow myself to love you. You were white. Those who had caused my heartaches were white. I feared loving you, a white woman."

"I understand all of that," Mariah said, her reserves melting, in truth ecstatic to know that without a formal ceremony she was already his wife! The mother of the children they planned to have! "But why did you take so long to tell me? After you realized that your fears were invalid, you could have told me everything. That would have lifted much guilt from my heart, Echohawk. In the white people's eyes, I would be considered a wanton whore for having shared a bed with you before vows were spoken. I fought against such feelings, knowing that you had more than a marriage to me to worry about. Always there were interferences."

"My woman, that is why I did not take the time to tell you," Echohawk said glumly. "So many things kept clouding my mind. Yet now I see that I was wrong to place other things before you." He drew her close, her legs straddling his waist. He kissed her, then embraced her sweetly. "You will never be second in my heart again. Forgiven, No-din?"

"Always, my love," Mariah said, easing from his arms so that she could brush his lips with a kiss. Then she held away from him and smiled mischievously into his dark eyes. "I, too, have kept a secret from you," she said.

"But not for as long as you," she quickly added.

His eyes gleamed into hers. "This secret," he said, cocking an eyebrow. "Is it the sort that will make my heart soar even more than it already has today?"

"I believe so," Mariah said, moving closer to him, twining her hands around his neck. "Echohawk, darling, you have spoken often of children. Of sons. Have you not?"

Echohawk's heart began to race, knowing that she would not bring up the subject of children between them unless . . .

"Ay-uh," he said, "and you have spoken of having many children, like the Snellings."

Mariah nodded, her eyes twinkling into his. *"Ay-uh,"* she murmured. She pressed a soft kiss to his lips, then whispered against them, "My darling, handsome Chippewa chief, we are going to have a baby!"

A sudden joy leapt through Echohawk. He lifted Mariah into his arms and rose quickly to his feet. He swung her around as she clung to him, laughing. "A child!" he shouted. "A *child*!"

"Ay-uh," Mariah giggled. "And, like Nee-kah, my firstborn will be a son."

Echohawk stopped and eased Mariah from his arms, then gazed at her abdomen. Almost reverently he placed a hand there. "A child grows there, yet it is too early to see the growth in your body," he said, nodding. Then his gaze moved to her breasts. He placed a hand under each, cupping them. A slow smile tugged at his lips.

"I should have known before you even told me that you held this secret," he said, smiling down at her. "My woman, your breasts lie much heavier within my hands than that first time I touched them. Already, No-din, they are filling with our child's milk."

Mariah relished his hands on her breasts, and his admiration of them. "In time our child will be suckling from my breasts. Surely nothing can compare with that." She snuggled into his embrace. "Except, my love, for being with *you.*"

Echohawk held her for a moment, and then she stepped away, looking up at him without a smile. "My breasts have already changed," she said warily. "Soon my whole body will look different. Will you still be able to look at me with favor, Echohawk?"

"*No-din,* you will look radiant while heavy with child," he said, flashes of his Fawn there before his mind's eye, unable to cast the thought away as quickly as he wanted. He was recalling how beautiful she had been while carrying their child. He was recalling how he had enjoyed placing his hand to her abdomen, feeling the child kicking against it from deep within her womb. It had been a miracle of miracles, until . . .

Deep shadows fell upon Echohawk's face, the memories so painful—memories that he thought he had left behind.

He turned from Mariah, the pain gripping his heart, as though he had only yesterday witnessed Fawn's death, having lost more than her on the day of the raid.

His child.

His unborn child!

Mariah grew numb inside when she saw the sudden change in Echohawk. It did not take much to realize what had come over him at the mention of children. He had come so close to having a child, until Tanner McCloud had devastated Echohawk's village.

Trying to understand Echohawk's grief at this moment, when he should be so happy, Mariah stepped around and looked up at him, his eyes soon locking with hers.

"Darling, I understand," she murmured, leaning up on tiptoe, giving him a soft kiss on the lips. "It is only natural that you would be taken back in time, remembering another wife . . . another child. And I do not resent this, Echohawk. It only proves how devoted a husband you were. And how devoted a father you would have been to the child that was denied you."

She eased into his arms and pressed her cheek against his smooth broad chest. "Let me help you, darling," she whispered. "I am always here to help you."

Guilt swam through Echohawk's consciousness, guilt for having brought this sadness to his No-din, when she had only moments ago given him the world.

He placed his arms around her waist and drew her closer, molding her naked body into his. "No-din, my No-din," he whispered, then kissed her with a gentle passion and laid her back on the mats beside the fire.

With skillful hands and lips, and a body aroused anew, he showed her all over again how much he loved her.

Only her.

31

Our lives would grow together
In sad or singing weather . . .
If love were what the rose is,
And I were like the leaf. . . .

—SWINBURNE

Two Years Later, Early Winter of 1828

Outside, the wind whistled around the wigwam, the first snowfall of winter upon the Chippewa village, the creeks choked with ice. Mariah settled herself down next to Nee-kah beside the warm and inviting cook fire in Mariah's wigwam.

"Are they not the most handsome and healthy sons?" Mariah commented, turning her eyes to Night Hawk, hers and Echohawk's one-year-old son, and Nee-kah's son, Strong Branch, as they played with their miniature bows and arrows close beside them.

Mariah had watched Echohawk make their son's bow and arrows with their flint heads, wood shafts, and hawk feathers at the tails. He had used deer sinew to string the bow, but had explained that the skin from a snapping turtle's neck was the best bowstring because it wouldn't stretch or shrink, no matter the weather.

"Silver Wing would have been proud of his son," Nee-kah said, busying her fingers making herself a new pair of moccasins with her prized metal sewing needle, the special gift that Mariah had brought to her from Saint Louis. "Strong Branch already walks with the stance of a chief, so tall and erect. He will one day make his people proud. He will lead them as nobly as his chieftain father."

Her flaming red hair lustrously long again, hanging loosely across her shoulders instead of in two braids, as Nee-kah wore her raven-black hair, Mariah resumed her task of painting a new cradleboard for her second child, which was due in five months. "Strong Branch will be assuming the duties of chief before you know it," Mariah said softly. "The years pass quickly."

Nee-kah nodded and rested her needle and buckskin on her lap as she silently admired the colorful rainbow that Mariah was painting above where her child's head would rest on the cottonwood cradleboard.

"You paint well the 'arch above the earth' " Nee-kah then said. "You've learned well the beliefs of our people."

Mariah smiled at Nee-kah. "Echohawk taught me the meaning of this design," she said. "He explained to me that the Chippewa believe that if mothers decorate the cradleboards in this manner, their papooses will be watched over by the 'Powers of the West.' I think that is such a lovely thought."

A young maiden came into the wigwam, clutching a buckskin robe around her shoulders, the cheeks of her round face rosy from the bitter cold temperatures of the early afternoon. "A lone rider was seen on the horizon," she said in warning. "He is a white pony soldier. Several braves rode out to meet him, to see what his mission is here at our village."

Mariah's eyes widened as she laid her paintbrush aside. "He is white?" she said, rising to her feet, unsure how to feel about this bit of news. Since Colonel Snelling had left and a new commandant been assigned at Fort Snelling, communications between the soldiers and the Chippewa were rare.

Yet she could not help but feel anxious at the prospect of perhaps William Joseph or Colonel Snelling returning to the Minnesota wilderness to see her and Echohawk again.

They *had* been fast friends.

She regretted that she had given up her quest to see her true father, at least once before one of them died. Even if he was a cheat and a liar, she had decided long ago that she above all wanted to see him.

Mariah turned anxious eyes to Nee-kah, whose fear was evident in the way she sat so tense, looking guardedly back at Mariah. Mariah understood why. Not only did Nee-kah have the Sioux to blame for her losses, but also white men!

"In my husband's absence, while he has gone to check the traps in the forest, I shall go and see what business the soldier has at our village," Mariah said, grabbing up a buffalo robe and swinging it around her shoulders. She went to Night Hawk and kissed his soft copper cheek, then left the wigwam with the young maiden who had brought her the news.

Just as she stepped outside, the soldier, dressed in full uniform, rode into the village, flanked on each side by braves armed with rifles. Mariah met their approach, walking toward them, her chin held proudly high. When the horses came to a stop and the soldier dismounted, the two braves quickly at his side, he smiled with recognition at Mariah.

"Mariah, it's good to see you again," the young lieutenant said, snatching his hat from his head. "I hope you have been well?"

"I do not know your name," Mariah said, offering a hand of friendship.

"Osborne. Lieutenant Dan Osborne. I served under Colonel Snelling," Lieutenant Osborne said, shaking her hand eagerly. "I was in line to dance with you at the ball." He laughed heartily, casting his eyes bashfully down to his boots. "But it seems you disappeared before I had a chance to ask for that dance."

"Why are you here?" Mariah said, remembering the ball, her face coloring with a blush when recalling how clumsy she had been that night, trying to learn to dance.

Lieutenant Osborne clasped his hat behind him, his smile fading as he brought his eyes back up, meeting Mariah's. "Ma'am, we at Fort Snelling have received word that Colonel Snelling has passed away," he said gently. "Colonel Snelling died in Washington on August 20."

The news came as such a shock to Mariah, it was as though someone had thrown ice water on her face. She paled and her hand flew to her throat, stunned to the core by the news. "Colonel Snelling is dead?" she gasped. "How can that be? He was not an old man. And the last time I saw him, he . . . he was healthy."

"Ma'am he was forty-six years of age," Lieutenant Osborne

said, his voice drawn. "His death was attributed to chronic diarrhea, and/or its remedy, opium."

"You . . . you are so kind to take the trouble of coming to break the news to me and my husband," Mariah murmured, her heart aching in her sadness.

"It was not I who made the decision to come," Lieutenant Osborne said sheepishly. "William Joseph Snelling asked me to. He thought that perhaps you and Echohawk would like to know of Colonel Snelling's passing."

Mariah's heart skipped a beat, her eyes widened. "William Joseph sent you?" she murmured. Her color began to return at the hope of perhaps seeing him again. "Is he at Fort Snelling now? Will he be there for long? Or will he be leaving, to return to Washington for his father's burial?"

"William Joseph isn't at Fort Snelling," Lieutenant Osborne said softly. "He wired us the news. Ma'am, he hasn't been back to Fort Snelling since he left for Boston to become involved in politics."

A keen disappointment swept through Mariah. She lowered her eyes. "I see," she said, her voice breaking. Then she squared her shoulders and firmed her jaw. "Lieutenant, I thank you so much for coming to us to tell us of Colonel Snelling's passing," she said, reaching out for a handshake again. "Perhaps you would like to stay the night? It's a long ride back to the fort. And the temperatures are just barely above freezing."

Lieutenant Osborne looked uncomfortably from one brave to the other at his side, and smiled shakily at Mariah. "I appreciate your offer . . . your kindness," he said, shaking her hand vigorously, then placing his hat back on his head. "But I think it's best if I get back to the fort to see to my duties."

"You might want to at least have a bite to eat before leaving," Mariah said, yet wanting to be left alone to her thoughts—to her own silent grieving. Her father never knew of this daughter who could have loved him oh, so much, had she been given the opportunity!

"I've brought along enough provisions for myself," Lieutenant Osborne said, turning to swing himself quickly into his saddle. He tipped his hat to Mariah. "Sorry to be the one to bring you such sad tidings. Perhaps the next time we meet, it will be under more favorable circumstances."

Mariah smiled weakly up at him. "Yes, perhaps," she murmured, then waved as he gave her a last look over his shoulder and rode away at a gallop.

Unable to hold back the tears, Mariah let herself shed those for what had not been—for a father's love that had been denied her—and then she wiped her eyes clear of tears over one sadness, to be troubled by something else. She peered into the forest at the snow-laden limbs of the trees.

Echohawk.

Where is he? she worried to herself.

He had left early in the morning to check the rabbit and bird snares in the forest, but she knew that he should have been back by now. Yesterday they had received their first snowstorm of the season, but during the night the storm had ceased. At sunrise the cold had been extreme. The smaller twigs had beep covered with a thick rime, and the atmosphere had held only minute glittering particles of snow.

That was when Echohawk had gone out into the forest, even though Mariah had feared for his safety. It had been a fretful night of wolves howling eerily. She had had nightmares of the rabid wolf that had come close to attacking Echohawk so long ago.

And also there was always the renegade Sioux White Wolf to worry about. Still no one had found him to make him pay for his wrongful deeds. And while he was still free, hating Echohawk as he did, Echohawk was not safe.

Her heart pounding out her fear, Mariah rushed back inside the wigwam, breathless with her need to go and search for Echohawk. "Nee-kah, can you watch Night Hawk for a while longer?" she asked, bending over her son, smoothing her hands through his coarse black hair, the child an exact replica of his father.

"Where are you going?" Nee-kah asked, rising slowly to her feet, panic filling her eyes. "You aren't leaving with the white pony soldier, are you? I thought I heard his horse leave already. And why was he here? I did not hear all that well what was being said. The children were laughing and carrying on so!"

"*Gah-ween,* no, I am not leaving with the pony soldier," Mariah said, drawing on heavy fur mittens and strapping snowshoes on her feet. She stopped and turned sad eyes to Nee-kah. "The soldier brought word of Colonel Snelling's death. I am saddened terribly by the news, Nee-kah. But I am suddenly worried about someone else far more dear to me. Echohawk. I must go and find him. He has been gone for too long. I fear . . . I fear . . . something is wrong."

"I did not know Colonel Snelling," Nee-kah said softly. "But I hear he was a fine man." She went to Mariah and placed a hand on her arm. "As for you leaving, No-din, I do not see it as wise. Echohawk will be home soon. Do not worry so!"

"I cannot sit here warmed by the fire, laughing and watching our children, while Echohawk might be out there somewhere alone and in danger," Mariah said, grabbing up a rifle and slipping extra bullets into the pocket of her dress. She turned and walked toward the entrance flap. "I must go, Nee-kah. I must."

After stepping outside, Mariah pulled her fur hood farther forward to protect her face from the bitter cold, then trudged through the snow to her toboggan, feeling that it might be needed, in case she found her husband injured and unable to ride on his horse. She placed the rifle in the toboggan, then with eager steps began dragging it through the snow.

Since very little fresh snow had fallen since Echohawk's departure, she found the tracks of his horse, leading farther and farther into the forest. The cold nipping at her nose, the forest quiet, Mariah moved steadily onward, the sled behind her. The longer she walked, the less she could find the tracks. The winds had become brisk, shaking snow from the trees onto the ground cover of snow beneath them, erasing the tracks.

Her heart pounding, her legs becoming weak in her weariness, Mariah began to think of how foolish this search might have been, after all. The ache of her back was a reminder of her pregnancy.

Should she lose this child . . .

She came to an instant halt when she heard gunfire echoing and ringing through the trees from a short distance away to her right.

Panic filled her when there was then a strange sort of charged silence.

She took her rifle from the toboggan. Then, leaving the toboggan behind, she began running through the forest, forgetting everything but her desperate need to see if Echohawk had been the one to fire the gun, and at what.

She paled and felt suddenly weak-kneed when a short distance away she saw Echohawk lying in the snow, a wolf stalking him, two lying dead close beside her husband.

Then she stifled a scream when she saw the blood on his arm, and his torn buffalo robe revealing a rip in his flesh. His wounds must have rendered him too helpless to reload and fire a third shot against the remaining wolf.

Mariah watched the wolf snarl and draw back when he turned his silver eyes to her. Trembling, she raised her rifle and fired one shot and downed the last surviving wolf. Dropping her rifle to the ground, she ran to Echohawk and lifted his head onto her lap, cradling him, as she rained kisses on his face.

"A healthy wolf does not stalk a human," Echohawk said, leaning away from Mariah as he looked at the slain animals. "The wolf is brother to the Indian."

He paused, then said, "It was not I the wolves hungered for, but the dead rabbit I had just taken from one of my snares."

Echohawk reached his good arm to Mariah and circled it around her neck, drawing her lips to his mouth, and kissed her softly, then whispered against her mouth, "My No-din, again I am in your debt."

Mariah looked down into his dark eyes. "*Ay-uh,* you are in my debt," she murmured. "And your debt to me is to stay alive!"

Echohawk chuckled, then groaned as he tried to lift his injured arm.

"Echohawk, I had thought that perhaps White Wolf had . . . had stalked and killed you," Mariah said softly.

"Do not fill your thoughts with that snake!" Echohawk grumbled. "Never will he be the cause of my death."

Mariah's eyes wavered; then she helped him from the ground. "I've brought the toboggan," she said softly. She spied his horse tethered close by to a low tree limb. "This time you will ride much more comfortably on the toboggan than on Blaze."

"But you can't pull the toboggan with my weight on it," Echohawk fussed, cringing again when a sharp pain shot through his injured arm. "No-din, you are with child."

"I am strong," Mariah argued. "So is the child that grows within my womb."

Echohawk struggled free from her grip and went to Blaze. He uncoiled the reins from the tree, then managed to get himself into the saddle. "Get the toboggan. Attach it to the horse. We will ride together on Blaze into the village."

"You are a very stubborn man," Mariah said, sighing. She shuddered when she stepped around the dead animals, then went to the toboggan and did as Echohawk asked. When she climbed into the saddle behind him, and clung to his waist, a sudden fear gripped her. In his eyes she could already see signs of a fever, surely caused by the wound.

32

Under the arch of life . . . I saw
Beauty enthroned; and tho her gaze struck awe,
I drew it in as simply as my breath. . . .

—Rossetti

This was so familiar to Mariah, as though it were only yesterday that she had sat beside Echohawk in his wigwam, he in a fevered state and she bathing his heated brow. She had managed to get a medicinal drink made of dogwood bark between his lips, a concoction used against fevers.

She had learned many more ways of healing since Nee-kah's earlier teachings—a sharp bone instrument was used for pricking medicine into the skin; sphagnum moss was used for wound healing because of its absorbency; and sumac leaves were used to stop bleeding.

The fire's glow the only light in the wigwam, Mariah gazed down at Echohawk, who lay beneath many blankets, asleep by the fire. Her eyes saddened as she bathed her husband's fevered brow again, as she had all through the long, weary night.

Before, when he had not known her identity, only that she had cared for him with compassion, he had recovered. And she kept praying to her Lord that this time would be no different. She had cleansed and wrapped his wounds. She had forced medicinal herbal liquids through his parched lips. She had allowed a Mide priest to come and speak over him. She had bathed him with cool compresses all night.

Now all that was left was the waiting, and her continued silent prayers. . . .

She looked beyond Echohawk at the crib where their young son lay sleeping. She was filled with pride and love as she listened to his steady breathing, recalling that first night after he had been born and how strange it had been to have another person breathing in their wigwam.

But, ah, how she had cherished the sound!

Their son!

Oh, how he filled their lives, even more than she had ever expected. For many months her life had been centered only around Echohawk. Now she had two people who relied on her, and this was wonderful, for while she had been growing up, it had been only herself, fending for herself.

She had been so very alone as a child and young woman.

She looked up at the smokehole, seeing shadows softening into a light orange glow. "It's morning," she whispered. "It's another Chippewa sunrise."

"No-din?"

Echohawk's whisper drew Mariah's eyes back to him. When she found him looking at her, a slow smile fluttering on his lips, she almost shouted with joy. She reached a hand to his brow, gasping with delight. His fever had broken! The crisis had passed. He was going to be well again.

"Echohawk, oh, darling," Mariah said, tossing her cloth aside. She twined her arms around his neck and kissed him softly on the lips, then drew only slightly away from him, gazing lovingly into his eyes. "You gave me a scare, you know."

"Did I not tell you that I always pay my debts, my darling No-din?" he said softly. "My debt to you, always, is to stay alive, is it not?"

"Always, my love," Mariah said, beaming. She eased her lips to his mouth and kissed him sweetly, content, yet still fearing the day that White Wolf and Echohawk would come face-to-face, weapon-to-weapon. . . .

Wild Rapture

With much love I dedicate
Wild Rapture
to my sister Judy Decker,
who is no longer with us,
except in wonderful,
precious memories.

A Warrior's Heart

White woman,
Can you not hear the faintness of heart crying in the wind?
Do you not see my eyes cascading upon your beauty?
You are the princess in the vision of all tomorrows.
Do you not know that I am without completion
If you do not become as one within my life circle?
The stars are naught but reflections of you.
How can this man in me endure, without the woman in you?
Do you not taste my tears?
Do you not feel this emptiness that divides us?
White woman,
I am truly haunted.
Can you not understand that it is only I who can love you?

—NICOLE R. JOHN

1

I will be the gladdest thing under the sun,
I will touch a hundred flowers and not pick one.
I will look at cliffs and clouds
With quiet eyes.

—Millay

O-day-ee-min-ee-gee-zis, Strawberry Moon Minnesota Territory, June 1857

The flames spread over the cabin like waves on an ocean, the fire coughing black belches of smoke into the sky, hiding the sun behind its death pall. Whooping and hollering, several Indians rode away on horseback into the early morning light, heavily laden with stolen firearms and ammunition.

A hawk hovered low over two bodies sprawled scalpless at the edge of the forest. Not so far from where they lay, the first shoots of corn sprouted from the rich black earth of an abandoned garden. . . .

* * *

At peace with herself and the world, having just finished what could be her favorite painting for her upcoming art showing at the St. Paul Art Museum, Briana Collins guided her horse and buggy carefully along the narrow forest path.

Although the sun's rays shone like a tongue of flame among the stately Norway pines, the air was cool beneath the arch of trees. Briana's blue-and-white-striped floor-length sundress, worn over white cotton eyelet pantaloons and camisole, did little to ward off the chill. The straw bonnet perched upon her flowing honey gold hair gave her some comfort, as did her net gloves and cotton knit stockings.

The pure, sweet smell of the cedar and pine trees filled Briana with pleasure, and all around her the activities and songs of nuthatches, sparrows, wrens, and chickadees thrilled her with the wonderful sounds of nature.

Smiling, she thought of her productive day. She had found the perfect, serene spot for her latest painting. Ethereal blooms limned in muted watercolors were her secret pleasure, painted on her most restless evenings in the privacy of her bedroom. But on her outings, she chose to paint in oils, to recreate the soft, clear light of Minnesota. Through extensive study and practice, Briana had developed the subtle palette and delicate brushwork that had made her reputation as one of America's most promising young painters.

Snapping her horse's reins, Briana urged him into a gallop as they broke from the trees into open land. The buggy carried her across a meadow of softly blowing grasses and wildflowers that turned their colorful faces toward the warmth of the afternoon sun. She held her chin high and her blue eyes sparkled as she considered her chosen profession, and what a commotion her work had already caused. Most American painters celebrated the beauty of European cities and landscapes. Most Americans saw little subject matter of artistic merit in their own country, and didn't care to depart from traditional themes.

Briana considered her decision to paint her homeland a worthy and patriotic gesture, but it was seen as an act of artistic rebellion, a challenge to the artistic establishment of America. She was devoted to promoting greater appreciation of American art in her own country, trying to overcome the prevailing preference for all things European.

Briana had studied in New York, and when her parents moved to Paris to establish their permanent residence, she spent two years studying in Paris's finest art academies. But she had missed her homeland, its grandeur . . . its wonders!

When her Uncle Arden invited her to live with him, she grabbed the chance, even though she knew that his reasons for having her there were selfish ones. Surely having a niece of Briana's talent to brag about and to show off at his political rallies would draw more attention to himself and his aspiring political career.

"Blackie," she whispered, her eyes dancing. "Governor Blackie Collins."

She laughed aloud, throwing her head back so that her laughter wafted across the land like a melody.

In the far distance, the dome of the capitol building rose grandly and statuesquely over the frontier city of St. Paul.

"No," she murmured to herself, "my uncle would not want to be known as Blackie by his constituents." The name Blackie had a less than sterling reputation, but she had known him for so long as Blackie, she found it hard to think of him as Uncle Arden.

Yet she must. He now insisted that she address him only by the name Arden while in public.

Briana's thoughts were jolted from her uncle as she was thrown violently sideways and her buggy came to a sudden, pitching halt.

Caring more for her paint paraphernalia and the treasured painting that was still drying on canvas than her own well-being, Briana looked quickly over her shoulder. Upon discovering that she had secured everything well enough, and that her painting had not been smeared in the mishap, she sighed with relief and turned back to the problem at hand.

Letting the reins go slack against the seat of her buggy, Briana slid to the ground and walked slowly around the buggy until she found the cause for the delay.

"Oh, no," she groaned, bending over the wheel that had fallen into what appeared to be a gopher hole.

She spread the knee-high grasses to get a better look, to see just how locked the wheel was in the dreadful hole. She quickly realized that she was helpless in the dilemma. The depth of the hole covered half the wheel. She did not have the muscle required to lift it back to level ground.

The sun was beating down on Briana, making her wish that she was back beneath the cool umbrella of trees in the forest. Turning, momentarily resting her back against the buggy, she wiped a bead of perspiration from her brow.

Suddenly her heart stood still, her throat went dry. A lone rider was approaching her from the distance. Alarm filled her as she realized how foolish she had been for leaving home without the protection of a firearm. She had been so anxious to be on her way, to enjoy her day of painting in the wilds of the forest, she had simply forgotten.

"White Wolf . . ." she whispered aloud, dread creeping over her. She now realized by the color of the approaching man's skin, and the clothes he wore, that the lone rider was an Indian. Her uncle had spoken of the renegade Sioux, White Wolf, and how, after many years in hiding, he was on the warpath once again. There had been several raids on settlers these past months. The first man to be suspected was White Wolf, for the soldiers at Fort Snelling were all familiar with this Indian's ruthless reputation. Never in the history of the Minnesota Territory had there been an Indian as elusive and as deadly as White Wolf.

Oh, Lord, Briana wondered with despair. How can I have been such a fool?

Having no choice but to stand her ground, she watched the Indian with unwavering eyes of courage as he came closer on a beautiful white-faced bay with white hind legs.

When the brave got close enough for her to see his face, she exhaled a quivering sigh of relief. This was not White Wolf. The renegade Sioux that everyone dreaded was an Indian well along in years. The Indian brave approaching her was much younger, perhaps somewhere in his mid- or late twenties.

As he came to a halt beside her, she realized, with her heart skipping a beat, that he was strikingly handsome. He was at least six feet tall and sheathed in a light buckskin garment which revealed the shape of his lean, muscular limbs and powerful chest. He had long, luxurious hair as black as a raven's wing, and wore a fillet of beads at his brow to keep his hair in place. His skin was a smooth copper, and there was a surprising gentleness in his dark, proud eyes.

It was this that Briana's heart answered to, making her trust him immediately.

"Hello," she said, extending a polite gloved hand to the brave. "My name is Briana. And you are?"

Amazed to find a white woman unescorted and so far from St. Paul, Night Hawk was almost too in awe of her to speak.

Then he recalled his father's tales by the evening fires about Night Hawk's pale-skinned mother, Mariah, having been daring in her youth—as carefree and courageous, it seemed, as this woman.

And, he thought, as his eyes roamed over Briana, she is so *mee-kah-wah-diz-ee,* so beautiful! Her voice was like the cooing of a dove, her body as slight and slender as a sapling. She had perfect features, delicate cheekbones blooming with color, thick golden lashes, and sky blue eyes as big, round, and soft as a doe's.

His gaze drifted to her honey gold hair that flowed from beneath her straw bonnet in soft swirls around her shoulders. He wanted to reach out and run his fingers through it, knowing that surely nothing could feel as fine to the touch.

"*Boo-shoo,* hello," he blurted, accepting her offer of friendship, eagerly wrapping his fingers around her small hand. "Night Hawk. I am called Night Hawk, the son of Chief Echohawk."

His solid grip and piercing eyes warmed Briana inside and caused a strange sort of weakness in the pit of her stomach that she had never before experienced in the presence of a man. Despite her various escorts both in Paris and St. Paul, it was not until she had touched Night Hawk that her pulse raced with such alarming speed.

She knew this handsome Indian brave was of Chippewa descent. Chief Echohawk was known for his gentle ways and considerate leadership. Surely the son must be the same, made in his father's image.

And she was not at all surprised that he spoke the English language so fluently. Everyone who knew of Echohawk also knew of his white wife, Mariah—Night Hawk's mother.

"It is very nice to make your acquaintance," Briana finally managed, blushing, keenly aware of the admiration in Night Hawk's eyes as they swept over her again.

She slipped her hand from his and nervously twined her

fingers together behind her. Suddenly the woman who spoke her mind at any cost was at a loss for words.

Night Hawk slid easily from his saddle and stood towering over Briana. "It is *mah-nah-dud* to be alone away from the city," he observed, his eyes narrowing down into hers. "Your parents? Your husband? They allow this?"

She puzzled over the Indian word that he had used, but she was certain it was a word meant for scolding, as his tone implied.

"I am not married and my parents do not know my every move," she said in defense, her upper lip stiffening. "In fact, they only know my activities by way of letters. They live in Paris. I am living temporarily with my uncle in St. Paul."

"It is your uncle who is the foolish one, then," Night Hawk again chided, walking away from her to bend beside the lodged wheel. He ran his hands over the wheel as he studied it, then stood to his full height and turned to her.

"You can soon be on your way," he said, their eyes locking, stirring his heart to a strange sort of throbbing. This was not usual for him when he was in the presence of a woman—any woman. He had never allowed himself to feel many emotions toward any one woman; his life was too full to want such interferences.

"Think twice before heading out alone again," he continued. "There are those along the trail who will not be as kind as I. Remember that, and live longer for it."

"I was foolish only in that I forgot to bring a firearm for protection," Briana answered, whipping the skirt of her dress around her and going to stand beside Night Hawk as he bent to lift the wheel from the hole. She could not help but admire the muscles of his shoulders and upper arms that were flexing powerfully as he managed quite easily to get the wheel back on level ground.

Night Hawk rose to his full height and wiped the dirt from his hands on his fringed buckskin breeches. "Let me escort you on to St. Paul," he said, his gaze rediscovering the sweetness of her lips, the softness in her eyes, and creaminess of her flesh. He could hardly repress the desire to take her in his arms and kiss her, with her lips only a heartbeat away, so tempting, so alluring.

It seemed to Night Hawk that he had been taken as quickly by a white woman as his father had those many years ago. He did not see any wrong in such feelings, perhaps only a bit *gee-wah-neh-dis,* foolish! It was apparent that this was a woman of purpose, and that she would not have time for a Chippewa brave. She surely would only allow one passion in her life. He had seen the painting in the back of the buggy and could tell by the feelings transferred to canvas that this painting was that passion. Seeing this had made him realize that no matter how many times he scolded her for being away from the city, she would not be able to resist the beauty of the forest which supplied her heart and soul with ideas for her art.

Somewhere in that knowing there was a reason for being pleased—for was he not a man of the forest? Somehow, whenever possible, he would try to protect her from the likes of White Wolf.

"I appreciate your kind offer," Briana said, becoming unnerved by Night Hawk and the way he continued to look at her, as though his eyes were branding her. She could not deny that this made her feel sweet inside, and she could not help but greedily absorb the sight of him also. In all of her fantasies she had never felt as alive as now. And even as he bent slowly over her, his hands softly clasping her waist to draw her near, she could not speak against it.

She melted against his broad chest when his tongue brushed her lips lightly, and he pressed his mouth softly against hers.

His touch was scorching!

Her heart threatened to beat out of control!

She began to push herself away, but not because of being kissed by this extraordinary man, but because she heard the thundering of an approaching horse.

Easing away from Night Hawk, her lips parted and eyes wide, Briana stared up at him momentarily, her knees scarcely holding her up.

When she turned away from him at last, a sudden panic rose within her when she recognized the bulky shape of her

Uncle Blackie riding toward her like all hell and brimstone had been set free on this earth.

She covered her tingling lips with her hand, wondering if Blackie had seen her in the gentle embrace of Night Hawk. If so, she knew what to expect. He did not hide the fact that he hated Indians. He had spoken openly against Chief Echohawk, when everyone else had nothing but praise for the gentle chief. If her uncle knew this was Echohawk's son, all the freedoms she enjoyed would be put to a stop. He might even place guards at her door, all hours of the night and day! She knew that he felt responsible for her welfare, but sometimes he carried his guardianship just a mite too far.

Trying to put Night Hawk momentarily out of her mind, Briana lifted her chin stubbornly and faced her uncle as his black stallion wheeled to a halt before her. She shuddered when she saw that her Uncle Blackie's attention was fixed fiercely on Night Hawk.

At first glance it seemed that they knew each other, as both men exchanged looks that were filled with a fiery hatred. Sadness surged through Briana. She feared that her uncle would create problems for her and this handsome Indian brave whom she felt certain was meant to be a part of her life.

2

I'll tell you how the sun rose—
A ribbon at a time.

—Dickinson

Briana looked guardedly from her uncle to Night Hawk, and back again to her Uncle Blackie. Having never truly seen the dark side of her uncle, only having heard from close friends that he had not always maintained the cool composure he displayed in public, a shiver raced across her flesh. His eyes were filled with silent rage as he slipped down from his saddle to place a possessive arm around her waist, never taking his eyes off Night Hawk.

Attired in fawn-colored trousers, a black coat, black satin vest, and a black cravat on his high shirt collar, and with his black hair slicked down, except for his bushy, broad side whiskers, Blackie looked like the man of prominence he had become after marrying a woman of wealth and standing in the community many years ago. His marriage seemed to have transformed him overnight from a riverboat gambler and man of ill repute, having once aligned himself with renegades and highwaymen, to a man with aspirations in politics.

Since the death of his pretty Agnes five years ago, he had become driven even more energetically than before to his work, his ambitions taking the place of his lovely wife.

Briana wanted so badly to look past the dark side of her uncle, and admire the part of him that had become respectable. His heart was set on winning the governorship of Minnesota one day, but he was happy enough now with the prospect of becoming a congress-man for this territory that soon would be a state.

"Briana, after making my rounds of campaigning today, I

found you gone when I returned home. I've been looking for you for hours," Blackie said, his voice steady, his eyes still locked with Night Hawk's. "And I find you here. With an injun. What do you have to say for yourself?"

"This is Night Hawk," Briana said, smiling weakly at the handsome Chippewa brave as he gave her a quick glance and focused his attention on Blackie again. She had not missed the gleam of a pistol beneath the flap of her uncle's coat as the wind momentarily whipped at its corner.

"I have been on an outing, painting," she said cautiously. "I was on my way home when . . ."

She paused, exasperated that her uncle only seemed to hear half of what she said, his gaze still intent on Night Hawk.

"Uncle Arden, Night Hawk came to my rescue," she persisted more loudly, trying to keep from showing her anger at her uncle's attitude toward the kind Chippewa brave. "Uncle Arden, the buggy wheel became lodged in a hole. If not for Night Hawk—"

"Night Hawk?" Blackie said, interrupting her as he glared even more heatedly at the Indian, recognizing the name, knowing who his father was. He could not help but recall with much bitterness the humiliation Echohawk had caused him on a riverboat many years ago.

Blackie remembered quite clearly that first time he had encountered Chief Echohawk on an excursion to Saint Louis. Blackie had not been able to stop himself from taunting the Chippewa chief over wearing eye-glasses—a strange sight, to say the least.

And Blackie had also taken great delight in tormenting Mariah, a white woman, for being Echo-hawk's traveling companion, having gone so far as to call her a whore.

Echohawk had reached the limits of his endurance then and wrestled Blackie to the floor. When Blackie drew his knife in defense, Mariah hit him over the head with a whiskey bottle, rendering him unconscious.

On the return journey to Minnesota, Blackie had tried to avenge his earlier humiliation by cornering Echohawk, but he was too quick and was soon holding Blackie by his heels over the ship's railing, threatening to drop him into the cold, muddy water.

The incident ended when Blackie was incarcerated on the riverboat like a common criminal. Eventually, he had managed to escape.

It was many years later, but the humiliation Blackie had suffered then had not diminished.

He had not pursued his revenge only because he had met his beloved Agnes shortly after that incident on the riverboat. She had become his life—and then politics. Echohawk had been the last thing on his mind, until now.

"Night Hawk?" he said again, this time through clenched teeth. "The half-breed who mingles with the whites in town, as though he's one of them? Once I'm congressman for this proud land, I'll do something about that. An Indian has no place among whites!"

Briana stepped back from her uncle, dislodging his arm from around her waist. She paled as she stared disbelievingly at him. She had heard his bigoted remarks against the Indians in conversations with other politicians, but never had she seen him act this way before her very own eyes.

It was embarrassing!

So much so that she could hardly stand there with him, claiming to be his kin.

She finally found the composure to speak again. "Uncle Arden, I believe you owe Night Hawk an apology," she said, her eyes squinting angrily into her uncle's. "He—he does not deserve such unkindness!"

Blackie's cruel mouth twisted into a grin. "Just because his mother is white makes him no better than the rest of the Injuns who beg for handouts day in and day out at Fort Snelling," he said, slipping his hand beneath his coat, resting it on the pistol thrust into the waistband of his trousers. "An Injun is an Injun. They are all liars, beggars, and scalp takers."

Briana gasped and looked guardedly over at Night Hawk, seeing a seething hatred in the depths of his dark eyes. She was amazed at how he could possess the restraint to just stand there and let this man talk down to him.

Yet she was proud of Night Hawk for having the willpower not to lash out at her uncle. The Chippewa brave knew the dangers in speaking out against a white man of Arden Collins's standing in the community. He did not want his careless actions to cause his people harm.

The word of a man as politically powerful as her uncle would always be believed over an Indian's, even if the Indian was the son of the most respected chief in the region.

Briana felt helpless. She could not offer more assistance to this handsome Indian whose lips had stirred passion deeply within her. Her heart cried out to him. Her body longed for his touch in ways she did not understand.

Night Hawk doubled his hands into tight fists at his sides and had to restrain himself from wrapping his fingers around the smug politician's throat. He wanted to show him exactly what this Chippewa brave was capable of doing to such an arrogant and merciless man who was driven by ambition and who would let nothing stand in his way of becoming a congressman.

Night Hawk had found many friends among the white community, and he tried to understand men like Arden Collins. He knew Arden was called Blackie among those who frequented the back rooms of saloons and gambling halls. They laughed at the pompous man who had been no better than a snake in his younger years.

The hardships and perils of the raw frontier seemed to repel men of culture and sensitivity, Night Hawk thought bitterly. For the most part, the territories attracted misfits. The ignorant and the bigoted, like Arden Collins, were the ones who flocked to this land of sky blue waters to steal from the original people—the Indians!

This man standing before Night Hawk was like so many others, the brave continued to ponder. Arden Collins had more ambition than ability *or* sense. It was his type who were most frequently elevated by necessity to offices of responsibility that they were totally unfit to hold.

They were the men most frequently responsible for the shameful massacres and inhumane treatment of the red man.

Night Hawk, for the first time in his life, felt the savage instinct to murder a man, and this troubled him more than the man and his ugly words. He gave Briana a troubled gaze, pitying her for being kin to such a black-hearted man, then spun around on a heel and mounted his horse in one leap, riding away in a hard gallop.

Night Hawk's heart pounded. He wondered how he could ever find a way to see this woman again, whose fiery spirit and big, soft eyes had stirred passions deeply within him.

He knew that her uncle would try to keep them apart.

He smiled to himself, sensing that nothing would keep Briana from the delights of the forest.

Gah-wee-geh-goo, nothing!

"Or from my beckoning arms," he said, shouting to the heavens. "She will be my *ee-quay,* woman. She will be mine!"

Then he frowned, knowing that some day something would have to be done about Blackie. The Chippewa had been tolerant of him and his kind for much too long already.

He flicked his reins and sank his moccasin heels into the flanks of his horse and turned him away from the direction of the city, no longer in the mood to seek out friends in St. Paul.

He needed to be alone.

He needed time to think.

* * *

Briana stomped to her buggy and pulled herself up onto the seat. "What you did today is unpardonable, Uncle Arden," she said, glaring at his unwavering eyes as he came and stood beside the buggy. "How could you? Night Hawk did you no harm. And he was quite a gentleman to me. If not for him, I could have been stuck here all night! What then, Uncle Arden? Would you rather I be food for wolves or bears? Or—or even be left to the mercy of that renegade Sioux, White Wolf?"

"You wouldn't have been stuck anywhere," Blackie said, trying to take her hand, flinching when she jerked it away. "I came for you. I would have gotten the wheel out of the hole. You didn't need that Injun."

Briana's eyes filled with rage. "There!" she cried. "You did it again. Did you hear what you said? You do not even have the decency to call Night Hawk an Indian. You have to refer to him as an Injun. That's disgusting. Do you hear? Disgusting. Next you'll call him a savage, and, Uncle Arden, he is anything but a savage."

Blackie arched a thick black eyebrow. "Oh?" he said, clasping his hands tightly behind him. "You were with him long enough to know that much about him?"

Her face flooded with color, recalling the kiss shared with Night Hawk. Still not sure if her uncle had witnessed it, Briana looked away from him. She picked up her reins and rested them on her lap, afraid to speak, fearing that she would reveal too many feelings that were washing through her. Already her knees grew weak and her heart began a strange sort of thudding just remembering his lips on hers.

Her uncle could never know that Night Hawk had that sort of effect on her. She was afraid of what her uncle was capable of doing.

She looked warily at him, wondering just how safe she was living with him. Little by little she was witnessing the side of him that made her afraid.

"Briana, I think it's time to get a few things straight between us," Blackie declared, sensing her hesitation in answering him. "This is not Paris. You are not with your doting parents who spoiled you outrageously. You are my responsibility now, at least as long as I am your appointed guardian, so you must do as I say."

He paused and took a step closer, leaning into her face so that she could not help but look him squarely in the eye. "Do I make myself clear?" he growled. "Do you understand?"

Briana stiffened. She had no intention of being trapped. If she wished, she could flee back to Paris tomorrow.

But now, in addition to her love of painting this beautiful land, she had another reason for wanting to stay.

She had to see Night Hawk again!

Yet how could she tolerate living under her uncle's strict regimen? How could she stand living with this man who had proven to her that he was little more than an ignorant bigot? How could this man be her wonderful father's brother?

Yet they were brothers, and respect for her uncle was expected of her, for this was what her father would want. And she did appreciate her uncle having taken her in.

"I understand, Uncle." She paused, then leaned farther into his face and said, "Blackie."

She flicked her reins and sent her buggy racing across the flower-spotted meadow. Smiling, she realized that she could not help but call her uncle the name that fitted him best.

Respect her uncle?

Perhaps.

Sometimes.

She would pretend.

Sometimes.

Briana stiffened when she heard her uncle's horse fast approaching her from the rear. When he began shouting at her, his words pierced her heart.

"I forbid you ever to leave St. Paul again to do your damnable paintings!" he shouted. "I forbid you ever to see that damn injun again. Do you hear? Forbid!"

Briana bit her lower lip with frustration and her eyes burned with tears. Never in her life had anyone refused her anything, for she had never been selfish.

Nor was she now.

She would not let her uncle rule her life!

When he rode up beside her, she ignored him. But she could feel his cold, steely gaze on her, sending currents of dread and foreboding throughout her body.

* * *

The sun was casting its last rays of light through the leaves of the birch trees. Night Hawk was following the Mississippi River through the forest, having learned long ago this was the quickest route to his village. He was troubled, but was distracted by another object of concern when he spied Chief

Strong Branch and a number of Chippewa braves just up ahead, also following the course of the river toward their home.

Before letting Strong Branch and his braves discover his presence, Night Hawk fell back and urged his horse into a soft canter. He watched Strong Branch from a fair distance, having only recently begun to suspect him of dirty dealings, but not knowing with whom. Except in the presence of his friend, Gray Moon, Strong Branch's attitude had become haughty, self-assured, and cold, while in the past he had been humble and a kind leader of his people.

Of late, it seemed to Night Hawk that Chief Strong Branch wanted more: he wanted leadership of all the Chippewa. If he succeeded, Echohawk would no longer be chief. Strong Branch, the son of the dearly departed Nee-kah and Chief Silver Wing, was now the chief of his people. Before reaching adulthood, he had relinquished his claim on this leadership to Echohawk, who had, upon the request of Chief Silver Wing on his deathbed, accepted the duties of leading both Chief Silver Wing's people and his own. But that had been many years ago, when Strong Branch was just a child. Now he was a man.

Until recently Strong Branch had even been Night Hawk's closest friend and ally, and Night Hawk had given him the right hand of his heart.

But envy and greed had changed that. Strong Branch no longer wanted to share this leadership with Echohawk, who remained the main voice of both their peoples. And he certainly did not wish to share leadership of two bands of Chippewa with young Night Hawk upon the death of Echohawk.

Strong Branch's plans were to take over all of this leadership, Night Hawk realized, but he did not know how or when, which made him uneasy in the company of this Chippewa whom he no longer considered a friend.

Worried, Night Hawk wanted to get to his village, to be at peace with himself in the privacy of his wigwam. He needed to devise a way to see Briana again—without having to shoot her uncle first. Night Hawk thrust his heels into the flanks of his horse and rode ahead, drawing the reins when he reached

Strong Branch. They exchanged fierce glances. Night Hawk was the first to speak.

"So, Strong Branch, where have you been with Gray Moon and so many other braves?" Night Hawk asked, his voice taut with suspicion he hoped he had not revealed. He looked warily at Gray Moon, who rode at Strong Branch's right side, then glanced over his shoulder at the braves who followed, most of them friends who were slowly turning into his enemies, thanks to Strong Branch.

"My *bay-bay-shee-go-gah-shee,* horse, is not lathered too much, would you say?" Strong Branch said, glowering at Night Hawk.

"That does not mean you have not ridden far today," Night Hawk said, glowering back at him. "What, but the *gee-wee-sayn,* hunt, takes you from your people for days at a time, Strong Branch? You are their *chee-o-gee-mah.* A chief does not go wandering all over the countryside, unless there is a good reason. What is your reason, Strong Branch? Or do you dare tell me?"

Strong Branch's dark eyes matched the midnight dark of Night Hawk's, and his features were as genuinely Chippewa as Night Hawk's. Yet Strong Branch was leaner, even taller in stature, and less muscular. He had a sour, pinched look which revealed his less generous nature.

The small scars on Strong Branch's body proved that he was also more warring than Night Hawk, always ready to skirmish with anyone, for any reason.

"You are not my *gah-nah-wayn-dun,*" Strong Branch said, bitterly. "Nor are you anyone's keeper. You are not even chief of your people yet."

Strong Branch chuckled, his eyes flashing fire as he looked even more intensely at Night Hawk. "Your father is an old man, yet he still does not die," he taunted. "You will never be chief, Night Hawk. You will always only be a *nin-gwis,* son, answering to a *gee-bah-bah,* father. Do you not feel just a little bit *wah-yay-szhim,* cheated, Night Hawk?"

"Strong Branch, you are a young man, a youthful leader of your people, yet you speak with the tongue of one who is old and *mah-shee-po-gwud,* bitter, with life," Night Hawk said, holding back the words that he truly wanted to say yet would surely regret. "Why is that, Strong Branch? Once you and I were inseparable. We enjoyed the hunt. We enjoyed the secrets of *nee-gees,* friends. There are no more hunts. But there are many secrets, and none are shared between us. What do you hide within your heart that you cannot tell me?"

"What do you hide in your *gee-day*?" Strong Branch challenged. "You are friends with too many white people. That is *mah-nah-dud,* bad, for the Chippewa!"

"You speak of false friendship with white people, yet you have confessed to loving my sister, Lily, whose skin is as white as alabaster," Night Hawk chided.

"Her skin is white, but her heart, her very soul, is Chippewa!" Strong Branch hissed between tight lips. "Her white mother is the only reason her skin is white."

"You say you look past my sister's white skin, yet you have yet to marry Lily," Night Hawk pressed.

"When I marry Lily is of no concern of yours," Strong Branch said sourly. He flicked his reins and rode on ahead of Night Hawk, who soon caught up and rode beside him again.

"Leave me in peace," Strong Branch said flatly. "If I wanted your company, I would request it."

"You have it without the request," Night Hawk said, laughing lightly. "Old friend, soften your mood. Let us talk as we once did. Tell me, what has taken you from your village today?"

Strong Branch challenged him with a set stare. "What has taken you from yours?" he questioned, his lips curling into a sly grin. "From a distance, I believe I saw you with a white woman. You were giving her assistance. You even kissed her. Do you not realize that one day the white people will send the Chippewa from Minnesota, as they did the Sioux? Then will you defend them? Where is your loyalty to your people Night Hawk? As I see it, there is none."

"The 'enemy people,' the Sioux, were chased from this land by the white pony soldiers *and* the Chippewa because they were snakes in the grass who killed innocent people, both red- and white-skinned alike," Night Hawk defended. "The Chippewa can never be accused of such unjust actions. They will be a part of Minnesota's history until the end of time. *Ah-pah-nay,* forever!"

Strong Branch frowned, but said no more. He and Night Hawk had not seen eye to eye on many things for a long time now, and Strong Branch felt superior enough not to care. He was the chief of his band of Chippewa. Night Hawk was only the son of a chief.

Strong Branch smiled to himself, knowing that one day both Night Hawk and Echohawk would no longer be in the way of his idea of progress.

Feeling uneasy, Night Hawk rode away, realizing that his friend was no longer someone he knew.

Strong Branch needed to be watched. How shameful for the son of the late, peace-loving chief, Silver Wing, who had sought friendship with everyone, using the word *enemy* only when referring to the Sioux.

Gray Moon rode up to take his place at Strong Branch's side. They exchanged troubled looks.

"Gray Moon, do you think Night Hawk knows more about our activities than he says aloud?" Strong Branch asked, his dark eyes searching Gray Moon's.

"My friend, only time will tell," Gray Moon said solemnly. "Night Hawk was never someone to be taken lightly."

Strong Branch nodded. "*Ay-uh,* that is so," he mumbled. "That is so."

3

Now summon the red current to thine heart—
Old man, thy mightiest woe remains to tell.
—Anonymous

Sitting tall on his mighty steed, Night Hawk rode into his village. It had been constructed in the image of the other Chippewa village near the outskirts of his own. Many moons ago, two chiefs had brought their people together as one heart, mind, and soul. Chief Silver Wing and Chief Echohawk had been brought together by Chief Echohawk's chieftain father, Gray Elk, when his people had fallen on hard times and sought help from his old friend, Silver Wing.

From that time on, the two bands of Chippewa had shared everything—laughter as well as pain.

Night Hawk's village sat serenely beside the Mississippi River, shaded by many tall oak, elm, and cottonwood trees with their leaves rustling in the breeze. He was proud to be a part of this land, and of these people. He surveyed his village, made up of a number of wigwams which were built on a framework of poles and saplings covered with the most suitable material the Chippewa could find in this beautiful land of sky blue waters.

Horses grazed at the far edges of each village. Gardens prospered. The people were content—the women moving to and fro, performing their daily chores, while the elderly braves sat amongst themselves beside the large, communal outdoor fire, sharing their long-stemmed calumet pipes and tales of long ago.

Night Hawk reined up beside his parents' wigwam and dismounted. A young brave dressed in only a breechclout scampered over to him, eager to help, to please. Night Hawk handed his reins to the lad. He smiled at the boy.

Ay-uh, to Night Hawk it was the best of times. All that was lacking in his life, it seemed, was a woman to warm his bed at night. Until now he had not thought much about it. He had busied his mind and hands while walking in his father's shadow, readying himself for the day when he would become the chief of their people.

Night Hawk's future *was* his people.

Yet he could not be expected to deny himself the pleasures of a wife. Had not his father reigned proud and sure with a woman at his side?

He could even remember times when his mother had helped his father with crucial decisions.

Night Hawk lifted the entrance flap to his parents' wigwam. The first person he saw was his mother, and a deep sadness engulfed him. Though she had been a strong force in the Chippewa village in the past, this was no longer so. Called No-din by his father, which meant "Woman of the Wind," and Mariah by the white community, his mother's skin was no longer the beautiful white of her youth. Now it was gray from a long, lingering illness.

Before going to the fire to sit among his loved ones, Night Hawk studied his mother a moment longer. Although she was busying herself close beside the fire, sewing beads onto a moccasin, he could tell by the trembling of her fingers that even this small chore had become almost too much effort for her.

His pitying gaze swept over her, seeing how her red hair no longer had a lustrous glow but hung limply over her frail shoulders. And having lost so much weight, her buckskin dress almost seemed to swallow her whole.

Her skin was drawn tautly across her face—a face that at one time had been so beautiful that Night Hawk had loved just watching her, so proud to boast of his *gee-mah-mah*.

He was as proud now. Yet he was troubled by how she continued to waste away from recurring bouts of malaria. The fevers sapped her strength, and sometimes even her will to live.

Standing in the shadows, still unnoticed by his family, Night Hawk's gaze moved to his *gee-bah-bah,* father.

The powerful, cherished, peace-loving Chief Echohawk.

Night Hawk's anxieties mellowed, as always, at the sight of his beloved father. He had been the best of teachers, as well as a friend *and* father. A man who knew how to guide with gentle words and his own example, Echohawk stood tall among his people as well as his family.

Night Hawk smiled, so very proud of his father of sixty winters who was still muscular and virile. Only a trace of wrinkles on his brow and around his eyes betrayed his age. Only a thread or two of gray wove through his thick, shoulder-length black hair.

Night Hawk's smile faded as he saw his father's glance settle sadly on his mother. There was something in the depths of his father's eyes that revealed a lonesomeness that Night Hawk understood, although it had never been spoken aloud between father and son. Night Hawk knew that his mother no longer warmed his father's bed at night. Being ill for so long had caused her to lose her desire of the flesh, it seemed.

Night Hawk had expected his father to take another wife long ago, yet Echohawk had remained faithful to his No-din.

Night Hawk noticed how his father's attention had turned to his daughter, Lily. His pride was quite evident as he watched her beading a doeskin robe.

"Night Hawk!" Mariah said, suddenly noticing him standing in the shadows. She lay her beadwork aside and rose unsteadily to her feet. She began walking slowly and shakily toward Night Hawk. "*Nin-gwis,* son, how long have you been standing there in the shadows?"

When she reached him, she stood on tiptoe and kissed him softly on the cheek, then ran her thin fingers over his smooth copper face, always relishing her son's extraordinary handsomeness. She did not know how much longer she would be alive for such enjoyments. Every time she became ill with the fever, more and more of her strength was drained away. Even now it took much effort to stand, her knees almost buckling beneath her as she tried to look strong in her son's eyes.

"I only just arrived, *gee-mah-mah,*" Night Hawk answered, folding his arms around his mother, hugging her gently to him.

Mariah enjoyed the warmth of the hug, then stepped away from Night Hawk and looked up into his midnight dark eyes. "Surely you have not been to Fort Snelling and back so soon," she questioned. "I expected you to spend the night away from the village. What caused you to return so soon? Did you run into difficulties? There are many rumors about White Wolf being in the area, stirring up problems with the settlers. You know how he would love to bring grief to our Chippewa people."

Echohawk looked up quickly at the mention of the Sioux. "White Wolf?" he said, laying his calumet pipe aside. "What about him? *Nin-gwis,* did you come across White Wolf while on your journey to Fort Snelling?"

Night Hawk walked arm in arm with his mother to the fire, then helped her down onto a pallet of pelts, seating himself between his mother and father. "*Gah-ween,* no," he said, staring into the fire. Seeing his white mother had stirred thoughts of another woman with white skin. It was hard not to think about Briana. Her body had been slight and slender, her eyes so big, full, and soft. Her voice had touched his very soul.

"I did not see White Wolf, or even speak of him with anyone," he finally said, feeling not only two sets of eyes on him now but three, as his sister too had begun to look to him for answers.

"Then why have you returned to the village so soon?" Echohawk prodded, leaning closer to Night Hawk. "In your eyes, my son, I see something I have never seen before. What happened today? Who did you meet while traveling to Fort Snelling?"

Night Hawk's shoulder muscles stiffened, and his jaw became tight. He did not want to talk about his feelings for this white woman whom even he did not yet understand.

And then there was also this politician, Blackie. Echohawk would not like the fact that his son had come face to face with an enemy of his past.

"It was not so much who I met on my journey that made me turn back, but perhaps the awkwardness I now feel when I am there," he said, in a sense telling the truth. He looked from his mother to his father. "Of late, there has been much tension among the soldiers at the fort. I believe it is caused by the tales of White Wolf and his renegades being in the area, stirring up trouble for the white community again. In some soldiers' eyes, an Indian is an Indian, even if he is from a peaceful Chippewa village. Even if he is the son of Chief Echohawk." He glared into the fire again. "My people are best served with me here, not there."

Echohawk nodded, he too staring into the fire. "*Ay-uh,* this I understand," he said somberly. "It is sad that the soldiers still see us as the enemy. For many years now there has been no reason to call us that wicked name. And now it is because of the aging renegade Sioux White Wolf! Why has he chosen to come out of hiding again?"

"Let us not talk of White Wolf or the soldiers at Fort Snelling," Mariah said, always saddened at the mere mention of Snelling. Her true father, Colonel Josiah Snelling, had never known that she was his daughter. Even her brother, William Joseph, had never known her true identity.

And now both were dead.

The name Snelling cut into her heart, always, as though an arrow were lodged there.

"So we shall talk of my darling sister, Lily, and how she so dutifully sews beads onto her doeskin robe which is meant to be worn on her wedding night," Night Hawk said, looking at his sister, loving her so much sometimes it hurt. "Lily, when will you and Strong Branch marry?"

Even the thought of his sister marrying Strong Branch made Night Hawk's insides knot. Since Strong Branch's personality had changed he did not deserve anyone as kind and sweet as Lily. She was a slight little maiden of sixteen summers, with sleek black waist-length hair, the facial features of the Chippewa, and the darkest eyes of all midnights, yet her skin was lily white, like her mother's.

Lily was a blessed one, the daughter that had filled the aching vacancy after Night Hawk's parents lost a son during childbirth. Night Hawk had been so young, he could not even recall his mother being swollen with child.

Because of her rare charm, Lily had not only become the darling of his family, but also of the tribe.

She had been the last child born to Night Hawk's mother, and her dream of having many children stopped with this daughter.

"Do not fret so much over your sister's welfare," Lily scolded, laying her sewing aside. "Strong Branch and I will be married soon." She gave her father a sweet smile, one that always got her way with him. "May I be excused, *gee-bah-bah*? I would like to take my evening walk."

Echohawk did not reply immediately. Instead he sat thinking about his daughter, and the reasons for her evening strolls. Though she was not aware that her father knew it, Echohawk did realize that she met with Strong Branch every night. And, without complaint, Echohawk allowed his daughter to go to him. He had once been a young lover, with young, fresh desires of the heart. And he had wanted a brave who could prove himself worthy of his daughter. He had wanted him to be strong in the swim and race, and courageous in the hunt. All these things Echohawk had seen in Strong Branch.

Before Echohawk had begun to suspect that not everything was right with Strong Branch, he had even encouraged his daughter to marry him. Only recently had Echohawk wavered in such encouragements.

But tonight, when everything seemed at peace within the world of his village, Echohawk chose not to voice doubts about Strong Branch to his daughter.

He had to have proof. Once he had evidence of any wrongdoing on Strong Branch's part, then Echohawk would say his piece—even forbid his daughter ever to see Strong Branch again.

"*Ay-uh,* you can go for your walk," Echohawk finally said. "But do not wander far."

Lily scurried to her feet. With one long braid hanging down her back to her waist, dressed in a colorfully beaded buckskin dress, she was a vision of lovely innocence. She hugged her mother and father.

After embracing them, she turned to Night Hawk and hesitated. Of late, she had become aware of tension growing between them. This was something she could not understand, and regretted with every beat of her heart.

"Night Hawk, my brother, will you hug your sister tonight?" she asked softly.

Night Hawk looked down at her silently for a moment, realizing that she was aware of his misgivings about Strong Branch and that she did not understand. He could not find the courage to say the word *betrayal* to her, so he said nothing at all.

He quickly embraced her and held her tightly, as though this mere gesture could protect her from all harm, then gave her up to her world of fantasies. He watched as she left the wigwam with haste.

Night Hawk glanced at his father, whose eyes were trained on him, and they seemed to exchange the same doubts about Strong Branch.

Then Night Hawk turned and left, and went to his own wigwam at the far edge of the village. The fire in his firepit had burned down to low embers, casting weaving shadows on the walls of his dwelling.

After placing several logs on the fire, Night Hawk stretched out beside it and let himself get caught up in remembrances of Briana. How might he arrange to meet her again? It was obvious that it would not be an easy task. Because of the damnable politician there just might not be a way to get to know her better.

"Perhaps that is best," Night Hawk sighed, turning to lie on his back and stare at the curved ceiling of his wigwam. "She is from a different world. And she has her love of painting to fill her days and nights."

He tossed himself back on his stomach, holding his chin in his hands as he once again stared into the dancing flames of the fire. His jaw became tight with determination. Nothing would keep him and Briana apart.

He even welcomed a reason to go up against Blackie. No Indian ever dared to speak up against him. It was time that someone of the Chippewa community did.

"And that will be Night Hawk!" he whispered harshly to himself. "Somehow I will find a way to show that politician's true colors to the people of Minnesota Territory."

He smiled to himself, thinking that through Briana Collins, many things were possible—even achieving the long sought-for revenge against Blackie Collins for his father.

* * *

Using a high white bluff as a trysting place with Strong Branch, Lily melted into his arms as he lowered her to the ground. In a wild embrace, they made passionate love. Lily writhed beneath him, never getting enough of Strong Branch's lovemaking. Her dress was hiked up above her waist, and Strong Branch's fingers were tight around her buttocks, lifting her so that she could meet his every hungry thrust. She groaned in whispers against his neck.

"My darling," she said, feverish with the intense, building passion, "say that you will marry me soon. Please say it!"

Strong Branch placed a finger to her chin and lifted her lips to his, silencing her words with a fiery kiss.

She clung to him, but was aware that again he was ignoring her questions.

Yet at that moment she did not care. The ecstasy was all that mattered, the wondrous wild rapture that being with him evoked.

She cried out against his lips as he buried himself even more deeply inside her, his strokes becoming maddeningly faster until her head was swimming, and the flood of bliss washed through her in wild torrents of pleasure.

And then they lay there, panting and clinging to each other. Darkness had fallen and the moon was a sliver overhead, taking on the appearance of a canoe in the sky. Lily knew that she could not stay much longer. She did not want her father coming to search for her and finding her in the midst of such questionable behavior.

"Strong Branch," she said, easing from his arms, "I do not think I can continue meeting with you in such a way much longer." She pulled her dress down, to hide her nakedness beneath it, while Strong Branch repositioned his breechclout around his hips. "Even now I suspect my father knows about us meeting."

She badly wanted to tell him that she had missed her monthly weeps, but she wanted the mood to be right when she told him that she was with child—their child. She wanted him to be less moody, less subdued. Yet this was something that she could not keep secret from her beloved for much longer.

Strong Branch framed Lily's pale face between his copper hands and drew her lips to his, and gave her a gentle, soft kiss.

Then he held her away from him at arm's length, his fingers clasped to her shoulders. "My woman, you know that I am now practicing chief of my people," he said thickly. "My decisions are many. When we will marry is not as important at present as other things that concern my people. But soon, Lily, I shall concentrate on you and our marriage only. Be patient. Things must be right in my village before I bring a wife to them to accept."

"Your people and my father's people have lived as one entity for as long as you and I have had breath in our lungs," Lily argued softly. "They would not resent having me as your wife. They see me as one of them already. You know that, Strong Branch. Your argument is not enough!"

"But it is the one I give you tonight," Strong Branch said firmly. "Let us talk no more about it. I am the man. I am chief! My word is final!"

Lily stared disbelievingly at him, fighting back tears. She stiffened as she leaned her face into his. "You are not my chief yet," she said sourly. "So do not tell me that your word is final with me. Strong Branch, you marry me soon or not at all!"

She turned and fled from him, holding her tears back until she was out of his sight, then let them rush down her cheeks in torrents. She placed her hand to her abdomen, thinking of the child that was growing there.

Would the child have to be raised without a father? Would she be forced to have the child in shame?

She stopped and turned, looking back at Strong Branch's silhouette against the dark sky, thinking that perhaps she had spoken in haste to the man she loved. He was the only answer to the dilemma in which she now found herself.

She bit her lower lip and began running blindly again toward the village, never before having felt so terribly confused.

Fort Snelling

There was a commotion in the courtyard as several soldiers arrived on horseback and quickly dismounted.

His saber clanking at his side, Lieutenant Braddock hurried to the commandant's office and stood over a huge oak desk, saluting Colonel Hawthorne.

"What is it?" Colonel Hawthorne asked, forking a shaggy gray eyebrow as he stared up at Lieutenant Braddock through thick-lensed eyeglasses. "Why the flurry in the courtyard? My God, man, your eyes are wild. Your clothes are filthy."

"It's another massacre, sir," Lieutenant Braddock announced, stopping to catch his breath. "An Indian attack on another settlement. As in the other attacks before, there were no survivors."

"Good Lord," Colonel Hawthorne declared, sinking lower in his leather chair. "What's the Minnesota Territory coming to? And what's the cause of this sudden unrest among the Indians?"

"I think it's for guns and ammunition," Lieutenant Braddock offered, wiping a bead of perspiration from his brow. "Those items are always taken."

"Of course that would be part of the stolen loot, you dimwit," Colonel Hawthorne growled. He placed an unlit, half-smoked cigar between his thick lips. "But you can't say that's the only reason for the raids on the settlers." He chewed on the cigar for a moment, staring into space, then lifted his gaze back to Lieutenant Braddock's. "By damn, we've got to find out who and why."

"White Wolf," Lieutenant Braddock said, narrowing his blue-gray eyes. "You know damn well it's probably White Wolf. That renegade has eluded us for too many years to count."

"Yes, as before, I strongly suspect it is White Wolf back to his old tricks," Colonel Hawthorne mumbled. He placed his fingertips together before him and rocked his desk chair slowly back and forth. "Yet it could be any Indian." He glared up at

Lieutenant Braddock. "Tell the men to keep an alert eye at all times. Bring in any Indian that stirs up problems of any sort."

"Yes, sir," Lieutenant Braddock said. He saluted the colonel, then spun around on his heels and left the office.

Colonel Hawthorne rose to his feet and went to look at a large portrait that hung in a gilt frame above the mantel of the fireplace. "I wonder what you'd do about the uprisings," he said, staring at the portrait of Colonel Josiah Snelling, Fort Snelling's founder. "What was your magic formula for keeping peace with the Indians? Josiah, seems I need some advice about now."

He turned and gazed slowly around the room, always feeling a presence there other than himself. He felt it now, even though the room was quiet, except for the popping and crackling of the fire.

The shelves were lined with books that had been Colonel Snelling's. The desk had been custom made for him, as well as the large desk chair. The maps that hung from the walls still held Colonel Snelling's markings, as did the hardwood floor—streaked with the wear and tear of Colonel Snelling's relentless pacing.

"You're here now, aren't you, you restless sonofabitch?" Colonel Hawthorne chuckled. He nodded and smiled. "Josiah, it's good to have your company. But damn it, I'd sure like to have the honor of you talking back to me sometime!"

The flame of the kerosene lamp on the desk flickered low momentarily, then burned again in a steady blaze. Colonel Hawthorne bowed and kindly saluted the flame.

4

Under a sky of blue with a leafwove
awning of green,
We placed our basket of fruit and wine
By the runlet's rim,
Where we sat to dine.

—HARDY

The hills in the distance were mantled in mist. The morning dew glistened on blades of grass like shimmering teardrops. A great bell in the distance clanged the morning hour of six from the slender tower of the church steeple, then quivered into silence.

Briana's uncle's stately mansion on Snelling Avenue was behind her. It was a grand Victorian home, rectangular with a wide porch, stained glass windows, and a mansard roof. Snuggled beneath a warm shawl in her buggy, Briana snapped the reins, sending her horse into a steady trot along the cobblestone street. She smiled victoriously as she glanced behind her at what lay at the back of her buggy—her painting equipment, plus a wicker picnic basket brimming with delicacies and plates as pretty as the flowers that bordered the walkways of the city.

Sighing leisurely, Briana looked straight ahead at the forest that was unfolding before her. She had managed to elude the men that had been ordered to stand guard outside her uncle's house so that she could not venture again into the forest. The men had stood watch for several days, but they finally grew lax in their assigned duties, perhaps thinking that her Uncle Blackie had been wrong to suspect his niece of having an adventurous nature. They had slipped away earlier last night and she suspected they were asleep in the arms of women, or sitting at a poker table in the dark back room of a saloon.

It was a beautiful, clear morning. The sky was blue with little white clouds floating about, the sun just peeping over the hilltops in the east. As Briana drove her buggy into the shadows of the forest, the birds were waking and chirping their morning songs, filling her with the anticipation of surrounding herself with nature again, painting.

Briana peered ahead into the darker depths of the forest, where in its thick underbrush the gentle deer reared their young, the great bear stalked about in search of food, and wolves stealthily crept about, endeavoring to surprise their prey. Briana hoped that the wild beasts of the night had entered their dens. She did not want to have to use the pearl-handled pistol that she had brought for protection this time to shoot anything two- or four-legged that might endanger her. She was not practiced in firearms, yet her uncle had insisted that she have one since he was a celebrity of sorts, which drew all sorts of questionable people to their doorstep.

Her heart grew cold at the thought of the true reason why her uncle had given her the firearm.

To keep her safe from Indians.

And he had warned her not only of White Wolf, but also of being friendly with any men with red skin, which regrettably included the wonderfully handsome Night Hawk.

As she rode alongside the waters of a lake that were clear and calm and reflected the blue of the sky, Briana's thoughts were catapulted back to the last time she had ventured from the city to paint. She could even now feel Night Hawk's lips pressed against hers, and his powerful hands at her waist, drawing her body against his. Although it had been just a brief kiss and embrace, never had she experienced such rapture, such bliss.

She glanced down at what she was wearing today for this outing, knowing that she had purposely dressed for the handsome Chippewa brave should they meet again, yet feeling foolish to even think that they might. Beneath her warm shawl she wore a fully gathered soft cotton dress resplendent with lace, and lavender iris designs embroidered on a white backdrop. The bodice was low, revealing the upper, gentle curves of her breasts, where a cameo necklace lay against her pale white skin.

Her golden hair was drawn back from her face and tied

with a lavender satin ribbon, so that it hung in long, lustrous waves down her straight back.

Her blue eyes sparkled and her cheeks were tinged pink from both the chill of the morning and the excitement of being free from her uncle to paint—and possibly to see Night Hawk again.

Briana rode for a good portion of the morning, then chose to stop at an attractive spot with shade and cool breezes off the water. As she stepped down from her buggy, she feasted on the serenity beneath the grand trees spreading their leafy boughs to curtain the day. The water in the lake was clear and teeming with fish. The great forest trees seemed to reach almost to the clouds which were mirrored in the water.

Briana eagerly unloaded her supplies from the buggy, not taking long at all, for when she painted out of doors she always put herself in as light "marching order" as possible.

After setting up her easel and folding seat close to the lake, she noticed the abundance of wildflowers in a variety of shapes and colors that grew along the ground for as far as she could see. Always anticipating finding wildflowers on her outings, she carried a lace bag with her, as light as a dandelion seed, in which to collect the flowers. She had a scrapbook already half filled with flowers she had found in France, England, and all corners of America.

Yet her fondness for her wildflower collection always came second to her love of painting.

As the noon sunlight shone down through the high canopy of elm leaves, dappling the shaded ground with shimmering light, Briana plucked several small dogtooth violets, pale blue bird's foot, and delicate moccasin flowers, placing them in her bag.

Sensing motion behind her, she stopped. Her heart thudding from fear, unsure of who the intruder might be, she bent gingerly to one knee and placed her bag of wildflowers on the ground. Slowly she slipped her trembling fingers inside her dress pocket and circled them around the handle of the small pearl-handled pistol.

She slipped the pistol from her pocket, her finger quickly

poised on the trigger as she rose to her full height and spun to see if this was all in her imagination, or if someone was truly there.

Night Hawk stepped out of the shadows, his piercingly dark eyes locking quickly with hers. Briana's heart did a quick leap, then her lips quivered into a relieved smile.

"You frightened me to death," she said, breathing out a heavy sigh as she lowered her pistol to her side. "My mind conjured up all sorts of things that might be ready to jump out and devour me," she laughed.

"And seeing that it is an Indian does not frighten you?" Night Hawk tested, already having seen in her eyes that he was welcome. "Did I not warn you about being so far from home alone? There are renegade Sioux who are not as friendly as I. White Wolf is stalking the forests again, earning his name, the vicious wolf!"

"I would never be afraid of you, and as for White Wolf and others like him, I brought a firearm along with me for protection this time," Briana defended, showing him the pistol that lay in the palm of her hand. "If I were threatened, I would not hesitate shooting it."

"Your uncle. He is the one who gave you this firearm?" Night Hawk asked, taking the pistol and gazing down at it mockingly. He thrust it back into Briana's hand. "He knows nothing about firearms if he thinks you can defend yourself with this thing that does not even have the capacity to fell a frog!"

Briana's eyes wavered and her lips parted in a gasp as she also gazed down at the almost weightless pistol in her hand. Then she looked up at Night Hawk. "I imagine my uncle did not think that I would truly ever have a need to use it," she said softly. "He did not know that I would be this far from home again unescorted. I came on my own while he slept. Perhaps I should have brought his rifle instead?"

"*Ay-uh,* that would have been the wisest thing to do," Night Hawk said, his gaze now moving over Briana. As when he had seen her before, his insides warmed at the sight of her slender body, but this time an even fiercer heat was enveloping him, tightening his loins.

She was so perfectly feminine in her lacy dress with the curves of her well-formed breasts revealed at the low bodice, and with her honey gold hair drawn back with a satin ribbon. Again he was swept into waves of desire when her round, soft eyes locked with his, her delicate cheekbones blooming with color.

"I will be sure to do that the next time," Briana said, almost breathless beneath his steady stare. He stirred many strange yet delicious feelings within her. Although there was a gentleness in his large, bright eyes, there was something else there that she felt was reserved only for her.

She could not help but feel that again he wished to kiss her. She could not deny that she wished he would.

Yet how foolish this was! she silently scolded herself. The fact that he was there again was pure coincidence, and it was just the chivalrous side of him that had made him stop, to be sure that she was all right.

She looked past him. She could see his white-faced bay with white hind legs grazing lazily, tethered close by to a low limb of a tree. She had not heard the approach of a horse. He must have been there before her and she had not realized it.

Fate seemed to have drawn them together a second time.

Night Hawk bent to his knee and picked up Briana's lace bag of flowers, then rose to his full height over her again and handed it to her. "I did not mean to frighten or disturb you," he said huskily. "I was just beyond the trees resting my horse, before traveling on into St. Paul, when I saw you arrive. I watched you unload your painting equipment, and then collect the wildflowers."

Briana accepted her small bag from him, the scent of the flowers wafting between them, sweet and spicy. "You then chose to let your presence be known," she said, turning to walk slowly toward her buggy. She cocked her head toward him as he fell into step beside her. "Why did you?"

In one sweep of the eye she was again in awe of his solidly built body, sheathed in fringed buckskin leggings. His limbs were long and muscular, his chest and shoulders powerful. Again she was overpowered by the sensation of having been held in those arms, so strong, so protective.

"Had it been you, would you have been content just to watch?" Night Hawk asked, following her to the buggy, his eyes gleaming into hers. "Would you have had no desire to speak to me? To become more acquainted? As I recall, our other meeting was cut short by the arrival of your uncle."

"Yes, it was," Briana said, feeling suddenly shy beneath his steady gaze and the sensual way he disturbed her. "And no, I would not have been content just to watch you silently. I too would have come to you and introduced myself again."

Night Hawk smiled, and as Briana placed her wildflowers in her buggy, he went back to her easel and stood over it, noticing that it was blank. She had come to the haunts of the forest again to begin a new painting. Knowing that, he expected her to stay quite awhile longer and he was glad.

"I haven't yet started to paint today," Briana said, going to stand beside Night Hawk. "First I wanted to collect the flowers—I guess, in a sense, to get the feel of the setting that I am going to paint."

"And do you feel that you are now ready to place your brush to the canvas?" Night Hawk asked, arching an eyebrow toward her. "It would please me to watch you, to see how you capture the sky and the trees. It is a talent known by my people for generations, yet we do not use canvas. We use the hides of buffalo and elk and other such animals. And we do not paint just to be painting. There are meanings behind each symbol painted on our dwellings and clothing."

"You truly wish to watch me paint?" Briana asked, clasping her hands behind her as she stared up at him, her knees growing weak as he gazed warmly at her from his great height.

"Some," Night Hawk said, nodding.

Briana unclasped her hands and eased down onto her folding seat, lifting the brush from her easel. She had to force her hand not to tremble as she dipped the brush into a tiny vial of color and began painting beneath his watchful eyes. He saw her create a whisper of sky blue, a blush of rose, the white touch of a butterfly wing after her eyes had followed an adventure-bound butterfly, and again the summer's softest and gentlest blues.

"My paintings are small in scale and usually completed in a half day's time," she explained, finding it hard not only to paint under his close scrutiny, but also to think. "I feel that the best paintings are those candid views which are executed on the spot. It is my opinion that this is the only way to rightly interpret nature as it truly is."

"It is most beautiful," Night Hawk said, admiring how the different colors seemed to rush against one another like the competing reds, golds and purples in a shifting wall of flame.

"I like everything I paint to fight for space on my canvases," Briana further explained. "It is impossible to exaggerate the abundance of nature."

Thoughts of her upcoming art show suddenly came to her. She paused and turned anxious eyes up to Night Hawk. "Very soon my work will be displayed at the art museum in St. Paul," she said, laying her brush aside on the easel. "Do you think that you could come? It would please me so much if you would."

Night Hawk frowned at the suggestion, having never been welcome at the social functions of the white people. Nor had he ever wanted to attend such gatherings.

Not until now.

"Perhaps Night Hawk will come," he replied, his jaw tight.

"Oh, how wonderful it would be to have you there!" Briana exclaimed, her stool toppling over as she rushed to her feet. She laughed nervously and bent to right it, then turned her eyes up to Night Hawk again. "It will be two weeks from today. Please don't forget."

He smiled at her exuberance, yet did not offer any more encouragement, for he truly doubted that he would go. His presence would most likely disrupt the showing. All eyes would be on him, wishing him away.

"Strange how I am so suddenly exhausted," Briana said, laughing lightly. "And hungry. Would you share a picnic lunch with me, Night Hawk? Are you hungry? Perhaps thirsty?"

"Picnic lunch?" Night Hawk said, painfully remembering times with his mother long past. "My mother made many picnic lunches before she became ill. *Ay-uh,* I would enjoy sharing with you."

Briana was thrilled by his acceptance. She felt strangely giddy and lightheaded as she went to the buggy and got the basket, then walked beside him until they reached the edge of the lake.

"Your mother," she murmured. "You said that she made picnic lunches for you until she became ill." She bent to her knees to spread the lace-trimmed tablecloth on the ground. "I hope that she is well again."

"My *gee-mah-mah* will never be totally well again," Night Hawk said, marveling over how Briana had prepared her picnic, which she had most surely thought she would be eating alone. "She has been weakened over and over again by malaria. Each time she is gripped with a fever, I think it might be the last moments of her life."

"I'm so very sorry," Briana said, giving him a tender glance, then busying herself again setting out the food.

She plucked a handful of wildflowers and placed them in a small vase and set it in the middle of the tablecloth.

She placed two peaches along with bread and cheese on delicate china plates, then offered Night Hawk pink, shimmering lemonade in a cut-crystal, long-stemmed glass.

Night Hawk took the glass and eased down on the ground opposite Briana. "You are a woman of wonder," he said, chuckling. "Even lemonade? My mother first drank this special drink many moons ago while living for a short while with Colonel Josiah Snelling and his wife, Abigail, at Fort Snelling. She treated me to lemonade when I was very small. I have craved it ever since."

"It is also one of my weaknesses," Briana said. She eyed him over the rim of her glass as she slowly sipped her drink.

"Have you many?" Night Hawk mused, setting his empty glass aside.

"Many what?" Briana asked, also setting down her empty glass.

"Weaknesses," Night Hawk replied, drawing his knees to his chest, clasping his arms around his legs.

"I am not sure what you mean by weakness," Briana said, picking up a small knife, slicing first her peach, then his.

"Your love of painting?" he said, smiling at her. "Would you call that a weakness?"

"No," Briana said softly. She lay the knife aside. "I see that as one of my strengths."

"That is good," Night Hawk said, grabbing her hand before she could reach for a slice of peach. He urged her to her feet as he rose to his, moving around the tablecloth until they were in a sweet embrace.

"Would you say my wanting to kiss you is a weakness?" Night Hawk asked huskily, lifting her chin with a finger so that their lips were only a heartbeat away.

"I don't think so," Briana whispered, her heart pounding.

"Would you consider it a weakness on your part should you want to kiss me?" Night Hawk further teased, brushing her lips with a slight kiss, his tongue flickering against them.

Briana almost swooned from the sweet currents coursing through her. "No, never," she breathed, twining her arms around his neck.

Their lips met, bodies straining together hungrily.

Then Night Hawk wrenched himself away, and for a moment he gazed with a strange foreboding into her eyes. He then turned and fled.

Briana covered her mouth with one hand, her eyes wide, as she watched him mount and ride away on his beautiful horse, shaken and stunned by his quick escape, but even more overcome with how he had affected her again.

She realized that she was falling in love with him.

And he surely felt the same—it was clear in the way he had kissed her. It had been there in his eyes.

But she was confused by why he had kissed and then left her so suddenly.

It must be because of the differences in their cultures, she concluded. She was from an affluent family. Perhaps because of this, he was afraid that she could never live the life of an Indian's wife.

Yet the thrill of being with him forever gave her cause to believe that she could live anywhere, and endure any hardships. It would surely be paradise with Night Hawk.

And isn't his mother white? she suddenly remembered. Hadn't his mother adapted?

Smiling, she went back and sat down on her folding seat to resume painting, but she could not keep her mind on what she was doing. It kept drifting to Night Hawk, and how she felt about him—and he most surely about her. Immersed so deeply in such thoughts, she found it impossible to paint anymore today. She gathered up her things, returned to her buggy, and was soon heading back toward St. Paul.

"My art show," she whispered. "Will he truly come?"

She would anxiously be watching for him, for something told her that he would be there, if only outside, awaiting her departure from the museum after everyone else had left.

From somewhere north a loon laughed hysterically, startling Briana. The tall pine forest around the lake bounced the eerie cry back across the water, where it echoed until it died in a soft quaver.

Then she heard another sound which sent spirals of fear through her. She yanked her reins, drawing her horse to an immediate halt, her face paling as she heard the thundering of hoofbeats drawing closer and closer across the nearby meadow, the trees around her blocking her view.

She searched around her desperately, needing better cover, for she did not want to be at the mercy of a gang of men—recalling the highwaymen and Indians that were ravaging the countryside with their hideous raids!

Seeing a cluster of lilac and forsythia bushes that were not only thick but also tall, she snapped her reins and led her horse behind them. With wide, frightened eyes she watched the men come into sight and go past her, then suddenly they stopped. "Indians," she whispered harshly to herself. "My Lord, there are so many!"

She held her breath as she watched them enter a cave not

far from where she was hiding. Everything became still—except for her whirling thoughts, wondering what these Indians were doing in a cave.

A sudden thought gripped her insides like clutching, squeezing fingers.

Night Hawk!

Had he left her so quickly so that he could come to this cave to meet with his braves? Were they in some sort of council? It had looked innocent enough.

She wanted to go closer, to see if she could hear them talking, yet thought better of it. These Indians could be renegades. They could even be participating in the raids. They could be led by White Wolf! If so, surely Night Hawk was not a part of this. He obviously hated White Wolf. He had said so often enough.

For more than one reason Briana couldn't confide in her uncle about what she had seen. She would be confessing to having left the house, and the city, without his permission. And her uncle hated all Indians, especially Night Hawk. This would give him the perfect opportunity to seek him out and kill him, convincing the authorities that he was the leader of the marauding renegades, without Night Hawk having the chance to defend himself. Then his people would certainly suffer.

No, she could not tell anyone what she had seen. Not until she knew that Night Hawk was innocent of belonging to any renegade band of Indians.

She couldn't even tell Night Hawk what she had seen. If he was not one of the renegades, she did not want to see him getting involved in the dangers of fighting them. She would protect Night Hawk at all costs.

She eased her horse and buggy from the bushes and snapped the reins, soon finding herself far away from the cave. She kept looking over her shoulder, not feeling at all safe until she finally entered the outskirts of St. Paul.

She inhaled a quavering breath of relief, yet she was still troubled over whether or not Night Hawk was involved in the tragic crimes against the white settlers of Minnesota.

5

And I will make thee beds of roses,
And a thousand fragrant posies.

—Marlowe

Two Weeks Later

Briana had placed the incident at the cave at the furthest recesses of her mind. She was all aflutter about her art showing, an elegant selection of her rich oil paintings in carved gilt frames spaced evenly along the walls of the St. Paul Art Museum.

Having wished upon a star the previous night that Night Hawk would attend the exhibition, Briana had tried to make herself as beautiful as possible tonight. She had chosen a pale blue gown of rich satin, her breasts curving just slightly above the plunging neckline, the bodice coming to a point in front, emphasizing the smallness of her corseted waist. The little puffed sleeves of her dress were trimmed with a lace ruffle that draped to the elbows, and her glorious hair cascaded from a topknot of flowers and ribbons.

Around her neck she wore her cameo necklace, a treasured gift from her mother at their last parting in Paris.

Briana glanced over at her Uncle Blackie and sighed heavily. She could not keep from being somewhat embarrassed over his antics tonight. He was forever mingling with the people at the museum, trying to win favors for votes on election day, his tuxedo and his forced manners making him appear to be a man of distinction. But Briana had to wonder just how many people knew the real man behind the false toothy smile. It was apparent from some sly glances that his clever schemes to get votes might not be working.

Not wanting to think further about her uncle using her popularity as an artist for his own personal gains, Briana turned her eyes from him. She sipped on a long-stemmed glass of wine and stared at the closed double doors at the far end of the room with dwindling hopes that Night Hawk was going to arrive.

Yet she could understand why he would not come, and felt foolish for having harbored even the smallest hope that he would. She did not allow herself to have any suspicions about Night Hawk being a part of what might have been renegades at the cave. She was going to force this from her mind. She was going to trust him. One could not build a relationship on mistrust—and she badly wanted a relationship with him.

When people came to her, complimenting her on her paintings, she smiled politely and thanked them, yet could not help but look past them, again staring at the doors. Every time one would open, her heart stood still for a moment, then, disappointed, she would nod more thank-yous and accept more warm, affectionate hugs from those who truly did care about what she had achieved in the art world.

She painted a false picture of warmth for her uncle when he came to her and gave her a hearty hug, almost causing her to spill her wine down the front of her dress in his eagerness to display his affection for his niece. Briana set her glass on a table and forced a smile as Blackie moved to her side and placed a possessive arm around her waist. Her face became splashed pink with blush as he began complimenting her in a loud voice. Everyone turned to stare at the man whose thunderous voice drowned out everyone else's.

"Now, who among you would not agree with me that my niece's paintings are veritable little jewels?" he proclaimed, his dark eyes gleaming. "They are marvelous little masterpieces. They are brilliant, strong, and joyous works!"

He bent and gave Briana a wet kiss on her cheek. She was suddenly aware of a change in his mood as his arm stiffened around her waist and he gazed past her with intense hatred toward the doors that had just opened at the far end of the long gallery.

There was a sudden hush in the room as everyone turned to see the cause for her uncle's silence.

Briana's knees grew weak and her heart leapt with joy when her eyes locked with Night Hawk's. He entered the room proud and square-shouldered, and so very handsome in his porcupine-quilled embroidered shirt, fringed leggings and moccasins, and beaded headband.

She also noticed that he was wearing bands of fur around his wrists and ankles, the ends hanging and decorated with beads. And his long black hair was glossy and arranged in two plaits, with otter skins braided into them.

Briana's insides grew warm knowing that just for her Night Hawk was defying many people by appearing at a social function normally frequented by white people. Plus, he had gone to a great deal of trouble to make himself more acceptable in the eyes of the people who were now staring at him.

She saw him as courageous. They were aghast that he was brazen enough to mingle with them.

Again she forced herself to forget what she had seen at the cave, although she knew he must be innocent of all wrongdoing. A man with the compassion he had showed could not perform heinous acts against humanity!

"What is *he* doing here?" Blackie growled, his eyes filled with rage. He glanced down at Briana. "Did you know he was planning to come?"

"No," Briana lied, her eyes never leaving Night Hawk as he moved in a slow, dignified manner toward her. "How could I have, Uncle Arden? You made sure that I couldn't by posting men around the house, as though I were your prisoner."

"Do you think I don't know that you managed to elude them?" Blackie hissed, leaning closer to her face so that no one else could hear their conversation. "But since it was only that one time, I didn't bother scolding you. Now I see that I should have! Surely you met with the Injun again. Tell me the truth. Have you seen him since the day you broke the wheel? Have you?"

Briana didn't have the chance to respond. Night Hawk was there, standing over her, making her forget everything but him.

"You came," she said, her heart fluttering with a wild rapture within her chest.

"Did you think that I would not?" Night Hawk said, looking into Briana's soft eyes, ignoring Blackie's cold stare. "I hope it is not an embarrassment that I have come to celebrate your success with you."

"An embarrassment?" Briana said, smiling up at him. "I think it is an honor that you have taken the time from your many duties to share this special event with me."

She stepped away from her enraged uncle, ignoring his gasp as she locked her arm through Night Hawk's and walked away. The silence in the spacious room was strained as the gawking crowd stepped aside, making room for Briana and Night Hawk to go to the broad wall of paintings.

Blackie was so incensed by Briana's outrageous behavior, he could hardly get his breath. His face was beet red with embarrassment as everyone's attention slowly turned back to him, a strange sort of questioning in their eyes.

"That you came tonight is such a wonderful surprise," Briana said as she slowly walked with Night Hawk beside the paintings, still ignoring the stares and the disfavor in her uncle's eyes. "I had hoped that you would, yet I did not believe it. There are many bigoted people in this room who would just as soon shoot you as look at you. You are brave to come up against such odds as this."

"It has nothing to do with being brave. Perhaps I'm a bit careless," Night Hawk said, chuckling. "I owed it to a certain lady whose eyes are the color of the sky and precious lakes of Minnesota."

"Oh?" Briana said. "And why is that?"

"Did you not share your picnic lunch with me?" Night Hawk said, his eyes dancing. "Did you not share your lemonade?"

"Yes, and it was my pleasure to do so," Briana said, tingling inside when she thought back to something else that they had shared—a sensual kiss and embrace!

"I did not yet thank you for those special moments," Night Hawk said softly. "And I must apologize for later—when I kissed, then left you without an explanation."

"Why *did* you leave so quickly?" Briana whispered so that

only Night Hawk could hear. She did not want to hear the truth if it had anything to do with the cave. No! She would not allow herself to continue thinking about it. To do so was perhaps dangerous, for herself and Night Hawk.

"It was so sudden," she quickly added. "I could not help but think that I—that I had done something wrong. Did I, Night Hawk? Was it because of me that you left?"

"It was because of you, *ay-uh,*" Night Hawk returned in a whisper. "Twice now I have rushed into kissing you. I felt that perhaps that was not best. I did not want to frighten you."

In truth, he thought to himself, he had left her so suddenly because he had begun to feel somewhat guilty. *Ay-uh,* in his heart he truly wanted her, yet a part of him wanted to use her, to achieve a revenge so long sought for by his chieftain father.

Ay-uh, that was what had troubled him while kissing her.

But after days of deep thought and sweet remembrance, he had overcome that guilt, knowing that he had kissed her only because it was Briana that he wanted, not how she could help in achieving vengeance.

It was his duty to show her this truth. But not now. Not among a crowd of white people.

Later, when they would be alone, he could tell her many things that were meant to be spoken in private.

"You were right to think that I was frightened," Briana whispered back. "But not because of you having kissed me. But because of my response to the kiss. I thought that perhaps you saw me as—as a loose lady for responding so passionately to you when, in truth, we scarcely knew each other. Please never think that I do this with every man that chances along in the forest!"

"Do not fret so," Night Hawk said, his insides tightening when, out of the corner of his eye, he saw Blackie deliberately pushing his way through the crowd toward him and Briana. "I see you as a genuine lady, nothing less."

Briana also caught sight of her uncle coming. She cleared her throat nervously and changed the conversation to something less intimate. "How is your mother?" she blurted, looking away from her uncle and up into Night Hawk's eyes again. "I hope she is better. I would love to meet her someday. I have heard so much about her—that she is a special lady."

"The bouts of malaria have weakened her. She is scarcely at all what she used to be," Night Hawk said, his voice filled with sudden emotion. "She rarely has the strength to do anything but sit and sew. It saddens me to see this. I can recall when she joined in the hunt with my father and me. She was quite spirited. I can safely say that before her illness she could shoot a firearm as well as any man and ride a horse even better. Now—"

Blackie grabbed Briana by the arm and jerked her away from Night Hawk. He took her aside and glowered down at her. "Briana, I can't stand any more of your insulting behavior," he said, his teeth clenched. "Get rid of that Injun. Quick! Do you hear?"

She leaned up into his face, her nostrils flaring angrily. "I will do no such thing," she said, placing her hands on her hips.

"Then you are forcing me to see to it myself," Blackie said, doubling his hands into fists at his sides to keep himself from striking Briana. Her sudden bouts of insolence were something he could not understand, or tolerate.

Briana's eyes wavered as she backed away from Blackie. "Uncle Arden, please don't embarrass me or Night Hawk by ordering him to leave," she begged.

"Tonight you are the embarrassment," Blackie said, then turned and stomped away.

Briana stood by herself long enough to regain composure and to swallow back the bitterness that had risen in her throat over her uncle's crude behavior toward Night Hawk and even herself.

She was glad when Night Hawk came to her, and even happier when her uncle was no longer in sight, surely having decided not to create a scene by forcing Night Hawk to leave.

Briana lifted her chin and, with Night Hawk at her side, began saying her good-byes to everyone that had been kind enough to come and view her paintings. Her heart was not in it, and having to force a smile, she began mingling with the crowd, shaking hands and receiving warm hugs. She ignored the icy stares and forced handshakes from those who did not approve of her choice of friends, and was glad when the room was cleared of everyone except for herself and Night Hawk.

He clasped her shoulders with his hands. "I have a sad heart that my being here has made your special night an awkward one," he said thickly. "It would have been best had I not come. Perhaps my place, always, is with my people, in the forest. Never are the Chippewa welcomed at functions such as these. But my heart grows tired of giving into the wishes of white people. And my heart was anxious to see you again, no matter how or where."

Briana placed a hand to his smooth copper cheek. She smiled sweetly up at him. "And I was anxious to see you," she murmured. "Although awkward at times tonight for both you and me, I am glad that you came." She giggled. "You showed them, didn't you, Night Hawk? The damn bigots!"

"Perhaps so, but I hope it does not cause you to lose face in the community because of your association with me," Night Hawk said, taking her hand from his face and holding it endearingly over his heart. "Although I am part white, I am at heart a full-blooded Chippewa."

"And such a kind and generous Chippewa," Briana said, sighing. "And so very, very handsome."

"I want to kiss you," Night Hawk said, framing her face between his hands.

Briana stood on tiptoe and slowly twined her arms around his neck. Their lips met in a tender kiss, and then Night Hawk drew his lips away and placed an arm around her waist and walked her outside. His horse was tethered to a low-hanging branch of a maple tree, and he started walking her toward it.

Suddenly Blackie gripped Briana's arm firmly and jerked her away from Night Hawk. "Get outta here, Injun," he snarled. "Haven't you done enough harm for one night?"

Night Hawk and Blackie exchanged looks of hate for a long moment that seemed an eternity to Briana. Then Night Hawk walked away like a noble prince—tall, stately, and proud.

Briana placed her hands to her throat, stifling a sob in its depths, as she watched Night Hawk grab his horse's reins, mount his steed in one leap, and ride away.

She turned and glared at her uncle. "How could you be so cruel?" she said, her lips trembling.

"I warned you about such loose behavior," Blackie said hotly. "I forbid you to see the Indian. Why can't you understand why? No one will vote for me if they know my niece is an Injun lover!"

"Of all the bigots in this city, you are the worst!" Briana said, sobbing. Tears splashing from her eyes, she ran to her buggy, and in a flurry she was soon heading for home.

"I'm so sorry, Night Hawk," she whispered, wishing that he were there to hear her.

6

Quick!
I wait!
And who can tell what tomorrow may befall—
Love me more, or not at all!

—SILL

As Briana wished that Night Hawk were there to hear her apologies, he suddenly appeared on his horse in the shadows at the side of the road, and came to ride beside her buggy.

"It seems I am always leaving you too suddenly," Night Hawk mused, his gaze meeting hers in the soft glow of the moon. "I should not have left you with your uncle. I should have swept you away in my arms and defended you against that tyrant."

"I appreciate the thought, am even thrilled by it, but that wouldn't have been wise," Briana said, startled at the thought of him whisking her away into the night in full view of her uncle. "You would have been the loser, Night Hawk. My uncle is a powerful man. No Indian dares go against him in public. Not even you, Night Hawk, the son of the beloved Echohawk."

"Does that not remain to be seen?" Night Hawk said, his lips lifting into a slow, confident smile.

"Please don't do anything foolish on my account," Briana said softly. "I would never want to be the cause of you getting in trouble with the white community. As it is now, you are somewhat accepted. As you saw tonight, only a few people gave you frowns. In some ways, Night Hawk, you have already won against my uncle."

"Your home," Night Hawk said, turning from her to look ahead at the streets lined with houses on both sides. "Is it near?"

"Very," Briana said, dreading to have to go there, especially so soon after the confrontation with her uncle.

A sudden thought came to her. She jerked on her reins and led her horse in another direction, on a road toward the forest.

Night Hawk nudged his horse's sides with his knees and rode up next to her again. "You are no longer going toward the houses," he said, questioning her with his dark eyes. "You will soon be in the forest."

Briana straightened her back and heaved a heavy sigh. "It is too beautiful a night to go directly home," she said, giving him a quick glance. "It is so deliciously warm tonight, I do not even need a shawl. And look at the winking fireflies: don't they look like the eyes of ghosts? Before going on to my uncle's home, I would love to spend a few moments in the forest among the fireflies. Would you come with me? Would you sit with me and talk? It is the only way we will ever achieve privacy from the probing eyes of my uncle."

"*Ay-uh,* I will go with you. There is no need for me to get back home quickly," Night Hawk said, his pulse racing at the thought of being alone with her again. While with her at the art museum, it had been hard not to wrap her in his arms and hold her to him, never to let her go.

She was quickly stealing his heart, as well as his soul.

He found it hard to envision a future without her.

Yet achieving this goal could mean much heartache for her. Except for her uncle, she seemed quite content with her life. If she hungered for the attention of people to view her paintings, how could he ever expect her to be content living away from the city, in the haunts of the forest with the few people of his village?

Ay-uh, having her forever seemed an impossible dream. But it was a dream worth fighting for.

And he would do it. She *would* be his!

An awkward silence ensued in which they rode together into the darker shadows of the forest. When the moon's reflection could be seen in a body of water only a short distance away, Briana steered her horse toward it. She arrived at the small lake surrounded by low-hanging branches of willows and drew her horse to a halt.

As Night Hawk reined in his horse beside Briana's buggy,

she gazed up at him, her heartbeats like crashes of thunder within her. She felt wicked for having invited him to come into the forest with her, yet it had been as though an unseen force had compelled her to do it.

As she watched Night Hawk dismount and tether his horse to a low branch of a tree, she had the urge to flee. Yet the promise of another kiss from this adorable man made her stay.

When he came to her and placed his strong hands on her waist and lifted her from the buggy, she felt the beginnings of the same sort of warm feelings soaring through her that his presence always evoked. She hardly felt her feet meet the ground, for his hands were now framing her face, drawing her lips to his mouth.

His kiss caused a tingling sensation to engulf her. And when he lowered her body to the ground, she did not even feel its hardness against her back. A blissful ecstasy overwhelmed her as one of his hands touched her breast, kneading it through her dress, while the other hand inched along one of her legs beneath her skirt. When his hand cupped her mound at the juncture of her thighs, she became aware of intense feelings that she had never experienced before, frightening her.

She pushed him away and rose to a sitting position, breathing hard.

"Night Hawk, please . . . don't . . ." she murmured. "I was wrong to encourage this." Her hands went to her hair, discovering that her ribbons and flowers were no longer there. Her hair had fallen from its bun and was now hanging loosely around her shoulders.

She began to push herself up from the ground. "I . . . really . . . must go." She faltered, her words untrue to how she felt and what she wanted to do.

He gently took one of her hands and helped her up from the ground. "Night Hawk's feelings are too strong for you," he said thickly. "I regret that I have frightened you. But please do not leave just yet. If you leave in this state of mind, I fear we will never see each other again."

Briana was aware of the hurt in his voice and felt guilty for having caused it. She turned to him and placed a gentle hand on his cheek. "It was not you I was frightened of," she murmured. "It was myself. Never before has a man caused me to feel foreign to myself. That frightened me, Night Hawk. Only that. Although we are from different cultures, and although I live in a community which sees the love between a white woman and a red man as forbidden, I must confess that neither matters to me. But my feelings do. I want to love you without feeling . . . shame for giving myself to you so easily."

"This shame you say you do not want to feel," Night Hawk said, taking her hand and placing it on his chest, over his heart. "If you love someone, truly love him, there should never be feelings of shame while with your beloved. As now, only moments ago, what I did to make you feel ashamed is a natural thing shared between two that are in love. Did you truly not enjoy the sensations caused by my lips and hands?"

A blush colored Briana's face a soft pink. Her eyes wavered as she gazed up at Night Hawk, disbelieving that she was with a man, talking so openly about such things!

But as time went on with him, it seemed only natural to say what she pleased, and perhaps even do what she so badly wanted.

"I enjoy everything you do," she finally said, her heart thumping wildly within her chest, knowing that to continue with this conversation was to continue with that which she had just denied him.

"Did you feel shame while confessing your feelings to me?" Night Hawk asked, drawing her against his hard body. "Do you feel shame while being held within my arms? Would you feel shame should I decide to kiss you again?"

"No, not shame, Night Hawk, just an intense yearning for you," Briana admitted, her knees weakening as he lowered his mouth to her lips and consumed them in a long, fiery kiss.

Sculpted against him, she could feel the hardness of his manhood through her clothes. She knew that this should frighten her, but it only excited her.

And she did not fight him off when he eased her to the ground again.

She even allowed it when he began to busy his fingers disrobing her.

Her pulse racing, allowing everything as though she had never breathed a denial across her fevered lips, Briana reached her arms out to him as she now lay nude on the ground, an offering to him.

Night Hawk stood over her and slowly removed his clothes, his eyes locked with hers, so as to hold her there with the sheer force of his will.

Never had he wanted a woman as fiercely!

And he knew that her need for him was just as intense, and that they would be linked together forevermore, as though one heartbeat.

Briana's breathing was shallow as she watched him lower his fringed breeches, revealing this part of a man that was only somewhat new to her. During her studies in Paris, many men had posed nude for the aspiring artists during class. At first she had been embarrassed by seeing the most private part of a man's anatomy, but eventually it had become commonplace.

But this time—this man—was different. Seeing his satin hardness made her want him even more. And as he moved his hand over himself for the moment it took for him to kneel down over her, Briana was mystified by how even this made her feel. A spinning sensation flooded her entire body, feeling oh, so close to going over the edge into total ecstasy.

"Say that you want me," Night Hawk said, nudging her legs apart with a knee. "We have not gone so far that it cannot be stopped. If you wish to leave, leave now. If you wish to stay, I will take you to paradise with me."

"I feel like I am already there," Briana whispered, twining her arms around his neck as he lay down over her, his hardness resting against her thigh.

His lips close, she ran her tongue slowly over them, then gasped with pleasure when he again kissed her.

His hands at her hips, she could feel him lifting her from the ground. She tightened her hold about his neck and cried out with pain against his lips as he entered her with one hard thrust.

Night Hawk smoothed his lips over to her ear. "The pain was brief, was it not?" he whispered, concerned. "The enjoyment I shall bring to you will be forever."

He held her close and started his rhythmic strokes within her. His mouth lay against her cheek, where he could breathe in her sweetness as he felt pleasure mounting deeply within his loins. He smiled to himself when he felt her relaxing more and more in his arms and beginning to move her body with his, opening herself to him so that he had full access to loving her. Surges of tingling heat flowed through him. He was not sure how long he could hold back the pleasure, yet he knew that he must. This time, the first for her, had to be unforgettable. That she was a virgin, having never been with a man before in this sensual way, made him know that from now on she would be his, a woman he wished to give the world to.

And he would not let himself think about the fact that she already had so much in her life—so much that she just might not want to turn her back on it all once he asked her to be his *ee-quay,* woman.

But, he had decided, he would turn heaven and earth to have her with him. He would make her want him, not the rich life of white people.

The air heavy with the inevitability of rapture in Night Hawk's wild embrace, Briana let herself enjoy these wondrous moments with the man she adored.

Who was to say they would ever get the chance to be together again? If her uncle had his way, she would be tied to her bedpost, the key to her locked bedroom door thrown away—until he wanted to show her off to his constituents! That was all that her uncle wanted her for—to use her.

Yes, tonight was hers and Night Hawk's. She would take from this night all that she desired, and never look back. Shame no longer filled her. Rapture was carrying her away on silver wings into the night. She so badly wanted it to continue.

Her body reacted even more wildly to Night Hawk now. Ecstasy spilled over within her and was spreading, deliciously spreading . . .

She cried out and clung to Night Hawk as that most wondrous instant of pleasure overwhelmed her, drenching her with a lazy, unforgettable warmth.

Night Hawk felt her release and let himself go now. He moaned throatily against her cheek as his thrusts within her became fast and deliberate. His body stiffened momentarily, and then he clung to her as his body convulsed into hers.

She rocked with him until he lay still above her, their bodies slick with perspiration glistening like dew beneath the silvery beams of the moon.

"I have a hold on your heart," Night Hawk whispered against her lips. "In Chippewa, that means 'I love you.' "

Tears of happiness came to Briana's eyes. She looked up into his dark depths and touched his lips. "I also have a hold on your heart," she whispered back.

They gazed into each other's eyes for a moment longer, and then kissed again, this time more softly, more sweetly, more devotedly.

7

> She could feel as if she were out for the day,
> As she had not done since she was a little girl.
>
> —James

Her painting paraphernalia left in the downstairs study, Briana almost floated up the spiral staircase, the ecstasy within her was so intense.

She could still taste Night Hawk's kiss.

She could still feel the crush of his hard body against hers.

As she took the last step to the second-story landing, she stopped and inhaled a quavering breath and placed a hand over her pounding heart, closing her eyes as she allowed herself to recall that very instant that she had found total paradise within Night Hawk's passionate embrace.

It had been no less than a wild rapture that had overwhelmed her, and there was no shame, no remorse at all that she had allowed the handsome, wonderful Chippewa brave to teach her how it truly felt to be a woman.

The distinct sound of someone clearing his throat caused Briana's eyes to open in a nervous flutter, her thoughts flooding back to the present. When she peered toward her bedroom door, she saw that it was open, lamplight pouring out onto the floor of the corridor.

"Uncle Blackie," she whispered, alarm setting in at the thought of him waiting for her, afraid to wonder why.

She knew the answer already. She should have been home hours ago! Her uncle was keenly aware of when she had left the art museum.

She touched her trembling fingers to her hair, checking to see if it was in place and not too mussed from the rapturous moments with Night Hawk in the forest, and then smoothed her hands over the skirt of her dress to make sure it lay in place over her crinoline slip. She moved slowly toward her bedroom.

Just outside the door she inhaled a nervous breath and squared her shoulders, then with a lifted, proud chin, went in. The room would have pleased a queen in its decoration of lacy curtains, bed skirt and spread, velveteen chairs, and a gilded mirror that hung over her dressing table, which was crowded with assortments of fancy bottles filled with even fancier perfumes, most of which were French.

"And so my wandering niece is finally home," Blackie said, folding his arms angrily across his chest. He peered at Briana with his dark, glaring eyes, slowly assessing her. His look became one of utter contempt as his eyes locked with hers.

"Uncle Arden, I-I . . ." Briana said in an attempt to explain, but the words wouldn't come.

She had not thought to think up an excuse for her late arrival. She had not expected that her uncle would be there waiting for her. Then again, she had never given him cause before. She had always come right home after her outings, which had never lasted this long into the night.

"I'm not going to waste my time questioning you as to where you've been, or with whom," Blackie said, taking two angry strides toward her.

He raised a hand and slapped her hard across her face, causing her head to jerk sideways with the blow. "The flush of your cheeks and the glow in your eyes give me all the answers I need," he growled, his voice filled with disgust. "You are a disappointment. A trollop."

Stunned, her cheek burning from the blow, Briana turned and watched her uncle leave in a huff, disbelieving that he had actually hit her!

That he had called her a trollop made a rush of tears flood her eyes. She ran across the room and threw herself onto her bed, sobbing. She was so confused.

She had never been wanton before. No man had ever stirred such uncontrollable passion within her before. Her passion had always been her painting, but she realized now that painting did not feed certain hungers.

Nor had her uncle treated her cruelly before.

Not until she had met Night Hawk.

Firming her lower lip, Briana wiped the tears from her cheeks, realizing that she could not please everyone. She would have to turn her back on either her uncle or Night Hawk.

She wished that such a choice had not been forced upon her, but now that passion for something besides painting had been unleashed within her, she did not want to deny herself of it, or the man who had awakened her into loving.

She did love Night Hawk, and would chance anything to be with him.

Rising from the bed, Briana went to the window and drew the sheer curtain aside. Peering toward the moon-drenched forest, she wondered what Night Hawk was thinking, if he was still feeling the afterglow of the ecstacy they had shared. Now that she had been able to sort through her feelings and realize that nothing her uncle said or did would stop her from seeing Night Hawk again, she was reliving the delicious rapture all over again.

Oh, but if only he was feeling the same about her, and would not allow anything to stand in his way of feeling free to love her.

Her uncle. If he dared interfere again . . .

She shook her head desperately, not wanting to think ahead to what her uncle might do to keep her from the handsome Chippewa brave—her love, her desire.

Her hand went to her cheek, still feeling the imprint of her uncle's hand and the heat from the blow. A shiver coursed through her. She knew that if her uncle had the nerve to slap her, he was capable of doing anything. Yet surely he wouldn't, for he knew that if his brother ever found out, he would live to regret ever having loosed his rage on his niece.

That thought made Briana smile.

* * *

Deep in thought, Night Hawk rode in a slow trot through the forest. His mind was filled with the shared moments with

Briana, still in awe of her. She had made him forget all of the women he had ever had in his lifetime, and the fact that she was white.

It had been hard for him to leave Briana after having found such wondrous bliss within her arms. He had wanted to ask her to go with him to his village, to stay with him forever.

Yet he had not spoken.

He never wanted to give her cause to say no to him again. And she would not have had a choice this time but to say no, for he knew that she had to set things right with her uncle before ever embarking on something with Night Hawk which would be for eternity.

"In time," he whispered to himself. "Until then I shall take what I can, when I can, and give back twofold."

Although a half-breed himself, he had always thought that he would not allow his eyes to stray to a woman other than that of his own skin coloring, as his father had all those long years ago.

Ay-uh, he argued to himself, his mother was beautiful! She was special. Yet so were the Chippewa maidens.

But there was no more arguing with his heart. None of the Chippewa maidens had stirred his insides into wanting them for a lifetime.

Only Briana, whose skin was lily-white.

The first time he had laid eyes on her, he had known. Oh, how he had known!

He frowned darkly at the thought of her uncle, who was called Blackie in the back rooms of the saloons, where cards were dealt over felt-covered tables and cigar smoke hung like thunder clouds low and thick in the room.

This man pretended to be something to the people that he in truth was not. His reputation had been an unsavory one even before settling down in St. Paul. This uncle, whose heart was cold toward all Indians, would be an obstacle that Night Hawk would have to deal with.

This man who Night Hawk's very own father despised would not be allowed to stand in the way of Night Hawk's happiness. Somehow he would find a way to deal with him.

Riding out into an open meadow, Night Hawk sank his heels into the flanks of his horse and sent it into a hard gallop, then slowed it back down to a lope when the moonlight allowed him to recognize several soldiers advancing on him from the front.

Having no cause for alarm, since almost all of the soldiers at Fort Snelling knew of his peaceful nature, Night Hawk rode onward and drew the reins as the soldiers stopped, only one coming to Night Hawk's side. His jaw tightened when he saw the soldier reach for his pistol, and by instinct, his own right hand started to reach for his firearm in the gunsling at the side of his horse.

"I wouldn't do that," Lieutenant Braddock warned, yanking his pistol from its holster and aiming it at Night Hawk. With his free hand he leaned over and eased Night Hawk's rifle from the gunsling, then rested it on his lap. "Come along with us to Fort Snelling. And I'd advise you to go with us without complaint. Several of the soldiers have an itch to shoot an Injun. I might be obliged to allow it should you try to run."

"I guess I can't ask you to have the courtesy to explain what this is about," Night Hawk said, his voice void of emotion. "Lieutenant Braddock, isn't it? I know of you. I have seen you many times at the fort. You have seen me. You know that I am a peace-loving Chippewa. You know that my father is Chief Echohawk, and that my mother is Mariah, who was close friends to the Snellings."

"I know all of these things," Lieutenant Braddock said, slipping Night Hawk's rifle into the gunsling with his own. "And, yes, I am Lieutenant Braddock. But none of this changes the fact that Colonel Hawthorne has asked all of the regiments of Fort Snelling to round up any Indian that looks suspicious. So get along with you, Night Hawk. Being the son of a chief makes no difference to me. None at all."

"What have I done that is suspicious to you?" Night Hawk said, arching an eyebrow.

"It's not so much that you look suspicious," Lieutenant Braddock said, motioning with the barrel of his pistol for Night Hawk to move ahead of him. "Word has spread of the commotion you caused at the art museum earlier this evening. What are you turning into? A rebellious renegade? We can't have that, now, can we? We can't have you bursting into all functions of the St. Paul elite, now can we?"

"No, we would not want the dark skin of an Indian brushing against the snow white skin of the St. Paul elite," Night Hawk said in a feral snarl. He moved on ahead of Lieutenant Braddock, his head held high, yet his feelings severely injured by the bigotry of the world. He had to wonder just how far this would go against an Indian who was guilty only of loving a white woman.

As he rode along with the regiment of soldiers in the direction of Fort Snelling, he once again became lost in thoughts of Briana, and the fact that she was very much a part of that elite group of socialites in St. Paul.

Yet she had proven to be different. She did not see him as anything but the man whose heart had been lent to her. While with her, it was easy to forget the bigots—the prejudices against his people as a whole.

And he was also reminded of his mother—how she had turned her back to such prejudices and become as one with the Chippewa culture without a glance backward at how the white community lived so differently in houses, with furniture, curtains, and stoves for cooking and heating. She had accepted, and learned to love, the simple life of the Chippewa.

But he was not sure if Briana could ever go that far. She was from a different sort of world. She had been across the large body of water, where she had attended the finest of schools in a land they called France. How could living simply in the forest ever be enough for her?

How could she accept the fact that her Chippewa lover could not ride through the forest without being accosted and accused unjustly by the white pony soldiers as though he were no better than the "enemy-people," the Sioux that had once roamed the land in droves, killing and maiming all of the white settlers, putting fear in their eyes and hearts at the mere thought of stepping outside their cabins on a dark winter's night.

But even though Night Hawk had only known Briana for

a short while, it was enough time to know that she would let nothing shadow her feelings about him. She knew that his heart was peaceful toward whites, and that he would do nothing to stir up bad feelings between his people and the soldiers at Fort Snelling.

Night Hawk just had to convince the person in charge, and it would only be a matter of moments before he was standing face to face with Colonel Hawthorne. Night Hawk rode beneath the tall shadows of the stone walls that surrounded the fort, then through the open gate. Except for one, there was hardly any lamplight in the windows of the establishments within the fort's walls, which meant that most of the soldiers were in bed.

Night Hawk dismounted and, flanked on both sides by soldiers, went into the central headquarters building. He soon found himself standing before a huge oak desk piled high with papers and journals. Lamplight glowed brightly on the bald head of a man in a chair behind the desk, bent low over his ledgers, inking figures onto the pages.

"Sir, we've brought you a suspect," Lieutenant Braddock said, standing at attention beside Night Hawk and clearing his throat nervously when the colonel did not look immediately from his journal. "Sir, we found Night Hawk. We brought him to you for questioning."

Colonel Hawthorne finally responded. He slowly lay his journal aside, then turned his ocean blue eyes up at Night Hawk. He frowned for a moment, then began speaking in a succinct manner, his voice deep and mannerly. "What's this I hear about the commotion you caused at the art museum tonight?" he asked, stretching the fingers of one hand out atop the journal, as though not wanting to part with it for even one second.

Night Hawk folded his arms across his chest, his midnight black eyes flashing at Colonel Hawthorne's. "It is not written into law that a Chippewa brave cannot go and view paintings," he said, obviously trying to keep his anger at bay. "It is hard for me to understand why you would have your soldiers search for me because of my interest in art, when it is known by many that even you sometimes dabble in painting. Why were you not among those attending the art show tonight? Was it because it was a lady whose paintings were being celebrated instead of yours? Did you have to find someone to punish, to help alleviate some of the anger within your heart because your artistic abilities have been ignored by the white community?"

Colonel Hawthorne rose slowly from his seat. He leaned over toward Night Hawk. He splayed his fingers against the top of his desk and leaned on them. "You'd better watch your tongue," he grumbled. "I am the authority here. I say who is arrested and who is not. I would think twice before humiliating me in front of my soldiers."

"The humiliation is well earned," Night Hawk said, not wavering in his determination to put the colonel in his place. "You see, it is a widespread fact that there are many raids being carried out in Minnesota. Should your White Father in Washington hear that you are wasting your soldiers' time bringing in an Indian because he is interested in art instead of searching for those responsible for the killings of innocent settlers, I believe your position would soon be filled by somebody more deserving."

"I could easily accuse you of those ghastly deeds and order my men to stand you before a firing squad tonight," Colonel Hawthorne said, his lips tugging into a smug smile.

"That would work for only a short while," Night Hawk said, returning the half smile. "When the raids continued after my death, then who would be blamed?"

Colonel Hawthorne's smile faded. He eased back down in his chair. He picked up some papers and began absently stacking them, all the while looking up at Night Hawk. "Perhaps you have an idea who is behind these raids?" he asked, his voice shallow. "Of course I have never blamed you. It is known that you walk in the shadow of your father, who is a man of peace, and that your mother is white, another reason why you would not turn to murdering white settlers in cold blood."

Colonel Hawthorne cleared his throat absently. "Also, the rumors spread quickly to me about your, ahem, interest in Arden Collins's niece," he said smoothly. "You wouldn't be making eyes at one white woman while with your next breath you were killing others, would you? So, Night Hawk, who is responsible? We are never there in time to catch the sonofabitches red-handed. They are as elusive as the wind!"

"I do not know why I would offer you any assistance after being treated as though a renegade myself," Night Hawk said stubbornly.

"The part of you that is white would lead you into assisting me," Colonel Hawthorne grumbled. "Now, Night Hawk, who do you think it is? Who hates so much that they must kill over and over again?"

Night Hawk paused for a moment, searching through his heart for answers as to whether or not he should help or even trust the white colonel. Then knowing that he would like to see the killings stopped, he decided to give the only clues that he knew.

"It is my belief, as I am sure it is yours, that your search should end when you find the renegade Sioux, White Wolf," Night Hawk said solemnly. "He is a crafty, cruel, and bitter old man with unflinching endurance. He is surely at the root of most of the trouble in the Minnesota Territory today. Find White Wolf, and the massacres will stop."

He turned and started walking away. Lieutenant Braddock drew his pistol, but Colonel Hawthorne rose from his chair and went quickly to Braddock, taking his pistol. "Let him go," he said, politely placing the lieutenant's pistol back into his holster.

Night Hawk walked out into the splash of moonlight, and without looking back, mounted his horse. With a jerk of the reins and a nudge of his heels into the flanks of his steed, he quickly rode away from the fort, a cold, mean bitterness eating away at his heart.

* * *

Lily lay on her pallet of furs in the far recesses of her parents' wigwam, watching in the dim glow of the fire for her parents to go to sleep. As soon as she was sure they were, she drew a blanket around her shoulders, crept toward the entrance flap, and hurried outside.

The moonlight lay a silver path across the ground as she fled from the village and into the darker recesses of the forest. Her heart pounded out her anxiousness to be with Strong Branch again, loving him so much she felt possessed by such a love.

And tonight. She would tell him tonight. Now that she had made up her mind, she could hardly wait.

Yet a part of her feared telling him this sweet truth. He had turned his back already too often when she had spoken of marriage. What if he saw the child as interference with his plans to better his life as chieftain?

"Perhaps I should not tell him," she whispered to herself. Tears pooled in her eyes as she found him waiting for her at the foot of the bluff, his hand extending to her.

She ran to him and took his hand, and her breath was taken away when he swept her fully into his arms and gave her a long, passionate kiss. She felt his anxious hands on her, and she allowed it. His need for her seemed greater tonight, for he did not lead her up to their usual trysting place. Tonight he eased her to the ground beneath the giant sycamores and oaks, one hand lifting the skirt of her dress above her knees, his other lowering his breechclout.

He began kneading her throbbing center with his skilled fingers, then knelt down over her and curled his tongue around it, so warm, wet, and soft. All her thoughts of truths tonight melted away into the wonders of how he was sending her heart into a sensuous spinning.

Tonight was meant for loving. Only loving.

Perhaps tomorrow night she would tell him, she found herself thinking amid the joyous bliss of building pleasure.

Or perhaps the next?

At this moment, like the other times with him, all she wanted was the passion. The wild rapture!

She did not want to do anything to spoil these times with him. She had plenty of time to tell him about the baby before she began showing.

Repositioning himself, Strong Branch nudged Lily's legs apart with his knee, then entered her with a deep, thick trust. She lifted her hips, welcoming how he so magnificently filled her. She closed her eyes and tossed her head back and forth with ecstacy, her whole body quivering as he pressed endlessly deeper within her.

At this moment they were the only two people in the universe.

There wasn't even a child to consider.

8

> My conscience hath a thousand several tongues
> And every tongue brings in a several late,
> And every late condemns me for a villain.
>
> —RICHARD III

Clouds were floating across the moon like great puffs of gray cotton. The wind had picked up and was howling through the pines as a lone traveler rode his horse to higher ground, where the river wound like a narrow ribbon below, in the shadows of a great cliff.

Dressed in black riding gear and dark, heavy boots, Blackie blended well into the darkness of night. A pistol was thrust into a holster at his waist, and a rifle rested in the gunsling at the side of his black stallion.

A wide-brimmed black hat pulled low over his brow, his dark eyes peering through the night, Blackie left the higher ground again and began watching for a cave. He had been there more than once. Lately, in fact, he had been there quite frequently with White Wolf, the two of them inciting the terrorism that was being spread across the land.

There was a part of him that would not let go of his past—that which lived for the excitement of not only gambling but of seeing people bend to his will.

By entering politics, he had felt the power that came with the reputation of being a politician—bending people's will in that more genteel way. And by joining forces with White Wolf, he was able to bend other people's wills with force—a thrill no woman ever gave him!

But he had not been able to actually participate in the raids as much as he would have liked. It was too risky. His face had become too well known to take a chance at being recognized. He had helped the cause mainly by backing it with his money.

He had even encouraged White Wolf to set up camp elsewhere, in a fortress, where he and his men could live more comfortably, even though White Wolf had not wanted this sort of life. He was happier living off the land, in a cave.

Blackie's eyes narrowed as his thoughts drifted to Briana and her obvious feelings for Night Hawk. He was not upset that Briana had fallen in love with an Indian. But the whole affair brought Night Hawk too close to Blackie and his illegal activities with White Wolf.

Night Hawk was a threat, a threat that had to be eliminated.

The clouds had slipped past the moon, leaving it bright and round in the sky. It sent down enough light for Blackie to make out the shape of the entrance of a cave only a short distance away. He rode onward until he came to a thick stand of cottonwood trees. Reining in his horse, he slipped out of the saddle and walked his stallion the rest of the way.

Just inside the mouth of the cave, Blackie tethered his horse with several others. Squinting, he began feeling his way along the wall of the cave, and as it made a bend, he finally got his first sight of a campfire up ahead.

Blackie walked onward, farther and farther into the cave, the rocks crunching beneath his boots, the musty aroma of the damp walls curling his nose. Every once in a while he would hear the squeak and flap of a wing as a bat became frightened and scrambled from its dark hiding place.

In the far distance, Blackie heard the sound of splashing water, and he knew that at the very far end of the cave was a stream that had cut its way through the heavy rock, giving White Wolf and all of his renegades a good supply of fresh water every day.

Overhead, he saw occasional winks of moonlight through the cracks in the cave ceiling. Those cracks made it possible for White Wolf to build a camp fire, so that the smoke would have an escape.

Blackie listened to the hum of voices as he grew closer to the campsite, recognizing many of the men that were sitting around the evening fire, chatting and planning the next strike of terror against humanity. He recognized White Wolf's voice, and several of his renegade warriors, none of which had ever fit into any way of life.

"Misfits, all of them damn misfits," he snickered to himself. "Especially that damn White Wolf."

Blackie went on into the cave and arrived at a torch-lit area. He stopped and looked slowly around him at the stacks of firearms piled high at each side of the cave, the flames from the torches glistening on the barrels of the rifles. Boxes of ammunition were spread about, along with some sticks of dynamite, which gave him cause to be unnerved.

As he approached, White Wolf embraced him, then stepped back, folding his arms across his chest. "Why have you come tonight?" he said, his voice deep and resonant. "Do you carry with you bad tidings?"

Blackie tossed his hat onto a pile of bearskins. He laughed gruffly as he went with White Wolf to the campfire and the circle of Indian renegades lounging beside it, some smoking their long-stemmed pipes, some eating.

"Well, in a way, I guess you might say that," Blackie said, settling down onto a thick layer of blankets beside White Wolf, the fire warm against his face. He reached inside his coat pocket and pulled out a leather pouch of tobacco, handing this over to White Wolf.

"Tell me about it," White Wolf said, lifting a long-stemmed pipe and resting it on his lap. He opened the drawstrings of the buckskin pouch and sprinkled some of its tobacco into the bowl of the pipe.

The pouch laid aside, White Wolf placed the stem of the pipe to his lips. Bending close to the fire, he lifted a burning twig from its periphery and placed its glowing tip to the tobacco, inhaling deeply as it became lighted.

"Of course, since we have both allied ourselves with Strong Branch and Gray Moon, you are familiar with Chief Echohawk," Blackie said in a low growl.

"Who is not familiar with the Chippewa chief?" White Wolf said, his voice filled with annoyance. He looked over at Blackie and handed him the lit pipe. "He is my same age. We are bitter enemies, he and I. But we have not come face to face for years. There was no need to. He went his way—I went mine." He narrowed his eyes as he leaned closer to Blackie, who puffed slowly from the pipe. "Tell me, why do you mention his name to me now? Has he become an irritation to you?"

Blackie gazed over at White Wolf as he leisurely enjoyed the pipe, seeing him as surely sixty years of age, yet still virile and muscular. He wore his graying hair long and past his waist, secured by a fur headband. His attire, no matter whether it was winter or summer, was only a breechclout. He had explained to Blackie that his body had been trained to tolerate the extremes of both heat and cold.

The soft sound of a baby crying a short distance away, where lamplight flooded the low, damp ceiling of the cave with its golden light, made Blackie turn his attention from White Wolf. "Your squaw and child?" he asked, resting the bowl of the pipe on his knee. "They are well?"

"Both are well," White Wolf said, nodding.

Blackie caught sight of Gentle Fawn as she rose to her feet, strolling back and forth with her baby. The child nursed from a breast where Gentle Fawn had lowered her buckskin dress only low enough so that the child could have benefit of her sweet milk.

Blackie saw Gentle Fawn as young and beautiful, knowing that she could hardly be more than twenty years old. He knew that she was not there of her own free will, yet he had done nothing about it. He never interfered in anything that White Wolf felt strongly about.

And what did it matter to him? he thought, shrugging. She was no concern of his. He had his hands full enough keeping his niece at bay.

Anyway, he concluded to himself, once the squaw's child had been born, it seemed Gentle Fawn had settled in and accepted her fate, never trying to escape from her "keeper" any longer. The child had made her afraid to leave. She was frightened that White Wolf would seek her out and kill the child for spite should she ever manage to flee from him.

But he would kill both her and the child, Blackie thought

to himself, having heard White Wolf lay this threat on her many times.

Blackie turned his eyes back to White Wolf and gave his pipe to him. He raised his legs before him and, hugging them, scowled at White Wolf. "I need your help," he said, his voice low and threatening. "It seems my niece has become a nuisance, to say the least."

White Wolf forked an eyebrow, again sucking on the stem of the pipe, inhaling a deep whiff of smoke, then exhaling it slowly. He placed the pipe aside and leaned back on an elbow. "You want me to kill your niece?" he said casually. "Is that why you have come to me tonight?"

Blackie felt the sudden silence on all sides of him and looked slowly around, seeing that everyone had begun listening alertly to the exchange. Blackie cleared his throat nervously, then looked into White Wolf's midnight dark eyes again. "That isn't what I want at all," he said thickly.

"Then what?" White Wolf said, straightening his back and folding his arms across his chest. "You speak in circles tonight."

Nervously, Blackie ran his fingers through his dark hair, then placed his hands on his knees as he leaned closer. "My niece has fallen in love with an Indian," he said dryly. "I want you to make sure he's no longer a problem." He leaned his face into White Wolf's. "I want him killed, White Wolf. I want you to do the killing."

"You spoke of Echohawk earlier," White Wolf said blandly. "Is he the Indian your niece is infatuated with?"

"No, it isn't Echohawk," Blackie mumbled. Yet deep inside his heart he knew that Echohawk would be a problem for him as long as he was alive, although the threat seemed to have lightened through the years. Now the son was his main concern.

"Oh?" White Wolf said, obviously confused.

"It's his son," Blackie said in a snarl. "Night Hawk. He's made his way into my niece's heart. Soon he will be trying to squirm into her life totally. He's a half-breed, you know. Perhaps he's tired of living with his Indian half, and wants to make a life with the whites. How better to worm his way into my life and try to take advantage of my money? I can't allow that. Nor can I allow him to get closer to me and discover how I spend my time when I am away from St. Paul. If it was ever discovered that I was associated with you and your men, I'd be finished. Do you hear? Finished!"

"I know of Night Hawk," White Wolf hissed. "He sees all Sioux as snakes in the grass. He is my enemy as well as his chieftain father. Tell me what to do. I shall do it."

"It's plain and simple," Blackie said, shrugging. "Kill him."

A slow smile tugged at White Wolf's thick lips. "That will be a pleasure," he said smoothly. "As long as I can do it at my leisure, and in my own way."

"However it is done does not concern me," Blackie said, rising slowly to his feet. He glared down at White Wolf. "But just be sure to take him out of commission soon. Get him away from my niece."

White Wolf rose to his feet and placed a hand on Blackie's shoulder. "Why not let me also kill your niece and get her out of your way?" he said thickly.

"You don't get the point, do you?" Blackie said, brushing White Wolf's hand from his shoulder. "She's important to me. Having a devoted niece at my side makes me look legitimate."

"I see," White Wolf said, kneading his chin thoughtfully.

"Can I trust you to do this for me?" Blackie asked, picking up his hat and placing it on his head.

"It is as good as done," White Wolf said, walking Blackie away from the camp fire and into the dungeon darkness of the outer part of the cave.

"You owe me, White Wolf," Blackie said in a growl. "Damn it, you owe me good for what I've done for you and your renegades. On those lean weeks when you didn't net enough loot from the raids, who was it that gave you food to eat and tobacco for your damn pipes? Damn it, White Wolf. Never forget that you owe me."

There was a strained silence when White Wolf didn't offer any response to this different sort of threat.

Blackie spoke again. "I hear you have another raid planned

soon," he said, taking his horse's reins, leading him out into the moonlight.

"That is so," White Wolf said, following beside Blackie.

"Are Strong Branch and Gray Moon planning to go on this raid with you?" Blackie asked, peering intently at White Wolf.

"As far as I know, yes, they are planning to ride with me and my men," White Wolf said, his gaze locking with Blackie's. "And what does that matter?"

"Do not reveal our plans for Night Hawk to either of them," Blackie flatly ordered. "I've never trusted them."

"They feel the same about you," White Wolf said in a low grumble. Then he nodded. "Nothing will be said to them about our plans to kill Night Hawk. But it is not necessary to keep it from them. They both would benefit from the death." His lips lifted into a smug smile. "And also, if anything should happen to Echohawk, it would make the life of those two young braves much more comfortable. Perhaps after I see to Night Hawk's death, I will also see to Echohawk's."

"Whatever. That sounds fine to me," Blackie said, mounting his horse. "But one thing—one person at a time. Take care of Night Hawk. Do you understand? Soon!"

Blackie did not wait for a response. He nudged his horse's sides with his knees and rode off into the darkness, feeling as though he had just signed a pact with the devil tonight, and feeling comfortable with it.

His laughter rolled into the hills and treetops as he sent his stallion into a hard gallop across the meadow.

9

So teasing!
So pleasing!
Capricious!
Delicious!

—IRVING

It was a June night, scorching and breathless. As twilight fell on the small city park, drummers, tuba players, and saxophonists in black uniforms with bow ties and gold braid took their seats beneath the ginger-bread of a bandstand. At the conductor's cue, they struck up a venerable American traditional song, setting hands clapping.

Among those who were enjoying the concert were small children sitting in the front rows of seats that had been placed close to the outdoor platform, picnic parties at tables along the sides of the park, and others sitting comfortably on blankets beneath the deepening shadows of the trees.

Briana was standing away from the crowd beneath a tree, trying not to be noticed and hating every minute of being there, acting out the role of the dutiful niece for her uncle's political rally. She gazed with contempt at Blackie sitting smugly on the platform in his dark suit and tie. He was tapping his foot in time with the music, papers clutched in his left hand—his speech carefully prepared for tonight, with hopes that he might pull more voters into his political arena.

Briana knew that as soon as the band ceased playing her uncle's favorite patriotic tunes, he would stand up behind the podium and pretend to be the people's savior, pretend to be something that he was not.

Shaking her head with disgust at the thought of her uncle's pretenses and his forced smile and aloof snugness, Briana leaned her back against the rough bark of the tree, then eased away from it again, not wanting to muss her dress. Today she wore a floor-length, soft silk dress dappled with tiny petals, the floating tiers of lace on her dropped sash designed to waft as she walked, creating a floral whirl. She also wore a big hat with a brow full of bows, and was clutching a beaded purse in her gloved hand.

Yes, she had dressed the part of a niece who should want to look uncommonly pretty for her politically aspiring uncle, but as she dressed, she had felt anything but glad to help him in his aspirations. She knew that he did not deserve to be involved in the formation of Minnesota as a state, or anything else that might decide the good of the land or the people.

Her gloved hand went to her cheek, recalling how her uncle had slapped her, realizing then that he was a vicious, unpredictable man. She was only pretending to be a dutiful niece now because she needed time to chart out a future that would not include him. If she wrote her parents of her unhappiness, they would send her the money required to return to Paris.

But she did not want to leave St. Paul. Her heart was there. She could never leave Night Hawk.

As the band ceased playing and her uncle rose to the podium to begin his speech, Briana tried to focus her mind elsewhere so that she would not have to listen to his lies. She centered her thoughts on her paintings, for even while not painting she always carried with her the memories of a certain golden light, the delicious hues of rivers and the sky, of fields and flowers.

She could not concentrate long on her painting, because something about her uncle's speech tonight puzzled her. For some reason he appeared to be more fired up, more priggish, and more self-assured.

She looked up at the platform, seeing that lanterns were now lit on both sides, darkness having fallen like a velvet cloak draped across the heavens. A chill coursed through her as her uncle's eyes searched for her, and then singled her out in the crowd, making eye contact with her.

She blinked nervously when she saw an even stranger sort of smugness in the way he gazed intensely at her as he talked about why he would be the best man for Congress for this land that was moving quickly into statehood. He spoke of the railroad that was being planned that would stretch from coast to coast, saying that the people of Minnesota knew that the chances of the railroad passing through their wonderful land were much better if Minnesota was a state and had a vote in Congress.

He spoke more loudly when he declared that he would be the best man for that vote.

Trumpets blared and people shouted, his approval quite pronounced tonight by the attitude of the citizens who were there rooting for him!

And then there was silence again, enough for him to resume his speech.

Briana cringed when he raised a hand and pointed at her, causing heads to turn when he introduced her to the crowd, saying that she was a renowned artist who had studied abroad, someone he was proud to call his niece, and who was herself bringing attention to their proud land—her reputation as an artist was spreading far and wide across the vastness of the United States.

Briana saw his smugness fade and a dark frown crease his brow when she smiled awkwardly at the crowd and began slipping back farther into the shadows, no longer able to play the game with her uncle. She knew that her dodging the gawking crowd would infuriate him, and that he would accuse her of trying to spoil everything for him.

But at this moment it did not matter. Tonight she just could not stand any more of his lies.

Turning to leave the park and the drone of her uncle's voice as he continued speaking behind her. Briana gasped when she found Night Hawk on his horse, reined in at the roadside.

"Night Hawk, you frightened me," Briana said, holding her hat as she tipped her head to look up at him. Fear crept quickly into her heart. "You shouldn't be here. If my uncle knew that you were, there would be hell to pay."

"For him perhaps, but not for Night Hawk," the brave said stiffly.

"How long have you been here?" Briana asked, his mere presence stirring her insides passionately. "Why are you here?"

"I followed you here and have been waiting," he said thickly. "I could not stay away. I have thought of you day and night. Come with me, Briana. Let us be together again. Let us talk."

Briana glanced over her shoulder toward the lamp-lit platform, able to see that her uncle was occupied, his audience staring raptly up at him as he spoke fluently and moved his hands in the air like a preacher to keep their attention.

She turned back to Night Hawk. "I really shouldn't," she murmured, recalling her uncle's fury and his threats over her feelings toward Night Hawk.

"You should," Night Hawk teased, reaching a hand to her. "Come. Let us go and sit by the Father of Waters. We will not stay long if you wish not to."

"It's only because of my uncle," Briana said, casting her eyes downward. Suddenly she felt a strong arm around her waist. She inhaled a quivering breath as she felt herself being lifted onto Night Hawk's lap. She did not fight his decision to do this as he held onto her and began riding away.

They rode for a while, then Night Hawk reined in his horse at a secluded spot overlooking the river. He eased Briana to the ground and quickly dismounted.

After securing his horse's reins to a low-hanging tree limb, he took Briana's gloved hand and led her beneath the trees toward the shine of the Mississippi River. They made their way down the winding path to the river's edge, and once there they stood side-by-side, content to just be there together.

"Tonight the stars are so soft, the river so quiet," Briana whispered, the first to break their silence. She removed her hat and dropped it to the ground, dropping her purse beside it.

"Tonight you are all that is truly beautiful," Night Hawk said, releasing her hand to place his hands at her waist to turn her to face him. Yet he did not kiss her. He urged her to sit on the ground, where he then drew her to his side and held her next to him.

"I love being here with you," Briana said, gently leaning against him.

"But first you fought this decision to be with me," Night Hawk said, peering down at her. She seemed so delicate in her dress of lace and frills.

"I know," Briana said, turning her eyes up to him. "But I was wrong." She laughed softly. "No matter what, I will never again let my uncle, or my fear of him, stand in the way of our being together." She removed her gloves and cuddled closer. "Night Hawk, I've missed you so much."

The brave turned to her and placed his hands on her shoulders, easing her onto her back on the ground. When his lips came to hers in a fiery kiss, she no longer worried about mussing her dress, or what her uncle might do when she came home with grass stains on its skirt, or perhaps a piece or two of dried leaves in her hair.

This was her life. Her uncle would not control it!

Night Hawk was her life, her very breath, it seemed.

A noise behind them startled them to their feet. Breathless, her heart pounding in fear that perhaps her uncle had followed them there, Briana watched as Night Hawk drew his pistol and began stalking around the high bushes and trees, searching for the intruder.

Briana raised an eyebrow and her heart slowed when she heard Night Hawk utter a sudden, deep laugh, then came into view carrying a raccoon with its bandit eyes peering through the darkness at her.

"It was only a raccoon?" Briana said, her shoulders relaxing with her relief.

She did not dare go any closer to Night Hawk as long as he held the wild animal in his arms. "They are known to bite," she murmured.

"The forest animals are as one with me," Night Hawk said, bending to a knee and releasing the raccoon. "None has ever bit me."

After placing his pistol on the ground beside Briana's hat, Night Hawk went to her and began taunting her. "You are afraid of a mere raccoon?" he mocked, lifting her up in his arms. He held her over the water and began swinging her back and forth teasingly. "Are you also afraid of the Father of Waters and the fish with their large teeth and mouths?"

Briana turned her eyes to the river, knowing its reputation of being muddy. That was what she truly feared—not the innocent fish. "Night Hawk, let me down," she said, laughing softly and clinging to him with all of her might. "You might drop me. Please . . . let—"

Night Hawk teasingly took another step closer, but suddenly he tripped over a rock and found himself toppling over the edge, carrying Briana with him into the water.

Briana didn't have time to scream from alarm. She was already in the depths of the water. She loosened herself from Night Hawk and swam to the surface. Coughing and gasping for air, she stood on the muddy bottom of the river, her hands smoothing her hair back from her face.

Night Hawk came to the surface beside her, his long black hair floating around his shoulders as he placed his feet on the bottom.

"You!" Briana cried, seeing the lace of her dress floating ugly and wet in the water. "Night Hawk, why did you do that? How am I to be expected to go home? My dress is ruined. I-I look like a drowned rat!"

Night Hawk chuckled. "I do not think the comparison is accurate," he said, reaching for her wrist, bringing her close, anchoring her against his hard body. "You are much lovelier."

He held her in his embrace with the strength of one arm, while his free hand roamed over her, feeling the suppleness of her curves through her wet dress, and the tempting triangle at the juncture of her thighs. "And you do not need to go to your uncle's home," he said huskily. "Return to my home with me. Be my woman. Stay with me *ah-pah-nay*, forever."

Briana was only half hearing what he was saying. His fingers were awakening her to the wild rapture that she always found while with him. As he caressed her through her dress, his mouth so temptingly close, she closed her eyes and let the euphoria claim her.

When he brought his lips to hers in a frenzied kiss, she clung to him and wrapped her legs around him at his waist. Night Hawk somehow released his throbbing need from his fringed breeches, and tore her under-garment away. He found her open and ready for him, his thick, hard manliness moving within her with powerful, rhythmic strokes.

His lips moved away from her mouth, down her neck, and to her breast, stopping to suck on the nipple through the soft, textured silk of her dress. Briana held her head back and sighed with bliss. Her hair swirled around her in the water, her shoulders swaying in her passion. Her gasps became soft whimpers as she felt the pleasure growing.

And when she felt a great shuddering in Night Hawk's loins, she strained her hips to accept his seed inside her, crying out at her own fulfillment the same moment he groaned out his own wild ecstasy.

Afterward, her heart still beating soundly, Briana clung to Night Hawk, savoring his closeness. As he slipped himself from inside her, she placed her feet on the bottom of the river, steadied herself, then reached and found his limpness and began caressing it with her fingers. She felt the first stirrings as it began to grow within her hand. She could feel him groan and she looked up at him, at his eyes hazy with renewed passion.

She was not at all surprised when he moved her hand away from his newly aroused pulsing need of her and swept her into his arms and carried her to dry land.

He lay her down, his fingers quickly disrobing her. He began disrobing himself. She watched, loving it.

He tossed all of his clothes aside and knelt down over her, worshiping her body. It seemed his tongue left no dip or crevice untouched. She breathed hard, closing her eyes, enjoying it.

As his tongue stopped at her throbbing mound, she parted her legs and twined her fingers through his thick, dark hair and led him on to what he sought. She became lost in the sensual pleasure that swam through her like soft waves on an ocean, needing it.

She was soon overcome with the shocking sensations of sheer bliss.

And then she reciprocated. As he rolled onto the ground,

she moved toward him, the flesh of her thighs rippling in sinuous hollows. Her hands moved over his body, until they cupped his buttocks. They were smooth and hard as she clung to him, her mouth giving him pleasure that seemed to make him mindless.

His groans filled the night air.

And when it seemed that he could no longer stand this sort of loving, he turned her beneath him and plunged his throbbing shaft deeply within her.

Their naked flesh became one as they rocked and swayed in a gentle pressure of bodies. It did not take long for them both to go over the edge into total ecstasy again, leaving them breathing hard, laughing softly as they clung to each other.

"It was maddeningly beautiful," Briana said as Night Hawk rolled away from her and onto his back. "Always with you I am awakened to so many feelings that until now I could never, in my wildest dreams, fathom." She turned to him and smoothed a hand across his flat, tight stomach. "Was it as wonderful for you, darling? Will you love me forever?"

"Did I not ask you to return with me to my village and be my woman?" Night Hawk said, smoothing some of the wet strands of her hair from her face. "I would want you there with me, *ay-uh, ah-pah-nay*. Marry me. Be the flower of my wigwam."

"Marry you?" Briana gasped incredulously. "Be the flower of your wigwam?"

The clouds shifted and rays of the moon fell upon the two. Night Hawk looked heavenward, smiling. "See?" he said. "The Great Spirit is pleased with our togetherness and is smiling upon us."

He turned to her and grasped her shoulders, drawing her atop him so that her legs straddled him. "We are good together, you and I," he said huskily, shifting his body so that his arousal was probing for entrance inside her again. He clung to her rounded hips, smiling as Briana gasped with pleasure as he thrust himself inside her, finding her tight and willing. He lifted himself more deeply into her with steady thrusts.

"Tell me that you do not wish to be mine, to live with me

until I am old," Night Hawk said, his heart pounding as his own pleasure mounted. He did not slow his strokes within her. He kept them steady and demanding. "Tell me that you would not desire awakening to these sorts of pleasures every morning, when my body aches to be touched and kissed. Is it not the same for you?"

"My body never felt much of anything until you awakened it to these sensual pleasures," Briana said, sucking in a wild breath when his hands moved to her breasts, cupping and kneading them.

"And now?" he urged huskily.

"Now all of my soul cries out day and night for what we are now sharing again," Briana said, choking back a sob as the passion began to peak. She covered his hands with hers, causing his fingers to press more tightly into her breasts. "Oh, how it would delight me to live with you—to be your woman. I love you so much! Oh, so much!"

"You will tell your uncle tonight?" Night Hawk said, slipping himself from inside her, turning her so that she was now beneath him. He spread himself atop her and plunged inside her again, his whole body stiffening as he found himself so close to that brink of joyous bliss, so much so that he scarcely heard what she said, her words seeming to come from deep within a tunnel as his body spasmed, for a moment blotting out everything but the sheer pleasure.

Briana responded in kind, everything within her warming from the ecstasy anew within her.

And then she lay with him, side by side, her head cradled between his arm and chest. "Didn't you hear me?" she whispered. "I'll marry you. But first I must write my parents. I-I mustn't rush into anything as serious as this without first sharing the news with my parents. Do you understand?"

Stunned that she had actually agreed to marry him, Night Hawk leaned away from her, his eyes wide, his lips parted. And then he shouted to the wind, the stars, the heavens, and the moon as he picked her up and began dancing around in a circle, she in his arms, clinging and laughing.

When he finally placed her on the ground, the grass cold

beneath her bare feet, she sobered, knowing what lay ahead of her.

She gazed down at her wet, ruined dress, then up at Night Hawk.

"How on earth am I going to get past my uncle without him seeing me in such disarray?" she said, her voice breaking at the thought of how he might react. He had given her a slap only on his *suspicions* of her and Night Hawk having been together. Seeing her like this, he might react even more violently. Yet she had no choice but to return to his house.

But it thrilled her heart to realize that soon she would never have to face him again. Night Hawk was giving her a place to go—a haven—in his arms forever.

"You do not have to face him ever again," Night Hawk said, stooping to pick up her dress, then handing it to her.

"Yes, I must," she murmured. "If I didn't go home tonight, Uncle Blackie would come looking for me, and I do not want to give him any excuse to bring a rifle and use it on you."

Even though the night was still deliciously warm, she shivered as she slipped into the wet garments. Soon, riding on Night Hawk's lap on his horse, her uncle's house came within view.

"You'd better let me go the rest of the way alone," she insisted, turning wistful eyes up at Night Hawk. "Please, I'd best face my uncle alone."

He drew a tight rein and stopped his horse. He eased Briana to her feet and slipped out of the saddle, standing beneath low-hanging branches of an elm tree. He circled his arms around her waist and drew her against his hard body.

"Go with care, my beloved," he whispered. He gave her a long and feverish kiss before releasing her.

Her heart fluttering wildy within her chest, Briana broke free and began running toward her uncle's great mansion, dying a slow death inside when she heard Night Hawk riding away in the opposite direction. She ran her hands down the front of her wet dress and then through her hair, knowing what a sight she was. She dreaded what awaited her, but she rushed onward.

When she reached the house, she tiptoed as softly as she

could up the steep front stairs, gently opened the heavy oak door, and crept into the dimly lighted foyer.

Before climbing the spiral staircase, she stopped to get her breath. She looked up the stairs, toward the second-floor landing, and noticed that hardly any lights were on, except for the candles glowing softly in the sconces along the corridor walls.

Sucking in a breath of air, she crept up the stairs. Then, just as she reached the landing, she almost toppled backward when she found her uncle suddenly standing there, holding a razor strop in his right hand, smacking it threateningly against the palm of his left hand.

"Uncle Arden, what are you doing there, with—with that thing?" Briana said, inching around him, wanting to get to the safety of her bedroom. Yet she knew that while she was in this house, there was never anything akin to safety. It was as though she had just entered the pits of hell—and the devil was there awaiting her, glaring.

"Go to your room at once," Blackie snarled, continuing to slap the razor strop against his hand.

Frightened nearly to death, Briana walked backward, inching her way to her room. When she reached it she rushed inside and slammed the door.

But she did not get it bolt-locked quickly enough. Her uncle burst the door open with one shove of his shoulder.

Blackie pushed Briana, which made her lose her balance and fall across the bed on her stomach. When the razor strop fell across her back, the pain almost made her black out. She screamed and clawed her fingers into the bedspread.

Then her pain changed to anger.

She flew from the bed and, surprising her uncle, jerked the razor strop from his hand before he had a chance to stop her. Raising it, she brought it down across his face, instantly drawing blood.

Realizing what she had done, Briana gasped, dropped the razor strop, and tried to run.

But a tight hand on her wrist swung her around and her whole body shuddered as Blackie hit her across the face.

Briana's body doubled over with pain, and she crumpled to the floor. She lay there sobbing as Blackie stood over her.

"You bitch," he grumbled, then walked away.

Briana lay there for a while, then rose slowly to her feet. She wiped a trickle of blood from the corner of her mouth and stumbled to the door, bolt-locking it. She rested her back against the door for a moment longer, then went to the desk and sat down shakily at it.

Opening the drawer, she found a pen, ink, and paper. Sobbing, she began penning a letter to her parents. She first explained about her uncle's behavior toward her, and then told them that she soon would be married, and to whom.

Once the letter was sealed and ready to take to the post office on the morrow, she went to the window and drew back a sheer curtain, thinking that perhaps she should escape into the forest tonight, away from her demon uncle.

Yet another thought came to her that made her smile. She was going to wait at least another twenty-four hours before mailing the letter, or leaving this house of horrors. That was the date of her uncle's next political rally. She was going to be at his side, but this time when she was introduced, she was going to step boldly up to that podium and make an announcement that would ruin her uncle's political career forever!

She would tell all of the ugly truths about this man who most did not know as Blackie.

"Yes, my dear uncle, I'm going to make you pay for what you've done to me," she whispered to herself. "Pay dearly."

10

There are loyal hearts, there are spirits brave.
There are souls that are pure and true.

—Bridges

After leaving Briana, Night Hawk rode hard to get to his village by midnight, the designated time for the council meeting of the elders of not only his village but also Chief Strong Branch's village, whose people were as one with Chief Echohawk's.

Night Hawk swung himself out of his saddle and gave his horse's reins to a young brave who took his steed swiftly away to the corral. Night Hawk walked somberly toward the great outdoor fire that was reaching its flames toward the sky, lighting the heavens as though it were midday instead of midnight.

Night Hawk's troubled mood was caused by what he expected from Strong Branch tonight. Echohawk had given his son the duties to preside over the council meeting, having told him proudly that he soon would take over the full duties of chief of their people. Echohawk had taught him well, and his preparations for stepping down to let his son become chief were almost completed now.

Echohawk wanted more time with his ailing wife, a luxury that being chief did not allow him.

Night Hawk knew that Echohawk's announcement at the last council meeting—that his son would soon be chief—also had stirred jealousy within Strong Branch's heart, for it was known by everyone that Strong Branch was not happy with being chief of just his band of Chippewa.

Suddenly, it seemed, Strong Branch had become obsessed with power, and he would not be pleased at all when he had to sit by and watch Night Hawk preside over this meeting tonight, when Strong Branch had never been allowed to.

Until tonight, Echohawk had been in control of such meetings. He was the elder of these two chiefs of the adjoining bands of Chippewa, and respect for his age gave him more authority than Strong Branch was comfortable with.

Needing time to collect his thoughts, Briana still sweet on his breath and in his heart, Night Hawk stepped into the shadows of a wigwam and inhaled a shaky breath. Tonight it was important to show his father that he was worthy of soon becoming chief. He must run the meeting with a calm reserve, and should Strong Branch or Wise Owl, an elderly spokesman of Strong Branch's band who spoke his mind more often than not, stir up resentment tonight, he knew that he must be prepared to meet this challenge head-on.

It was sad that this was even a worry to him. In their youth, Strong Branch and Night Hawk had been the best of friends. Strong Branch had been the chief of his people even then, with Echohawk having full control of Strong Branch's people, until Strong Branch had grown old enough to realize what the title of chief meant, and what powers were needed to take over the role that was meant to be his upon the death of his father, Chief Silver Wing. Chief Silver Wing's last dying words had been to Echohawk—asking him to assume the powers of chief over his people until his infant son grew into them.

Bitter and old, and having never agreed with Chief Silver Wing's decision to allow Echohawk to reign as chief over Strong Branch's band of Chippewa, Wise Owl had pressed Strong Branch into the decision to try to oust Echohawk from power. This had changed the younger chief's life. He was no longer a carefree person who laughed a lot. He had turned into a suspicious, greedy young man that frowned now more than he laughed.

Now it was only Lily, Night Hawk's sister, who seemed to find any goodness left inside Strong Branch's heart.

"Perhaps that is for the best," Night Hawk grumbled to himself. "Perhaps this marriage between Strong Branch and Lily could bring our people together again with much love, compassion—and respect." Yet he doubted that and wished that his sister would look elsewhere for a husband—for a man that would treat her like the jewel that she was instead of just something to use.

"Big brother Night Hawk?" Lily said suddenly from behind him.

Night Hawk turned with a start, yet he knew that he should not be all that surprised to find his sister standing there, and that she was not in bed, as was usual for girls her age at this time of night. "Lily, do you plan to sit in council with the men of the two adjoining villages?" he said, chuckling low as he placed a gentle hand on her lily-white face.

"You know that I would not do that," Lily said. "It was just as usual . . . I am too restless to sleep. I plan to take my nightly stroll through the forest." She lifted the fringed hem of her dress, displaying a knife that was sheathed at the calf. "And, yes, big brother, I am weaponed in case I find myself face to face with danger during these hauntingly late hours."

Night Hawk drew her to him and gave her a gentle hug. "Then you have listened well to your brother's worries about you," he said. "But if you would listen even more attentively, you would not leave your dwelling at all after the moon replaces the sun in the sky. You would sit beside the fire and do your bead-work with *gee-mah-mah*."

"There is more on my mind than mere beadwork." Lily sighed heavily. She leaned away from Night Hawk. "As there is more on your mind than your sister and the council meeting tonight." She touched his cheek with her fingers as she peered into his eyes. "My brother, I see something about you tonight that is different. It is in your eyes. It is in your voice. My brother, you are courting a woman? Who is she, Night Hawk? Is she beautiful?"

Night Hawk took her hand from his cheek and pressed his lips against the palm, kissing it, then held it as he smiled down at her. "Baby sister, you think you see and hear all," he said softly.

He glanced over his shoulder, at the men in council awaiting his arrival, knowing that he was delaying the meeting much too long. In preparation for this meeting, a great outdoor fire had been built and lighted at noon when the sun was high so that by midnight there would be many red coals. The Chippewa believed that great wisdom was to be found in the embers of a fire.

The village was brightly lit by these burning embers, and all of the braves were sitting with their knees drawn up against their chests, held in that position by wrapping their robes tightly around their loins and knees. This fixed them somewhat in the fashion of a rocking chair during this meeting of neighboring bands of Chippewa, sharing plans for the summer activities.

"I must go," Night Hawk said, releasing his sister's hand. He frowned down at her. "Go home. Go to bed. Forget this foolishness about marrying Strong Branch. Do you not know that I realize this is why you are not able to go to sleep peacefully? He is the cause. You deserve better, Lily. Do you not see that he has changed into someone neither you nor I know? He would not be a good husband, Lily. Choose someone else from another band of Chippewa. Will you consider this, for your brother?"

Lily's hand moved to her abdomen. She swallowed hard, thinking that if her brother knew about this child growing within her womb, he would not be asking her to seek another man to marry! She must marry the child's father, for the child's sake. And for hers—for she loved Strong Branch with every beat of her heart—and also her baby's!

But she could not share her secret with anyone except Strong Branch. She would be shamed in the eyes of her people if they knew that she was with child before her wedding vows were shared with the Great Spirit's blessings.

And she had lied to Night Hawk. She was not planning to venture into the forest tonight for her nightly walk. She was going to stand in the shadows until the council meeting was over, and then follow Strong Branch to his dwelling and demand that he hear her out—and this time before he was able to kiss her senses away!

"You do not answer me," Night Hawk said, placing his hands on her shoulders. "Will you, Lily, consider searching for another man to be your husband? Will you?"

"I cannot make you such a promise," Lily said, her voice breaking. She flinched when he jerked his hands away, within his eyes a deep, angry hurt.

Night Hawk glared down at her for a moment longer, then turned on his heel and went to the circle of men and made his way to the place assigned him, beside his chieftain father, and sat down.

Lily moved into the shadows of the wigwams, her heart anxious, her eyes intently on Strong Branch. Her insides froze when she saw his utter contempt as he glared at Night Hawk. Her brother accepted the lighted, long-stemmed calumet pipe that a young brave brought to him. She watched Strong Branch as he accepted the pipe as it was passed around to him, his eyes never leaving Night Hawk, the hatred increasing, it seemed, as each minute passed.

Lily placed a hand to her mouth, stifling a sob of remorse, knowing that her brother was right about Strong Branch, yet knowing there was nothing she could do about it now. She moved farther into the shadows, tears flowing down her cheeks.

The pipe was passed around the complete circle of men, each brave taking a puff, or if a particular brave did not care to smoke, he touched the tip with his lips or laid his hands gently and respectfully on the stem. Another way of conducting devotion was to blow the smoke in the mouth into cupped hands, then rub the hands over his head and arms, as if pouring water over his body.

Then the pipe was laid aside.

"Summer is upon us, my friends," Night Hawk said, smiling at those in council. "Let this summer be a festive one. Let us share many dances, feasts, and songs! The crops are planted. The hunt has been good. The maple trees gave us much sugar last autumn which will last until the next sugaring season. There is much to be thankful for. It is a time of prosperity for both our bands of Chippewa."

He wanted to speak even more loudly and say that perhaps even a wedding would be celebrated—his and Briana's. But that would wait. *Ay-uh,* that would come later, at a different sort of council.

Wise Owl, bent and haggard, who had sat close-mouthed and narrow-eyed while waiting for Night Hawk's arrival, pushed himself up from the ground, clinging to his robe, which was draped over his lean shoulders. "I wish to be heard," he announced, his voice a low rumble.

Night Hawk peered up at him, trying to show consideration for the old man, since respect was always shown to the Chippewa elders, and because at one time he had been Chief Silver Wing's best friend and most devoted brave. But it was difficult.

Wise Owl had become a nuisance, a troublemaker, not only for Night Hawk's tribe of Chippewa but Wise Owl's own. Until his interferences, for the most part these two bands of Chippewa had lived side by side for more than twenty-five winters in peaceful coexistence.

Night Hawk glanced over at Strong Branch, seeing his smug sneer, knowing that he was behind coaxing the elder Chippewa into interfering, for only Strong Branch would benefit from it.

Knowing that he must give Wise Owl his time to speak his mind, Night Hawk turned his gaze back to him and nodded.

Wise Owl's eyes moved around the circle of braves as he began talking in a low drone. "It is time that our two neighboring villages become truly one entity," he said. "One chief should be named to rule over all, and that chief should be a younger man, with younger ideas and ideals." He raised a shaky hand and pointed toward Strong Branch. "This young chief should be Strong Branch! He is dependable! He has proved his abilities as chief!"

He lowered his hand to his side and narrowed his eyes on Echohawk, and then Night Hawk. "It is known that Echohawk will soon hand over his title of chief to his son, saying he is worthy of it, but I say that he is not. He is half white. Most have labeled him a half-breed! Do you wish to be led by a half-breed who is mocked behind his back?"

Again he looked at Strong Branch. "Strong Branch is Chippewa through and through. His father was the great Chief Silver Wing. His mother was Nee-Kah!" he said more loudly. "He deserves to be chief! Only he!"

Night Hawk was stunned by Wise Owl's obvious dislike of

him and lack of respect for Echohawk. He was speechless that Wise Owl seemed willing to do anything to keep Night Hawk from becoming chief at all.

He sat there for a moment longer, then turned his head slightly when he felt eyes on him. His heart ached when he saw his father staring at him, within his eyes a strange sort of embarrassment that Night Hawk had never seen before. At this moment he almost felt hatred toward Wise Owl for what he was trying to encourage both bands of Chippewa to do. It was a moment of humiliation for both Night Hawk and Echohawk.

Strong Branch squirmed uneasily on his pallet of furs, his sneer erased from his face almost as soon as Wise Owl began speaking. Strong Branch gave Gray Moon a fleeting, troubled glance, knowing that if their secret was ever disclosed, Strong Branch would not even be chief for his own people, much less both bands of Chippewa. Not unless their plans were first carried out to the fullest.

And they had only just begun to sketch out the future for both bands of Chippewa. They had to have time. And now Wise Owl was interfering.

Strong Branch ducked his head. Wise Owl was his elder and had to be shown respect by not telling him the wrong he was doing the tribe as a whole. Strong Branch just sat there, stiff and silent.

Echohawk was shattered by Wise Owl's declarations tonight, yet he did not respond to his comments, realizing that he himself was growing old and might one day say things that he might just as quickly regret. He hoped Wise Owl was regretting his words even as he eased back down on his thick cushion of furs.

These past years Echohawk had spent much time sitting by his lodge fire, smoking his pipe, and watching his tall, stalwart son grow into manhood. He had felt great satisfaction that his son was even now efficiently managing the affairs of their band of Chippewa, though not yet bearing the title of chief. The day would soon come when Night Hawk would be proclaimed chieftain, and no one would rob his son of this honor!

Not even Strong Branch, the Chippewa who would one day be the husband of Echohawk's beloved daughter, Lily.

This thought brought Echohawk to his feet. He nodded at Night Hawk for him to rise and stand beside him. Proudly he placed an arm around his son's shoulders and faced the others.

Then he glared at Wise Owl. "Old man, you have interfered in my people's affairs one time too many!" he grumbled. "Through the years, since Chief Silver Wing's death, I have tolerated these interferences only to keep peace between two bands of Chippewa that have joined together as one, yet were ruled by two separate chiefs. The younger chief, Strong Branch, has too often been guided by your suggestions. But, Wise Owl, you have overstepped your challenges of power this time. Any more interference and I will see to it that you are banished from the Chippewa tribe as the troublemaker that you have become!"

There were rumblings and gasps of shock among those being witness tonight to the battle for power. Yet no one offered any argument. They became silent again, just in time for Echohawk to say one more thing to Wise Owl before returning to his pallet of furs.

"Wise Owl," Echohawk said in a low, measured voice, "You ought to follow the example of the wolf. Even when the wolf is surprised and runs for his life, he will pause to take one more look at you before he enters his final retreat. So should Wise Owl take a second look at everything he sees, and even more important, have a second thought about everything he speaks."

Night Hawk smiled at his father as they both eased down onto their comfortable cushions. Wise Owl humbly lowered his head in a pretense of humility, but to himself vowed revenge.

The rest of the meeting concerned ordinary matters which did not stir up confrontations. The meeting came to a close and everyone began disbanding. Echohawk walked Night Hawk to his wigwam.

"My heart is heavy that this happened tonight between myself and Wise Owl," he said, more in apology than a statement of fact.

"It was not just between you and Wise Owl, *gee-bah-bah,*" Night Hawk said, stopping at his wigwam. He turned and faced his father, placing a hand on his shoulder. "You spoke for us all. Wise Owl spoke for only himself and Strong Branch. His heart is not good toward those who look to him as a man that can be trusted. He surely knows that Strong Branch is no longer the caring, kind person that he was when he first became chief. Wise Owl has to know that Strong Branch is no longer fit even to be chief of his own people, let alone be chief of ours." He lowered his eyes, then looked slowly back up at his father again. "I believe it is time that you forbade Lily to see Strong Branch," he said thickly. "It is no longer in her best interest, or that of our people."

Echohawk kneaded his chin, then nodded. "Perhaps I shall tell her tomorrow," he mumbled. With his head somewhat bowed, he walked away, dreading having to deny his Lily anything. Perhaps he would give it awhile longer, this relationship between his daughter and Strong Branch. Surely the young chief would come around to the ideas that would truly be better for these two bands of Chippewa as a whole.

Perhaps Lily in her sweet kindness could persuade him.

* * *

Lily shied into the darker shadows of the wigwams, waiting for Strong Branch to go past so that she could reach out for him and draw him into the shadows with her. She had to speak to him tonight. These delays were driving her wild! Surely once he heard about the child, everything would be changed back to how it was before. She wanted to be the one to bring him back to his senses so that her brother could step up into the status of chief without further interference from Wise Owl or Strong Branch.

She sorted through the disbanding figures that moved from the outdoor fire in groups, searching for Strong Branch. When she finally found him, she frowned.

Again he was with Gray Moon! The brave seemed to mean

more to Strong Branch now than Lily, and she could not help but resent him with a passion.

She watched as they made a quick escape from the others into the corral, quickly loosening their reins and mounting their horses that were already saddled.

She started running after them, but too quickly winded, stopped, sobbing when she realized that she could not catch up with them. They were already lost to her in the dark depths of the forest. Another night, it seemed, they were taking flight to do whatever consumed them away from their people.

This mystery she was not sure she wanted to unravel, afraid of what she might discover.

Sullenly she headed back toward her wigwam. She wiped the tears from her face before going inside, not wanting her family to question her about why she was crying.

In truth, they would not really want to know.

11

Give me a mind that is not bound,
That does not whimper, whine or sigh.

—WEBB

Having seen his father's distress during the council meeting, and torn with feelings himself about life in general, Night Hawk did not go directly into his wigwam. He needed to go and commune with Wenebojo, the Great Spirit, in the aloneness of the forest, where he would be as one with the night, stars, and sky.

On foot, he broke into a soft run away from his village, the night noises soft and filled with melancholia. A renewed rage filled his soul when he thought back to Wise Owl's insistence on challenging Night Hawk and Echohawk's right to be chief! Night Hawk realized that his father had humored Wise Owl through the years, having allowed him to believe that he had been in more control of things than he actually was, thinking there was no harm in it, especially if he was always in agreement with Echohawk's suggestions to the young Chief Strong Branch.

But Night Hawk now realized that the humoring had been wrong. Wise Owl had become too prominent a figure in the Chippewa community, taking away some of the powers of Echohawk. Night Hawk's jaw tightened, knowing that Wise Owl had to be stopped, but how? Strong Branch was the chief of Wise Owl's band of Chippewa. If Wise Owl was banished, it should, in truth, be Strong Branch's decision.

But now that both Night Hawk and Echohawk had begun to have uneasy feelings about Strong Branch, should not they make sure Strong Branch no longer made decisions that might affect Echohawk's people? Strong Branch had changed, and these secret meetings in which he was involved were a great, troubling puzzle to Night Hawk.

"I will follow him soon, to see where he goes and who he meets," he whispered to himself. "Also, Gray Moon. He is involved in the same mysterious secrets as Strong Branch. They have become inseparable."

His eyes became two points of fire, knowing that secret meetings could involve many ugly things, perhaps even the renegade Sioux, White Wolf!

He shook such a thought from his mind. Strong Branch could never be that deceitful—the Sioux had always been arch enemies of the Chippewa, especially White Wolf. Night Hawk ran onward. He came to a path that led upward, taking him to a high limestone bluff.

He stood there, tall and square-shouldered, his chin lifted proudly, his senses alive and alert to the myriad forms of life about him. Much depended upon the senses of hearing, seeing, and smelling. Half-dormant senses meant to be only half alive.

As before, he drank in the marvelous beauty of the night, the river winding like a silver ribbon toward the horizon, again finding peace, as he had so often found peace along the shores of the broad, silent river.

He loved the river, its flow music to his ears. Ah, but was it not a beautiful sight tonight as the water shimmered with moonlight? How he loved this valley filled with towering trees and clear, cool running springs.

And it was all there because Wenebojo allowed it. Wenebojo, the maker of all things of earth, sky, and water, had breathed life and motion into all things, both visible and invisible. He was over all, through all, and in all. Wenebojo's greatness and goodness could not be surpassed. All of the mysteries of birth, life, and death, all the wonders of lightning, thunder, wind, and rain were but evidence of his everlasting and encompassing power.

Ay-uh, all that he gazed upon tonight was a blessing from the Great Spirit, he thought to himself, feeling most grateful.

Yet did his people not deserve such blessings? They had

been a peaceful and home-loving group, not seeking fame in war. And now there were those who were trying to spoil the peace, even take away the chief that had guaranteed it.

The leaves of several white birch trees trembled in the breeze behind him as he knelt down on a soft bed of grass and reached for a small buckskin pouch that was tucked inside the waistband of his fringed breeches. He took the pouch and loosened the drawstring. He shook some tobacco out onto the ground, his offering to Wenebojo, then lay the tobacco pouch aside.

His hair streaming down his back, he raised his face and voice to the sky and began a soft prayer, asking for guidance.

"Oh, thou Father of Waters, thou who has been such a friend to me and my father's people, stay with the Chippewa forever and ever," he whispered.

"Oh, thou beautiful valley, thou who has been such a joy to me and my father's people, be a home to the Chippewa forever and ever."

"Oh, thou great and mighty Great Spirit, thou who has led me and my father's people wisely and lovingly for many years, stay with the Chippewa forever and ever—"

His prayer was brought to an abrupt halt when a blow across his head rendered him quickly unconscious.

When he awakened, he found himself gagged, blindfolded, and his wrists and ankles bound tightly. The first thing he was aware of was the throbbing of his head, and then the gurgling of water from somewhere close by, a musty smell, and a dank sort of coldness enveloping his face.

Otherwise, there was a strained quiet that surrounded him. He heard the crunch of rocks and sensed a presence, realizing that he was not alone.

When his gag was roughly removed, he heard someone chuckling beneath his breath. He tensed, then spoke. "Who is there?" he asked, wrestling with the bonds at his wrists, trying to loosen them. "Where have you brought me?"

When there was no response, Night Hawk's thoughts went quickly to Wise Owl and how the old Chippewa had been humiliated in front of the others at the meeting when Night

Hawk's father had threatened to banish him. Wise Owl could have abducted Night Hawk for revenge, yet he was too old to see to such an abduction alone.

Night Hawk could not believe that Strong Branch had helped Wise Owl, yet it was true that Night Hawk hardly knew Strong Branch anymore, and that, *ay-uh,* perhaps he could stoop this low to fulfill his aspirations.

Yet there was always White Wolf. And there was Briana's Uncle Blackie!

Night Hawk was suddenly aware of having many enemies, when he had tried so hard not to have any.

He stiffened and listened intently to the sound of voices and laughter in the distance, and then only footsteps as they came closer. His ears picked up the sound of not only one person but many.

His head snapped to one side as someone slapped him across the face.

"And so we have us a prisoner, eh?" an unfamiliar voice said. "White Wolf, is he of blood kin to you?"

"He is Chippewa, not Sioux," White Wolf growled. "Were he Sioux, he would not be here to be tortured, then sentenced to death. He would be treated as though he were my brother."

Night Hawk turned his head slowly, now realizing who had abducted him.

White Wolf.

Night Hawk was not sure exactly why White Wolf had done this now, when he could have done the dirty deed many winters ago!

Night Hawk had rode, prayed, and hunted in the forest alone many times. It was his second home. There had to be a reason why White Wolf would act upon his hatred for him now.

And to speak of torture and then a death sentence? Why would White Wolf hate him this much, unless his hatred was being transferred from someone else, for him to do the dirty deeds for them? He had to wonder if it was Wise Owl, or his childhood friend, Strong Branch, or perhaps Blackie.

If it was Strong Branch, it stung his heart to realize that the love that he had shared with Strong Branch could have turned to such hate.

He lifted his chin proudly, fear foreign to him, for he had been taught that it was not honorable to be afraid even when faced with possible death.

"And so it is you, White Wolf," Night Hawk said, his voice slow and emotionless. "And who else stands beside you tonight, just as guilty of kidnapping as you?"

"It is enough that you know that White Wolf has finally achieved a measure of vengeance," White Wolf said, bending to a knee, grabbing Night Hawk's hair at the back, yanking it hard. "The torture I spoke of? It will not begin just yet, I will give you time to wonder what sort of Sioux torture I will choose for you. Tonight White Wolf has better things to do."

Night Hawk straightened his back when White Wolf released his hair. "And so you leave me to go raid innocent white settlers?" he said, his voice drawn. "It is you, is it not, White Wolf? *You* are responsible for the raids and killings."

"This is not confession time," White Wolf said with a feral snarl.

"You do not need to admit to these unspeakable actions for me to know that you are responsible for them." Night Hawk said smoothly. "My father told me many moons ago about you. He also warned me never to believe that you had cowered away into the hills, a beaten man. It seems that he was right. But this time your days are numbered, White Wolf. Once my father hears of my abduction, and searches and finds you, your life will be ended as quickly as my father can plunge a knife into your dark heart!"

White Wolf laughed boisterously, then walked away. Night Hawk listened and realized that everyone had left along with White Wolf. And as he listened more closely, he could define the sound of many horses' hooves in the distance, strangely muffled by something.

And then he heard a sound that made his heart jump with surprise—the sound of a baby crying from somewhere close by.

He turned his head in the direction of the sound, wondering why a woman was there with a child—and if she was also a captive. He could not envision any woman loving a man like White Wolf or any of his renegades that rode with him.

Soon the baby's cries became muffled, making Night Hawk feel alone again. His shoulders slumped as he leaned up against the cold wall behind him, at least glad that neither Strong Branch nor Wise Owl had anything to do with his abduction, feeling guilty for having silently accused them of it.

Now he had no choice but to wait and see what fate awaited him, wondering if Briana would ever know why he never came to her again, filling his arms with her, smothering her lips with his kisses.

* * *

Echohawk awakened with a start, as though someone were there, pressing a heavy hand on his shoulder. He leaned up on an elbow and looked at Mariah, finding her sleeping soundly on the platform next to his, the low embers of the fire casting faint golden shadows on her frail face.

He looked over at Lily, who lay beautifully asleep, her thick lashes closed over her lily white skin, her hair having tumbled down, to hang in a black sheen on the floor.

He looked slowly around him, finding no one else there, yet he still felt the presence that had awakened him. It had to be for a reason.

His thoughts went to Night Hawk, almost numbing him in the sudden fear that perhaps something had happened to him!

He bolted from his sleeping platform, jerked on his fringed breeches and shirt, and stepped into his moccasins. He took a lingering look at Mariah, hurting deeply inside when he saw how she had changed so much in appearance since having been ravaged by her lingering illness. It was as though he were looking at someone else; not a trace of her loveliness remained from the debilitating malaria.

Turning away, the pain too great to gaze for any length of time at his beloved wife, Echohawk grabbed his rifle and left the wigwam in long, even strides. He hurried to Night Hawk's wigwam. He wasn't there. He sighed heavily, fear building inside his heart with each footstep as he then went to the corral and found his son's horse there. This was not normal if Night Hawk had not left the village.

He left the corral and walked determinedly into the darkness of the forest, knowing where Night Hawk went to commune with the Great Spirit. Surely that was where he had gone on foot this time of night. Echohawk prayed silently to Wenebojo that he was right, and that he would soon feel foolish for having left his warm bed tonight to follow his fears.

Onward he trudged, the rifle clasped in his hand, his heart heavy. When he reached the path that led up to the butte, he inhaled an unsteady breath, then went onward. Daybreak was just lighting the world in its violet glow when he reached the top, revealing nothing.

His heart pounding as his fears for his son mounted, Echohawk went to the edge of the butte, where he could look down upon the beauty of the land, knowing that was where even he had paid homage to Wenebojo with offerings of tobacco.

His heart stopped dead cold when he found something lying at his feet.

He knelt quickly to a knee and picked up the empty buckskin pouch. He recognized it, now knowing for certain that his son had been there. His offerings of tobacco was still there on the ground, slight wisps of wind stirring it around, spreading it farther and farther into the tall grasses. Echohawk held the pouch to his heart and let out a loud cry to the heavens, flooded with emotions that made him suddenly weak all over.

His son. His beloved son! Surely he had beep abducted!

"*Ah-neen-dush,* why? Who would do this thing?" he cried, unashamed of the tears that rushed from his eyes.

Anger soon replaced fear and hurt as he recalled the council meeting the night before and Wise Owl's bitterness. Yet although Wise Owl was filled with resentment and jealousy, Echohawk could not envision the elder Chippewa being capable of anything as horrendous as this.

And Strong Branch? he wondered, arching an eyebrow.

Gah-ween, no. Strong Branch did not *hate* Night Hawk.

He just wanted to steal what was his so that he would be the most powerful of the two in the eyes of the Chippewa.

"White Wolf," Echohawk said, the words bitter even as they crossed his lips, as though having bitten into a sour grape. "Could it be White Wolf? Has he waited until my son got to his prime and then taken him away? Would he not know that this would hurt me more than if he had stuck a knife into my heart?"

Frustration set in and a dull ache knotted within his chest. Even though he truly believed that White Wolf could be responsible for his son's abduction, no one knew where White Wolf was. He had been elusive for years. And even though White Wolf was suspected of being responsible for the raids on the white settlers, the white pony soldiers had not been able to find his hideout.

Echohawk's eyes widened and a small ray of hope flashed within his troubled mind. He knew of a man whose reputation had been joined with White Wolf's many years ago.

Blackie. Blackie Collins! The gambler and highwayman turned politician.

"Blackie, after all these years, it is time for us to meet again," he said, recalling the last time they had come face to face, clashing. It had been many, many moons ago, yet it seemed as though only yesterday.

Rushing down the path that led him from the butte, Echohawk realized that perhaps Blackie, who no longer went by that name, was an upstanding man, yet Echohawk did not think so. Once a lying, cheating crook, always a crook. And back then, no man could have been more crooked or dirty-dealing as Blackie Collins.

With the sky splashed crimson in the morning sunrise, Echohawk went on through the forest. He would tell his wife that he would be traveling into St. Paul, yet he would not tell her the reason why. As far as she would know, Night Hawk was safe, doing his daily chores that often kept him from his mother's wigwam now that he was an adult with his own life to lead.

She would never know that her son was in *nah-nee-zah-ni-zee,* danger.

Hopefully, there would never be a need to tell her, Echohawk worried to himself.

12

Be strong!
Say not; The days are evil,
Who's to blame?

—Babcock

Her paintbrush steady in her hand, her fingers deftly adding the final touches of color to a painting that she was completing, Briana sniffed the tantalizing aromas wafting from the kitchen and up the staircase outside her room, realizing that it would soon be time for lunch. She planned to take it alone in her bedroom, as she had her breakfast. She not only lacked the stomach to take meals with her uncle after last night and his fit of violence, she did not want to show off her black eye more than was necessary.

One maid was enough.

Briana had recruited Maria, her personal maid, to see to her needs.

But soon, no matter how embarrassed Briana would be to stand before the people of St. Paul with a blackened eye, she was going to walk determinedly to the podium and allow everyone to see exactly what her uncle was capable of. Surely they would decide that a man of violence had no place representing them in Washington.

This gave her cause to smile, knowing that this chance to ruin her uncle would come tonight. There was to be another political rally close to the capitol building. It had been highly advertised in the city's two newspapers.

A sudden commotion below in her uncle's study caused Briana's eyes to widen and her paintbrush to drag out the color of orange on a sunset into a wavering smear, disgruntling her. She sighed heavily, knowing that no amount of effort could repair this blunder—it was ruined! Absolutely ruined!

She slammed her paintbrush onto her palette and started to remove the painting from her easel, but stopped, alarmed, when the commotion became louder beneath her, the voices in a heated debate. And when the name Night Hawk could be distinguished from the rest of the words being shouted, Briana paled, and for the moment stood frozen to the spot.

With an anxious heartbeat she rushed to the door and opened it. She stepped gingerly out into the corridor, hoping that this would enable her to hear what was being said more clearly.

Why was her uncle discussing Night Hawk? Who was so angrily discussing Night Hawk with her uncle?

The thought frightened her. She knew that her uncle was capable of anything, especially if it had to do with Night Hawk. He surely would go to any lengths to see him dead—and that thought sent spirals of terror through her, knowing that he had the means and the money to pay someone to see the deed done.

Stepping lightly, she went to the head of the staircase and leaned against the banister, peering down at the closed door to the study. Her eyes widened and her pulse raced listening to the angry debate, now realizing that the man with her uncle was Night Hawk's father—Echohawk!

She was stunned, having never before seen any Indians at her uncle's mansion, knowing that the bigot would never allow it. This had to mean that Echohawk had arrived unannounced, and that her uncle had been forced to listen to what the Chippewa chief had to say.

She grew numb and covered her mouth with a hand, gasping when she heard Echohawk demanding to know where White Wolf's hideout was, for he was surely responsible for Night Hawk's disappearance!

"Night Hawk has been abducted?" Briana whispered, paling, her knees weakening. Hardly able to stand there just listening, wanting to demand answers from her uncle herself, almost certain that he was responsible for her loved one's disappearance, she held herself back and listened.

Echohawk leaned his face into Blackie's. "Many years ago you were in alliance with White Wolf," he said, his voice steady yet threatening at the same time. "Although you now hide behind the mask of a politician, Echohawk knows that you still mingle with renegades. Now tell me, Blackie, where can I find White Wolf? There I will find my son!"

Blackie went to his desk, lifted a cigar that he had left resting on an ashtray, and placed it between his lips. Smoke spiraled upward, his eyes squinting behind it. "Your son and White Wolf may have become friends, working for a common cause—to scare the hell out of the settlers, stealing from them," he said out of the corner of his mouth, the cigar fat and obtrusive in the other corner. "Who is to say that maybe they got caught while raiding and were lynched on the spot?"

Blackie gestured with a hand, as though drawing a picture before Echohawk's eyes. "I can see it now," he taunted. "The rope tight around Night Hawk's broken neck, his tongue hanging out with flies buzzing around it. His raven black hair is blowing in the breeze, his body swinging back and forth, his bare toes pointing down to the ground. . . ."

Hearing such a horrible description of Night Hawk's possible demise, Briana felt faint. She grabbed the banister and steadied herself, tears flooding her eyes. Then she jumped with alarm when she heard Echohawk's explosive reaction below.

Echohawk moved as quickly as a panther across the room and reached across the desk. Grabbing Blackie by the throat, he lifted him from the floor. "You go too far, *chee-mo-ko-man,* white man!" he growled, tightening his fingers around Blackie's throat, causing the cigar to pop from his mouth and his eyes to bulge.

"Let . . . me . . . down!" Blackie gasped, grabbing at Echohawk's fingers. "I'll . . . call . . . the law on you! I should've the minute you stepped inside my house!"

"But you did not," Echohawk said, jerking his hands away, letting Blackie fall back to his feet. "You wanted to have some fun first with an *ah-nee-shee-nah-bay,* Indian. Is that not true?"

"No time spent with an Injun is fun," Blackie said, rubbing his raw throat. He walked quickly to the door and flung it open. "Leave now, or by God, you'll be the one hanging with a noose around your neck. I'll see to it, Echohawk. Do you hear? Now get out!"

"Echohawk leaves, but only because it is my duty to think of my people first, myself last," he grumbled, walking slowly toward the door. "Without me, and now my son, they would be lost." He stepped up to the door and glared at Blackie. "You know my son would never ride with White Wolf in raids. His heart is peaceful. If he is with White Wolf, it is because White Wolf forced him!" He took a threatening step closer. "If anything happens to my son, I will be back. And your death will not be quick. I shall take you far away and take my time killing you!"

Blackie swallowed hard as he watched Echohawk stroll in a dignified manner from the room and down the narrow corridor. He inhaled a heavy breath of relief as Echohawk then left the house, yet he was already weaving a plan that would finally rid the land of the cocky Chippewa chief.

He smiled, knowing that Echohawk would never have the chance to enter this mansion again. Soon, Echohawk would be walking among his ancestors in his "Land of the Hereafter," hopefully with Night Hawk walking along beside him.

Briana stood like a stone as she watched her uncle finally return to his study, slamming the door behind him. She sighed deeply, her mind spinning with how she might be able to help Night Hawk, knowing that nothing could keep her in her bedroom, safe, while the man she loved was out there somewhere in danger.

She went to her bedroom and closed the door softly behind her, then began pacing back and forth. Her heart pounded out the seconds that she was not with Night Hawk, knowing that time was wasting while she stayed there in her room.

"Perhaps he's even dead!" she worried aloud, stopping to peer out the window toward the beckoning forest. "I can hardly bear not knowing!"

She turned and glowered at the closed door, so badly wanting to go to her uncle and force answers from him, but she knew that was impossible. He would never tell her anything that might help her find Night Hawk.

Yet she knew almost for certain that he was behind Night Hawk's disappearance. As far as she knew, her uncle was the only one to truly gain from Night Hawk's absence.

"I can't go to Uncle Blackie and ask him," she kept reminding herself. "I must stay calm and collected so that I can think of what to do, how, and when. I must try and find Night Hawk. I must!"

She had a flash of insight. She stopped in mid-step. "The cave!" she whispered harshly. "The cave where I saw all of the Indians go. Perhaps that is where he's being held prisoner. It did seem a likely place for hiding something or someone."

She went to the window and drew the sheer curtain aside again, looking toward the forest in the distance. "I must go and see," she whispered. "And if he's not there, I will look elsewhere. I won't give up my search until I find him."

Cold fear gripped her at the prospect of what she was planning for herself. She had never been the adventurous sort, having only lived the serene life of an artist.

Yes, that had taken her beyond the city, yet it had not been the adventure she had been seeking. It had been that perfect setting—that perfect sunset, that perfect sky, that perfect flower.

Again she started pacing, wringing her hands as she continued to work out a plan. She had to wait until she could leave the house without her uncle knowing it. He now seemed to be aware of her every move. She suspected that even now he was in his study, listening to her footsteps overhead as she paced, wondering about her sudden restlessness.

"Unless he knows that I heard the confrontation between him and Echohawk, and wonders now what I plan to do about it," she whispered, stopping dead in her tracks, not wanting to get her uncle's suspicions aroused. She wanted him to forget that she was even there. Then she would sneak out of the house, take her uncle's beloved stallion, and ride free of him and his wicked ways.

Once she was gone, even having to leave her beloved painting paraphernalia behind, she knew that she could not return.

She reached a hand to her black eye, feeling the soreness as she pressed her fingers into the bruise beneath it. "No, I can't return, ever," she murmured to herself. "Who is to say what he might do to me next?"

Tiptoeing around the room, avoiding the sections of flooring that she knew creaked when stepped upon, she started gathering clothes from her drawers and chifforobe, placing what she could into a paisley-embroidered satchel.

She eyed her canvases and paints hungrily, yet knew for certain they had to be left behind. Sacrifices had to be made if she were to go searching for Night Hawk. And she was willing to make them.

She eyed the letter that she had penned to her parents, but had not yet mailed. It was too late for such a letter, it seemed, but hopefully not for her and Night Hawk to have a life together.

Her jaw set, her eyes flashing angrily, she tore the letter to shreds, then changed into a heavy riding skirt and long-sleeved blouse, and tied her hair back with a ribbon. She slipped into boots her uncle had recently bought for her riding outings with him, glad for at least this one generous gesture. Unknowingly he had prepared her for leaving him. The riding clothes and boots, and even the wide-brimmed felt hat, were perfect for her escape into the forest.

"And these gloves," she whispered, slipping butter-soft leather gloves onto her hands.

Sighing resolutely, she went to the full-length mirror at the end of the room, grabbed up her hat and plopped it onto her head, and then eyed her reflection in the mirror, smiling.

"Yes, that'll do just fine," she whispered to herself.

She grew tense when she heard the sound of a single horse's hoofbeats leaving the estate grounds. She twirled on a booted heel and rushed to the window. Her eyes widened when she discovered that it was her uncle leaving, goading his beautiful black stallion into a hard gallop.

"He's making it easy for me," Briana said, smiling smugly. "There's more than that stallion in the stable. I'll get the beautiful brown mare that was bought just for my use."

She turned and eyed the drawer in the nightstand. Her heart thundered as she went to it and opened it, eyeing the pistol that lay there. "Uncle Blackie bought it for my protection, so that's exactly how it shall be used," she said, yanking it up, slipping it and several spare bullets into the depths of her deep pocket at the right side of her skirt. "If I'm forced to, I shall even use it to protect myself from my uncle!"

Then a thought came to her that made her heart skip a beat. "Where else could Uncle Blackie be going but to where Night Hawk is being held?" she whispered, a shiver coursing across her flesh to think that she might not get to Night Hawk in time.

She hoped that the route she had taken that day of her outing was closer than the one her uncle was taking. She crept down the stairs, thinking that her uncle might have ordered someone to stand guard. When she found no one, and even saw that she was free to go to the stable without being stopped, she had to believe that it was because her uncle felt that he had the upper hand with her—that he had frightened her into obedience.

"He couldn't be more wrong," Briana laughed, running now, the satchel heavy in her hand, the gun bouncing in her pocket.

* * *

Night Hawk could not tell whether or not a day and night had passed. He had not allowed himself to fall into the trap of sleeping. To survive, he knew that he had to stay alert and find a way of possible escape. Thus far he was helpless, in that each time he tried to work the ropes loose at his wrists, this only caused them to become tighter.

And as he had tried to get to his knees to crawl away he fell back down clumsily to the rock floor of his prison.

Night Hawk's stomach growled almost unmercifully as his nose picked up the scent of food wafting from somewhere close by. His ears picked up the sound of men talking and laughing boisterously, surely around a campfire, eating.

And when his abductors got into a more serious discussion, their laughter fading, he did not have to strain his ears too much to pick up the voice of White Wolf. He spoke more often, and Night Hawk heard him handing out orders about a raid that was to take place tonight.

Then there was silence, except for the crunch of rock as someone came and stood over Night Hawk. Still blindfolded, he could not see who was there, but soon knew why. He felt the heat of a burning stick on the back of his hand, causing the smell of burnt flesh to rise into his nostrils. He winced, yet held back the cry of pain that had risen from his gut to the tip of his tongue.

"What is it you would like to say to White Wolf?" the renegade Sioux said, chuckling low as he continued holding the flaming stick to Night Hawk's hand. "Do you beg White Wolf to stop? Does not your hand pain you? Would you prefer it to be your neck instead?"

Sweat was pearling on Night Hawk's brow as the pain worsened, yet he clenched his teeth together, proving to White Wolf that he would never allow a Sioux to hear this Chippewa show his pain, for this would be humiliating. The pain was much easier to bear than humiliation.

Night Hawk was relieved when White Wolf took the stick away. When he heard the crunch of rock, he realized that White Wolf had decided not to play with him any more this time.

Then, willing himself to bear the pain, Night Hawk tensed and leaned his ear toward the sound of White Wolf's voice as he made a low threat to someone other than his men. He was talking to a woman, ordering her to stay hidden in the depths of the cave with her baby until he returned. He threatened her, telling her that should she do anything to help Night Hawk escape, he would search and find her and cut out her tongue, kill her slowly and unmercifully, and then he would kill the child.

The woman's low sobs tore at Night Hawk's heart, making him forget his own pain. It was obvious that the woman was a prisoner, and more than likely, one forced to share many things sexual with White Wolf, and even perhaps all of the low-down renegades!

The thought of this filled him with intense rage. He vowed

to somehow get loose and not only set himself free but also the woman.

And he had to wonder who the father of the child was. If it was White Wolf, it was apparent that he had no feelings for it.

Night Hawk sucked in his breath and held it for a moment when he heard the other men approaching, their feet crunching loudly in the rocks, their voices low.

When they had passed and everything was silent again, he listened to see if he could hear the woman or the child, but sighed heavily when he heard neither.

It was obvious that White Wolf had frightened the woman into total obedience.

"Set me free and I'll take you out of here," Night Hawk began shouting. "Wherever you are, come out of hiding. I will take you and your child with me. You will be safe. No harm will come to you. I would not allow it."

The ensuing silence disheartened Night Hawk. He again worked with the ropes at his wrist, scooting along the rock floor until he found one sharp enough that he felt might cut the ropes in half. He tightened his jaw as he began to saw the rope back and forth across the jagged rock, hope rising within him.

* * *

Blackie rode hard across the flat stretch of meadow, now seeing Echohawk up ahead. Smiling, he turned his horse in another direction, knowing how he could cut off Echohawk, then take him prisoner.

Echohawk would sit beside his son and they would die together!

Finally, Blackie would get his revenge for those many years ago when Echohawk had humiliated him on the riverboat. He could still feel it now—Echohawk's hands on his ankles, the damn Indian holding Blackie over the sides of the boat while everyone on the riverboat watched, surely feeling Blackie's humiliation.

Blackie had carried this hatred inside him for too long. If

it hadn't been for getting so involved in politics, his main goal in life would have been to go after Echohawk and make his life miserable.

Now riding through the protective covering of the forest, Blackie could see a short distance ahead through a break in the trees where Echohawk had just entered the forest himself. Riding hard, Blackie went onward, then snatched his pistol from its holster at his waist and lifted it, aimed, and fired.

He laughed into the wind and slipped the pistol back inside its holster when he saw that the bullet had hit Echohawk, even if only grazing his right arm. It had been enough to cause Echohawk to fall from his horse. He clutched hard at the wound, blood seeping between his fingers.

Blackie rode up to where Echohawk lay on the ground and reined in his horse. Leaning on the pommel of his saddle, he smiled crookedly down at Echohawk. "Seems we meet again," he said, chuckling.

Echohawk glared up at him, his dark eyes narrowing in hate. *"Geen-gee-wah-nah-dis chee-mo-ko-man,"* he hissed throatily.

The hair rose at the nape of Blackie's neck, not so much because of what Echohawk had said to him but the manner in which it had been spoken. His smugness quickly waned.

13

> Who walks with beauty has no need of fear;
> The sun and moon and stars keep pace with him.
>
> —MORTON

The brown mare was lathered into a sweat. Briana snapped the reins more determinedly and rode hard across the land, first across a stretch of meadow, and then in a slow trot through the denseness of the forest, now almost certain that she was near the cave. She was seeing the setting around her as she had painted it on the canvas, recognizing a certain tree, a certain outcropping of rocks, the silver stream winding across the land beneath the low-hanging branches of elm trees.

Her heart was pounding, her anxiousness to find Night Hawk and save him outweighing any fear that kept trying to edge into her heart at the thought of being caught by either Blackie, or White Wolf!

But the risks were worth it if she was right in her assumption, that those who had abducted Night Hawk were the same Indians that she had seen enter the cave. Or, she despaired to herself, she could be wrong on all counts, and then where would she go? Where would she search? And where would she go when it became dark?

She had left her uncle's home knowing that she could never return. This time he could be waiting for her with a rifle clutched in his hands, a bullet with her name on it waiting for her in its dark chamber.

Briana's heart skipped a beat when she heard hoofbeats of many horses approaching her. Frantically she drew a tight rein on her mare, bringing it to a shuddering halt. She dug the heels of her boots into the flanks of her horse and raced into a thick stand of trees.

Breathless from fear, she quickly slipped out of the saddle. Taking the horse's reins, she led it behind the denseness of some brush and hunkered down, waiting for the riders to pass.

She held her breath as they came closer and closer, then uttered a heavy sigh when they were finally past, the hoofbeats soon fading into the distance.

When she turned around, she was surprised, and grateful in the same heartbeat, when she found that she was within walking distance of the cave. With her pulse racing, she tethered her horse to a low limb of a tree, took the pistol from her pocket, then moved stealthily and breathlessly onward. She constantly surveyed the land around her, watching for any sudden movement, or the signs of someone hiding, guarding the cave.

When she saw that no one was near, she rushed to the cave's entrance and stopped short as she peered inside. Its darkness made her clasp her fingers more tightly around the pistol and swallow back the building fear. The one other time she had discovered the cave, she had not entered it, having viewed the Indians as too dangerous to do anything but flee.

It was the same now as then. She knew too well the risks of being discovered. But she would do anything to find Night Hawk.

Her pulse racing, her knees somewhat weak, Briana tiptoed lightly into the cave, suddenly blind in the darkness. Yet that would not stop her. She would travel the full length of the cave if necessary. She would not give up until she knew that she had searched every inch of it. Even if she had to do it in pitch darkness!

Reaching around until she found a side wall, she began inching her way along, grimacing when the mossy dampness of the wall caused her fingers to become cold and stiff. Listening, she could hear water dripping somewhere in the distance. Her eyes widened when she caught the distinct smell of food cooking over an open fire.

As she made a turn, still letting the wall guide her, her heart fluttered wildly within her chest when she saw the first signs of a fire up ahead.

She lifted her eyes and stopped to give a soft prayer that she was not entering her own death trap, and that she would find Night Hawk alive and well.

Pursing her lips tightly, she moved cautiously ahead, again watching for any signs of movement, relieved when she still saw none.

Determinedly she moved onward. The fire was still quite a distance away, yet its dancing gold light had spread to where Briana was now walking. She gasped as she peered on both sides of the cave passage up ahead, seeing stacks and stacks of firearms. Her heart tightened within her chest when she discovered stacks of dynamite lying around also.

Her legs almost buckled beneath her when she first caught sight of Night Hawk. He sat slumped against the wall, his ankles and wrists bound, his eyes covered with a blindfold.

"Night Hawk!" Briana screamed, throwing all caution to the wind as she began running toward him. "Oh, dear God, Night Hawk, I've found you. Darling, I've found you!"

Night Hawk's head jerked up and he looked sightlessly around him. "Briana?" he gasped, his heart thudding like drums being beaten within his chest. "You are there? How did you know where to find me? Briana, it is not safe! Go! Go now!"

His words of warning were falling on deaf ears. Briana dropped her pistol into her pocket and fell to her knees before Night Hawk. She so badly wanted to hug him, yet knew that she had to hurry. Her uncle could arrive at any moment! He would not hesitate to shoot her as well as Night Hawk. She was more of a threat to her uncle now than an asset he could flaunt before his constituents.

At this moment she realized that by taking flight, she would never get the opportunity to go on the podium with her uncle at his next political rally and expose him for what he truly was.

But there were other ways to do that. Hopefully she would be given the opportunity. If she got out of this cave with Night Hawk in one piece!

Briana's fingers trembled as she untied the blindfold, letting it drop to reveal his midnight dark eyes that had mesmerized her the very first moment she had lain eyes on him. Her eyes locked with his for a moment, and then she bent over him and began untying his wrists. She paled when the light of the fire revealed his tortured hand to her.

"Oh, Lord," she cried, lifting the hand, examining the wound. It was red and raw. "They tortured you!"

She wanted to take the time to doctor his wound, but knew that time was running out for them.

Her uncle. He could arrive anytime!

Somehow the villain would pay for what he had done to Night Hawk. She knew that he had to be responsible. Who else would gain so much by Night Hawk's absence . . . or death?

Tears near, she quickly untied Night Hawk's ankles. His powerful hands were suddenly at her shoulders, drawing her directly before him. She could see in his eyes that he had discovered the black eye that proved her uncle's abuse.

"Who did this to you?" he growled.

"Perhaps the same person that did that to your hand," Briana said, holding back a sob.

"Your uncle did not burn my hand," Night Hawk said, loosening his grip on her shoulders. He framed her face between his hands and drew her lips close to his. "My beautiful Briana. You came in the face of danger to rescue me. How did you know about the cave? It belongs to White Wolf and his renegades. He is the one who abducted me. Of course, I do not hold your uncle blameless. He is in cohoots with White Wolf. He is as guilty!"

"I'll tell you later," Briana said, slipping away from him. She rose to her feet, taking him by the hand, urging him up. "My uncle left before me. He could be arriving soon. We must be gone!" She looked down at his hand again. "We must doctor that wound. It—it could become infected. You—you could lose the hand."

Frowning, Night Hawk looked past her, at the cache of firearms and ammunition. "My concerns are not for my own welfare," he said, taking her by the elbow, hurrying her away into the outer darkness of the cave. "If your uncle can hit an innocent woman, there is no telling what he would do if he found you here, obviously where the loot from the raids is being stored. We will leave now and I will tend to him later. He will regret the day he was born—especially the day he laid a hand on you!"

Then Night Hawk abruptly came to a halt. He turned and stared at the distant soft light of the flames from a campfire, where the woman had surely prepared the food for the renegades—where she had probably sat while nursing her infant.

She was White Wolf's prisoner. Night Hawk had to save her and the child.

He turned to Briana. "You stay here," he flatly ordered. "I've something to do. Someone to get. *O-wahbum-ow-way-nayn-yah-ow,* I must go look for her."

Briana's eyes became wild and wide, fearing that they had already taken too much time. "No," she cried, grabbing him by the arm and trying to pull him onward. "We can't. My uncle could arrive at any moment. Please, Night Hawk. So far we've been lucky. Let's get out of here. Now!"

Night Hawk brushed her hand aside. He started walking away from her toward the light of the fire. "You go on outside," he said over his shoulder. "I will follow soon. *Wi-yee-bah,* soon! Leave now. Who can say why no guard was watching the entrance of the cave when you arrived here? Perhaps he will return at any moment. Go to safety while you can!"

Frustrated, Briana chewed on her lower lip, then broke into a run and moved up beside him. She walked with him, pleading with him. "Who are you going after?" she asked. "I saw no one but you."

"There is a woman," Night Hawk said thickly. "There is a child. I cannot leave them behind. They are *gee-tay-bee-bee-nah,* captives, also. I must release them from their captivity."

"A woman?" Briana said softly, lifting an eyebrow. "A child?"

Night Hawk said no more. He hastened his steps and moved through the part of the cave where he had been imprisoned, stunned anew by the number of firearms there, and then moved past them, finally arriving at the campfire. He stood with his hands on his hips and looked around, seeing the bedding, the clothes, and the cooking utensils. He gazed at the pot of stew cooking over the fire, then past this into the deeper depths of the cave.

"I know you are there!" he shouted. "*Mah-bee-szhon,* come. I am free now. I can take you to safety!"

When there was no response, Night Hawk cupped a hand over his mouth and shouted again. "There is not much time!" he said. "Come now, or I will be forced to leave you and the child. You will be again at the mercy of White Wolf and his renegades. Surely you wish for a better life than this!"

Again there was silence. Briana moved to Night Hawk's side. "She's too afraid to come out of hiding," she murmured.

"She has good reason to be," Night Hawk grumbled, moving quickly around the fire.

He began looking for them, but soon discovered that the cave separated into different avenues at this point, giving the woman and child many opportunities for hiding. He was losing hope of ever finding them.

Sighing, he returned to Briana. "She does not want to be found," he said, shaking his head slowly. "Her future and the child's is bleak. And that is *gee-mah-szhan-dum,* said. There is no need for it. I could take her to my village. She would be welcomed. Whether she is red-skinned or white, she could stay there forever, her child being raised among the best of people."

Briana was getting edgy. "Let's go," she pleaded. "You did all that you could. Now let us try to save ourselves." She glanced down at his injured hand. "And I've got to find a way to medicate your hand as soon as possible."

Looking back over his shoulder a last time, Night Hawk hurried alongside Briana through the cave. When he saw the weapons again, his jaw tightened. "My hand is *way-way-nee-ee-shee-ah-yah-mah-gud,* fine," he grumbled. "What we must do now is go to my village, get many armed braves, then come back to the cave and get these weapons. We will also search the cave from end to end and find the woman and child. Once they and the firearms are taken to my village, many Chippewa braves will go after White Wolf."

He paused and added, "And soon, your *gee-szhee-shay,* uncle," he growled. "If he thinks he is going to escape the wrath of Night Hawk, he is mistaken!"

Together they stepped out into the twilight of evening. Briana took Night Hawk to her horse. Together they rode away, Briana snuggled on the saddle behind him, her arms wrapped solidly around his waist, so glad that she had been given the opportunity to be with him again. Through the traumas of this night, she had discovered that Night Hawk was most definitely not involved with renegades. For this she was most grateful.

* * *

Blackie gave Echohawk a shove into the cave. "Just keep walking," he snarled. He stepped up behind Echohawk and pushed the barrel of his rifle into his back. "Move slowly ahead of me. If you try anything, you will have more to worry about than a mere flesh wound in the arm."

Echohawk said nothing, his heartbeat anxious. Blackie had said that he was going to join Night Hawk. That had to mean that his son was being held in this cave. Echohawk was allowing Blackie to feel smug in his abduction, biding his time until he was with his son. Together they could take flight—with Blackie finally dead!

"White Wolf isn't here to greet you," Blackie said, laughing softly. "Nor are any of his renegades. Their horses are usually corralled just inside the entrance of the cave." He chuckled. "It seems they're out having some fun at the expense of some of my constituents. I guess losing a couple more voters won't interfere in my being elected."

"You will not live long enough to see election day," Echohawk threatened. "In fact, I would say that you are taking the final breaths of your life. You have to know that you cannot get away with abducting two powerful Chippewa. If I do not kill you first, my braves will tear the countryside apart until they find you."

"Who says I abducted two Injuns?" Blackie said, giving Echohawk a nudge with the rifle barrel as they walked farther into the dank darkness of the cave. "As I see it, I have only one damn Injun on my hands, either to hang or shoot."

"You spoke of my son earlier," Echohawk said, his jaw tightening.

"Yes, I think I did," Blackie said, his voice filled with amusement. "But I only ordered the abduction. I didn't actually do it."

"White Wolf did the deed for you," Echohawk said, his gaze picking up a slight wavering of light from a fire on the cave ceiling a short distance away. His trained ears picked up the sound of trickling water of a spring, and his nose, the aroma of food cooking.

"Let's just say that it's done and soon you'll both be dead," Blackie said. "Now just shut up and move on. I don't like debating anything with you, a dumb Injun. I leave that for my cohorts in St. Paul."

Echohawk walked softly in his moccasins, looking anxiously ahead. When he turned a corner and got his first sight of the firearms, his insides tensed. It was apparent now that White Wolf and his renegades *were* responsible for the raids that were terrorizing the countryside. And it was obvious why they raided—to build their supply of firearms!

But why? he wondered.

"And so you see the firearms?" Blackie said, shoving Echohawk into the main chamber of the cave. "Does it make fear grab your guts? I guess you have to know that I agree with White Wolf about how he plans to use them. He's going to rid the land of a few Injuns for me!"

Echohawk turned and glared at White Wolf. "You are an *gah-gay-go-gee-kan-deh-zeen-ee-mee-nee,* ignorant man," he said, his teeth clenched. "You think White Wolf will stop at just killing innocent Chippewa? He will also kill as many whites as he has ammunition for. That means he will probably take over Fort Snelling and the city of St. Paul." He laughed softly. "He will probably make your house his *en-dah-yen,* lodge!"

Blackie paled and he took an uneasy step backward, his eyes flashing as he thrust the rifle barrel into Echohawk's chest. "Just shut up with your Chippewa mumbo-jumbo," he growled. "Do you hear? I don't want to hear any more of that nonsense. White Wolf is my partner."

Blackie glanced away from Echohawk, slowly around the cave, feeling a sudden absence. Where the hell was Night Hawk? he wondered, panic rising within him.

Keeping a steady aim on Echohawk, Blackie began slowly walking around, thinking that perhaps White Wolf had hidden Night Hawk behind some of the stacks of ammunition.

"Night Hawk, where are you, you sonofabitch?" he finally shouted, knowing that Night Hawk could not answer, having been gagged.

Echohawk was beginning to fear that something was wrong. It was obvious that Blackie had expected to find Night Hawk there. The thought that White Wolf had possibly gone ahead and killed him caused his knees to grow unsteady and a bitterness to rise into his throat.

When Blackie shouted another name, a woman's name, Echohawk's eyebrows rose in surprise.

"Gentle Fawn, damn it, get out here," Blackie shouted. "It's me, Blackie. Now get out here this minute, or by God, I'll come shooting. Both you and your kid will be killed. White Wolf can always find himself another broad to keep his bed warm at night. One that doesn't have a brat sucking on a tit morning till night."

Echohawk scarcely breathed as he watched a beautiful woman step into view a short distance away. A child wrapped in soft doeskin was held protectively within her arms. He was taken quickly by her loveliness, her innocence.

A slow ache crept into his heart as he continued gazing at Gentle Fawn. He felt as though he was being catapulted back into time, as though his beloved first wife, Fawn, were there. This young woman who bore half of his dearly departed wife's name was almost a mirror image of Fawn.

That she carried a child in her arms made the comparison twice as painful—it was as though this child was the unborn child that had died at the exact moment his wife had been slain, but was now miraculously alive.

He ached to rush to her, to hold her, to say endearing things to her.

And then shame engulfed him, for while he had been transported back in time almost forty winters, he had forgotten his present, beloved wife, Mariah.

Gentle Fawn walked slowly toward Blackie, her heart pounding out of fear of what he had threatened to do. She had learned to live in fear, yet had no choice but to stay. White Wolf's threats were never idle.

"What do you want with Gentle Fawn?" she asked meekly. She held her daughter more tightly to her bosom when Blackie gave an ugly snarl as he looked at the bundle with utter disgust.

Gentle Fawn turned her sad, wondering eyes on Echohawk, seeing the kindness in his eyes, mingled with a strange sort of anxiety. She gazed slowly down at his injured arm, knowing that it needed attention, then back at Blackie, thinking that the evil white man had different plans than offering any sort of medical assistance. He more than likely planned to kill this handsome Indian, as he had planned to kill the Chippewa called Night Hawk.

She smiled to herself, glad that at least he had been able to escape.

"Where's Night Hawk?" Blackie said, holding a steady aim on Echohawk.

"Gone," Gentle Fawn said thinly, flinching when Blackie's face turned grotesque in his anger.

"You removed the ropes that bound him?" he said darkly. "You let him go?"

Tears flooded Gentle Fawn's eyes, fear revealed in their depths. "No!" she cried. "I did not do that. Someone else. A lady. She came and set him free. I could not stop them. Please. Please do not blame me!"

"A lady?" Blackie said, arching a thick, dark eyebrow. "What lady?"

"She was called Briana by the captive," Gentle Fawn said, swallowing hard.

"Briana?" Blackie gasped, paling. "My niece?"

Blackie was stunned at first; how had Briana known to

come to the cave and rescue Night Hawk? Then anger quickly seized him at the thought of her going this far over her love for the Indian, no matter how she had discovered him or where he had been held hostage.

How could she have done this? She was risking her whole future as an artist over an Indian.

Then another thought came to him that seized him with panic. Surely she would discover his role in this abduction, if she hadn't already. He had to wonder what she would do about the information. Would she use it against him? Or would she keep quiet for the sake of the family name?

He glared down at Gentle Fawn. "You dumb broad," he said. "If my future is ruined because of what happened here today, you will pay. Do you hear?"

He inhaled a desperate breath as he looked around the cave at the supply of firearms, ammunition, and dynamite. His fingers began to tremble, realizing that if Night Hawk was free, he would be returning with his Chippewa braves to take the firearms and to finish off White Wolf and whoever was in the cave. And also to point an accusing finger at Blackie!

"How long has White Wolf been gone?" Blackie asked, his eyes narrowing as he looked over at Gentle Fawn.

"A short while," Gentle Fawn said faintly.

"Enough time for me to catch up with them, I hope," Blackie said, giving Echohawk another nudge with his rifle barrel. "Go over there. Sit down against the wall."

He gazed angrily down at the ropes that had held Night Hawk captive, then glanced over at Gentle Fawn. "Put the brat down and tie up the chief," he ordered. "Tie his wrists and ankles. And do a good job. If he escapes, by God, you'll be sorry."

Trembling from fear, Gentle Fawn carefully laid her child on the ground, then went to Echohawk and knelt down before him. She quickly tied his wrists together and then his ankles, then stopped and gazed into his eyes.

"*Gee-mah-szhan-dum,* I am sorry," she murmured. "Truly I am."

Echohawk realized by the language she spoke that she was

of Chippewa descent. Remembrances of his first wife again pierced his heart. She had been Chippewa! She had been as sweet and innocent!

He was deeply touched by this young woman, and what she must have suffered at the hands of White Wolf and his renegades. Somehow he would find a way to release her from her misery.

And if the day came, he would take her back to his village with him and try to make all wrongs right for her.

"If I don't get back here soon enough with White Wolf, and I'm forced to go into hiding with him because your son escaped today, I'll be back. I won't stop, Echohawk, until I see both you and your son dead," Blackie growled.

With that statement he spun on a heel and ran from the cave.

Gentle Fawn reached a hand to Echohawk's wounded arm. "I will make it *nah-wudge-o-nee-shee-shin,* better," she said, smiling warmly at Echohawk—a smile that touched his soul with a remembrance of what it was to be young again.

He returned the smile and nodded.

14

Serene I fold my arms and wait.

—Burroughs

Night Hawk rode into his village and passed the outdoor fire that was lifting its light into the dark heavens. He drew his reins before his wigwam. He slid easily from his saddle, and Briana dismounted before he could offer his assistance. It was obvious to her that his hand was paining him more than he would admit.

She moved to his side, wanting to take another close look at the hand, but was stopped when several braves approached Night Hawk with questions, everyone speaking at once.

"My friends, we have no time for discussing where I have been, or why I have returned with a white woman," Night Hawk said, interrupting them, causing a strained silence. "Saddle your horses. We have much to do, and there is little time in which to do it!"

He turned and saw his mother step into view at the entrance of her wigwam. She was so thin and frail in her cotton nightgown, she looked no more than something the wind might grab up and send floating away in the breeze.

Mariah moved slowly toward her son, each step obviously an effort. When she reached him, she placed a trembling, weak hand to his cheek. "My *nin-gwis,* son," she murmured. "Where have you been?" She looked slowly around her, her gaze stopping momentarily on Briana, then peered up at Night Hawk again. "Your father? He is not with you? I missed you both all day. I thought you may have decided to join in a hunt."

"*Gee-mah-mah,* I have not been with Father," Night Hawk said, fear suddenly gripping his insides. "He has been gone long? Did he not tell you where he was going? Mother, this is not like *gee-bah-bah*. He never leaves without first telling you about it."

"Sometimes he does not tell me everything," Mariah said, swallowing hard. "You see, Night Hawk, he doesn't want to worry me." She looked slowly over at Briana again. "Who is this woman? Why is she here?"

Night Hawk reached for Briana's hand and drew her close to his side. "She saved my life," he said. "Her name is Briana Collins." He frowned down at her. "She has yet to tell me how she knew I was in the cave, being held prisoner. But that she did is all that is important now."

Mariah swayed and placed a hand on her throat, alarmed that her son had been held captive. Night Hawk caught her and drew her into his arms. "It is all right, *gee-mah-mah,*" he reassured her. "I am safe now. Father will be also. I promise you that."

He held her for a moment longer, then eased her out of his arms and turned to face his braves, who had brought their saddled horses and were standing beside them, awaiting Night Hawk's orders.

"My friends, it seems we have another reason for riding tonight," he growled. "My father is missing. We must search and find him!"

A warm hand in his made Night Hawk turn wondering eyes down to Briana.

"Night Hawk, the reason I came searching for you was because your father came to my Uncle Blackie. He demanded that my uncle tell him where you were," she said. "I heard your father saying that he knew that my uncle had been in cohoots with White Wolf many years ago, and suspected that he was now. I heard him threaten my uncle, and in return, my uncle threatened him. Your father left when he could not get the answers he sought." She paused and swallowed hard. "My uncle left shortly after your father left. Perhaps he was going after Chief Echohawk? Could he be the reason your father hasn't returned?"

Night Hawk's jaw tightened and his eyes narrowed angrily.

"The cave," he said. "He has probably taken my father to the cave, thinking that I would still be there. What a triumph for him if he could abduct and kill both Chief Echohawk and his son."

He turned to a young brave. "Go to my dwelling quickly!" he shouted. "Get my rifle and gunsling. Bring them to me. *Wee-weeb,* quickly!"

Without further thought, even forgetting the pain in his hand, Night Hawk swung himself into the saddle of Briana's horse, not taking the time to go and get his own trusted steed.

Time was of the essence. And although he was weary from lack of sleep, and hungry from lack of food, nothing was important to him now—only his father!

He knew the importance of arriving at the cave before his absence was discovered. Once it was, and if his father was a prisoner of the same gang of renegades, Chief Echohawk might not live this night out.

The young brave brought Night Hawk his rifle and gunsling. He then slipped Briana's satchel from the side of the saddle, where she had placed it, and handed it down to her. He then secured his gunsling to the horn of the saddle and thrust his rifle into it.

"You will be all right here with my people," he said softly to Briana. He smiled over at his mother. "Go with Mother. She will welcome you as though she has known you forever. She is that sort of woman, compassionate and caring."

Mariah stepped to Briana's side and placed a frail arm around her waist, proof that Night Hawk knew his mother well. Briana smiled at her, then, clutching the handle of her satchel, she nodded her head and smiled through a haze of tears up at Night Hawk.

Yet she knew that at the first opportunity she would flee into the night herself, knowing that she would never be able to wait to see if her beloved came out of this ordeal without further wounds. She wanted to help him in his fight.

"God speed," she said, sniffling as tears crept down her cheeks. She mouthed the words "I love you" in a whisper that she saw pleased him.

Reaching her free hand inside her skirt pocket, she circled her fingers around the small pistol. She held onto it tightly as she watched Night Hawk and his braves ride away. Mariah gently placed a hand under her elbow and guided her to the warmth of her wigwam, settling her down beside the fire on a pallet of pelts.

Briana gazed at a sleeping platform in the dark shadows of the wigwam. Someone was asleep on it. She had to believe that was Lily, Night Hawk's sister. She then looked back at Mariah as the older woman leaned down and whispered to her.

"I wish I felt like talking," Mariah said, wheezing, the exertion of having gone outside to see Night Hawk having taken its toll. "But I must go on to bed. Please understand. I-I'm not at all well."

"Please don't worry on my account," Briana said, sad to see this lady who had traces of once having been beautiful, now so thin, almost to the point of death. "I'll sit here for a while beside the fire, and then I'll stretch out and go to sleep myself."

"Tomorrow when I am rested, I would like to talk to you at length about what has happened, and about how you happen to know my son," Mariah said, getting more breathless by the moment. She placed a hand on her throat, gasping for air. "I-I must lie down."

Pityingly, Briana watched Mariah go to a sleeping platform piled high with comfortable blankets and pelts. She saw the effort it took for the woman to get onto the platform and position the blankets comfortably over herself.

Briana then watched and listened, hardly able to wait until she knew that Night Hawk's mother was asleep. She wanted to be able to find Night Hawk before he reached the cave.

She wanted to be with him, no matter what transpired between the renegades and the Chippewa braves. She wanted to be there for him if he needed her.

Laying her satchel aside when she realized that Mariah was finally asleep, Briana crept to her feet. She looked guardedly from Mariah to Lily, then lifted the entrance flap and stepped outside into the stillness of night.

Somewhat disoriented, she stood there for a moment. Then the neighing of horses drew her in the right direction.

Soon she was riding away from the village on a horse, the night air cold against her face. But she continued onward, hoping that she was going in the right direction. While on the horse with Night Hawk, he had been the one leading the way. She had not thought to see exactly which route he took.

She continued riding for a while through the forest, across meadows, and then suddenly she felt herself being thrown across the horse's head, realizing that it had tripped in a gopher hole.

When she hit the ground, her head cracked hard against it, knocking her unconscious.

* * *

Blackie drew his reins as he saw White Wolf approach in the splash of moonlight. When the Sioux reined in beside him, Blackie explained why he was there, and the urgency in returning to the cave.

"You found Night Hawk gone?" White Wolf hissed, reaching over to grab Blackie by the throat. "Do you think I will believe that you are not responsible? You are a coward! You went and set him free because you thought over what you had ordered me to do and feared his father's wrath, then pretended he escaped!"

"You damn Injun, let go of my throat," Blackie said, coughing. "Let me tell you the rest. I abducted Echohawk. I only went to the cave to take him there, to let him join his son! I was handing him over to you, White Wolf, to do with him as you pleased. He's still there, damn it! At least you still have him to toy with."

White Wolf dropped his hand from Blackie's throat. His eyes gleamed. "You abducted Chief Echohawk?" he said, laughing. "He is in the cave?"

"That's what I said, isn't it?" Blackie grumbled, frowning. He rubbed his raw throat, his hate for White Wolf swelling, not sure how much longer he would tolerate him. He put up with him only to get him to do his dirty work. But when White Wolf became more of a threat than a help, Blackie would kill him.

"That is good," White Wolf said, rubbing his chin. "We will soon have Night Hawk again as prisoner. He will come for his father. We will be ready!"

Blackie edged his horse closer to White Wolf's. "You damn idiot, the first thing we've got to do is move the ammunition," he growled. "We can worry about Night Hawk and Echohawk later."

Anger flared in White Wolf's eyes. "How did Night Hawk escape?" he hissed. "Is Gentle Fawn responsible? She was the only one there to help with the escape."

Blackie swallowed hard, not wanting to disclose that his niece was responsible. Yet he could not cast the blame on Gentle Fawn, either, for once White Wolf discovered the truth, Blackie would be the one to pay, and he did not want to imagine the ways in which he would. He had seen White Wolf's ways of torturing those from whom he wanted obedience.

"I questioned Gentle Fawn," Blackie said guardedly. "She said that she didn't release Night Hawk. God, White Wolf, you know she wouldn't. Your threats lie heavy on her heart. She's scared to death of you!"

"Then how?" White Wolf cried.

"Night Hawk is a crafty sonofabitch," Blackie said hoarsely. "He could probably escape from a pit of rattlesnakes." He chuckled. "As for Echohawk, it won't be that easy. I wounded him."

"That is good," White Wolf said, also chuckling. "That is very good." He raised a fist in the air. "Let us ride! Let us go to the cave and move the firearms to our next best hideout—to the other cave that we have used from time to time. No one will ever find it." He smiled over at Blackie. "As for Echohawk, we will take him with us. We will keep him alive awhile longer, at least long enough to see his son die. Night Hawk *will* be our prisoner again! Soon!"

Blackie smiled, yet could not help but worry about Night Hawk being free, and about his niece possibly knowing about his secret alliance with White Wolf. Both could ruin his political career.

As he slapped his reins, sending his horse into a gallop beside White Wolf's, he became calmer. Who would believe an Indian over him? As for his niece, he doubted if anyone would listen to her once they saw that she had joined up with an Indian, for in the eyes of most white people, it was forbidden for a white woman to love an Indian. They would look down their noses at her and pity her uncle.

He smiled broadly, feeling confident that everything would work out after all. Somehow, for him, it always seemed to. He shrugged, thinking that now was no different.

And what did they know, anyhow? Only Echohawk knew the truth, and he was being held prisoner. Yes, besides Echohawk, there was no actual proof. And Blackie knew the art of playing the role of an innocent man to the hilt.

When they arrived at the cave, much haste was made to load the firearms onto the horses, leaving the dynamite and some of the ammunition scattered along the floor of the cave.

After everyone was safely out of the cave, Echohawk was tied onto a horse on his stomach. Gentle Fawn walked beside his horse, clutching her child to her bosom. Finally, a torch was pitched into the cave.

As they rode away, they soon heard the explosion, felt the ground shake with the force of it, and saw the sky light up with the crimson flash of the fire.

Blackie slapped White Wolf on the back, laughing, then they fled into the depths of the forest.

* * *

Night Hawk heard the explosion and saw the sky light up. A gnawing agony swept through him, knowing that anything that exploded with such force had to be caused by dynamite. And that meant that the cave had just exploded. In that cave could have been his father!

He hung his head, hoping that he was wrong, then more determinedly rode through the forest until they came close enough to see the fire that had spread to the banks of the river, twisting cool and serene just below the cave entrance.

He jumped from his horse and searched as close as he could to the hot debris of the cave, yet saw nothing akin to the remains of a body. He wondered about the woman and child, and whether or not they had been out of the cave at the time of the explosion. Had it gone off by accident? Or had someone purposely set it?

He then quickly remounted his horse and rode away with his braves, back in the direction of his village. Hopefully he had been wrong to think his father had been abducted. Hopefully, it had just taken him longer to get home today, perhaps having been sidetracked by something more innocent than White Wolf or Blackie.

His heart pounded with a dull throbbing as each mile was traveled. Finally, he was back at his village. He slid quickly out of his saddle and went to his parents' wigwam. He grew frantic when he discovered that not only was his father gone, but so was Briana!

He went to his mother and gave her a gentle shake. "Where is Briana?" he asked, his voice hollow. "Mother, where is she?"

Mariah leaned up on an elbow and looked around her. "She was here when I fell asleep," she said, wiping her eyes sleepily. She looked with alarm up at Night Hawk. "Your father? Did you find him?"

Night Hawk shook his head, despair filling him.

He left again, this time alone, and searched the forest until he almost dropped from hunger and lack of sleep.

Downcast, and shaken to the core by his losses, Night Hawk returned home. He went to his wigwam and fell into a restless sleep.

15

Let wish and magic work at will in you.

—DRISCOLL

The aroma of rabbit stew awakened Night Hawk from his troubled sleep. His stomach responded to the smell with a low, rumbling growl, and he leaned up on an elbow. By the dim glow of his lodge fire, he made out a figure sitting beside the fire pit, hanging a pot over the flames, and then adding more wood to the fire. Night Hawk's first thoughts were of Briana.

Through the golden haze of his wigwam he saw the petiteness of her straight back as she leaned over closer to the fire on her bent knees. He saw the swirl of hair across her shoulders, then her delicate fingers.

But when she turned and faced him, he was quickly awakened from the illusion, a wish so deep that even now it seemed lodged in his heart. He realized that the young and beautiful thing looking after his interests this morning was not Briana at all, but his sister, Lily.

She crawled to his bedside and placed a gentle hand on his cheek. "You are awake," she said, smiling sweetly at him. "Did you sleep well, my brother?"

"Well enough," Night Hawk said, not wanting to tell her that he tossed most of the night, dreams of various things haunting him—especially of his beloved father and woman being somewhere out there in the forest in danger.

"I have brought you food," Lily said. "I have built you a fire." She glanced over her shoulder, then back at Night Hawk. "I have gone to the river and brought you fresh water for bathing. I have also brought new moccasins that I beaded for you."

"You are too kind to your brother," Night Hawk said,

brushing his blankets aside. "Is there a reason for you being this attentive to Night Hawk?"

Lily cast her eyes downward, guilt washing through her, yet she knew she could not reveal to her brother what troubled her day and night.

She was concerned about her unborn child and ached to confide in Night Hawk about it, yet she could not. He no longer approved of Strong Branch. He would shame her for allowing herself to get so intimate with him.

No, she could not share this secret with her brother. She could not share it with anyone, except the father of her child.

She would have to tell Strong Branch soon. Or it would be too late. She would soon be showing.

"Lily?" Night Hawk said, placing a finger under her chin, lifting it so that their eyes met. "What are you not telling your brother?" His gaze swept over her face. "You are pale this morning. Why is that, Lily?"

"There are many reasons," she murmured, her throat tight. "Most of which trouble you also my brother. Yes, my heart lies heavily within my chest today, as I am sure it does in yours."

"Yes, very," Night Hawk said, swinging his legs over the sides of the sleeping platform.

He held his face in his hands a moment, trying to sort out exactly what his first move would be today.

He had to search for Briana and his father. He would send braves in different directions. Surely someone would find his woman and father.

He looked anxiously up at Lily. "Father?" he said. "Tell me that he arrived home safely last night. Tell me, Lily, that Briana has found her way back to our village. I cannot believe that she returned to St. Paul. It is not a logical thing for her to do, and she is quite a logical person."

Lily lowered her eyes. "Neither have returned," she said softly.

Night Hawk emitted a low moan of regret, then stormed to his feet. With his fringed breeches that he had worn the past few days still on, having been too tired to remove them the evening before, he went and knelt on his haunches beside the fire and lifted a bowl, ready to dip stew in it. He needed stamina to do what was necessary today.

He must find his loved ones.

Lily came to him quickly and dipped the stew into his bowl, handed him a wooden spoon, and sat down beside him as he ate ravenously.

It was then that she saw the wound on his left hand. "My brother, what happened to your hand?" she gasped. She reached for it, but he pulled it away from her.

He frowned as he placed the bowl aside. "During my abduction I was tortured," he said, seeing the sudden alarm in her eyes. "These men who ride with White Wolf are less than human, my sister. But soon, if the Great Spirit lends a hand, all of the renegades will be found and dealt with. Never will they be able to ravage the land again, killing and maiming."

Thinking of her brother being tortured made a sudden bitterness rise into Lily's throat. And as she had these past few days, she felt the urge to retch. She rushed to her feet and stumbled from the wigwam. Going behind it, she vomited until her stomach ached from its emptiness.

When she felt a warm hand on her arm, she turned, startled, and saw Strong Branch. But she did not have a chance to say anything to him, for Night Hawk was suddenly there, concern in his eyes as he moved past Strong Branch and framed her face between his hands.

"You are not well," he said. "I knew it by your paleness." He glanced over his shoulder at Strong Branch and glowered at him, then swept an arm around his sister's waist and led her away, toward their parents' dwelling. "Tell me, little sister, what is ailing you?"

"It is *gah-ween-geh-goo,* nothing," Lily murmured, her knees trembling and weak. She glanced back at Strong Branch as he stepped into view, her heart crying out to him, so badly wanting to him to be happy about their child yet fearing that he would perhaps even think that she was tricking him into marriage by having allowed herself to get pregnant.

Oh, how she still loved him—but she feared that he would

turn his back on her forever once he knew of this burden she was carrying in her womb.

Trying to behave as though there was nothing wrong, Lily went inside her parents' wigwam with Night Hawk. She knelt beside the fire and added some wood as her brother went and knelt beside his mother's sleeping platform.

"*Gee-mah-mah?*" Night Hawk said, smoothing his hand across her cool brow. "How are you today?"

Mariah did not want to worry her son. She reached a hand to his cheek and gently caressed it. "I am *nay-mi-no-mun-gi*, fine," she murmured. "Just somewhat tired." She swallowed hard. "Go and find your father, Night Hawk. He has never been gone this long unless he told me where he would be. Please, Night Hawk? Go and find him for me."

Night Hawk took her hand and kissed its soft palm. "This I will do for you," he said, his voice breaking.

"Thank you, my sweet one," Mariah said, soft tears rolling down her cheeks.

Night Hawk rose to his feet and took one last, lingering look at his mother, then turned and gave Lily an appraising look, knowing that she was hiding something from him. He then left the wigwam and began rounding up his braves.

Today he would ride until he dropped from the saddle, if need be! He would not rest until both his father and woman were safely with him again.

* * *

Her hair tangled, her dress torn, Briana awakened from a restless night of sleep beneath a covering of leaves that she had swept over herself to keep her body warm as best she could through the long and dreary night in the forest. Shivering, she rose on an elbow and looked around her, seeing the gleam of the river, hearing the rustling of cottonwood leaves above her, like softly falling rain.

She had wandered until she almost dropped from exhaustion late the night before. Since her fall from the horse, and its ensuing escape from her, it seemed to her that she had been going in circles, everything looking the same to her one minute to the next.

She was lost. She doubted if she would ever find her way to civilization again. And to survive, she had to find food.

Scraping the leaves aside, she groaned and placed her hands at the small of her back as she rose slowly to her feet. Except for the aching of her body, she had survived the fall without mishap.

As she began walking aimlessly beside the river, allowing this to be her guide today, her thoughts went to Night Hawk and his father. Had Night Hawk found him? Had Night Hawk returned to his village unharmed himself?

Was he even now searching for her?

She raised her eyes to the sky that peeked through the dense foliage overhead. "Please, God," she prayed. "Let him be searching. Let him find me! I-I don't want to spend another night alone in the forest!"

She hooked her fingers around the pistol in the pocket of her skirt, having not used it—for protection or for food. She feared that she would have to soon. But the thought of killing an animal or bird sickened her. She would not do this unless absolutely forced to.

A cool fog began rising from the river as Briana stumbled onward through a maze of thickets, briars and thorns, and great mats of vines. She was about to give up ever finding anything to eat when up ahead in the mauve light of dawn, she saw huge vines hung with cluster after cluster of grapes!

"Thank the Lord," Briana said, tears spiraling down her cheeks as she broke into a run.

She fell to her knees before the grapevines and began picking the delicate clusters of grapes from the vine tendrils. She ate ravenously, unaware of horse hooves stopping a short distance away, or of someone approaching her from behind.

When strong arms snaked around her waist and drew her to her feet, she turned and found herself looking up into Night Hawk's dark eyes. She flung herself into his arms, sobbing.

"Night Hawk, I didn't think I'd ever see you again," she cried, clinging to him. "Thank you, darling, for finding me."

He held her close, his heart pounding with hers, then held her away from him, frowning. "Why was it necessary for me to search for you?" he grumbled. "Why did you leave the security of my village? Did you not know the dangers?"

He looked her over, seeing her total disarray, then gazed into her eyes again. "What happened?" he said more softly. "Why are you here without a horse? Are you all right?"

"Yes, I'm all right," Briana murmured. "Now that you are here, I am. I'm just a bit weary from wandering in the forest, and eager to have a substantial meal to fill my stomach."

She glanced down at herself, cringing, then smiled up at him. "I am a sight, aren't I?"

"You still did not say why you are here instead of my village," Night Hawk said. "Were you on your way to St. Paul? Had you decided that you wished to live under the tyranny of your uncle instead of living with Night Hawk and accepting the love he offers you?"

"No," Briana said, her voice breaking. She crept into his arms again, relishing his closeness. "My darling, I never want to even see my uncle again, unless it is behind bars, much less live with him."

She leaned away and gazed up at him. "Night Hawk, I left on horseback shortly after you left your village to follow you to the cave, searching for the firearms and your father," she murmured. "But—but my horse threw me, and here I am, a mess."

She frowned up at him. "Your father?" she murmured. "Did you find him? Were you able to transfer the firearms from the cave to your village?"

Night Hawk cast his eyes downward, recalling the instant of the explosion and the fear that had swept through him for his father.

Then he looked at Briana again. "There was a great explosion," he murmured. "The cave was destroyed, and most surely the firearms that were inside it." He swallowed hard. "I am not sure if my father was in the cave. My heart tells me that he was not. Many braves are searching for him now. I was among them until I saw you kneeling here, eating. I told them to keep searching and I came for you."

Briana lowered her eyes. "I am sorry to be such a bother," she said. "If not for me, you could still be searching for your father."

Night Hawk placed a finger under her chin and lifted her eyes to him. "You know your importance to me," he said. "It is good that I found you. Now, together, if you are able, we will resume the search for my father. If he is not found by this evening, we will return to my village. There we will eat and rest, and I will resume the search again the next day."

Her stomach and thirst both quenched by the grapes that she had stuffed into her mouth, Briana eagerly nodded. "Yes, let's go," she said anxiously. "I want to help you. Thank you for allowing it."

When he started to lift his left hand to her cheek, she saw the redness of the burn on the back of his hand. She gasped and looked quickly up at him. "Night Hawk, I believe it's infected!" she said.

She took his good hand and began half dragging him to the river. "Before we go anywhere, you are going to let me cleanse and wrap the wound," she said stubbornly.

He smiled and went with her.

After she had bathed the wound for him, he left her and went beneath the trees and began gathering different herbs. Taking them back to Briana, he showed her how they worked as medication. After crushing them between the palms of both of his hands, he spread the crushed leaves atop his wound, pressing the mixture into it, then smiled again as she ripped away a portion of her petticoat and wrapped it.

"Now, isn't that better?" Briana said, sighing as she looked into his dark eyes.

Night Hawk said nothing. He drew her into his arms, his mouth meeting hers as he kissed her long and hard, feeling the press of her breasts into his chest, wanting her yet knowing that this want must be delayed until later.

Thanks to the Great Spirit he had found his woman.

Now he hoped to be as blessed a second time—and find his father.

* * *

The long procession of horses heavy-laden with firearms, and the renegades riding alongside, keeping close watch for any approaching horsemen, wove its way through the forest.

Echohawk, whose wound pained him little and who was now riding tall and square-shouldered on his assigned horse, kept watch himself, trying to memorize every detail of the forest they were traveling through. He was also glancing over his shoulder, checking often on the welfare of the beautiful woman and child traveling on foot beside the horse.

A father's affection for Gentle Fawn made Echohawk want to offer her his horse. A lover's affection made him want to have her on the horse with him so that he could hold her tender body against his. Then he turned away, again ashamed for allowing himself to become caught up in feelings for another woman when his sweet No-din was surely weeping over him even at this moment. But she did not mourn the loss of him as her husband. She only treated him in a motherly fashion now, all the while his body was crying out, was burning to be caressed—to be loved!

A soft, tiny hand was suddenly in Echohawk's, making his heart leap. He turned his gaze back down to Gentle Fawn. When she smiled up him so endearingly, he knew that loving her was not impossible. Had not his very own father loved two women at once? One white-skinned, the other red? Was he not his father's son, borne to him of his Chippewa wife?

He circled his fingers around Gentle Fawn's hand, no longer hesitating to return her affection. When he asked her to get on the horse with him, a warning shot rang out over his head and Gentle Fawn resumed walking beside his horse, fear deep in her wife eyes.

Again, Echohawk tried to work the ropes loose at his wrists, at least glad that his ankles had been untied to let him ride the horse, instead of being forced to lie across the horse's back, as though something worthless. But no matter how hard he tried, he could not loosen the bonds at his wrists, and his flesh was now raw from having tried so often.

Suddenly looming before him was another massive cave that he was not familiar with. He had hoped the journey would take longer, for being out in the open heightened his chances of being found.

Echohawk's jaw tightened and his eyes narrowed with hate when Blackie rode up next to him.

"Now that I've seen you've arrived without mishap to your next dark prison, it's time to bid you adieu, Chief," Blackie said, laughing loudly. "My constituents await me."

He leaned closer. "Don't ask me what awaits you," he taunted. "I'm leaving it all up to White Wolf. He has much more interesting ways of dealing with people like you!"

White Wolf came to the other side of Echohawk's horse and glared at him, then rode on away, leading the procession into the cave.

Echohawk had no choice but to follow.

16

> To nestle once more in that haven of rest—
> Your lips upon mine, my head on your breast.
>
> —Hunt

Briana's head nodded, only half awake when she entered Night Hawk's village on his horse with him. She was only vaguely aware of being lifted from the horse and carried into Night Hawk's wigwam, lit by the flickering glow of a cedar fire.

When he lay her down on a thick pallet of furs beside the low-burning embers, she was barely aware of him gently drawing a blanket over her. Though every bone in her body seemed to be aching from the lengthy time spent on Night Hawk's horse, searching for his father in vain, she felt content in the fact that she was with Night Hawk again.

And it felt so good to be safe!

While she had been lost, wandering aimlessly about, she had begun to think that she would die out in the midst of the wilderness, alone. She had doubted she would ever see Night Hawk again, much less be with him.

Her eyelashes fluttered partially open, and she smiled drunkenly at Night Hawk as he slipped beneath the blankets beside her, allowing her to snuggle into his embrace. "I love you," she whispered, twining an arm around his neck. "I adore you."

He swept her against him, their bodies straining together. He kissed her passionately, then drew away. He turned his back to Briana as he stared into the dying embers of his lodge fire, unable to make love to her—his disappointment of not finding his father haunted him.

Sensing his pain, Briana fitted her body against his from behind, her hand reaching over to gently touch his face. "I'm sorry you didn't find your father," she murmured. "But, Night Hawk, no one could have been so persistent in his search as you. It seems that White Wolf has more than one hideout. Surely the firearms and your father have been transferred there. Can you think of a section of the forest that you are not familiar with—where White Wolf could go, realizing that you do not know of the place?"

"Minnesota is a vast land, with many lakes and forests," Night Hawk grumbled. "It would be impossible to know every secret place. But perhaps I know someone who might know of this one."

He turned to her. "Tomorrow I will ride to St. Paul," he said, smoothing a fallen lock of hair from her brow. "I will question your uncle."

Panic seized Briana. She sat up quickly, her eyes wild. "Please don't," she said, her voice filled with fear. "You could be walking into a trap, Night Hawk. Surely there are other ways of finding answers. Please try anything but going to my uncle. He could have you seized and jailed. He could say you are responsible for my disappearance! He would say anything to anybody if it would bring harm to you. And what will you say about me should he ask if you've seen me? I don't want him to know where I am now—or ever!"

Then she lowered her eyes. "My one regret is that I was forced to leave my painting equipment and my paintings behind," she said sullenly. "Without them, I-I feel so empty."

Night Hawk turned and pulled her into his arms. "I would hope that my love for you would banish all of your emptiness," he said, his gaze locked with hers. "But if that is not enough, I promise you that I will manage to get anything that you ask." He kissed her eyes closed. "I want you to be happy. Totally, unconditionally happy."

"Darling, never think that my love for you comes second to anything else in my life," Briana whispered, feeling secure in the warmth of his arms. "You are everything to me. Everything."

"I saw your passion for your painting," Night Hawk said,

his hands caressing her back. "Such a passion must be fed. I shall see that it is."

Briana leaned back and smiled. "My passion for you is greater, my love," she murmured. She laughed softly. "But tonight I am too tired to prove it to you." She sighed heavily and snuggled against him again, pressing her cheek against his chest, feeling his strong, rapid heartbeat through the buckskin fabric of his shirt.

"No proof is needed tonight, or any other night," Night Hawk said, easing her down on her back, stretching out beside her. "You have already proved it to me, in many ways. Remembrances of sweet times with you are locked within my heart, to draw from at times like these. I will go to sleep and you will be there in my dreams, kissing me, holding me, making love to me."

When she didn't respond, he leaned over and pressed a soft kiss to her cheek, thinking that it was hard to tell when she was the lovelier. Now, when she slept so beautifully beside him? Or when she was awake, laughing, her eyes twinkling into his?

"You are always lovely," he said, snuggling down beside her, his eyes heavy with sleep himself.

When, in her sleep, her hand sought his and held it, he brought it to his lips and kissed it, then held it above his heart, finding at least this moment of peace while the rest of the world beyond his wigwam seemed to be crashing down.

* * *

The moon was high in the sky, and the treetops were silvered with its glow as Lily stood on her secret limestone bluff that overlooked the river way down below.

Falling to her knees, she looked heavenward, tears burning the corners of her eyes. Sorrowful over her father's absence, her mother's health, and Strong Branch's desire for the company of Gray Moon over hers, she began to sing to the nightly spirits, hoping to find some sort of peace within herself.

Lily was unaware that Strong Branch stood apart, watching and listening.

He stepped closer, clasping his hand on the handle of his knife, thrust in a buckskin sheath at his side. A lump grew in his throat, for he was a lover of songs, and each pretty song that Lily sang thrilled him with delight, then shame. He knew what Lily expected of him, and it was not yet his to give. He had plans that did not include a wife at this time. He wanted to better himself before taking a wife—especially not one whose father was the chief of the opposing band of Chippewa!

"He is not chief for long," Strong Branch whispered to himself. "He is now a captive, and soon a corpse."

He shifted his feet nervously in the loose rocks, frowning at the fact that Echohawk was still a captive at all. He would have slit Echohawk's throat the moment he arrived at the cave. But White Wolf had forbade it, as well as forbidding Strong Branch and Gray Moon to enter the cave lest Echohawk see them.

That was a part of White Wolf's devious plan—just before Echohawk died, he would see at last who was going to kill him—who had betrayed him! As he took his last breaths he would realize that Strong Branch had won the battle of chiefs. As the knife lowered to Echohawk's heart, he would be told that Night Hawk's death was next.

Strong Branch would finally be chief of both bands of Chippewa. There would be no one else to question it. The two villages would finally become as one under one leadership—Strong Branch's!

White Wolf would benefit by having a Chippewa chief as an ally. As far as Strong Branch knew, it would be the first alliance between the Sioux and Chippewa of Minnesota in the history of these two warring tribes.

Strong Branch refocused his attention on Lily as she sang to the rippling waters, the dancing stars, and the shifting winds. He hated disturbing her. He too loved the moon, the night noises, the call of the birds as they sought their mates, the calming waters, and the swish of the night breeze in the tree tops. Yet he knew that time was wasting. He must go to Lily and hope that she would understand when he told her that tonight they could not be together. Gray Moon was waiting. They were going to ride into the night again.

His moccasin-padded footsteps as soft as a panther's, Strong Branch went to Lily and bent down beside her. He took her hand. "Lily?" he said softly. "My love?"

Lily's heart leapt into her throat, having not heard his approach. She turned startled eyes to him, then laughed softly as she crept into his arms. "Strong Branch," she whispered, clinging tightly. "I am so glad that you came. I was beginning to think that you had forgotten, or—or just had not wanted to."

"I have come, but I cannot stay as long as usual," Strong Branch said, easing her out of his arms, his fingers on her shoulders as he urged her to her feet. "Gray Moon is waiting."

Lily was quickly overcome by jealousy, and not for a woman. It was for Strong Branch's strong, questionable alliance with Gray Moon. It was always Gray Moon that stood in the way of their togetherness—of their discussions of their future.

She looked bitterly at Strong Branch, this time determined not to allow him to leave. Now, she thought, was the time to tell Strong Branch about their child. It was time for him to take on the same responsibility as her—that this child that she was carrying was his! She would not allow him to leave tonight until he agreed on a wedding date. He knew the disgrace brought upon a woman if she gave birth to a child, unwed.

"I understand, Strong Branch," Lily said, forcing a smile. "I do not need much time to say what I have wanted to say so badly to you, the man who will be my husband." Her smile wavered. "You are still planning to marry me? Tell me, Strong Branch, that you are."

Strong Branch shaped his hands around the soft curves of her face, the sheer beauty of Lily causing the usual ache in his loins. Her pure white skin was touched tonight by a soft pink, which he had grown used to seeing when she was excited. Her hair was loose and billowing across her shoulders, the breeze causing it to shimmer down her back. Her eyes were soft and round, and fringed with thick, dark lashes.

Her lips, he marveled to himself, ah, her ruby lips, how

they beckoned to him even now for a kiss—one that would surely delay his night's events if he gave in to the temptation.

"I have promised myself to you, have I not?" he finally said, a touch of annoyance in his voice. "Why must I always be forced to tell you this over and over again?"

Stung by the sharpness of his voice, Lily took a step away from him. "Why must I always be reminding you?" she said, almost bursting into tears. "It is because you say that you love me, say that you will marry me, yet you do not! What am I to expect, Strong Branch? What? Do you expect me to wait forever?" She firmed her jaw and squared her shoulders. "If you do not tell me tonight a set date for our marriage, I absolutely refuse ever to speak to you again!"

Stunned by Lily's outburst, yet knowing that he shouldn't be, since she had done this more often than not lately, Strong Branch's eyes widened. But seeing the seriousness of the situation, and not wanting to lose these special, sensual moments with her just yet, he placed gentle hands on her shoulders and drew her into an embrace.

"My beautiful Lily," he murmured, gazing warmly into her eyes. "I do want you for my wife. But I want more time." He could feel her tense up again, so he hurried his words:

"But if it will make you happy, sweet Lily," he said, "let us say that we will be wed in seven sunrises. Does that please you, Lily? Is that soon enough?"

Happiness instantly seized Lily's heart. She began laughing and crying at the same time. She hugged Strong Branch tightly. "Seven sunrises is fine with me!" she said, her heart pounding.

"Then that is the way it will be," Strong Branch said. He placed his hands on her waist and eased her gently from his arms. "But promise me something, Lily?"

"Anything," she said, beaming.

"Let us not tell anyone just yet," he said, his brow furrowing.

Lily's face became shadowed with doubt again. "Why would you ask me not to tell?"

"It is something that we should do together," Strong Branch said. "Give me two sunrises. You secretly plan a celebration for when we make our announcement. Surprises are nice, do you not think so, Lily?"

He smiled weakly down at her, hoping that he was being convincing. What he truly needed was more time to make things right not for them, but solely for himself. He wanted this time to achieve the full power that he sought.

Most of all, he needed her silence to enable him to achieve this goal.

Things were finally going his way. Finally! He could not, would not, allow her to ruin it!

Looking at her, being near her, made a slow ache grow in his heart, for he did love her so much. Yet in truth, he did not plan to marry her at all.

"That is wonderful!" Lily said, clasping her hands, smiling again. "It will be much fun making plans!"

Then a thought came to her that saddened everything that she wanted to be wonderful and gay.

Her father was still missing. And her mother was so ill.

But she had to place such sadness from her heart. Because of this child growing within her, she had plans to make for her future. Her child's future, and she would not make them with a sad, burdensome heart.

She grabbed Strong Branch's hands and squeezed them. "My darling, I have the most wonderful news to share with you," she said, her voice lilting.

"And what might that be?" Strong Branch said, filled with regret, knowing that this happiness that she was showing would soon be turned to remorse—and hate.

"My darling Strong Branch, I am with child!" Lily burst out, her eyes searching his face for shared joy over this wondrous news that she had held close to her heart for so long. Her smile wavered when she saw how shaken Strong Branch was by the news.

"Strong Branch?" she murmured, putting a hand on his cheek. "Are you not happy? Soon we will be married. We can then tell everyone that we are expecting a child! Our child. Is that not wonderful, Strong Branch?"

He forced a smile and drew her into his arms. "*Ay-uh,*" he said flatly. "Wonderful."

He now felt his world slipping away. He felt completely trapped.

17

I would ask of you, my darling,
A question soft and low,
That gives me many a heartache,
As the moments come and go.

—Anonymous

The early morning light was spiraling through the smoke hole in the ceiling. The fire in the fire pit had burned to shimmering orange embers.

Briana awakened, thrilled when she felt hands cupping her breasts through her dress and warm lips pressing into hers in a kiss savagely sweet and long.

All of her aches and pains of the prior night quickly faded into lethargic bliss as she twined her arms around Night Hawk's neck and returned the kiss. His hand crept up her skirt and found her wet and ready for him as he began caressing the core of her womanhood.

She sucked in a wild breath when he plunged several fingers inside her, thrusting heatedly, taking her to a world that knew no bounds of pleasure.

Night Hawk's lips slipped down her neck, then sucked her hard nipple through the cotton material of her blouse, until she felt faint with the pleasure he was arousing within her.

When he leaned away from her, she opened blissfully hazy eyes and beckoned with open arms for him not to leave her. She quickly saw that was not his intention at all. He was lowering his fringed breeches, his throbbing hardness springing forth as he dropped them to the floor.

He put his hand on himself, moving his fingers slowly over his hardness. She swallowed hard as he knelt down over her, soon straddling her. She lifted her skirt and opened herself to him, her lips parting when his mouth came on hers again, his tongue darting within. As his tongue danced within her mouth, he plunged his hardness within her and began his heated strokes.

Loosening Briana's blouse and lifting it away from the waistband of her skirt, Night Hawk slid his hand beneath it and cupped a breast, squeezing the nipple between a thumb and forefinger, drawing a heavy sigh from Briana.

She lifted her hips, twined her legs around his waist, and rode with him, thrust for thrust, stroke for stroke. Surges of warmth flooded through her body. Tremors cascaded down her back when he moved his lips to her breast and his tongue began circling the nipple, his teeth teasingly nipping it.

As he braced himself above her, his hands caught Briana's and held them slightly above her head against the soft pelts, his buttocks moving rhythmically, his strokes heating up within her.

Briana groaned throatily when he kissed her again, this time more hungrily, more demandingly. She knew that the passion was peaking, and that soon they would once again share the ultimate of wild rapture.

When his lips went to her breast again and he sucked a nipple between his lips, she drew in a sharp breath, and released a cry of sweet agony from the depths of her throat.

His hand then moved over her breasts, down her ribs, and across the soft, tremoring flesh of her belly. He found her throbbing center again and caressed it as he continued his rhythmic strokes inside her.

Hardly able to bear the building ecstasy, Briana circled her arms around his neck and again drew Night Hawk's lips to hers, kissing him fiercely. When she felt his body stiffen, she knew that he was nearing that peak of pleasure that they both had been seeking. Their bodies jolted and quivered. For the moment they were the only two people in the universe.

Night Hawk pressed endlessly deeper. Briana clung to him, sculpting herself to his moist body, running her fingers along his tight buttocks, then clasping them as again she felt the pleasure grabbing her.

There was a great shuddering in Night Hawk's loins. Briana

strained her hips up at him, crying out together at their shared fulfillment.

Sighing, wonderfully shaken by the experience, they lay exhausted together.

"This is a wonderful way to greet a new day," Briana said, giggling as Night Hawk, breathing hard, rolled away from her to stretch out on his back.

She then grew sober and stroked Night Hawk's perspiration-laced stomach. "But today there are more things to do than make love," she murmured. "You are going to see my uncle. You are going to search for your father. I shall fear for you until your return, my darling."

"My mother!" Night Hawk said, jumping to his feet. He drew on his breeches. "I must go and check on Mother. When she worries, her body weakens."

He brushed a kiss across Briana's brow. "I shall return soon," he said. He glanced down at the fire pit, then back up at Briana. "Upon my return I shall tend to the fire. I shall ask Lily to bring us food. And then, my love, I must leave."

He knelt before her and framed her face between his hands. "Leaving you is not something I wish to do," he said. "Were we ever to have a full day for making love, I would not stop to eat or rest. I would make love to you until there was no breath left in me, or a beat left in my heart."

"That would be a bit drastic, wouldn't it?" Briana said, laughing softly. "My darling, when things are better, we will have a lifetime of sharing wonderful, blissful moments together. We would not have to use them all up in one day."

A frown creased Night Hawk's brow. "Sometimes I do not think life will ever become uncomplicated," he said, his voice drawn. "If it is not the interference of the white man or the Sioux, it is from the people of our own tribe of Chippewa! Greed causes many to become foreign to themselves."

"You are speaking of Strong Branch?" Briana said, stroking his broad back as she leaned up against his chest.

"*Ay-uh,* Strong Branch and Gray Moon," he growled. "They plot together for Strong Branch to be chief. It is becoming more and more evident that they would do anything to rid themselves of my father and myself. Perhaps they are in part responsible for my father's disappearance, and that saddens me."

He rose back to his feet, drawing on his fringed shirt. "My sister, Lily?" he grumbled. "She wishes to marry Strong Branch. Is not that the worst sort of complication?"

Briana nodded, then sat down beside the glowing embers of the fire and watched him leave, her heart heavy for him.

* * *

Night Hawk hurried to his mother's wigwam and found Lily sitting vigil at her side. When Lily lifted sorrowful eyes up at Night Hawk, he looked at their mother. Anger rose in his heart for those responsible for his father's disappearance, for this had caused his mother to worsen.

He knelt down beside Lily and drew her into his arms. "I see that Mother is worse," he said, stroking his sister's back. "And I will find the one responsible!"

"*Gee-mah-mah's* malaria has returned," Lily cried, clinging to him. "She is in the grip of a fever and melancholia over *gee-bah-bah*. Night Hawk, you must find Father! You must!"

Lily closed her eyes, trying to blot out everything ugly and unpleasant in the world, trying to concentrate solely on Strong Branch's promises that were fresh in her heart.

Night Hawk held her close, his eyes focused on his mother. Her breathing was shallow. The fever was almost consuming her.

He yanked away from his sister. "I must leave now," he said, more determined than ever to find his father. If not, he might lose his mother and father at the same time.

He clasped his sister's shoulders. "Briana is in my dwelling," he said softly. "Go to her. Lend her a hand with the fire. Take her food. I do not have time. I have someone to see and it cannot wait any longer."

"The white woman?" Lily said softly. "She is in your dwelling? I thought—"

"I found her and brought her home late last night," Night

Hawk said. He looked over at his mother again. "Send for a Mide priest. See that he performs his magic over *gee-mah-mah.*"

"*Ay-uh,* soon," Lily said, almost choking on a sob.

"Explain to Briana that I had to leave," Night Hawk said, then swung around and rushed from the wigwam.

Lily wiped tears from her eyes as she gazed down at her mother, guilt awash throughout her for having kept the secret of her child from her. What if her mother died, never knowing that she was going to be a grandmother?

She knelt down beside her mother and began saying a soft prayer, asking the Great Spirit for a way to find forgiveness within her mother's heart.

* * *

It was high noon. Blackie was on a podium near the capital building, hoping to draw a crowd of people as they came and went in their buggies and fancy carriages along the busy thoroughfare. He was making a speech to those who had already stopped and were standing around the platform, listening. His eyes wavered, realizing that his speech was lacking its usual spark. He couldn't get his mind off Briana, wondering what he would tell her parents if she didn't surface again; wondering where on earth she was.

But, of course, he suspected that she was in Night Hawk's village, having become his willing whore. And he could not do anything about it, because he could not draw any undue attention to himself that could lose him the election. He was too close to winning to worry about her whereabouts.

He had labored hard and long to make a name for himself. He would not let anything or anyone stand in his way.

At least he had succeeded in helping get the firearms moved to another hideout. Plus, he had made sure that Echohawk was still captive. He hoped that White Wolf would soon succeed at capturing Night Hawk again. That would be the icing on the cake. He would not only win an election with the white community, but also gain a firm hold on the Indian population as well.

Seeing that his speech was not going well, Blackie soon left the platform and stepped into his buggy. Snapping the reins, he sent his horse on through the crowded streets, needing the solace, the privacy of his house for the rest of the day.

* * *

Another successful raid behind them, Strong Branch and Gray Moon were riding together through the forest toward their village.

Gray Moon edged his horse closer to his chief's. "No matter what Wise Owl says, I feel that it is best that our band of Chippewa break completely away from Chief Echohawk's," he said stiffly. "Is now not a perfect time? Chief Echohawk is not there to interfere. I have thought long and hard about this, Strong Branch. This is truly the only way you will ever achieve any true peace as a leader."

Strong Branch had not been able to focus on much else besides his unborn child since Lily had broken the news. This changed everything, it seemed. He could not turn his back on a child. Because of his father's and mother's untimely deaths so long ago, he had been forced to be raised without parents, and he knew the emptiness that brought into one's life, especially a son's. He would not allow his child to live such a life. It seemed that he would have to marry Lily after all.

And if so, his plans to achieve the full powers of both bands of Chippewa would go awry. He could not go against his wife's very own people, could he?

Seeing that Strong Branch was not responding, Gray Moon sneered at him. "You allow a woman to shadow your vision of the future," he chided. "Our people's future! Not Lily's chieftain father's. Do you not realize that should Night Hawk be allowed to live, he will soon be chief—and he is part white, a lover of white skins. You should want no part of that band of Chippewa! You should want no part of Lily. White blood flows through her veins. Her skin is white. Her mother is white. What if she were to bear you white children? Could you live with such disgrace?"

A coldness grabbed Strong Branch in the pit of his stomach, having never even considered the possibility of his child having any skin coloring other than his own. But until last night he had not even considered having children by Lily. He had not planned to marry her.

He turned angrily to Gray Moon. "You have said enough," he shouted. "I need no one to tell me anything of my mind. I will make my own decisions, and that is final!"

Gray Moon quickly turned his eyes away, to hide the seething anger in their depths.

* * *

Concerned about Night Hawk, wondering why he had not yet returned, Briana went to the entrance flap and lifted it to look for him. But just as she did, Lily appeared with buckskin clothes draped over an arm and moccasins hanging from the fingers of her left hand.

"Night Hawk is gone," Lily said softly, seeing how Briana's eyes left her to again search the village. "My brother sent me to tell you that he had to leave. I am to help you with the lodge fire. I will soon bring you food." She held out the buckskin clothes, smiling. "I have brought you a change of clothes."

"That is kind of you," Briana said, trying to hide her disappointment at not seeing Night Hawk again, her heart pounding with worry for him.

She looked past Lily, and sighed, finding everything at the village so peaceful. It was hard to think that anything was amiss today.

"I can see in your eyes that you find my village pleasant," Lily said, stepping up to Briana's side, turning slowly to survey everything around her as well. "My village is noted for its sunny days and its cool nights, a paradise where children may gather pebbles in the beautiful river. It is the nesting place for many varieties of songbirds."

Lily uttered a sigh. "I love this valley filled with beautiful trees and clear, cool running rivers. It is a perfect place to raise children."

Smiling, her secret of soon having her own child held sweetly within her heart, Lily went on inside Night Hawk's wigwam. When Briana came and stood beside her, Lily placed the buckskin garments in her arms.

"These are mine, beaded and fringed by my own hand," Lily said softly. "Please enjoy them. They are now yours."

"Thank you," Briana murmured. "You are very kind."

As Lily worked with the fire and continued talking, Briana slipped out of her torn and soiled clothes, planning to bathe in the river as soon as she felt she could slip away. She put on deerskin leggings, tying them around her legs just under her knees. She slipped into a buckskin garment that displayed beads set in leaf and flower designs that came to her calves. The moccasins were soft and pleasant to her sore and tired feet.

"With our alert people, nothing is without purpose," Lily said, turning to face Briana. "The rattle of a rolling pebble or stone; the whirr of bird wings disturbed at their rest; or the warning snort of a horse—"

She paused in her chattering when Briana tried to smooth the tangles from her hair with her fingers. "Allow me to make your hair pretty," she said. Briana smiled and silently nodded her approval.

Using her own personal hairbrush—the tail of a porcupine attached to a decorated handle—and instead of a comb, a hair parter—a slender painted stick, also with a decorated handle—Lily parted Briana's hair. She then carefully brushed and plaited it into two braids, tying the ends with strings of painted buckskin, called hair strings.

"Again I thank you," Briana said, drawing one of her braids around and admiring the hair string. It was a work of art, tipped with ball tassels of porcupine quills and fluffs of eagle feathers. "It is so very pretty, Lily."

"You look lovely," Lily said, stepping back and clasping her hands as she admired Briana.

"I feel lovely," Briana said, smiling. Then her smile faded when someone's chanting wafted into the wigwam.

"That is the Mide priest," Lily said solemnly, bowing her head. "My mother has worsened. The Mide is performing his magical cures over her."

Briana went to the entrance flap and lifted it, peering outside to see a crowd assembling around Echohawk's wigwam. A shiver coursed across her flesh. Now she felt a strange sort of doom hanging over the village, replacing what she had only moments ago thought was so beautiful, so serene.

She looked into the denseness of the forest, wishing Night Hawk were there, dreading what might happen to him while he was gone.

And, she wondered, where was Night Hawk's father?

* * *

Echohawk leaned against the cold, dank wall of the cave as he watched the renegades celebrating the victory of another night of raiding. He had also watched the firearms being brought into the cave, and the ammunition being stacked against the far wall.

It was apparent that they had found whiskey among the loot. Most were too drunk to stand now, many falling to the ground, having passed into a whiskey-induced sleep.

The night had been long and he could not tell even if it was now day. The cave was always dark, always cold and damp.

Moving to lie on his side on a blanket, he was starting to drift off to sleep himself when a body slid in behind him and arms circled around him. He could not find the courage to send Gentle Fawn away. He hoped that White Wolf would not awaken and find her there. She was White Wolf's woman, a possession to be used but not loved.

White Wolf was sitting in the shadows, watching drunkenly, a sly grin on his face. Letting Gentle Fawn warm up to Echohawk was just part of the misery he wished to create for Echohawk before he killed him. He could tell that the temptation was becoming too great for the old chief, even for a man who had a wife and two children.

Gentle Fawn's hands wandered slowly over Echohawk, until she could feel the arousal of his manhood. She had seen him watching and wanting her. She wanted him no less. He was a gentle, beautiful man. She had never been with such a man, and wanted him now as she had never before in her life wanted someone.

She began stroking his hardness through his buckskin breeches, but when his hand circled hers and eased it away, she knew that he was not the sort to be with another woman so easily when he had a woman of his own awaiting his return at his village.

She did not move away from him, in awe of White Wolf allowing her to stay. She snuggled closer, fitting her body into the curve of Echohawk's body from behind.

Having become aroused from watching Gentle Fawn try to pleasure Echohawk, White Wolf jerked her away and threw her to the cave floor. He yanked her dress up to her waist and plunged his throbbing tightness into her, his grunts of satisfaction reaching Echohawk like stab wounds to his heart.

Echohawk closed his eyes and tried not to hear, but how could he not when each of White Wolf's forceful thrusts inside Gentle Fawn made her cry out with pain? Echohawk gritted his teeth, vowing to get free somehow to see that White Wolf never touched the lovely woman again.

Echohawk knew that he shouldn't, that he was not free to, but he was falling in love with Gentle Fawn. He knew that this would have never happened had he and Mariah had the chance to share a healthy relationship these past years. But after having the sensual side of their marriage die when she had become weakened by her illnesses, he had ached many a night.

Now that he had been awakened anew with thoughts of desire, he knew that he could not deny himself the pleasure of it much longer.

Gentle Fawn. He wanted Gentle Fawn so badly. His whole soul cried out for her.

18

The moonlight of a perfect peace
Floods heart and brain.

—Sharp

Night Hawk waited in the shadows of the forest until the moon had replaced the sun in the sky. Then he ventured onto the streets of St. Paul until he reached Blackie's mansion. Dismounting, he left his horse a short distance away, then moved stealthily through the darkness until he reached the protective shadows of a towering elm tree. From that vantage point he watched Blackie's house, trying to sort out which room the politician was in by the splash of golden lamplight in the windows. When he saw a light flicker on in a room on the lower floor, he smiled, tapping his fingers nervously against the pistol thrust into the waistband of his fringed buckskin breeches.

He waited only a moment longer, giving himself time to peer cautiously around the estate grounds, watching for movements and seeing none.

Then springing forth like a panther, he ran across the flat stretch of yard, up the steps to the wide veranda that reached around three sides of the house, and then flattened his back against the house. He edged himself along, hugging the wall with his back, until he came to the window where he had seen the lamplight flicker on.

Scarcely breathing, he leaned away from the wall, only enough to be able to look in the window. Through a thin gauze curtain he saw Blackie sitting at a massive oak desk, leisurely smoking a fat cigar, intently reading a book.

Night Hawk nodded, knowing that now was the time to make his move. Blackie was lost in another world—the one that "talking leaves," books, created within one's mind. Blackie would not hear the door open, or the approach of his enemy.

Going to the door, he slowly turned the knob, opened the door, then crept inside a dimly lit foyer. He stopped and stared down a long corridor, seeing the flood of light on the floor from only one room, and knew that was his destination. Night Hawk moved down the corridor, his moccasined feet silent. When he reached the study he burst into it, his pistol drawn, aimed at Blackie's heart.

Hearing the rush of movement, Blackie looked up quickly. When he saw Night Hawk standing there, a drawn pistol in his right hand, he gasped and dropped the book to the desk, the pages fluttering closed.

"What are you doing here?" Blackie asked, inching up from his chair. He moved behind it and fixed his fingers tightly on the back of the chair. "You crazy Injun, put that gun away."

"Tell me where my father is," Night Hawk said in a threatening snarl, his eyes having narrowed into two dark slits. "Tell me now, politician, or you'll soon be joining your ancestors in the land of the hereafter."

"I know nothing," Blackie said, his heart pounding as he looked down the barrel of the pistol, then slowly at Night Hawk's finger resting on the trigger. "Why can't you Injuns leave me alone? I'm—I'm a peace-loving, God-fearing man!"

"That is what you pretend in the public eye, but those who know you as you truly are know better," Night Hawk said gruffly.

He glanced to one side, seeing row after row of books along the side wall. Strange, he thought to himself, how a man of ill-breeding like Blackie Collins could have such a collection of "talking leaves." But that he did, Night Hawk decided, proved that Blackie must have acquired a love of them somewhere between being a gambler and politician.

Night Hawk stepped quickly and purposely to the front of the bookcase, and with his free hand he began knocking the books to the floor. His wounded hand pained him as he jerked each stack of books to the floor, yet he did not show his pain to his enemy.

He laughed when he heard Blackie gasping, obviously horror-stricken over his precious books being abused in such a way.

Keeping his aim steady on Blackie, Night Hawk chose a book, and with his one hand, let it fall open, then spat on the pages.

"Stop that," Blackie said, eyeing the soiled book with a bleeding heart, loving books almost as much as he had once enjoyed gambling. "Those are precious things. Leave them be." His face became suffused with color when Night Hawk dropped that book to the floor and took another one from the shelf, repeating the performance.

"You heathen," Blackie said, his teeth grinding together in his mounting anger. "You don't even know the importance of books. How can I expect you to realize what you are doing when you abuse them in such a way?"

"You speak of abuse?" Night Hawk said, kicking books aside as he stepped closer to the desk. "Did you not strike Briana? Did you not see the bruises—the blackness of her eye that was left as evidence of that abuse? You, who pretend to be a pillar of the community, are no better than a snake. I should force you on your stomach and make you slither down the streets of the city, so that the people who you wish to vote for you on election day could see you as you truly are!"

Blackie paled as Night Hawk inched himself even closer. "Stay away from me," he said, taking a step backward.

"Tell me where my father has been taken," Night Hawk said flatly. "I saw the explosion at the cave. Do you think that fooled me into believing that everything was destroyed—even my father?" He laughed. "For a moment, *ay-uh,* I was fooled. But then I realized it was a tactic to draw off my guard."

"What cave?" Blackie said, trying to be convincing. "What explosion? You crazy Injun, how would I know about either?"

"Because, just as you were in the past, you are again in cohoots with White Wolf," Night Hawk said, standing just on the other side of the desk from Blackie. "And don't tell me that you don't know anything of White Wolf's whereabouts now, or that I am wrong in assuming White Wolf is behind my father's abduction."

Night Hawk stepped quickly around the desk and aimed the pistol directly at Blackie's temple. "Do not tell me that you did not know of my abduction and that I was held captive in the cave," he said with another snarl. "I am sure it was you who ordered the abduction."

Paling, the pistol much too close for comfort, Blackie inched away from it. "You—you are wrong," he said, sweat pearling his brow. "Please don't do anything you'll be sorry for, Night Hawk. Leave. If you do, I promise I won't inform the authorities about your craziness tonight."

"Do you think I am concerned about the authorities?" Night Hawk said, laughing. "You could draw undue attention to yourself, and then your unscrupulous activities would be uncovered."

"I'm innocent," Blackie whined. "Innocent!"

Realizing that he would be unable to get answers from Blackie short of torturing him, and not wanting the coward's screams to attract any attention from passersby on the street, or the servants who were surely asleep in their quarters, Night Hawk began slowly taking steps away from him.

"I will find the answers," Night Hawk said. "Somehow. Then I will be back to finish what I started tonight."

Blackie sighed heavily and ran a finger around the tight white collar at his throat. "My niece," he blurted out before Night Hawk fled from the room. "You have been with her. Where is she?"

Night Hawk stopped and glared at Blackie. "You did not give me answers about my father, so I shall not give you answers about your niece," he said.

"I know you didn't abduct her because some of her personal belongings were gone," Blackie said, his voice drawn. "Did she come to you willingly?" He wanted to shout at Night Hawk and tell him that he knew that his niece had helped him escape from the cave—but that was a truth that he had to keep to himself, for it would condemn him for sure in the eyes of the Chippewa brave—and the entire community of St. Paul.

The mention of Briana's belongings brought something to Night Hawk's mind. Briana had pined over having left her beloved painting paraphernalia behind. He had promised to bring at least a portion of her painting equipment back with him. This was a promise that he was going to keep, for he wanted nothing to sadden her ever again.

"Where is Briana's room?" Night Hawk said, ignoring Blackie's question. "Take me to it."

"I told you that—that she isn't there," Blackie said, his words stumbling clumsily across his lips.

Night Hawk's lips formed a slow smile. "That is true," he said. "Now take me to her room."

"Why would you want to—to go there?" Blackie said, not having budged.

Night Hawk aimed his pistol at Blackie again. "Do as I say, politician," he threatened.

Blackie's knees trembled as he moved slowly from behind his chair, around the desk, and then past Night Hawk. Swallowing hard, he went out into the corridor, walked slowly to the spiral staircase, then began slowly walking up the plushly carpeted steps.

"What the hell are you up to now?" Blackie said, giving Night Hawk a glance over his shoulder, paling anew when he saw Night Hawk so close behind him, the pistol aimed at his head.

"Just do as you are told and ask me no more questions," Night Hawk said icily. "Take me to Briana's room."

"Then what?" Blackie asked, ignoring Night Hawk's demands to be quiet. He gasped when he suddenly felt the thrust of the barrel against his back.

Blackie said no more. He rushed up the steps and went to Briana's room, then stood back as Night Hawk moved stealthily and quickly around him and into the room.

Night Hawk's gaze roved slowly, feeling Briana's presence in the room, the aroma of the perfumes that he had become familiar with on her soft skin. He saw the painting paraphernalia that he had seen while in the forest with her.

"Get together Briana's paints, brushes, and everything that she needs to do her paintings," Night Hawk flatly ordered, giving Blackie a cold stare.

Blackie's eyes widened. "Why?" he asked, his voice faint. Then his lips parted in another gasp. "You're taking this to her, aren't you? Damn you, Injun, she is going to shack up with you, isn't she?"

"Do as you are told and say no more about Briana to me," Night Hawk said, smiling to himself as Blackie began scrambling around the room, getting everything into Briana's painting satchel that she used on her outings in the forest.

When this was done, Blackie set it down in the middle of the floor. "How many of her canvases do you want?" he grumbled.

"None," Night Hawk said. "She will paint on the canvas of the Chippewa—on stretched and bleached hides of animals."

"God," Blackie said, a shiver racing across his flesh. "She won't only be living like a heathen, she'll be acting like one."

Ignoring Blackie, Night Hawk backed toward the door. "Grab the satchel," he said, motioning with his head toward it. "Take it down the stairs and set it beside the door."

After Blackie did as he was told, he stepped aside. "Now what?" he said sarcastically.

"Allow me to leave without drawing attention to me, or you will die soon after," Night Hawk warned. "If I am not able to come and shoot the arrow into your heart, one of my most devoted braves will." He smiled darkly. "You will not know when or where it will happen. Only that it will."

Night Hawk picked up the satchel with his free hand, gave Blackie another threatening stare, then turned and fled into the night.

Briana's satchel secured at the side of his horse, Night Hawk rode away from the city, his heart heavy.

How was he ever to find his father?

* * *

Echohawk gazed intently into Gentle Fawn's dark eyes. "The renegades are gone again," he said softly. "Help me escape. I shall take you with me. I will make all wrongs right for you."

Gentle Fawn rocked her child back and forth in her arms, tears pooling in the corners of her eyes. "I cannot do this thing you ask," she murmured. "Although I tended to your wound, I can do nothing else for you. I-I am too afraid of White Wolf. No matter how much you tell me that I will be safe with you, I cannot truly believe so. White Wolf would search until he found me. He would make me pay for disobeying him."

"I would kill him before he had a chance to get near you," Echohawk growled.

"I am sorry, Echohawk," Gentle Fawn said. "I am too familiar with White Wolf's cunning ways. I would die quickly, and also my child. I do everything now for my child!"

Seeing the futility in trying to talk Gentle Fawn into doing anything that frightened her so much, Echohawk settled back against the wall of the cave. "It is good to know at least that you are not here because you love the renegade," he said, sighing heavily. "You did not seem the sort to choose such a man for a husband."

"Nor did I choose this man for the father of my child," Gentle Fawn said sullenly, her eyes deepening in regret. "But he is. Moonstar is his, but also by force."

She unfolded the corners of the soft doeskin that was wrapped around her child and took the naked child from the blanket. She held her daughter out for Echohawk to see. "Although she is the renegade's child, she is beautiful and sweet."

Echohawk was immediately taken by the child, by her soft brown eyes, her tiny copper facial features, her tiny fingers and toes. He remembered when Night Hawk and Lily had been born. He doubted if White Wolf had given his child a second glance.

"She is most beautiful," Echohawk said, wondering where Night Hawk was, and if he was safe.

Pleased with Echohawk's response, Gentle Fawn placed her child's tiny hand on Echohawk's face. "Does she not have the softest skin?" she said. "Does she not smell so fresh and clean from her bath in the spring at the back of the cave?"

"She is both of these things, and even more," Echohawk said, relishing this time alone with Gentle Fawn and his acquaintance with Moonstar. "It is obvious that you have been a good *gee-mah-mah*."

Gentle Fawn smiled broadly as she wrapped Moonstar in the doeskin blanket again, then laid her aside on a pallet of furs.

Echohawk was stunned when Gentle Fawn crept to her knees before him and placed her soft hands on each of his cheeks, drawing his lips to hers in a sweet, wondrous kiss. Guilt splashed through him when he felt himself responding to the kiss.

He was even more stunned when she drew away from him and lowered her dress so that it rested around her waist. Soon her well-rounded, milk-filled breasts leaned against his bare chest, and then his lips.

"Kiss them," Gentle Fawn whispered. "Please?"

Echohawk sighed from the wondrous feel of her breasts, yet he could not help it when a mixture of sadness and shame engulfed him. Being with a woman, even in this small way, made him miss those carefree days of loving his No-din when she had not been ill, when she had wanted him as much.

His heart bled to see his wife, to touch her breasts! It had been too long since they had shared anything intimate. It had been many winters. And he needed a woman for these needs—for these hungers.

The guilt overwhelmed the pleasure he felt from the feel of a woman's breasts against his lips again, and he recoiled from Gentle Fawn.

"Do not do this thing," he said huskily, his heart pounding. "It is wrong!"

Gentle Fawn jumped with a start away from him. With lowered eyes she drew her dress back onto her shoulders. She lifted her baby and fled to the darker depths of the cave, leaving Echohawk alone, his thoughts troubled.

He lifted his eyes upward and silently pleaded with the

Great Spirit to give him the strength required to have no feelings for this young, tempting woman.

He prayed that Night Hawk was all right, and that he would soon find this cave with many braves accompanying him. Many would be needed to fight off the bloodthirsty, greedy renegades. Echohawk found it hard to believe that they had allowed him to live this long, wondering what the purpose of this decision was.

He expected to die soon.

19

Now folds the lily all her sweetness up,
And slips into the bosom of the lake.

—TENNYSON

The sky was lightening overhead as Night Hawk rode into his village, having been forced to return home without any news of his father's whereabouts. His shoulders were slightly hunched, the regret heavy within his heart.

After placing his horse in the corral to graze with the others, he carried Briana's satchel to his mother's wigwam. He set it just outside the entrance flap and went inside. He found two maidens sitting vigil at his mother's side, both attentively awake as they took turns bathing Mariah's brow with soft, wet compresses. He knelt down beside one of the maidens, absorbing the sight of his mother as she slept fitfully, her breathing having taken on a rattle somewhere deep within her lungs.

"*Gee-mah-mah* has worsened," Night Hawk said, placing a hand on his mother's brow, feeling how fevered it was.

"*Ay-uh,* she has worsened," one of the maidens said. "We are doing all that we can. And the Mide priest? He has performed all of his magic over her. Now we must wait and see what Wenebojo has planned for your mother."

Night Hawk placed a kiss on his mother's cheek, then turned. "My *gee-bah-bah*?" he asked quietly. "Is there any news of him?"

"*Gah-ween,* none," the maiden said, her eyes revealing her sorrow.

Night Hawk nodded, then rose to his full height and left the wigwam, knowing that before he could gather many braves to search for his father again in the haunts of the forest, he had to rest—and he had to be with his Briana.

She knew ways to soften the pain in his heart.

He picked up Briana's satchel and went to his wigwam. Once inside, he placed the satchel on the mat-covered floor just inside the entrance flap.

He jerked off his fringed shirt, his moccasins, and his breeches, his gaze sweeping slowly around him. The fire in his fire pit had burned down to glowing coals, yet gave off enough light to see Briana. She was asleep on soft pelts, a blanket casually thrown aside, revealing the delicate curves of her shapely legs where her gown was hiked up past her knees.

Night Hawk's gaze worked higher, seeing the swell of Briana's breasts where her gown dipped low in front, then higher, seeing her sensually shaped lips parted slightly in her sleep, her eyelashes like golden veils where they lay spread thick and long above her delicate cheekbones.

Now naked, Night Hawk moved to his knees and crawled to Briana. He knelt down over her, resting himself with his knees on each side of her. He bent low, his hands framing her face between his hands, and drew her lips to his. He kissed her with passion, glad when she had awakened and began reciprocating with a fiery kiss, her arms twining around his neck.

Drawing one hand away, he swept it slowly down her curves, until he reached the hem of her gown, then slowly lifted it up past her thighs. He drew the gown over her head and eased it away from her.

Tossing it aside, he looked down at her with a fierce need, his heart pounding as he let his gaze roam over her, his hands following the path of his eyes, touching, caressing.

Briana sucked in a wild breath as his hand moved between her thighs and found her swollen bud and began moving his fingers over it until it throbbed against his fingers.

"Night Hawk, when did you arrive home?" she finally found the sense to ask, yet breathlessly as the sensations began to burn within her like molten lava.

"Only moments ago," he said huskily, his other hand kneading her breast. He lowered his mouth to one of the breasts and teased the nipple with his teeth, then softly chewed on it.

"Your father?" Briana asked, removing his headband. She

wove her fingers through his long, coarse, dark hair. "Did you find anything out about your father? Did—did my uncle cause you problems?"

"My father?" Night Hawk said, drawing away from her, turning his back on her, the magic spell that had been weaving between them momentarily broken. He hung his head in his hands. "No, no news of my father. And, no, no serious confrontation with your uncle." He turned glowering eyes to her. "Except that he lies over and over again. He said he knew nothing of my father."

"You don't believe him, do you?" Briana asked, running her fingers down his smooth copper back.

"Never," Night Hawk hissed. "But I could not get answers out of him, short of torturing him, and that is not a tactic I have practiced. I will have to find answers by other means."

"I'm sorry," she murmured. She rose to her knees and fitted herself behind him, pressing her breasts into his back.

She wove her arms around his chest, then moved her fingers across its broadness, then down to his flat belly, stopping where she found his half-shrunken manhood resting against his thigh. She circled her fingers around it, realizing the pleasure it caused him when he emitted a low growl.

He allowed the caresses for only a moment. Then he turned around quickly and placed his fingers on her shoulders, urging her on her back onto the plush pelts. "Let us talk no more of sorrowful things," he said, his eyes filled with dark need. "Fill my heart and mind with only you, my darling. Make love to me, Briana. Let me enjoy being with you before I am forced to leave again."

Briana placed her hands on his shoulders and urged him to roll onto his back. She leaned over him, smiling, her hair trailing along the flesh of his stomach as she kissed her way down to that part of him that was now hard and erect.

She circled her fingers around him and moved them slowly up and down, then placed her lips to him. She asked for nothing, this time only giving. And when he gently shoved her away and the proof of his pleasure spilled within the palm of her hand, she was glad that she was there, the woman he could depend on for eternity.

They lay there, not saying anything, their bodies touching. In a few minutes he eased her down beneath him, revived and needing her again.

She saw the plea in his eyes and answered it. She spread her legs and slowly lifted them around his waist as he thrust his heavy shaft within her.

His lips were demanding as he kissed her hard and long, his hands all over her, teasing, caressing, touching, loving—all at once.

She clung to him, lifting her hips to receive him more fully within her. He moved in short, confident thrusts as her hands cradled his hips, pulling him deeper, deeper, deeper.

And then the peak of pleasure was met. The wondrous bliss that ensued caused them to cling together, not wanting to part.

Finally Briana caught sight of the satchel just inside the entrance flap. "Night Hawk," she gasped, causing him to roll away from her. "You brought my supplies!" She flung her arms around his neck. "Thank you! Thank you!"

She gave him a quick, wet kiss, then rushed to her feet excitedly and grabbed the satchel. She took it and sat down beside Night Hawk. She opened it and began bringing out that which was precious to her, when a sudden thought struck her.

She looked over at Night Hawk. "It is all so very wonderful," she murmured. "But, darling, how can I paint without my—my canvases?"

"You will paint on the canvases used by the Chippewa," Night Hawk said, reaching a hand to her hair, drawing his fingers through its softness.

"The hides that I have seen hanging outside the wigwam entrance flaps?" Briana said, eyes wide. She smiled and nodded. "Yes, that will do. I will stretch them between strips of wood. Yes, that will do just fine."

Night Hawk smiled at her sweet innocence, and was touched by how easy she was to please. He felt guilty, though, for this private moment with the woman he loved, while his father was—where could he be?

* * *

Having not slept the whole night through, Lily decided that it was futile to stay on her sleeping platform any longer. She had only moments ago seen Night Hawk come in to check on their mother. She had heard him say that he had not found their father.

This, and oh, so very much more, saddened Lily early this morning. All she had to do was look at her mother and her heart seemed to turn inside out. She had not told her about the child that she was carrying within her womb, and now perhaps she would never have that chance.

And Strong Branch.

Although he had promised that he would marry her soon, there was something in the way he had said it that made her uncomfortable.

Gray Moon. He was the thorn in her side that she could not shed. He would stop the wedding, she was sure.

Pulling a dress over her head, slipping into moccasins, and grabbing her fringed shawl, Lily smiled at the two maidens sitting vigil at her mother's bedside, then crept on around them and outside. She gazed up at the heavens, seeing the beautiful streaks of orange and pink suffusing the sky, a tiny sliver of the moon still evident in the far distance.

"I must go and commune with Wenebojo," she whispered, determinedly turning toward her secret trysting place. "I must get my mind settled, at least on one of my worries. Surely the Great Spirit will give me a small measure of comfort this morning."

She went through the tangled vines of the forest, over the damp leaves beneath the trees, and amid the stirrings of birds and animals awakening all around. Every once in a while she would stop and listen, when she heard something behind her that she did not think was made by the forest animals and birds.

When she would turn and search but find no one following her, she would shrug and go on her way, determined to find solace in her morning prayers.

When she was finally on the butte high above the farthest stretches of the forest, the river winding through the trees way down below her, she started to kneel but was stopped when someone suddenly came up from behind her and placed their fingers around her throat.

She grabbed at the fingers that were choking the life from her, but the strength of her attacker was twice her own. Choking and gagging, tears streaming from her eyes, the thing she thought of as she began to see a haze of black was her child. Her heart cried out for her child, a child that she would never hold!

And then she grew limp, the breath and heartbeat gone from her.

His heart beating soundly, torn with emotions over what he had just done, Gray Moon lifted Lily up into his arms. When he felt and saw her limpness, he held her for a moment, staring down at her lily white face, hating her for having interfered in his life so much. Because of her, Strong Branch had not moved ahead in making decisions for his people. Lust for this white woman born into the Chippewa tribe had blinded Strong Branch too much.

He had let his duties to his people take second place to Lily.

"But never again!" Gray Moon growled, carrying Lily to the edge of the bluff. He held her over it and then released her. He leaned over and watched her frail, limp body tumble over and over again in the air, then land with a thump on the rocks below, echoing back to his eager ears.

Smiling, wiping his hands on his fringed buckskin breeches, he started to turn but stopped abruptly when he heard someone approaching.

His heart skipping a beat, he dived into a thick stand of bushes and hid, his eyes narrowing as he discovered Strong Branch.

He watched his chief go to the edge of the butte and begin pacing, kneading his brow thoughtfully all the while. Then he knelt and picked up several pebbles. Rising to his full height, he began tossing these over the side of the butte.

When he stepped closer to the edge, to watch the pebbles

fall through the air, his sudden wails were so loud, it seemed as though the heavens might split open with the remorseful sound.

"He has seen her," Gray Moon whispered to himself, his lips forming a smug smile.

He waited a moment, then made a wide half circle so that he could approach Strong Branch from behind, to draw undue attention away from himself, and the possibilities of being accused of the crime.

"My friend!" Gray Moon shouted, rushing toward Strong Branch. He turned him to face him. "What is wrong? I was passing by. I heard your wails."

Strong Branch could not hold back the tears, not even to save face in front of his friend. Without turning to look again at his beloved, he pointed at the butte. "She—she fell to her death," he said, finding the words hard to say, since that made what he wanted to deny a reality. "Lily! She is dead! She lies down below, dead!"

"What a tragedy!" Gray Moon said, easing his hands from Strong Branch's shoulders. He went and peered down at Lily's body, then turned and gazed at Strong Branch again. "Lily has been here too often to lose her footing. She knows every inch of this butte. You know that, Strong Branch. You have been here with her often enough. Strong Branch, she must have been too distraught with life to carry on another day. She must have killed herself, Strong Branch."

Hearing Gray Moon be so matter-of-fact about his beloved's death, and seeing that the brave was even smug about it, Strong Branch recalled just how much Gray Moon had always hated Lily. He had begged Strong Branch to forget his feelings for her.

A sickening thought came to him, making him dizzy with rage.

"You wanted her dead," he said, taking a slow step toward Gray Moon. "You are glad that she is dead."

Not having expected this reaction, Gray Moon stood frozen on the spot for a moment, then tried to circle around Strong Branch, away from the edge of the butte. He suddenly did not feel safe with his longtime friend. He seemed more the enemy at this moment, and perhaps had been for a long time, and Gray Moon had not recognized it.

"Strong Branch, stay away from me," Gray Moon said, his hand automatically reaching for the knife sheathed at his waist. "You—you have a wild look in your eyes. Why? I am not at fault here. It was Lily! She jumped to her death! Do you not see?" He stumbled backward. "Or she fell. That is it, Strong Branch. She stumbled and fell!"

"Lily did neither," Strong Branch, snarled, moving closer to Gray Moon. "She did know this bluff like the back of her hand. And she would not kill herself. She had no reason to. She recently discovered that she was with child. We set our wedding date. She thought that we would be married soon."

"You told her you were going to marry her?" Gray Moon mumbled. "She was with child?"

"You fool," Strong Branch hissed. "From the very beginning I never planned to marry Lily. I just told her this to give myself more time to make adjustments for our people's future. Your people, Gray Moon, as well as mine! But murdering Lily was not in the plan! She was sweet and innocent! And—and I did love her, Gray Moon. I could have never loved another woman as much! I had changed my mind. I was going to marry her! For the unborn child she carried within her womb, I was going to marry her!"

"You are talking in circles!" Gray Moon said, his eyes wild. He yanked his knife from its sheath, brandishing it between himself and Strong Branch. "Is this the way you want it? That one of us dies today?"

"She died," Strong Branch said, moving stealthily around Gray Moon, avoiding the knife as Gray Moon started stabbing toward him. "And so shall you. You should not have killed her, Gray Moon."

"It had to be done," Gray Moon said, crouching, spinning around as Strong Branch spun around behind him, grabbing for his wrist. "She was in the way of our progress."

The actual confession was what set Strong Branch's emotions into a tailspin. He lunged for Gray Moon and began wrestling with him. The knife plunged into Gray Moon's chest, making him lose his balance. He toppled from the butte, clutching the knife and screaming.

Pale and shaken, Strong Branch looked downward and found Gray Moon lying beside Lily on the rocks, his eyes staring upward accusingly.

Turning away, holding his head in his hands, Strong Branch burst into tears, his whole body wracked with the hard crying.

After he was drained of tears, Strong Branch began walking slowly down the path that led to the forest below, where his horse was tethered. He looked at the gleam of the river through the trees and wanted to take the time to get Lily and take her back to her people for proper burial rites, but he knew there were dangers in that.

He could be accused of both deaths!

Tears flooded his eyes again, and he quickly mounted his horse, slapped his reins, and rode in the opposite direction. His whole body was empty over having lost Lily and Gray Moon, whom he had thought his best friend and adviser.

At this moment he was void of hopes and desires for his future—unless he could work it out, and he did not see how that was possible now.

He would try, though. Surely there was a way. And somehow he would find it. But now all that he could think about was escaping.

He must flee the wrath of Echohawk's family once Lily's body was found.

"I have lost everything today," he cried, hanging his head.

* * *

Wise Owl had seen both Strong Branch and Gray Moon leave the village on their horses, yet at different times. Earlier, he had seen Lily leave, and he had guessed then that she was going to her secret trysting place, which in truth was not a secret at all. Wise Owl had followed her there one night. He had witnessed the shameful lovemaking between Strong Branch and Lily, yet kept his silence.

Until now.

If Gray Moon was going to become involved also, it had to be stopped! Lily was becoming too strong a force to reckon with. And Wise Owl was going to put a stop to it, no matter how.

Hardly able to mount a horse anymore, his bones aching and swollen, he grunted and groaned.

Then finally comfortable enough in the saddle, he rode into the forest and dismounted next to the winding path that led up to the butte. He started to make the climb but decided first to quench his thirst. As he walked toward the river, he saw something strange on the rocks—then grew faint when he realized exactly what it was.

Shakily he rushed along the rocky shore. His eyes widened and he gasped when he saw Gray Moon, a knife still protruding from his chest, his body crushed from the fall.

He then gazed down at Lily, and turned cold inside when he saw the blood on her crushed body.

"Strong Branch! You did this!" he whispered, realizing that of late Strong Branch had become uncontrollable, even strange.

At first the shock was so intense, he could not think further than the fact that two murders had taken place. Then when his sense of logic began to reassert itself, he smiled. "Perhaps it is better this way," he said, strolling softly away from the bodies.

He nodded as he kneaded his chin contemplatively. "*Ayuh,* it is better this way. I will become chief of my people. I am most deserving, because I am the eldest and wisest."

Somehow in time, he flatly decided, he would convince both villages of Chippewa that he was the wisest of them all.

20

She sleeps! My lady sleeps! Sleeps!
—Longfellow

Sometime during the night, Mariah had heard a voice singing woefully and softly in the distance. Night Hawk had explained that this meant that sorrow was present.

The delicious aroma of steaming broth filled the wigwam. The two maidens had left Mariah's side to get their rest. Briana and Night Hawk were there, one on either side of Mariah's sleeping platform.

Briana's heart warmed at the sight of Night Hawk's devotion to his mother. He smoothed a damp cloth across her fevered brow, and she could tell that there was much between them that was good. She hoped that she could feel as close to a son, once one was born to her.

She smiled weakly at Night Hawk as he gave her a somber look. His time with his mother had to be short today, for he planned to leave soon with his many braves to search the forest for Echohawk once again. Briana had agreed to sit vigil at his mother's side for as long as it took for him to return.

Mariah's eyelashes fluttered against her pale cheek, and then rose slowly, revealing even paler eyes. She lifted a trembling hand to Night Hawk's copper cheek. "Echohawk, my darling," she murmured. "You have returned to me. You are safe."

A sob was wrenched from the depths of her being when she just as quickly discovered her mistake. It was her son sitting there, not her beloved husband!

"*Gee-mah-mah,* it is I, Night Hawk," he said, his voice breaking. "Do you not recognize me?"

Mariah cleared her throat and wiped tears from her cheeks with her free hand. "My son, for a moment I thought you were Echohawk," she whispered. "But now I see that it is you." She patted his cheek. "I am always glad to see you, my son. Always."

Her eyes wavered and her hand crept down beneath the blanket again. "Your father?" she said, her voice quavering. "You did not return home with your father?"

It tore at Night Hawk's very being to have to deny his mother anything, especially good news about his father. Yet he had no choice. Even in her weakened state, she had to face reality.

"*Gah-ween,* no," he said, softly kissing her fevered cheek. "I am sorry. Father has not returned." He leaned away from her, glancing over at Briana, then back down. "But I am leaving soon with many braves. We will search the day through again. We will find Father!"

"I will stay with you until Night Hawk's return," Briana said, taking the damp cloth as Night Hawk handed it to her. She began bathing Mariah's brow. "I shall feed you some broth soon. You need your nourishment, as well as rest."

"Food doesn't sound good to me," Mariah said, her eyelids heavy as they closed again. "Sleep. All I want to do is sleep."

The sound of piercing wails outside the wigwam startled Briana and Night Hawk to their feet. Mariah's eyes opened wildly and she grabbed for Night Hawk's hand. "Go and see who wails, and why!" she cried. Tears flooded her eyes. "Oh, Lord, what if someone has found your father—and he is dead?"

His heart pounding as the wails grew louder, Night Hawk pulled his hand from his mother's and stepped around the sleeping platform. Together he and Briana went outside, discovering Wise Owl standing in the center of the village, close to the great outdoor fire, his hands reaching to the heavens. His wails continued on and on as people gathered around him.

Night Hawk rushed to Wise Owl and stood square-shouldered beside him. "Wise Owl, why are you doing this thing in my village?" he asked, now scanning slowly around him, relieved when he did not see any bodies—especially his father's. Yet this made him even more confused by Wise Owl's actions.

Wise Owl turned his eyes into Night Hawk's. His lined face became even more furrowed as he frowned and placed a gentle hand on Night Hawk's arm. "I have brought disheartening news for you and your people, and then I must go and spread the same news to my village, for my people have lost one of their most valiant braves today," he said thickly. "Gray Moon. He is dead!"

"Gray Moon . . . is dead?" Night Hawk gasped. Then he tightened his jaw. "Who else is dead, Wise Owl? Who? And where are their bodies?"

Wise Owl lifted his chin and folded his arms across his narrow chest. "While going through the forest I stopped for a drink at the river," he said somberly. "I did not quench my thirst as planned. Something distracted me."

His patience running thin, Night Hawk took a step closer to Wise Owl and locked his fingers on the elderly man's bony shoulder. "Tell me what you found," he said flatly. "Now, old man. Now!" He swallowed hard, then said, "Did you find my father's body? Is that what you are taking so long to tell me?"

"Not your father's," Wise Owl said, a strange gleam in his eyes. "It was Lily. Your sister. She was lying beside Gray Moon on the rocks. They were surely shoved from the butte overhead." He narrowed his eyes and yanked himself free from Night Hawk's burning grasp. "Strong Branch must be responsible! He has disappeared. Does that not point to his guilt?"

Night Hawk's mind was swirling with what Wise Owl had said—Lily was dead? That Gray Moon had died with her?

And Wise Owl was accusing Strong Branch of murdering them. The chief that Wise Owl had always backed, even fought for, short of being banished from the tribe because of his strong viewpoints. Now Wise Owl was accusing Strong Branch of such a heinous crime?

To Night Hawk, it made no sense.

And then the full brunt of the news grabbed him at the core of his being—his beloved sister was dead.

Dead!

Dizziness overcame him and he would have fallen to his knees had not Briana caught him and supported him as he hung his head and fought back the tears that were battling to be set free.

Then Night Hawk regained his composure somewhat. "My sister," he said, gazing at Wise Owl. "You—you left her there, to be food for the bears?"

"I am an old man," Wise Owl said, pretending sadness as he lowered his eyes. "I could not lift her or Gray Moon to bring them to our villages."

Night Hawk erupted in snarls as he walked away from Wise Owl and headed for the corral. Briana ran after him, breathless. "Night Hawk, don't go alone," she cried. "Don't go at all. Send some braves. Night Hawk, it won't. . . . it will be such a terrible sight to see your sister like that."

Night Hawk stopped in mid-step and turned to Briana. He gazed down at her, then drew her into his embrace. "Help me to understand this," he whispered, holding her tightly to him. "She was so young, so vital. If Strong Branch did this, he will pay. He . . . will . . . pay."

"Night Hawk, darling," Briana said, easing from his arms. "Let someone else go for Lily. Right now you have your mother's welfare to consider. You have to tell her about Lily before she hears it from someone else. Hearing it from you will be easier—and you will be there to comfort her the instant she becomes grief-stricken."

Night Hawk sucked in a deep breath, then nodded. "You are right," he said, placing a gentle hand on her cheek. "You are always right."

He gave orders to several braves to go for his sister and Gray Moon, then he placed an arm around Briana's waist and drew her to his side. They walked together to his mother's wigwam. As they sat down beside Mariah, her eyes searched their faces for answers.

She discovered so much there that she turned away and began softly crying. "He is dead?" she murmured. "My darling husband is dead."

Night Hawk placed a finger under her chin and turned her

head around, their eyes locking. "*Gah-ween, gee-mah-mah,*" he said, his voice breaking. "It was not Father."

Briana's hand crept beneath the blanket and circled around Mariah's and held on for dear life as Night Hawk told her the full story.

Mariah's screams filled the village, and then there was an ensuing silence as she subsided again into a sad, deep slumber.

Briana flung herself into Night Hawk's arms, sobbing. "It is so sad," she cried. "Night Hawk, darling, I am so sorry. So very sorry!"

He held her for a moment, then rose to his feet. "I must prepare for my sister's burial," he said. He gazed down at Briana. "Please stay with my mother. Come to me if there is a change?"

Briana nodded, then turned back to Mariah as Night Hawk left the wigwam. A coldness seized her. Would she someday be forced to face such sadness about a husband? About a daughter? About a son?

The life of the Chippewa seemed one of constant trials and tribulations, continually wrought with losses.

* * *

Fairly bent over his saddle by the burden that he was carrying within his heart, Strong Branch drew his reins outside White Wolf's cave. Dismounting, he tethered his horse to a bush, then walked disconsolately toward the cave entrance. His head rose when he realized that he was no longer alone.

He made instant eye contact with White Wolf, who was leading his horse from the cave, ready to go on a morning hunt. Strong Branch remembered when life was sweeter, when every morning he had awakened with plans to ride with Night Hawk, to share their hunting adventures.

Back then, the rolling yellow plains had been checkered with herds of buffaloes. Along the banks of the streams that ran down from the mountains there had been many elk, which usually appeared in the morning and evening, and disappeared into the forest during the warmer part of the day.

Deer, too, had been plentiful, and the brooks had been alive with trout. Here and there the streams had been dammed by industrious beavers.

In the interior of the forest there were lakes with many islands where moose, elk, deer, and bears were abundant. Waterfowl gathered in great numbers, among them the crane, swan, loon, and many of the smaller kinds.

If he listened now, he might hear the partridges drumming their loudest, while the whippoorwill sang with spirit and the hooting owl reigned at night.

This land of Minnesota was a paradise, he thought. Then, as now.

It had been shared with Night Hawk, a friend then, an enemy now.

"What has brought you here this time of day?" White Wolf said, walking toward Strong Branch. He stopped beside him, his eyes narrowing when he saw the pain etched onto the chief's face. "Gray Moon. Where is he?" he asked guardedly. "You usually ride together when you come to meet with White Wolf."

Rage filled Strong Branch at the thought of Gray Moon and what he had done. The camaraderie they had shared—the excitement of the raids, the thrill of taking the firearms and storing them in the cave for future use—had vanished. It was easy to banish the love he had had for Gray Moon, as though he had never even existed.

But never could he forget his feelings for Lily—and she had been taken from him because of Gray Moon's misguided jealousy.

"He is dead," Strong Branch hissed.

"Dead?" White Wolf said, forking an eyebrow. "And how did this happen?"

"My knife moved as though it had a mind of its own into the body of Gray Moon," Strong Branch said in a snarl. "He is dead—lying in the rocks along the river."

White Wolf's lips parted in a quiet gasp. His eyes widened. "Your voice and the look in your eyes tells me that you did this thing out of hate," he said, running his hand along the withers of his horse. "Why would you? You worked together to make life more tolerable for your tribe. Did he do something that did not suit you in your scheme of things? Is this why you killed him?"

"*Ay-uh,* he did something that did not suit me," Strong Branch cried. "He murdered my woman—my Lily."

"Chief Echohawk's daughter?" White Wolf said, glancing over his shoulder at the cave entrance, since Echohawk was still his prisoner.

"*Ay-uh,* Echohawk's daughter," Strong Branch said solemnly.

"She was an extraordinarily beautiful woman," White Wolf said, his eyes taking on the appearance of one in deep thought. "I saw her more than once. She was a half-breed, her skin as white as alabaster."

Then he regarded Strong Branch closely. "You say she was your woman," he said thickly. "You were going to marry her?"

"No . . . yes . . ." Strong Branch mumbled. "Now I am not sure! But still I loved her no less than if she have been my wife, the woman to warm my bed *ah-pah-nay,* forever."

And then another thought came to him, causing him to sway. When Lily had died, so had the child—his child. Keen sadness swept through him again, at the thought of having lost so much, so quickly.

"I had planned to kill Echohawk today, after my hunt," White Wolf said matter-of-factly. "Now I will delay his death. I will give him much time to live through his suffering once I tell him about the death of his daughter. He will wish he were dead."

He laughed and mounted his horse. "You can have the pleasure of telling him, if you wish," he said, gathering his reins into his hands.

"I do not wish to inflict that sort of pain on anyone, not even Echohawk," Strong Branch said. He looked up at White Wolf. "I have come today to tell you that I am surely going to be blamed for both deaths, Lily's and Gray Moon's. I feel that it is best for everyone—all of the Sioux renegades, White Wolf, and Strong Branch—to part ways. The soldiers are searching for you even now, and the forests soon will be filled with many Chippewa braves searching for Strong Branch. When things clear up, my friend, we can get together again."

"You go on your way, and yes, I will tell my comrades to scatter to the far hills for now, and you and I will meet again soon. But White Wolf does not flee like a coward," he growled. He dismounted and began leading his horse back into the cave. He smiled over his shoulder at Strong Branch. "It is time to begin Echohawk's true suffering."

Strong Branch swallowed hard, then mounted his horse again. Just as he started to ride away, he flinched as though he had been shot when Echohawk's wails pervaded the air with its agony.

Hanging his head, Strong Branch snapped his reins and urged his horse into a slow trot toward the darkness of the forest, not allowing himself to feel pity for Echohawk or to feel wrong about his association with the Sioux. White Wolf had been there for him, to assist him in getting ammunition and guns for an eventual battle with the white pony soldiers *and* Echohawk's village of Chippewa. All of this had been required for Strong Branch to gain eventual total control over this land of lakes. He craved total power.

And he would still have it.

He had vowed to himself long ago that he would be the voice of this land, over everyone else's. Still this would be true. But he knew that it would now be harder gained than ever before. The odds were slowly stacking against him.

21

We want each other so.

—Alford

Briana slipped from the sleeping platform and began tiptoeing soundlessly toward the embers in the fire pit, hoping to get the morning fire going before Night Hawk awakened.

She glanced over her shoulder. He was still asleep, the first time she had seen him sleeping this peacefully since the death of his beloved sister. He had presided over Lily's burial and had taken several days since to sit vigil at his mother's bedside, to comfort her should she awaken from her strange, drugged sleep. But she had not awakened, not even when Briana succeeded at getting some broth through her lips and down her throat.

Today Night Hawk was going to end his period of mourning. He was going to focus on his father again, on the search that he had said would not end until he had his father at his side, or answers about his abduction.

Her cotton gown hardly enough this morning to ward off the chill, since the month of August was more than normally cool, Briana shivered and hugged herself, then knelt down before the fire pit and began laying twigs across the smoking, glowing embers. At first they sent sparks into the air, then slowly began to catch fire.

After they were burning substantially, Briana placed several larger pieces of wood in the flames, then sat down and held her hands close to the fire, soaking up the warmth into her flesh.

And then she felt another warmth, this one more delicious than that caused by the flames. Hands crept around from behind her and cupped her breasts through her thin cotton nightgown. She shivered in delight when Night Hawk's breath became hot on her cheek as his mouth brushed against it.

"You leave my bed without awakening me with a kiss, or touches from your hands?" he said huskily, softly kneading her breasts. "My woman, every morning we should warm each other with our bodies, *then* worry about a fire in the fire pit. The fires created within our hearts should be enough, do you not think so?"

"I didn't want to disturb you," Briana whispered, moving in a slight twisting motion to help Night Hawk slide her gown down from her shoulders to around her waist. She sucked in a wild breath as his hands cupped her breasts, his thumbs circling the hardened nipples. "Darling, you needed your rest before . . . before leaving. Who is to say when you will be able to sleep again?"

"That is true," Night Hawk said, turning her to face him. He sat down and lifted her onto his lap, her legs wrapping around his waist. He looked at her, adoring her. "But being with you, loving you, is more important to me than sleep. Because of the recent sadnesses, it has been many nights now since we made love. It is important never to allow our lovemaking to become commonplace. We must nurture it, as though it were food for our body."

Briana's eyes closed with ecstasy. She flung her head back when he thrust his thick hardness within her. His hands enfolded her breasts again and he stroked them as he lifted her up with each of his thrusts.

She leaned toward him and clutched his shoulders and began moving her own body in fluid motions, while Night Hawk slowed his strokes and let her take charge.

Briana rode him, giving her all this morning to this man that she would die for. She rose up and down in rhythmic movements, his shaft impaling her over and over again—deeper and deeper. She leaned her mouth to his lips and sucked his tongue as he thrust it inside her mouth, their kiss deepening.

Night Hawk placed his hands on her waist and lifted her away from him. He lay her down on the mat-covered floor and rose over her. Nudging her legs apart, he positioned himself inside her again and began his strokes within her, his hands trailing over her, seeking, finding, and caressing her every secret place, causing her to whimper with pleasure.

His mouth closed over her lips again. They kissed wildly, their bodies on fire as they moved with an intense searching for that realm of mindless bliss that was close to erupting within them.

And then their bodies quaked together.

They clung and rocked against each other.

They rolled over and over again across the floor, their bodies still locked together, their passion unfolding within them in wondrous, repeated climaxes of sexual excitement.

Finally their bodies became calm, yet Night Hawk's strong arms still enfolded Briana within them, she on top, her breasts crushed against his chest.

She smiled down at him through eyes hazed over with the afterglow of rapture, loving the feel of his hands as they stroked the swell of her buttocks. "Everything you do to me, every time you touch me, causes me to melt inside, my darling," she whispered, brushing a kiss across his lips.

She inhaled a sudden breath when she felt his renewed male energy filling her again as he thrust upward into her.

She moved with him, biting her lower lip to stifle the cries of passion that were building within her. He filled her magnificently. As he bucked into her, she felt her whole body tremble with the pressure within her.

And his hands were everywhere, stroking, caressing. His teeth were teasing the lobes of her ears, nipping, his hot breath stirring her into a frenzy of pleasure.

And again, in one quick turn, she found herself below him. She wrapped her legs around his waist and rode with him, her hips responding to his every thrust within her. She closed her eyes in ecstasy as his tongue slithered down her neck and stopped at her breasts. She twined her fingers through his hair as he sucked on one nipple and then the other, his hands gently squeezing the breasts.

Before she reached that height of joy that she was drawing near, Night Hawk rose from her. With warm hands against her waist, he guided her into a different position that was foreign to her.

She did not question him when he asked her to move onto her hands and knees.

She did not question him when he moved behind her and she could feel him probing with his hardness, soon entering her, his thickness filling her and moving in rhythmic strokes within her again, his fingers locked on her buttocks.

She could hear his guttural moans, knowing that this new way of loving her was pleasuring him. She soon closed her eyes and became lost in her own wondrous pleasure, gritting her teeth so that she would not scream, the rapture was so wild and intense.

Soon she felt the peak of his desire as he thrust more wildly within her. She responded in kind, pushing back against him, receiving him more deeply, the bliss intense as it flooded through her, touching her every nerve ending with the ultimate of pleasure.

Night Hawk stayed on his knees a moment longer, shaken by the intensity of their lovemaking this morning, as his manhood ebbed within her. Then he eased away from her and drew her down beside him.

Briana cuddled close, her eyes wide with questioning as she peered into his passion-dark eyes. "You never cease to amaze me," she murmured, smiling devilishly at him. "My darling, the way we just made love. It—it seemed so forbidden, yet I cannot deny the pleasure I found while doing it."

"It is not a forbidden way to make love," Night Hawk said, chuckling. He drew her lips close to his. "It is just because it was new to you. My sweet, innocent woman, the flower of my wigwam, nothing we choose to do together should ever be labeled forbidden. If our hearts lead us into it, then it is right, for we are as one, are we not? Soon we will seal that bond with a marriage ceremony."

Briana eased away from him and sat up, reaching for her buckskin dress. She had left it folded on the floor beside their sleeping platform, and she slid it over her head. "So many things keep us from what is most important to me," she murmured. "I feel so wanton sharing these sensual adventures with you since we are not married."

She wriggled the dress down the full length of her body. She turned to Night Hawk, whose nudity caused her heart to flutter anew, wanting him no less now than moments before. She was always filled with need for him!

Night Hawk took her hands and together they rose beside the slowly burning fire. "Before your God and my Great Spirit, we have been joined at the heart from the first moment we saw each other," he said softly. "So never feel wanton. Although no ceremony has been performed, we are man and wife. No love could be greater, or more sincere, than ours. That is what makes it right that we love one another as freely as we do. Never regret it. Regrets and doubts burn holes into one's soul."

She crept into his arms and snuggled close, her cheek resting on his muscular chest. "I do love you so," she murmured. "You are my soul, my darling."

"Keep that thought with you while I am gone," Night Hawk said.

He stepped away from her and began dressing. Briana watched him, admiring how his suit of fringed buckskin set off his splendid physique to advantage. When he lifted his rifle and stared down at her, she stifled a sob behind a hand, fearing that when he left this time, she might never see him again.

"Please be careful," she said, her voice breaking.

"I will not return this time unless my father is with me," Night Hawk said.

Briana locked her eyes with him, then turned quickly away and went to a buckskin bag that she had prepared for his trip—having filled it with an assortment of foods that would last for many days of travel.

"I wish you would stay long enough for us to share a warm breakfast," she said, handing him the heavy bag of food. "But I understand. You told your braves to be ready at sunup."

Night Hawk slung the bag over his shoulder, then with a bold sweep took her in his arms again, holding her tight against his hard body. "Do nothing foolish while I am gone, like leave this village unescorted," he said. "There are many things to fill your time. You can sit with my mother. Other times, you can paint. The children of the village would enjoy being taught your unique way with brushes and paints."

"It would delight me to show them how I paint," she said, beaming at the thought. "I shall paint a picture for each of them and give it to them to keep."

Night Hawk smiled warmly down at her. "Always you think of others," he said. "That is one of the many reasons I love you."

He crushed his mouth down upon her lips and kissed her with a savagery she had never known before, yet she understood why.

This might be their last good-bye.

* * *

The cave was dark and silent, the fire having burned down to glowing embers. Echohawk sat with his back resting against the cold wall. He had tried to lie down without success, aching with the want of sleep, not having been able to since he had received the news about his daughter. White Wolf had found the perfect sort of torture for his captive, for every breath was now torturous for Echohawk.

With each heartbeat he saw his lovely daughter: her dancing eyes, her soft white skin, her innocent smile, and the way she would duck her head when shyness overcame her. . . .

Hearing a slight stirring somewhere close by in the darkness, he stiffened, yet realized that he had not much to fear anymore. White Wolf's gang had disbanded, leaving White Wolf as his only threat. And White Wolf had not approached him much since he had given him the news that had shattered his heart into a million pieces.

But Echohawk expected White Wolf to grow tired of playing with him soon. Perhaps then Echohawk's miseries would be over, he thought bitterly to himself.

His daughter was dead!

His wife was lost to him, in many ways.

Ay-uh, perhaps it was time for Night Hawk to assume the duty of chief. It was for the better, it seemed.

Not far away, a torch flamed suddenly into view, drawing Echohawk quickly around. With a shallow-beating heart he watched White Wolf approach with Gentle Fawn. Lighting the renegade's face, the torch revealed a leering sort of smile. He kept one hand on Gentle Fawn's arm, forcing her to walk beside him.

When White Wolf shoved her to the floor on her back, he stood spread-legged over her. Echohawk's jaw tightened and he felt himself becoming filled with life and energy again as anger fused the wick that seemed to have died within him.

He wrestled with the ropes at his wrist, drawing blood as they bit into his flesh, his eyes wavering as he realized what White Wolf's intent was. He was going to torment Echohawk by forcing himself on Gentle Fawn—the woman that Echohawk now cared for. Although he knew the wrong of it, he had fallen in love with Gentle Fawn. Hopelessly in love.

And this was another reason why he had begun to feel that he did not care if he lived or died. He also loved Mariah and felt ashamed for having the needs that caused his heart to thunder within his chest every time Gentle Fawn came close to him.

When she touched him, everything within him cried out to kiss her. To hold her.

Dying a slow death inside, he watched the performance being acted out before him.

White Wolf lodged the torch into a hole in the cave's wall. He slowly, teasingly lowered his breechcloth, revealing his swollen need at the juncture of his thighs. He kicked the breechcloth aside and knelt down over Gentle Fawn, thrusting his hardness within her, his mouth slobbering over her face and down to her breasts.

Gentle Fawn grimaced and sobbed, having to lie limply and be raped before the eyes of the man that she had grown to love.

Echohawk growled, his eyes two points of fire as he helplessly watched the sweet, innocent young thing be defiled, as though she were no better than an animal.

White Wolf bucked more wildly into her, and then his

spasms subsided. He collapsed away from her, breathing hard, totally spent.

Gentle Fawn was allowed to rise. She gave Echohawk an ashamed, downcast glance, then fled to the darker depths of the cave, her sobs wafting through the air like softly falling rain, hurting Echohawk through andthrough.

White Wolf lay there awhile longer, panting, then moved slowly to his feet. Slipping his breechcloth back in place, he leered down at Echohawk. "She is very *o-nee-shee-shim,*" he said, chuckling.

Then White Wolf grabbed the torch, extinguished it by covering it with a damp buckskin covering, and went back to his sleeping platform.

Echohawk breathed hard, hate seething inside him. He eased down onto the blanket on the cave floor, and with his teeth he drew another blanket over him. Chilled not so much from the cold, but from what he had just witnessed, he closed his eyes and tried to go to sleep. He tossed from one side to the other, trying to get comfortable, trying to forget so much that pained him. Then he stopped, his eyes flying open widely when he felt a slender body slip beneath the blankets with him.

He melted within when a soft hand touched his cheek.

"It is I, Gentle Fawn," she whispered. "White Wolf is asleep. I have come to you, my love. But not to make love. I have brought you something even more valuable tonight."

Echohawk's pulse raced maddeningly when Gentle Fawn's hand left his cheek and he felt her begin cutting through his ropes with a knife. He scarcely breathed, fearing that she would get caught, but sighed heavily with relief when his hands were finally free.

He took the knife and leaned over, and soon the ropes fell away from his ankles. He placed his hands on Gentle Fawn's arms. "Return to your child," he whispered harshly. "Stay with her. Do you hear?"

"I will get her," Gentle Fawn whispered back, her eyes wide and anxious. "Let us escape. Tonight! I am finally brave enough to do this that I have feared for so long. With you, I feel safe. Please! Let us escape now!"

"Nothing is ever as easy as it seems," Echohawk said. "Do you truly believe that White Wolf would allow you to steal the knife? It is a trap. Now return to your child. When he looks my way, I shall pretend that I am still tied up. Do you not know that he perhaps is waiting for us to try to escape? I am the wiser. I will fool him, pretending that I am still bound. When White Wolf approaches me in the morning, I will then take advantage of my unbound hands and feet."

"Echohawk, I am so afraid," Gentle Fawn said, her eyes frantic.

Echohawk framed her face between his hands and drew her lips close. He had ached for her for so long, yet was still unable to have her in the way his loins ached for. "My sweet one," he whispered. "Trust me. Tomorrow we both will be rid of this snake."

He wrapped her in his arms and kissed her, the intensity of his feelings for her stirring a memory of how it had felt when he was a young man. It had been too long since those needs had been fulfilled.

His life was a gamble, it seemed, always a gamble.

Gentle Fawn's lips quivered against his. Her fingers crept up inside his fringed shirt, slowly caressing his bare, muscular chest, then lower. She started to touch him through his breeches where he had risen in response to his feelings, but his hand clasped onto hers, stopping her.

"Go now," he whispered, his voice husky with passion. "*Wah-bungh,* tomorrow. Things will be different tomorrow."

Gentle Fawn gave him a final hard hug, then fled into the darkness.

Echohawk stretched out beneath the blanket again, his eyes open the rest of the night. When he heard footsteps approaching him, and the flare of a torch being held high as White Wolf came into view, a keen questioning in his eyes, Echohawk clasped the knife beneath the blanket and waited.

He closed his eyes and feigned sleep. First he sensed White Wolf standing over him. Then he felt the heat of the torch as White Wolf slowly knelt down beside him. Echohawk sprang up like a panther and knocked White Wolf to the cave floor, the torch rolling away from him.

White Wolf was as quick as Echohawk. He sprang to his feet and began to wrestle the chief, holding his wrist, trying to keep the knife away from him.

They fell to the floor. In what was supposed to be a death plunge, Echohawk brought the knife down, but White Wolf rolled out of the way. The knife grazed the flesh of his upper left thigh instead of his chest.

When Gentle Fawn came into view, the bundled child in her arms, Echohawk looked her way long enough for White Wolf to scramble to his feet and flee toward the cave entrance, where he had his horse tethered. Seeing the quick exit, Echohawk moved to his feet and started to run after him but stumbled, realizing that having been left bound for so long had taken away much strength in his legs.

He stopped, took a deep breath and steadied his legs, then ran onward. As he arrived at the cave entrance, he found that he was too late. Angrily, his hand doubled into a tight fist at his side, he watched White Wolf gallop away on his horse.

Gentle Fawn came up behind. "Echohawk," she murmured, clutching her wrapped baby to her bosom, "we are now safe? He is gone?"

Echohawk turned to her, forgetting White Wolf for the moment. He beckoned to her with opened arms and when she came to him, he hugged both mother and child to him. "It is going to be all right," he said. "I will take you to my village. There you will begin a new life—a life that will include much love and warmth."

"I will be your *ee-quay,* woman?" Gentle Fawn asked, gazing up at him with her dark, doeful eyes.

Echohawk's eyes wavered and he swallowed back a fast-growing lump in his throat.

He was torn between two loves. He could not give up one or the other. Somehow he would have to work it out so that neither were hurt.

"I have a wife," Echohawk said, his voice drawn. "But I will still care for you and your child." He stroked her delicate, soft face. "But I will not be there at night to warm your bed. You understand, though, that I will be there for you other times."

Gentle Fawn's eyes misted with tears. "I understand," she murmured. Then she lay her cheek on his chest, feeling his quickened heartbeat through the buckskin fabric of his shirt. "You are the first man I have ever loved. I shall never love another, Echohawk."

He inhaled a shaky, deep breath. He closed his eyes as he burrowed his nose into the depths of her silken hair. "I have loved two other women in my life before I met you," he said softly. "My first wife is dead, but my second wife awaits my return even now. I still love my No-din, yet I love you also, Gentle Fawn. My woman, it is hard—this loving two women with only one heart to give. I want you with all of my being, yet I must deny myself this want. I must be true to my wife. She is ill. She depends on me."

"You are an honorable man," Gentle Fawn said, smiling sweetly up at him. "That is admirable." She touched his cheek. "But, my beloved, when your hungers become too hard to bear, remember that I will be there to satisfy them."

Echohawk took her hand and kissed her palm, then turned and surveyed the cave around them, suddenly struck with the knowledge that although free, there were no horses to ride to freedom.

He turned back to Gentle Fawn. "Give me the child," he said. "It is a long walk to my village. Allow me to make your burden and walk easier. I will carry your child."

Gentle Fawn shook her head. "No, it is enough that you will be at my side," she said. "Your presence is all the strength from you that I need."

Echohawk saw the wisdom in this younger woman's logic, then stared into the darker depths of the cave, remembering the firearms. He must equip himself well. White Wolf could return and find them. Echohawk would be ready.

This time he would send a bullet through the renegade's heart.

22

Your mouth that I remember
With rush of sudden pain.

—Russell

Downcast, with his braves following behind him on horseback, Night Hawk rode beneath an umbrella of elm trees, peering upward through their thick branches of leaves. He frowned. The sun was lowering in the sky, ending the day much too quickly for him. Although he had covered much territory, he still had not found any signs of White Wolf's new hideout or his father.

Night Hawk swallowed hard, beginning to doubt that he would ever see his father again. Perhaps, even, his father had died in the explosion at the cave and Night Hawk had just not wanted to accept it.

The ashes were cool now. If he went and sorted through them more carefully, would he find that which would wrench his heart from his chest?

He shook his head desperately back and forth, in an effort to loose his mind of such thoughts. He would find his father. Perhaps not today, but *wah-bungh,* tomorrow. If not then, the next day, for he had made a vow to himself that he would not return home again unless his father was riding at his side.

A shout stirred his thoughts back to the present. He turned to the brave at his right side, seeing an anxiousness in his dark eyes as he pointed to something up ahead.

Night Hawk turned and followed the path of the brave's vision, and his heart stopped when he caught sight of someone walking toward them, recognizing the proud stance of his father!

Then he saw someone else—a beautiful woman at his side,

a bundled child clutched to her bosom. His throat went dry when he recalled the woman and child in the cave when he had been held captive. Could these be . . . ?

Too glad to have found his father, he brushed away any wonder about the woman and child and sank his heels into the flanks of his horse and rode on ahead at a gallop. When he reached Echohawk, he swung himself out of his saddle and flung himself in his father's strong embrace.

"*Gee-bah-bah,*" he said, so humbled by his father's presence he was at this moment a child again. "I have finally found you, Father. I had begun to think that—that I never would. That you were dead."

Echohawk hugged Night Hawk to him, having had many fears about his son as well. "My *nin-gwis,* my son," he said hoarsely.

Night Hawk clung to his father a moment longer, then stepped away, resuming a dignified stance as he squared his shoulders in the presence of his braves that had followed him here to this place of an emotional reunion of son and father.

"*Gee-bah-bah,*" he said, growing cold inside as his gaze settled on the rip on his father's shirt sleeve and the blood dried on it. "You were injured?"

"I was shot," Echohawk grumbled. "But the wound has healed adequately enough."

"You were shot?" Echohawk said, the very thought paining him, as though the bullet had entered his own flesh.

"It was only a flesh wound, my son," Echohawk reassured him. "Nothing to concern yourself about." He glanced down at Gentle Fawn, recalling her gentle ways of bathing his wound, taking the heat from the very core of it. He recalled the mixture of herbs that she had concocted from the few she had found just outside the entrance of the cave. Because of her, the arm was almost healed.

"Then you are well otherwise?" Night Hawk asked. "You were not tortured?"

"*Ay-uh,* I am well otherwise," Echohawk murmured. "Physically I was not tortured, but . . ." He glanced down at Gentle Fawn again, remembrances of having been forced to watch White Wolf rape her filling him with renewed rage. Then he looked back to Night Hawk. "But mentally I was tortured—in many ways."

Night Hawk had seen his father glance down at the beautiful woman more than once, then had noticed something hidden in the depths of his eyes as he had looked again at Night Hawk. "Father, when I was held captive in the cave, I recall hearing a woman and a child, but because I was blindfolded, I never saw them," he said guardedly. "Is this them? Did she allow you to rescue her? I tried. When I did, she did not even show her face to me. She remained hidden in the depths of the cave. I had to leave without her."

Echohawk possessively placed an arm about Gentle Fawn's tiny waist and drew her close to him. "*Ay-uh,* this is that woman and child," he said. "This is Gentle Fawn and her daughter, Moonstar. While I was held captive, she was not allowed to stay hidden. She was forced to do many things in my presence." He swallowed hard, then gave her a soft look filled with gratitude. "But what she did for me was out of the pure kindness of her heart. She saw to my wound. That is why it is not festering now with infection."

Night Hawk's eyebrow arched when he saw the affection between his father and the woman. It was as though they held secrets within their hearts—perhaps those which would condemn his father in his son's eyes, since his father already had a wife.

He felt the dire need to change the subject from the woman, not wanting ever to resent his father. "Who besides White Wolf was responsible for your abduction?" he said, his eyes wavering as his father still did not release his hold on the woman at his side.

"Blackie," Echohawk said, his voice cold.

Night Hawk's jaw tightened. "So Blackie *was* responsible for all of this," he said through clenched teeth. "If I had resorted to his own tactics and forced the truth out of him, I would have found you sooner!"

Echohawk stepped away from Gentle Fawn and placed a gentle hand on Night Hawk's arm, urging him away from the others to talk in private. "My son, it was known that you were being held captive just before my own abduction," he said. "Gentle Fawn was forced to tell Blackie how you managed to escape. She said that a woman came for you. In Blackie's rage he said something about his niece having done it. Is that true, my son?"

"*Ay-uh,* that is so," Night Hawk said, nodding. "Briana. She awaits me even now at our village. My father, she and I will soon wed. And I know that you will be pleased with my choice."

Echohawk wanted to question his son at length about this woman—a woman of much courage. He wanted to ask how she had known where the cave was, and how Night Hawk had met her, and when he had become enamored of her. But another woman was now in his mind—his sweet wife, Mariah, his No-din.

"Your *gee-mah-mah*?" Echohawk asked. "How is she, my son? How has she taken my absence?"

Night Hawk glanced over at Gentle Fawn, in his mind's eye still seeing his father's arm so possessive around her tiny waist.

He turned back to face his father, his eyes narrowing. "Mother has worsened in your absence," he grumbled. "She is suffering another bout of malaria, and she is filled with melancholia from worrying about you. We must tarry no longer, Father. We must return to our village. You must go to mother and show her that you are alive and well. This will give her a reason to smile again. Perhaps she then will recover from her latest bout of illness."

Echohawk lowered his eyes, his heart aching with mixed emotions. He was anxious to see his wife, hoping that she would soon recover again, yet he was torn with wanting to make everything right for Gentle Fawn. She had already suffered a lifetime of insults and humiliation. He had to make sure she suffered none of this at the hands of his people. Especially from his son, who would one day be her chief.

Night Hawk saw that his father was battling something within his heart, and suspected what, for he himself had noticed how sweet and lovely Gentle Fawn was, and he knew that his father had not had a wife that was a lover for many years now. So he placed all resentment of his father loving another woman from his heart and placed an arm around his shoulders.

"Father, whatever it is that is troubling you, I shall make it easier for you to cope with," Night Hawk said, squeezing his father's shoulder. "Have we not always shared our minds and hearts? It is no different now. I understand you, *gee-bah-bah,* as though we were of one heartbeat. That is the way of devoted sons to fathers. No matter what, Father. No matter what."

Echohawk turned to Night Hawk and embraced him. "You are a good son," he said, his voice breaking. "Thank you, Night Hawk. *Nee-gway-chee-wehn-dum,* thank you."

They remained in each other's embrace a moment longer, then swung away and started walking back toward the others. Suddenly, however, Night Hawk realized that he had news of someone else to relay to his father. Lily! His father had to be told about his daughter. And seeing his remorse would surely be the same as reliving her death all over again inside Night Hawk's heart.

Yet he had to tell his father now and allow the pain to lessen somewhat before he entered the village to go to his ailing wife. But Night Hawk feared that too many hurts at once might devastate his father, perhaps even age him many moons.

He placed a hand on his father's elbow and stopped him. He looked at him morosely, then knew that he could not hold in the terrible truth any longer. It was paining him as though someone were plunging a knife into his heart over and over again.

"*Gee-bah-bah,* there is something I must tell you that you will find hard to bear," he finally said.

"It is about your sister?" Echohawk said, gazing into his son's eyes.

"*Ay-uh,* it is about Lily," Night Hawk said. "How . . . could you know?"

"My son, I know that your sister is dead," Echohawk said, placing a gentle hand on his son's shoulder. "I grieved for her long and hard. But now I am looking forward to the welfare of those who are alive. So should you, my son. Life is short. So very, very short. It is for the living, to be lived."

"Father, how did you find out?" Echohawk asked softly.

"White Wolf," Echohawk grumbled. "It gave him much pleasure to tell me."

"But how did he know?" Night Hawk asked, his mind aswirl with wonder.

"*That* he did not share with me," Echohawk said, then dropped his hand from his son's shoulder and resumed walking toward those who were waiting. "That he told me was enough at the time. I could think of nothing else but my grief, my son. Nothing else."

When they reached the others, Night Hawk went to his horse while Echohawk went attentively to Gentle Fawn and placed a gentle arm around her waist, ushering her toward the mounted braves.

Echohawk smiled up at one of his most devoted braves. "Perhaps you could allow me the use of your horse today?" he said. "Perhaps you could ride with Blue Heron."

The brave looked questioningly at Gentle Fawn and his chief's attitude toward her, then nodded and slipped easily from the saddle.

Night Hawk stood back and watched the expressions of the many braves as Echohawk very gently took the child from Gentle Fawn's arms and held it to his bosom as she placed a foot in the stirrup and swung herself into the saddle. Night Hawk had many mixed emotions when he saw the sweet smile that Gentle Fawn gave his father as she reached for the child and took her into her arms. His gut wrenched when his father swung himself into the saddle behind her, again showing his possessiveness of her as he placed an arm around her waist to hold her against him as he prepared himself for the long trek through the forest for their return home.

Night Hawk sighed heavily, realizing now that for certain his father had found someone else to warm his bed at night, and prayed that his mother would never find out. If she did not already have enough that caused her life to be slowly ebbing away, this would perhaps cause her to take her last breath.

He mounted his own horse and rode up beside his father. His mouth parted in a quiet gasp as he watched Gentle Fawn lower a portion of her dress and offer her breast to the tiny lips awaiting it. He quickly looked away, this scene seeming to be much too intimate for him to witness, yet his father was behaving as though it were his own child now suckling at the nipple, for in his eyes there was much adoration.

Fighting back the urge to be jealous for himself and his mother, Night Hawk rode with a straight back and lifted chin beside his father. He had to remind himself that only a few short hours ago he had been losing hope of ever finding or seeing his father again. He had reason to rejoice now, for his father was riding at his side, scarcely harmed by his abduction.

And he knew his father well enough to realize that he would not do anything to hurt his mother. Even if he loved Gentle Fawn, he would not flaunt it. Nothing would make his father waver from being a devoted husband, especially now, when his wife needed him the most.

This made him more relaxed with the woman and child being held protectively close by his father. And Echohawk was known for his gentle ways. It would not be his nature to treat the woman and child any other way than with kindness.

Except that Night Hawk knew beyond a shadow of a doubt that his father's feelings for this woman reached much deeper than mere kindness. Hopefully he was the only one that would recognize it.

He glanced over at Gentle Fawn and saw the innocent beauty of her face; yet when Gentle Fawn turned his way, he recognized the look of one who had suffered much at the hands of her captors. Even when she smiled, there was a shadow of pain. He could see how his father had been moved to such protective feelings for the woman and child.

Night Hawk returned a soft smile to Gentle Fawn, wanting her to relax in his presence, as he would try to accept what she had become to his father. Deep down he wished that she had let *him* release her from captivity. Then she would have never met his father, perhaps avoiding much pain in the end, for Night Hawk knew that his father would never leave his wife for another woman. Not as long as his father's wife had an ounce of breath left within her weakened lungs.

Night Hawk looked straight ahead and urged his horse into a steady gallop, anxious to return to the woman *he* loved, finally able to have some semblance of peace within her arms before he and his father set out to avenge what her Uncle Blackie had done to them.

* * *

Their entrance into the village was met with much jubilation. Even though Echohawk carried a woman and child on his horse, people crowded around them, touching him, their eyes filled with much happiness and relief to see him again. He smiled down at them all, nodding a silent hello to those whom he favored—true friends of his since he had been a child.

He drew the reins before his wigwam. He dismounted, then helped Gentle Fawn from the horse.

Night Hawk acted quickly. He went to Gentle Fawn and took her by the elbow. "You will stay at my dwelling until my father makes arrangements for you and your child," he said. Hesitantly she glanced with desperate eyes over her shoulder at Echohawk.

"Do not fear me," Night Hawk urged, moving her onward, wanting to witness his mother's reaction to Echohawk's return. Hopefully, this would draw her from her self-induced sleep.

Quickly formulating explanations to offer Briana before rushing back to his father's wigwam, Night Hawk was surprised when he lifted the entrance flap and found that she was gone. He expected now to find her sitting vigil at his mother's bedside. She had done this willingly, not only out of the goodness of her heart, but because she was Night Hawk's mother, soon to be her mother-in-law.

He helped Gentle Fawn down on a soft cushion of pelts beside the low embers of the fire. "You must be tired, please rest," he said. He nodded toward a kettle of food that hung over the hot coals of the fire. "You must be hungry. Eat. Father or I will return later."

Gentle Fawn lifted her soft, doe eyes to him. "Thank you," she murmured. "You are a mirror of your father not only in appearance, but also in your behavior. Your kindness is most appreciated."

Night Hawk returned her smile, finding it hard to resent anyone as sweet and as vulnerable as this woman. He turned and fled the wigwam. He broke into a run, panting hard when he entered his father's dwelling. His gaze took in a sight that warmed him through and through. His woman was on one side of his mother's sleeping platform, his father on the other. His mother's eyes slowly opened as his father continued to speak of his love for her.

Night Hawk crept into the dwelling and sat down beside Briana. He reached for her hand and held it tightly as he watched his mother look adoringly up at Echohawk, trying to mouth her first words in many days.

"My . . . darl . . . ing . . ." Mariah finally managed to say, reaching for Echohawk's hand, clutching it weakly with her frail hand. "You—you . . . have come back to me."

Echohawk softly kissed her cheek. "No-din, my wife," he said, fighting back the urge to cry. His wife was hardly a trace of what she had been. The flesh of her face was drawn tautly across her bones. Her eyes were dark beneath, her breathing was shallow.

"Hold me, Echohawk," Mariah whispered, reaching out her free hand to him. "Please hold me."

Echohawk leaned over her and swept her frail body into his arms. He held her cheek close to his chest as he stroked her dry, lifeless hair. "You must get well," he whispered, choking back a sob. "My darling, you must get well!"

"I promise that I will," Mariah said, stroking his muscular back with her bony hands. "You shall see. I will be well soon. For you, my darling. For you."

Mariah drew away. Tears streamed down her cheeks as she gazed woefully into her husband's eyes. "Lily," she sobbed. "Our Lily is . . . dead . . ."

Echohawk choked back a sob. He took Mariah's hands and squeezed them softly. "I know," he murmured. "I know."

He then leaned over Mariah and enveloped her within his arms and held her, their tears mingling.

Filled with emotion, Night Hawk urged Briana to her feet and ushered her outside. He swept an arm around her waist and drew her to his side as he walked her toward their wigwam.

"That was so sad," Briana said softly.

"Ay-uh," Night Hawk said, nodding.

"But I do believe Mariah is going to be all right," Briana said, giving him a reassuring smile. "And, darling, you are home safe, along with your father. I'm so relieved and so . . . so happy."

Night Hawk tried to feel as content, yet the very sight of his wigwam made him suddenly remember who awaited inside. Gentle Fawn and her child. Right now they were his responsibility, soon to be his father's! He had to explain to Briana before she entered the wigwam.

He stepped in front of her. He placed his hands on her waist and drew her against him, their eyes locked. "There is something I must tell you," he said. "There is a woman and child—"

He stopped abruptly when his father walked past him and entered the wigwam. Wide-eyed, his jaw slack, Night Hawk watched as his father soon emerged from the wigwam, Gentle Fawn walking beside him, her child clutched to her bosom.

Echohawk said nothing to his son. He took Gentle Fawn to a nearby wigwam that had been vacated when one of the elders of the village had died. Once inside, with a comforting fire burning, he turned to Gentle Fawn.

"You will be seen to," he said, his voice resonant as he took one of her hands and held it. "But understand that I cannot come to you. My wife is quite ill. She needs me."

Gentle Fawn lowered her eyes as tears rolled down her cheeks.

Echohawk placed a finger under her chin and lifted her eyes to his. "This is the only way it can be," he said, his voice strained.

He turned from her and left the wigwam. His gut twisted as he heard her soft weeping, his heart torn between two women, both adored by him.

Briana and Night Hawk went on into their dwelling, Briana questioning him with her wide eyes.

Night Hawk sat down beside the fire pit and drew his knees to his chest. "My father seems to have duties to two women now," he grumbled. "This I find hard to accept, for I do not believe in sharing my heart with but one woman. So should it be for my father."

Then he turned sadly to Briana. "Yet I can understand how he can be swayed by Gentle Fawn's sweet loveliness," he said, his voice breaking. "My mother has not been a wife for many years now. My father is a virile man who has denied himself the hungers of the flesh! Perhaps he has reached his limits of restraint. I must not judge him for this hunger, for I hunger just as much for what we share."

"Night Hawk, is she possibly the woman in the cave that you tried to encourage to come with us when I rescued you?" Briana asked, now recalling Night Hawk worrying about a woman and child.

"They are the same," Night Hawk said, nodding. "It seems she trusted my father more than she did me."

Briana eased into his arms. "I believe I am relieved that she did," she said, laughing softly. "If not, perhaps she would have cast her spell over you."

"*Gah-ween-wee-kah,* never," Night Hawk said huskily, easing her to the soft furs beside the fire pit. "You are my woman. Always and forever." He sealed that promise with an all-consuming kiss.

Then Night Hawk drew away from her and looked at her questioningly. "You have never told me how you knew about the cave on the day of my rescue," he said, placing a gentle hand to her cheek.

Briana smiled up at him and told him everything.

23

Out of a world of laughter,
Suddenly I am sad.

—Russell

The Chippewa village was well into the mourning period for Mariah, who had died the very next morning after Echohawk's return to the village. In memory of Mariah, a tipi shrine had been especially erected at the far edge of the village on a slight knoll, where on a clear day the sun would always bathe it with its warmth.

A strand of Mariah's hair, symbolizing the living spirit of the buried dead, was the object of adoration. The hair had been wrapped in a bundle, the covering of which was made beautiful with paintings, porcupine quillwork design, and then hung on a tripod which had been painted red.

Just prior to the day of the memorial service, many gifts had been taken and tied to the tripod inside the tipi. The gifts had then been distributed among the people of the village on the day of the memorial service.

Briana was sitting beside her lodge fire, sewing beads on a new pair of moccasins for Night Hawk that she had fashioned from buckskin. She was deep in thought of the memorial service and how beautiful it had been. It had left her with the feeling that Mariah was at complete peace, and happy wherever she was—in Heaven or in the Chippewa's Land of the Hereafter.

Briana's thoughts shifted to Night Hawk and his dark mood ever since the burial. He and his father were carrying around too much blame—too much hatred toward her uncle, blaming him in part for having brought on Mariah's death so suddenly. They felt that if not for her uncle, she would still be alive.

And they vowed to find and kill White Wolf as well.

Briana stiffened when Night Hawk's and Echohawk's voices grew close outside as they walked toward the wigwam. Again they had been together, walking and communing with their Great Spirit in the forest, making plans that soon would be acted out once the mourning period for their loved one was over.

Briana cast Night Hawk a worried smile as he came into the wigwam, his father beside him. Night Hawk was so immersed in thought, his brow knitted into a frown, he did not even notice her sitting there. He went to the kettle of stew hanging over the lodge fire and dipped some out into two wooden bowls. He handed his father one of the bowls and a wooden spoon, then took a bowl of stew and a spoon himself and sat down close to the fire.

Briana was hurt that he did not even offer her a hello, but soon realized why. He and his father had just made plans that Night Hawk apparently did not believe she would understand or accept. And, surely, she concluded, because of this they did not include her in their further conversation about it.

Briana tried to relax, knowing that Night Hawk's decisions always came from the deepest recesses of his heart. Knowing that thus far he had been right in all of his decisions, Briana continued her beadwork, yet eavesdropped on the conversation anyway.

"Tomorrow we will place our mourning behind us," Echohawk said, then scooped another spoonful of stew into his mouth.

"*Ay-uh,* tomorrow," Night Hawk said, nodding his head in agreement. He also scooped a spoonful of stew into his mouth, chewing eagerly.

"We will bring him back to the village, Night Hawk, and let all of our people witness his punishment," Echohawk said, setting his empty bowl aside.

"*Ay-uh,* that is best," Night Hawk said, setting his own empty bowl aside. He wiped his mouth free of grease with the back of his hand and glowered over at Echohawk. "But, *gee-bah-bah,* I expect him to have taken flight, like a tiny sparrow trying to escape the claws of a mighty hawk. I doubt we will achieve our vengeance anytime soon because of his cowardice."

Echohawk managed a slight laugh, although his heart was still bleeding over the loss of his Mariah, his "Woman of the Wind." "If he is smart he will have become that sparrow," he said, stretching out a long, lean leg before him. "My son, we are the hawk, are we not? When we do find him, we will quickly and unmercifully snatch him up into our claws. He will only wish his death could come as swiftly as the sparrow whose neck is broken almost the moment it enters the claws of the hawk!"

"And how will we hand out his punishment, *gee-bah-bah*?" Night Hawk said, too matter-of-factly as far as Briana was concerned.

Whose punishment? she wanted to ask. What sort of punishments do you usually use?

Listening intently, growing more uneasy by the moment over what she was hearing, Briana gazed from father to son, suspecting that the only man they could be talking about was her Uncle Blackie, or perhaps White Wolf.

Nonetheless, it gave her a sense of foreboding, as though a dark cloud was settling over this village of Chippewa as the conversation grew more dedicated to abduction and punishment.

"Perhaps we will let our people choose the punishment," Echohawk said, frowning over at Night Hawk. "Or do you think it should be the council's decision? What do you think, my son? You soon will be chief. Your voice in the matter is the most powerful of all the people who are linked with our band of Chippewa."

Night Hawk coldly turned toward Echohawk. "Until you appoint me chief of our people, you are still the voice of this band of Chippewa," he said. "And, *gee-bah-bah,* the choice of punishments for Blackie should be yours alone, for you have been the target of his hate for too long now."

"Blackie?" Briana said, finally voicing her feelings aloud.

She dropped her beadwork onto her lap, paling. Although she had suspected that her uncle was the subject of the conversation, she had held to the hope that somehow it was not so. Although she hated her uncle almost with a vengeance, she did not want to think that she had even the slightest part in harming him. What's more, if Night Hawk had a part in her uncle's death, surely the authorities would come and take him away. He could be hung, or shot by a firing squad. The thought sent spirals of dread through her.

"What you are saying, Night Hawk, about my Uncle Blackie?" she managed to say as two sets of dark, piercing eyes turned her way. "You can't mean that you are going to abduct him and drag him away into the night, and—and hold him hostage, and then kill him."

Night Hawk glowered at her. "Do you forget so easily what your uncle is responsible for?" he said, his teeth clenched. "Both my father and I were taken captive. My mother is dead because of this act of vengeance. It is the code of the Indian that it is an eye for an eye, a life for a life. Your uncle must die!"

Briana rushed to her feet and went to Night Hawk, kneeling down before him. She took his hands and held them tightly. "My darling, don't you see? Although it is true that I do not like to think of you killing anyone, even my dreaded uncle, it is not my uncle that I am concerned about," she said. "Think of the consequences, Night Hawk, should you manage to steal my uncle away and then kill him. The white community won't stand for it. They will come for both you and your father. You will be taken back to Fort Snelling. They will either put you before a firing squad, or they will place nooses around your necks!"

Night Hawk eased one of his hands from Briana's. "My woman, I know that what you are saying is from the heart," he said softly. "But, Briana, you are interfering where women should not. These decisions reached today were made between a chieftain father and son, and well thought out. Should the white pony soldiers come and investigate, no signs of your uncle will be found. Our scouts will have alerted us. So rest easy, my woman, that everything will be done that will bring no harm to me, my people, my father, or you."

With a nod he gestured toward the beadwork that had dropped to the floor when she scrambled to her feet. "Resume your beadwork," he said, more as an order than a suggestion.

Briana stared disbelievingly at him. She jerked away and plopped down by the fire, across from him and his father. "No, thank you," she said stubbornly, folding her arms across her chest. "I have lost interest tonight in my beading. And I may never do beadwork again! That is done to keep the fingers and minds of the women busy so that they do not interfere in the matters of the men! I am not a typical woman who sits obediently, voiceless and brainless, Night Hawk, to everything you expect of me. Perhaps—perhaps I will not even become your wife. I have freedoms, Night Hawk, that marriage to a Chippewa chief might cause to become stifled. I doubt if I can be stifled in any way, Night Hawk. I doubt that very much!"

Her gaze met his. "I have many passions, Night Hawk," she murmured. "Freedom of speech and movement is one of them!"

Her eyes slightly wavered. "Until tonight I had not minded sitting by, trusting your judgment in everything," she murmured. "But this, Night Hawk? The decision to bring my uncle here for punishment? I see it as perhaps bringing tragedy to your people, not vengeance. I chose to speak out tonight, Night Hawk, only because I fear for you and your people."

Not used to women speaking their mind so strongly, Night Hawk peered at her with a slack jaw. He turned his eyes from her and met an amusement in the depths of his father's.

He realized why. It was a well-known fact that his mother had been a stubborn, strong-willed person when she had been younger—a lady with a fiery spirit. His father was seeing this in Briana and enjoying it—and obviously accepting it, for he was not chiding her now for her outburst.

Night Hawk turned back to Briana. He went to her and knelt down before her. "Briana, you worry needlessly," he tried to reassure her. He placed a hand on her cheek. "Trust me. Trust my father. We are both known for seeking peace. No one will come looking for your uncle here."

Briana gazed into his eyes, wanting to believe what he said, yet doubts kept creeping into her mind.

Finally she realized what she must do. She had to warn her uncle.

She had to believe that he would flee the Indians' wrath instead of going to the authorities to stop the Chippewa. Knowing her uncle as she did, she expected him to take the quietest way out of this to keep from drawing attention to himself that could harm his chances in politics. A skirmish with Indians would make people ask why, and when they found out all of her uncle's dirty secrets, he would be ruined.

She wanted the worst for her uncle, yet she wanted to assure Night Hawk's safety more than she wanted to see her uncle finally pay.

Yes, she decided to herself, even now, while Night Hawk was looking into her eyes so trustingly, she knew that she had to sneak away from the Chippewa village and go to her uncle and encourage him to take flight—a flight that would take him far, far away from her, and the man she loved, and the beloved Chief Echohawk, hopefully forever.

"I understand," Briana said, keeping her unblinking eyes steady with his, the lie having slipped across her lips so easily. "Please go ahead and discuss what you must in my presence. I-I shall resume my beading. You will be very proud of your new moccasins, Night Hawk. They will keep your feet warm during the long winter days while hunting."

Night Hawk's eyebrow arched, finding her sudden change of heart hard to believe. Although she seemed to be accepting what was planned for her uncle, he doubted that she did. He did not want to believe that she was capable of lying, yet he suspected that she had—and he knew that he must keep a close watch on her.

"I will accept the new moccasins with a happy heart," he said, trying to keep the wariness from his voice. He turned to his father. "We have spoken enough today of our plans. Let us meet at sunrise tomorrow, *gee-bah-bah,* and finalize them."

Echohawk pushed himself up from the thickly matted floor. He swung an arm around Night Hawk's shoulder and gave him a warm hug, then went and lifted the entrance flap. "*Wahbungh,* tomorrow, my son," he said somberly.

Night Hawk went to Echohawk and stopped him. "There is someone else we must now search for and make pay for wrongful deeds done to our family," he said sullenly. "It is time to search for Strong Branch. His absence this long is proof of his guilt. My thoughts were burdened by too much until now. But now my vision is clear and I see Strong Branch as guilty—and one who must pay!"

"If you are that positive of his guilt, I shall send many braves to search for him while you and I go in another direction to bring Blackie back for his punishment," Echohawk said, nodding. "*Ay-uh,* all those who have brought pain into our lives will pay, my son. And soon."

Night Hawk nodded, gave his father a warm embrace, and watched him walk away. He turned and went back to sit beside his lodge fire.

There was a strained silence in the wigwam after Echohawk's departure. Briana forced her fingers to string beads onto a long length of string, to store them for future use, knowing that to look at Night Hawk now might reveal that she had deceived him, even though thus far in intention only. She had never thought herself capable of deceiving the man she loved, even if it meant that what she had planned might ensure his safety.

She wanted him to trust her always, not have cause to doubt her during their lifetime together. But, she had already decided, if ensuring his safety meant losing him, so be it. His life was more important than having a lifetime with him. And hopefully, he would understand her motives and forgive her.

Night Hawk gazed with wonder down at Briana for a moment, her silence proof to him that she was either still angry at him, or she was trying to hide the truth from him—that she could not live with what he planned for her uncle. He hoped it was not the latter, yet he would not let down his guard. If she tried to flee to her uncle, he would make sure that she was stopped.

Thinking that there was any tension between them made a

grievous ache circle Night Hawk's heart. He could hardly bear it.

He went to Briana. He took the string of beads from her fingers and lay them aside. Placing his hands in hers, he urged her to her feet, then led her to their sleeping platform, piled comfortably with warm pelts.

Without saying anything to her, he began slowly disrobing her. Within them rose a need that momentarily erased all sadness, doubt, and misunderstanding from their minds. All that mattered to them was their undying love for each other.

After her clothes were removed and she felt the warmth of the lodge fire caressing her flesh, Briana grabbed Night Hawk's fringed shirt and drew it over his head, revealing to her a copper chest all muscular and tight, the nipples on his breasts tautly erect.

She tossed the shirt aside, then placed her fingers on the waistband of his fringed breeches. Her eyes devoured his nudity as it was slowly revealed to her, his manhood springing free as she swept his breeches on down across his stomach, his thighs, and then dropped them to rest around his ankles.

Night Hawk drew in a wild breath and closed his eyes as Briana circled his hardness with her fingers and started moving them around him, squeezing and fondling as she continued this up-and-down movement.

Night Hawk reciprocated by placing a hand at the juncture of her thighs and caressing the center of her passion. Briana closed her eyes. She sighed as the pressure of his fingers increased, sending her into a world that only knew pleasure—that only knew Night Hawk.

He then placed his hands on Briana's waist and eased her down onto her back on the sleeping platform. He kissed his way down her body. She was almost beside herself with pleasure. She twined her fingers through his glossy dark hair and urged him up.

As he stretched himself above her, his one hand guiding his shaft within her, a sensual shudder rocked Briana. She sighed and lifted her hips to take him more deeply inside her.

At first his strokes within her were gentle, but soon they

became faster. Briana clung to his neck, his mouth seizing hers in a fiery kiss, his hands kneading her breasts.

The explosion of rapture came quickly. And after their passionate trembling had subsided, Night Hawk rolled away. She leaned on an elbow and watched him gather up his clothes and get into them. Never before had he left her so abruptly after having made love.

"Where are you going?" she murmured, drawing a fur robe around her shoulders.

"I feel as though I must go and be with my father for a while longer," Night Hawk said, not actually telling a lie. He did have to go to his father. He knew that he was torn. Echohawk wanted to go to Gentle Fawn and take comfort from her arms, yet had denied himself this pleasure until the mourning period was over for his beloved wife. Night Hawk had grown to accept his father's feelings for the young Chippewa, knowing that much of his feelings were because he felt her sadness that she still carried with her. She had been raped time and time again. Who could not pity her?

And she *was* lovely in features and personality. Who could not stop themselves from allowing her to find her way inside their hearts?

Ay-uh, Night Hawk could understand his father loving her. Night Hawk could have himself if he had not met Briana first.

Fully clothed, he went to Briana and kissed her. "I love you," he whispered. "You are a most beautiful flower for my wigwam."

He then turned and left. He did not go far. Instead of going to speak to his father, he went to the edges of the forest, positioning himself close to the grazing horses, where he could keep a close eye on his wigwam—and Briana.

If she fled into the night, he would be there to stop her. If she hated him for it, then her love for him had not been strong enough in the first place.

Knowing that this was the opportunity she needed to leave and warn her uncle, Briana scurried into her clothes. She was glad that it was growing dusky when she peered cautiously from the wigwam. That would make her escape much easier.

Slipping a fringed shawl around her shoulders, she left the wigwam, scarcely breathing. She stopped and looked guardedly around her, and when she saw that no one was noticing what she was doing, she broke into a mad run toward the fenced-in horses. When she reached them, she almost fainted. Night Hawk stepped out into plain view, his arms folded across his chest, his eyes narrowing angrily.

Briana then squared her shoulders. "Night Hawk, let me pass," she said. "If you persist with this plan to abduct my uncle, I have no choice but to go and warn him. If a confrontation can be stopped, no lives will be taken. Yours especially, Night Hawk!"

"Briana, either you return with me to our dwelling peacefully, or I will take you by force," Night Hawk said flatly. "You cannot be allowed to warn your uncle. The evil man deserves what is planned for him."

Softening her stance, Briana began pleading with him. "Please, Night Hawk," she cried. "Tell me you won't go after my uncle. Everything we have planned could be lost! Is it worth it, Night Hawk, to seek vengeance when you are possibly jeopardizing everything we have together?"

"Do you return with me peacefully, or do I take you by force?" Night Hawk growled, refusing to listen to her pleas.

"You would actually force me?" Briana said, gasping.

"If it is required," Night Hawk said matter-of-factly.

Enraged by his cold indifference, Briana stared up at him for a moment longer, then turned and ran back to their wigwam. She tossed her shawl aside and threw herself down on the pelts before the fire and began crying.

When Night Hawk came to her and drew her into his arms, she jerked away.

"Just leave me alone," she said icily.

She stamped to the sleeping platform, placing her back to Night Hawk. When it came time for him to go to bed, he slept on the floor on the opposite side of the wigwam. Tears flooded her eyes, missing him, fearing what this meant for their future.

She, in truth, knew that she could not live without him.

24

I will have my revenge.
I will have it if I die the moment after.
—Spanish Curate

The fire was burning brightly, casting dancing shadows along the wall and the curved ceiling of the wigwam. The smoke was rising through the smoke hole, meeting the splash of morning sun as it rose upward into the sky.

Having lain stiffly silent as Night Hawk dressed for his journey of vengeance, Briana watched him slip on his war shirt, its breast containing a prayer for protection, and on the back the symbols of victory woven in beaded tapestry.

She shivered beneath her blankets when she noticed something else on the shirt—fringes of human hair—wondering . . . whose.

Briana pretended to be asleep as he finished preparing himself for the journey, and only when he finally left did she bolt from the sleeping platform, her own journey stretching before her.

Breathless from hurrying, knowing that she must ride hard to get to St. Paul ahead of Night Hawk, his father, and the many braves that she heard leave on horseback with them, she changed into fresh clothes.

She had one advantage today. Earlier in the morning, when Echohawk had come to Night Hawk's wigwam and they had stood outside talking in guarded whispers, she had crept to the wall and listened to what they were saying. She managed to hear Echohawk tell his son that before going to St. Paul, and before sending their braves out to search for Strong Branch, they should ride to the cave with their braves, and if the weapons were still lodged there, they would be confiscated.

Night Hawk had agreed, and Briana had just had enough time to rush back to her sleeping platform before he had come back into the wigwam to complete his wardrobe before leaving on his mission of revenge.

"Thank God Echohawk remembered the weapons in the cave," Briana whispered, slipping into soft moccasins beaded by her own hand. "That will give me the time I need to encourage Uncle Blackie to flee their wrath. Hopefully, that's what he will do—*not* go to the authorities."

Fear grew inside her heart at the thought of her uncle going to Fort Snelling and giving them the reason why he was pleading for their protection. Then her only hope would be that those at the fort would not believe him. They would ask for proof. There would be none, because she had to believe that Night Hawk's and Echohawk's vengeance would not lead them into such a foolish act as going on to Fort Snelling to achieve their vengeance.

Not only would their lives be in jeopardy, but also those in the village that depended on their leadership.

Her buckskin dress fit her like a glove. The fringes at the hem swayed as she went to the weapons leaning against the wall and chose a rifle. She quickly dropped a handful of bullets into the pocket of her dress. She lay the rifle on her sleeping platform and grabbed a fringed shawl and placed it around her shoulders, tying the ends together in front.

Taking up a narrow strip of leather from the floor, she gathered her hair together at the back and tied the thong about it, preventing her hair from constantly blowing in stinging wisps around her face while on horseback.

Swallowing hard, Briana eyed the entrance flap warily and reached with trembling fingers for the rifle. She knew what the consequences of her actions today could be. Night Hawk could turn his hatred of her uncle on to her. He could turn his back on her forever, even though what she was doing was to preserve his love—and his very own existence.

He would never understand. Never! He would see her as an interference.

And she knew that not only he, but no future Indian chief

would tolerate such disobedience in a wife. She knew that it could make him lose face with his people, yet she had no choice but to do what she knew was best for everyone, except for herself.

Either way she would lose.

With a racing heart she took a determined step toward the entrance flap.

* * *

Echohawk drew his reins tautly. His horse came to a shimmying halt, Night Hawk drawing up beside him.

Night Hawk edged his horse closer to his father's. "Why do you stop?" he asked, seeing that their braves had also stopped behind them. "It is far to the cave. We must make haste. We must get that chore behind us, then hurry on to St. Paul. We want to arrive there just as it is turning dusk so that we can watch Blackie's movements before entering his house for the abduction."

"And that we will do," Echohawk said, nodding. His dark eyes narrowed. "I was wrong to encourage going to the cave before going to St. Paul. It was a foolish notion of mine to think that the weapons would be abandoned there, for the taking. As before, White Wolf will have removed them. Along with the weapons, he will be our next target of vengeance. But later, my son. Later. Besides finding Strong Branch, it is imperative to get to Blackie before word reaches him that we are coming."

"And how would it, when only our trusted braves know of our plans?" Night Hawk said solemnly.

Echohawk put a steady hand on Night Hawk's shoulder. "My son, there is one among our people who I am not so sure can be trusted," he said, his voice drawn. "Did you not say that Briana tried to leave once to go to her uncle with a warning? Who is to say that she will not try again? She has torn loyalties, my son. I fear that the white blood running through her veins will guide her into that which could go against the Chippewa."

"*Gee-bah-bah,* please understand that what I say is not out of disobedience of a son to a father, but I believe I understand

Briana's motives much more clearly than you," Night Hawk said in her defense. "In her heart, deep in her soul, she thinks that telling her uncle about the planned abduction is a way to protect the future of the Chippewa. She fears there will be a confrontation between the white man and the Chippewa if we succeed with our abduction. And, partly, Father, that is true. We are taking a risk. Yet a risk that must be taken. *Ay-uh,* we must achieve our vengeance, or live the rest of our lives cowering in the shadow of that evil man and his evil ways that always go against the Chippewa."

"At least in that your thinking is clear," Echohawk said, his voice a low grumble. "And I hope, for your sake, the future chief of our people, that your thinking is clear about your woman's motives. If not . . ."

His words faded into the wind, since he did not want to speak of threats or foreboding this morning. He wanted to think of hope and inspiration. Of a sought-after peace that only Blackie's and White Wolf's deaths might achieve for his people. And now also Strong Branch's death.

Echohawk turned to his braves and told them of the changed plans and urged them now to concentrate on finding Strong Branch.

He and his son then rode away from the braves, for the first time in their lives feeling a strain between them.

* * *

Briana lifted the entrance flap and peered outside, looking cautiously around her. When she saw the usual morning activity in the village, she sighed in relief. She had feared that perhaps Night Hawk had left one of his braves to stand guard outside their wigwam to stop her escape.

What she saw was innocent enough—the women taking wood from their piles inside their wigwams to get the cooking fires built, others going to the river for their early morning bath, despite the cool breezes of autumn that were on them. She gazed at the children, who were rowdy and playful as they chased one another or their dogs, causing them to yelp and howl if one or the other was caught by the tail.

She scarcely saw any braves at all wandering through the village, only the elders, who sat in clusters, smoking and chatting. Most of the young, virile braves who had not joined their chief and his son on their journey of vengeance had surely gone to strategic points in the forest to keep watch for any possible intruders during the absence of their chief and his heir. These braves were the worst threat to her escape from the village today. She would have to keep alert for them as she fled on horseback through the forest.

Not seeing anyone looking in her direction, Briana stepped quickly from the wigwam, then froze in her path when a muscular brave stepped in front of her, peering down at her with his dark eyes, his jaw tight and his arms folded across his chest.

She had not thought that a brave would be hidden in the shadows of the wigwam.

"You cannot leave," the brave said flatly. He pointed at the closed entrance flap. "Go back inside. Night Hawk's orders!"

Briana paled and her eyes wavered. "He ordered you to stand guard?" she said, her voice breaking.

Her eyes became two points of fire as she gazed brazenly at the brave. "I don't care what he said, I'm leaving," she said, the strength returning to her voice.

She placed her free hand on her hip, her other hand clutching the rifle that she was almost determined to use if she did not get her way. "Step aside!" she said, lifting her chin stubbornly.

When the brave did not move and only stared angrily down at her, Briana started to lift the rifle, but was quickly shaken when the brave grabbed it from her hands and dropped it to the ground.

"Go inside," he said, nodding toward the wigwam. "Or I will take you there!"

Seeing that she had no choice, and frustrated that she was being held prisoner in Night Hawk's village, Briana turned around and stamped back inside the wigwam. She began to pace, growing angrier by the minute. She sighed heavily and plopped down beside the fire, gazing disconsolately into the flames. She truly couldn't blame Night Hawk for having her guarded. He felt as strongly about abducting her uncle as she felt against it.

They were at opposite ends of the spectrum this time, and it threatened to destroy everything that had blossomed between them so sweetly, so wonderfully.

Briana held her face in her hands. "Where is this going to end?" she said, unable to stop the tears from streaming from her eyes. "Where?"

She gazed around her, eyeing everything of Night Hawk's that was so familiar to her now. Strange how everything that she had known with him was so distant now, as though it had all been a dream. Yet there was his hunting gear, his breechclouts, his headbands, his bows and arrows, to remind her that it was real—she was here, and he had held her in his arms, professing his love for her time and time again.

"Now how will he feel after he hears that I tried to escape again to warn my uncle?" she whispered, panic seizing her, at the thought of him ever hating her.

* * *

As night fell over the Chippewa village, a lone figure ambled toward the council house. Wise Owl was seizing the opportunity to have council with the elders of both bands of Chippewa, to try again to convince them who their leader should be.

As Wise Owl entered the council house, the lodge fire was burning brightly in the center, lighting the faces of those who gazed up at him with questioning in their old, wisdom-filled eyes. He had called the meeting.

He felt lucky that they had complied with this request since Night Hawk and Echohawk were gone. Yet Wise Owl was acting chief on behalf of Strong Branch in his absence. It was only right that he should have a voice in the affairs of the two tribes. In fact, he hoped to convince the elders that he should have full control—the only chief over both villages.

He gathered the tail end of his long bearskin robe into his arms and settled himself down beside the fire where room had been left for him. All was silent as the calumet pipe was passed around to those in council, then all eyes were on Wise Owl again.

He nodded from brave to brave, then began his proposal in a monotone, his dark eyes almost hidden in the folds of his face. "It is good to be in council with you all again," he said. "It is important, this that I have to say, as an extension of what I have said before, yet I have never been filled with as much determination as tonight."

He did not cower before the frowning at his introductory comments. Instead he kept on talking, wanting to have his say before someone interrupted him, forbidding it. He knew the dangerous waters in which he was now treading. But he also knew that this was his best opportunity to convince the council that what he said was the best for everyone concerned.

Ay-uh, this was the best time to speak his mind—having purposely taken this opportunity while Echohawk and Night Hawk were away, the two who fought his every decision and suggestion, as though he were not present. Hopefully, when they returned to the village, they would see just how important he truly was.

"Elders of the council, Echohawk has proven his weakness as your leader by allowing himself to be abducted, and Night Hawk is no better," he began, his voice rising in pitch as each word was spoken. He lay the pipe aside. "He was also abducted. And he is a half-breed. White blood flows through his veins. Is this not a weakness in character in all Chippewa's eyes? I urge you to let Wise Owl be your leader. Wise Owl has never let you down. Never!"

Everyone seemed to rise at once, leaving Wise Owl sitting alone, his eyes wide, his mouth open as he gaped up at them. He flinched when one of the elders clasped his arm roughly and forced him to his feet. Then he led him from the council house, half dragging him to the center of the village, where the outdoor fire was burning brightly toward the dark heavens.

Against his will he was made to stand there until a crowd

had gathered around to stare at him and listen as each of the councilmen began speeches that shamed Wise Owl for his disloyalty to the reigning chief and his son, causing everyone to scorn him and turn their backs to him as they went to their dwellings.

Wise Owl began backing away from the councilmen, his heart pounding.

"Leave and never return," one of the elders ordered. "Banishment is what you have earned tonight. Leave and do not look back. You are responsible for many ugly things among our people. These actions can no longer be tolerated. As is Strong Branch, who hides like a coward since the death of Lily and Gray Moon, you are no longer of our people. You are now destined to walk alone."

Wise Owl was trembling and his eyes were downcast as he turned to leave, not even allowed to take his personal belongings with him. As he walked solemnly into the dark shadows of the forest he hung his head in shame, yet his heart was crying out for vengeance—and somehow he would have it!

25

Honor will honor meet.

—BRIDGES

When Night Hawk and his father ventured into the outskirts of St. Paul, the streets of the city were quiet. Only an occasional horse-drawn carriage clopped along the cobblestones, making an eerie sound as the hollowed clatter wafted into the night air.

The two tethered their horses in the trees at the far back of Blackie's estate grounds, and moved stealthily toward the house. The hour was late, yet a lone light remained shimmering golden in a window of the two-storied mansion.

Together, their breathing shallow, their movements hushed, Echohawk and Night Hawk rushed up the steps to the veranda that reached around three sides of the house. They moved stealthily to the window where they had seen the light and looked inside. Blackie was stretched out on a sofa before a roaring fire in the parlor, reading a book.

Father and son exchanged satisfied smiles, then crept to the door and tried the knob. Their smiles waned when they discovered that the door was locked.

Night Hawk needed no persuasion as to what he should do next. He went brazenly to the parlor window, took his pistol from the waistband of his fringed breeches, and crashed the butt of the firearm into the pane of the glass. Swiftly he cleaned the window of any glass as he moved his pistol all around it, scattering the glass in all directions.

Blackie bolted with alarm to his feet, dropping the book to the floor. He blanched, his face becoming ashen as he watched Night Hawk quickly climb through the window, his father following behind him.

"You . . . !" Blackie gasped, unable to back up, his back to the fireplace. "Night Hawk! Echohawk!"

He stared disbelievingly at the chief. "Echohawk, how did you get away from White Wolf?" he gasped.

"That I did is enough for you to know," Echohawk growled. "But I have come to you for answers, and if you are a wise man, you will give them to me."

"What . . . answers?" Blackie stammered.

Knowing that haste was needed to achieve their planned revenge without getting caught, Night Hawk slipped his pistol back at his waistband and grabbed a leather thong from his pocket. He hurried to Blackie and grabbed him by a wrist, twisting it as he turned him around.

"What are you doing?" Blackie managed to say between frightened breaths. His heart skipped several nervous beats, and he tried to get away when Night Hawk began binding his hands at his wrists with the leather thong, but found that escape was impossible.

A strangled sound came from the depths of his throat when Night Hawk just as quickly jerked a rope from his pocket and pulled it around Blackie's neck, tightening it, causing his eyes to bulge.

Echohawk went to Blackie and glowered at him, then nudged his chest with the barrel of his pistol. "You were easily found," he said. "But my son and I need assistance in finding White Wolf. He has become at large again. Tell me where he is. Now!"

"I don't know," Blackie breathed out anxiously, unable to move his head with the rope tightening around his throat. His eyes bulged even more and his tongue seemed drawn sideways inside his mouth.

"Please . . . have mercy," he said, his voice now barely a squeak. "Don't kill me."

"Perhaps not now," Night Hawk hissed. "But in time you will die, after you come to our village so that our people will be audience to your miseries!"

"God, no . . ." Blackie said, close to blacking out as the rope tightened even more snugly around his throat.

"If you tell us where White Wolf is hiding, I will loosen the rope around your neck," Night Hawk said, his fingers gripping the rope tightly. "Tell us. You will be spared some of the humiliation we have planned for you."

"I tell you, I don't know," Blackie whispered hoarsely. "He's gone his way . . . I've gone mine. My—my political career. Please let me go. I am so close to seeing my political aspirations fulfilled."

"You should have thought about that before siding with White Wolf," Echohawk said, leaning his face into Blackie's. "Those many years ago, when your life lay in balance on the riverboat, I should have ended it for you then. My wrong decision that day has been the cause for many hardships among not only the Chippewa community, but also the white! You have spread your evil far and wide. But now, it will finally stop. I will spare you nothing, Blackie. Nothing!"

"Oh, God . . ." Blackie shrieked as Night Hawk began dragging him across the floor, the rope cutting into the flesh of his throat. "Please . . . don't!"

Echohawk placed a gentle hand on his son's arm. "We must silence him before taking him from the house," he said, smiling at Blackie as he emitted a groan of fear.

Night Hawk nodded and watched matter-of-factly as his father raised the butt of his pistol and smacked Blackie on the head, rendering him unconscious.

Echohawk moved on ahead of Night Hawk, out into the corridor, looking guardedly from side to side, then peered up the spiral staircase, then down the dark corridor. When he saw no signs of anyone having been aroused, he nodded for Night Hawk to come ahead and follow him from the house. . . .

Soon they had Blackie tied across the back of Night Hawk's horse and were riding into the wind, the first step of their planned revenge achieved.

* * *

Briana was brooding beside the fire, only half-heartedly eating an apple. It seemed to be the only food that she could tolerate this morning after having been forced to stay in Night Hawk's village. The braves had returned during the night, but without Night Hawk and Echohawk—or her Uncle Blackie. Nor had their search uncovered Strong Branch.

She stiffened and dropped the apple core into the blazing fire pit when she heard horses arriving in the village. Her heart beating loudly, she rose to her feet and went to the entrance flap and lifted it. She grew cold inside as she watched Night Hawk and Echohawk arriving at the village, her Uncle Blackie tied across Night Hawk's horse. His eyes grew wide with fright as he noticed her standing there, watching him.

"No," Briana whispered, covering her mouth with a hand. "They did abduct him. Oh, dear Lord, now what are they going to do with him?"

She was thankful for one thing. It seemed they had gotten away with the abduction, for no one had followed them—yet. She feared that this would be short-lived. Her uncle was too well known in the community for his absence to be ignored.

Yet, she realized, there would be no reason for his absence to be blamed on the Chippewa. A man like Blackie Collins surely had many enemies.

Briana pursed her lips tightly when Echohawk turned and caught sight of her standing there, his gaze momentarily burning into hers. He continued with his chore of loosening the ropes that had held Blackie into place during the long night journey from St. Paul.

It took all the willpower Briana could muster not to rush out to Night Hawk and pound his chest with her fists, to berate him for having imprisoned her—supposedly the woman he loved! But all thoughts of harshly scolding him were erased by astonishment as she watched a brave place a stake in the center of the village. Her uncle then was tied to the stake. Then a pile of tree limbs and split wood were stacked around her uncle and the stake. . . .

"Oh, my God," Briana gasped. "Surely neither Night Hawk nor his father will burn my uncle alive! That is the work of savages! They aren't savages!"

When torches were brought to the wood and sparks began

lifting into the air as the flames began to spread around the stake, Briana felt nauseated and her knees were weak. Now she realized the seriousness of Night Hawk and Echohawk's decision to achieve their vengeance—to finalize it today.

"Tell us where White Wolf is and your life will be spared!" Echohawk said to Blackie as the Chippewa amassed around them.

"How can I when I don't even know myself?" Blackie cried, his eyes feverishly watching the flames eating away at the wood, drawing closer and closer to his boots.

He then looked past Echohawk, again locking eyes with his niece. "Briana! Don't allow them to do this to me," he pleaded. "We're blood kin! Doesn't that mean anything to you? What will your parents think when they find out that you allowed these savages to kill me in such a way? Please, Briana! Do what is right! Save me!"

Torn by his pleading, knowing that what he said was true, Briana choked back a sob. When she felt other eyes on her, as though hot brands were touching her flesh, she shifted her gaze and met the anger in Night Hawk's as he seemed to be daring her.

Then her whole body flinched when Blackie let out a scream of pain. She became faint when she saw that the fire was lapping at his boots. The smell of scorched leather was filling the air.

She gasped as she watched the fire reaching up toward the legs of his breeches, his screams seeming to split the heavens in half.

Seeing the utter savagery of what was happening to her uncle, Briana rushed from the wigwam and went to Night Hawk. She clutched his arm, looking wildly up at him. "Let him go!" she cried. "This is wrong, Night Hawk. Even though I know you feel you have cause to do this terrible thing, it is wrong! Please, darling. For me, let him go. I don't think I could live with the memory of my uncle dying such a horrible death, especially since you will be the one responsible for it!"

When Night Hawk did not respond, still staring angrily at her, she clutched his arm more feverishly. "Say something!" she cried. "Do something! Don't just stand there and allow this to continue!"

When he still did not respond in any way, Briana wrenched herself away and turned and looked pityingly up at her uncle. When she saw that his head was hung, that he had fainted clean away, his breeches smoldering, she realized that she had no choice but to defy the man she loved for a man she abhorred!

It was the humane thing to do. She must!

She ran toward the circle of flames and without stopping began to run through them to get to her uncle and set him free. But almost immediately the lightweight fabric of the skirt of her buckskin dress caught fire. The intense heat against her calves alerted her to the danger. She looked down and a lightheadedness swept through her when she saw that her dress was on fire!

She tried to run on, to get to her uncle, her hands trying to beat out the fire on her dress, but felt suddenly trapped, seeing that she would burn long before her uncle would.

A muscular arm wrapped around her waist, and she felt herself being swept out of the fire. She was thrown onto the ground, Night Hawk covering her body with his to snuff out the fire on her dress.

Breathing hard, the flames at last extinguished, Briana gazed into Night Hawk's eyes as he leaned away from her. "Should I thank you?" she said sarcastically, then looked back at her uncle, panic rising within her.

He was now hidden behind the screen of billowing smoke!

She had no idea if he was burning, or if it was just the smoke causing this illusion.

She shoved at Night Hawk's chest. "I must go and save Uncle Blackie!" she cried, sobbing. "Please, Night Hawk. Please allow it!"

Night Hawk moved quickly to his feet and turned to his father. "Perhaps Blackie's punishment can be a less drastic one," he said, suddenly seeing that Blackie was important to Briana, yet not understanding why.

Father and son exchanged troubled glances, then Echohawk nodded to a brave. "Release him," he said.

They all jumped with alarm as a gunshot rang out, and as the smoke separated, they could see blood spiraling from a wound in Blackie's chest, where he'd been shot square in the heart.

Echohawk turned with a start and looked up at a butte overlooking the village. That was where the shot had to have come from, since no one in the village would have cause to shoot Blackie, or have even seen through the smoke to do it. Up high on the butte, though, someone would have a clear shot through the spirals of smoke.

Briana felt faint when she was able to see through the smoke and saw the blood and how limp her uncle hung from the ropes of the stake. She did not have to go any closer to know that he had died instantly from the bullet.

She turned away, tears flooding her eyes. The grief was not so much for her uncle, but for how it could have been between them if he had not been a heartless cad. His was a life wasted.

She spun around, eyes wide as she wiped them free of tears. "Who shot him?" she asked, peering up at Night Hawk, at least glad that he was not responsible for the crime.

Echohawk had already ordered several braves to go search for the killer, and their horses' hooves sounded like distant thunder as they galloped from the village.

"Hopefully, we will soon see," Night Hawk said, placing a gentle hand on her shoulder.

A brave stepped forward. "Perhaps it was Strong Branch," he cried. "We failed in our search to find him. Though I do not understand why he would kill Lily and Gray Moon, he must be guilty, for he is eluding us now with much trickery. Perhaps he has come now and killed the white man to prove his cunning again to us!"

Another brave stepped forward. "Perhaps it was Wise Owl," he said, clutching a rifle.

"Why would you say that?" Night Hawk said. "Why would Wise Owl kill Blackie?"

"His aim may not have been for Blackie," the brave said. "It may have been for you or your father."

"I do not understand," Night Hawk said, his voice edged with irritation.

The brave then explained about Wise Owl's banishment while Night Hawk and Echohawk had been gone. Night Hawk's jaw slackened as he looked quickly over at his father.

"The killer is more than likely White Wolf," Echohawk said. "Always the elusive renegade of the forests. I doubt if we will ever find him."

The fires around the stake were splashed out by buckets of water. Blackie was taken down and placed on the ground, a buckskin cape thrown over him.

Briana stood over him, silent for a moment, then she turned to Night Hawk. "I must return him to St. Paul for a proper burial. I must do this for my parents, who would expect no less from me," she said, her voice drawn. "And then, Night Hawk, I-I will prepare myself for a journey to France. I imagine that is the best for both of us."

And then a sudden panic seized her. "Lord," she said, gasping, "you will be blamed for my uncle's death."

And then she set her jaw firmly. "I won't allow that to happen," she murmured. "Although I was against you becoming involved in this abduction from the beginning, I cannot allow you to suffer because of it—for, in truth, my uncle was the one who carries the burden of his own death, because of the pain he caused you and your people. I shall tell a convincing lie, Night Hawk. I will tell the authorities that White Wolf abducted both me and my uncle and that—and that he killed my Uncle Arden. You think he did, anyway. Perhaps it will lessen the lie somewhat in my heart to think so."

"You would do that for me—for my people?" Night Hawk said. Then what she had said about a journey to France hit him like a blast of cold air. "And then you will leave for this place you call France? You will leave me forever, Briana?"

"I have no choice," Briana said, trying to keep her voice steady, to hide the trembling she was feeling inside to know that their final good-bye was so near. But she did not see how she could stay with him, for more than one reason. She had seen a savage side to the man she loved, and he had seen that she could defy him. Under these circumstances, she was not sure if they could ever feel the same about each other.

"You always have choices," Night Hawk said, drawing her closer, yet not completely into his arms. Many eyes were on them. Many ears had heard that she had said she was going to leave him. He had to protect his pride. Even if she were gone, he would have to face his people forever.

"Yes, I do," Briana said, gulping hard, trying to fight off the attraction that, as always, his mere presence aroused within her. "And I am doing what I feel is best."

She eased from his grip and looked regretfully down at her uncle's covered body. She went to the wigwam and began gathering up her things. When she felt a presence behind her, she stiffened, then turned and faced Night Hawk. When he took her into his arms and kissed her, she melted from the ecstasy that the kiss evoked, then wrenched herself free and continued getting her things together for leaving.

"I am leaving," she murmured. "Please prepare my uncle for the journey."

Night Hawk glared at her back, then spun around and left, his heart bleeding, his pride wounded. He knew that he had no choice but to let her go, but he would go for her again soon, and in private. When it was just the two of them, he would convince her to return with him.

She was too much a part of him to let go.

* * *

Strong Branch drew his reins tight and stopped his horse to rest beside the river once he was far enough from the scene of the shooting to feel safe. He patted the rifle sheathed on his horse, relieved that Blackie was dead. He had been the one who involved Strong Branch and Gray Moon in White Wolf's schemes in the first place.

Strong Branch realized now that Blackie, the evil man that he was, had deliberately stirred up this sort of Indian trouble to give himself a cover—if any of the people in the area possibly attacked him for hating the Indians, he would point out the reason why everyone should hate them. By doing this, he would be adding votes on election day, not taking them away.

Strong Branch held his head in his hands and sobbed, also knowing that he had had his own, selfish reasons for having joined with the Sioux. It seemed that Strong Branch's lust for power equaled Blackie's. He now realized the wrong he had done. And it was too late. He was no better than the renegade Sioux and the white politician. He himself was now branded with the ugly name "renegade."

Lifting his head and peering in all directions in the forest, he knew that, for his survival, he still had to depend on the likes of White Wolf. It was best to find him. He had to encourage him to get his men back together again.

In truth, no matter how much shame he felt, Strong Branch missed the excitement of the raids. The daring. He must be a part of it again.

He also hoped that he would die amid such a raid, and soon. He could not take his own life. He had been taught from childhood that a suicide never entered paradise.

He sank his moccasined heels into the flanks of his horse and rode onward, feeling the aloneness around him as though the world was closing in on him from all sides.

26

I need so much the quiet of your love.

—Towne

The morning sun was dappling the trees outside the window as Briana stood in the sun room of her mansion, gazing upon the peacefulness of the morning. Yet it bore no resemblance to the way she felt inside. It seemed an eternity since she had seen Night Hawk on that fateful day of her uncle's shooting, and as each day passed, she knew that she had made a mistake by leaving him.

But still she had not summoned the courage to go to him and confess to being wrong. She had hoped he would come to her.

She had concluded that although he had asked her not to leave him, he had more than likely decided that it was best—he could get on with his life as a proud Chippewa leader without the interference of a woman who had tried, in a sense, to betray him.

She turned and began strolling slowly around the room, touching things that, yes, were now hers. The white rattan sofa with its plush, flowered cushions. The tables and plant stands that were made from Chinese bamboo. Among the needlepoint pillows on the sofa were Indonesian batiks, all set against the languor of white canvas and linen.

Yes, surprising to her, on the day of the reading of her uncle's will, she had learned that all of his worldly possessions had become hers. She had been his sole beneficiary. She was now rich.

She settled into a plushly cushioned rattan chair and stared into the flames rolling like satin across the logs on the grate of the fireplace, realizing that being rich was not important to her.

She missed Night Hawk with all of her being!

She rose slowly to her feet again and went to a closed trunk beneath a window. She bent to her knees and opened it and began removing what she had placed there for her long journey to Paris. She had come as close to leaving as ordering her trunk carried to her private carriage—then had stopped the driver as he lifted it from the floor to carry it outside.

In a flash she realized that she could not run from her feelings. She would stay in St. Paul and battle them out within her heart.

Hopefully, Night Hawk would also be grappling with these same feelings, and somehow they would be drawn together again, in mutual love, mutual trust.

Until that day came, Briana had decided to put her other passion and this mansion that she had inherited to good use. She was going to transform the house into guest rooms. She was going to open a boarding-house for artists, hopefully attracting a generation of America's finest painters. She was going to turn this into a school for aspiring artists. She would hire the best teachers.

She had more than enough money to contribute to these studies. She would even offer scholarships for those who did not have the money to attend.

These thoughts made her remorse over losing Night Hawk somehow more bearable. She would throw herself into this project. It would make her come alive again, although not in the way that she felt while within Night Hawk's arms.

But it just might be the best substitute.

Hearing a movement behind her made Briana move quickly to her feet and turn around. Her heart stopped when she found Night Hawk standing there in his full-fringed buckskin attire, his shoulder-length, raven black hair drawn back from his brow with a headband that she so vividly recalled having beaded for him. She looked quickly at his feet. He also wore the moccasins that she had sewn and beaded for him.

She looked up and melted inside when his gaze locked with

hers. Within his dark eyes she saw such feelings of love, and yet also she could see the hurt in their depths—a hurt she had surely caused.

She bore the same pain in her eyes, the same longings within her heart.

Something compelled her to brush aside all doubts. She broke into a mad run and flung herself into his arms, so glad when he wrapped her in a tight embrace. She lifted her lips to his and closed her eyes as the kiss stole her breath and her senses away.

She clung to him as he picked her up and carried her toward the spiral staircase. She placed her cheek against the soft buckskin fabric of his shirt and could hear and feel the pounding of his heart against her flesh.

Tears of joy leapt into her eyes as once again his mouth found her lips. He stepped up to the second-floor landing and began carrying her down the corridor. She did not stop the wondrous kiss when they entered her bedroom and he placed her on a bed.

They wrenched their lips apart and he began to undress her, as she was undressing him.

He moved over her, their bodies meeting in a sweet reunion as he sculpted himself to her. When he looked down, their eyes met, locked in unspoken understanding, promising ecstasy. She twined her fingers through his hair and pulled his head down, and once again they kissed.

When he plunged into her, she arched and cried out, shuddering at the intense pleasure at how magnificently he filled her. Slipping her hands down to his buttocks, she gripped him tightly and strained into him, abandoning herself to the rush of feelings that were overwhelming her. Their naked flesh seemed to fuse, their bodies yearning for each other, their lips parting in a mutual sigh as the passion mounted.

It was as though they had never been separated. And she knew that nothing mattered now, except that they remain together for eternity. She would require no apologies for his long absence. She did not expect him to demand any from her. Today was the beginning of the rest of their lives. Neither one would allow any more interference.

Night Hawk pressed endlessly deeper within Briana. He buried his face into the sweet curve of her throat, inhaling the familiar scent of her. His tongue slid down her throat, to her breasts. She drew in a wild breath of pleasure as he locked his lips over one of her nipples and began flicking his tongue around its tautness.

He rolled away from her, his hands caressing their way down her body, his lips and tongue following their lead, finding and stroking her every pleasure point. Briana lay there and closed her eyes, enjoying these moments of sheer ecstasy again with the man she loved.

When his tongue found the bud of her desire, she arched her hips to give him more access to that sort of lovemaking that made her head swim with pleasure. As he stroked her with long sweeps of his tongue, she tossed her head and chewed her lower lip to keep from crying out.

Just as she felt that she was beyond coherent thought, he moved around, positioning himself so that she could reciprocate the same sort of pleasure. Moving to her knees, she leaned over him, her hair hanging over his thighs in silken waves, and placed her fingers around him. She ran her fingers slowly along his pulsing satin hardness as her lips began a soft pleasuring that caused him to groan and his body to stiffen with pleasure.

When she felt his body begin to tremble, she knew that it was time for them to join again so that the pleasure that had built up to such a peak of excitement could culminate in something even more wondrous, even more blissful.

He molded himself perfectly to the curved hollow of her hips. She locked her legs around him and moved with him as his thrusts became more determined, more maddening. She clutched him, pulling him closer and closer, and cried out as he made a last plunge. Their bodies quivered into the other, merging as though one mind, one heart, one soul.

Afterward, they lay still in each other's arms. Then Night Hawk rolled away, still gazing at her.

"I could not stay away," he said hoarsely, his hand moving

across her body, stopping at a breast. He cupped it and drew its nipple between his lips, sucking it.

Briana's heart was pounding. She closed her eyes: the rapture was still so intense, it blocked out all rhyme and reason.

"I thought I had stayed away too long, that you might have left for that place you call France," Night Hawk continued, his hands now framing her face. As her eyes opened, he gazed into them with devotion and love. "But I took the chance that your love for me would be too strong for you to leave me forever. I felt that you needed time to sort everything out in your heart and mind. Now I see that you have."

He kissed the tip of her nose. "Your body relayed the message to me that you still love and want me," he murmured. "But I need to hear this also from your lips, my woman. I need to hear you say that you still wish to be my wife . . . that you will return to my dwelling and be the flower of my wigwam forever."

Briana took his hands and urged him into a sitting position. Smiling at him, she moved onto his lap, relishing the feel of his naked thighs against her body, and that part of him that always sent her into a tailspin of joyous bliss rising in its turgid strength again and touching the core of her womanhood with its renewed heat.

She placed her arms around his neck and leaned her lips close to his, her breasts just barely touching his chest. "Night Hawk, my beloved, I have never stopped wanting to be your wife," she whispered. "My darling, I need so much the quiet of your love. Oh, how I do love you."

"You will return with me to my village?" he asked, gently smoothing a lock of her hair from her eyes. "You will give up your world for mine?"

"Yes, except for . . ."

She paused and did not finish her sentence, leaving Night Hawk wondering why she hesitated at all. He lifted her from his lap and lay her beneath him, stretching out above her, the velvet tip of his shaft teasing her.

"You are not ready to commit fully to the man you love?" Night Hawk grumbled.

"No, that is not at all what I was going to say," Briana said, placing her hands at his neck, drawing his lips close to hers again. "My darling, this house is now mine. Uncle Blackie left everything to me. I-I don't want to give it up altogether."

Night Hawk eased his lips away from her, giving him room to glare down at her. "Are you saying that you wish to live here instead of in my village, in a wigwam?" he said. "Is a wigwam too crude for you now? Before, you seemed to accept the way I live. Why have you changed your mind?"

Briana laughed softly. "I am not planning to stay here in my house," she said, smiling up at him. She placed a hand on his cheek. "I am going to live with you wherever you are, however you live."

"Then what are you saying about this house?" he asked, confused.

"You know my love of painting," she said softly. "My darling, I am going to share that *and* this house with others who have the same sort of passion. I am going to turn this house into a boardinghouse for budding artists. I am going to turn it into a school for artists. Doesn't that sound wonderful? It seems that Uncle Blackie's evil scheming came to some good, after all." She giggled. "I imagine he will turn over in his grave when he realizes what I have planned for his mansion. His interest in my painting was only for show, for everyone to see. In truth, he cared nothing at all for it."

A wave of melancholia swept through her. "But, Night Hawk, his having named me his sole beneficiary has proved that he did care for me," she said solemnly. "I truly never knew how much. He—he was not a demonstrative person in that way. Only when he was on a podium preaching politics."

"How could he not have cared for you?" Night Hawk said, brushing a soft kiss across her brow. "My woman, how could anyone not love you?"

His mouth covered hers in a warm kiss. She sighed as she received his lips, so glad that things had once more come together for them.

She could not think of anything that could postpone their happiness again.

* * *

Echohawk stood outside Gentle Fawn's wigwam for a while, contemplating life as it had been handed him. His first wife, Fawn, and their unborn child had been taken from him long ago. His beloved Mariah had been taken from him only a short while ago, and with these losses a portion of his heart.

Yet there was still so much of his heart that he was ready to share with Gentle Fawn now that the mourning period for his No-din was past. It was something ready to be left behind. He was eager to push such thoughts from his mind.

He had waited long enough to speak his mind to Gentle Fawn. He had waited long enough to hold her in his arms. He had not kissed her since before his wife had passed away. He hungered for her lips and the sweetness of her flesh.

She had made him feel young again, so very much a virile brave who had denied himself for too long the pleasures of being with a woman.

Not wanting to tarry any longer, he lifted the entrance flap. The mere sight of her sitting beside the lodge fire, the child sucking from the nipple of her abundantly filled breast, made his heart begin to pound like a young brave getting his first thrill from being near a girl of his desire. He went to her and sat down beside her.

Soon Gentle Fawn slipped the baby's mouth from her breast and laid the child aside on a thick layer of pelts. Moonstar's eyes were peacefully closed, her stomach comfortably filled.

Gentle Fawn then rose to her feet, and as her eyes met his, she slipped the dress down her body, stepping free of it as it fell around her ankles.

She beckoned to him with outstretched arms. Echohawk removed his clothes, then placed his hands on her shoulders and spread her out beneath him. With a rapid heartbeat, and desires that had been stifled for much too long now, he plunged inside her. His eyes closed with the pleasure and he groaned, her tightness squeezing his hardness as he stroked rhythmically within her.

His mouth covered her lips with a feverish kiss. His hands were exploring, touching and fondling her every secret point of pleasure. And just before his seed exploded into her, he drew his lips from her mouth and whispered something soft and endearing in her ear.

"Marry me," he said. "Marry me soon, Gentle Fawn. I want you every waking moment. Please allow it."

Tears streamed from her eyes. "*Ay-uh,* my love, I will allow it," she whispered back.

Their lips sealed the promise, their bodies responding as they swayed and rocked with the explosion of rapturous bliss.

27

I have thee by thy hands
And will not let thee go!

—Bridges

It was so cold the trees were crackling all about the wigwams like pistol shots. The day was now gone; the moon had risen; the cold had not lessened. The trunks of the trees were still snapping all around the council house where Briana sat with many of the village children, close to one of the four great lodge fires, showing them her types of canvases and how she applied her paints to them in wondrous designs of the forest, the sky, the rivers, and then a sketch of the village of which they were so proud.

She smiled at the children as they talked occasionally in mixed languages of English and Chippewa. They were excited as she allowed each one of them to take up a brush and apply some paint to the canvas, their eyes wide and bright as they made their own drawings of what pleased them.

A mischievous young brave sketched the moon with a face on it, evoking giggles from the others. A petite girl sketched a dog with several puppies trailing after it. Another lad sketched a young brave notching an arrow onto a bow.

All of this caused a serene contentment to wash through Briana, as well as what she had accomplished at her mansion in St. Paul.

It had taken some time, yet she had finally filled the rooms with artists. She had found talented teachers who were eager to spread their lessons of art to those who were just as enthusiastic to learn.

She had hired a cook to keep food hot on the stove for those involved in this project. And she had also hired meticulous maids to be at the beck and call of all those who lived at the boardinghouse, all hours of the night and day. She had instructed the maids and the cook to do everything they could to please the students, for this would ensure their best work.

She smiled, realizing that she had perhaps gone to extremes in her plans, knowing that surely there was no other such boardinghouse or art school that could boast of having maids and a cook that only prepared meals that the budding artists requested.

A soft sigh escaped her lips when she thought of how soon her first art scholarship would be awarded to a young person who would not have the means to attend an art school otherwise. Being able to offer such a scholarship made her proud. Strange that it was her uncle's monies that made all of this possible, while all along she had regarded him as a selfish tyrant, always concerned for his best interests.

But of course, she thought further to herself, had he known how she would use her inheritance, he more than likely would have never named her his sole heir. And he had probably not had a chance to change his will after realizing that she loved an Indian. With his thoughts so filled with other things, it had probably not entered his mind to change the will.

She listened as the children conversed excitedly among themselves about how they had been taught to paint before Briana had introduced these sorts of new skills to them. They were talking about how their mothers had to dig in the earth for their paints and how they had always made their paintbrushes from the inner spongy portion of a socket bone of an animal.

They chattered on about how their mothers' paints were stored in bags instead of jars, and that the only artwork they had known before was the language of symbol and design that was employed in the decoration of wigwams, clothings, skin, and rawhide articles in flaps, banners, and tomtoms. This symbolism was rich and interrelated with legends, stories, songs, and ceremonies.

They each bragged about their mothers being talented decorators—their mothers' bags, purses, war bonnets, awl cases, and robes decorated in beautiful designs and colors.

They boasted of how their fathers decorated the outside of the wigwams—drawing figures of men and animals and objects of nature by which they told of historic events such as travels, battles, captures, and various other exploits.

A strong arm, suddenly thrust around Briana's waist, caused her attention to leave the children. Her insides became warm, knowing whose arm was claiming her.

She turned and looked up at Night Hawk. "The Chippewa children are quite talented on my canvases," she said, smiling up at him. "Do you see their sketches? I will enjoy working with them, to help them hone their skills. We will then display their paintings among those being painted by my students in St. Paul. Everyone will see their talent. I would say that many of the children could become well known for their paintings."

Night Hawk gazed past her, noting the impatience of the children as they waited for their turn to paint on this new sort of canvas. It was good to see not only that they were enjoying learning from Briana, but also that they had accepted her without question as the future wife of the next chief. He was as proud of their mothers and fathers who had also accepted Briana into their hearts.

"It is good to see this camaraderie that has formed between you and all of my people," he said, smiling at Briana. "Tomorrow our celebration of marriage will be one that will live within my people's minds and hearts for many moons."

Briana's gaze lowered, seeing how he was dressed—wrapped snugly in a buffalo robe, with the hair inside, a wide leather belt holding it in place about his loins. The winter winds were blowing and there was a smell of snow in the air. She had feared that the snows might come and ruin their wedding day. Many Chippewa braves had taken invitations of bundles of tobacco to the other Chippewa villages, requesting their presence at the wedding, and many acceptances had been sent back in similar fashion.

Briana raised her eyes to Night Hawk. "You have returned from taking the invitations to some of the neighboring Chippewa villages?" she said, gently smoothing a hand across his cheek, still rosy and cold from the blustery winds of November. "Did you bring with you many acceptances?"

"As many as I took to them," Night Hawk said. "Many will come early tomorrow and pitch their tipis along the edge of the forest, in groups, or semicircles, each band distinct from the others by the paintings on their temporary dwellings. My woman, your artistic talents will be seen by many Chippewa tomorrow. They will be in awe of not only your talents, but also your beauty. I will be the envy of every brave who looks upon you."

"Darling, please . . ." Briana said, laughing softly. She could not stop a blush that was suffusing her face with its heat, yet she was so happy that her fiancé was proud of how she had helped with the preparations for their wedding day. Just for him, over the entrance of their wigwam she had painted in red and yellow a picture of a pipe and, directly opposite this, the rising sun. He had explained to her that this painting was symbolic of welcome and goodwill to men in the full light of day.

She prayed that the sun would shine brightly tomorrow, and that the snows would be delayed at least until after the ceremony. She wanted nothing to stand in the way of this wondrous day. She had waited too long to be his wife.

"My father also feels your painting on his dwelling is something special," Night Hawk said.

Briana, seeing something akin to pain enter his expression at the mention of his father, asked, "Haven't you yet accepted the fact that your father and Gentle Fawn are going to be married along with us?" Her question was guarded, for she was unsure of whether or not Night Hawk would ever completely accept Gentle Fawn as his stepmother. He still carried the pain of his mother's death inside his heart.

Briana was not sure if he would be able to accept the thought of his father making love to anyone but his mother.

"It is what my father wants," Night Hawk said sullenly. "He deserves happiness, too. How can I, a mere son, speak up against it?"

His lips formed a smile. "*Ay-uh,* I do accept what is to be, as well as accepting Gentle Fawn as part of my family," he said. "She also deserves some happiness in her life. For so long she was a victim of abuse. My father has erased the ugly memories from her mind."

He placed a hand on Briana's cheek, his expression sweet and caring. "And there is also Gentle Fawn's child," he murmured. "She deserves a chance at happiness also. My father will give her that chance. He already loves her as though she were his own."

Briana eased into Night Hawk's arms, placing her cheek against the warmth of the buffalo robe. "Just keep those happy thoughts, my darling," she murmured. "It is best for your father. He is happy."

Night Hawk stroked his fingers through her flowing hair. "But never will I call Gentle Fawn *gee-mah-mah,*" he said. "Never."

Briana leaned away from him. "No one would expect you to call her Mother," she said softly.

She swung away from him and turned to watch the activity in the council house beyond where she and the children had positioned the canvases. "Everything is so exciting," she said, clasping her hands before her. "I can hardly believe it is truly going to happen, Night Hawk. We are finally going to be married."

"It has been too long in coming," Night Hawk said. "But there will be no more interferences."

"No," Briana murmured. "None."

She watched the women scurrying around, preparing for the great feast that would be shared by all on her wedding day. Hunters had brought fowl and fish and fresh meat from the hunt. The meat of wild game had been put aside with much care during the previous fall in anticipation of such a feast. There was wild rice and the choicest of dried venison, as well as turnips and berries that had been stored in holes that had been dug deeply into the ground.

Her attention was drawn elsewhere when a brave came into the council house carrying something that she was not familiar with. As he came and stood before Night Hawk, she curiously eyed the bundle of arrows tied tightly together.

"Night Hawk, instead of bringing back a gift in response to the invitations carried to our people, I bring you something ugly," the brave said, handing the bundle to Night Hawk.

A pained expression entered Night Hawk's eyes as he took the arrows and closely examined them. "Where did you get these?" he grumbled, turning his dark eyes up at the brave. "Who sent these in response to our invitation?"

"It is a strange thing," the brave said, scratching his head. "It was not given to me, actually, from anyone in particular. I found it hanging from my saddle after I paid a visit to one of your closest friends in the Chippewa community. When I took them to him and questioned him about it, he said he knew nothing of them, nor would any of his people, for they held only good feelings for you and your father within their hearts."

"Then how?" Night Hawk said, his jaw tightening. "Who?"

"No one saw it being placed on my horse," the brave said, his voice strained. "The person responsible must be as elusive as a ghostly vision one imagines while traveling the dark haunts of the forest. This person moved quickly, Night Hawk. First he is there. And then he is gone. Poof. Like a breath of wind!"

Determinedly, Night Hawk strolled in a dignified manner toward one of the roaring lodge fires. He broke the arrows over his knee, then dropped them into the fire and watched them being consumed by the flames. "White Wolf," he said tightly. "This is the work of White Wolf."

"Or it might be Strong Branch," the brave offered. "He has become just as elusive as White Wolf, and perhaps as deadly. Will we ever know, Night Hawk, what caused him to turn against his own people? Killing Lily and Gray Moon makes no sense to me at all."

"Nor to me," Night Hawk mumbled, never liking to be reminded of his sister's murder, or of the man who had killed her.

Briana paled. She went to Night Hawk and placed a hand on his arm. "White Wolf? Strong Branch?" she cried. "Do you truly think one of them did this? Is one of them planning to ruin our wedding day? Is he planning an attack on our village?"

Night Hawk looked down at her with fire-lit eyes, then took her hands and squeezed them reassuringly. "Nothing will ruin our wedding day," he said. "Nor will anyone attack our village during the celebration. I promise you that, my woman. With every beat of my heart, I vow to you that nothing will stand in the way of our marriage."

He turned to the brave. "It is a warning," he said. "Alert everyone. And send many sentries out. Tell them to place themselves at strategic points so that no one can get past them. Shoot anyone that looks suspicious. I am weary of such intrusions."

"But there will be many arriving for the celebration," the brave said, his brow creased with worry. "This will make it hard to keep watch for an attack."

"Not so," Night Hawk argued. "All of the braves of our village are aware of who is and who is not their enemy. It will be easy to choose who is to be shot, and who is to be allowed to come on into our village."

The brave nodded in agreement, then turned and hurried from the council house.

Briana looked up at Night Hawk. "You called the arrows a warning," she said, fear creeping into her heart. "In which way, Night Hawk?"

"When a bundle of tied arrows is found at one's doorstep, in Indian language this means 'war to the teeth,' " he said solemnly. "The only difference is, the recipient of this dark gift usually knows who has sent them. This time Night Hawk is forced to guess. And of course, my heart tells me it is White Wolf."

Briana tightened her hands into fists at her sides. "I wish that renegade would drop dead," she said, rage engulfing her at the thought of the Sioux renegade ruining the most beautiful day of her life.

"If given the opportunity, I will make that wish come true," Night Hawk said, chuckling at how beautiful she looked even while angry.

"Briana! Briana!" one of the young braves suddenly said from behind her. "Look what I have sketched on your canvas!"

Together, Briana and Night Hawk went and looked at the drawing. Briana was quickly taken by the artistic talent of the young man. She was looking at the most vivid colors of a rainbow arched across a sky that was half sun and half rain, and at the end of the rainbow he had sketched a young brave on his knees, reaching his hands to the heavens as he seemingly prayed to his Great Spirit.

It was a touching sight, and at this moment Night Hawk took it as an omen—of peace and happiness for the generation of young braves this painting seemed to represent.

He placed his arm around the young man's shoulders. "Two Stones, you speak well through your painting," he said. "I can hear the message as clearly as though you were speaking the words from your mouth. It is good, Two Stones, that you have such feelings within your heart that leads you to draw such a painting. Perhaps you will even learn the ways of a shaman, and when you reach adulthood you can be the shaman of our tribe. You can speak then, and teach the ways of the Great Spirit, if you wish, through such paintings. Does such a suggestion please you?"

Two Stones turned his wide, dark eyes up at Night Hawk. His lips were parted in awe of what Night Hawk had said. All he could do was nod his head anxiously. Then he ran from the council house. His shouts of happiness proved that his voice had soon returned to him.

Tears were shining in Briana's eyes as she turned to Night Hawk. "That was so lovely," she said, wiping a tear from her eye as it swam to the corner. "So very, very lovely."

"At this moment Two Stones gives me cause to hope again for our future generation of braves," Night Hawk said, taking her hands and holding them. "But the fear of someone planning to make war against my people takes so much of my hopes away. I fear true peace will never come. There is always someone whose heart is dark with greed and hate. Peace! If only it could be achieved and kept."

"I imagine as long as there is man on the earth, there will be war," Briana said, heaving a sigh.

Together they walked from the council house out into the chill of the night. Briana looked heavenward when she felt the softness of snowflakes on her face. Earlier in the day she had prayed that it wouldn't snow. Later, when she had heard wolves howling, whose cries always portended a snowstorm, she had known that her prayers had not been heard, and she had expected the worst.

But now?

She thought that it might delay any warring against Night Hawk and his lovely people. A deep snowfall would not stop the marriage, but perhaps it could stop the enemy's approach.

28

The winds of heaven mix forever,
With a sweet emotion.

—SHELLEY

The heavy snowfall failed to materialize, and the visiting bands of Chippewa were received with much enthusiasm. As soon as the visitors had arrived and begun putting up their tipis, the women and girls of Echohawk's village built fires close to the visitors' campsites and cooked great quantities of food.

They then carried the food over and spread the feast for the visitors, waiting upon them with every attention.

The council house was filled with Chippewa braves who had donned their finest belts of wampum and their finest feathers, and women who had put on their best beaded garments. Before the wedding ceremony there was much dancing, singing and hugging.

But there was total silence when the wedding vows were exchanged. The ceremony itself was as simple as the touching of the hands, a few words spoken, and gentle embraces.

As with Echohawk and Gentle Fawn, Briana read in Night Hawk's eyes, and he in hers, the plighting of their troth.

And then the feast was enjoyed by all. Assortments of meat were strung on a pole over the fire to cook. The food was served on wooden platters, and soup passed in horn spoons of different sizes, some of them capable of holding enough to fill a large bowl.

Before the food was served, a small portion was placed in the fire as a blessing for the meal.

The feast was followed by more dancing and singing. Briana giggled as though having consumed too much wine as she tried to mimic the dance that Gentle Fawn was trying to teach her.

Dressed in his finest beaded garment of white doeskin and fancy headdress of feathers, matching the attire worn by his father, Night Hawk stood back from Briana, watching her sway to the beat of the tomtoms. Her doeskin dress, beaded beautifully with seashells and porcupine quills, clung to her voluptuous figure, making him want to reach out and grab her up into his arms and carry her away to their wigwam.

Tonight he wanted to make love endlessly to her. Until the morning sky became flooded with the sunrise did he want to whisper in her ear how much he loved her.

Even then it would be hard to let her go, for she was now his. She made his heart take flight and soar like the *mee-gee-see,* eagle.

He glanced over at his father, whose eyes were as intent on his new bride. Only a twinge of bitterness came to Night Hawk today in realizing that his mother had been replaced in his father's heart. But this resentment he quickly placed behind him. It was good to see his father happy again, to see some life in his eyes, and to see the spring he once again had in his step.

And Night Hawk found it easier to accept Gentle Fawn as each day passed. Like his Briana, Gentle Fawn was sweet like the songbirds in the trees in the spring.

And it was good to see how Briana and Gentle Fawn had become friends so quickly. This had also helped ease the tension between father and son.

Night Hawk cast a troubled glance toward the entrance of the council house. He had not been able to relax and enjoy the day as much as he would have liked. He still feared an attack. Even though he had sentries posted all around the village, White Wolf could arrive with so many warriors that no amount of sentries would stop him and the devastation he could cause.

Although Night Hawk's heart was here in the council house, he still kept his ears alert to all sounds outside it.

He gazed back to Briana, seeing her as nothing less than exquisite today. As she laughed and danced, the wisps of her long, flowing hair whipping about her flushed face, her well-rounded breasts bouncing beneath the soft fabric of the doeskin, he could not help but go to her and take her in his arms.

He led her away from the dancers and sat her down on a soft pile of bear pelts beside one of the four lodge fires, while Gentle Fawn and Echohawk settled down across the fire from them.

"You exhaust yourself before going to bed with your husband on your wedding night?" Night Hawk teased, flicking a strand of her hair back from her eyes with a finger. "That is not wise, my woman. Not wise at all."

Briana threw her head back as she laughed softly, allowing her hair to hang in long waves down her back. She marveled to herself over this dress she wore today. After the tanning procedure, the skin of the dress was exquisitely white, richer in sheen than fine broadcloth, and softer than velvet. It had been beautifully painted by her own hands, and trimmed with fringe and quillwork and lovely seashells.

Then she gazed over at Night Hawk. "My darling, don't you ever worry about your wife not having enough energy for you," she said, scooting over close to him, reveling in the strength of his arm as he swept it around her shoulders and held her close. "Don't you know that I live for our private moments together? Even now I wait with bated breath for you to carry me to our love nest."

Night Hawk chuckled. "I see that I have taught you well," he murmured. He held her close as everyone left the floor and sat down in a large circle around the great lodge fire.

Young braves stripped to their breechclouts and painted bodies then rose and began dancing around the fire. The agile and graceful use of their bodies these young men made was a marvel to see. They danced in quick-paced, flashy steps, their intent to keep pace with the drum while using a wide variety of hand, arm, leg, and body movements. This dance reflected the athletic ability of the dancers as they attempted to distinguish themselves from the other dancers that had already performed.

When these young braves concluded their performance, one

by one several partially clad braves came into view and leapt into a circle, amid the larger circle of viewers, chanting songs and dancing to the beat of the tomtoms. Their breechcloths bounced, their headbands of feathers seemed to take flight, as they shook their bodies and bobbed their heads, their chants becoming louder, their dance becoming more frenzied.

Wild sage, the symbol of cleanliness and purity, was wrapped around the ankles and wrists of the dancers. Small sprigs of wild sage were also tied to the eaglebone whistles next to the mouthpieces of some dancers, and when they began to feel thirsty, they bit off small pieces of the sage and chewed on it.

Briana noticed that all of the children were shuffled from the council house as several scantily clad maidens entered the circle of dancers and joined the dance. Their breasts swelled almost free of the band of fur wrapped around them, bouncing, it seemed, in time with the music. They wore a scant strip of fur around their lower abdomen, reaching down only far enough to cover their uppermost thighs.

Briana watched as the rhythm of the women dancers became more frenzied, soon joined by several braves who had only moments ago been observers. She watched as these braves joined the women in the frenzied movements.

Briana drew in a shaky breath when Night Hawk jumped to his feet and motioned for her to come with his outstretched hands.

She blushed and timidly shook her head, but that did not dissuade him. He reached down and grabbed both of her hands, pulling her to her feet before him.

Out of the corner of her eye Briana saw Gentle Fawn and Echohawk joining the dancers, their bodies almost locked as they swayed in rhythm with the tom-toms and chanting.

Soon Briana also felt her body responding to the drumbeat. She drifted toward Night Hawk, and soon moved into her husband's arms without any more coaxing. She twined her arms around his neck and pressed her breasts against him, finding it easy to forget her bashfulness while becoming entranced by the magic of the dance and the eyes of her beloved. She felt his thick arousal pressing against her stomach through their clothes and slid in a gyration of movements against him.

Becoming consumed herself with wild rapture, she closed her eyes and held her head back, his lips hot as he kissed the hollow of her throat.

Then when she felt that she was too close to that realm of pleasure that she wanted to enjoy only in the privacy of her bed, she stepped back from Night Hawk and reached a hand out to him, in her eyes a pleading that he understood.

He lifted her fully up into his arms and carried her away from the council house.

When they were inside their wigwam, and all was quiet except for their heavy breathing, they quickly disrobed each other.

They both groaned as their bodies met hurriedly. Briana gasped with pleasure as he drove his thickness deeply within her and began his heated strokes, which began lifting her up above herself, it seemed, as though she were floating.

Briana's nipples became taut and pleasure flowed through her as Night Hawk ran his fingers over the creamy curves of her flesh. She moaned against his chest as she placed her lips against his flesh. Night Hawk's hands slipped farther down her body and furled the hair at the juncture of her thighs, touching her swollen bud of desire, caressing it as he continued to move rhythmically within her.

Briana reciprocated by strolling her fingers across his muscular body, across his deep chest and straight shoulders; along his hard stomach and large and powerful thighs; and to that wonderful place between his legs. She splayed her fingers out between her thighs and where he was moving himself in and out of her, reveling even a moment's touch of that part of him that always set her body aflame.

She then moved her hands around him and locked her fingers into the flesh of his buttocks, urging his hips to press harder into her loins, the full length of him buried within her, yet wanting him to fill her even more deeply.

His strokes were strong and long, his face pressed within the soft pillows of her breasts, his breathing raspy.

Briana closed her eyes and let the euphoria claim her. As his body tightened and hardened, she arched and cried out, and together they shared the explosion of ecstasy.

* * *

Echohawk carried Gentle Fawn into his wigwam. Before placing her on a pallet of furs on the floor beside the fire pit, he gave her a kiss, finding it sweet and wonderful.

He lay her on the furs, and as she smiled up at him, he removed her clothes. Then he bent down over her as she removed his garments.

When both were naked, Echohawk drew her up onto his lap, easing her legs around him and thrusting his thick shaft into her. As she clung to him around his neck, he ran his fingers over her smooth copper body, stopping at her abundant, milk-filled breasts.

She closed her eyes and sighed as he kneaded them, then lowered his mouth over one, flicking his tongue around the nipple. Then Echohawk lifted her away from him and lay her down on her back and knelt beside her, his tongue and lips paying homage to her every secret place.

She placed a hand on his head and urged him away. She moved to her knees beside him, pleasuring him in the same way, smiling up at him when the flick of her tongue drew a guttural sigh of pleasure from the depths of his throat.

Finding himself too close to that brink of bliss that he wanted only while deeply imbedded in her, Echohawk lifted her again away from him and lay her down beneath him, soon thrusting his hardness deeply within her again. Their bodies strained together and their lips burned from their heated kisses.

Soon they went over the edge into total ecstasy. They laid together, clinging, their bodies still tingling from their joyous moment—their first sexual joining as man and wife.

"You make Gentle Fawn so very happy," she murmured, kissing Echohawk gently on the cheek. "You are so good to me. Gentle Fawn will forever be grateful."

"You are my wife now," Echohawk said huskily. "I am the one who is grateful."

Gentle Fawn smiled sweetly and snuggled against him again.

* * *

Wrapped warmly in buffalo robes, Briana and Night Hawk sat beside the fire, feeding each other pieces of sliced apple. "Can this truly be happening?" Briana said, beaming with the bliss of being married after having thought she might never see Night Hawk again. "Are we truly husband and wife?"

"Although the ceremony was a simple one, *ay-uh,* we are married," Night Hawk said, chuckling. He reached his hand inside Briana's robe and brought one of her breasts within his fingers, drawing an ecstatic sigh.

"You had better remove your hand, or my darling, you will have to give me more of what such caresses promise," Briana said, daring him with a flashing smile.

She leaned into his hand as he moved it from her breast, smoothing it along her ribs, down the flat plane of her stomach, and then between her thighs, where she was still tender from their previous lovemaking.

She gasped as he pushed his finger up inside her and began thrusting it gently, over and over again.

"My darling, please . . ." Briana whispered, her face becoming flushed from rising passion.

She laughed throatily when he suddenly clasped his hands on her shoulders and half threw her on the pallet of furs, casting off her robes and his gaze feasted on her velveteen softness. She tossed the apple aside and closed her eyes, trembling with pleasure as again Night Hawk began kissing his way down her body. Her eyes suddenly flew open with alarm when a gunshot broke the reverie, and the sounds of the celebration at the council house stopped.

Night Hawk bolted to his feet and pulled on his breeches. He hurried into his moccasins and shirt and grabbed a fur robe around his shoulders before stepping out into the chill night wind.

Briana hurried into her own clothes and raced after him, stopping when one of the village braves came into the light of the great outdoor fire, carrying a limp body in his arms.

"Wise Owl," Night Hawk said, gasping as he recognized the old Indian.

Echohawk stepped up beside Night Hawk, his gaze locked on Wise Owl's death stare. "Wise Owl," he said, his voice drawn.

With a nod of his head Night Hawk motioned to the brave to place Wise Owl on the ground.

"He was moving stealthily toward our village with a loaded rifle," the brave explained. "When I yelled at him to ask him why he was there, since everyone knows of his banishment from our tribe, he turned his rifle on me. But before he got the chance to shoot me, I shot him first."

"And so *he* is the one responsible for the gift of bound arrows," Echohawk said, his jaw tight. "He hated us so much that he returned to kill his own kind."

"*Ay-uh,* it is sad. Yet I am much relieved to know that only he was the threat. Everyone can sleep in peace tonight," Night Hawk said, trying to find something good about the unfortunate circumstances of someone who was once a beloved brave of the Chippewa.

"Finally the old man has found a semblance of peace, even if death was the only way he could achieve it," Echohawk grumbled. He nodded toward the brave. "Take him away. See to his burial."

Echohawk turned to another brave. "Send word to the sentries they can be relieved of their posts and return to the village," he said. "It is safe now for everyone to resume their normal activities."

Echohawk returned to Gentle Fawn and held her close as he fought back tears of regret over Wise Owl and how he had become someone unknown to him.

Night Hawk walked with Briana back to their wigwam,

and clung to her beside their lodge fire, fighting back his own tears.

* * *

The gunshot in the distance had sounded like a lone clap of thunder echoing through the forest. White Wolf and Strong Branch hovered over a camp fire. "Today dual marriages were performed in Echohawk's village," White Wolf said, squinting over at Strong Branch. "To get them off guard, I allowed it. Tomorrow we will arrive at sunup at their village, when they least expect it. They will then know who sent them the gift of arrows."

White Wolf laughed boisterously, his breath like white silver against the dark shawl of the night.

Then he grew serious as he glanced over his shoulder at the many renegades that he had managed to round up for the attack. He gazed intently into Strong Branch's eyes. "When you found Wise Owl wandering in the forest, it was clever of you to give him a rifle, suggesting he use it to achieve his vengeance," he said, smiling crookedly. "This drew the attention away from us, the true danger. And you knew he'd get shot before he got anywhere near the village. Yes, Strong Branch, that was clever."

Strong Branch offered no response, in his eyes a strange, haunting sadness.

29

I saw the arrow from the bow-string part;
I heard the hoarse, blood-freezing war-whoop well;
I heard the victor shout—the dying yell.

—Anonymous

Night Hawk awakened with a start, sweat pearling his brow. Briana leaned up on an elbow, eyes wide, the morning light spiraling down from the smoke hole in the ceiling, giving enough light for her to see the fear etched onto her husband's face.

"Good Lord, what is it?" she gasped, reaching a hand to his brow and smoothing the perspiration from his flesh with her fingers. "You awakened as though you were shot."

Night Hawk turned troubled eyes to Briana. "In my dream I was," he said. "And also my father." He clasped her and drew her into his embrace. "Also you, my love."

Placing her cheek on his bare chest, Briana clung to him, feeling his rapid heartbeat thudding. "I'm sure you dreamed that because of Wise Owl's death," she murmured. "Please forget it, darling. We've so much to be happy about. Let us enjoy it."

"*Ay-uh,* I am sure you are right," Night Hawk said, easing her out of his arms. He urged her back down onto the pelts which covered their sleeping platform. He swept the covering of pelts away from her, his gaze warming her flesh where his eyes touched her with a caress.

"I never get enough of you," he said, smoothing his hands across her stomach, eliciting a low moan from deep within her. "Perhaps we shall spend the day making love. We would not be missed among our people. Not today, the second day of our marriage."

Although every nerve ending in her body cried out for his

tender caresses, and feeling as though she would be neglecting him by refusing to stay with him for a day of lovemaking, Briana crept away from him and rose from the sleeping platform. She sighed with regret for the plans that she had made for early this morning when he gazed up at her with keen disappointment and puzzlement in his eyes.

"Why do you say no to Night Hawk, your new husband?" he said, reaching toward her, beckoning for her to return. "It is not what I would expect of you the second day of our marriage."

"And I am sorry," Briana said, moving back onto the platform, kneeling beside him. She kissed him sweetly on the lips, then took his hands and held them. "I promise never to let this happen again. Every morning from now on will be yours. But today I can't. Yesterday, while painting with the children of our village, somehow I got drawn into agreeing to take many of them into the forest with canvases today, to paint the wondrous scenes of winter. When they asked, even begged, how could I say no?"

"There is not enough of you to share," Night Hawk teased, laughing softly. Then he nodded. "*Ay-uh,* today is the children's. Tonight and tomorrow are mine."

Briana threw her arms around his neck and gave him another kiss, then bounced from the sleeping platform. She went to a peg on the wall on which hung her buckskin dresses and chose one with long sleeves and also warm leggings to wear beneath them.

Night Hawk rose from the platform, yawning and stretching his arms over his head, then grabbed a pair of fringed leggings and jerked them up his muscular legs. "If my life were guided by my dreams I would not allow you or the children to go into the forest today," he said, giving her a troubled glance as he reached for his long-sleeved buckskin shirt. He also yanked this on, soon positioning his headband around his brow. "But as it was only a dream, it would be foolish to deny the children their day in the forest with you. Wise Owl sent the bundled arrows. And he is now dead."

"But have you so easily forgotten White Wolf?" Briana

asked, drawing her hairbrush through her long hair. "Where do you think he has made his new hide-out, Night Hawk? Perhaps he has even fled to Canada. You may never have him to worry about again."

"The Chippewa never forget any Sioux that have been a threat to them in the past," Night Hawk said, slipping into his moccasins, then squatting on his haunches beside the glimmering coals in the fire pit. He began stirring them and placing fresh wood on. He fanned them with his hands as they began to smoke and sputter.

"The Sioux never forget their enemy the Chippewa," he said. "Especially the Sioux renegade White Wolf. He hates all Chippewa, especially those with the names Echohawk and Night Hawk. He will come one day and prove how deeply this hatred is imbedded in his heart. He will come to kill and maim our innocent people. My father and I will not truly rest in this lifetime until White Wolf is dead."

"But, darling, I was told that White Wolf caused your people no problems for many years," Briana said, trying to ease his doubts. "Perhaps it will be the same again. Perhaps he is gone again until, let's say—maybe another twenty or so years?"

"He does not have enough years left," Night Hawk hissed. "Although my father's heart seems younger today because he is bedding a young wife, he is a man of sixty winters—and so is White Wolf. If he waited twenty winters to achieve his vengeance, he might be too old even to lift his bow and arrow against his arch enemies."

He rose to his full height and turned to Briana, whose hair was now free of tangles and hanging lustrously glossy and long down her back. He placed his hands on her waist and drew her against his hard body. "My woman, no matter when he comes to face his enemy, I will be here to protect you," he said, brushing a kiss across her lips. "Also the children that seek teaching from you, like they are your own children, for they are the future of our people."

"Night Hawk," Briana said, gazing unblinkingly up at him. "You speak of children with so much affection. I hope to become with child soon. That will complete my happiness, my darling."

"A child would please me very much," Night Hawk said, then jerked away from her, his eyes wide with alarm.

"What is it?" Briana asked, his alarm causing icy chills to run up and down her spine.

"Listen!" Night Hawk said, his jaw tight. "Do you not hear the hoot of an owl? I hear it sometimes in my sleep, for my father taught me long ago that it is deemed wise to impress the sound of an owl early upon the mind of a child."

"But why?" Briana whispered, stepping closer to him, flinching when she herself heard the distinct sound coming from somewhere in the nearby forest.

"The hoot of an owl is commonly imitated by Indian scouts on a warpath," he said, grabbing his rifle. "So often in the past with the Chippewa, a dreadful massacre immediately followed the call."

Concerned, he turned back to Briana. He thrust the rifle into her hand. "You stay in our dwelling and if the enemy somehow gets past me, kill him," he flatly ordered.

Briana swallowed back a lump of fear that had lodged in her throat. She nodded anxiously, then watched as he grabbed another rifle, then rushed from the wigwam.

Briana felt faint when war whoops suddenly filled the air, followed by much gunfire and cries of pain. She could not stand to stay inside the wigwam, like a coward, when she heard some of the Chippewa screaming, so many silenced, surely by either arrows or bullets as the massacre became widespread throughout the village.

Briana did not stop to pull on a robe to ward off the cold of the day. She knew that her gunpower was needed. And as she stepped outside, what she saw caused a keen lightheadedness to sweep through her. Many innocent Chippewa had been killed, both women and children. Some braves were lying wounded on the ground.

Desperately, Briana looked around to see if Night Hawk was all right, and also Echohawk. But she saw neither in the confusion of the fighting.

Her gaze was wrenched to a scene that made her almost faint dead away. Somehow she found the strength to lift the rifle, aim, and shoot a Sioux renegade in the back just after he had scalped a woman and leaped away with a whoop, her bloody scalp held tightly in his hand.

Briana watched the Sioux renegade's body lurch with the impact of her bullet. She was glad when he finally fell forward, his face hidden from her view as it went straightforward onto the ground.

Other high-pitched war cries split the air.

Torches sputtered and flared to life.

A horde of screaming Sioux renegades began running through the village, tossing the torches onto the wigwams. Others sent their bullets crashing through the smoke flaps and pole tips of the painted lodges, toppling buffalo hide walls into the cooking fires.

Although shaken by the experience, filled with a keen sadness for those people that only last night had celebrated her marriage to Night Hawk, Briana aimed over and over again at the warring renegades, smiling triumphantly when she hit her target and was able to stop at least some of the vengeful acts of the Sioux.

She took a step back, gasping, when only a few feet away from her a woman staggered. She caught herself momentarily to stand tall and unafraid beside her husband as he then was also shot.

Briana sobbed as both victims crumpled to the ground, and her heart ached as she watched their hands seek each other's. Just as their hands became tightly clasped, both convulsed, their eyes staring blankly into each other's.

Briana lowered her rifle and covered her ears with her hands. She closed her eyes as the deadly hail of gunfire screeched all about her. She could not help it when she began screaming, for the infernal tumult was now too much for her to bear.

A strong arm around her waist drew her back into herself as her eyes opened widely and found Night Hawk there, drawing her protectively behind him.

"You were told to stay in the dwelling!" he shouted, standing in front of her, aiming and firing. "Do you not see the women and children? The Sioux have no pity! They have come to totally annihilate the Chippewa!"

"Your father! Gentle Fawn and Moonstar!" Briana cried. "Have they been killed?"

"My father led Gentle Fawn and Moonstar into the forest for safety and then returned. Until now he stood beside me, father and son, fighting the Sioux as though one heartbeat," he shouted, then began smiling as he watched some of the Sioux retreating.

"My father is fine!" Night Hawk added. "He will not allow death to claim him so soon after becoming alive again with a new wife!"

He proudly watched as the Chippewa braves went after the Sioux renegades, not allowing them to advance farther than the edges of their village without first becoming the recipient of a poisoned arrow.

Then his smile faded when he caught his first sight of White Wolf among those who remained in the village alive. In the fierceness of the beginning battle, Night Hawk had not seen any recognizable faces. To him the enemy was the enemy. To him, as he fired his rifle, they were nameless. They were faceless.

But now he was focusing on the face. White Wolf was approaching Echohawk from behind! His tomahawk was raised. . . .

Briana caught the terrifying sight almost at the same instant as Night Hawk. Quickly, as though some hidden spirit had drawn her there, Briana stepped around Night Hawk, lifted her rifle, and fired. She missed White Wolf's body, but instead shot the tomahawk from his hand.

His hand bleeding, White Wolf whipped around and stared disbelievingly at Briana, who still stood poised with the rifle, frozen at what she had achieved!

Night Hawk smiled down at her, then ran to White Wolf and knocked him to the ground, placing a moccasined foot on his chest, to hold him there.

Briana noticed an abrupt silence around her. She glanced

on all sides, seeing that no more Sioux remained alive in the village. They were dead—the recipients of poisoned arrows and gunshot wounds. But she noticed that unlike the Sioux who had viciously removed many scalps today, none of the Chippewa had scalped their enemies.

Suddenly she spotted one of the injured renegades moving. She watched as this person reached for a rifle, leaned up on one elbow, and aimed at Night Hawk.

Briana was too stunned this time to react with her firearm. She began screaming. "Night Hawk!" she cried. "Fall to the ground, Night Hawk!"

Echohawk scanned quickly around him. Catching sight of the renegade whose aim was on his son, he lifted his rifle, aimed, and fired.

Night Hawk turned with a start and saw the renegade's rifle fall limply from his hand. Then he recognized the face as the Indian gazed up at him with wide eyes and blood curling from his nose and lips.

"Strong Branch!" Night Hawk gasped, allowing his grip on White Wolf to loosen.

Before he realized what was happening, White Wolf had grabbed his leg and yanked him to the ground, soon straddling and choking him.

Night Hawk grabbed a knife from its sheath at White Wolf's waist and lunged upward, thrusting it deeply into White Wolf's groin. At almost the same time two gunshots rang out, the bullets lodging in White Wolf's back.

Echohawk and Briana exchanged knowing glances as their rifles smoked in the early morning air.

Night Hawk brushed White Wolf's limp body away from him and rose nobly to his feet. He went to Strong Branch, who was gasping for breath and clutching his chest. He knelt down beside the fallen young chief and lifted his head from the ground.

"First Wise Owl betrays his people, and now you? You hated your people so much you would bring such disaster to them?" Night Hawk cried. "Strong Branch, as children we were friends. When did you decide to be not only my enemy but also our people's? You even killed my sister, the woman who you were to marry. Why, Strong Branch? Your actions became that of a madman, not someone who once was my devoted friend."

Strong Branch coughed fitfully, spewing blood from his mouth, then gazed sadly up at Night Hawk. "Strong Branch did not become your enemy because of hatred," he said breathlessly. "But out of love of power instead." Through a broken speech he admitted many truths to Night Hawk: about Gray Moon killing Lily, that she had been with child; about his having killed Gray Moon, and about his and Gray Moon's roles in the raids, and why he had done these things against the Chippewa.

Strong Branch reached for Night Hawk and clasped his shoulder. "From . . . the . . . depths of my heart, I am sorry," he rasped. "Today I became witness to what my drive for power caused. I became . . . a part of something that will keep . . . me . . . from entering paradise."

Strong Branch clutched desperately at Night Hawk's shoulder as his tear-filled eyes became locked in a death stare.

Briana stifled a horrified gasp behind her hand, then slowly turned and gazed at the death and destruction in the village.

A sudden thought seized her—that she was, in part, responsible. Had she not defied her uncle by coming to live with Night Hawk, perhaps none of this would have happened. Blackie had planted the seed of the Chippewa's destruction inside not only White Wolf's heart but also Strong Branch's. She could not help but think that had she never allowed herself to become involved with Night Hawk, none of this would have happened. For many years White Wolf had kept his distance from Echohawk's people. There had to have been a cause for his changed mind, to wreak havoc on their lives.

"I am that cause," she whispered to herself. Tears rushing from her eyes, she turned and ran blindly away from the death scene. Panting hard, unaware of the harshness of the cold penetrating her thin buckskin attire, she ran into the fringes of the forest.

When a hand gripped her arm, stopping her, she turned

weeping eyes up at Night Hawk as he spun her around to face him.

"Let me go!" she cried, trying to wrench herself free. "I have brought nothing but heartache to your people. Everything is my fault! Everything! I should've never allowed feelings to develop between us. Especially—especially after seeing how my uncle felt about you. I should have known that he would do everything within his power to cause problems for you because of your feelings for me."

She lowered her eyes. "Let me go, Night Hawk," she softly pleaded. "I wish to go to Paris, to be with my parents. I should've never come to Minnesota in the first place."

Night Hawk gave her a soft shake, causing her to look quickly up at him again. "What you are saying are words your uncle would want you to say," he murmured. "If you leave me, that is what he would want you to do. Are you going to allow him, even in death, to tear us apart?"

"I don't want to," Briana said, her voice breaking. "But—"

"I will not hear any more about it," Night Hawk said flatly. "Nor will I allow you ever to speak of blaming yourself again. Everything you have done has been in the best interests of your husband and his people. They know this. I know this. And so shall you, my woman, for I will not allow you to think otherwise."

Gentle Fawn stepped into view, snug in a buffalo robe, her bundled child pressed to her bosom. Her eyes were filled with fear as she moved slowly toward Night Hawk and Briana.

"My husband?" Gentle Fawn whispered. "Is he alive?"

Seeing the fear etched onto Gentle Fawn's tiny face made Briana quit thinking of herself. She knew that the young Chippewa maiden was again experiencing the terror that Echohawk had hoped he had saved her from.

Briana went to her and placed a comforting arm around her waist. "Echohawk is just fine," she murmured, casting Night Hawk a nervous glance as she recalled the bloody remains that lay strewn across the ground at the village. "But, Gentle Fawn, I don't think you want to go to the village. What you would see is not a pleasant sight."

"Gentle Fawn is strong," she said, determinedly walking straight ahead. "In my lifetime I have seen much death. I want my husband. I want to see my husband!"

"Let her go," Night Hawk said, stepping back to stand beside Briana. She turned to him and accepted the warmth of his embrace as he held her close to him. "Today will live within my mind forever," she whispered, shuddering.

"I shall help erase the memory, my love," Night Hawk whispered back.

Then he held her away from him, realizing that she was not wearing proper clothing to protect her from the cold. He picked her up in his arms and began running back toward the village with her.

Once there, he took her to their wigwam—one of the few that had not been destroyed by the enemy. He lay her close to the fire and covered her with several pelts. Her chills reached clean into his soul as he watched her shivering. "You stay here while I go and help see to the wounded and dead," he said. "I do not want to add your body to the burial grounds also."

Briana nodded anxiously, glad to be able to escape the gruesome sights. She relished the warmth of his lips as he kissed her, then turned toward the fire, shuddering anew when within the leaping flames she saw a reenactment of the grueling, bloody battle.

She pressed her eyes tightly closed, her sobs filling the awkward silence of her home.

30

Sing me a sweet, low song of night
Before the moon is rising.
—Hawthorne

The rebuilt Chippewa village basked in the heat of July. Wild rice was growing in abundance in the river beds, and the crops were knee high in the garden patches.

Briana and Gentle Fawn waddled toward the council house, their shadows on the ground beside them revealing their swollen abdomens. Both were now eight months heavy with child.

Briana wheezed and wiped beads of sweat from her brow, each heavy footstep an effort. She placed her hands at the small of her back, laughing lightly when she saw Gentle Fawn follow her lead, her own discomfort matching Briana's.

"I wish I hadn't gained so much weight," Briana said, groaning.

"I gained even more weight with my first child," Gentle Fawn said, giggling as she peered over at Briana with her dark eyes. "And then I thought I was so miserable. Perhaps this time I will have a boy child, do you think, Briana?"

Briana turned her gaze to sweet Moonstar as the child walked in short, awkward steps beside her mother, clinging trustingly to her hand. She was touched deeply by Moonstar, having become as close to the child as if she were her own. "I don't think you would be all that disappointed if you had another girl, would you?" she said, smiling as the tiny, delicate thing smiled widely up at her. "Moonstar is so sweet. Surely boys aren't as sweet or adorable."

Gentle Fawn laughed softly. "Boy children are not supposed to be sweet and adorable," she said. "They must be taught ways of men from the beginning—to be strong, brave, and noble.

Boys would not want to be cuddled, for that would make them feel as though the elders would look at them as no more than a girl."

Briana's smile wavered, hardly able to imagine any child of hers not being cuddled. She could remember her father singing her lullabys. Her mother had taught her nursery rhymes while she had cozied on her lap. She would want no less attention for her child, even if he were a son.

"I see your smile is not as bright at my mention of a boy child," Gentle Fawn said. "Do not worry so about what is expected of them. They learn by watching, listening, and imitating their fathers, by observing ways of their fathers, imitating examples placed before them. Slowly and naturally the faculties of observation and memory become highly trained in the manners, lore, and customs of our people without a strained, conscious effort. Body and mind grow together."

"That is such a lovely explanation," Briana said, smiling again at Gentle Fawn. "A son born to me and Night Hawk would surely be very wise and self-confident, for his father is filled with much wisdom and patience to teach it."

"The world of the Indian boy child teems with life and wisdom," Gentle Fawn explained. "From childhood their life is filled with a great desire to do, to be, and to grow. They all yearn for wisdom. They feel if they grow wise, their people will honor them. If they become very brave, they should be like their father; and if they become a good hunter, it would please their mother."

"I hope one day I will be as knowledgeable of children, and of what is expected of me, the mother," Briana said softly.

"Always remember that just as tiny roots of a plant silently absorb the earth food, so does the consciousness of the child absorb the influences which surround them," Gentle Fawn said. "Also, Briana, you will learn the ways of Chippewa mothers by watching and listening to those who already hold the proud title of *gee-mah-mah.*"

As they approached the entrance to the council house, all talk of children ceased. Chippewa men and women were entering the large dwelling, their faces solemn. Although several months had passed since the massacre, this was the first meeting of the Chippewa to discuss their future. Until now, everyone had concentrated on mourning their loved ones and rebuilding the village. And now that both were done, Echohawk had called his people together so that they could put their hearts and minds together and gain hope for their future from one another.

If they could forget that tragic day, they would now get a sense of sweetness and peace in the joined villages. But these were times of false fronts, everyone pretending that all was well in their worlds, while deep within their souls they were crying for all that had been taken from them.

Briana waited for Gentle Fawn to grab Moonstar up into her arms, and then they went together into the large council house, where no fires had been lit in the fire pits due to the sweltering heat that hung over everyone as though the fires of hell had been set loose around them.

The lighting for the dwelling was from the opened holes in the ceiling where the smoke usually escaped. These holes had been widened to allow more light and air into the spacious room. Briana soon spotted Night Hawk and his father, who sat together on a platform high above everyone.

As Briana sat down beside Gentle Fawn, she could hardly take her eyes off her husband. He was sitting with his legs crossed and his arms folded across his muscular copper chest, his raven black hair held back with a headband that she had just finished beading for him that day. Breechcloths were his and his father's only other attire.

Even though she was a very married and pregnant woman, the mere sight of Night Hawk could send her heart into a tailspin of passion, her pulse racing as proof of her feelings for him. Oh, how she was physically attracted to him! It would be an easy task to have many children with him. She could hardly imagine a night without showing him just how much she loved and adored him.

Briana was aware of the total silence around her. By now everyone was in the council house, each one sitting on mats on the floor.

A long-stemmed calumet pipe was passed from man to

man, a tangible link that joined man to Wenebojo, every puff of smoke that ascended in prayer unfailingly reaching his presence. With the pipe, faith was upheld, ceremony sanctified, and the being consecrated. It signified brotherhood, peace its greatest significance of all.

As the last man smoked from the pipe, then laid it aside, Briana looked slowly around her and saw the intensity with which everyone stared up at Night Hawk and Echohawk, trusting that they were going to lead them into a brighter future that hopefully would no longer involve surprise attacks from their enemies.

Echohawk rose tall and erect over his people, looking slowly around the room, from man to man, woman to woman, and child to child, his eyes lingering a moment longer on his wife.

Then, as he again gazed around the room, he began speaking softly and eloquently, as though his words were touching them in a caress. "My beloved Chippewa," he said, "it is with sadness that I have witnessed these past months of mourning brought upon you by those who were our enemy. But the time of mourning is now past, and it is time to rebuild faith and hope within our hearts. You are a strong, compassionate people. You have endured everything with squared shoulders and straight backs. And so will you endure whatever else befalls you, be it good or bad. But, my beloved Chippewa, we must think with a smile, and know that what lies before us is good. There are among you women blossoming with children within their wombs; my wife and my son's wife are also sweet with child. These children will be born into a kinder world and will carry on the peace-loving name of the Chippewa even after we, the parents and grandparents, are walking the roads of the hereafter."

He turned toward Night Hawk and placed a hand on his shoulder. "Rise, my son," he said. "I have something else to say that our people must be witness to."

With much grace and ease Night Hawk rose to stand beside his father. When their eyes met and held, Night Hawk saw such wisdom in the depths of his father's, yet something else—a soft gleam, as though something wonderful was just about to be released from the depths of his soul.

"My son, it is now time for me to step down from my duties as chief of our joined villages and proclaim you chief," Echohawk said, his voice steady. "I do this with much pride, for in you there is much compassion and wisdom that has been carried down through the generations of Chippewa before you, through blood ties of your forefathers. In your hands now lie the future and hopes of our people. I see this as no risk at all."

Touched deeply by what she was witnessing, Briana wiped tears of joy from her eyes. She smiled over at Gentle Fawn as she glanced her way, realizing that in part Echohawk's decision at this time was because of her. He wanted to spend more time with his young wife. His time with Gentle Fawn was surely more precious because of his age. His time with his children was also more precious.

When Night Hawk began to talk, Briana turned her head and gazed at him, at this moment idolizing him as never before.

"I accept the title of chief with a warm heart and much gratitude," Night Hawk said, reaching a hand to his father's shoulder. "I will carry the title with a lifted chin and squared shoulders. I will never give you cause to regret having lent me the title you have carried so graciously for so long. Like your father before you, you are cherished by everyone. I hope that at my age of sixty winters, I will be as cherished."

"And that you will, my son," Echohawk said, drawing Night Hawk into his embrace and giving him an earnest hug.

Echohawk whispered into Night Hawk's ear, "My son, one more thing. You must endeavor to equal your father and grandfather as peacemakers."

Night Hawk returned his promise in a whisper. "You have my word," he said, then they broke away from each other, standing arm in arm as everyone stood and broke into loud chants, proclaiming their acceptance of what Echohawk had chosen to do that day.

They stepped down from the platform side by side and received the warm hugs and kisses from their people. When the council was over, and the people had gone to their own corners of their private worlds, Briana and Night Hawk stood with Echohawk and Gentle Fawn. The former chief was holding Moonstar in his arms, his child in almost every sense of the word.

"It is done," Echohawk said, smiling over at Night Hawk. "My son, it has been good to watch you grow into a man. It will be good to watch you preside as chief over our people. I saw no need in delaying the process of son following father into chieftainship until I was on my journey to the hereafter. Now I have the opportunity to witness firsthand how you choose to use my teachings. *Ay-uh,* you will have your own views on things in council that will bring changes to our village, and the lives of our people. But that is how it should be. You are of a young mind and heart. Youthful thoughts and ideas will be welcomed."

He grew solemn for a moment as he looked into Night Hawk's dark eyes. "It is true that Strong Branch wanted to bring young ideas to the council, but his were twisted, as was his loyalty, it seems," he said, his voice drawn. "And of course we know who we must blame for this. Wise Owl. He was Strong Branch's adviser long before he began to seek ways to oust me from power. Wise Owl placed hatred and greed inside Strong Branch's heart, I am sure, as early as when he took his first step in this world. Had Nee-kah lived, she would have never allowed Wise Owl's interference in her young son's life."

"Nee-kah?" Briana said, raising an eyebrow. "Who is Nee-kah?"

"Nee-kah was Strong Branch's mother, and Mariah's best friend after she came to live as my wife among the Chippewa," Echohawk said, giving Gentle Fawn a troubled glance, relieved that she did not show any signs of resentment over him speaking about his second wife. Yet he knew that she was not the sort to be jealous. Her sweetness was genuine.

"And she died young?" Briana asked, slipping an arm through Night Hawk's, at this moment so enjoying this time of camaraderie with her husband's father, this moment seeming to draw them closer, yes, into a true family.

"*Ay-uh,* she left this earth much too soon," Echohawk

grumbled. "It was a strange death. One day she was well. The next she was dead." He tightened his jaw and anger filled his eyes. "I suspect she was poisoned."

"Poisoned?" Night Hawk said, shock registering in his eyes. "You have never spoken of that theory to me before, *gee-bah-bah.*"

"My son, never had I thought of it before," Echohawk said, his voice shallow. "But now it all fits together as though one fits pieces together of a puzzle. Wise Owl never approved of Nee-kah as Silver Wing's wife. She was headstrong. Wise Owl accused her of being a woman of defiance. Then when Strong Branch was born, and Silver Wing was dead, Wise Owl wanted full control of Strong Branch. As long as Nee-kah was alive, she would not allow it—even though Wise Owl was the wisest of Strong Branch's tribe and a close adviser of Chief Silver Wing. Nee-kah became wary of Wise Owl's intentions. Wise Owl saw her as a threat. I am sure he placed poison into her food."

Echohawk hung his head. "And what a loss it was," he said softly.

Moonstar started to wail, bringing everyone out of their saddened reverie. Echohawk was jolted somewhat by the sudden blast of lungs, then laughed and gazed down. He touched Moonstar's cheek gently as he looked into her beautiful eyes fringed with thick, dark lashes gazing up at him, not even tears spoiling their loveliness.

"And so you are always hungry, it seems," Echohawk said, placing a gentle kiss on Moonstar's brow. "I think you need your mother for that, not your *gee-bah-bah.*"

He handed the child to Gentle Fawn, and although Moonstar was now past her first birthday, Gentle Fawn slipped a corner of her dress down and let the child's tiny hands clutch the proffered milk-swollen breast, her perfectly shaped lips already sucking on the taut nipple.

"Her supper is always available," Night Hawk said, chuckling as he watched the child. He placed an arm around Briana's waist and leaned down into her face. "Soon we will be an audience to our own child feeding from its mother. What a joyous sight that will be!"

"My darling, I want to keep a child suckling at my breast forever," Briana said, smiling up at him. "We shall have to build a monstrous wigwam to make space for all of the children I will have for you."

Night Hawk chuckled again, realizing that, of course, she was speaking out of inexperience. Perhaps two children would do for her once she realized the responsibilities involved in raising a child.

She needed time for her other passion—her painting. And he was going to see that she had it. He did not need a brood of children to prove his virility. Having Briana as his woman was proof enough, for what man would not give his right arm to have such a woman for a wife?

Night Hawk and Briana bid Echohawk and Gentle Fawn a pleasant good-bye, then took a long, leisurely stroll through the forest. Evening was nigh. The air had cooled to a tolerable level. The breeze was sweet and filled with the fragrance of the blossoms of a wild crabtree and lilacs, which grew heavy in bloom on many bushes throughout the forest.

The birds overhead were making a racket as they settled into their nests for the night. A squirrel scampered from tree limb to tree limb, taking flight, it seemed as though it had wings.

"I so love the forest," Briana said, taking small steps, all that her large belly would allow. "It is as though I were born here, myself, a part of it. It touches my very soul with its loveliness." She closed her eyes and inhaled deeply. "The fragrances are so sweet, as though someone has opened many large bottles of French perfume and sprayed fine mists into the air."

Her eyes opened quickly as she felt Night Hawk's hands on her waist, stopping her from going any farther. She smiled up at him. "My darling, in your eyes I see something quite familiar," she murmured. She placed a hand to his cheek. "It is the look you get when you desire me."

"Flower of my wigwam, I desire you always," Night Hawk said huskily, leaning down to flick his tongue across her soft lips. He drew her as close as her tummy would allow and kissed her, touching her tongue through her parted lips.

Briana knew that soon she would not be able to make love with Night Hawk until after the birth of their child, but that time was not yet upon her. So she welcomed his arms as he lowered her slowly to the ground on a soft cushion of leaves.

As though in a gesture of worship, Night Hawk knelt over her and smoothed her dress up, past her stomach, then framed the large, tight ball between his hands. Bending lower over her, he kissed her stomach, then placed a cheek against her flesh as she twined her fingers through his hair.

"Do you feel our child's moving within me?" Briana murmured, herself feeling the slight kicking movements. Some days they were more energetic than others. Today, the child seemed to sense the peace within her heart, for its movements were soft and sweet inside her womb.

Night Hawk pressed an ear against her abdomen. His eyes widened as his lips spread into a smile. "I hear so many strange sorts of sounds," he said. "Our child is eager to begin its journey of life with its *gee-mah-mah* and *gee-bah-bah*."

"And it will soon," Briana whispered, placing her hands to Night Hawk's cheeks, urging his lips to hers. "Kiss me, my darling chief. Hold me. I love you so much."

As Night Hawk kissed her, he managed to remove his breeches, then he felt her breath catch as he very gently shifted the strength of his arousal within her. In a shared, spiraling need, their bodies moved rhythmically together.

Soon they joined on another flight of bliss, as though once again on the widespread wings of an eagle, soaring high into the heavens, reaching the moon, the stars.

Afterward, Night Hawk lay beside Briana, cuddling her close. The stars were fresh in the sky, the Milky Way creating a wave of light above them. "My woman, you are everything to me," he said, caressing her swollen abdomen, again feeling the movements of his child within it. "And soon we will be a family."

Briana snuggled closer. "I am so proud of you," she whispered. She smiled up at him. "And I have been remiss in saying something to you that needs saying."

"Oh, and what is that?" Night Hawk said, turning to face her, his hands cupping her heavy-laden breasts as he reached higher up inside her dress.

"Congratulations, my darling," she whispered, leaning up to kiss his cheek. "You are now the chief of your people. My sweet chieftain husband, congratulations."

"It means much more to me now that I have you at my side," Night Hawk said, smoothing her dress down to ward off the chill of the night.

Night Hawk offered her a hand and helped her up from the ground. "Come," he said softly. "Let us return to our dwelling. Let us lie down together. Let me hold you the whole night through, Briana. I remember a time when I hungered for just that and it was not possible. Now it is. Everything is possible for us now, my love."

Briana leaned against him as they walked with wondrous peace through the forest, toward the beckoning outdoor fires of their village. She hoped that now that peace had been won among Night Hawk's people, it would always be as it was at this moment—forever paradise.

31

Love? I will tell thee what it is to love!
It is to build with human thoughts a shrine,
Where Hope sits brooding like a beauteous dove;
Where Time seems young, and Life a thing divine!

—Swain

Like golden waterfalls, lemonade was pouring from pitchers into many crystal goblets. Finger foods, cakes, and cookies were heaped on huge platters on the oak dining table of Briana's artists' boardinghouse. At least a hundred candles burned from a crystal chandelier above the proffered delicacies.

Her cheeks rosy, her eyes shining in her moment of triumph, Briana stood back and watched the flurry of those who had participated these past three years in her dream of seeing her boardinghouse and art school become a success.

And to her delight, it had.

Aspiring artists of all ages and from all corners of the world had come to the state of Minnesota, where today they were chatting among themselves in Briana's mansion about this artists' "colony," as it had come to be known. She had created a haven for those who were scorned in the more public schools and colleges. Their interest in painting was called trivial; those who cried loudest against artists called them too lazy to make an honest living.

"The pride shows in your eyes," Night Hawk said as he came to stand beside her. "And you have cause to be proud. You wanted a dream, and now you have it. I feel the excitement. I see it. It was right, Briana, what you have done for these people who share your passion of painting."

Several squealing children running past them drew Briana's and Night Hawk's attention. "Our children are enjoying the day as well," Briana said, watching their twins, Spotted Eagle and Precious Dawn, and Echohawk and Gentle Fawn's twins,

Yellow Bird and Dancing Star, running past them, then out the opened French doors at the far end of the room to romp in the large yard.

On the morning of the birth of their twins, Night Hawk had shouted the news to the village and given away two horses. He then had explained to Briana that twins were special among his people—they were regarded as mysterious beings who had lived with the tribe at some past time and had come back again to live life over.

He had further explained that the spirits of little twins would hover above a wigwam, lifting up the entrance flap and peeking in. They were looking for a place in which to be reborn. They were visible only to certain people, and when the person who saw them shouted or called for someone else to look, the twins disappeared. These little twin spirits always appeared about the wigwam tied together with a rope.

Last, he had explained that twins had habits boys and girls born singly did not have. Though it was forbidden for brothers and sisters to speak freely with each other, twins were closest of companions—ties that did not exist between other brothers and sisters.

Since the twins' births, Briana had seen how proud Night Hawk was of them both. Often she had watched her husband lie on the ground on his back, and with his legs crossed, he tossed first one child, and then the other, up and down on his foot. It was the children's delight, and Night Hawk's, to play horse in that manner.

Briana had listened to him sing warrior songs to his children so that they would grow up loving the songs of his people. She had listened to him teaching his children of his ways, telling them there was no such thing as emptiness in the world, and that even in the sky there were no vacant places. Everywhere there was life, visible and invisible, and every object possessed something that would be good for the Chippewa to have—even to the very stones. This gave a great interest to life.

It was his firm belief that one was never alone.

"Does it disappoint you that as yet our son and daughter have not one serious bone in their body?" Night Hawk said, laughing softly as he placed his arm around Briana's waist. "They rarely stop long enough to take up a brush to paint on the canvases that you leave out for them in hopes that will stir them into painting."

"No, I'm not disappointed," Briana said, sighing deeply. "They have plenty of time to realize their dreams for the future. That they are strong and healthy, both our daughter and son, is enough for me right now."

Night Hawk leaned close to her ear. "Are you ready to fill the wigwam with more children?" he teased.

Briana rolled her eyes skyward. "Heaven forbid!" she said. The twins kept her hopping from morning till night!

"Briana, look in the next room," Night Hawk softly encouraged. "Look at Moonstar."

Arm in arm, husband and wife strolled into the adjoining room, where many paintings were on display. Briana felt warm through and through when she found Moonstar studying the paintings closely, her mother and father following close behind her. In her right hand Moonstar held several paintbrushes, gifts from some of the teenage artists who were taken by her interest in their work, revealing her own deep passion for painting.

"When I look at her, I see myself as a four-year-old," Briana murmured. "She has already found her dream, Night Hawk. I will build on that dream for her, and see that she has all of the advantages that I had. Perhaps I shall even take her to Paris!"

Night Hawk swept her out of the room and led her up the grand spiral staircase to the second floor where she kept a room for herself and her family on their visits to the boardinghouse. Night Hawk walked her to it.

After entering, he turned and locked the door, then swept Briana into his arms and gave her a heated kiss.

Together they moved to the bed and stretched out on it. Slowly, almost meditatively, they removed each other's clothes. Briana then moved her body sinuously against his as he thrust himself inside her.

"Let me hear no more talk about Paris," Night Hawk whispered huskily against her lips. "It is not a part of our world." He moved gently within her. "This is."

She felt no need to complain. This wild rapture that was always there waiting for her within her husband's arms was more grand, more wonderful, than a place called Paris.

Briana nestled close to Night Hawk, their bodies rocking and swaying together in their building passion, truly never wanting more than what her Chippewa chieftain husband's embraces promised.

Briana was fulfilled, and oh, so gloriously happy. Night Hawk had told her often how content he was in his world that forever included her. The peace, the ideal which man sometimes reaches, was always there for him while he had her.

Wild Embrace

With affection I dedicate
Wild Embrace to:
Sheila Bilbrey
Marion Campbell
Kathy Stone
Stella Alexander
Aurora Gonzalez
Damita Lewis

also: Bruce and Ruth
and Mike and Nancy Girot

I thought you savage
You thought me uncaring,
Desire has a mind of its own
As passion brings forth sharing.

Your hands so strong upon me
Warm and gentle as they seek,
A desperate quake begins within me
I stand vulnerable and weak.

You proceed to imprison my heart
All my resistance is torn asunder,
I can see only you before me
And hear your voice, that sounds like thunder.

To you, I will constantly come running,
Of shame, I have not a trace.
Your open arms are a haven,
I cherish the feel of our wild embrace.

—Sheila Bilbrey,
a fan, poet and
sweet friend

1

> No soul can ever clearly see
> Another's highest, noblest part,
> Save through the sweet philosophy,
> And loving wisdom of the heart.
>
> —PHOEBE CARY

The Pacific Northwest September, 1875

A fireplace dug out in the middle of the planked floor of the longhouse reflected the wavering light of its fire onto cedar walls hung with mats and various cooking and hunting paraphernalia, and onto sleeping platforms spread with several layers of bark, and soft, furry pelts. Overhead, berries and fish hung to dry from the crossbeams under the rafters. The smoke from the lodge fire was spiraling slowly toward the open cedar boards overhead, its gray wisps escaping upward, into the morning sky.

Chief Moon Elk rearranged his robe of black sea otter fur more comfortably around his lean shoulders, and pulled up his legs and squatted close to the fire. His steel-gray eyes were not large, but were bright and steady in their gaze, the skin of his copper face was fine in texture, although age and weather had wrinkled it.

"Remember always to walk softly, my son," Chief Moon Elk said as he peered at Strong Heart, who sat beside him feasting on a bowl of soup made from clams and wild vegetables. "While you are helping Four Winds escape from the white man's prison in Seattle, you must not shed blood. No good ever comes of killing whites. Our Suquamish people always suffer in the end."

Strong Heart paused momentarily from eating. "This I know," he said, nodding his head with grave dignity. "And no blood will be shed. I would do nothing to lead trouble to our village. By choice, our clan of Suquamish have kept ourselves from those who were tricked by the white man's treaties and promises. Because of this, ours has been a peaceful existence. So shall it continue to be, Father."

Chief Moon Elk's gaze moved slowly over Strong Heart, admiring his muscular son attired in fringed buckskin. "Your plan is to dress as a white man during the escape, and you will ride your horse instead of traveling by canoe to Seattle?" he asked, wiping his mouth with a cedar-bark napkin, his own stomach warmed comfortably with soup.

"*Ah-hah,* yes, that is my plan," Strong Heart said, leaning closer to the fire to ladle more clam soup into his elaborately carved wooden bowl. The ladle was decorated with the crest of his family: the red-tailed hawk.

Strong Heart began eating the soup again, needing his fill now, for he was not planning to stop for anything until he reached the outskirts of Seattle. His plans for Four Winds were several sunrises away. He had other chores to do before freeing his friend from the cruel clutches of the law.

Moon Elk studied his son for a moment without offering a response to what Strong Heart had said. It was like seeing himself in the mirror of the clear rivers and streams those many years ago when he could boast of being his son's age of twenty-nine winters. Moon Elk had begun to shrink with age, so he was no longer as tall as his son. Strong Heart was more than six feet in height, a giant among his Suquamish people, and most whites.

And not only was his son tall, he was powerfully built, broad shouldered, thin flanked, and lithe. His light copper-colored skin was smooth, with muscles that rippled beneath the flesh. He wore his dark brown hair long and loose, past his shoulders, and his gray eyes held strength and intelligence in their depths.

Ah-hah, Moon Elk thought proudly, there was a steel-like quality about his son.

His son was a man of daring and courage.

"My son, not only will the color of your skin give away

your true identity, but also your dignified gracefulness. You are a noble man who towers over the white man," Moon Elk said. "This can perhaps betray your plans, my son. No white man walks with the dignity of my son, nor carries within their hearts such compassion."

Moon Elk leaned closer to Strong Heart and peered into his eyes. "My son, is Four Winds worth risking your life for? The world would be void of a much greater man should *you* die."

Strong Heart was unmoved by his father's steady stare, or his words. "Even now I am sure the white people are building a hanging platform for my friend, Four Winds," he said flatly. "My friend will *not* die with a noose around his neck. Do you not recall *his* dignity, Father? Being caged and awaiting his death, his dignity has been taken from him. And *I* see his life as no less valuable than mine. I will set him free, Father. And do not fear for my safety. I have faced worse odds in my lifetime than a *cultus,* worthless sheriff, who is blinded by the power he feels by caging men the same as some might cage a bird for entertainment's sake. It is *he* who should be caged, and put on display in a white man's circus!"

"Such a bitterness I hear in your voice," Moon Elk said, shaking his head sadly. "Now, when the autumn salmon harvest is near, and when your heart should be happy and your very soul should be filled with song, you are filled with bitterness over another man's misfortunes. That is *me-sah-chie,* bad, my son! *Me-sah-chie!*"

"*Ah-hah,* it is regrettable, yet is it not as regrettable that Four Winds was arrested unjustly?" Strong Heart said, setting his empty bowl aside. "You, as well as I, know his innocence. Although we have lost touch these past moons after his Suquamish clan moved north to Canada's shores, I know that his heart remains the same toward life. He could never ride with outlaws, killing and stealing! Never!"

"Who can say what drives a man, even to insanity?" Moon Elk rumbled. "The same could apply to a man who takes up the ways of a criminal. Is it not the same? Men are driven by many things to become who they are. As I recall him, Four

Winds seemed a driven young man. You did not also see this, my son?"

Strong Heart arched an eyebrow and fell deep into thought as he peered into the flames of the fire. He was remembering many things about his friend Four Winds from when they were youths together. Some good. Some *me-sah-chie,* bad.

Strong Heart had overlooked the bad, for Four Winds's goodness had always outweighed his shortcomings.

"Ah-hah," Strong Heart finally said, looking back at his father. "I remember that Four Winds was in a sense driven, but not much more than I, Father. In games of competition, we *both* strived to excel."

"Do you not recall the times he would avoid you for days after losing at games with you?" Moon Elk persisted. "*This* is why I fear he may have changed now into someone you do not know. Or should not risk your life for."

"Father, this is not at all like you," Strong Heart said, rising. He then knelt on one knee before his father and placed a gentle hand on his shoulder. "Trust my judgment, Father. Never before have you doubted me."

Moon Elk turned his eyes to Strong Heart and placed a hand over his son's. "It is not you I doubt," he said softly. "It is Four Winds. Remember this, my son, as you take the long ride to Seattle. I trust your judgment in all things. It is only that I worry too much over my son who is destined to one day be a great chief. Remember always the importance of being a *tyee,* chief. He is a man whose opinion carries more weight than his fellow tribesmen."

"I remember all of your teachings, Father," Strong Heart said, rising to his full height. "And I understand the importance of being a *tyee.* But that is in the future. I must do what I must now for a friend."

Moon Elk rose to his feet also. He walked with his son to the large cedar door and swung it open. Together they stepped outside to a blossoming new September day, the air heavy with the sweet fragrance of the cedar-and-pine forest which lay just beyond the village.

Moon Elk walked Strong Heart toward his *san-de-lie,*

horse, a magnificent roan. "You will also search again for Proud Beaver, your grandfather?" he asked, his face drawn. "Your mother still grieves so over him, fearing that her father is dead."

Strong Heart turned and saw his mother coming toward them, having left the longhouse so son and father could speak in private about things that would only trouble her. She had busied herself by going to the river for water and walked with a huge earthenware jug balanced on her right shoulder.

It saddened Strong Heart to see his mother's change since the disappearance of her father. Her eyes were no longer filled with laughter. She scarcely ate, and had become frail and gaunt.

Then Strong Heart smiled as he looked at her pert nose. It had remained the same—tiny and *toke-tie*, pretty—the reason her parents had called her Pretty Nose on the day of her birthing.

Pretty Nose set her heavy jug on the ground and went to Strong Heart. Tears filling her eyes, she embraced him. "My son, return safely to me," she murmured. "This that you do is courageous, yet I cannot say that it pleases me. Courage is just a word. It cannot fill my arms if you are dead!"

"Mother," Strong Heart said, placing his hands at her tiny waist, holding her away from him so that their eyes could meet. "You worry too much. This son of yours will return soon. And I promise to search for Grandfather. I shall go back once more to our ancestral grounds where our village once stood. We all believe that is where Grandfather went when he disappeared a moon ago. He felt as if the spirits of our dead ancestors were beckoning him there. He spoke of that often to me."

Strong Heart lowered his head momentarily, then looked back at his mother. "Had I heeded the warning in his voice and words, *never* would he have left our village. I would have kept watch. I would have stopped him."

"Do not blame yourself, my son," Pretty Nose said, gently placing a hand to his cheek. She looked adoringly up at him. "How could you know that his mind was aging more quickly than his body? We have not lived beside the waters of Puget Sound for *many* moons now. Many moons ago, even before

Chief Seattle signed treaties with the white people, our people took money from white people for their land. Those who did were ignorant enough to think the value of the money was worth more to them than the land. It was a mistake. It ate away at your grandfather like an open wound festering with disease. His regrets turned him away from us. *Ah-hah,* it has surely carried him 'home,' to our ancestral burial grounds."

She flung herself into her son's arms and clung to him, sobbing. "Please find him, Strong Heart," she whispered. "Please?"

"I shall try is all that I can say," Strong Heart said, easing her from his arms. He framed her face between his hands. His mouth went to her lips and he kissed her softly.

Then he turned and, with an easy grace, he mounted his horse, settling himself comfortably on the saddle stuffed with cottonwood and cattail down. He reached for his rawhide reins, and took a last look at his village before leaving. Rectangular houses built solely of cedar wood without the benefit of nails sat side-by-side facing the Duwamish River. All were supported by frameworks of massive posts and planks. The large, gabled houses were adorned with carved house posts and door poles, painted with the owners' crests, the animal spirit guardians and ancestors of each clan. Lines of totem poles stood before the houses, those dramatic columns of carved animals and birds.

Strong Heart then shifted his gaze to the saddlebags on his horse, his thoughts sorting through what he had packed to ensure the success of this venture that he was embarking upon. He was taking a change of clothes which would give him the appearance of a white man—a flannel shirt, leather breeches, and jacket, and high-heeled boots. He was carrying a pair of Colt revolvers with seven-inch barrels and pearl handles. A sombrero hung from the saddlehorn.

Ah-hah, he thought smugly to himself. All of this would be used when the time came for his masquerade.

Strong Heart patted the knife sheathed at his waist, then placed a hand on the rifle that was resting in its holster at his horse's flank. He valued this repeating rifle as if it were his right arm. It had gotten him through many scrapes when gangs of bandits had lurked beside the trails, waiting to attack any traveler who looked as if he might have something worth stealing.

Until recently, when they had been forced to go into hiding due to the many posses chasing them, the desperadoes had swarmed the countryside, attacking stations along the trail where travelers stopped to exchange tired horses for fresh ones for the next lap of their journey.

The robberies had lessened at the same time of Four Winds's arrest, yet Strong Heart still would not believe that his friend had any connection with the outlaws. It was surely a case of mistaken identity that made the posse think that Four Winds was a desperado.

Strong Heart looked at his parents, seeing the concern in their eyes for the dangers of his mission. Yet not even this could change his mind.

"I must go now," he said.

"Strong Heart, take many braves with you," Moon Elk said, in a final plea to his son. "They will ride beside you. They will help you."

"Father, as I have told you before, I must ride alone," Strong Heart said shortly. "Less trouble comes with lesser numbers. Many braves would draw attention—not avoid it. I, alone, can move about without being noticed."

Moon Elk nodded in acquiescence. Pretty Nose stepped closer to Strong Heart. Tears streamed from her dark eyes as she reached a hand toward him. "*Kla-how-ya,* good-bye, my son," she said, sobbing. "*Hy-ak,* hurry! Make haste in returning to me!"

"I will, Mother," Strong Heart said, then urged his horse away in a gallop, not looking back. He kept his eyes straight ahead as he left his village behind him, savoring the wild, deep free feeling of being alone on a journey of the heart. He loved the quiet power of it.

He soon forgot the heartache that he had left behind and enjoyed this land that was precious to him. It was a wild yet peaceable land, sunny and quiet. Strong Heart urged his horse in a steady pace along the trail. The wind was soft today, and the mountains beyond were misted and breathtakingly beautiful. There was fullness to everything.

* * *

When the haloed fire of the setting sun was fleeing before an ashen dusk, Strong Heart rode through familiar terrain. With his horse breathing heavily, he topped a rise.

Drawing rein, he took in the familiar sight. Out of the east rose the mighty Cascade Range, shawled in a dark-green weave of cedar, hemlock, and firs, dominated by the eternally white cone of Mount Rainier.

Below, the city of Seattle stretched out before him. He recognized Skid Road, a steep slope along the Seattle waterfront where logs were skidded to waiting ships, and where brothels and saloons did a roaring business.

Looming high above Seattle on another slope of land, yet just below where Strong Heart stood, was a long, ugly and ramshackle wooden building, with the name COPPER HILL PRISON written on a large sign at the front. He squinted his eyes, watching the men hammering outside the prison, the tell tale signs of a hanging platform taking shape.

Heaving a long sigh, Strong Heart shifted his eyes to where the Sound lay. He knew that among its sheltered coves and winding channels, salmon were swimming peacefully through the kelp forests. Soon they would be making their journey upriver. He would be there waiting for them, meeting them at the canyon for the autumn harvest.

Then something else caught his eye: a huge, four-masted ship approaching Seattle. He watched its movement through the choppy waves made by the cool northwest breeze. He always felt awe for these large vessels with their white sails catching the wind. He could not help but wonder whom this ship carried to the land that once belonged solely to the Suquamish.

His jaw tight, he wheeled his horse around and followed the slope of land that took him away from Copper Hill Prison.

Tonight and tomorrow he would renew his search for his grandfather.

Then he would return to study the prison, and how often people came and went from it.

2

> We have made no vows, there will be none broken.
> Our love was free as the wind on the hill.
>
> —Ernest Dowson

The wind was damp and chilly as it blew across the deck of the four-masted schooner, whipping Elizabeth Easton's elegantly trimmed black cape about her ankles. Her luxuriantly long, red hair whispered in the breeze around her face. Her impudent green eyes watched the ship pass Seattle, to go to a private pier a mile or two down the Sound.

Elizabeth clutched her gloved hands to the ship's rail, and although it was growing dusk, she was able to study the city. From this vantage point, she could not deny that it was a lovely setting. Seattle was framed by mountains and water, the dark forest crowning the hilltop above the city. If she inhaled deeply enough, she could smell the mixed, pleasant fragrances of roses, pine, and cedar. If she could forget her resentment for having been forced to come to the Pacific Northwest with her father, she would regard the land as nothing short of paradise.

In the dimming light of evening, her eyes locked on something that gave her a feeling of foreboding. She had been told about the prison, its reputation having traveled as far as California.

"Copper Hill Prison," she whispered, shivering at the thought of the kinds of criminals that were known to be incarcerated there. She feared that this city of Seattle might be even worse than the one she had left behind, San Francisco.

As the moon rose bright and beautiful in the sky, Elizabeth turned her attention from the city, and watched the land creep by on her left. Soon she would be reaching the place that she would call 'home.' She didn't look forward to it, for she had not wanted to leave her home in San Francisco. But leaving San Francisco had been a part of her father's plan for more than two years now. He had gone on many scouting expeditions in the Pacific Northwest, searching for just the right spot to build his fishery. After much study, he had found that the area around Seattle abounded in shellfish and other fish, making it possible for him to procure fresh fish year round for his planned business.

He had heard that much profit could be made in salmon, which were in abundance in the autumn. He planned to double his wealth on salmon alone, by exporting packed salted salmon to all corners of the world.

Elizabeth grasped the rail harder as the ship edged close to a pier. The water was deep enough here so the ship could dock without the need of longboats to carry cargo and passengers to shore.

In a flurry of activity, Elizabeth was whisked along with the others to the pier. She watched guardedly as her trunks were being taken from the ship and brought to land.

She sighed heavily, still not believing that her father was not going to take the time to go up to the house with her. Instead, he was going to join the ship's crew to help unload his own supplies to begin constructing his fishery tonight. Once he began, she knew not to expect his company, except for short visits, until it was completed.

Except for Frannie, her devoted maid, Elizabeth would be spending her every moment alone. Long ago, Elizabeth's mother, Marilyn, had fled the life Elizabeth's father had given her, leaving behind much bitterness and hurt. Elizabeth didn't think that she could forgive her mother, ever, yet deep down inside she had feared that when she and her father left San Francisco, it would cut the ties with her mother forever. If her mother decided to return, to be a part of the family again, she would not know where to find them.

And Elizabeth knew that she should not care. She had been eight when her mother had left her. She was now eighteen and had learned, in the many absences of her father, to fend for herself.

If she allowed herself, Elizabeth could understand why her mother had left to seek a new life elsewhere. Elizabeth had felt the same abandonment many times. Surely her mother had felt the same, when her husband had traveled the high seas.

A slim, muscled arm slipped around Elizabeth's waist as her father stepped to her side. She stiffened as she was encouraged to lean against him. These rare shows of affection were always brief. She was well aware that her father only paid her these attentions because he knew that it was expected of him, not because he actually wanted to be open with his feelings. He was one who shied away from revealing feelings of any sort. He had become a cold, embittered man since his wife's departure.

"So, daughter, do you think you can survive the transition without your father?" Earl asked, hugging Elizabeth to him. He looked down into defiant eyes, yet shrugged it off because he did not wish to take the time to question it. Though Elizabeth was petite, she was not frail and could withstand any change without his pamperings.

"I'll never understand why you had to move to what I feel is the end of the earth," Elizabeth said, drawing away from him. "Father, that is the only description that comes to mind when I try to describe this wretched place. And you aren't even going to take the time to go to the house with me. Just how long would that take, Father? But I'm wasting my breath, aren't I? You are determined to leave me to find my own way in this new place, and in a strange house, no matter what."

"Elizabeth, if I'm ever to succeed in my new venture I must get right to constructing the fishery," Earl said, clasping his hands behind him. "Try to understand, Elizabeth. Although I won't be suppin' with you each night, I'll always be near. Soon we'll get acquainted with our house and land together."

"Yes, soon," Elizabeth said, her voice bitter. She hugged herself, her gaze sweeping around her. The moon was high now, lighting everything with its silver light. Elizabeth could see that the whole face of the country seemed covered with trees, with huge, looming bluffs making up the sides of the Sound.

Her gaze shifted upward and she shivered when she looked at the monstrosity of a house that she would soon be entering. Tremendous in size, with its towers and turrets and rough stone construction, it stood high on a cliff, protected by a grotesque, iron fence.

Its great stone edifice overlooking the waters of the Sound looked like some unblinking, unmoving sentinel. She had been told that it had survived Indian attacks, two earthquakes, and a fire.

Trees crowded around the dark bulk of the house, crackling in the wind.

"I know the house seems grim," Earl said, following her gaze, then looking back at her again, seeing her disapproval—even traces of fright in her wide, green eyes. "But it has to do for now. One day soon we'll replace it with a new one. But first, let me make this the greatest seaport in the Pacific Northwest."

Elizabeth moved her eyes to her father, wondering about a man who already had so much money he could retire to live comfortably for the rest of his life, yet hungered for more. Anyone that looked at him could see that he was a man of wealth. Tall and thin, he wore his clothes well. Tonight he sported a tan suit with a gold satin, embroidered waistcoat, and a white ascot with a diamond stickpin in its velvet folds. His golden brown hair was clipped immaculately to his collar line, his golden mustache was bold and thick, hiding his upper lip.

His eyes were the same soft green coloring as hers, yet in them were no warmth—no feeling.

"Elizabeth," he said, nodding toward the Sound, "there's no other place like this on the face of the earth. The water's alive with fish. And as I've told you before, salmon is the prime catch. We'll pay the Indians to catch 'em, and we'll sell 'em at a greater profit."

"Father, what if the Indians don't agree to catch the salmon for you?" Elizabeth asked softly. "They will surely look to you as an intruder. Most are still angry over having been forced to live on reservations."

"Not all Indians live on reservations," he said matter-of-factly. "There are some who weren't tricked by treaties. It's these free Indians that I plan to approach—that I plan to take my offer to."

"That doesn't seem like good logic, Father," Elizabeth argued. "If they couldn't be paid off then, why would you think they could be paid off now?"

"Things were different then," Earl scoffed. "It's a new day, a new time. Surely the Indians are more sensible in their thinking now and will be able to see a good way to make a profit when it is shown to them in black and white. All men want to make money, even Indians."

Elizabeth didn't respond, having never won an argument with her father in her entire life. She could not help but think that he was perhaps the most bullheaded man in the world.

"I hope you're right," she said sullenly. "I've sacrificed enough for this new idea of yours that is supposed to make you wealthier. I found it very hard to say a final farewell to my friends in San Francisco."

Earl embraced Elizabeth again. "Baby, you're going to inherit all of this one day," he said huskily. "It'll be worth the sacrifice of leavin' friends behind." He patted her on the back. "You'll see. You'll see."

Elizabeth slipped her arms about him, this time relishing this moment of closeness. She knew that it would be short-lived. She had seen her father looking nervously at the activity of the crew on the ship and the pier. He wanted to join them.

"Perhaps something good will come of this move after all, Father," she murmured. "If you establish a business here on land, you won't be out at sea as often. I so worried about you when you took those long sea voyages. I'm glad you are no longer planning to carry cargo as far as China. Now the ships will come to you."

"Baby, had I not gone to China, how could you have boasted of having some of the finest silk dresses in San Francisco?" Earl teased. He pulled away from her arms. "You know there won't ever be as fine a fabric hauled aboard my ship again, don't you?"

"Yes, I know," Elizabeth said, slipping her hands inside her cape, to smooth them along the skirt of her silk dress. "But I truly don't care. I'd much rather have you than any foolish silk fabric brought from China."

She wanted to shout at him, saying that had he not gone to all corners of the world, neglecting his wife for his business, his wife might have never fled for a better life elsewhere. Her mother was surely with a man who now catered to her every whim. As Elizabeth could recall, her mother had been absolutely, ravishingly beautiful.

But Elizabeth thought better of mentioning her mother now, seeing no need to spoil her father's mood.

She had already done that, time and time again.

Earl cast another nervous glance toward his ship and his eager crew. He watched as the last of the trunks were placed on the pier.

Then he again looked into Elizabeth's troubled eyes. "Baby, I really must get back to the ship. The men are awaiting my orders. They are almost as anxious as I am to begin building the fishery. We are going to begin as soon as the supplies are sorted out and ready." He placed a gentle hand on Elizabeth's cheek. "I'll be gone more than I'll be seein' you, but I'll be up at the house lookin' in on you from time to time."

He grew frustrated when he could tell that she still did not understand any of this. Why couldn't she see that it was imperative to get his fishery built as soon as possible?

"But, Father, even after you go and make the Indians an offer, what will happen if they don't agree to catch the salmon for you?" Elizabeth asked, fear gripping her when she gazed up at the massive fence that had been erected around the house. Indians were the cause. Elizabeth's father had told her that many years ago a whaling captain had been determined to have his house on this land that overlooked the Sound. For some unknown reason the Indians had not wanted the house built on that site. They had first killed several of those who had built it, and then had tried to burn it.

The captain had not let anything, even Indians, stop him.

Now another man, just as determined and stubborn, had taken possession of the house and land, and Elizabeth had to wonder what she truly had to fear, since she was this man's daughter and had to live there, also.

"Indians are driven to find means of survival just the same as the white man," Earl said, shrugging. "Most are dirt poor and will surely be happy to hear the clink of coins in their pockets after I pay their wages. That will keep 'em in line. You'll see."

Earl went to his waiting servants. He eyed them speculatively, then began handing out orders. One by one they turned and began dragging their trunks up a briar-laden path that led to the house.

Earl singled out a hefty, towering black man and ordered him to take Elizabeth's trunks to the house. Earl had left his own on the ship, knowing that he would be spending more time there than in the house.

Then Earl gently took an old black woman by an elbow and took her to Elizabeth. "Frannie, you see to Elizabeth while I'm busy building my fishery," he said to her. "See to it that she's made comfortable enough to forget San Francisco, her friends, and her damn mother."

"Yas, suh," Frannie said in a slow, calm drawl. "My baby'll not want for a thing."

Earl gave Elizabeth a troubled, yet stern stare. "Elizabeth, I don't want to receive word that you've left our estate grounds, unescorted," he said flatly. "This is a wild land, filled with savages and ruthless desperadoes. Let's not tempt any of them with your sweet, pretty face, do you hear?"

Elizabeth gave him a long and frustrated glare.

Frannie locked an arm through Elizabeth's. Short and plump, with tight gray ringlets of hair framing a fleshy face, and dark, sparkling eyes, she looked up at Elizabeth. "Come along, honey chil'," she soothed. "Let your papa go and tend to his business. We've lots to do ourselves. But first, when we get to the house, I'll draw you a warm, comfortable bath. We'll get that saltwater washed clean outta yo' pores and hair. Then we'll see what we's can do to make your room pretty and delicate like you'se is."

Understanding what Frannie was attempting to do, and appreciating the effort, Elizabeth smiled down at her. Then she looked sullenly over her shoulder at her father as he lumbered back toward his ship. He was in another world now—one that no longer included her.

Sometimes as a child, she could hardly bear moments like this. But now, all grown up, she had learned to bear anything. Even this move to a new land and a new life. She would cope, or die trying.

"Miss Elizabeth, we must hurry on to the house," Frannie encouraged, tugging on Elizabeth's arm. "You'll get a death of a chill. Bes' forget your papa for now. He'll check in on you from time to time. He promised, and Massa' Easton do keep his promises to his daughter."

Nodding, Elizabeth followed Frannie, half stumbling. The steep path leading up to the house was not a path at all. It was a maze of vines and briars, and it took all of Elizabeth's concentration to make her way through them. As the briars annoyingly grabbed her cape and pierced it, she jerked it free.

Ignoring Frannie's heaving breaths brought on by the climb, Elizabeth stubbornly moved onward, not wanting to look behind her again. Without looking, she knew that the shoreline was way below her now, the slap of the waves sounded like a great heartbeat, alive and threatening. She shivered as the hissing whine of the night wind swept about her, chilling her to the bone.

The fence now loomed high before her, morbid in its scrolled details and with its spikes lining the top. Behind it stood the mansion outlined against the moonlit sky, as if it were some dark, sinister monster ready to swallow her whole.

"Not to show disrespect to your papa, Miss Elizabeth, but I don't think I'm goin' to enjoy livin' in that house," Frannie said, suddenly clutching one of Elizabeth's hands. "It looks too ghostly to be lived in. How long has it been vacant?"

"I'm not sure," Elizabeth said, squeezing Frannie's hand reassuredly. "But we must make the best of things, Frannie. We shall make this house a grand place in which to live."

She eased her hand from Frannie's. Her fingers trembled as she gave the gate a shove and it squeaked as it slowly opened.

She gazed once again at the monstrosity of a house, then walked through the gate. Frannie hesitated behind her. Elizabeth ignored the other servants who had arrived at the house before them, hovering together at the foot of the steps.

"Come on, Frannie," she said softly. "Let's get this over with."

Frannie scurried to her side.

Elizabeth proceeded to walk toward the house, grimacing as she made her way through a thick tangle of trees and brambles. Her father had not said how long it had been since the house had been occupied, but it did seem to have been quite a long time.

Perhaps it should be even longer, she thought bitterly to herself. As far as she was concerned, she would as soon dive into a sea of sharks than live in this gloomy house.

Elizabeth stopped at the steps that led up to a leaning porch, and looked upward. She felt overwhelmed by the size of the house. The wind sounded lonely as it whistled around its corners. Shadows and silence seemed to close in on her. And then a shutter banged, causing her to start.

Swallowing back the fear building inside her, Elizabeth climbed the rickety steps and went to the massive wooden door with its ornate brass ornamentation, and found it ajar. With her heart pounding, she pushed the door open, squeaking hinges greeting her, echoing into the house.

Elizabeth and Frannie entered and searched for candles and matches. Elizabeth finally found a branch of candles on a table and lit several white tapers. She then looked slowly around her.

She was standing in a huge foyer that led to an ornately carved archway and down a broad, columned corridor that was broken at intervals by doors, and a wide, winding staircase that led upward to the second and third floors.

Elizabeth shuddered, feeling a sense of evil lurking inside the house. The corridor held too many dark shadows.

"This ain't a fit place to be," Frannie said, her eyes wide as she looked cautiously from side to side. "It ain't a place to be at all."

Elizabeth breathed shallowly. The house smelled dank and

musty. The walls were paneled with dark wood. The beamed ceiling rose dim and high above her. The oaken floors were bare, and silky with age.

Determined not to let a mere house intimidate her, Elizabeth jerked her cape from around her shoulders and lay it across the back of a sheet-shrouded chair. Then she walked boldly toward the staircase, the skirt of her dress rustling in her haste.

"I ain't goin' up there," Frannie said, staring with fretful eyes up the dark staircase.

"Hogwash, Frannie," Elizabeth said, casting Frannie a quick glance over her shoulder. "Come on. Let's find a room that I can call mine."

Frannie hurried to Elizabeth's side. They ascended to the second floor, and walked slowly from room to room until they found one that was less dismal than the rest.

Yet even in this room the plaster had crumbled off the walls, showing the white laths behind it. The only furniture was an iron bedstead painted white, a nightstand on one side, and a washstand with a chipped China basin on the other. A cracked chamber pot peeked out from beneath the bed.

Frowning with distaste, Elizabeth went to the only window in the room. It was curtainless, small, and barred, and spotted on the outside with bird droppings. It looked out onto a gray gulley in the roof. Yet beyond, Elizabeth could see the estate grounds.

As she peered from the window, a movement from below, beneath a tree, drew her attention. She removed a handkerchief from her dress pocket and rubbed it over the pane of glass, removing enough of the filmy dust to enable her to see better.

Leaning closer, she peered intently toward the spot where she had seen the movement, thinking that perhaps it had been one of the servants exploring.

Again she saw movement beneath the trees, and with the aid of the bright moonlight, she was able to see that it was no one she knew. Her heart skipped a beat when she realized that she was staring down at an elderly Indian clutching a tall staff in his right hand.

"An Indian!" she gasped quietly, placing her hand to her throat, recalling the tales of the Indians' hatred for the house. She had hoped that those troubles would remain in the past.

Yet, it seemed not. Elizabeth watched, stunned at how quickly the Indian disappeared from sight.

"Who?" Frannie asked, edging close to Elizabeth, trying to also see from the window. "Who might you be seein', honey?"

"An Indian," Elizabeth stammered. "An old Indian. And he was carrying a staff."

Frannie gasped and placed her hands to her cheeks, her dark eyes wide with fear. "An Indian?" she cried. "Lord have mercy, Elizabeth. Has he come to take our scalps?"

"I don't know why he's here," Elizabeth murmured.

When she realized how frightened Frannie was, she turned to her and drew her into her arms. "It's best not to tell anyone about this," she softly warned. "I don't need a whole household of servants too frightened to sleep at night."

"You'd best tell your father," Frannie said, pulling away from Elizabeth. "He'd do away with that Indian real quick like."

"No, I'm not going to tell Father," Elizabeth said, turning to the window again. Her eyes scanned the land for signs of the Indian, yet didn't find any. "No. Don't tell Father. He's got enough on his mind. Let me take care of this."

"But how?" Frannie cried. "It's too dangerous! What if the Indian sets fire to the house?"

Elizabeth turned back to Frannie and took her hands. "Frannie, if this Indian had wanted to burn the house down, he'd surely have done it long before we arrived," she said, her voice much calmer than her insides. She could not deny that she was afraid, yet she was also intrigued. Perhaps a little bit of excitement was what she needed to fill her days. She would try to find the mysterious Indian and discover why he was there.

3

If ever any beauty I did see,
Which I desired, and got,
'twas but a dream of thee.

—DONNE

The next day Elizabeth slipped into her dress of pale green cotton organdy with its embroidered designs of white lilies on the skirt. Her lovely breasts swelled above the low, round neckline.

Standing before a full-length mirror, she began pulling a hairbrush through her long red hair. She yawned. She had spent a restless night hearing creaking sounds in this strange house, and listening to the surf pounding against the walls of the bluff below her window.

Wondering again about the mysterious Indian, she turned and walked to the window. Raking her gaze across the land below her, searching again for any possible signs of the elderly Indian, she lowered her hairbrush to her side. She knew that she should be more afraid of the Indian's presence than she was, but for some reason she was more curious than frightened.

And he had seemed harmless enough. He was an elderly man, surely only wandering aimlessly about because he had nothing else to do.

Through the filmy haze on the window, Elizabeth peered into the distance, thinking that anything as beautiful as this land could mean nothing but a peaceful existence for its new inhabitants. She admired the forests of white pines and hardwood sweeping down the flanks of the mountains, and saw by the water, the dark green leaves of white birches trembling in the morning breeze.

She stretched onto her toes to look at the brilliant sunlight flickering on the waters of the Sound.

"My, oh, my, Elizabeth, I thought you were going to sleep the mornin' away," Frannie said, as she came into the bedroom. She puffed and fluttered around the bed, fussing over the blankets. "Honey, you'd best get yo'self downstairs and get a warm breakfast. This mausoleum of a house makes one's bones ache somethin' fierce."

Elizabeth turned a warm smile to Frannie and lay her hairbrush on the nightstand beside the bed. "Frannie, it's still early," she said, securing her hair back from her face with a pale green satin ribbon. "What did you do? Get up at the crack of dawn?"

"Earlier than that," Frannie said, giving Elizabeth a frown. "The noises in this place kept my eyes wide open mos' the night. I'm sure the house is haunted, Elizabeth. You watch yo'self. Somethin' might grab you as you go explorin' from room to room."

Elizabeth giggled as she swung away from the window and began walking toward the door. "Frannie, you seem to have survived the morning without being assaulted by ghosts," she teased. "And I would wager that you have already been in all of the rooms, cleaning. It's not like you to let anything go long without a thorough dusting."

Frannie pulled the last of the blankets up over the plumped-up pillows. Then she went to Elizabeth and gave her a soft swat on her behind just as Elizabeth started to step out into the corridor.

"Get on with you," Frannie said, chuckling. "And I must admit, honey chil', you'll soon see that things don't look all that bad. Now that I've seen the rooms in the daylight, with the sunshine comin' in at all of the windows, and with the dustcovers removed from the furniture, I think we can be comfortable enough here. The furniture is plush and the hardwood floors will be beautiful once they get a good polishing." She clasped her hands. "And the rooms is grand."

Frannie then thrust her hands inside her apron pockets. "But it's still too cold for my liking," she said, giving a glance toward the marble-faced fireplace in the room. "But once we get all of the fireplaces goin' with a fire, I'm sure it'll soon be warm enough."

Elizabeth gave Frannie a hug. "Frannie, you know that you'd be happy anywhere as long as you had a roof over your head and me to spoil," she said, laughing softly. "I love you, Frannie. I don't know what I would have done without you after . . . after Mother left."

Frannie patted Elizabeth's back. "Now, now," she murmured. "Let's not get to talkin' about your mother. She's a part of your past. Let it go, honey. Let it go."

Elizabeth stepped away from Frannie. She nervously ran her hands down the skirt of her dress. "Just when I think I have forgotten her, she's back on my mind again," she said cheerlessly. "I have never given up hope that Mother would return and my life would be normal again. But that is such a hopeless thought—I must stop thinking it."

"Yes'm, you must," Frannie said, then placed her chubby hands at Elizabeth's tiny waist and led her into the corridor. "Now you go on and eat some breakfast. There are plenty of eggs, bacon, and biscuits. And I unpacked a jar of honey just for you. That'll sweeten your thoughts if nothin' else will."

Elizabeth turned and planted a quick kiss on Frannie's cheek. "You're such a dear," she said, then bounced down the staircase.

When she reached the first floor, she was amazed at how much of the mustiness of the house had already cleared. The house now smelled of clean linens and furniture polish.

Before going to the kitchen to eat, Elizabeth went from room to room, smiling when she saw how Frannie had already made them presentable, even inviting. Even the shadows seemed to be lifting.

And Frannie had been right. The furniture was plush. And someone had paid a lot of money for the fancy tapestries that hung along the walls with the many gilt-framed portraits.

Elizabeth then went to the library and stopped short, appalled by the array of horns bristling on the far wall, overwhelming the rows of books that lined the room on three sides.

As Elizabeth looked slowly from horn to horn, she recognized those of the deer, antelope, and longhorn steer. Then she paled and placed a hand to her throat when her gaze found a perfect specimen of a bobcat. It was perched on a stand, as if ready to pounce on her.

She grimaced, thinking that the taxidermist who had prepared this animal for viewing had been quite skilled and exact. The eyes of the animal were gleaming into hers, and its sharp teeth were glisteningly white and bared.

She could not help but feel threatened by this room that reeked of death and danger, so she fled to the parlor and felt no less unnerved. No matter how much Frannie had tried, this room retained its mustiness, the sweet fragrance of the furniture polish unable to overcome the stale aroma of cigar smoke and smell of mildew that hung heavily in the air.

"This won't do," Elizabeth said. "This won't do at all."

She walked briskly to first one window, and then the next, lifting them open so that the room could have an airing.

A brisk, chilly breeze blew in, ruffling her dress and the bow in her hair. She hugged herself, shivering.

Yet she did not want to close the windows until the room smelled better. So she turned and eyed the fireplace. Wood was stacked neatly on its grate, old and yellowed newspapers wadded between the logs, to be used to help start the fire.

"That's what I'll do. I'll build a fire," she whispered to herself. "That might also help lift the rank odor from the room."

Spying matches on a table, Elizabeth picked up a few and took them to the fireplace. She knelt down before the hearth and struck a match and held the flickering flame to the newspapers until several of them caught fire. Then she stood, patiently waiting for the flames to ignite the logs.

Once they did, she turned to go get the breakfast that awaited her.

But she didn't get far. She was stopped by billows of smoke quickly filling the room. The smoke from the fire wasn't drawing up the chimney. Instead, it was escaping into the room in great puffs of black.

Elizabeth realized that the chimney must be clogged with

something, more than likely a bird's nest. Her eyes burned from the smoke. Her throat was closing up with it.

Coughing and choking, she tried to feel her way to the door that led to the corridor, to escape to the outside. But before she reached the door, her hand touched something—*someone.*

Startled, she looked up and peered through the screen of smoke and found herself face-to-face with an Indian. And it was not just any Indian. Nor was it the elderly Indian that she had seen the previous night.

This Indian was handsome. His piercing steel-gray eyes mesmerized her as he stared back at her with what seemed as much surprise at seeing her, as she had at seeing him.

Her sight swept quickly over him, seeing how muscled he was in his clinging buckskin attire, and how tall he was.

Her gaze returned to his face. She was struck speechless by his handsomeness. She had heard that there was such a thing as love at first sight, in which one look weds two souls in everlasting devotion. She wondered if she was now experiencing such a phenomenon.

He *was* causing strange sensations to flood her insides.

Stunned by her reaction to the Indian and where her thoughts had taken her, Elizabeth remembered the past history of the house. How the Indians had obviously hated it.

She took a quick step away from the Indian, his handsomeness not enough to quell her fear of him.

"Who are you?" she managed to ask. "Why are you here?"

Strong Heart was shocked, having never expected to find a lady in the house. From a nearby high bluff he had watched the activity on the beach. He had seen the moored ship, and several white men erecting some sort of building on the beach. He had thought that all of the white men were there, having not suspected that someone else might be here—in the *house.*

When he had looked toward the house and had seen the smoke billowing from the windows, his first thought was of his grandfather, and that he may have finally found him. His grandfather could have set fire to the house to keep the intruders on the beach from living in the old house that sat on the hallowed grounds of the Suquamish. Strong Heart knew that many years ago some of his ancestors had tried to burn the house down, but white people had stopped them by slaughtering them.

Since then, none of Strong Heart's people had tried to rid the land of the house. They had found peace and harmony elsewhere, on land far from this place of death and sadness.

Only recently had Strong Heart become acquainted with the house and grounds, when he had returned to search for his missing grandfather. But the house had been empty the other times Strong Heart had gone through it.

Now it seemed it was lived in again.

And, he thought to himself, the house was now inhabited by someone as entrancing as the roses that grew wild in the forests.

The woman's hair was as red as the most lovely of the wild roses. Her eyes were as green as the grass that blanketed the earth and the sides of the bluffs. Her cheeks were as pink as the interior of the conch shell that could be found along the shores of the Sound.

He looked down, seeing the swell of her breasts and the way they were heaving. She seemed to fear him. That he regretted, for he had not come to harm her. Nor would he ever.

She was not the sort of woman any man could harm.

His gaze lifted and he saw such innocence in her eyes and delicate face.

Then his mind returned to sanity. He must ensure his safety. Fearing that the white men on the beach might also be drawn to the house by the smoke, and not wanting to be seen there, Strong Heart knew that he must leave.

But first he would remove the lovely lady from the smoky house, no matter that her mere presence on this hallowed ground should anger him.

When would the white people ever realize that this land could never belong to anyone but the beloved dead of the Suquamish? When would they ever realize they desecrated this land?

But having fought this battle inside his heart more times than he wanted to count, and never winning, Strong Heart cast the sorrowful thoughts from his mind and whisked Elizabeth up into his arms and carried her outside to the porch.

Breathless, and aghast at what the handsome Indian had done, Elizabeth pushed at his chest. "Let me go," she cried. "What on earth do you think you're doing?"

Strong Heart didn't set her to her feet right away. Instead, he stood there and stared at her face. Elizabeth swallowed hard, wondering if he was going to carry her away, and hold her captive, perhaps even for ransom.

And then suddenly Strong Heart released her and fled into the deep shadows of the forest.

Elizabeth was breathless from the experience, in wonder at this Indian who had appeared out of nowhere, and who had left just as quickly and mysteriously.

And it was obvious that he had meant her no harm. He had actually carried her from the house.

Had he thought that it was on fire, she wondered? Had he thought that he was saving her?

She wanted to run after him and demand that he tell her why he was there, and why he had felt the need to rush away so quickly.

But she did not have the opportunity.

Her father was suddenly there, winded from running.

"Good Lord, Elizabeth," Earl said, gasping for breath. "I saw the smoke. I thought . . . I thought—"

"No, Father, the house isn't on fire," Elizabeth said, interrupting him. "I'm sure it's just a faulty flue. I imagine a bird's nest. I wouldn't be surprised if all of the flues aren't the same." She laughed softly. "Imagine how Frannie will be fussing over the damage the smoke has done to the parlor."

"To hell with the parlor," Earl said, wiping beads of sweat from his brow. "Just as long as you're all right."

"I assure you I am just fine," Elizabeth said. Her heart was pounding recklessly within her chest, but not from danger. It pounded from the excitement of having been with the Indian, even if for only a few moments.

"I'm damn glad that everything is okay," Earl said.

Then he shifted his feet nervously, his eyes not meeting hers.

"Baby, I . . . uh . . . was coming to the house for another reason," he said with a stammer. "I've got several dependable men working on the fishery. I feel that I can leave for a spell without being here to oversee every nail pounded into wood . . ."

Before he could finish, a stocky man, with brindled side-whiskers, sporting huge pistols holstered at each hip, came and stood beside Earl.

Earl swung an arm around the man's hefty shoulder. "Elizabeth, this is Morris Murdoch. You know. I've talked about him often enough. He's my partner in the fishery venture," he said, a smug smile across his face. He nodded at Morris. "Morris, this is my daughter, Elizabeth. Isn't she everything I bragged about?"

"And even more than that," Morris said in a flat drawl. He cocked his wide-brimmed hat aggressively at Elizabeth, then reached out to shake hands with her. "Pleased to meet you, Ma'am."

Elizabeth stared down at Morris Murdoch's huge pistols, stiffened, then looked up at him as she reluctantly shook his hand. When he released it, she wiped her palm on the skirt of her dress. Morris's hand had been so clammy and cold.

She nodded at him, not wanting to say that she was pleased to meet him, for, in truth, she wasn't. She *had* heard her father speak often of Morris Murdoch, ever since her father had chosen Seattle for his fishery.

But this was the first time she had met him and she could not help but take an instant dislike to him. A tall man, surely over six feet in height, he had eyes of a peculiar shade of blue that glinted menacingly down at her.

She could not help but equate such eyes with those of a killer. Then she shrugged off such a thought. She knew her father would not align himself with a man of questionable reputation.

"Elizabeth, what I was saying, is that I'm too eager to wait any longer before going to speak to the Indians," Earl said, interrupting her wary thoughts. "Morris and I are going to leave now, to talk business with the Indians—*salmon* business."

Elizabeth gasped at the news as she turned her eyes back

to her father. First he had dumped her on these faraway shores, and now he was going to travel to unknown territories, leaving her alone, waiting to see if he returned alive or dead.

She feared that he might not return one day from his reckless adventures. This could be the time, the worst time of all for her to be left without a father. Without a protector.

But she was silent. She had said all that was possible that could be said to such a father. She would have to wait again to see what fate handed him—and in turn, her.

She watched disbelievingly as Everett, their black groom, brought two saddled horses to the outside of the fence, dutifully holding them by the reins at the gate. Bulging saddlebags were on each of the horses. Her father was leaving her so soon, and she knew that he planned to be gone for several days and nights.

An emptiness filled her, the same feeling that she had always felt at her father's departure on his lengthy journeys.

Earl turned and followed Elizabeth's stare, then smiled when he saw the readied horses. "Ah, I see that my orders have been promptly followed," he said, glancing over at Morris. "Are you ready to ride, Morris?"

"Anytime," Morris said, his voice a silken, lazy drawl which rankled Elizabeth's nerves.

Earl turned back to Elizabeth and took her hand in his. "Baby, please understand why I must leave," he said. Elizabeth recognized the words he always spoke before heading out on an adventure. "It's business, Elizabeth. Business."

He cleared his throat nervously when he saw her set jaw and her eyes fill with defiance.

"I'll be gone for several days," he said, releasing her hand, not wanting to feel her reaction when he gave her a particular order that he knew that she would resent. "Elizabeth, I don't want you leaving the premises under any circumstances while I am gone, unless escorted by one of the servants. Do you hear?"

Elizabeth tilted her chin stubbornly, not wanting to give him the satisfaction of agreeing to anything he asked of her at this moment.

And what did it matter to him, anyway, she wondered.

Surely if something happened to her he would be better off. He would be free to do as he damn well pleased without having to offer awkward apologies or explanations to anyone.

She knew that she should have told him about having seen the two Indians, but she was glad now that she hadn't. She had something of her own that she could keep from her father. The secret about the Indians.

No. She would not tell him anything. He didn't deserve knowing her secrets—intriguing secrets that she could fill her lonely hours with. She would search for both Indians, to see why they were on the property that was now owned by her father. Although she knew that she might be placing herself in danger, she felt an excitement that she had never felt before at the thought of seeing the handsome Indian again.

"I understand your silence," Earl said. He looked with wavering eyes at his daughter for a moment longer, then spun around and walked hurriedly to the horses.

Flicking a tear from the corner of her eye with a finger, Elizabeth watched her father and Morris ride away on their horses. She watched them until they were no longer in sight. Then she looked with interest at the dark, silent forest. She quickly decided that this was the perfect opportunity to go exploring, hoping to find clues as to where the Indians had come from, and why—especially the young Indian.

Frannie came lumbering from the house, coughing and wiping at her dark eyes. "There you is," she said, moving to Elizabeth's side. "Lordy, lordy, I neva' thought I'd eva' get that room cleared of smoke. That fireplace needs a cleanin' bad. Don't neva' lights a fire in it again, honey, until we sees that it's cleaned first."

Elizabeth laughed softly. "I don't think you have to worry about that," she said, again studying the forest. The chill of the morning breeze caused goosebumps to rise on her flesh, as well as the apprehension she felt at wandering alone where she knew that she shouldn't. She shivered.

Frannie placed a chubby hand on Elizabeth's arm. "Come back inside the house," she said, trying to move Elizabeth along. She tilted a heavy, gray eyebrow up at Elizabeth when she refused to budge. "Elizabeth, honey. You come in the house. You gonna catch a chill standing out here without a wrap."

"I'm fine," Elizabeth said, easing from Frannie's grip. She gazed down at her sweet and caring friend. "I'm going exploring, Frannie. This is my new home—one that has been forced upon me, so it is my decision to acquaint myself with it and the grounds that surround it. I can't be expected to sit in that dreadful house every day and night, rotting away doing nothing."

"You ain't goin' nowheres," Frannie fussed, again grabbing Elizabeth's arm, " 'cept in the house with me, where you belongs."

Elizabeth detached her hand again. "Frannie, I'm not going inside the house until I'm good and ready," she said stubbornly. "I'm going exploring. That's final!"

"It ain't safe," Frannie grumbled. "It just ain't safe for a young lady to be wanderin' alone away from home. If you insist on goin', then ol' Frannie goes with you."

"No, Frannie, you're not," Elizabeth argued, her patience running thin. "But you can go and fetch my shawl. It's apt to be much colder in the forest than here. I would prefer my wrap, if you please."

"If you please," Frannie echoed, angrily folding her arms across her thick bosom. "If you do as I please, you'd stay here with me and not out there where Indians can take your pretty hair from your scalp."

Elizabeth paled somewhat at these words, having read many novels in which Indian scalpings had been described in gory detail. But all that she had to do was remember the handsome Indian, and his gentle arms and eyes, to know that she surely had nothing to fear from him.

Especially being scalped!

"I'll get my wrap myself," Elizabeth said, wanting to end this debate with Frannie.

"There ain't no need in that," Frannie said, sighing resignedly. "I'll fetch it. But mark my word, Elizabeth, if you don't get back home when I'm expectin' you to, I'se comin' after you. Does you understand?"

Elizabeth placed a gentle hand to Frannie's fleshy cheek. "Yes, I understand," she said, filled with much love and gratitude for this woman who had become a substitute mother to her. "I'll try not to stay long. I don't want to worry you."

"Huh! If you don't want to worry me none, you stay home with me," Frannie said, then shook her head and marched inside the house for the shawl. When she saw the stubbornness in Elizabeth's eyes, she knew that it was useless to argue with her. She had never seen anyone as stubborn as Elizabeth, except perhaps Elizabeth's mother. Now that was one redheaded stubborn woman who knew her mind better than she should have. She had walked away from her daughter because of her stubbornnesses.

Frannie took the shawl back outside to Elizabeth and devotedly placed it around her shoulders. She then watched with a heavy heart as Elizabeth began making her way through the brambles that stretched out across the lawn to the grotesque fence. She watched Elizabeth until she was out of sight. Then she moved back inside the house, unable to shake a feeling of doom that seemed to have suddenly come over her. She wanted to run after Elizabeth and beg her to return to the safety of the house, yet she knew that would be a futile attempt.

Frannie had to accept that although Elizabeth loved her, the child had her own mind and would do as she wanted, for, in truth, Frannie was only Elizabeth's maid, not her keeper.

* * *

Holding her shawl securely around her shoulders, Elizabeth moved into the deeper gloom of the forest, where the musty aroma of rotted leaves arose to her nose, stinging the tender flesh of her nostrils. She looked guardedly from side to side, everything too eerily quiet, as if she had stepped into a tomb. Except for herself, there seemed to be no life in this section of the forest. No birds sang and no squirrels scampered about collecting acorns for the long, cold winter vigil that was just ahead. She felt as if she might be intruding on some deep, dark secret, and that the trees surrounding her resented her presence.

She saw a break in the trees up ahead, which could mean that she had reached the Sound. Welcoming anything besides what she had found so far in her explorations, Elizabeth hurried her pace. As the sunshine began spiraling more vividly through the umbrella of trees overhead, and she could see even more light just up ahead, she began softly running toward the opening.

But when she finally reached the cleared land, where the sun drenched its warmth on all sides of her, what Elizabeth saw made her heart leap into her throat, and her mouth go dry. She stopped and stared at the many posts that had been driven into the ground, skulls topping each one of them, their eye sockets all facing her, as if looking at her accusingly.

Finding the courage to move again, Elizabeth edged her way around the skull-crowned posts, her heart pounding.

As she circled the hideous sight, she was able to think more clearly. She guessed that she had just found the graveyard of some Indians—burial grounds she may have desecrated by her intrusion. Burial grounds that were much, much too close to her house for comfort.

Breathing harshly, Elizabeth turned and fled onward, toward the welcome sight of a grass-covered bluff that overlooked the Sound. When she arrived there, she tried to blot the horrible sight of the skulls from her mind by looking at the beauty of the view.

She stepped closer to the edge of the bluff, gazing down at the thundering surf. But there was something foreboding in the rhythm of the waves and their steady splashing seemed for a moment to mesmerize, then disorient her. She found herself weaving, feeling as if she were going to fall. Then she cried out with alarm when she felt strong hands on her waist, stopping her.

When those powerful hands drew Elizabeth away from the edge of the bluff and turned her around, she was stunned to find herself again looking up into the steel-gray eyes of the handsome Indian. Although she knew that she should be wary of him, a stranger—she could not deny that being near him again made her heart take on a crazy, erratic beating.

His hands on her waist were like fire, scorching her clothing, burning her flesh.

Elizabeth shivered from the boldness of his hold. Then she found the strength to speak to him. "Thank you for stopping my fall," she murmured. She glanced down at his hands which still held her, then looked up at him. "You can let me go. I'm . . . I'm safe enough now. I've regained my balance."

"Your husband is *pel-ton,* foolish, to allow you to move about alone on land that is not familiar to you," Strong Heart finally said, scowling down at her from his tall height. "Does your husband not know about the bandit gangs and warrior bands that are known to roam the forests and the unguarded valleys? These men stop at nothing to get their pleasures and lusts fulfilled."

Elizabeth cast her eyes downward, her face coloring with a hot blush.

Then she boldly lifted her chin and met his steady stare with one of her own. "I'll have you know that I answer to no husband, because I have none. And under normal circumstances I am capable of taking care of myself," she blurted. "Furthermore, I have the right to wander on property that is owned by my father. Why are *you* here? Do you make it a habit to trespass, to go where you do not belong?"

When he did not answer her, she saw anger in his eyes, which changed quickly to pain. She wished that she could erase all that she had just said. Again she reminded herself that this land had once belonged solely to the Indians. This man's very ancestors might have lived here.

In truth, she was the intruder. In truth, all white people were the intruders.

"I'm sorry for being so abrupt . . . so thoughtless," she said in a rush of words. "Please allow me to once more thank you for being so caring that you would rescue me twice in one day."

Strong Heart was surprised that the white woman had apologized for having spoken harshly to him. She seemed to be a lady with compassion.

And he could not deny that he was glad that she was not married. Although he saw her as an interloper on what was once his people's land, he could not stop his eyes from devouring her loveliness.

Her luminous green eyes stirred feelings within him that he had willed himself to ignore when in the presence of women whose beauty captivated him. His goal in life was to prepare himself to be a great chief, like his father. A commitment to one woman had been the last thing on Strong Heart's mind.

It still was, yet the longer he was with this intriguing woman, the more he felt his reserve weakening.

Then he remembered the reason he had come to the bluff. It had been to watch the white men who had gone to the house to check on the smoke. When they had left on horseback, he feared they had gone after him. Surely this woman had told them about him. Yet they had traveled away from the mansion and the Sound, as if not in search of him but something else.

"Did you tell those two men that I was at the house?" he asked quickly.

"No, I did not see the need," Elizabeth said slowly, not sure if she should trust him enough to be this truthful with him. She still did not know his intentions. She feared to ask him.

What if he was there scouting the place, to take back the news to his people that there were white people who should be slaughtered and a house to be burned?

What if she was falling into a trap by innocently befriending him?

Her father had always told her that she was the sort who trusted too easily.

At this, Strong Heart arched an eyebrow, again surprised by her. "Why did you not see the need?" he asked, watching her expression. "Did you not see me as the enemy?"

"How could I see you as the enemy when only a short while ago you thought you were saving me from a house that was on fire. And now? To have rescued me from a fall?" she offered quietly. She swallowed hard. "As for why I did not tell my father, I . . . I . . . am not quite sure, myself."

Frannie's voice reached up to the bluff and broke the spell

that had captured Elizabeth and Strong Heart, causing Elizabeth to jump. She turned away from Strong Heart to peer down at the old house whose roof towered high above the treetops, knowing that it was best that Frannie didn't see this new Indian. She had been too upset over the other Indian the night before.

Her eyes wide with the wonder of having met the young Indian again, Elizabeth turned back to question him, but he had fled into the forest. Then she heard a horse's hoofbeats, and knew that the Indian was gone. She realized she had missed her chance to find out who he and the elderly Indian were, and why they were there. Apparently Frannie's voice had frightened him away. Perhaps she would never see him again, and that filled her with regret. She had not had the chance to tell him why she was there, or what her father was constructing on the beach.

She decided it was for the best. She did not know what his reaction would be if he ever found out. She feared that no Indian would be happy to know that her father was going to interfere in their lives for his own personal gain.

She then recalled the horrid skulls perched atop the poles. Perhaps she had found the graveyard of this handsome Indian's ancestors.

Frannie's voice called to Elizabeth again, this time filled with anxiety. Elizabeth fled from the bluff and hurried through the forest, avoiding the burial site, and, breathless, met Frannie at the fringes of the forest.

"Elizabeth Easton, I told you not to stay in the forest so long," Frannie scolded as they walked toward the house together. "You done went and frightened ol' Frannie outta ten years of her life! You ain't goin' alone into the forest again. No sir, honey chil'. Neva' again!"

Elizabeth listened patiently, yet not hearing, for her thoughts were on the Indian. She could not help but feel that something unspoken had passed between them, and somehow, some way, she had to find out exactly what.

She went back inside the house, and Frannie followed, still chastising her.

4

> Her face, it bloomed like a sweet flower
> And stole my heart away complete.
>
> —JOHN CLARE

Another long night of restless sleep had passed. Bored and frustrated, Elizabeth had a buggy readied, and ignoring Frannie's pleadings against journeying away from the house again alone, she was now traveling toward Seattle, to acquaint herself with the city. As the horse trotted in a leisurely fashion along the dirt road, the sun shone brilliantly in the midmorning sky. Elizabeth sat comfortably on a cushion in her buggy, the brim of her lace-trimmed bonnet shading her eyes.

The day was warm. The air was perfumed by roses and wild flowers blooming alongside the road. A monarch butterfly drifted past overhead, riding a south wind. The white branches of sycamores broke the dense green foliage of the towering hardwood forest, and a symphony of birdcalls pervaded the leafy halls.

Elizabeth smiled, thinking that this day, indeed, was perfect for an outing. Yes, it *was* another day. Another adventure!

She had been torn between whether to return to the bluff and, perhaps, meet the Indian again, or to go on into Seattle and see the sights.

She had decided to take advantage of her father's absence while she could, and had chosen Seattle for this day's explorations. Anyway, she scoffed at the thought of the Indian reappearing, especially after he had fled so quickly the previous day.

Twice he had disappeared as if no more than a mysterious apparition. He would surely not materialize all that quickly again—for her or anyone else.

"In time," she whispered to herself, "I surely *shall* see him again. In time. For he *was* real—*very* real!"

And what she had seen in his eyes told her that he had been as intrigued by her as she had been by him.

Foreign feelings that felt oddly delicious swept through her as she recalled her two encounters with him, being so near to him . . .

Lifting the reins, and slapping them against the back of the gentle mare, Elizabeth urged her horse to hurry onward, anxious now to get to Seattle. She had not been able to see all that much from the ship's deck, but from afar it had been lovely. She knew to not expect it to be any sort of paradise, for its reputation was not that much better than San Francisco's. She knew she would find many saloons, and wild and rough men lounging outside them, and also the bright skirts and painted faces of fallen women.

She feared none of it. She had learned to cope with almost anything while living in San Francisco. In truth, nothing much was left to shock, or frighten her.

A turn in the road brought the horse and buggy alongside the Sound, the rocky beach only a slight drop from the road. Elizabeth squinted her eyes against the glare of the sun as it shone brightly in the water.

Something drew her attention to the water, and what she saw gave her cause to straighten her back.

It was the strange sight of a young woman walking into the waters of the Sound. Elizabeth wondered why the woman seemed so intent on wading this morning, fully clothed. She was looking straight ahead, her gait determined.

And although the day was warm, Elizabeth realized the water had to be cold. No one in their right mind would go wading today. No one in their right mind would go wading *any* time in their clothes, whether it was summer, *or* autumn.

Elizabeth knew in a flash what the woman's intention was. She was going to walk until there was no bottom. She was planning to kill herself by drowning.

Elizabeth tightened the reins and drew her horse to a quick halt. She tossed her shawl aside as she scrambled from the buggy. Running toward the water, she began waving her hands and shouting at the young woman, who ignored her.

At the water's edge, Elizabeth shivered as the breeze blew damply against her face, her heart thumping inside her chest as she watched the woman go farther. Then she suddenly dropped out of view, her body now immersed in the water.

"Good Lord!" Elizabeth said, paling. "I've got to do something!"

She untied her bonnet and threw it aside. Without thinking about the danger, or the cold temperature, she began running into the water.

When she reached the deeper depths, Elizabeth began swimming steadily toward the victim. The woman was now splashing around, screaming for help, having suddenly changed her mind about wanting to die. She screamed and floundered wildly in the water, calling out that she could not swim.

Elizabeth reached the woman and tried to grab her, to tow her back to land. The young woman panicked and desperately clawed at Elizabeth, her eyes wild with fright.

Elizabeth tried to fight off the woman, realizing that if she allowed her to get a firm grip in her struggles to be saved, she would, instead, pull both of them to their deaths.

But the young woman's fear gave her frightening strength. She succeeded at wrapping her arms around Elizabeth's neck, pulling her beneath the water with her.

Swallowing great gulps of water, Elizabeth fought harder so that at least *she* could get back to the surface. Already her lungs felt as though they were going to burst. She felt lightheaded, as if at any moment she might pass out. She was losing the battle of survival.

Suddenly Elizabeth was aware of a third person in the water beside her. She felt, and welcomed, strong arms around her waist. She and the other young woman were drawn to the surface.

Elizabeth clung to the muscular arm that held her in place against a hard body. She coughed and spewed water from her mouth, until she could breathe. Her eyes cleared of their watery haze.

When she turned to see who was holding her safely from the depths of the Sound, she was stunned.

"You!" she managed to gasp, her voice weak from her ordeal. "Again, it . . . is . . . you who saved me?"

Strong Heart was just as stunned to see whom he had rescued from drowning.

The same woman that he had carried from the house that was smoking, but strangely not burning.

The same woman he had saved from toppling from the high bluff into the Sound.

It seemed to him that she was the most accident-prone person that he had ever encountered.

And he wondered if it was fate that caused him to rescue her again.

He gazed into Elizabeth's eyes, ignoring the other woman.

Yet that one, the total stranger, did seem to be the most helpless of the two as she clung to his arm with a wild desperation.

Still his attention remained on Elizabeth. "Are you all right?" he asked softly. "Are you able to swim to shore?"

"Yes, I'm sure that I can," Elizabeth said, nodding anxiously. She trembled, now quite aware of how cold she was. It felt as if she were immersed in a tub of ice water.

She glanced over at the young woman, remembering what she had shouted while flailing her arms in the water. "*I* can swim to shore," she quickly said. "But this young lady will need your assistance. She can't swim. Please take her to shore. I shall be right behind you."

"*Kloshe,* well enough," Strong Heart said, releasing his hold on Elizabeth. He noticed the blue tint of her lips, now realizing the cold temperature of the water. "But *hy-ak,* hurry. It is *me-sah-chie,* bad, to stay in the water much longer. Go to shore. I shall lend you and the woman a blanket to warm you."

"Thank you," Elizabeth said. "That would be very kind of you."

She was already swimming alongside him, yet found it hard to keep up with him. Although slowed from transporting the woman, this handsome Indian's strong body seemed unaffected by its burden. In a matter of moments he would be on dry land.

Elizabeth envied the woman, and how the Indian held so possessively to her as he took her to shore. Elizabeth recalled the strength of his arms, having now been held three times in their steely grip. If not for the emergency of each of these times, she could look upon them as sheer heaven. This was how the Indian affected her—as no other man had, in her entire life.

Glad to have finally reached shore, Elizabeth rose shakily to her feet and stumbled out of the water. The breeze nipped at her wet flesh like clawing, icy fingers and her wet dress clung to her, causing her to shake and tremble.

Strong Heart thought her just as lovely soaking wet, as dry. His loins stirred as his gaze moved from her enchanting eyes and face, to her breasts that were so evident under the wet dress. He could even see the outline of her dark nipples, and he had to look away, for he could not help but want to possess such breasts with his lips and tongue.

He cast such thoughts aside, knowing that this was not the time, or the place, if there ever would be one.

Elizabeth glanced over at the young woman, seeing how purple her lips were, and how she was shivering uncontrollably herself from the chill.

Elizabeth went to the frail young woman, thinking her perhaps only sixteen years old, yet well grown for her age. Her large swell of breasts heaved as she breathed hard and coughed into her hands. "Everything is going to be all right now," Elizabeth tried to reassure her, glad when the young woman gave her a flicker of a smile.

Elizabeth wanted to ask the young woman why she had tried to kill herself, but the Indian was there suddenly with his offering of blankets. He slipped one around Elizabeth's trembling shoulders, and then the young woman's.

Clutching the blanket closely around her, Elizabeth smiled up at him, and again thanked him. It seemed that he was giving her many reasons to repay him for his kindnesses. She wondered how this could ever be possible.

Strong Heart stood over Elizabeth, and their eyes met. "Do

you think you can get home all right?" he asked, a hint of amusement in the depths of his intriguing, gray eyes. "You have yet to prove that you are capable of taking care of yourself. You did say that you were able to, did you not, after I saved you from falling from the bluff?"

Elizabeth was embarrassed by his teasing, yet more relieved at him having been there again for her. And though she was captivated by him more than ever, she knew that she must return home quickly for a change to warm clothes. She was already tempting fate by lingering even this long drenched to the skin.

Pneumonia was the last way she wanted to spend her time in this land that now held such a fascination for her.

Not the *land,* she corrected herself. The man. The Indian.

"I can make it home just fine, thank you," she said politely, swallowing hard as he continued giving her a quiet, lingering stare.

Then he spoke slowly and eloquently to her. "When a favor is shown a white man, he feels it in his head and his tongue speaks," he said. "When a kindness is shown to an Indian, he feels it in his heart and the heart has no tongue."

He gazed at her a moment longer, then turned and walked away from her, leaving as abruptly as he had the other times.

Shaking from both the chill and her latest encounter with the handsome Indian, Elizabeth watched him ride away on a lovely roan horse. Yes, he was mysterious, but not at all dangerous.

He had proven more than once that he was a compassionate, caring man—and ah, so exquisitely handsome!

Then she wondered about his riding a horse. The Indians around Seattle were known as 'canoe Indians,' for most of their travel was done by canoe.

And, again she wondered about his name. Why did she always forget to ask him his name?

The young woman's coughs drew Elizabeth's thoughts from the Indian. Seeing that the young woman was as cold as herself, she went to her.

"Allow me to take you home," she offered. "You should get out of those wet things as quickly as possible."

Dark brown eyes, veiled with even darker, thick lashes, peered up at Elizabeth, tears springing forth in each. "I . . . I . . . have no place to go," the young woman said, a sob escaping from her throat.

Elizabeth was not surprised by this confession, realizing that anyone who had chosen to take their own life could not have a loving home with caring parents. It was plain and simple: She was alone.

"I'm sorry," Elizabeth soothed, placing a comforting arm around the younger woman's shoulders. "Then come along with me. I shall share my home with you. We shall both get into warm clothes and Frannie will prepare bowls of soup for us. Soon we shall forget about ever being in that dreadful, cold water."

The woman's eyes wavered. "I'm not sure if I should," she said, in hardly more than a whisper. "I . . . I . . . don't want to intrude."

"I insist that you come with me," Elizabeth said, guiding the girl by an elbow to her horse and buggy.

After the buggy was turned around and headed back toward home, and blankets were wrapped not only around their shoulders but also their laps, Elizabeth studied the young woman.

"Do you want to talk about it?" she blurted out. "Do you want to tell me why you had decided to end your life? Surely you have someone, somewhere, that cares about what happens to you."

"Yes, I do have someone," the young woman replied. "But not here. My parents live in San Francisco."

Elizabeth's eyebrows shot up. "Then why on earth are you here in Seattle?" she asked, glancing at the road, then again at the woman.

"I was wrong to come," she whispered, casting her eyes downward in shame. "Had I known . . . had I known . . . what I know now, I never would have come."

"Known what?" Elizabeth prodded. "What happened to

make you leave home, and then want to kill yourself? Did someone take advantage of you? Is that it?"

"In a sense, yes," the young woman said, nodding.

There was a brief pause. Then Elizabeth reached a hand to the young woman and took her hand. "Well, no one is going to take advantage of you again," she reassured. "I'll see to that. You can stay with me as long as you wish. We've plenty of room, and I'm new in these parts and quite lonesome."

"You'd do that for me?" the young woman gasped. "You'd be that kind?"

"It'd be my pleasure," Elizabeth said, not venturing to guess what her father would think about bringing a total stranger into the house. He was never home to lodge a complaint, anyway. "My name is Elizabeth Easton," she offered, smiling at the young woman. "Care to tell me yours?"

"Maysie," she said softly. "Just Maysie."

"No last name?" Elizabeth asked, again raising an eyebrow.

"Not one I feel free to use right yet," Maysie said, giving Elizabeth a cautious glance. "Please just call me Maysie."

"All right, Maysie," Elizabeth said. She patted Maysie's hand. "But one day I hope you'll tell me everything." She paused, then added, "Like where you've been living since you left San Francisco, and who has put such fear in your heart."

Maysie ducked her head and swallowed hard, then turned blinking, apologetic eyes to Elizabeth, as though what she wanted to tell her was too shameful to share.

* * *

Strong Heart rode onward to the outer fringes of Seattle. He made his way up the butte to his camp where he could continue to watch and study the activity at Copper Hill Prison below.

After securing his horse where it could graze peacefully beneath a towering oak tree, Strong Heart changed into dry buckskins. He was disappointed that he had not found his grandfather, yet he had not actually thought that he would. The old Indian was too elusive for his own good, it seemed. So tomorrow he would go for Four Winds.

But tonight he would think about the lady whose name he had not asked. It would have allowed her to ask too many questions about him, and he had already drawn too much attention to himself in meeting her and the other woman.

He settled down on a blanket and drew his knees to his chest, hugging them, smiling as he continued thinking about the lady whose hair was the color of a flaming sunset. Yes, she was worth taking risks for. Even though he did not approve of her living on Suquamish soil, the woman had fascinated him from the first moment they had met.

And today, he had been a witness to her courage. He had seen her fiery spirit, which matched the color of her hair.

And her eyes! They were as green as the panther's that stalked the trails of the forest. Somehow he had to find a way to meet her again—when danger would not overshadow their meeting.

He must learn her name, and soon. It must have been their destiny to meet. Chance had thrown them together now not only once, but three times.

Yes. Sometimes destiny worked in strange ways, he mused.

The dried buckskin warm against his flesh, Strong Heart glared down at Copper Hill Prison and thought, first things first.

He *had* come to Seattle for a purpose.

5

> They spoke as chords do from the string,
> And blood burnt round my heart.
>
> —John Clare

Dwarfed by the many monumental totem poles that stood on all sides of them, Earl and Morris entered the Suquamish village. Their horses moved in a slow lope between two long rows of Indians who stood with spears in their hands, apprehensively watching their arrival.

Earl and Morris exchanged troubled glances, then looked guardedly at the Indians, most of them men dressed only in loincloths. The women and children seemed to have disappeared into thin air—the village seemed void even of dogs.

And then suddenly, at the far end of the double row, a single man stepped out from the others and stood with his arms folded tightly across his chest, his jaw set, and his eyes narrowing as the horses bearing the white men came closer to him.

Earl gave Morris a quick look. "I think we'd best dismount and go the rest of the way on foot," he said, his voice a whisper. "I think we're just about to make acquaintance with the chief. And what I see doesn't make me feel too confident about our mission. I'd be surprised if we don't end up as that damn Indian's dinner. He looks like he'd as soon eat us as look at us."

"He's not a bad sort," Morris tried to reassure him. "From what I've heard about him, Chief Moon Elk's one of the most congenial of the chiefs in the area. That's why I suggested that we come to him first. He'll listen to reason. You'll see."

"I sure as hell hope so," Earl said, wiping nervous perspiration from his brow. "And soon. I'm not as confident as you are about these transactions. This is my first experience with Indians. I'll take the Chinese over Indians any day."

"The Chinese don't fish for salmon," Morris grumbled, "so keep your mind on who does. The Suquamish."

Earl nodded, then slipped easily from his saddle. He walked on wooden legs beside Morris until they reached the chief. Then he let Morris make the introductions.

"Chief Moon Elk, my friend and I have come in friendship to have council with you over an important matter," Morris said, his eyes steady on Chief Moon Elk. He extended his hand to the chief, then lowered it slowly to his side when the chief refused to shake it.

Chief Moon Elk looked sternly from Morris to Earl, then back at Morris. Then he turned and nodded for them to follow him.

Earl stayed close to Morris as several Suquamish braves fell in step beside them, their spears still clutched threateningly in their hands. His thoughts went to Elizabeth, hoping that she had obeyed him and hadn't wandered alone from the house. At this moment he knew the true dangers. He could see such hate and mistrust in the eyes of these Indians. It was enough that *he* was having to deal with them. He wanted to make sure that his daughter had no dealings with them, ever. With her brilliant red hair, she would be a novelty for them.

Earl and Morris were ushered inside a large, cedar long-house, the interior lit by a crackling fire in a firepit in the center. They were offered seats on mats of woven grass. The chief sat down on a platform opposite them, keeping the fire between them.

Earl swallowed his rising fear as several Suquamish braves positioned themselves behind him and Morris. Then his full attention was on the chief as a brave brought the man a robe of black sea otter fur, and placed it devotedly around his lean shoulders.

Chief Moon Elk studied the white men suspiciously. He had had no close connection with white people for many moons now. Chief Moon Elk had broken away from those who had agreed to live on reservations and that had earned him much respect among the white community. They left his people in peace, to live their lives as they would have it—away from the rulings of the great leader that the white people called their "president."

"And what brings you to my village?" Chief Moon Elk asked. He pulled up his legs and squatted on his platform. "Do you bring tidings from your president?"

Earl and Morris exchanged quick looks. Morris nudged Earl in the side, prompting him to speak now—to explain their plan to the chief while he was willing to listen.

Earl cleared his throat nervously and crossed his legs, resting the palms of his hands on each knee. "We have come to talk business with you," he said, his voice sounding foreign to himself with its frightened timbre.

He could not help but be unnerved. The chief's eyes were bright and steady in their gaze, seeming to see clear through Earl. He was afraid that the chief could even see his fear.

"Business?" Chief Moon Elk asked, lifting a shaggy eyebrow. "What business could white men and Suquamish talk about? We mind our own business. It is best that you mind *yours.*"

"I know that is the way it has been between the white men and the Suquamish for many years, but now it is time for change—a change which could be profitable for your people," Earl said, his fingers now digging into his knees, his fear changing to determination. He had come for a purpose, and he could not fail. Nothing, and no one could thwart his dreams. Especially not a dumb, savage Indian chief, he thought smugly to himself.

But the look of defiance in the chief's eyes was telling him that he may have come up against a brick wall—a wall that Earl would somehow have to tear down.

"My people do not seek change," Chief Moon Elk growled. "Especially changes suggested by white men. Our lives are filled with enough purpose, without any interference from white men!"

"But what I have to offer could make your people have more purpose in life," Earl softly argued. "At least listen to what I have to say. Think it over. Once you do, you will see that what I offer is good for your people."

"Nothing any white man has ever offered to the Suquamish has ever been good for them," Chief Moon Elk answered. "*Nah,* look here! If that is why you have come to have council with Chief Moon Elk, the meeting is now over. *Kla-how-ya,* goodbye!"

Not to be dismissed that easily, Earl rose to his feet. Morris scrambled to his feet beside him. "We will leave and *soon,* but I first will quickly tell you my plan," Earl said in a rush of words. "Please allow it. What can it hurt just to listen?"

"*Kloshe,* well enough," Chief Moon Elk said, standing, also. He nodded. "Speak. *Hy-ak,* quickly. Then be gone with you."

Earl explained his plan—that the Indians would use their skills at catching the salmon for him, and he, in turn, would pay them a high price. He also told Chief Moon Elk that he would like to hire several of his braves to work in his fishery, and that he would pay them well for a day's work.

After Earl had given his presentation, there was a long pause before Chief Moon Elk offered any response.

The chief moved around the fire and stood eye to eye with Earl. "Many moons ago my people labored for the white man, catching and selling salmon to them, but they were cheated. Now my people catch salmon only for themselves. My people rely on salmon for their main food. They share with no one!"

"That was unfortunate that your people dealt with men who cheated them," Earl said, becoming unnerved again by the chief's steady, penetrating gaze, and by the presence of the braves as they moved closer behind him. "But that wouldn't happen if they were under my employ. I cheat no one. I give you my word."

"A white man's word is no better than that huge boulder that perches on the edge of the butte close to our village. It threatens to fall at any moment and crush my people beneath it," Chief Moon Elk said, his voice tight. "No. I will not allow my people to participate in this white man's venture. My people will continue to catch salmon, but only for themselves."

Earl was at a loss for words. He looked over at Morris for support, but the chief began speaking again.

He turned his eyes to Chief Moon Elk, seeing his hopes in his fishery venture fading. There weren't that many Suquamish who had chosen to live away from the reservations. It was imperative that he convince *this* chief, for he was the most important and admired of those who chose to live a free existence.

"*Nah,* look here," Chief Moon Elk said, his voice taking on a softer tone. "The salmon to the Suquamish are what the buffalo once were to the plains Indians. If angered, the spirits that control the salmon will cause a failure of this autumn's run. It would anger the spirits if white men joined with the Suquamish in the salmon run."

Earl tried to dissuade him. "I'm sure your spirits would understand that there is more than enough salmon for everyone. Your spirits will see that my plan will help the Indians. Those who work for me will have a steady income."

"I have spoken," Chief Moon Elk said, lifting his chin proudly, and folding his arms across his chest. "My people will remain free like the *mee-gee-see,* eagle. The Suquamish people's lives and religion are tied to the salmon, whose migrations mean sustenance. And the salmon's autumn arrival is sacred. I will not take that away from my people—now or ever!"

Morris nudged Earl in the side again, and nodded toward the door. "We'd best leave," he whispered in Earl's ear. "But don't fret. I've my own plans. Chief Moon Elk will change his mind. You'll see."

Earl gave Morris a harried look. He looked one last time at the chief then turned and walked from the longhouse, escorted by the braves. Disappointed, frustrated, and angry, he mounted his horse and gladly rode away from the village. Usually, he was able to convince anyone of anything. He was known as a wheeler and dealer.

But he had never met anyone as stubborn and strong willed as Chief Moon Elk. He wasn't quite sure now how to deal further with him, but he must. He would not give up hope this quickly. He had not become a rich man by allowing himself to be stopped by discouragement and doubts.

"You sure are a quiet one," Morris said, edging his horse closer to Earl's as they rode beneath a massive umbrella of trees. "The chief's got you tongue-tied, eh? Well, that won't be for long. I've got a plan."

Earl glowered at Morris. "It's a little late for that, isn't it?" he spat out. "I could've used a little support back there in that damn Indian's longhouse. You just sat like a bump on a log, letting me do the pleading. Damn it, Morris, you're my partner. Why didn't you act like it back there when you saw me cornered? You've got a big mouth, usually. Did you lose your nerve, or what? Did the spears at your back make you yellow? Damn it, I don't need no partner that don't know how to think under pressure."

Morris's face became red with anger. His cold, blue eyes flashed into Earl's. He said in a low and controlled voice, "I'd watch my mouth if I were you. You wouldn't want me to back out on my deal. Without me, it's no deal at all. And just because the chief got the best of you, don't give you the right to jump on my ass about things. Just let it lay, Earl, or you'll have more than you bargained for."

Earl paled, not liking the implication behind Morris's threat. Morris was absolutely necessary for his fishery.

Yet, Earl was not sure if his choice had been a wise one. He had not been able to find out much about Morris before agreeing to a partnership with him. His credentials had been sketchy. Earl suspected that Morris had a dark side, but he did not want to find out what it was.

"All right, so I mouthed off a bit too much," Earl conceded. "Just forget that I did and tell me what you meant back there. How are you going to convince the chief to join up with us? What's on your mind, Morris? Tell me about it."

"There's no need in my going into detail about it," Morris said, shrugging casually. "Just relax. Things have a way of working out." He swung his horse away from Earl's. "This is where I leave you, my friend, to find your way back to Seattle alone. I've something to do—someone to see."

Morris rode away without further explanation. Earl headed in the direction of Seattle. His future seemed bleak. He had wanted the fishery for Elizabeth. Although, she did not know it, he was driven to succeed only because of her. She was all that was left in his life that was important to him. For her, he must succeed.

"Elizabeth," he whispered to himself. "I wonder what you're doing right now?" He smiled. "Frannie is probably fussin' over you, makin' you beautiful."

* * *

Elizabeth snapped the reins, goading the horse to hurry its pace. Her wet clothes were not only cold, but made her skin itch. She looked over at Maysie, whose shoulders were still weighted with her secret shame.

"I'm sorry for acting as though I don't trust you," Maysie suddenly blurted. "There is no need, whatsoever, in you not knowing my last name—or why I am in Seattle." The girl paused, then continued in a rush, "My name is Maysie Parker. I'm sixteen. My parents are poor. There was hardly ever enough food on the table for me and my five brothers and sisters. I came to Seattle after I read several leaflets that had been handed out in San Francisco—saying that the opportunity for young women in Seattle was great. I sneaked aboard a freighter and came here hoping to make my own way in the world. Hoping to make lots of money. Once here, I discovered that the leaflets had been distributed by brothel and saloon owners. The opportunities that lured me here were nothing more than having to live as a whore, to make enough money to exist from day to day."

The shock of this revelation showed on Elizabeth's face. She remained speechless as Maysie went on telling her sad tale of a young life in trouble.

"I grew tired of selling my body," Maysie said, lowering her eyes. "But with no hopes of ever being able to do anything better with my life, I . . . I . . . decided to end it."

Maysie looked up quickly, and met Elizabeth's pitying eyes. "This sort of thing happens to many innocent girls and women of Seattle," she softly explained. "Some have ended up in Copper Hill Prison for killing the men who led them into a life of prostitution. I could not bear ever to think of . . . of . . . being in a prison. Once there, one rarely ever leaves alive."

"Well, you are one young lady who will never have to worry about that," Elizabeth said, squaring her shoulders. "I will see to that."

Elizabeth was glad when, through a break in the trees, she caught sight of the old mansion. She had never thought that she would be glad to see it.

But now was different. After hearing Maysie's sad tale, Elizabeth knew just how lucky she was. Even though her mother had rejected her all those years ago, she at least had a father who kept her clothed and fed—and sometimes loved her.

Not everyone was this fortunate.

Her thoughts returned to the handsome brave, wondering what sort of life *he* led, and if there was someone who saw to his every wants and needs—a wife, perhaps?

The thought of a woman being a part of the Indian's life made a keen jealousy stab at her heart.

6

> A day of days!
> I let it come and go,
> As traceless as a thaw of bygone snow.
> —CHRISTINA ROSSETTI

The next day, her stomach warmed with oatmeal, Elizabeth took another slow sip of steaming tea, marvelling over the brim of her cup at how Maysie still continued to eat. Maysie, her hair drawn back from her pale face with a blue satin ribbon, was scooping up big bites of egg, and stuffing her mouth with jellied biscuits as if she hadn't eaten in days.

And last evening, when Elizabeth had offered Maysie a bath and perfumed soap, and then a fresh, clean dress with frilly laces at the throat and at the cuffs of the sleeves, Maysie had looked as if she thought she had entered Heaven.

At that moment, Elizabeth had almost understood why Maysie had stooped to selling her body for money. Just as Maysie had said, she had found it the only way to survive in a world that had forgotten she existed.

Elizabeth's heart went out to Maysie, hoping that it was not too late for the young woman to begin a new life of decency.

Frannie entered the dining room in a flurry, huffing and puffing, a scarf with bright designs wrapped around her head. She was carrying a huge bowl of fruit, which she set down on the middle of the table.

"Help yo'selves to the fruit," Frannie said, stopping long enough to place her hands on her hips, to give Elizabeth an annoyed stare and then a slight nod toward Maysie.

Elizabeth smiled weakly up at Frannie, realizing that Frannie did not altogether approve of her having brought home a total stranger to stay with them. Elizabeth had tried to explain

Maysie's plight, but couldn't tell Frannie that Maysie had been living the life of a prostitute. Elizabeth had just told Frannie that Maysie was homeless.

Elizabeth understood that it was not so much that she had brought home a stranger that Frannie was concerned about. It was Elizabeth's father and his reaction to Elizabeth being so free in offering her charity.

"I done been to the market this mo'nin'," Frannie said, untying the scarf from around her head and laying it across the back of a chair. "This city boasts of its fine apples. I can see why. They are plump and they smell delicious."

"Thanks, Frannie, I believe I'll have one," Elizabeth said. She was glad when Frannie left after giving Maysie another troubled glance.

Maysie wiped her mouth clean with a monogrammmed napkin, washed down the last bites of her food with a large glass of milk, then leaned back in her chair and sighed. "I haven't eaten that good since I left San Francisco," she murmured, lowering her eyes timidly. "My mama, when she had the makings, she baked the most delicious biscuits. But . . . but . . . we never could afford jams and jellies to eat on them. Nor could we afford butter."

Then Maysie's eyes looked up. "I can't thank you enough for taking me in," she said. "But what about your papa? When he comes back home, will he turn me out?" She glanced toward the door. "Your maid, she . . . she . . . doesn't like me. Perhaps your father won't either."

Elizabeth took an apple from the bowl, then shoved the bowl toward Maysie, silently offering her one. "It's not that Frannie doesn't like you," she tried to explain. "It's just that I've never brought strangers home before. She's finding that hard to accept. And don't fret about my father. At first he may behave gruffly, but deep inside his heart he will understand and allow you to stay for as long as you wish." She paused, then added, "He will, Maysie, because that is what I want, and he owes me, Maysie. He owes me."

Elizabeth took a bite of her apple. Maysie only eyed those left in the bowl, her mind elsewhere. "I wish everyone could be as lucky as me," Maysie said. "The poor women at Copper Hill Prison never had this sort of chance. I'm so, so lucky. I'm so grateful."

She leaped from her chair and gave Elizabeth a hearty hug. "Thank you from the bottom of my heart," she whispered. "Thank you, thank you."

Elizabeth lay her apple aside and rose from her chair. She embraced Maysie, then placed an arm around her waist and walked her out of the dining room to the sitting room. Elizabeth chose a plump, overstuffed leather chair before the roaring fire in the fireplace and sat down. Maysie chose the divan.

Elizabeth shook her hair back from her shoulders. The fire cast a golden glow on her face, and her bare neck. Her yellow dress was cut low in front, emphasizing her soft swell of breasts. The bodice was softly pleated to the tight waist and the skirt billowed out in yards of luxuriant silk.

Elizabeth turned and silently admired Maysie. She was a lovely girl, one could see, even though she was now much too pale and wan looking. Elizabeth had chosen a silk dress from her wardrobe for Maysie and it fit her perfectly as it clung to her large bosom and tiny waist. The full gathered skirt spread out on the divan on each side of her.

"Tell me more about Copper Hill Prison," Elizabeth said.

"I've visited the women at the prison as often as I could," Maysie answered softly. "Whenever it was possible, I'd steal some fruit at the market, or from apple trees in people's yards, and take it to the women prisoners. They never get decent food there. Just . . . just watery soup with no meat in it, and barely a trace of vegetables. With the sort of . . . profession that I was in, I met many of the women before they ended up in Copper Hill. They are mostly God-fearing women who had nothing in life, and no one who cared about what happened to them."

Maysie paused, then added, "They are the victims of the evil men who misused and abused them. Now they are with men who taunt them endlessly, and not only the sheriff and his deputy. Some are also at the mercy of the male prisoners whose cells they are forced to share when the prison is too crowded. These women are treated like animals—animals!"

Elizabeth listened sadly, finding it hard to accept that in any civilized community women could be treated so callously. It gave her a helpless, sick feeling at the pit of her stomach. Then her eyes brightened with an idea.

"Perhaps you and I could do something that could help lessen the women's burdens," she said, smiling at Maysie. "Of course I know that we can do nothing about their actual incarceration, but we *can* take them fruit. And books from my personal library to help while away their lonesome hours."

Elizabeth felt somewhat guilty for her suggestion, for she knew that she was not thinking only about the women's welfare, but also her own. Spending time helping them would give her something to do.

Maysie scooted to the edge of the divan. "You would do that?" she breathed, touched to the core by the generosity of this woman who had only yesterday been a total stranger.

Elizabeth pushed to her feet, the skirt of her dress rustling around her legs. "*We* shall do that, *together,*" she said, going to Maysie. She placed an eager hand to Maysie's elbow and urged her up from the divan. "Come on. Let's choose which books we can take to the women. They are still in packing crates. I have yet to take the time to place them on shelves in the library. Then we shall ready a basket of fruit and be in Seattle before the dinner hour. Isn't it exciting, Maysie, to think that we might help lessen the women's misery somewhat?"

Maysie pulled away from Elizabeth's grip. She began slowly shaking her head, a guarded fear in her eyes. "I shan't go with you," she said, her voice breaking. "I'm . . . I'm still tired and weak from my dip in the Sound. Please. Please go on without me."

Maysie looked away from Elizabeth, for she knew that she was not being altogether truthful. Deep inside, where her darkest fears lay, she was afraid of the man who had employed her at the brothel. She was afraid that Frank might see her and drag her back with him, or worse, throw her in prison for running away from him.

No, Maysie thought sullenly, she had best not be seen by

anyone for a while. While she was safely away from the city, she had best stay hidden.

Elizabeth drew Maysie into a gentle embrace. "I should've known that you wouldn't be up to traveling into Seattle just yet. You stay here and rest. I shouldn't be gone long."

Maysie slipped from Elizabeth's arms. "I'm not sure you should even go to the prison," she said, her eyes averted. "Elizabeth, the sheriff, Jed Nolan, can't be trusted. What if . . . what if . . . he tries to accost you? He's a despicable man with no morals. If he tried to rape you, there'd be no one there to stop him. If his deputy is there, he'd just laugh, any maybe even take a turn once the sheriff was through with his fun." She began to wring her hands. "No, Elizabeth. I don't think it's good that you go. You wouldn't be safe at all."

"Go wheres?" Frannie said from behind Elizabeth, her voice so loud that Elizabeth jumped as if she had been caught stealing cookies from a cookie jar.

"I didn't know you were standing there," Elizabeth said, nervously smoothing the front of her dress.

"And what if I was?" Frannie said, giving Elizabeth a look of impatience. "What is you plannin' behind my back, Elizabeth Easton?"

"So you *didn't* hear all that was said," Elizabeth said, trying to hold back a sigh of relief. Yet she knew that Frannie would have to be told, no matter that she might scream and yell, that she would not allow it.

"I hears enough to know that you're up to no good. Don't you get it in your head that you're leavin' this house again unescorted." She gave Maysie a haughty glance, then peered up at Elizabeth. "Who's to say what you'll be draggin' in the house the next time if you is allowed to run loose like, like, a trollop?"

That word made Elizabeth blanch and glance at Maysie. When she saw the look of shame in Maysie's eyes, she looked angrily back at Frannie.

"Frannie, I don't know what has got your dander up this morning," she scolded. "It can't be only because I felt compelled to bring Maysie home. What else has rattled your nerves, Frannie? Was it something you saw while you were in Seattle?

Did someone scold you for something? If so, tell me who, and I will see to it that this person never does it again."

Frannie wrung her hands, then answered somberly. "It ain't nothin' anyone said to me. It's . . . it's what I *saw.*"

"Well? What did you see?" Elizabeth said, her voice filled with impatience.

"It was high on that hill close to that prison," Frannie said, her eyes wide. "They was buildin' a hangin' place, they was. I ain't neva' seen such a sight. To think that soon a man will hang there, with a noose chokin' the life from him. I don't likes it one bit. Livin' near a city that has criminals bad enough they must be hanged."

Her words sent involuntary shivers through Elizabeth, especially now that she had decided to go into Seattle, *to* the prison. She was having second thoughts, yet she knew that if she put off going now, she more than likely never would.

And the idea of going to the prison to share some of her blessings with the women was too compelling not to do it.

But how was she going to tell Frannie? Especially since Frannie was so obviously frightened of the place. Yet she had never kept secrets from Frannie. Nor would she now.

"Frannie, would you prepare me a large basket of fruit for traveling?" Elizabeth asked, deciding on a direct approach. The sooner she got this settled with Frannie, the sooner she could leave and begin her mission.

Frannie seemed taken off guard. She raised her eyebrows. "A basket of fruit? What evah for?"

"I've decided to take fruit and some of my books to the women prisoners at Copper Hill Prison," Elizabeth said nonchalantly as she walked past Frannie into the corridor. She winced and tightened her jaw as Frannie fell into step beside her.

"You ain't goin'," Frannie said angrily. "You ain't goin' nowheres. You're going to stay put beneath this roof until your father returns. Then you tells *him* this crazy plan of yours. He won't allow you to go near that prison and you knows it! Lordy, lordy, Elizabeth, why would you even want to?"

Elizabeth went into the library, where stacks of boxes

awaited her. Lowering some boxes that were marked hers to the floor, she opened one and began sorting through it. "There are many less fortunate than I," she said calmly, laying books aside in two separate piles—those she would take, and those she would keep. "I intend to share my fortune with others." She rested a book on her lap and gave Frannie a stern look. "And, Frannie, I'm not about to wait on Father for anything. He is doing his work. I shall do mine."

"Elizabeth, the dangers," Frannie said in a whine, bending to place a gentle hand to Elizabeth's cheek. "Honey, don't do it. The hangin'. What if they hang the man while you're there? Does you want to see a man take his last breath? Does you?"

Elizabeth swallowed hard and blinked her eyes nervously, knowing that, no, that would not be something that she would ever want to witness. Yet, she had a mission, and she would not allow anything to stand in the way.

And, she thought with a rush of passion—she might at least catch a glimpse of the handsome Indian. She seemed to have a better chance of that in Seattle than here in the house.

"I'm going, Frannie," she said firmly. "No matter what you say—I'm going."

Frannie shook her head helplessly. She knew from Elizabeth's eyes, there was no use arguing. With a sigh, she left Elizabeth alone.

Maysie came in and knelt beside Elizabeth. "Perhaps she's right," she ventured. "Elizabeth, what you're doing is generous to a point—then it becomes dangerous."

Elizabeth smiled weakly at Maysie. "I know," she admitted. "I know."

They gazed at length at one another. Then Elizabeth returned to sorting through her books. Her heart beat quickly at the prospect of perhaps seeing the Indian again, and the danger that she might be facing to chance it.

* * *

Strong Heart had eaten pemmican for breakfast, a food that required no fire for cooking. It was dried meat pounded fine and mixed with melted fat. To this he added fresh apples that he had picked from an orchard not far from where he had made camp. He changed slowly and methodically into clothes that would help him to blend in with the white men on the streets of Seattle. He would look more like a white man on horseback than an Indian. Along with the white-man clothes, he would wear a bandanna to hide his face and a sombrero to hide his long, brown hair during the escape.

His effects gathered up and secured in his saddlebags, he slapped a gunbelt around his waist and fastened it, and pulled the brim of his hat low over his gray eyes. Then he swung himself into his saddle.

Pausing for a moment, he stared down at Copper Hill Prison. Then he began making his way down the side of the hill which would lead him to the city.

While inching his horse down the steep grade of land, memories of the green-eyed seductress plagued Strong Heart. He recalled her ravishing curves as her wet dress had clung so sensually to her body when she had stepped out of the water yesterday. She had disturbed him in many ways that were dangerous to him.

Yet he knew that he would search her out again, one day. He must have her. He *would* have her!

7

Wait not till tomorrow—
Gather the roses of life today.

—Ronsard

The sky was gray and the air damp as Elizabeth rode into Seattle in her buggy. With one hand she held on to the horse's reins, with the other she secured her fringed shawl more comfortably around her shoulders and adjusted her lace-trimmed bonnet. All the while her gaze swept around her, this being her first time in Seattle.

While on the ship she had not been able to see the tawdriness of the city—the saloons and gambling establishments, and the houses of ill-repute blossoming, it seemed, at every street corner. It was a bawdy seaport town, well known to sailors, loggers, and transients.

Holding the reins with both of her gloved hands, she directed her horse down First Avenue. At first she thought it was snow lying along the ground. Then she realized that it was, instead, piles of sawdust that had scattered and blown there from nearby Yesler's Mill.

This reminded her that Seattle was a lumber town. Every building, even the large public structures such as Squire's Opera House and Hotel were constructed from wood.

As she rode onward, she noted that among the commercial establishments were several miners' stores, ready to outfit prospectors bound for the new gold strike on the headwaters of the Skagit River.

On the left side of the road hung a sign advertising spring beds, a retail enterprise undertaken by two morticians. On the right was Yesler's Hall, where town meetings were held.

Her inspection was broken as several men loitering on a street corner began jeering and tossing leering remarks her way.

Insulted by such behavior, Elizabeth impudently thrust her chin up and snapped her horse's reins, setting her sights on the prison. She was anxious to get there, do her good deed, and return to the quiet and safety of her house. She could now see why her father had forbade her to go to the city alone. If he ever heard that she had, and that she had even gone to the prison, she guessed that he might even lock her in her room and throw away the key.

When a man dressed in buckskin rode past her on a black mustang, she was struck by memories of another man in buckskin, whose eyes, whose handsomeness, had mesmerized her.

How could she have forgotten for even a moment that he was also her reason for coming so boldly alone into Seattle?

She had hoped to see him again, perhaps to find out his name at last.

She wanted him to know *her* name.

For a moment she studied the buckskin-clad man, until she determined it wasn't him. Then she looked at the men on horseback who rode past her, and at the men trodding along the wooden walks of the city.

She also squinted at the men leaning against the buildings. Yet she saw no one who even remotely resembled the Indian.

In fact, as far as she could tell, there were no Indians to be seen in the city at all. As if they were forbidden to enter here. Which puzzled her, since the city had been named after a powerful Suquamish Indian Chief—Chief Sealth. His name was misinterpreted as Seattle by those who had founded the city.

The mysterious, handsome Indian seemed to go and come as he pleased.

Or had he not gone into the city after rescuing her from the Sound, she wondered. If not, then what had been his destination?

More taunts and insulting remarks coming from the boardwalks and the shadows of the buildings caused Elizabeth to urge her horse into a faster gait. They turned a corner, and the horse and buggy now climbed a steep road—the road that led to the prison.

Elizabeth felt the strain of the buggy, and heard the wheels groan frighteningly the farther the horse traveled up the grade. She paled, fearing to look over her shoulder, realizing that if the wheels slipped, or the horse faltered, the backward plunge would take her straight into the waters of the Sound.

But soon that fear was replaced by another. The sound of hammers striking wood came to her.

Her eyes widened and she gasped when she first caught sight of the hanging platform that Frannie had spoken so fearfully about. It was being built directly in front of a long, dreary wooden building—Copper Hill Prison. Forests towered way above the site as far as her eye could see.

Her heart pounding, as though an echo of the hammers, Elizabeth was at least glad that the steep grade of land had leveled out. She was now driving along a level, narrow street that soon took her to the prison.

After climbing from her buggy and securing her horse's reins to a hitching rail, Elizabeth tried to will her knees not to shake, and her pulse not to race so fast, but failed. Being there made her realize the danger she was in. The men working on the hanging platform had caught sight of her, and one was lumbering toward her, a cigar hanging limply from the corner of his wide lips, his eyes raking her body.

"What do we have here?" the man said, circling Elizabeth, not allowing her to reach for the huge basket of fruit and books at the back of the buggy. "Come to see the hanging? It's not 'til sunup tomorrow. Want some entertainment to pass the time whilst waitin' to see the Injun hang? I can offer some mighty interestin' entertainment, if I do say so, myself."

"Indian?" Elizabeth said, even more fear gripping her heart at what he had said. They were planning to hang an Indian. She felt anxiety at the pit of her stomach.

For she knew only one Indian.

Surely he was not the one to be hanged, she despaired to herself. In her mind's eye, she saw the handsome Indian's body hanging from the gallows, spinning slowly in a dance of death.

"Sure," the man said, guffawing. He yanked the cigar from his mouth and spat across his shoulder. "An Injun called Four Winds. And it's about time we hung the renegade. He's been stinkin' up our prison long enough."

"Just how long has . . . has . . . he been incarcerated?" Elizabeth dared to ask, feeling the sudden tightening in her throat at the possibility that the condemned man was *her* Indian!

"Weeks," the man said, shrugging.

Elizabeth sighed, knowing that *her* Indian was not going to hang. He had been free yesterday, to save her from the Sound. He was surely as free today.

She started to ask the man about the prisoner, wanting to know what he had done to deserve hanging, but he had been called back by the others. She watched, wide-eyed, as he helped secure the rope and its noose on the cross beam. Her insides rebelled at the sight and what it meant—that soon a man would die there, and not only a man, an Indian! No wonder she hadn't seen any Indians in Seattle today. Being there was dangerous.

Elizabeth was jarred out of her unpleasant reverie when the man who had talked with her mounted a horse, and began riding away with the others. She stiffened when he yelled something over his shoulder at her—that he would look her up later, and he would like to "acquaint" himself with her body.

"The pig," she whispered, cringing at the thought of this crude man's rough hands on her.

Yanking the heavy basket from the rear of the buggy, Elizabeth stomped up to the prison door, then stopped and took a nervous breath before placing her hand on the latch.

When she composed herself she lifted the latch, and took a shaky step across the threshold. What she encountered made her want to turn around and seek the haven of her home as quickly as possible. Never had she seen such filth and gloom as crowded this small, outer room. A bearded man sat behind a crude desk piled high with yellowed papers and journals, his booted feet resting on the edge.

She grimaced when their eyes met, and she felt ill when he leaned his head sideways and spat a long stream of chewing tobacco into a large and tarnished brass spittoon that had strings of tobacco dripping down its sides.

Elizabeth stood stiff and unresponsive to how this man was looking at her as he slowly pushed himself up from his chair. He hooked his thumbs through red suspenders that held up soiled, black, baggy breeches. A red-plaid shirt was stuffed loosely into the waistband.

Elizabeth looked slowly around the room, at the peeling paint of the walls, and at the one filthy window that failed to let in any light through its dirt.

Her gaze stopped at the many small pegs along one of the walls. Keys hung from each.

She then saw a closed door, which surely led to the back where she would probably find the cells in even worse condition.

Her nose curled at the foul odor emanating from the sheriff as he stood before her, blocking her view. His beady eyes squinted above a thick, dark mustache that had chewing tobacco clinging to the tips.

"What's your business here?" Sheriff Jed Nolan asked, his voice a growl. He glanced down at the basket clutched in Elizabeth's right hand. "What's in that basket? Somethin' to help you break out one of your gentlemen friends, huh?"

Elizabeth didn't get a chance to reply. The sheriff grabbed the basket from her and threw the cloth aside, and peered down at the books and fruit.

Then he looked slowly up at Elizabeth. "Books?" he said, tossing the basket aside, spilling its contents. "Fruit? Who are you, anyhow? What do you want here?"

Elizabeth stared blankly down at the spilled contents of her basket. Then a slow burn began within her and she turned angry eyes up at the man. "You had no right to do that," she said, placing her fists on her hips. "I came here out of the goodness of my heart to help lighten the burden of those less fortunate. I pity those who are under your care. You don't deserve the title of sheriff. I would think it would have to be earned. What have you done, sir, to earn it? But I'm sure I don't want to know the answers. Such a man as you gets what he wants by—"

Elizabeth's words were cut short when Sheriff Nolan grabbed her by the wrists and quickly wrestled her to the floor, where he proceeded to straddle her. "What are you doing?" she screamed, squirming to get free. "Let me up, do you hear? Let . . . me . . . up!"

The sheriff brushed her lips with a wet kiss, his body holding her in place as one of his hands went to the swell of her breast and began mashing it through the silk fabric of her dress. "You've got a big mouth," Sheriff Nolan grumbled, staring down at her with lustful blue eyes. "Let's see what else you have that I might find more pleasant."

Elizabeth managed to get a hand free, raised it and slapped him across the face.

She sucked in a wild breath of air when she saw a sudden angry fire leap into his eyes. He in turn slapped her across the face, and followed by crushing her mouth with his hungry, wet lips. His tongue assaulted her as it pressed in and out between her unwilling lips.

And then, as quick as lightning striking, someone else was there in the room. Elizabeth saw a man, whose face was partially hidden behind a bandanna, strike the sheriff over the head with the butt of his pistol.

The sheriff collapsed unconscious on top of her. Elizabeth screamed and began pushing at his chest. The stranger yanked the sheriff off, tossing him away from her.

Elizabeth scrambled to her feet. Then she realized that she should still be afraid. It was apparent from his mask that the stranger who had saved her was not there for any good reason. When he stepped closer to her, she quaked.

Elizabeth stared at the hooded eyes above the bandanna, seeing something familiar about them. And when he told her in a whisper to leave, there was something about the voice that compelled her to want to see his face.

Without thought of the outcome of her action, Elizabeth yanked the man's bandanna down, revealing his face. She became weak in the knees when she saw that it *was* whom she had thought it to be: The handsome Indian!

Sighing resolutely, Strong Heart pushed the brim of his sombrero back from his brow with the barrel of his pistol. "What you have done is *me-sah-chie,* bad. You shouldn't have interfered," he said with annoyance. "Now that you've seen me, I have no choice but to take you with me. I can't leave you behind to describe me to the authorities. Why didn't you leave when I told you to?"

Elizabeth was numb from the discovery. She didn't understand when Strong Heart told her to get the keys from the sheriff's pocket, then take them to the cells, and release the Indian, Four Winds.

When Elizabeth did not obey him, Strong Heart took a step closer and gestured toward the sheriff who still lay unconscious on the floor. "*Hy-ak,* make haste," he grumbled. "Get the keys from the *cultus,* worthless man."

"I can't do that," Elizabeth said, her voice quavering. "That would be breaking the law. I would become a criminal." She gave him a glare. "Just like you. You're a criminal, aren't you? A renegade Indian, just like the Indian you want me to set free."

"*Nah,* look here," Strong Heart answered, bending to get the keys himself, "this is not the time to discuss who I am, or why I am here." He turned his gray eyes up at her as he handed her the keys. "If we don't get out of here soon, the deputy will arrive. I would soon be hanging alongside Four Winds. Is that what you want? That I die, also?"

The keys seemed like hot coals burning her palm. She glanced down at them, then up into Strong Heart's eyes as he rose slowly to his feet.

Then, knowing from the depths of her heart that she wanted nothing to happen to him, she spun around and moved quickly toward the closed door that led to the cells. Strong Heart was suddenly there, opening the door for her. She stopped long enough to look deep into his eyes. She felt as if she were drowning in them, they were so dark with feelings that she knew were for her, for he had looked at her in the same way before.

"Set Four Winds free," Strong Heart said, his voice soft, yet commanding.

Elizabeth swallowed hard and nodded her head, then stepped into a gloomy corridor lined with a long row of cells which housed both men and women. Hands reached out for her. Women cried and wailed as they saw her, begging her to set them free. Men cursed underneath their breaths. Then she caught sight of one who stood quiet, his eyes probing hers.

Elizabeth knew that this was Four Winds, for he was the only Indian inside this horror chamber. She stared at him, thinking that he looked no more dangerous than the other Indian. Yet being in jail was proof that he was a criminal—a criminal awaiting his death at the end of a rope.

Suddenly his face was replaced in Elizabeth's mind with the handsome Indian's. It was *he* who was hanging from the platform, not Four Winds. It was him swaying in the gentle breeze, the flies crawling on his dead eyes.

The vision spurred Elizabeth into quick action. She went to Four Winds's cell. Clumsily she tried one key after another, sighing with relief when she finally found the one that fit, and set him free.

Many cries and jeers followed Elizabeth and Four Winds as they fled to the outer room. Elizabeth dropped the keys on the desk, turned and stared up into the handsome Indian's face which was alight with admiration and gratitude. Then all three hurriedly left the prison.

Elizabeth didn't object when she was placed in the handsome Indian's saddle. She knew that she had no choice. She didn't object when he swung himself into the saddle behind her, his arm circling her waist to hold her as he and Four Winds rode away.

Again, she had no choice.

She couldn't believe this was happening.

These Indians were surely part of an outlaw gang.

Never would she have believed that he, this *compassionate,* caring man, could be an outlaw!

Strong Heart led his horse away from the streets of Seattle, and they were soon thundering through the dark reaches of the forest.

Suddenly Elizabeth panicked and began struggling to get free, but the more she squirmed, the harder the Indian held her. "Why do you insist in taking me with you?" she cried. "I can't tell anyone your name. I don't even *know* it. And after saving me from harm the other times, why would you harm me now?"

"*La-daila,* do you make it a habit to search for trouble?" he shouted over the sound of his horse's hooves. "First I find you choking to death in a house filled with smoke, then almost toppling off a bluff. Then I find you half drowned in Puget Sound. And now I find you in a hellhole of a prison. Why is that, *la-daila*. Why is that?"

"What is this *la-daila* you call me?" Elizabeth shouted back. "That isn't my name! My name is Elizabeth. Elizabeth Easton."

His chuckle made Elizabeth turn to stare up at him. "What do you find that's so amusing?" she asked heatedly. Yet, again, his handsomeness nearly stole her breath away. "At least I have no secrets about who I am. You have yet to tell me *your* name."

"Secrets?" Strong Heart said, smiling down at her. "My *la-daila,* which means 'woman,' I have no reason now to keep secrets from you. My name? It is Strong Heart. I am Suquamish. My father is Chief Moon Elk."

"Does your chieftain father know that his son has turned into a renegade who sets hardened criminals free?" Elizabeth taunted. She was now his captive but she decided that she would not cooperate with him one bit!

"*Ah-hah,* my father knows of my plans to set Four Winds free, and he approves," Strong Heart said, giving her a stern look. "For you see, Four Winds is innocent of the crime he is accused of."

Wanting to believe Strong Heart and not wanting to think he was just a criminal lying to her to make his escape from Seattle easier, Elizabeth turned her eyes away in confusion.

But she did know that she was now a captive, something that even Strong Heart could not deny, for it was he who was her captor.

She glanced over at Four Winds, his shoulder-length brown

hair flying in the wind as he leaned low over his horse. She had to wonder, what sort of crime had he been accused of? How could she not think that he might be capable of anything?

She looked away, fear freezing her thoughts. Strong Heart could be a liar. Although she had never seen him be cruel, she did not really know him. He could be a renegade.

If so, what would become of her?

He seemed adamant against setting her free. How long would he force this upon her?

What if it was . . . forever?

She had fantasized about being in Strong Heart's arms. But not under these conditions. The fantasy had lost its sweetness, as she was taken farther into the unbroken wilderness, a mist rising eerily from the floor of the forest.

8

> My heart has left its dwelling place,
> And can return no more.
>
> —John Clare

Bone tired from the long ride, Elizabeth was relieved when Strong Heart and Four Winds finally stopped for the rest of the night. Embarrassed that she had been forced to go into the bushes to take care of her most private needs, she strolled back to the campsite and ignored Strong Heart as he glanced her way.

Yet she had no choice but to sit down beside him on a blanket spread across a patch of soft moss.

Still not giving him the slightest inkling that she knew he was there, sitting so close to her, Elizabeth sat stiffly against a big, downed sycamore tree which was half buried in the ground. Her eyes feasted on fish skewered on sticks over the hot coals of the fire that Strong Heart had built. She had watched in awe as he started a fire without matches. He had used a flint and a stone to strike with and a spongy piece of dry wood. She had sat, shivering from the damp chill of night, as he had struck the flint against the rock until a spark flew out igniting the wood.

Then Four Winds fashioned a spear from a tree limb. His fisherman skills honed as a child became quickly evident after he had smilingly brought a string of fish to the campsite for their supper.

The aroma wafting from the fish cooking slowly over the fire caused Elizabeth's stomach to emit a low, lazy growl.

This had drawn both silent Indians' attentions to her. Embarrassed, she turned her eyes away and tried to focus her thoughts elsewhere—especially away from Strong Heart and how he sat so close to her, so close that if they should turn to face each other, their breaths would mingle.

But it was hard not to think about him. And although she was angry at him for having taken her captive, she could not deny that the excitement of the adventure of being with him was giving her strange, glorious feelings that until tonight she had never experienced.

But now she was in the wilderness, free from her father's watchful eye, and stern, commanding voice, and having been attracted to Strong Heart from the first made her fear her feelings for him. She was glad that Four Winds was a part of the group. For, if she were totally alone with Strong Heart, she did not know what she might expect from him, or herself.

She already knew the wonders of his touch, of being held in his strong arms, and the thrill of the heat of his breath on her face and lips. Alone with him, she might forget all that she had been taught about being a lady. She would perhaps learn what it meant to be a *woman,* with needs of a woman.

Shocked at where her mind had wandered, Elizabeth again tried to change her thoughts. It was a cool September night, with lightning flashing luridly over the mountains in the distance. Elizabeth gazed around her at the groves of tall, slim pines which stood majestically sprinkled with stars. Only a few feet away, a swift-running, sweet-singing trout stream coursed. Strong Heart had chosen this beautiful campsite which seemed like a woodland cathedral, roofed by the open skies, and where wave and rock and tall pine met.

It was a place of serenity, yet Elizabeth could not feel that serenity within her heart, for again her thoughts had traveled back to Strong Heart and the dilemma in which she had found herself.

Strong Heart had not said much to her during their flight from the prison. She had to wonder if he was reconsidering keeping her captive.

The thought that he might set her free frightened her, for they were now many miles from Seattle, and she would not be able to find her way back alone.

And he did not dare return with her, for surely a posse had

been formed to search for him and Four Winds and herself. It was possible that she was considered an accomplice. The sheriff would not know the truth, for he had been unconscious.

Elizabeth started when a stick with cooked fish at its tip was thrust toward her. She turned and looked up at Four Winds, who was offering it to her.

"Eat," was all Four Winds said.

Elizabeth accepted the skewer and nodded a silent thank you. Four Winds had been quiet since his release. He and Strong Heart had not even discussed the escape. There seemed to be a strain between them, and Elizabeth could only surmise that it was because Strong Heart and Four Winds were not so much friends as allies in crime. Surely if they were close friends, they would have been warmer to each other.

At the moment she only truly cared about the hungry ache in her stomach. Elizabeth tore at the fish with her teeth, giving Strong Heart a sideways glance as he also began eating from his stick.

When he looked her way, she turned away from him, embarrassed by how her hunger was making her forget her table manners. She was so hungry, she yanked the fish from the stick and began stuffing it into her mouth with her fingers, then blushed when she found two sets of eyes on her. She offered Four Winds and Strong Heart a weak smile.

Having eaten all of her fish, Elizabeth wiped her mouth free of grease with the back of her hand, then opened her ears to the conversation that had started between Strong Heart and Four Winds.

Four Winds squatted before Strong Heart and placed a heavy hand on his shoulder. He began earnestly, saying, "Strong Heart, *mah-sie,* thank you for what you have done for your childhood friend. Your silence since the escape proves that you do not yet fully trust that I am free of guilt for that which I was about to be hanged. Trust that I am. Feel good in your trust."

"My silence was caused by many things," Strong Heart said, giving Elizabeth a quick glance, then focusing his attention on Four Winds. "Many things trouble me, and, *ah-hah,* part of that is my doubt about your innocence. But knowing you from childhood, I cannot see you as anything but innocent. When I spoke with my father about breaking you free, he hesitated, yet agreed with me that you should be saved. Prove to me, old friend, that you have earned our trust. Do not allow yourself to be taken prisoner again by the white man. The hangman's noose would not go empty a second time, for this friend of yours would no longer be a friend."

"Four Winds will remain your friend, for Four Winds will never give you cause again to risk your life for his," he said, humbly lowering his eyes. Then he raised them and looked into Strong Heart's. "I must now go my way alone. I will flee high into the mountains until I feel it is safe to surface again. This I do not only for myself, but also for you. As long as I am with you, your guilt in helping me escape could be proved. Without me, you are just another Indian to the white man, for no one witnessed your part in the escape."

Four Winds's eyes focused accusingly on Elizabeth, then turned back to Strong Heart. "This woman's presence with Strong Heart can also prove dangerous," he said, his voice barely a whisper. "Her being with you could be proof enough of your guilt, not only for having aided an accused criminal in an escape from prison, but also for abducting a white woman. Once the sheriff regains consciousness, he will remember, and recognize her if his posse finds you."

Strong Heart rose to his feet. He placed a hand at Four Winds's elbow and led him toward the grazing horses. "*Ah-hah,* yes, it is best that you leave," he murmured. "As for the woman, she stays."

"But do you not see the danger in that?" Four Winds persisted, untying his horse's reins from a tree stump. "She can be the cause of *you* being taken to the hanging platform." He placed his free hand on Strong Heart's shoulder. "Consider carefully your decision about this woman. Is she worth the risk? Is she?"

"I have learned many ways of being elusive," Strong Heart said, setting his jaw. "No posse or sheriff will find me."

He glanced over his shoulder at Elizabeth. Her beautiful

eyes unnerved him. There was no denying the true reason why he would not set her free now that he had her to himself. It was for his own selfish needs that he held her in bondage. She was the embodiment of all temptation. And he never would allow her to leave.

Never.

Not even his father could shame him into releasing her. She had stolen his heart, a heart which until now beat for no woman.

Only her, only Elizabeth, who was now his *la-daila*.

Strong Heart turned his attention back to Four Winds. He squared his shoulders proudly. "You say that it is dangerous for the woman to be with me," he said, stubbornly. "The chances are worse for me if I set her free. She knows too much. And I cannot *kill* her to silence her. Do you not recognize me still as a man of honor?"

Four Winds could remember very well his childhood with Strong Heart, and could see that he had not changed. Strong Heart was still a bullheaded, stubborn man. Four Winds knew not to argue with Strong Heart when he had his heart set on something.

Four Winds looked over at the woman, seeing her loveliness, and was convinced now that his friend's heart was set on the white woman. Four Winds had seen how Strong Heart had looked at her, and had seen the gentleness with which he had treated her.

Four Winds knew that Strong Heart saw her as special, perhaps special enough to take as his *la-daila,* and there was no arguing with that, once *any* man chose the woman of his heart.

"*Ah-hah,* yes, Four Winds knows that Strong Heart is a man of honor, and Four Winds will say no more about your decision concerning the woman," Four Winds said, dropping his horse's reins as he stepped close to Strong Heart. He embraced Strong Heart. "*Kla-how-ya,* good-bye, my friend. Again, *mah-sie,* thank you."

Strong Heart embraced his friend, then stepped back and watched Four Winds mount his horse. They exchanged looks filled with deep emotion. Then Four Winds swung his horse around and rode away in a brisk gallop.

Strong Heart watched Four Winds until he was lost to the night, then turned slowly around to Elizabeth. She had drawn a blanket around her shoulders, and was staring into the dancing flames of the fire. Strong Heart's breath caught in his throat as once again he looked on her loveliness. His loins ached for that which he would deny himself until she invited him into her blankets.

9

Give all to love,
Obey thy heart. . . .

—EMERSON

Now that they were alone, Strong Heart did not know what to expect from Elizabeth. Would she demand to be set free? He moved cautiously to the blanket and sat down beside her. When he looked at her, she did not follow his lead and raise her gaze to meet his. Instead, she stared into the flames of the fire, her jaw set, her eyes filled with a defiant anger.

Even when Strong Heart began talking to her, she did not budge, nor did she show any sign of even hearing him. When he called her by the Suquamish term for 'my woman,' he thought he noticed a flicker of reaction, but just as quickly it was gone.

"*La-daila,* there is much to be said between us," Strong Heart began, his voice soft, yet measured. "Please listen while I tell you the truth about everything. Then if you condemn me, so be it."

A dull knot ached within Elizabeth's chest, she so wanted to be able to turn to him and tell him that she would willingly talk with him, that being with him was thrilling her through and through. But for too many reasons she did not feel free to speak her mind. Just the thought of Strong Heart being no better than the man he had set free from prison made her heart silently cry out to him in pain. For she had discovered this side of him just when she had begun to believe that she was falling in love with him!

Before the encounter at the prison, before she realized what he was capable of, she had loved the way his mere presence caused her heart to beat so erratically. Even now, while he was so close, she could not deny the wondrous, strange sweetness that seemed to be pressing in on her heart. And the more he spoke—the more sense he made, giving her cause to hope that perhaps all of these wrongs could be made right between them!

But how could he? she despaired to herself. He could never deny having helped an outlaw escape from Copper Hill Prison. She could never forgive him for forcing her to participate, then abducting her, an innocent bystander.

"*La-daila,* for so many years Four Winds and I were the best of friends who knew all the secrets of the silent forest; who, together, heard when the bluebird sang his wildest, clearest notes; knew where the scarlet wing hung his nest in the river rushes; and knew why the yellow beak sang his most beautiful song in the springtime."

He paused to place another log on the fire.

Although Elizabeth did not reveal to Strong Heart that she was listening, she was, intently, never offering him a nod or a glance. Her pulse raced and she was feeling more hopeful by the minute that he was that man of compassion she had first thought him to be. And perhaps she *could* forgive him, but only if he would escort her safely back home, she thought bitterly to herself, knowing how unlikely that was.

Strong Heart resumed his place beside her and she listened even more raptly, desperately wanting to believe him.

"As youths, Four Winds and I shared everything," he said softly. "We shared the hunt, bringing home to our clans our prizes of the day, boasting of each other's catch to our chieftain fathers. We are of two separate clans of Suquamish, and as we grew older and had to become more diligent in learning the ways of our fathers, we had to give up our childish friendship for the more serious side of life."

Again he paused, his eyes melancholy as he looked into the flames of the fire.

Elizabeth was touched by the sincerity of his words, and the emotion in his voice, yet she still did not reach out to him with words, or a gesture of sympathy.

When he began talking again, and gave her a slow glance, she jerked her eyes around, not wanting him to know that she had been studying him and imagining her flesh being warmed by his touch.

She swallowed hard and concentrated on his words.

"Four Winds and I meet from time to time, sharing talk and dreams of our futures," Strong Heart said, again turning his eyes away from Elizabeth, not sure if he was reaching her with his explanation. She was stubbornly hiding her feelings, whether they were in his favor or against him.

"But after Four Winds's clan of Suquamish moved far to the north toward Canada, we broke all our ties," Strong Heart continued. "Then I received word that Four Winds had been arrested for riding with criminals—something I could not, *would* not allow myself to believe. I decided to set my old friend free from the prison, having hoped—no, having *known,* without a doubt—that Four Winds had been accused unjustly, for I know the honor by which Four Winds guides his life."

Strong Heart's brow furrowed into a deep frown. His eyes narrowed as he spoke in almost a snarl. "The white men who imprison my people would cage eagles, chain the wolf, corral the moose!" he said sharply. "The white race is unable to order their lives into ways of peace and freedom, not knowing an innocent man when they see one, for most white men are guilty of one or more crimes against nature or humanity. From the Indian, the white man stands aloof, scarcely deigning to speak or touch his hand in human fellowship. He calls the Indian *savage,* meaning that he believes we are low in thought and feeling, and cruel in acts; and that we are incapable of a philosophical understanding of life and life's relations."

Elizabeth was stunned by the strength in his words, and his intense feelings against the white race, yet it did not show in how he treated her. He had risked his life more than once to save her. How could he have, when he obviously hated the white people so much?

And, oh, what he had said was so true! She had always been aware of the injustices against the plains Indians. She had never thought to consider that it was the same for those who lived elsewhere, such as here in the Pacific Northwest. Now, she realized that her father's hopes of winning the Suquamish over to his side must surely have been dashed when he met with them about his proposals.

Strong Heart moved to his knees before Elizabeth, blocking her view of the fire. He placed a finger under her chin and elevated her eyes to meet his. "Have you listened to what I have said?" he asked, his voice filled with kindness; filled with gentleness. "The white people are wrong about the Suquamish. Among my people there are many men of vision. There is great honesty and loyalty, noble sacrifice, unselfishness, and devotion to peace. Tell me that you hear me and understand, that you *believe.*"

Elizabeth felt deeply touched by his words, and overwhelmed with relief that she had *not* been wrong about him. He was a man of compassion, of deep understanding, a man of clear vision and intelligence.

And she could not control the beating of her heart when she gazed into his steel-gray eyes, his lips so close—his voice so suddenly soft and sweet.

"I have heard you," she murmured. "And . . . and . . . I believe you. Truly, I do."

"Do you understand now why I set my friend free?" he asked, leaning closer to her, placing his hands on her shoulders, drawing her nearer to him. "While caged, Four Winds was the *mee-gee-see,* the eagle, his wings no longer able to spread and fly. He had to be set free, for to cage an innocent man is a crime against all humanity!"

"I'm trying to understand everything," Elizabeth murmured, blinking her eyes nervously. "And I think I do. But please, Strong Heart, set *me* free. While you hold me captive, I too am like the eagle. You must allow me to return home, where I belong."

"You belong with *me,* not in the white man's world," Strong Heart said, drawing her even closer to him, their lips only a breath away. "Do you not see that? Do you not feel it? Your heart no longer beats only for yourself. It also beats for me, the man you are meant to be with."

A great heat rose to Elizabeth's cheeks; she was speechless over what he had just said. She knew she should be frightened of his declaration, yet how could she be, when she had such strong feelings for him?

She wanted to make her own choice, not be forced to be with a man—no matter how wonderful he made her feel.

"I cannot allow you to go free, and not only because I have never felt this way about any other woman," Strong Heart said. "I am to be chief of my people one day. I cannot allow you to jeopardize this that I have prepared for all my life. If you were to point an accusing finger at me and have me caged by the white man, I would not be the only one to suffer. Many Suquamish people would be punished."

His fingers dug more tightly into her arms. "No," he said determinedly. "I cannot let you go."

When he saw a defiant anger enter her eyes, he grabbed her wrists and lowered her to the ground before she had the chance to rise and run away from him.

"Everything that I have told you is true," he said, leaning in close to her. He feathered soft kisses along the lovely contours of her face. "Trust me. I mean you no harm. Remember that I gave you the chance to flee at the prison, after you stripped away my mask and discovered my identity. If I had meant you harm, I would have never given you the chance to leave. I would have taken you then as my prisoner, without any questions asked, or apologies for having abducted you."

Elizabeth could scarcely listen to his words as her senses were swept away by his lips and the press of his body against hers. She lay on her back on the dew-dampened grass, drinking him in, and her anger slowly waned. "Are you apologizing for having abducted me?" she asked, their eyes locking.

"If that is what you want, *ah-hah,* yes, I apologize," he said thickly.

"If you apologize so easily, why don't you let me go?" she asked, her pulse racing as his lips came close to hers again. "I promise never to say a word. Truly . . . I do."

"I'm sorry, *la-daila,* but your promises alone are not enough protection against being hunted down and arrested," he said, again brushing a kiss across her beckoning lips. "Did not the sheriff see you just prior to my arrival at the prison, and only moments before I knocked him unconscious?"

"Yes," she said, her voice weakening, the building passion making her feel crazed and confused.

"If you were to return to Seattle, the sheriff would ask you many questions," he said, urging her to appreciate the danger. "Under pressure, you might break down and tell everything."

He paused, every fiber of his being tense and poised for her response.

"Are you never going to allow me to return home?" she asked, her voice breaking.

"It's not possible," he said too matter-of-factly, bringing Elizabeth abruptly back to her senses. She began shoving at him, trying to push him away from her.

But the more she shoved, the more tightly he held her.

"You are more beautiful than all the skies," Strong Heart whispered passionately against her cheek, and when his lips came to hers, she forgot everything but how her body thrilled to his kiss.

Her breath quickened and she tilted her face back, letting herself feel the strange sinking downward, the wondrous swirling sensation deep within her. When his hands sought her breasts and kneaded them through the fabric of her dress, she felt aflame with desire for him. Blind to every risk, she melted against him and twined her arms around his neck, returning his kiss with complete abandon.

A great clap of thunder drew them apart. Elizabeth winced when a bolt of lightning split the sky above them, followed by another boom of thunder. When a few desultory raindrops began to fall, Strong Heart rose quickly to his feet and went to his belongings and began setting up a tent.

When the tent was erected and Strong Heart returned to Elizabeth, offering her his hand, she accepted it. He led her to the tent, her knees weak and her heart pounding, not knowing what would happen next, and afraid of how she might respond.

She was baffled when he left her at the flap of the tent and returned to his bedroll beside the fire. A part of her wished that he would stay with her; another part of her was glad that he hadn't.

Struggling with her feelings, she entered the tent and stretched out between the blankets, wondering about this man she could not help but love with all of her heart.

"Heart," she whispered to herself. "Strong Heart. What a lovely name."

She moved to her knees and crawled to the tent opening. "I adore your name," she said, glad to have something to say to break the silence between them.

Strong Heart rolled over to his side and smiled at her. "*Mah-sie,* thank you," he murmured, blinking raindrops from his lashes as the storm began to thicken the air. "The name means courage."

"My name also has a special meaning," Elizabeth said, glancing up at the sheets of gray falling from the sky. "My mother told me many years ago that my name means consecrated by oath to God."

They exchanged warm smiles and she returned to her blankets.

Strong Heart wondered about her name, and her god. He had always felt that God was where one finds him. And her god had most surely thrown away the mold when he had made her.

Elizabeth listened to the rain hitting the tent with such great force, she thought it might collapse on top of her.

But it was not herself she was concerned about. It was Strong Heart, still lying in the open, surely becoming drenched to the bone!

Determinedly, Elizabeth went to the tent opening again. "Please come in out of the rain," she said, wiping sprays of water from her face as she held the flap aside. "Strong Heart, there is room in here for both of us. Come on. There is no need for you to stay outside. You will catch a chill at the least."

Dripping and cold, Strong Heart went to the tent. Once inside, Elizabeth wrapped a dry blanket around his shoulders. "You must get out of those wet clothes," she said, blushing at the thought of him undressing in her presence. "I . . . I . . . shall turn my head. Please do it quickly, Strong Heart. You don't want to become ill."

Amused, Strong Heart watched her turn her head from him, then dropped the blankets away. Swiftly, he yanked the clinging white man's clothes off and tossed them from the tent. They were of no further use to him. He would dress in buckskin tomorrow for his journey through the forest toward his home. He was glad to be returning to his people and his familiar ways.

He drew on the blanket, wrapping it snugly around his body. "You no longer have to keep your eyes from me," he said lightly.

Smiling abashedly, Elizabeth turned her face back to him. She blushed again when she saw him dressed in only the blanket. "Are you warmer now?" she asked softly, sitting down on another blanket, wrapping it around her shoulders.

"*Ah-hah,*" Strong Heart said, settling down beside her.

"Well, I . . . I guess we'd best get some sleep," Elizabeth said, her eyes wide, wondering if he could hear the thunderous beating of her heart. She could feel it in her ears, pounding like a thousand drums.

"*Ah-hah,*" Strong Heart said, easing down onto his side, so that she would have plenty of room to lie down.

She followed his lead, stretching out beside him.

When another great clap of thunder shook the ground beneath her, she jumped with alarm and welcomed a comforting arm around her waist, yet knew the dangers in even this minimal contact.

She closed her eyes tightly, to try and block out the desire that made her ache for the feel of his lips on hers, his skin against hers.

And, as if he read her mind, he slowly turned her to face him, and she allowed it. . . .

10

In one another's being mingle;—
Why not I with thine?

—SHELLEY

His long lean fingers weaving through Elizabeth's hair, Strong Heart drew her lips to his. Never had she felt such bliss as when he began kissing her, his free hand at her waist, urging her closer to him, pressing her hard against his body—which was now nude, the blanket having dropped away from him.

Her senses reeled as he prolonged the meltingly hot kiss, his hand skillfully unfastening her dress at the back. She watched, feeling as if she were in some sort of magical trance, as he leaned away from her and slipped the dress over her shoulders, and down the full length of her.

She did not protest when he continued, not even when she was totally disrobed and could relish the feel of his skin on hers as he again drew her fully against him.

His hands were on her flesh, searching, caressing, fondling, causing Elizabeth's breath to catch in her throat. Just when she thought she could bear no more, Strong Heart's lips explored her body for her most sensitive pleasure points.

She stretched out on her back and closed her eyes, giving herself up to the rapture, fighting off the urge to tell him to stop—tell him that what she was allowing was surely wicked.

All rational thoughts she easily cast aside, having never been lectured against this beautiful thing that was happening between herself and the man she loved.

Her mother had not been there to explain this side of life to her.

Her father had never been able to speak of such things around her.

What she had learned had been from novels, and now, tonight, Strong Heart was her true teacher.

And, ah, how skilled a teacher he was. His tongue and lips were like flames against her flesh, scorching . . . burning. Desire rose high within her as he showered heated kisses over her taut-tipped breasts, his mouth sweet and hungry as he then kissed her lips with a lazy warmth that left her weak.

And then she became aware of something else. A thick shaft resting against her thigh, pulsing it seemed, with a life of its own.

Curious, she drew her lips away from Strong Heart's and peered down at him, blushing when she gazed upon this part of a man that she had never seen before.

She was not as embarrassed as she was intrigued.

She slowly reached a hand toward the swollen shaft, Strong Heart's fingers circling hers, guiding her hand to his throbbing member.

"Touch it," Strong Heart said huskily, his heart thundering within his chest, desire filling him now as never before in his life. "Caress me. There you will find the center of my passions . . . my passions aroused by you, my *la-daila*. Only you."

Her pulse racing, every nerve ending within her feeling the exquisite tension of the moment, on fire with needs that were new to her. Elizabeth looked shyly up at Strong Heart.

Then, without losing contact with his eyes, she circled her fingers around the thickness of his manhood.

She was fascinated at how when his lean, sinewy buttocks began to move, he caused his manhood to move within her fingers.

But this seemed to cause too much pleasure for Strong Heart, for too soon he moaned throatily, then placed his hands at her shoulders and urged her away from him.

He drew her against him again, cradling her in his arms, the heat of his passion now pressing into her abdomen.

Holding her tightly, he turned her to lie again on her back. Brushing some strands of her hair back from her brow, he gazed at her with a look of possession in his eyes. "My love for you is new, yet strong," he said passionately. "My *la-daila*, tell me that it is the same for you."

"I have never loved before," Elizabeth said, pleasure spreading anew through her body as his fingers gently kneaded her breasts. "But I know it, now that I am experiencing it."

She framed his handsome face between her hands and drew his lips close. "Yes, Strong Heart," she whispered. "Although new to me, my love for you is strong. It steals my breath away, this love I have for you. It is a wonderful feeling, as if I am suddenly wrapped in a cocoon of deliciously warm cotton, my whole body responding to yours. You are lying with me in this cocoon, your body awakening mine to pleasure."

She clung to him as once again he kissed her. She felt a soft probing at the juncture of her thighs—something hot, something wonderful, and then she understood exactly what was trying to make entrance where no man had been before: His manhood.

One of his knees moved her legs apart, and then again she felt the probing. She closed her eyes tightly and clasped her arms around Strong Heart's neck, opening herself to him, making it easier for what he sought. Yet he pulled away, stopping what he had begun and she had agreed to.

Elizabeth's eyes opened in surprise as Strong Heart rolled away from her, his hands still at her waist, turning her on her side to face him.

He gazed at her naked splendor, his eyes filled with a drugged passion, then he looked into her eyes.

"Say that you want me," he said, tracing the line of her jaw with his finger. "I must hear you say it, before our bodies become as one. It is important to know that you understand this that we do, and want it as badly, as I. I want you to love me forever, my *la-daila*. Not just tonight."

"I'm not sure what want is," Elizabeth said, innocently. "As I said earlier, I've never been in love before."

"Listen to your body—the ache, the passions aroused within it," Strong Heart said, his one hand now at the core of her womanhood, slowly caressing it with his fingertips. "Do you feel it? The passions that need to be answered with mine?"

Desire was shooting through Elizabeth as his fingers so skillfully awakened her body to even newer sensations. She closed her eyes and threw her head back, sighing.

"Yes," she whispered. "The passion. Oh, such passion. I do feel it. Please, oh, please. I do need you, Strong Heart. Forever I will need you."

Strong Heart drew her beneath him. He bent down and kissed her, his palms moving softly and arousingly over her as he once again parted her legs with his knee and began pressing his manhood slowly inside her yielding folds.

Gently he entered her. When he reached that shield that stopped his entrance, he held her tenderly to him and kissed away her pain as he made the plunge that finally made her wholly his.

The pain was only brief, causing Elizabeth's body to wince, and then the pain smoothed out to something deliciously sweet.

She twined her arms about Strong Heart's neck and circled her legs around him, locking them at the ankles, and rode with him, taking from him all that he offered, his strokes within her a steady rocking movement now.

As Strong Heart's breathing quickened, he moved his mouth from her lips and pillowed his cheek against her full bosom. He closed his eyes and plunged ever more deeply within her, his fingers digging into the flesh of her hips, pulling her tightly against him.

The soft, melting energy was warming him, spreading throughout his body.

Overcome by the unbearably sweet pain, Elizabeth began rolling her head from side to side, the whimperings that came to her ears, her own. She trembled with excitement as Strong Heart began sucking one of her nipples, then flicked his tongue around its hardness.

She drew in her breath sharply and gave a little cry as he gave one last, hard thrust, his manhood filling her—oh, so magnificently filling her—causing the passion to spill over within her.

She strained her hips up at him when she felt a great shuddering in his loins, thinking that surely meant that he had also reached the same pinnacle of ecstasy that she had just climbed.

Breathing hard, Strong Heart's body subsided exhaustedly onto hers. He lay there for a long moment with her, stroking her womanhood, that still pulsed from the aftermath of her rapture.

And then he rolled away from her. His hands found the soft swell of her breasts. She arched toward him, her parted mouth and closed eyes an invitation to kiss her again.

With a groan he pulled her against him and kissed her, their tongues touching, their bodies straining together.

As she clung to Strong Heart, his kiss dizzying her, Elizabeth moved her body sinuously against his, feeling his renewed desire as his swollen shaft once again pressed into her warmed flesh.

In what seemed a dream, Strong Heart had her positioned above him and magnificently filled her again with his powerful need. As she straddled him, leaning back, her red hair streaming long and gleaming down her back, she rode him as he lifted himself into her with his thrusts. She awakened anew to the smoldering desire that she had discovered tonight with this man that she adored—that she loved.

As the rain poured against the tent and the thunder boomed, shaking the very earth beneath them, Strong Heart reached for Elizabeth's waist and urged her beneath him again. As he entered her and began his steady strokes, they once again found paradise together, their bodies locked together in a fierce, fevered heat.

And then they lay side by side, their hands entwined, their breaths mingling as they stared with bliss into each other's eyes.

"You now understand the meaning of want?" Strong Heart whispered, his one hand gently caressing one of her breasts.

"Yes," she breathed, her face flushed from the drunken pleasure that she had just experienced. "Oh, yes. I understand. Oh, so very much, my darling."

"Your needs were answered . . . fulfilled?" he prodded. He could feel her tremble sensually when he flicked his tongue out to again taste the sweetness of her breast.

"Yes, yes," she said, shivering with delight when he moved to his knees and bent over her, kissing the pleasure points of her body. "You are a masterful lover. So . . . so . . . very skilled."

She wove her fingers through his long, brown hair and brought his lips to hers. She kissed him softly, then sighed languorously when he moved away from her and lay on his back beside her.

"Come," he said, beckoning with a hand toward her. "Lie within my arms. Let me sing you to sleep, my *la-daila*. Listen. Relax. Enjoy. Sleep and dream of this man who loves you."

Smiling sleepily, Elizabeth snuggled into the warm nest of blankets with him. She moved into his arms and lay close to him, having never felt so much at peace with herself and her world.

And as he began to sing to her, he pulled her deeper and deeper into loving him.

"What did you think when you saw the trail we took?" he sang in a soft and lulling voice. "What did you think when you saw the trail we took? My dearest one, I thought of you when I saw the trail we took. I thought of you."

He paused before starting his next song. He glanced down at Elizabeth and smiled to himself when he saw her eyes were closed, sleep coming easily to her tonight, as it would to him. He was in a world now that transcended all troubles and pain. He was in a world that belonged only to him, and his *la-daila*.

He began singing again:

"I saw the moon rise tonight and my thoughts went to you.
I saw the moon rise tonight and my thoughts went to you.
Beloved, I wish I were there with you.
I saw the moon rise tonight and my thoughts went to you.
My beloved, I wish I were there with you."

Cradling Elizabeth protectively, he closed his eyes, a smile on his face.

11

Too late I stayed—forgive the crime,
Unheeded flew the hours.
—William Robert Spencer

Elizabeth's eyes flew open and she bolted to a sitting position. Then she paled and drew a blanket around her nakedness as she slowly looked around her, her sight stopping on Strong Heart. She remembered the previous evening as she looked at him lying so close beside her, his breathing slow as he soundly slept, his blanket having fallen aside.

Elizabeth could not deny the passion that flooded her when she regarded his nude body, seeing that part of him that had made her body thrill with pleasure.

Her heart beat wildly at the memory, yet now she regretted her wanton behavior with Strong Heart.

Last night it had seemed so right.

Today—she was confused about how she should feel!

She loved Strong Heart, yet a part of her tormented her, telling her that what she had done was wrong.

What she had done had surely been because she was under his spell. Strong Heart's presence had bewitched her from the moment they had met.

Even now, she felt it, the way he made her feel—oh, this wasn't her!

He turned on his other side, his face now away from her, his breathing still, even, and soft, indicating that he was still asleep. Elizabeth recalled something else—how he had said that he would never allow her to return home. How he seemed to want *total* possession of her.

She wanted nothing more than to be with him, forever. Yet there was this thing called "freedom" that nagged at her mind.

She did not want to be anyone's captive. She wanted him to understand that if she stayed with him, it was because *she* had decided to—not because *he* had made the choice for her.

Yet, he had seemed so determined in his decision, she saw no other option but to try and escape, even if it meant losing him. *And* the special love that he had introduced her to.

As her gaze lingered on his muscular body, every beat of her heart told her that she wanted to stay with him.

Yet these strong feelings for him were another reason she must try and escape from him. She did not see how a love between them could work. She began crawling on her knees, gathering her clothes into her arms. Then she scurried outside where she could dress without awakening him.

As she slipped into her clothes, she looked around her, and was glad to see that the morning mists had vanished. The sun was clearing the horizon, the dew sparkled on the grass.

She peered warily into the depths of the forest, a rush of fear stopping her. She wondered that even if she did escape from Strong Heart, could she, in truth, find her way back to Seattle?

There were no true roads. There weren't even any paths. And she would be at the mercy of all the animals roaming the land, four-legged and two-legged.

The thought terrified her, yet she saw no other choice but to take her chances.

Her future must be *hers,* not something planned and mapped out by someone else.

Finally she was fully clothed. She groaned as she glanced down at her silk dress and saw how wrinkled and stained it had gotten on her flight from Seattle.

And it was less than suitable for the return journey. Its yards of silk would constantly impede her movements. It was not the attire to wear while riding a horse.

"A horse," she whispered to herself, blanching. "I must steal his horse."

She glanced back guiltily at the tent. If she stole the horse, Strong Heart would be stranded without any transportation.

She set her jaw. It would serve him right! He had not

thought of her welfare when he had abducted her. Nor would she his!

Relieved that the air was warm, *that* at least in her favor, Elizabeth began moving toward the roan that grazed close beside the river. When she reached the lovely animal, she grabbed for the reins, then she felt a movement behind her.

Turning with a start, she gasped when she saw Strong Heart running after her, having not taken the time to dress when he had found her gone. She watched his muscular, copper body and recalled with a rush of passion how it had felt to be pressed against it. Then she shook herself free of her trance and again grabbed for the horse's reins, knowing that this was perhaps the only chance, ever, for her to win her freedom.

Her fingers worked clumsily with the knot of the rawhide reins, unable to untie them.

She glanced over her shoulder just in time to see Strong Heart lunge for her. Her breath was momentarily knocked out of her when he threw her onto her back on the ground.

"You leave me?" he said, holding her wrists to the ground as he straddled her. He thrust his face into hers, peering down at her angrily. "Why do you? You professed to love Strong Heart. You professed to *need* me!"

Elizabeth did not know how to explain to him why she was leaving him, for deep inside, where her desires dwelled, she knew that she was going against everything that her heart was telling her to do.

The sudden screech of a hawk overhead, and its loud flapping of wings as it dipped low, barely missing Strong Heart's head, caused him to flinch and loosen his grip on her wrists.

Taking advantage of his loss of concentration, Elizabeth jerked her wrists free and gave him a hard shove on his chest.

Wild-eyed, she watched him fall away from her. Then he grabbed her at the waist, bringing her along with him as he rolled threateningly close to the river.

"Let me go!" Elizabeth cried, struggling to get away from him.

But he was determined not to let her go. He rolled her over and started to straddle her again, then lost his balance and started slipping sideways into the water. At the last moment he grabbed her hand, pulling her into the water with him.

Stunned by the spill and the intense cold of the water, Elizabeth's wits were momentarily stolen away. When she regained her bearings, she found herself floundering just beneath the surface of the river, the sun pouring through the water like bright lamplight.

A muscular arm circled around her waist. She tried to pry it away, then rose with Strong Heart to the surface, coughing fitfully. He held her close to him as he stood, his feet planted firmly on the rocky bottom of the shallows. She again struggled to get free, slapping at his arms and chest.

"I can't believe this!" she shouted, coughing and gasping for air. "Let me go, do you hear? Haven't you done enough?" A shiver coursed through her. "I'm freezing. Let me out of this water!"

"Not until you tell me that you are sorry for planning to leave me," Strong Heart said, his grasp strong as steel, his face leaning into hers. "Only then will I let go of you."

"You will have to hold me in this water until it freezes over then," Elizabeth cried, wiping wet strands of hair back from her eyes. She shivered and shook and her teeth chattered from the frigid cold.

Strong Heart's eyes bored into hers. He saw how purple her lips were, but he still would not allow her to leave the water.

"When the waters turn to ice in the dead of winter, then both of us shall become lodged within it," Strong Heart said stubbornly. "I mean to have you. And I shall."

He lowered his face closer, smiling. "You are already mine, you know—body and soul. Why do you fight it? It is useless, this decision of yours to turn your back on Strong Heart. Because I know that it is not what you truly want. I shall not allow it. Ever!"

"No one wants to feel imprisoned, by *anyone*," Elizabeth cried, hugging herself with her arms. The silver minnows in the water seemed puzzled as they swam in circles around her and Strong Heart.

"You are not the only one held captive," Strong Heart said,

his eyes flashing into hers. "Strong Heart is also a captive—of your heart. Even if I would allow you to ride away from me, or I from you, *I* would *never* be free. Do you not understand this? Do you not believe it? As long as I have breath in my body, I am yours. Totally."

Frustrated, Elizabeth lowered her eyes. "Oh, Strong Heart, please don't confuse me any more than I already am," she said softly, her voice catching in her throat.

When his finger lifted her chin upward, and their eyes met, she even became more confused between loving him, and wanting not to.

But when his mouth came to hers, and he kissed her, everything began to fall back into place within her heart and mind.

And when he wrapped her within his powerful arms, the coldness of the water was forgotten. All that she felt was the heat of his flesh. She knew what she wanted.

To be with Strong Heart. *He* was her heart. Her soul. Her entire being.

She knew at this moment that she could never leave him—not as long as he wanted her with him.

She hungrily returned the kiss, moaning as his hands slipped from her waist up to her breasts, stroking them through the clinging wetness of her dress.

"I do need you," she whispered, as she pulled her lips away from his. "I do want you. I love you, Strong Heart. I no longer want to flee from you. I want to stay. I love you. I adore you."

Strong Heart framed her face between his hands and smiled down at her. Then he placed his arms beneath her and swung her up into them, and carried her from the water, his lips again sending her into a whirlwind of desire as he kissed her until they were inside the tent.

"Your wet clothes," Strong Heart whispered as he slid his lips down to the hollow of her throat. "You must get them off."

"So I won't come down with pneumonia?" Elizabeth said, her eyes twinkling into his as she raised her arms, allowing Strong Heart to pull the clinging dress over her head.

"I do not wish to see you get ill," Strong Heart said, tossing the dress aside. His long, lean fingers finished undressing her. "But the main reason for disrobing you is so that I can give you more cause to not want to leave me. Perhaps last night was not lesson enough. Today I will make love to you so that you will never, for even a moment, forget my feelings for you—and yours for Strong Heart."

Now splendidly nude, Elizabeth drifted into Strong Heart's embrace. His flesh quickly warmed hers as he held her and kissed her.

Then he led her to the blankets, spreading her out on top of one, while he drew another blanket over them, so that as they made love, the heat of their bodies would be warmer than the flames of any fire.

Elizabeth's breath quickened with yearning as Strong Heart's lips brushed her throat. His hands moved over her silky, satiny flesh, stroking her, teasing her.

Then he took her mouth by storm and engulfed her in his muscled arms. She trembled with readiness as she felt the probing of his manhood at the juncture of her thighs, then arched and cried out as he drove in, swiftly and surely, his body soon moving against hers.

She absorbed the bold thrusts, his lips drugging her, the intoxication of his kiss, and the caress of his hands, causing her to be overcome by an unbearable, sweet agony that was pressing in on her heart.

When he slithered his lips down her neck, and he flicked a tongue around one nipple, and then the other, she gave herself up to the ecstasy. She clung to him, her fingers grasping his long, wet hair, and then down his back. Then she splayed her fingers against his buttocks and wrapped her legs around his waist and thrust her pelvis toward him, drawing him more deeply into her. He pressed endlessly deeper, his mouth moving back to her lips, their tongues tangling through parted lips. Tremors cascaded down Elizabeth's legs.

Strong Heart paused and looked at her, their eyes locked in an unspoken understanding, and promise of rapture.

Then Strong Heart gathered Elizabeth to him, feeling the pleasure mounting within him, ready to go over the edge.

One last, deep plunge inside her, and the spinning sensation rose up and flooded him. He felt the intensity of his passion exploding through every cell of his body.

A surge of tingling heat spread through Elizabeth. Her head rolled and she emitted a cry of joy as the fire began exploding within her.

Afterward, they clung to each other, breathing hard, sweat pearling their bodies.

"I'm no longer cold," Elizabeth whispered, placing a gentle hand to Strong Heart's cheek. "I feel as if I'm on fire, my darling. What I just experienced with you was agony *and* bliss. How can that be?"

"Who can explain the wonders of the body when in love?" Strong Heart said hoarsely, leaning over to kiss the pink tip of one of her breasts. "Just accept it. Just enjoy it."

"I do love you so," Elizabeth said, snuggling closer to him. Then she gazed up at him and smiled. "Do you think it's time we ate something, then went on to your village?"

Strong Heart smiled back at her and nodded. "*Ah-hah,* it is time," he said, then grabbed her more tightly into his arms and kissed her heatedly, hungrily.

"But first, let us make love again," he whispered to her. "Then, my *la-daila,* I shall give you dry clothes to wear for the rest of the journey. It will not be any that you are used to. You will wear one of my buckskin outfits."

She nodded her approval, then lost herself in sensual frenzy again as he lowered himself onto her and began moving, loving her slowly and leisurely this time.

12

And now on the sky I look,
And my heart grows full of weeping.
—MRS. CRAWFORD

Disgruntled, and his clothes snug after shrinking from riding in the rain, Earl stomped into his house, slamming the large oak door behind him.

Dropping his saddlebags to the floor, he stared down the long corridor that led to the grand staircase, then at the doors which led from the corridor to the other rooms on the lower floor, anxious to find Elizabeth. Had she behaved while he had been gone? The long ride into the wilderness away from her had made him realize just what she meant to him. He had sworn to himself that he would pay more attention to her—make her feel more loved, more wanted. He had lost a wife due to his business concerns. He did not want to lose his daughter's love, as well.

"Elizabeth!" he shouted, smoothing his hands through his golden hair as he began walking down the corridor, toward the staircase, thinking that perhaps she was in her room this time of day, napping or sewing. "Baby, I'm home. Elizabeth, do you hear me? I'm home."

When he got to the foot of the staircase, he heard footsteps above him. He smiled and looked up, expecting Elizabeth to be there, glad to see him home safe and sound.

But his smile quickly faded and his mouth gaped open when he did not find Elizabeth there. Instead, a young lady—a total stranger—stood at the head of the staircase, looking down at him with an awkward smile.

Then Frannie stepped to this stranger's side, herself looking no less nervous as she twisted and untwisted the strings of her lace-trimmed apron as she peered down at him, her eyes wide.

"Frannie, who is that young lady and where is Elizabeth?" Earl demanded. When Frannie did not answer immediately, he began to feel unnerved.

He glanced from the young lady, back to Frannie, then doubled his fists at his sides. "By God, Frannie, explain this lady's presence here. Tell me why Elizabeth is not here to greet me," he said between clenched teeth. "If you have allowed my daughter to leave this house unescorted, so help me, Frannie, you may have to swim all the way back to San Francisco, for I doubt if I would be able to tolerate such foolery from you."

Frannie glanced at Maysie, then with a pounding heart she looked back down at Earl. "This here is Maysie," she said, her voice pitched high from fear. "Elizabeth . . . Elizabeth invited her to stay with us for a while. Our sweet Elizabeth done saved Maysie from drowning in the Sound."

Earl's eyebrows rose. "Drowning?" he said with a gasp. "Elizabeth risked her life for a total stranger? How, Frannie? When?"

Frannie twisted her apron strings more as she cast her eyes to the floor, fearing to tell him the whole truth. What she had told him already had condemned her.

Earl stomped up the stairs and when he reached the second-floor landing, he towered over Frannie and glowered at her. "So help me, Frannie, if you don't tell me what this is all about, I'll horsewhip you," he said, his voice edged with anger and frustration.

He glanced toward Elizabeth's door. It was open and he could see that she was not there.

Then he gave Frannie an uneasy look. "Damn it, Frannie, where is Elizabeth?" he half shouted.

Tears streamed in silver rivulets down Frannie's dark face. She looked slowly back up at Earl. "Massa' Easton, she's gone," she sobbed. "After Maysie here told Elizabeth about the poor women locked up in that prison in Seattle, Elizabeth, with her big heart an' all, she done take books and fruit to them women."

His shock was so keen, Earl had to reach for the bannister to steady himself. He clutched it, speechless for a moment. Then he forced himself not to shout at Frannie again. Right now all that was important was to get answers—answers about his beloved daughter. A frantic, hysterical Frannie would not be able to help.

He placed a trembling hand gently on Frannie's thick shoulder. "Hush up your crying," he said. "I'm not going to ship you off. I'm sorry I frightened you. Now tell me how long Elizabeth has been gone."

Frannie burst into loud wails, shaking her head frantically. "For too long, Massa' Easton," she cried, now looking pitifully up at Earl. "Too long. She left yesterday mornin' and hasn't returned. I sent Everett to look for her. He didn't find her. When he went to the sheriff to see if he'd seen her, the sheriff made no sense. He'd been hit over the head earlier by someone who helped turn the Indian loose from the prison. He was still not talking right when Everett asked him about Elizabeth. Seems no one knows about her, Massa' Easton. Oh, lordy, lordy, what has become of our Elizabeth?"

Earl's face twisted into a grimace, frightened by Frannie's words. There had been an escape at the prison, and the sheriff had been injured during it. If Elizabeth had been there at the time of the escape. . . .

"God," he said beneath his breath, panic filling him. He began running down the stairs. "I'm going to Seattle to find Elizabeth. I've got to. Surely someone's seen her!"

His horse was still saddled from his journey. Earl quickly mounted and sunk his heels into the flanks of the animal. Snapping the reins harshly, he urged the stallion into a hard gallop. Something terrible must have happened to his daughter for her not to have returned home by now. If anything had happened to her because of her foolish do gooding, he would have no one but himself to blame—and he would never forgive himself. He shouldn't have given her cause to be restless. He should have spent more time with her.

And Frannie had said Elizabeth had saved the strange girl

while wandering about the Sound. Who was to say where Elizabeth had wandered in his absence?

His jaw tightened and his eyes became lit with fire. "Damn it, Frannie," he grumbled to himself. "I thought you had more hold on her than that."

But he knew that he could not blame Frannie for any of it. Frannie had tried with all of her might to keep Elizabeth in line. Even in San Francisco, Elizabeth had given him and Frannie fits at times. Frannie had never been unable to stop her. His daughter had a mind of her own. She was even more stubborn than her mother had been.

And that gave Earl much cause for concern.

The ride to Seattle seemed to take forever, but finally he was riding up the steep hill that led to the prison.

When he arrived at the ramshackle building, he dismounted, his eyes locking on the swaying noose on the hanging platform. An involuntary shudder coursed through him at the sight. He had seen many hangings in his lifetime.

But the worst sight of all for him had been when he had been in China. The Chinese did not hang their condemned. Instead, they lined them up in a row in the center of the city, and chopped their heads off.

Shaking the memory from his mind, Earl walked quickly to the prison, and marched into the office. The sheriff was sitting with his feet propped up on the desk. What Earl saw on top of the desk made him pale and feel light-headed.

"Elizabeth's books," he gasped, knowing them well, for he had bought every one of them for her during his travels. He now knew that she *had* been there.

She *had* brought the books to the incarcerated women, as Frannie had said. But what then had happened to her?

"What'd you say about those books?" Sheriff Nolan said, rubbing the raw, aching knot at the base of his skull. "Do you know the woman they belong to?"

Earl sighed heavily as he shifted his gaze to the sheriff. "More to the point," he said dryly, "do *you* know her? Do you recall her being here?"

"Who wants to know?" Sheriff Nolan asked, rising slowly

from his chair. He ambled out from behind the desk and stood eye to eye with Earl.

Earl squared his shoulders. "I'm her father," he said, leaning his face into the sheriff's, repulsed by the foul odor of chewing tobacco and rotgut whiskey. "Now you tell me. Where is she? She didn't make it back home after comin' here with her books."

"Oh? Is that a fact?" Sheriff Nolan said, resting his hands on the handles of his pistols at each hip. "Describe this daughter to me and I'll tell you whether or not she's been here."

"Damn it, Sheriff, I already know she's been here," Earl said. He nodded toward the books. "Those are hers. You don't look like the sort that reads, or pays for books."

Sheriff Nolan shrugged and went to his desk, lifting up a book and slowly turning the pages. "She's an educated redhead, is she?" he asked. He recalled yanking her basket from her and wrestling her to the floor. Right after, he had been knocked unconscious. Ever since he had regained consciousness he had thought of hardly anything else but the redhead and that she had probably participated in the escape. She had been the distraction, and it sure as hell had worked.

Sheriff Nolan quickly decided not to let Earl in on his assumptions about Elizabeth. He had his own score to settle with the slut.

"So you *did* see my daughter?" Earl said, impatient with the sheriff's vagueness.

"Yeah, guess I did at that," Sheriff Nolan grumbled, slamming the book back down on his desk. "But that was short-lived. Soon after our introduction, someone knocked me out." He shrugged. "As far as I can figure, she's been taken captive by whoever hit me and set the Injun loose from his cell. Yeah, that's how I see it."

On hearing the sheriff say that Elizabeth had been abducted, the reality of the situation hit Earl hard. It was as if someone had slapped him across the face. He tottered, feeling a sudden queasiness. His sweet, his precious daughter's life was at the mercy of hardened criminals, one of them an Indian condemned to die!

It was hard for him to bear—the possibility of having lost his daughter forever.

Then he came to his senses, realizing that something had to be done.

A posse. Yes, a posse had to be formed. Why was the sheriff here when Elizabeth had to be found?

The sheriff moved behind the desk again and slouched down into his chair. He reached for a fresh plug of chewing tobacco and bit off a large wad, stuffing it into one corner of his mouth.

Earl had to work hard at controlling his temper at the sheriff's indifference. He leaned his hands on the desk and looked the sheriff square in the eye. "You say my daughter has been abducted and you just sit there twiddling your thumbs and chewin' that damn tobacco?" he said, his voice cold and steady. "Am I to expect nothing more from you? You allow an innocent girl to be abducted and you talk about it as if it is something that happens every day, and nothing to concern your ass about?"

"I wouldn't get myself riled up too much before knowing everything," Sheriff Nolan said, turning his head, to spit a long stream of tobacco juice into the stained spittoon. "There's a posse out there somewhere busy lookin' for the criminals, *and* your daughter. That's all that can be done at this point."

The sheriff leaned his elbows on the desk. "Now I'd suggest you go home and wait for the posse's return. Do you get my meaning? There ain't nothin' you can do here, 'cept get me riled, and I don't think you want to get me riled, eh? What did you say your name was?"

"I didn't," Earl said through clenched teeth, his eyes narrowed with anger.

"A name is needed if you want to know the results of the posse's findings," Sheriff Nolan said, smiling crookedly up at Earl, enjoying his fooling with the man. If the redhead *was* found, safe and sound, her father would be the last to know. Jed would take his turn with her before her father had a chance to even realize that she was alive. What he had planned for her would not paint a pretty picture.

She was worse than the outlaw who had been set free from the prison. She was a whoring seductress who had made a fool out of him. And no woman made a jackass out of Sheriff Jed Nolan and lived to tell it, he thought darkly to himself.

Earl wasn't quick to respond to the sheriff's command, seeing too much about the man that did not ring true. He seemed an untrustworthy sort. Earl was amazed that such a man had been elected to be sheriff.

Yet too often in bawdy seaport towns, these were the kind of men in power that he had run into. And he had no choice but to trust that this lawman would do right by his daughter.

"My daughter's name is Elizabeth," Earl said, his voice guarded. "Elizabeth Easton." He reached a hand to the sheriff. "I'm new in town. I'm establishing a fishery down the Sound a mile or two. At the old Pike Mansion. I'm sure you've heard about it. I'm Earl Easton."

Before accepting Earl's handshake, Sheriff Nolan turned to the spittoon and spat out another long stream of juice.

He wiped his mouth and mustache on the back of his right hand, then offered it to Earl. "Nice to make your acquaintance," he said, chuckling beneath his breath when he saw Earl grimace as he took the hand with traces of tobacco juice on the fingers.

Earl wiped his hand on the leg of his pants, then glowered down at the sheriff. "I'll be waitin' to hear from you," he warned. "If I don't hear soon, I'll take out after the damn outlaws myself."

"That wouldn't be wise," Sheriff Nolan said, placing his fingertips together before him. "You'd just complicate things. Let the professionals do the job. You just get back to your fishery. I'll send word as soon as I know."

Hesitating, yet knowing that he was only one man and did not know the countryside as well as those who made a living hunting outlaws, Earl nodded and left the prison.

With a heavy heart, he mounted his stallion and headed back for home. His thoughts were on Elizabeth, and how it had been between them through the years—how he had been the one to hold back on love.

It was her mother's fault. If Marilyn had not fled to parts unknown, Earl would not have had the need to reject his daughter.

He hung his head. He knew that he should hate his wife for having deserted him, yet he knew that he was the cause. Just as now, as he was the cause for his daughter's life to be in peril.

Before he realized it, he was home. The miles had been eaten up while his mind had been absorbed by thoughts of the past and the future.

He gave his horse's reins to Everett. Then he went inside the house, where he was met by an anxious Frannie.

"Elizabeth?" Frannie said, her eyes wide as she followed Earl toward the parlor. "Do you know any more about Elizabeth?"

Earl stopped and turned and gave her a watery stare. "As far as anyone can tell, she's been abducted," he said, his voice breaking.

Maysie stepped beside Frannie, just in time to hear the disheartening news. Her knees grew weak and she felt a desperation rising within her. Guilt pressed on her heart.

"No!" she cried, placing her hands to her cheeks, tears flooding her eyes. "Elizabeth has been abducted? No! Please, no! Oh, God, I'm to blame. If I'd never told Elizabeth about the women at the prison, she'd have not gone there! Who abducted her? Who?"

"Apparently the man who set the Indian free from prison," Earl said. Then he took a step toward Maysie and glared down at her. "And, yes, young lady, you *are* to blame. If not for you, my daughter would be home now, *safe*!"

Maysie stared up at Earl with stricken eyes. Then she bolted up the steep staircase, wailing distraughtly.

Frannie went after her, also wailing.

Earl hung his head, and went into the parlor. He walked lifelessly to a window and drew the sheer curtain aside, staring into the trees.

His beloved daughter. Where was she?

He tried to distract himself from his anguish with other

thoughts. He knew he must go back to the Suquamish Indian village. He had to convince them that what he offered was for their best interest, as well as his own.

"My fishery," he muttered to himself.

He wondered how he could make plans for the future now, when he did not know if it would include his daughter?

He was ridden with guilt for having neglected her.

First his wife, and now his daughter.

He had never been a God-fearing man. But now he could not help but think that God was punishing him for all of his transgressions against humanity, especially his own kin.

13

Ah!—With what thankless heart
I mourn and sing!

—Barry Cornwall

The sun was splashing the sky a brilliant crimson as it lowered behind the mountains in the far distance. Elizabeth sat in the saddle behind Strong Heart, clinging to his waist, apprehensive about soon entering his village and meeting his people, especially his parents. She knew Strong Heart's bitterness over white people well enough. Surely his people's feelings were even stronger against white people.

If so, they would not take to their chief's son having fallen in love with a white-skinned woman. Her mere presence might make life awkward for Strong Heart, and that was the last thing that she wanted.

Yet he was strong willed. Perhaps he would overlook any resentment toward her.

She glanced down at her clothing. The fringed buckskin outfit fit her loosely. A rope around her waist held the breeches up. She had rolled up the legs so that she would not trip over them as she walked, and she had rolled up the sleeves of the shirt to her elbows.

Although she knew that she must look comical, at least it had made traveling on horseback with Strong Heart more tolerable.

Strong Heart noticed hawks circling in the air up ahead. They must surely be flying above his village. It would soon be within sight once they rode up a slight butte. His roan's footing was sure on the loose and crumbling rock.

His keen senses picked up a faint odor of smoke and ash, sending a warning to him that all was not right.

He surveyed the soaring hawks, realizing that they only flew like this in a group, if death was on the trail. Or in a village, he thought grimly.

Elizabeth could feel how Strong Heart's muscles had suddenly tensed. His breathing had quickened and he was concentrating strangely on several hawks in the sky.

"What is it, Strong Heart?" she asked, clutching even more tightly around his waist as he kicked his moccasined heels into the flanks of his horse and sent it up the rise, to the top.

Strong Heart had not heard Elizabeth. All that he heard was the crying of his heart as he peered down and saw the destruction of so much of his village. Half of its cedar homes had been burned to the ground. The burnt totem poles listed crazily. The sight chilled his blood.

The devastation was everywhere.

He could see the people of his village roaming about, their heads bowed, their wails reaching clear into his soul. While he was gone, tending to his own affairs, his village had caught fire, somehow. And by the sound of the wailing, several of his people had died.

"Mother!" he gasped. "Father! Are *they* alright? *Aieee,*" he cried with a shrill yelp, sending his horse into a hard gallop toward the remains of his village.

When he arrived, he dismounted in one leap, and forgetting Elizabeth, began running toward his father's longhouse. It still stood proud and untouched by the ravages of the fire that had swept through the village.

As he continued to run, he also saw that *his* longhouse still stood, saved by the people who loved him and his parents so much. They had probably allowed their own dwellings to burn in order to save their chief's, and the one who would next be chief.

He was followed by many people who reached out for him, crying his name. Strong Heart did not stop until he came to the entrance of his parents' lodge. Then he hurried inside.

What he saw made him teeter, for his father was lying on his sleeping platform, his eyes closed, otter fur pelts drawn up to his chin. "Father," he cried out, rushing to kneel beside the sleeping platform. He could not understand how his father had been harmed when his dwelling had been saved. Unless, unless, being the kindhearted man that he was, he had gone to help the others, and perhaps falling debris had struck him.

Strong Heart's mother came into the longhouse with a jug of water balanced on her shoulder. When she saw Strong Heart, she sat the jug down and went to kneel beside him.

When Strong Heart felt her presence, he turned to her and, with tears splashing from his eyes, he quickly embraced her. "You were not hurt by the fire?" he asked, holding her tightly to him, her usual scent of sweet grasses now ruined by the stink of smoke.

"Your mother is well enough," Pretty Nose murmured, then coughed fitfully. She eased from Strong Heart's arms and covered her mouth with her hands, continuing to cough until she was red in the face.

When she finally stopped, she cleared her throat and gazed sadly up at her son. "The smoke," she said hoarsely. "It entered my lungs. Still I cannot rid myself of the burning feeling left by the smoke."

Strong Heart stared with pain for a moment at his frail mother. Then he looked at his father again, whose eyes were now open, watching Strong Heart. When his father's hand reached out, Strong Heart circled his fingers around it and clung to it.

"My father, how are you?" Strong Heart said, seeing much pain in his father's eyes. He wanted to believe that part of that pain was from the loss of some of his beloved people, and the devastation the fire had caused.

"Your father has a heavy heart," Chief Moon Elk mumbled. "So much hope was taken from me yesterday."

"Yesterday?" Strong Heart said, recalling the fierceness of the thunderstorm as he and Elizabeth had clung to one another beneath the protection of their tent. "You say this happened yesterday. Was it lightning, Father, that caused the fire?"

"No, not lightning," Chief Moon Elk said somberly. "The fire was set by—"

Chief Moon Elk stopped in mid-sentence and looked

fiercely into Strong Heart's eyes. "Four Winds?" he asked, his voice low and threatening. "You set him free? He is free to roam and do as he pleases now?"

"*Ah-hah,* that is so," Strong Heart said, puzzled by his father asking about Four Winds. What could Four Winds have to do with the fire?

If it had not been started by lightning, then by what? Or by whom?

"He is with you now? He has come to our village before riding on to his village in Canada?" Chief Moon Elk asked suspiciously.

"No, he did not come here. Once free, he rode separate from me," he said. His eyes widened when he remembered that, in his haste to check on the welfare of his parents, he had left Elizabeth alone. He wanted to rush to her now, but the matters of his people came first. Especially now that so much *me-sah-chie,* bad, had befallen them.

"That is as I thought," Chief Moon Elk grumbled, turning slowly away from Strong Heart. "He was probably among those who came and ravished our village. He was not recognized, but it was renegades like Four Winds who rode side by side with the white men as they tossed torches on our people's dwellings. They sent many of our people to their deaths with sprays of arrows and bullets."

Chief Moon Elk's eyes flashed with anger as he threw aside the otter fur pelts, and revealed a gunshot wound in his right leg. "Four Winds may have even sent the bullet into your father's leg!" he shouted.

Strong Heart sat there, aghast and speechless over what had happened while he had been gone. Chief Moon Elk drew the pelts back in place again and turned his eyes from Strong Heart.

"My son, you should have let the white man hang Four Winds," he said bitterly. "Four Winds is *me-sah-chie,* to the core!"

Pretty Nose placed a gentle hand on Strong Heart's arm. "My son, it is best now that you let your father rest. His wound has been treated well enough by me, but his heart—it still pains him, terribly."

She flung herself into Strong Heart's arms. "My son, it is so good that you are home again," she cried. "Pay no heed to your father's anger about Four Winds. I believe that you would not have allowed him to be set free just to come and harm us. I truly do not believe that Four Winds had any part in the attack on our people. It is just someone for your father to blame, so that he does not feel so to blame, himself, for our tragedy."

Strong Heart held his mother close. "If anyone is to blame," he said thickly, "it is I. I should have been home, protecting our people, instead of—"

He closed his eyes tightly, trying to block out thoughts of where he had probably been at the very moment of the attack. In Elizabeth's arms, his people and their concerns far, far from his mind. While he was making love to his *la-daila,* his people had needed him.

And he had not been there for them.

Pretty Nose pulled away from Strong Heart and peered up at him. "My son, you are only one person," she tried to reassure him. "You cannot be everywhere at once. No one expects you to be." She paused, then added, "While in Seattle, you did not find your grandfather? He is dead, is he not, my son? Your grandfather is surely dead!"

Strong Heart held her face between his powerful hands and leaned down and kissed her on her pert nose. "I searched and I did not find," he said. "But I do not allow myself to think that he is dead. I shall return to Seattle when I can, and search again, Mother."

Then his thoughts flew again to Elizabeth, seeing her sitting on the horse, afraid, as his people surrounded her. Perhaps they had even pulled her from the horse. She was white. And white men, accompanied by Indian renegades, had only yesterday come to their village and wreaked havoc in their lives! They could suspect her because her skin was white.

Without further words, Strong Heart left the longhouse at a run, then stopped in dismay when he did not find Elizabeth anywhere. His heart pounded as he looked in all directions. Seeing his longhouse, he wondered if she could be there.

With swift strides, Strong Heart went to his longhouse. He

found Elizabeth inside sitting beside a fire. There was even a pot of soup hanging over it.

Strong Heart's eyes went to the Indian who was kneeling beside the fire, slowly stirring the soup. It was Many Stars, a lovely, petite Suquamish maiden who served Chief Moon Elk and his son devotedly. Although the same age as Strong Heart, she had been widowed twice. She now spent her time helping others, warding off any man's attempt to court her. She had declared that she would never love again. She had experienced the pain of too many losses already.

When Elizabeth saw Strong Heart standing in the doorway, she bolted to her feet and ran to him. She flung herself into his arms and clung to him. "Thank God you've come. If not for Many Stars, I may have been slain. She grabbed me away from several of your people. They see me as the enemy, Strong Heart. They hate me."

Many Stars smiled up at Strong Heart. "It was just a few who reacted foolishly to seeing Elizabeth on your horse," she said, rising to her feet, her eyes as dark as midnight as she gazed up at Strong Heart. "I guessed she was your woman since she was riding on your horse, and wearing your clothes. I brought her to your lodge. I knew that was what you would want."

Strong Heart reached a hand to Many Stars's soft, copper cheek. "*Mah-sie,* thank you," he said softly. She was comely as always, in her mountain sheepskin dress that was beautifully ornamented with quill beads. Her hair was neatly plaited in large braids that hung down over her breasts. "Now return to your parents. Help them build a new dwelling. I saw that their longhouse was among those that burned, yet I was thankful to see that your parents were among the survivors."

Many Stars nodded. "*Ah-hah,* they survived and I will return to my chores alongside them. We were the lucky ones. We still have one another, while others have lost loved ones."

Guilt flooded Strong Heart's heart again, for having not been there to look after the welfare of his people.

Yet he felt blessed that it had not been worse than it was. All of the village could have been destroyed and all of his people could be dead.

His thoughts went to Four Winds, also wondering about his innocence or guilt in this. Yet it was just not logical to think that Four Winds would repay Strong Heart in such a way for having helped him to escape from the prison.

No. Four Winds could have had nothing to do with this. Strong Heart would keep that thought while trying to find out who *did*.

"Go with care," Strong Heart said to Many Stars as she slipped outside.

Elizabeth eased from Strong Heart's arms. "Your parents?" she queried softly. "Are they all right?"

"Both are alive, but my father lies with a leg wound."

"I'm sorry about your father," Elizabeth responded. "I hope it's not serious."

"In time he will walk again," Strong Heart said sourly. "But for now, when he is needed the most by his people, he is incapacitated. He needs my leadership now. I will lend it to him to lessen his burden. I will be his legs. I will be everything for him."

"How can I help?" Elizabeth asked, almost afraid to hear the answer. For that brief moment, when her life had been threatened by those few Suquamish, she had seen just how much she could be resented by the Indians. In truth, she was quite shaken by the incident. But for Strong Heart, in his time of need, she would have to brush her fear aside.

"It is perhaps best if you return to Seattle," Strong Heart said. Saying this to her made it feel as if a knife were cutting into his heart, for he never wanted to let her go. But for now, he had to put his people before his needs.

Elizabeth paled. "You no longer want me?" she said, gasping. "Now that I want to be with you . . . you will send me away?"

Strong Heart softly held her shoulders. "My *la-daila,* I have much to make right in my world. That includes *you.* I should have never taken you against your will. You are free to go. And I have much to do. I must help set things right for my people. And I trust you now, my *la-daila*. I know that you would never lift an accusing finger at me. I know that you love me too much to ever want harm to come to me."

"If you know that I love you, and I know that you love me, why then do you still send me away?" she pleaded.

Strong Heart placed a finger to her lips to silence her. "Listen to what I have to say," he said quietly. "*Ah-hah,* our love is strong between us. But there is more in life, than love between man and woman. I have always aspired to match the deeds of my father. I have spent much of my time hunting, fishing, wrestling, and swimming—preparing my mind and body for a worthy life, the life of a *leader.* So many of my people are now in their death sleeps due to the vile actions of the renegades and outlaws. I must guide those who are still alive!"

He paused, then added, "I must see to my people's burials, then go and try to find the ones responsible for the raid and deaths. Then I must help prepare my people for the salmon harvest."

Elizabeth was reminded of her father, and what he had planned for the salmon run. She suddenly felt protective of Strong Heart and his people, not wanting her father to come *here* with his hopes for his fishery! These people had already suffered enough at the hands of intruders.

"I would like to stay and help you in any way that I can," Elizabeth reasoned. "There are many ways that I could help. And, darling, must I remind you that if I do return home, it would be as you had earlier worried—the sheriff could come to me and question me about what had happened. He would order me to describe the man who had knocked him unconscious. The sheriff surely knows that I had to have seen you. And how could I explain my absence—where I have been since then? And with whom?"

The memory of the hanging platform was embedded in her mind. She must, at all costs, make sure that Strong Heart was never accused of any crime. She knew that the hangman's noose was always ready for the neck of an Indian, no matter if they were guilty or innocent.

Strong Heart nodded. "*Ah-hah,* what you say is true. It is

best that you stay. I will welcome anything that you might do to help lessen the burden of this grief."

"Thank you, darling, for allowing it," Elizabeth said.

But Strong Heart's mind was elsewhere. It seethed with anger at who might have done this thing to his people. His tribe lived separate from others because they wanted to live in peace.

Strong Heart pulled Elizabeth close to him. She could feel his sorrow and anger lessening, and she was glad. She knew that he had to be strong to live through the days ahead as he buried so many of his people and guided the living toward hope again.

"Such pain burns within my heart," Strong Heart whispered to Elizabeth, his voice choked with despair.

"My darling," Elizabeth comforted him. "My poor, sweet darling. I'm so sorry about everything. So very, very sorry."

* * *

As Earl stood dejectedly at the window in his new office in his fishery, he almost did not hear someone enter. When he looked up and found Morris there, his eyes narrowed in anger.

"Where the hell have you been?" he yelled. "Why has it taken you so long to get back here to see to business? We're partners, or do you find that hard to remember?"

"You'd better hope I never decide to forget," Morris said, coming to the desk and running his hands over the smooth texture of the oak finish. "I'd say my money even paid for this desk, wouldn't you?"

Earl's face flushed. He tried to ignore the constant reminders that Morris offered of who did not have the money to back this project and who did.

"How's it all look to you?" Earl asked, shaking off his anger and his worry about Elizabeth.

Morris sat down behind the desk, as if he belonged there. He smiled smugly up at Earl. "I'd say it's as fine as it ever will be," he said, chuckling. "And don't you worry about Chief Moon Elk either. Things have turned around in our favor. Let's go full speed ahead with the fishery. We'll wait a few days and go and talk with the chief again. He'll place his 'x' on the dotted line. I'm sure of it."

Earl lifted an eyebrow, wondering exactly what Morris would do to convince the chief, yet his thoughts were interrupted by a sight from the window of the office. He saw Maysie riding at the back of a wagon that was headed into Seattle.

He smiled to himself. Maybe she was gone for good. He hoped.

"And how's Elizabeth?" Morris asked, rising from the chair, to place an arm around Earl's shoulder.

Earl looked at Morris. The empty feeling rushed back. He had no answers at all about his darling Elizabeth.

* * *

Maysie clung to the wagon as it rattled along the dirt road. She had gotten permission from Everett to go with him into Seattle. Unable to bear being at Elizabeth's house in her absence and feeling guilty because of it, Maysie had decided to leave. She didn't believe that Elizabeth would ever return. She had been gone for too long. There were too many wicked men in the world to believe Elizabeth would come out of this abduction alive.

She sat listlessly on the tailgate of the wagon, wondering how she was going to live. It was better to die than to return to her former life! She could walk into the Sound right now, and no one would save her. She would not allow it!

Making her decision, she jumped from the wagon and ran toward the crashing waves of the Sound. She walked into the water without looking back. But again a voice yelling to her caused her to stop. She remembered how Elizabeth had yelled at her, and had then risked her life to save her.

She could not resist turning around, to see if it could possibly be Elizabeth.

The sky was darkening overhead, dusk coming on, so Maysie could not tell whether or not it was Elizabeth. But the hair coloring of the lady standing beside a fancy carriage was identical.

Hoping that somehow Elizabeth *was* there, safe and sound, Maysie worked her way back to the shore. She walked, breathlessly toward the road. The lady came forward to meet her.

"Child, why on earth would you want to kill yourself?" the woman fussed, lifting her shawl from her own shoulders and placing it around Maysie's. "You come with me. Let me get you warmed at my house and then we can talk this over."

Maysie was disappointed that she wasn't Elizabeth. But she was stunned by the resemblance. This lady was as beautiful as Elizabeth. Her hair was stunningly red. Her eyes were a soft captivating green. Their faces were almost identical, yet this lady had to be at least twenty years older than Elizabeth.

No matter how much Maysie wanted it to be Elizabeth, she had to accept that someone besides Elizabeth had saved her this time. She couldn't find it in herself to try again. And this lady seemed just as kind as Elizabeth.

The woman placed an arm around Maysie's tiny waist and led her to the fancy carriage, helping her inside. Once they settled on the plush cushions, the woman commanded the driver to return to her house "promptly."

Maysie shivered and accepted a blanket around her shoulders. "You are way too kind," she said, her teeth chattering. "Thank you."

"My name is Marilyn," the woman said softly, smoothing a stray lock of dark hair back from Maysie's brow. "Care to tell me yours?"

Feeling that she could trust this lady, Maysie replied, "Maysie. You can call me Maysie."

"Well, Maysie, it's good to make your acquaintance." Marilyn ran her hand down her fully gathered, silk dress. Its shade of green matched her hat trimmed with flowers at the brim.

Maysie smiled meekly at Marilyn. Then, so quickly it seemed, the buggy had come to a halt. "We're at my house," Marilyn announced, nodding a thank you to the driver as he opened the door and stepped aside. "Come. Let's see to getting you warmed."

Maysie started to leave the carriage, then stopped in confusion when she recognized the mansion. She remembered it well from when she had envied those women who worked there instead of in the tawdry places along the waterfront. She had heard that this brothel was the best in Seattle, its furnishings and its women breathtakingly beautiful.

But she no longer wanted such a life. Not after having met Elizabeth, and seeing her wholesomeness.

No. She would definitely die first!

"Why do you hesitate?" Marilyn asked, drawing Maysie's attention.

"Ma'am I don't want no part of a brothel," Maysie said, swallowing hard.

"Yes, I do manage a brothel," Marilyn said, placing a gloved hand to Maysie's cheek. "But that doesn't mean that you have to work in it just because I bring you here to make you warm and comfortable. You don't have to do anything you don't want to."

Marilyn gazed admiringly at Maysie's well-endowed figure, then at her angelic face. This young lady could bring top dollar from the men callers.

But Marilyn would never force this life on anyone—a life that even she did not totally approve of. She, herself, no longer took gentlemen to her bed. She supervised, only supervised.

"If you are sure," Maysie said, still hesitating.

Marilyn drew her gently into her arms and gave her a motherly hug. "Positive," she murmured. "Absolutely positive."

Maysie clung to Marilyn, her eyes filling with tears, grateful, yet afraid to totally trust again.

14

How many days, thou dove,
Hast thou been mine?
—Barry Cornwall

It was late afternoon. The sun dipped low in the sky as the muffled beat of ceremonial drums filled the air. The burial rites for the Suquamish dead had just begun. The survivors of the massacre stood on a butte that rose high over the Duwamish River. The cremated remains of the many dead were in one large communal jar. Some would be tossed into the river; the rest would be spread across the land.

Attired in a fringed buckskin dress decorated with seashells that Many Stars had sweetly lent her, Elizabeth stood among the Indians, with Strong Heart's sanction.

She had felt awkward until Many Stars had come to stand by her to give her moral support. Elizabeth gave Many Stars a grateful glance.

Elizabeth did not think that the lovely maiden was befriending her only because Strong Heart wanted her to. Many Stars sincerely seemed to care for her, even though Elizabeth was white-skinned, and red-haired, and quite different from anyone Many Stars had ever known.

Elizabeth gave Many Stars a warm smile. She was warmed through and through when Many Stars smiled generously back at her. At this moment, Elizabeth could feel that she belonged in this new world, in this new place with its foreign customs.

Chief Moon Elk was carried through the throng of people, his wife walking beside him, and carefully placed on a pallet of furs at the front of the assembly. Elizabeth could see Pretty Nose's devotion to her husband as she made sure he was completely covered by the furs before settling down beside him.

Elizabeth swallowed hard as she stared at Chief Moon Elk's wounded leg as he eased it from beneath the furs and stretched it out before him. His wound was covered with some sort of ointment that was green in color. Elizabeth hoped that it would heal quickly. At least then there would be one less burden that Strong Heart would have to carry.

When Strong Heart stepped before the crowd of silent people, Elizabeth melted inside at his noble appearance. A robe of sea otter pelts was hung from his broad shoulders. It did not hide the heavily beaded, fringed shirt that he wore beneath, nor the leg bands of shredded bark that were twisted about his fringed breeches.

When he began speaking from the heart to his people, his father and mother looked proudly up at their son. Elizabeth recalled what Strong Heart had told her just before the burial ceremony.

He had told her that today's ceremony was not the usual kind for those who had died. Today there were too many dead to eulogize individually.

And since most of the deceaseds' houses had been burned during the raid, it was impossible to perform a main part of the ceremony.

Under normal circumstances, the individual bodies would have been first wrapped in cedar-bark mats for burial. The relatives, torn between grief and fear of his ghost, would have removed the body from the house as soon after death as possible. The exit of the body was through a hole specially made in the wall so that the living would not have to follow the path of the dead as they walked in and out through the main door.

The body would then be placed in a canoe that was usually raised off the ground on a scaffolding, or placed in the limbs of a tall tree. The bow always pointed toward the setting sun which would light the way for the dead. The personal possessions would be placed with the dead or burned.

"Do you hear Strong Heart and what he says?" Many Stars whispered as she leaned closer to Elizabeth, her English quite proficient. The tribe had dealt with white men for many years. "He will one day make a great chief. I have known him since we were children together. Neither of us had brothers or sisters. I became his sister. He became my brother. I watched him as a boy. He out ran, out swam, and out wrestled all of his playmates. He also spoke well before people. Even when he was only fifteen winters of age, he practiced the art of speaking well. Then many of his speeches were devoted to restraining our people and allies from declaring war on the settlers. Today he again speaks to his people, sad though it is that he must."

Many Stars took Elizabeth by the hand. Elizabeth felt their bond of friendship strengthening. She squeezed Many Stars's hand in response. Many Stars further encouraged, "Listen to this man whose heart you now hold within your soul. Listen well, and you then will see how lucky you are that he has chosen you to be his *la-daila.*"

Feeling so grateful for so much, and at the same time feeling sad for these people and their losses, Elizabeth could not stop tears from springing in her eyes. She gazed proudly at Strong Heart. His words, translated by Many Stars, touched her deeply. He was skilled at making it seem that he was speaking to each individually.

She had never seen this side of her beloved. She felt filled with more love than she ever thought possible.

She leaned forward and soaked up his every gesture. The ceremonial drum still beat softly somewhere behind her. Many Stars's voice murmured in her ear.

"My people, the spirits of our dead have drifted onward, to the 'Land of the Dead,' " Strong Heart was saying. "What remains here with us today are pure white ashes, the essence of the good in those who have gone on before us. I shall fling the ashes to the winds and the waters. I shall scatter them on the rocks, the pines, the ferns, the sands, and the wild flowers. Forevermore, they will blend with the things that we all love so well. Would we not all want the spring rains to bathe us? To awaken to the fragrance of the forest, to the call of the birds from out of the sky, and to the lapping lullaby of the river? Would we not want to experience forever the leap of the frog and fish in the stillness of the dawn?"

He paused and smiled from person to person, stopping

longer at his parents. Then he shifted his eyes slowly to Elizabeth, causing her heart to lurch as she met his steady, loving gaze.

Then he continued his speech, still commanding complete silence from his people. "Our departed loved ones will still be warmed by the summer sun. Be as one to the joy of life and love, to the wonders of a canoe skimming between towering bluffs crowned with emerald and jade. They will still be able to experience the thrill of swimming in golden waters, surrounded by the trees and rock giants, and to know the serenity of twilight, and the infinite mysteries of night. It is with these thoughts that you watch as I scatter the ashes. Then your grief will be lifted to the sky, along with the spirits of those who have loved you while living."

Elizabeth's eyes widened as she watched Strong Heart reach into the white ashes. She sucked in a wild breath of air as he released the ashes into the river. Then he began walking along the bluff, spreading the ashes onto blossoming wild flowers, along the granite rock, the green grass, and into a brook that flowed down the sides of the bluff.

When the ashes were all scattered, Elizabeth stood mute as everyone returned to their dwellings, except for Strong Heart. He removed his sea otter robe, and dove into the Duwamish River, looking like a graceful eagle as he soared through the air, splashing into the sparkling clear waters.

Preoccupied with watching Strong Heart swimming masterfully in the water, Elizabeth did not hear the soft footsteps behind her. When a hand touched hers, she turned with a start, then swallowed hard when she found Strong Heart's mother standing there.

"My son will be a while," Pretty Nose said, glancing down from the bluff, watching Strong Heart taking wide and even strokes as he swam in the bone-chilling waters of the river. "He is saying his last good-byes to those whose ashes are now a part of the river. It is his farewell to friends and comrades. Come. Let him do this without an audience."

Elizabeth blushed, now thinking that she had been intruding on a private ritual. "I'm sorry," Elizabeth apologized. "I . . . I didn't know."

"No one expected you to," Pretty Nose said, urging Elizabeth to walk beside her as she moved slowly down the slope toward the village. "It is true that your customs differ much from ours. If you stay among us, you will learn quickly enough, for my son is a great teacher of many things."

Elizabeth was in awe of the kindness of these people, after having recently suffered so much at the hands of their enemies.

But she knew that Strong Heart had spoken with his mother and father about her, which might have made their acceptance of her more coerced than actual.

Elizabeth went with Pretty Nose to the longhouse of the chief and accepted a place beside where the lodge fire was blazing. Gazing across the fire at Chief Moon Elk who reclined on the platform piled comfortably with pelts, she smiled weakly as he offered her no more than a nod of welcome.

She then eased down onto a pillow pad of shredded bark. With a quiet nod of thank you, she accepted a *makuk* of roasted fish that Pretty Nose had taken from a flat tray of wood.

With a large bone spoon, Elizabeth attempted to eat the fish. She wished that she had a fork, which would have made it much simpler.

Pretty Nose sat down beside her and began eagerly eating. Elizabeth attempted to continue eating, but her heart wasn't in it. Today's rites had made her hunger wane. All that she wanted was to be with Strong Heart—to have his comforting arms around her again. Only then could she for at least a little while forget the savagery that had been done against his people.

She looked around her, examining the way in which the chief and his wife lived. It was quite simple, yet much better than she would have expected the Indians to live. The household furnishings were made of wood, or woven of cedar bark. She could see masks and ritual paraphernalia hanging on the walls. There were furs and clothing, trade blankets, and prized oils rendered from candlefish and whale blubber stored on low shelves.

At the far end of the large room, a rolled-up skin curtain

revealed a large bunk covered with several layers of furs and blankets of mountain goat wool. Bladders of whale oil, and long strings of *hiaqua* shells, considered money here, hung from the overhead rafters.

There were crest designs painted on everything, like the ones she had seen carved on the totem poles outside. Even the troughlike dishes, hollowed out from blocks of alder, were painted with these designs.

Elizabeth's attention flew quickly to the door when Strong Heart came into the longhouse, dressed in only a breechcloth.

He came to her and held out a hand, beckoning for her to come to him. She lay down the large wooden dish and took his hand, inhaling the heady fragrance of pine emanating from his muscled body. Strong Heart had dried himself with pine needles and the smell clung wonderfully to him.

Strong Heart offered his parents only a silent nod each, then walked with Elizabeth out of their longhouse to his.

After they were inside the privacy of his dwelling, Elizabeth noticed that the lodge was lit not only by the fire in the firepit, but also by several "candlefish," that were so rich in oil that a dried one with a wick threaded through it burned like a candle for hours.

Many Stars had been there in their absence. Clean grass had been spread on the floor and over this, rugs of rawhide were thrown, hair side up. Soft buckskin pillows with cottonwood floss lay beside the fire, and painted bags and clothes containers decorated with brightly hued quillwork hung against the walls of the home.

"The day was long," Strong Heart said, stroking Elizabeth's cheek with his hand. "The day was hard. But now it is night, and the night belongs to you and me. Love me, my *la-daila,* so that I may only think of now—of us. Today was sad. It is hard to shake away the sadness. Except with you, my *la-daila*. Except with you."

Overwhelmed by the joy of being with him again, his eyes mesmerizing her anew, Elizabeth stepped away from him and slowly began undressing herself. She watched with a tremulous excitement as he also began undressing.

When they were both nude, their hands reached out and touched, and caressed. Elizabeth crept closer and molded her body against his as he held her and lowered her to a thick bed of pelts beside the fire.

As Elizabeth lay there, Strong Heart leaning over her, she ran her fingers over his finely chiseled copper face, along his bold nose, his strong chin, and the line of his hard jaw.

She then ran her fingers over his wide shoulders, across the expanse of his sleekly muscled chest, and then smoothed her hands down and across his hard and flat stomach.

As she smiled up at him, she found his eyes smoky and dangerous, as her hand paused before going on. She could already feel the throbbing hardness of his shaft as it lay thick and heavy against her thigh, and to go on with her exploration of his body meant that was the place to touch next. She was reminded of the other time that she had touched it, and how it had felt the moment he had pressed it inside her.

The pain had been brief. The pleasure had been blissful.

"You stop now?" Strong Heart said, his eyes dancing. "You have yet to touch the center of my passion, and you stop?"

"A part of me is almost afraid to," Elizabeth murmured, her face flushing with a building arousal as Strong Heart cupped one of her breasts and circled his thumb around her taut nipple. "I'm not sure if I can stand such rapture again, Strong Heart. It stole not only my breath away, but also my senses. Surely there is danger in that."

"The only danger is in not answering the need that I have awakened inside you," Strong Heart said, his hand leaving a heated path in its wake as it moved from her breasts, across her stomach, causing her body to tremble with pleasure. Then his hand reached the juncture of her thighs where he began stroking her.

When he thrust a finger inside her, he smiled at how she moaned and how her eyes rolled with the pleasure. "Never deny yourself this that I so freely offer you," he said huskily. "Who is to say what tomorrow brings? Did you not see how quickly life was snuffed from those whose ashes I spread today? One can never be certain of tomorrow. So it is only right to take from life today, as it is being offered you."

Elizabeth's head swam as he lowered his lips to hers and gave her a fiery kiss. She returned the kiss and moaned against his lips as she felt the thrust of his hardness as he entered her, and then arched her hips to meet his steady strokes within her. His mouth urged her lips open as his kiss grew more passionate and demanding, his fingers teasing and stroking the supple lines of her body.

Her world melted away as his fingers moved purposely slow in circles around one of her breasts, then swept down her spine in a soft massage.

Elizabeth's pleasure bubbled from deep within as Strong Heart enfolded her in his solid arms and showered heated kisses over one breast and then the other. Anchored fiercely against him, in an embrace long and sweet, she was soaring—she was thrilling. She reached around and placed her fingers on his muscular buttocks, and urged him even more deeply within her.

And again he kissed her—a blazing, searing kiss that left Elizabeth weak with a delicious languor. She clung to him now in a torrid embrace, the air heavy with the inevitability of pleasure.

Tremors ran down Strong Heart's back and perspiration laced his brow, the bliss drenching him with warmth. He moved in steady strokes inside her, feeling the tightness of her encircling his throbbing member.

It was that tightness that he was answering, sending him to a world that was far from the sadness of this land of sudden heartache and death. He was delirious with sensation, feeling the last vestige of his rational mind floating away.

He pressed himself closer to her moist body and plunged more deeply inside her. Soon their bodies jolted and quivered, then grew quiet, yet still entwined.

"We are the only two people in the universe tonight," Elizabeth whispered, her hands skimming his perspiration dampened back. "There is no one else, Strong Heart. No one."

Strong Heart looked down at her, smiling. In the light of the fire, her body gleamed golden. He ran his hand across her curves. "If I died tonight, it would be with a smile on my face," he whispered, then again drew her into his arms and gave her a soft kiss. Their tongues touched as Elizabeth slightly parted her lips.

* * *

The moon was casting shadows across the land as Earl looked from the window. He felt the strangest, God awful loneliness tonight without Elizabeth. He had gone to the prison today and had checked with Sheriff Nolan, and the posse had still not returned with any sort of answer.

Hope was dwindling within Earl's heart that she would be found alive. And he felt as though he had let her down by not having searched for her himself. He had probably been wrong to listen to the sheriff's advice.

The sound of a horse approaching drew Earl away from the window, and he rushed to the door and swung it open. His heart pounded and his mouth went dry when he recognized Sheriff Nolan riding toward him. Surely the sheriff had some kind of news about Elizabeth, or why else would he be way out here this time of night?

Earl stood on the porch, clasping and unclasping his hands as he waited until the sheriff reined in and dismounted. Nolan ambled toward him, his hands resting on the heavy pistols at his hips.

"Posse's returned," Sheriff Nolan said, as he came eye to eye with Earl. He spat a long stream of tobacco over his right shoulder, then turned his gaze back to Earl. "They've given up. There's no sign of your daughter *or* the escaped renegade anywhere. Sorry, but the men refuse to look any longer. Those who have wives have gone home to them. Those who are itchin' to bed up with a whore, are probably smellin' their cheap perfume even now. I thought I owed it to you to come and tell you the news. Now I'd best get back to more important business." He turned and began to saunter away.

Anger quickly welled up inside Earl. He stomped to the sheriff and stopped him, swinging him around so that their eyes met again. "More important business?" he said, his voice threatening. "You call my daughter unimportant? You give up on finding her this easy? I think you'd best rethink things, sheriff, or I'll—"

Sheriff Nolan sneered at Earl and knocked his hands away from his shoulders. "Or you'll what?" he said, thrusting his bearded face into Earl's.

Earl swallowed hard and took a step back. "Surely there are other men that you can get together to continue the search? I'll personally lead the posse. I've got to find my daughter. If you can spare the men, I can damn well spare the time!"

Sheriff Nolan pulled his beard thoughtfully, then nodded. "That's fine with me. Come into town first thing in the morning. I'll see what I can do."

Sighing heavily, Earl nodded. He wiped the perspiration from his brow as the sheriff rode away. Then he turned with a start when Morris came out of the shadows, his gaze on the sheriff's back.

"I heard everything," Morris said, turning his eyes to Earl. "I don't think you have any business leadin' a posse. You'll never find your daughter, and might even get yourself killed in the bargain."

"I'm going to go, so save your breath," Earl said, turning to walk back up the steps. He stopped and gave Morris a stern stare. "And I expect you to cooperate. While I'm gone, I'm leavin' the business in your hands totally."

Morris didn't answer.

15

Come, live with me, and be my love!

—MARLOWE

Several days later, with everyone's feelings still raw since the burial, Strong Heart felt that it was still too soon to take warriors to seek vengeance for the devastation and deaths at the hands of the raiders.

But the village was being restored quickly, with all of the braves who were healthy enough working.

Elizabeth stood near Strong Heart as he helped construct a longhouse. She watched several young men carve figures into six-foot-tall cedar logs to support the roof.

"You are admiring the handiwork of my people?" Strong Heart said, moving to Elizabeth's side. He leaned on a tall, heavy wooden mallet that he had been using to pound cedar poles into the ground. "Some are carving the legendary guardian spirits of our tribe. Others are carving the cedar log into a story pole, which records the history of the Suquamish to instruct future generations."

Elizabeth glanced from one pole to another. On some of the poles were a number of carved toads, bears, blackfish, and other spirit guide symbols. But the ones that showed a red-tailed hawk, carved in detail at the top, drew her most keen regard. They looked real, as if they could take flight.

Strong Heart also admired the hawk. Above everything, he admired those whose hands were skilled enough to make the hawks look so alive, as if more than mere wood.

"These story poles are being built to replace those that were burned," Strong Heart quietly explained. "They are to remind our youngsters of their heritage. The hawk is the crest of my family, and thus of this clan. It is the heraldic emblem of nobility."

He glowered as he looked around at those totem poles that had been ravaged by the recent fire. "It was *me-sah-chie,* bad, that the raiders saw fit to destroy that which is so precious to the Suquamish," he grumbled. "But soon the desecration will be gone. These new story poles will not be robbed of their future teachings as those others have been. Warriors will forever guard our village now. It is understood that there will always be someone who chooses to be the enemy of the Suquamish. Those who do, will die."

Hearing Strong Heart talk in such a way, his words filled with such venom, caused an involuntary shiver to course through Elizabeth. She hugged herself and watched Strong Heart as he directed his eyes to something else—some*one* else.

In Strong Heart's eyes she could see pain as he stared at an elderly man. The man was reclining on the ground close to those who were laboring, too old to help with the regrowth of his village.

Elizabeth wondered what Strong Heart was thinking about the old man. His eyes were filled with longing.

Strong Heart was remembering another old man. He thought of his beloved grandfather who was still missing. His grandfather had often placed a hand on the ground, saying that the Suquamish sat in the lap of their Mother when they sat upon the earth. He could even now hear him saying, "From her, our Mother Earth, we, and all other living things, come. We shall soon pass, but the place where we now rest will last forever."

"What is it, Strong Heart?" Elizabeth asked, placing a hand on his arm. "What are you thinking about?"

"My grandfather," Strong Heart said, a haunted expression crossing his face. "He, in his beautiful eagle-feather headdress so long ago, taught me many things—how Indians loved the earth and all things of the earth."

With a nod of his head, Strong Heart motioned toward the elderly man. "See that Suquamish elder?" he said softly. "See how he lies upon the ground? It is with a feeling of being close to a mothering power that he does this. My grandfather, my mother's father, told me as a child that it is good for the skin to touch the earth. The old people like to remove their moccasins to walk with bare feet on the sacred earth. My grandfather told me that earth was the final abiding place of all things that lived and grew. He taught me that soil was soothing, strengthening, cleansing, and healing. When he sat or lay upon the ground, he could think more deeply and feel more keenly. He could see more clearly into the mysteries of life and come closer in kinship to other lives about him."

"That's so beautiful," Elizabeth said. Then she jumped when Strong Heart suddenly threw his wooden mallet to the ground.

When he turned to her and clutched her shoulders with his fingers, she looked wide-eyed up at him, seeing a determination in his eyes, replacing the haunted look that had only been there a moment before.

"I must go and find my grandfather," Strong Heart blurted out. "He deserves to know that so many of his beloved have passed away. It is my place to carry this message to him. It is *my* responsibility, for I am his only grandson."

"You have never mentioned your grandfather before," Elizabeth said. "Where is he? Why is he gone?"

"Over a moon ago, he disappeared from our village and no one knows where he went, or why," Strong Heart said, his voice filled with emotion. "I have searched for him more than once, but still I have not found him. It is my duty to search again, and *now*. He *must* be allowed to mourn the dead with the rest of our people."

"Where will you look for your grandfather?" Elizabeth asked slowly, afraid that he was planning to leave her behind in the village. Although she had made friends here, she did not relish being among those who still were suspicious of her.

"The first time we met," Strong Heart said, reaching a hand to her cheek, softly touching her, "I was searching for my grandfather. You see, your house sits on the hallowed ground of my tribe. It once belonged solely to our people. Where your house sits once housed many Suquamish longhouses. Close by, in the forest, are our burial grounds. It was my assumption that my grandfather had gone there to make peace with the spirits of the dead who were deserted by our people when we were forced to move north, away from land that was no longer ours."

Elizabeth listened with a pounding heart, now understanding so much. She now knew why the Indians had tried to burn down the old mansion in the past, and rid the land of any white intruders.

Then she suddenly recalled the old Indian walking outside her house with a staff in his right hand. It had to be Strong Heart's grandfather.

"Strong Heart, I wish you would have told me this earlier," she said eagerly. "Strong Heart, more than once I saw an old Indian close to my house. He carried some sort of staff. But he disappeared as quickly as he appeared, so I never did get to question him."

Strong Heart's eyes widened. He clutched Elizabeth's shoulders, almost desperately. "You . . . saw . . . an elderly Indian?" he gasped. "It was surely my grandfather! I must go now and find him! Come. Come with me. We shall search for him together!"

"Return with you?" she asked, searching his eyes. "Now? Have you forgotten why you took me away from Seattle in the first place?"

Strong Heart eased his fingers from her shoulders and dropped his gaze to the ground. There was danger in returning to Seattle so soon after the escape. And, especially, with Elizabeth.

"*Ah-hah,* yes, it is dangerous," he conceded, turning his eyes to Elizabeth. "But, *ah-hah,* yes, I still plan to go. This is the first time I have ever had true hope that my grandfather is still alive. I must go and search for him now, not later, no matter the risk."

Elizabeth stroked her fingers through her long hair as she pondered what to do.

She thought of her father, Frannie, and then Maysie. It was not at all fair for them not to know that she was alive.

And although she knew the risk of returning to Seattle, she saw that she must. She would just have to make sure she wasn't seen by the sheriff. She would not go into Seattle under any circumstances.

She must not be the one to lead the sheriff to Strong Heart. She knew what Strong Heart's fate would be, if she did. The memory of the gallows stayed in her mind.

"Yes, I will accompany you on this venture of the heart," Elizabeth decided. "While there, I must see my father, and others who are important to me. I must let them know that I am alive."

She paused, then added, "My darling, in no way will I endanger your life. If I am cornered by the sheriff, I will lie to save your life. In my eyes, you are innocent of any crime. I will not be the one to cause you to pay for a deed that even I see as being right."

Strong Heart took her elbow and they walked away from the workers to the edge of the forest. He drew her into his embrace, his eyes burning down into hers. "My *la-daila,* I do not want you to be forced to lie for me, ever. And I do not want you to leave me, ever. Once you see your father and reveal to him that you are alive, I want you to return with me to my village and become my wife. Share my blankets with me forever, Elizabeth. My people are impressed with your gentleness, intelligence, and beauty. They would accept you as my wife."

Elizabeth was not surprised by his proposal. She was thrilled, yet wondered how this could be arranged. "Strong Heart, I want nothing more than to say yes to your proposal. But how can I? If my father knows about you, he will also have to know how I happened to know you. It could prove dangerous."

He dipped his head and smelled the sweetness of her hair. "If your father loves you," he whispered, "*truly* loves you, he will do nothing to endanger your life. Bringing the sheriff to arrest Strong Heart would threaten your life. No, I do not think a father would do this to a daughter."

And then he paused, remembering that through all of the confusion of these past days, he had not thought to ask her about her father—why he had come to the Pacific Northwest in his great ship, and what he was building on the shores of Puget Sound.

He quickly asked her now.

Elizabeth paled, not wanting to reveal the full truth to her beloved, fearing that it would cause a confrontation between her father and the man she loved. Strong Heart could not afford an argument with any white man now that he was a fugitive.

"My father?" she said, easing from his arms. She turned her back to him and plucked a leaf from a tree. Nervously, she began shredding it into tiny pieces.

"My father came to Seattle because he was no longer planning to travel the seas with his ship. He found the Pacific Northwest a perfect place to enjoy fishing."

She turned quickly to him and looked innocently up into his eyes. "Yes," she said, her voice lilting. "That's why he came to Seattle. To enjoy fishing."

Strong Heart lifted an eyebrow as he regarded her, feeling that she was not being altogether truthful. But he did not want to think that she would lie to him.

"I will help you search for your grandfather, and then go alone to speak with my father," she said. "Perhaps it . . . it would be best for you to come back to the village alone, just in case my father doesn't react favorably to the news. I will come to you later, when I am certain that it is safe."

Strong Heart did not respond quickly. He mulled it over, then said, "That is not the way I want it to be, but if you feel that is best for *you,* then I will agree."

"Strong Heart, you have searched for your grandfather before and did not find him," Elizabeth said, as he placed an arm around her waist, walking her back toward the village. She gazed up at him. "What if you still cannot find him?"

Strong Heart frowned down at her. "Perhaps I will not be able to find him this time, but I *will* find him some day," he vowed. "It seems that my grandfather has learned the art of being invisible. Strong Heart hopes to find out why, and *how.*"

In Elizabeth's mind, she was recalling the times that she had seen his grandfather, and how quickly he had faded from sight.

And the mere fact that he had chosen to return to the grounds of his ancestors, gave her cause to be afraid for her father. What if the old man decided to set a torch to the house to finish what his ancestors had not been able to?

What then not only of her father, but of Frannie and Maysie?

Maysie, she thought suddenly. Elizabeth wondered if Maysie had stayed on at the house, or had been forced to leave. Perhaps to return to a life of sin again—or to die in the Sound?

Yes, Elizabeth decided. It *was* best that she return home, to tie up some *very* loose ends.

16

> Love's wing moults when caged and captured,
> Only free, he soars enraptured!
>
> —Thomas Campbell

As the sun was setting beyond the ever purple ridges of the distant bluffs, the crackling fire of lightning forked across the heavens above Elizabeth and Strong Heart as they dismounted. They looked warily at the display.

Elizabeth moved to Strong Heart's side and jumped with alarm as the cannon roar of the thunder reverberated all around her, the ground shaking ominously beneath her feet. "I have never seen such weather as I have found in this country," she said, shuddering. The heavens darkened to an inky blackness as the storm clouds moved in rapidly. "On our way to your village we were almost drowned by rains, and now, on our way back to Seattle, it storms again?"

She turned her green eyes up at Strong Heart. "Is the weather always this temperamental, Strong Heart? Or am I just worrying too much?"

Strong Heart placed a comforting arm around her waist, and gazed at Mount Rainier in the distance as lightning danced and played around its peak. "Rain is a natural thing in our land of trees, mountains, and rivers," he said, his voice hushed. "But thunder and lightning do not always accompany the rain. You have cause to be alarmed over the repeated storms. It is the spirits of the mountains that cause storms. They are angered. The spirits of the mountains speak of this anger tonight."

He paused and turned his eyes back to Elizabeth. "My people have long pictured the spirit of the storm as a huge bird known as the Thunderbird, flapping its wings, causing the sound of thunder. The lightning is the flash of its eyes. This bird is never seen, only talked about. It is known to live in a cloud above the highest peak that our tribe can see—which to us is *Dahkobeed,* Mount Rainier."

"I have heard about the Thunderbird. I have read about it. Thank you for sharing this with me, Strong Heart. I want to know everything about your culture, about your beliefs. It will make my being with you as your wife more complete."

The sky seemed to open up as rain began to fall in torrents, quickly drenching them.

Strong Heart grabbed a blanket from his saddlebags and held it over Elizabeth. He turned and searched quickly around him for a place to go for shelter.

When another lurid flash of lightning lit everything around them, he caught sight of a cave not that far from where he and Elizabeth stood.

"Come," he said, taking her by the elbow with one hand, and grabbing both horses' reins with his other. "Over there. We shall seek shelter in the cave. The spirits are kind to us. They have lit the sky enough so that I could see the protective sheltering of the cave."

Trembling from the cold of the rain, her buckskin dress clinging wetly to her skin, Elizabeth walked briskly beside Strong Heart as the horses followed. She sighed with relief when they stepped into the cave.

Hugging herself, her teeth chattering, Elizabeth watched Strong Heart quickly unsaddle the horses, tossing the saddlebags toward her.

"There is another blanket inside my bag," he said, running his hands down the flanks of his roan, settling him down as another crash of thunder echoed into the cave. It was as if someone had pounded a giant drum within the close confines.

"There is a change of clothing for you in your saddlebag," Strong Heart called, above the sound of the thunder. "Many Stars packed not only one clean buckskin dress in your bag, but two. Change into one. As soon as I get the horses settled down, I shall search for wood inside the cave, then build a fire."

Elizabeth was too cold to answer him. She fell to her knees on the damp ground of the cave. With trembling fingers, she opened his saddlebag and grabbed a blanket from inside it. She wrapped it around her shoulders, savoring its warmth.

She then reached inside her own bag and felt the softness of the buckskin dress and also some moccasins that Many Stars had been thoughtful enough to provide.

Elizabeth clutched the moccasins to her chest, and smiled, filled with such gratitude and love for a friend as kind as Many Stars.

Her smile wavered. She hoped that she would be able to see her again. This journey back to Seattle had many risks for Elizabeth—and her future with the Suquamish.

Before she was able to change into the dry dress, Elizabeth was amazed to see that Strong Heart had found enough wood and had a fire going. Its warmth touched her flesh like a soft hand.

She drew the wet dress over her head and lay it aside. Again she quickly drew the blanket around her shoulders to warm her nakedness.

While slipping her wet moccasins off, she peered up at Strong Heart as he hurriedly yanked his wet clothes off. Then he stood close to the fire, absorbing the warmth into his gleaming, copper body, his back to her.

Elizabeth felt wanton when her heart began to beat at the mere sight of his nudity. Never before in her life had she hungered after a man as she now hungered for Strong Heart.

It was a fact that he was in her blood. Her very soul cried out for him at this moment.

She looked at the planes of his shoulders, his straight back, slim hips, and muscled buttocks, recalling the rapture she had felt when she had explored every inch of his body with her fingers.

Her gaze caressed him now.

As Strong Heart turned to place his back to the fire, to warm it as well, the muscles moved down the length of his lean body, and his eyes caught Elizabeth's.

Elizabeth blushed. She was afraid that he could read her mind—her thoughts of wanting to go to him and run her hands down the full length of him, and then gather his manhood within her hands, to stroke it. She felt strangely light-headed.

Strong Heart reached a hand out toward her, beckoning her to come to him. She hesitated for a moment, then rose slowly to her feet and went.

When she reached him, she blinked her eyes nervously. Her heartbeat almost swallowed her whole as his hands went to the blanket around her shoulders and tugged at it.

He began pulling on both corners of the blanket, drawing her with it against his hard body. Both of them were enfolded within the warmth of the blanket. Elizabeth closed her eyes in pleasure. Never had anything felt as wonderful as to be with him in such a way, the blanket and their fiery need for each other warming them.

As he held the blanket in place, Elizabeth snuggled against him. Her arms wrapped around him, hugging him tightly.

Standing on tiptoe, she pressed her lips to his. He answered her silent invitation by crushing his mouth down upon hers, his tongue surging between her teeth, exploring the depths of her mouth. She melted into him, grinding her body against his, her breasts pressed hard into his chest.

Not even knowing how the transition had been made, just knowing that her back was now pressed hard against the cave floor, the blanket beneath her, his body warm against her as he nudged her legs apart with his knee, she welcomed the floating sensation as his hands stroked her sensitive flesh.

Breathless, longing to have him inside her, to fill her with his magnificent strength, Elizabeth opened her legs willingly to him and arched her hips. She moaned with pleasure against his mouth as he entered her with one, quick thrust.

Strong Heart began his even strokes within her. Her body moved with his, rising and falling as he plunged deeply in and out.

Elizabeth's hands thrilled at the mere touch of him. She reached down and touched his manhood as he withdrew it from her, circling the shaft as he paused before his next thrust, allowing her to give him this sort of pleasure for a moment.

As Elizabeth moved her hand on him more quickly, more

determinedly, Strong Heart slipped his mouth down to the hollow of her throat and moaned against it.

She could feel his body stiffening with his building pleasure. And when he reached down and moved her hand away from his throbbing hardness, and once again buried himself deeply within her, she tossed her head in excitement. Then the thrashing stopped when he caught her face between his hands and he kissed her.

Strong Heart was no longer aware of the lightning, the thunder, nor the torrents of rain that were falling just outside the entrance of the cave. All he could concentrate on was this vision that lay beneath him, her lovely red hair spilling away from her face, spread out beneath her like a fiery halo. Her flawless features were vibrant and glowing, her slim, white thighs now clutching to him as she locked her legs around him.

His hands framed her face as he smiled down at her, feeling he was drowning in passion, hardly able to hold back any longer.

His lips brushed the smooth, satin skin of her breast, and then again he kissed her lips.

As he thrust his tongue teasingly into her mouth, so did he press his manhood endlessly deeper within her moist channel. He could tell by her harsher breathing that she, too, was ready to ascend that same plateau as he, where a joyous bliss was awaiting them. He could feel the excitement growing, growing, growing.

And then his body jolted and quivered as for a moment he lost all sense of time, place, or even of being. All that mattered was that wave that rose through his whole body, making it fluid with fire.

Elizabeth sucked in a wild breath of air, then let herself go, to experience the ecstasy. It flooded through her, it seemed, with sweet agony.

Afterward, they lay together, their bodies still throbbing with the afterglow of love.

Then Strong Heart rolled away from her and drew the blanket over them again. "You are no longer cold?" he asked, his eyes smiling into hers.

"No," Elizabeth said, softly giggling. "I feel as though I'm burning up inside."

"It is a good feeling?" he asked, flicking his tongue across one of her breasts as he bent beneath the blanket.

Elizabeth closed her eyes and shivered. "Yes, a good feeling," she whispered. "As is what you are doing right now." She placed a hand to his head and urged his mouth even more closely to her breast. "My darling, how wonderful you make me feel, *always.*"

He moved his lips back to her mouth, yet did no kiss her—only whispered against it. "Remember what you just said, that when you reach Seattle and are tempted to stay behind, to live the life that you are more familiar with," he said huskily. "Remember that, my *la-daila,* always remember that."

"Always," she whispered. "How could I ever forget how you make me feel? I could never live without you, Strong Heart. You are my very reason for breathing—for getting up each morning. It is you I wish to see upon my first awakening. Only you."

"That is *kloshe,* good," he whispered back against her lips. "That is very good."

He kissed her softly, his hands plumping her breasts.

She slung a leg over him and trembled with pleasure as his manhood found her open and ready for him again.

* * *

Earl was cursing as he yanked off his wet clothes. "This damn weather," he grumbled. Members of the posse stood around the campfire in the cave, also taking off their drenched clothes. "I've never seen anything like the weather here. Why does it have to rain so often?"

"We're lucky we found this cave," one of the men said, totally naked and drying himself off with a blanket before the campfire. "So quit grumblin', Earl."

Another of the men came up next to Earl—a Suquamish Indian who had taken more to the life of the whites', than the Indians'. "You have angered the mountain spirits by traveling too far into land that one time only knew the footsteps of the Suquamish," Joe Feather grumbled, squeezing water out of his waist-length black hair. "That is also why your horse took a spill, and even now limps on its lamed leg. It would be better if you would shoot the horse. If you continue riding him, your journey back to Seattle will be slowed, and then you will have to shoot him anyway."

"We don't have any spare horses and I'm a damn sight better off riding my own steed, than saddling up with someone else," Earl snarled. He reached into his saddlebag and pulled out a dry change of clothes. "And don't fill my head with any more nonsense about the mountain spirits. I've had enough of your mumbo jumbo for one day. If you still believe in so many of the Suquamish customs, why the hell are you riding with the white men, as though you're one of them? Or don't you know where you fit in best? Huh?"

Joe Feather frowned at Earl as he stepped out of his fringed breeches, and then into dry buckskin. "A lot of me is still Suquamish," he said, his voice void of emotion. "*That* part of me speaks of spirits whenever it seems fit to do so. And tonight, when the storm warriors are throwing their lightning sticks to earth, I remember my beliefs."

"Save me from a lecture about Indians," Earl retorted, even though he wished that he knew of a secret potion that he could use on Chief Moon Elk, to sway him over to his plans. "I've got one Indian on my mind tonight. That's enough."

Earl buttoned his fresh, dry shirt, then stepped into his breeches and fastened them. Disconsolately, he sat down on a blanket close to the fire, wondering where Elizabeth was.

The search was going badly.

And now, with his hobbled horse, it would take him much longer to return home to see if any word had arrived there about her whereabouts.

Joe Feather sat down beside Earl. He drew his knees to his chest and hugged his legs. "There are many beliefs about why there are fierce storms," he said, ignoring Earl's agitated sigh. "One belief is that there are warriors who live in the sky who dash about on their spirited horses during a thunderstorm, their lances clashing with the thunder, and glittering with the lightning. Lightning does no harm to most Indians. Whenever it comes too close, the mothers of the tribes put cedar leaves on the coals of their fires, and their magic keeps danger away."

Earl turned angry eyes to Joe Feather. "Will you just shut up?" he growled.

"This cave that we are in?" Joe Feather said, looking over his shoulder, toward the darker depths of the cave. "It has another opening, on the far end. Would you want to go and see what might be at the other end?"

Earl glowered at Joe. "I like this end just fine," he said, his teeth clenched.

Joe Feather shrugged, then stretched out on his side, his eyes soon drifting closed.

Earl sighed heavily. "Finally," he whispered to himself. He had not been sure how much more of the damn Indian that he could tolerate.

He glanced over his shoulder at the darker depths of the cave. "Another entrance, hogwash," he said, soon forgetting about it.

17

> We parted in silence, we parted by night,
> On the banks of that lonely river.
>
> —Mrs. Crawford

The sun was low in the sky. The shadows lengthened around Strong Heart and Elizabeth as they rode silently through the forest. Up ahead, Elizabeth's house loomed through a break in the trees.

Elizabeth gave Strong Heart a downcast look. She was weary not only from the long travel, but also from searching for hours in this forest for where Proud Beaver might be hiding.

Elizabeth's muscles were sore from the many hours in the saddle, even though the Indian saddle was stuffed with thick layers of cottonwood and cattail down. She was not used to this sort of life—this life of adventure.

And although it meant being parted from Strong Heart, she looked forward to telling her father about her upcoming marriage to the handsome Suquamish brave. It would be a reprieve before she would have to make the long journey back to Strong Heart's village.

She glowed inside, thinking about what would happen once they were back at his village. She had agreed to be his wife. From that time on, they would never have cause to be separated. It would be like living a dream, to be with the man she loved from morning 'til night.

"The sun soon sleeps as the moon replaces it in the sky," Strong Heart said, drawing his reins and stopping his horse. Elizabeth followed his lead and her horse stopped beside his. "It is best that we give up the search for my grandfather. He knows the art of elusiveness too well. He does not want to be found. So be it. There is only so much a grandson can do for a grandfather. Now I must return to my people, to my duties to *them.*"

Elizabeth reached a hand to his bronze cheek. "Darling, you do understand why I won't be returning with you right now? That I must make all wrongs right with my father? I've been selfish until now to only consider my feelings. Although he does not always show how much he loves me, I am sure he does and is very concerned over my welfare."

"What man could not love you?" Strong Heart said, taking her hand, kissing its palm. "My *la-daila,* I am fighting jealousy over you putting another man before me. But I know that loyalty is owed to parents. This lightens the burden of jealousy within my heart. Go to your father. Stay as long as it takes to make him understand. Then return to me. I have been careful to map the way for your return. But do not travel alone. If your father is at peace with this that you wish to do, and has agreed, ask him to accompany you to my village. There I will pay him gifts for you. There he will join our wedding celebration. It will be a good time of camaraderie and understanding, this time spent with our people and your father."

Elizabeth smiled weakly at Strong Heart, easing her hand from his. "You make it sound easy," she murmured. "I shall try, Strong Heart. But if I do not return soon, please come for me. No matter if my father understands or not, I want to be with you. Come and take me back with you. Please?"

Strong Heart reached for her and placed his hands at her waist. He lifted her from her horse and placed her on his lap facing him.

Breathless from the surprise of what he had done, Elizabeth then laughed softly as she twined her arms around his neck, drawing his lips close to hers. "How foolish of me to even ask if you would come for me," she breathed, as he brushed her lips with a teasing kiss, his hands on her breasts, massaging them through the soft buckskin of her dress. "I'm surprised that you are allowing me to part from you for even one second. Our time together is so wonderful, Strong Heart. So wonderful."

She looked at him, a pout on her lips. "I'm going to miss

you so much," she complained. "I'm not sure I can stand being away from you."

"Then do not stay behind without me," Strong Heart urged, his hands now at the fringed hem of her dress, pushing it up her legs. "Return with me. Forget your father."

Elizabeth's face flushed hotly and she flung her head back so that her hair hung in silken red streamers down her back as she felt him slip his manhood into her. He began the sweet rocking rhythm.

Elizabeth moaned as she clutched Strong Heart about his neck. It felt wicked making love on a horse. Wicked doing it so close to her father's house, where he might even now be pacing the floor in worry about her.

But her insides were burning from the passion that her beloved always evoked in her. She knew that this was his way of saying good-bye. Strong Heart was such a sensual man, such a splendid, romantic lover. He had awakened in her feelings that surely no other man could have ever awakened.

Now, as she rode him, his body thrusting his satin shaft within her, so pleasurably filling her, she could not deny that he was the answer to all of her tomorrows—her need for him perhaps even stronger than his for her.

Yes, she would return to him, for without him, she would be only half a woman.

But first, she must see her father. She could not forget that without her, her father was alone. She hoped that he could bear his loss.

Then she felt foolish for thinking that, knowing that his business was all of his tomorrows—not her.

The heat building within her made Elizabeth feel euphoric. She could tell that Strong Heart was feeling the same, for his moans of pleasure filled the air, echoing into the forest that lay on each side of them.

And then that peak of bliss was reached.

Afterward, they clung to one another, Elizabeth still straddling him, their cheeks pressed together.

"You still say good-bye to Strong Heart?" he asked throatily, as he placed a finger to her chin and directed her eyes up to his. "I have not persuaded you to return with me?"

"Your ways of persuasion are unique," Elizabeth said, laughing softly. "But, darling, I still must stay and talk to my father. Please tell me that you understand."

"*Ah-hah,* I understand," Strong Heart said, tracing a finger down one of her cheeks. "And in your absence I will do what I must, to make things right for my people. As soon as I return to my village, I will get many braves together and leave to search for the culprits responsible for the raid. And this must be done soon, for the autumn salmon run must be prepared for. Without the salmon, the lives of the Suquamish are not as easy. *Ah-hah,* and when it comes time to participate in the harvest of the salmon, it will be done with you at my side as my wife."

Elizabeth sighed and hugged him. "It sounds so magical. I so want it to be that way."

"And why should it not?" Strong Heart challenged, again holding her away from him so that their eyes could meet.

"Strong Heart, I'm not able to forget the threat that lies over your head, should you be suspected of having set Four Winds free," Elizabeth said, her voice trembling. "That, alone, clouds my hopes for the future, Strong Heart. What if the sheriff discovers that I am home, and questions me? Will he be able to tell that I am lying when I tell him nothing about you? I have never been skilled at lying." She cast her sight downward. "Never before have I had *cause* to lie."

He placed a finger to her chin and brought her eyes to his again. "Knowing me brings too much pain in your life," he said sadly. "I am sorry for that."

"Never be sorry for this that you and I have found together," Elizabeth said, then kissed him softly and sweetly.

She drew away from him. "I must go now. The sooner I get on with this thing that I must do, the sooner we will be together again."

"That is so," Strong Heart said, nodding. He pulled her dress down, then lifted her over onto her horse. "Go. I shall watch until you are safely at the house. Then I shall search awhile longer for my grandfather. But only for a short while. My people await my return. I must not worry them needlessly."

Tears misted Elizabeth's eyes as she gave Strong Heart a lingering look, realizing how slim the chances were that they might be together again. Danger seemed to be lurking everywhere, not only for her, but also for the man that she loved. He could fall victim to evil white men and Indian renegades. She wondered if Four Winds was a man who could be trusted. What if he *was* a renegade, guilty of all sorts of horrendous crimes? Would he go as far as committing a crime against his own people? Against his friend?

Shaking these thoughts from her mind, afraid that if she thought much more about it, she might return with Strong Heart after all, and her father would forever worry about her. That was not fair of her, she decided firmly.

"I shall see you soon," Elizabeth said, tears rushing from her eyes. "Please ride with care, darling."

"*Kla-how-ya,* goodbye, my *la-daila,*" Strong Heart said, placing a fist over his heart. "My *tum-tum,* heart, already misses you."

Elizabeth brushed the tears from her cheeks, gave Strong Heart a feeble smile, then wheeled her horse around. Without looking back, she urged her steed into a hard gallop away from him.

When she rode through the open gate, she continued until she reached the stables behind the house. Dismounting, she led her horse inside the stables, and then jumped with alarm when Everett stepped from the darkness into the dim light of a lantern that hung just inside the door.

"You frightened me," Elizabeth said, placing a hand to her throat.

Everett took the lantern from its nail on the wall and held it above him, walking slowly toward Elizabeth. "You frightened *me,*" he said, his dark eyes wide. "You're the last person I expected to see. Your father is leadin' a posse even now, searchin' for you."

"Father is-is a part of a posse?" Elizabeth said, paling and looking past Everett, to the darkness outside. Her thoughts went to Strong Heart, now fearing more than ever for him. If a posse was out there somewhere searching for her, Strong Heart might come right into the midst of them!

Then she willed her heart to stop its racing, reminding herself that no one in the posse knew of Strong Heart's role in Four Winds's escape, or her abduction. Strong Heart would be just an innocent traveler on his way home.

No, she tried to convince herself—she had nothing to fear. Strong Heart would be all right. He would be all right.

Then she noticed Everett staring at her attire. He shifted his eyes slowly to the Indian saddle on the horse. Her heart plummeted to her feet, knowing those things were enough to reveal to anyone that she had been among Indians. And that might be fatal.

Trying not to show her uneasiness, Elizabeth went to the saddle and removed it from the horse. Boldly, she turned and handed it to Everett. "I want you to hide this for me," she said crisply. "And, Everett, if you value your position with my father, you will never tell anyone about the saddle. Do you understand?"

Everett gulped hard as he sat the lantern aside and took the saddle. "Yes'm," he said, nodding his head. "Whatever you say, ma'am."

She slowly ran her hand down the buckskin dress. "And don't you breathe a word, either, about this dress that I'm wearing. It is nobody's affair but my own. Do I make myself clear, Everett?"

"Yes'm," he said, again nodding. "I won't say a word. Not to no one."

"Thank you," Elizabeth said, exhaling a long breath and relaxing her shoulders. "I truly thank you."

She turned and left the stables, dreading having to meet Frannie and her curiosity when she saw how Elizabeth was dressed.

But Frannie had to know, as did her father, eventually. For now, she had been given a reprieve. Hopefully she would at least get a night's sleep in her bed before her father arrived home and she would have to face him.

18

How can I live without thee?
How forego thy sweet converse,
and love so dearly joined?

—MILTON

The sun poured through the bedroom window in streamers across the drab furniture and hardwood floor. The forest beyond was alive with the music of birds. The pulse of the waves crashing endlessly against the beach below seemed to echo Elizabeth's heartbeat.

As she brushed her hair in long strokes, Elizabeth stared at her reflection in the mirror. She had changed overnight, it seemed, to the person she had always been. She no longer wore a buckskin dress or moccasins. Today, for her planned outing on the beach, she had chosen to wear a light blue, eyelet wrap dress with white cotton-eyelet pantaloons and petticoat with crocheted trim.

"No matter what I wear, my heart will forever be changed," she whispered to herself. "Strong Heart, darling. Oh, how I miss you."

She shifted her gaze and looked with melancholy at the buckskin dress that she had laid ever so gently over the back of a chair the previous evening. Frannie had peppered her with questions as to where she had got the dress, and why she had been wearing it.

Elizabeth was silent, refusing to answer any of Frannie's questions. So Frannie's conclusion, that Elizabeth had been with Indians, had made Frannie almost faint with fright. She had grabbed the dress and announced she would burn it.

Elizabeth took back the dress and told Frannie that this dress belonged to a sweet Indian maiden, someone who was Elizabeth's friend.

But she hadn't explained any more to Frannie. That would have to wait until Elizabeth had been given the chance to first talk with her father. Once he understood that she was in love, then she would tell Frannie her secret. But not until then.

Elizabeth's thoughts went to Maysie. "Sweet Maysie," she whispered to herself as she lay the hairbrush aside. "If only I could go search for her."

When Frannie had told her that Maysie had left without telling anyone, a sudden ache had risen in Elizabeth's heart.

But she knew that she couldn't go into Seattle for anything, not even to try and find Maysie. Yet Elizabeth could not stop thinking about that day when she had found Maysie walking into the Sound, and had discovered Maysie's life of prostitution.

"And so's you still determined to keep that dress I sees," Frannie said, entering the bedroom with an armful of fresh linens. She laid the linens on the bed and turned to Elizabeth, folding her arms angrily across her thick bosom. "You still too stubborn to tell ol' Frannie where you've been these long days and nights?"

Elizabeth went to Frannie and placed a gentle hand to her plump cheek. "Isn't it enough for now that I am home safe?" she asked softly. "Please don't ask any more questions until I am ready to tell you everything. First, I must talk to Father."

Elizabeth turned and walked to the window and looked down at the yard below. "Father hasn't returned yet," she said, her voice full of concern. "I wonder what's taking him so long?"

She was worried not only about her father's delay, but also about Strong Heart's welfare because of it. What if they had met on the trail?

What if her father somehow knew of Strong Heart's guilt, and even now was ushering him into a cell at the prison?

Her imagination worked overtime. She felt that she must think of something else or she would go insane from worry. Elizabeth turned abruptly and walked determinedly toward the door.

"I need a breath of fresh air," she said, grabbing a shawl from a peg on the wall. She wrapped the shawl around her shoulders. "I'm going to take a stroll on the beach, Frannie. I shan't be too long."

Frannie rushed after her and grabbed her by the arm, stopping her. "Don't goes nowhere today, honey," she pleaded. "Stay in the house where's you'll be safe. Ol' Frannie don't trust this land, nor nobody. Lordy, Elizabeth, ain't you glad to be home, in the safety of your house? Why on earth would you trust leavin' it again, no matter that it's only to take a walk on the beach? Anything could happen to you. Anything!"

"Frannie, please quit worrying," Elizabeth said, taking Frannie's hand, clasping it tightly. "I'm not going to do anything to put myself in danger. All I want to do is take a walk and clear my head of a few things. Start my breakfast. I'll be back to eat it before you can flip a stack of flapjacks onto my plate."

Frannie sighed heavily and shook her head, then pulled her hand from Elizabeth's. "If that is as long as you plan to be gone, I sees no true harm in it," she said, her dark eyes concerned. "Go on. The sooner you get your strollin' over with, the sooner you'll be back here with me so's I can keep my eye on you."

"Frannie, I don't need anyone keeping an eye on me," Elizabeth said. "I can take care of myself."

"Hah!" Frannie said haughtily. "You sure do have strange ways of provin' it."

Elizabeth looked down into Frannie's face and tried to smile. "I'm here, aren't I?" she asked in a lighthearted manner. "I'm all right, aren't I?"

"For now," Frannie said, giving Elizabeth a disapproving stare. Then she walked past her and went downstairs with heavy footsteps.

When Elizabeth reached the first-floor landing, she took a straw hat from a hat rack and placed it on her head, tying its satin bow beneath her chin. Then without the usual spring in her step, she went on outside.

She crossed the estate grounds, through the wide gate, and walked toward the beckoning waves of the Sound. When she reached the steep incline that led down to the beach, she stopped momentarily to look at the large building that would soon be processing salmon for export.

Today there were men busy putting finishing touches to the building. She could even make out Morris Murdoch among them. She realized that he would have to have stayed behind instead of joining her father on the posse. He seemed to be enjoying having full control in her father's absence as he shouted curse words to the workmen.

Recalling his cold, blue eyes, and how being around him gave her a sense of discomfort, Elizabeth shivered with distaste. She was careful not to be seen as she moved down the rocky slope, and sighed with relief when she reached the sandy stretch of beach.

The wind was warm and soothing, the sprays of water from the Sound were salty on her lips as she began walking aimlessly along the beach. Her eyes looked across the water to the mountains in the distance. She recalled how the lightning had played across the peak of Mount Rainier, and how the thunder had shook the earth on her journeys with Strong Heart.

She remembered how wonderful it had been to lie in Strong Heart's sheltering arms during the storm after having just made maddening, exquisite love.

"This isn't making me forget anything," she murmured, feeling frustrated. She stopped and turned her face toward the sun, closing her eyes as she absorbed its warmth. The skirt of her dress lifted in the gentle breeze.

"Strong Heart, I wish I were with you now," Elizabeth whispered longingly. "Father, where are you? Please come home soon so that I can rejoin the man I love!"

She resumed walking, then sank down onto the soft sand and scooped up a handful, watching it run through her fingers. Time. Today it was dragging so.

Watching the sand as it collected in peaks beside her, she was reminded of when she was a child in San Francisco, and how her mother had taken her to the beach and had taught her how to build sand castles. It seemed as if her mother was there even now, laughing and playing with her. She remembered that there had only been the two of them, the rest of the world held at bay.

Smiling at the memory, she tossed her shawl aside, and without the aid of a bucket, she used her hands to scoop out a hole in the sand. Then she made a foundation for her sand castle with the moist sand she had dug out.

Skillfully, she formed pancake-shaped layers of sand, piling them up to make a dome. The secret was to keep the sand good and wet so that the castle did not topple.

After the dome had reached the desired height, it was time to carve the architectural details and add flourishes like winding staircases and graceful arches.

Pleased with how things were progressing, and how the castle looked so far, Elizabeth rose to her feet. She moved along the beach looking for small pieces of driftwood and tiny twigs for sculpting and smoothing the walls and carving everything from doors to balconies.

Bright sea shells and pebbles would be used to line the walkway. A handful of seaweed would be planted for the lawn.

Her arms and the pockets of her dress crammed full with treasures for her castle, Elizabeth turned to go back to her sand castle, then stopped. She dropped everything from her arms when she saw Sheriff Nolan standing beside her castle, his eyes glaring at her.

"You . . ." Elizabeth said, frozen to the spot. "What are you doing here? I-I didn't hear you."

"No, I guess you didn't," Sheriff Nolan said, taking a plug of the ever-present chewing tobacco from his shirt pocket and pushing it into a corner of his mouth. "Your mind is elsewhere, I'd say, Red."

Elizabeth swallowed hard, knowing the danger of revealing too much to him—not only by her words, but by her actions, as well. If she behaved guiltily, then he would have reason to suspect her. She had to act normal, as if seeing him didn't matter one bit.

She tried to act nonchalant as she gathered up her treasure and willed her feet to take one step after another until she reached her sand castle. The sheriff hovered over it like a monster ready to step not only on the castle, but also its sculptress.

"Pardon me," Elizabeth said, giving Sheriff Nolan an annoyed glance as she tried to make him step back.

When he did not budge, she gave him an icier stare. "If you please?"

"If I please what?" Sheriff Nolan grumbled, spitting sticky tobacco juice over his left shoulder. His blue eyes gave her a steely cold stare.

"Please step aside," Elizabeth said, trying to keep her voice steady. "I would like to resume what I was doing before your rude interruption."

"Red, I didn't come here to play house with you," Sheriff Nolan said, not moving. He even placed a hand on Elizabeth's shoulder.

Elizabeth paled and her knees trembled as she looked up at him. "Why *are* you here?" she found the courage to ask. "I'm minding my business. Why don't you?"

"I'm making *you* my business this mornin', Red," Sheriff Nolan said, easing his hand from her shoulder. He rested it on one of his holstered pistols. "I've been keepin' an eye out for you for days. Today I lucked out. As I was riding past your house I saw you coming to the beach. Now ain't that perfect timin'?"

His smug, throaty laugh unnerved Elizabeth. "Oh, I see," she murmured. "Since my father is gone with the posse, you've been watching for my return so that you can send word to them to return home. That's good. Please do it soon. I didn't think my father would be gone this long."

"How would you even know how long he's been gone when you've been gone so long, yourself?" Sheriff Nolan asked with a growl. "Where've you been, Red, since the prison breakout? Who've you been with?"

Elizabeth stiffened. Even though she had expected him to ask her these questions, it did not make it any easier for her. If she answered them wrong, she knew what the consequences would be.

"Where have I been?" Elizabeth said, fighting not to stammer.

"More to the point, I want you to identify the man who knocked me unconscious just before the breakout," Sheriff Nolan said, taking a threatening step toward her. His large boot toppled the sand castle. "I know you had to see the culprit. You were there, damn it. Now you identify him to me."

"I can't," Elizabeth said, her voice breaking. "I . . . just . . . can't."

He reached behind him and took a pair of handcuffs from his back pocket, and before Elizabeth could even blink, he had her wrists handcuffed together. "You leave me no choice but to take you into custody," he said gruffly.

"What?" Elizabeth said, gasping. "You have no right. I am innocent!"

"You're no more innocent than Four Winds who escaped the hangman's noose," Sheriff Nolan said, yanking Elizabeth close to him as he pushed his face into hers. "You were in on the plot from the start, weren't you? You were used as a diversional tactic for the one who planned the escape. Why else did you disappear at the same time? Why else are you home now, safe and sound, as though nothing happened? A few nights in jail will change your mind about confessing the full truth. It will loosen your tongue, all right."

He straightened his back and jerked her to his side as he turned to walk up the hill to his horse. But he was stopped when he found Frannie there, a shotgun leveled at him.

"You let my Elizabeth go," Frannie said breathlessly. "I sees you come to the beach. I sees you place handcuffs on my little girl. Now you just takes them off her again and leave. If you do, I won't pull this trigger. If you don't, I'll fill your stomach full of holes."

Elizabeth became light-headed at the sight of Frannie going up against the sheriff. Not because of her courage to defy him, but more because she was a colored person and it was dangerous.

"Frannie, put down the gun," Elizabeth begged, cringing when Frannie determinedly took a step closer. Her eyes were wild as she peered at the sheriff. "Frannie, there is no need in you going to prison, too. I won't be there long once Father finds out. Please, Frannie, go back to the house. Please?"

Frannie's eyes wavered. "Honey, I can't let this man takes you away like some . . . some . . . common criminal," she said.

"Frannie, I'll be all right," Elizabeth said softly. "It's all a big mistake. One that Father will correct as soon as he returns with the posse. That will probably be today sometime, Frannie. I'll be home in my own bed tonight. I promise you."

Frannie slowly lowered the gun.

Elizabeth saw the sheriff go for the pistol at his right hip. "Please let Frannie go," she cried. "Please don't blame her for wanting to protect me. I'm like a daughter to her. Please forget what she did. Let her go. Please?"

Sheriff Nolan eased his hand from the pistol as he glared down at Elizabeth. "You've been lapse in teachin' that fat thing her place," he grumbled. "You're lucky I don't blow her damn head off."

Elizabeth sighed heavily. Ignoring Frannie's wails, she went with the sheriff. She had to protect Strong Heart at all cost—even if it meant the loss of her own freedom.

When they reached the summit, she took a last glance over her shoulder at the remains of the castle that she had been building. When she was a child, her sand castles lasted for days.

Today's castle had been crushed, along with her hopes for tomorrow.

19

Some fears,—a soft regret,
For joys scarce known.

—Barry Cornwall

The next evening, worn and weary from the unsuccessful search, Earl rode his limping horse in a slow gait through the open gate of his estate. He peered at the monstrosity of a house. The window panes seemed to be on fire from the reflection of the sunset.

He shifted his gaze to the heavy oak front door. His shoulders slouched, knowing that if by chance Elizabeth had arrived home before him unharmed by whoever had abducted her, she would have already been at the door.

A low whinny, filled with pain, drew Earl's attention back to his horse. He would have to put the horse out of its misery. The animal was no longer useful to him. He felt lucky that the horse had gotten him back home instead of leaving him stranded out in the wilderness after Earl and the posse had parted ways earlier in the afternoon.

The stables now in sight, Earl rode his horse slowly onward, giving a mock salute to Everett when the black groom came toward him.

Everett peered intently at the horse's lame leg, then up at Earl. "He's doin' mighty poorly, Massa' Easton," he said, shaking his head. "Mighty poorly, indeed."

"Yeah, and I've been riding him for too long that way, that's for sure," Earl said, yanking on his reins to stop the horse. He slid out of the saddle, but did not offer the reins to Everett. "Never mind about him, Everett. I'll do the ugly task of shootin' him. You can have the job of getting rid of his body."

Earl walked the horse toward the stables and gave Everett a sidewise glance. "I don't guess my daughter's arrived home yet, has she?" he said, his voice thin and tired.

Everett lowered his dark eyes to the ground as he walked into the stable with Earl. He did not reply, just busied himself removing the horse's saddle.

Earl went to Everett's side and placed a heavy hand on his shoulder. "Have you gone deaf?" he asked irritably. "I asked you a simple enough question. Has Elizabeth returned home?"

Before Everett could answer, Earl saw something half hidden beneath some straw in the corner, the light from the lantern spilling onto it.

"What the hell is that?" he said, for the moment forgetting Everett's strange silence. He sauntered over to the pile of straw and kicked it aside. His eyes widened when he discovered that it was a saddle—an Indian saddle.

His head jerked around, his eyes questioning Everett. "Where did that come from?" he asked. Then he saw an unfamiliar horse in a stall to his right. "That horse. It doesn't belong to me."

He stomped back to Everett and gathered Everett's shirt front into his hand and leaned into Everett's face. "If you value your job, you'd best begin talking," he said, his words hissing through his clenched teeth. "Whose saddle? Whose horse?"

"I was told not to tell," Everett managed to say, his eyes wild with fright. "If I do, she'd make sure I was let go."

Earl's heart skipped a beat. He dropped his hand away from Everett, placing it on the handle of his holstered pistol. "She?" he said, an eyebrow rising. "Who, damn you? Who?"

"She'll not like me tellin' you," Everett said, dropping his gaze to the floor.

At the end of his patience, Earl now grabbed Everett by the throat, half lifting him from the floor. "If you don't tell me," he said, his eyes narrowing into Everett's, "I'll not only be shootin' my horse this evening, I'll use one of my bullets on *you.*"

"Elizabeth!" Everett shot out. "She told me to hide the saddle. She came home the other night. She was ridin' that horse there. It was saddled with that Indian saddle." He swallowed hard, then said, "And she was dressed in some kind of Indian dress!"

All of this was coming too fast for Earl. It was spinning around inside his head, not making sense. He jerked his hand away from Everett's throat and wiped it on his breeches. His breath came in short, raspy sounds.

"She's here," Earl mumbled, walking toward the door. "That's all that matters now. My Elizabeth. She's home. She's safe."

Everett hurried after him. "Sir, you'd best not go to the house just yet," he said, his voice hushed. "You'd best let me tell you what happened yesterday to Elizabeth."

Earl stopped and turned to face Everett. "What about Elizabeth?" he said, his voice ominous. "Damn it, what about Elizabeth? Tell me. What happened to her?"

Everett slipped his thin hands into the pockets of his loose, dark trousers. "The sheriff came," he said thickly. "He took her away. He arrested her. He took her to Copper Hill Prison."

Feeling his knees close to buckling beneath him, Earl grabbed for the door jamb and steadied himself. He blinked his eyes nervously, finding it hard to breathe.

Then he turned his gaze back to Everett. "Why would the sheriff arrest Elizabeth?" he said, his voice weak. "Why?"

"He said that she was in on the recent escape," Everett said, shifting his feet nervously in the straw. "He called her an accomplice, or something like that. He said she helped the renegade Indian escape."

Again Earl felt a weakness sweep through him. He concentrated on the Indian saddle, and then on the strange horse. "You say Elizabeth was using an Indian saddle on that horse, and she was dressed in Indian attire when she arrived home?" he said, his mind conjuring up all sorts of nightmarish thoughts about what Elizabeth may have gone through after being abducted by the renegade Indian and his partner.

And now the damn sheriff had cooked up some cockeyed idea that she had joined the escape party? That she had actually had a helping hand in it?

The thought filled him with a keen revulsion for the sheriff and his idiot logic.

"You know as well as I that Elizabeth had no part in anything," Earl said, doubling his hands into tight fists at his side. "She was taken captive."

Then his eyes wavered. "How'd Elizabeth look when she got home? Did she look as though . . . as though she may have been tortured by her abductors? Was she all right?"

Everett slipped a hand from his pocket and rubbed his chin thoughtfully. "Come to think of it, she looked better than I've ever seen her," he said, nodding. "There was something about her eyes—a happiness of sorts. No, I don't believe you have to worry about her having been tortured in any way. I'd say that someone took mighty good care of your daughter."

Earl lifted an eyebrow at his response. Then he hurriedly took a horse from a stall, slapped his saddle onto its back and fastened it. "I'm riding into Seattle," he said, stopping to eye his lame horse. "Do what's required here."

Everett nodded and went to grab a rifle that was propped against the stable wall.

Earl swung himself into his saddle and gave the Indian saddle another lingering stare. Then he slapped his reins and rode quickly away past the towering house and through the gate.

When the low blast of a rifle echoed from the stables, he flinched. Then he rode onward, not stopping for anything or anyone until he reached Seattle. He didn't slow his horse's gait as he made his way through the throng of traffic on First Avenue.

When he reached the street that led to Copper Hill Prison, he felt sick knowing that his sweet daughter was there among the most hardened criminals, at their mercy. He had heard tales of what happened to the women prisoners there:

They were used in every way unholy—they were used.

This torturous thought spurred him on. He didn't even notice the strain on his horse as it climbed the steep street. His eyes were set on the prison. If Elizabeth had so much as been touched by any of those vile men, he vowed to kill the sheriff. Then one day he would find the one who had made her life go astray—the outlaw who had set the Indian free, and taken his Elizabeth as captive.

Earl could not move fast enough when he reached the prison. He jumped out of the saddle, secured his horse's reins and rushed inside the prison. When he found the sheriff lazing behind the desk, chewing on his perpetual wad of tobacco, it almost threw Earl into a fit of rage. To think that this man could arrest his daughter without any proof of her guilt, then lock her up with the rest of the criminals, as though she was one, herself. . . .

Earl stormed to the desk and slammed his hands down on the paper-cluttered top. He leaned into Sheriff Nolan's whiskered face. "I hear that you have my daughter at this godforsaken place," he growled, his eyes red with anger. "You Goddamn idiot, go and set her free at once. Do you hear? Release her. Now!"

"That ain't possible," Sheriff Nolan said, turning his head so that he could let fly a string of tobacco into the spittoon. "She's there until her trial, and then we may have our first hanging of a woman in the history of Seattle."

Earl paled at the thought and his resolve weakened. "You can't be serious," he finally said. "My daughter isn't a criminal. And you know it. Why are you doing this? Why would you want to take your troubles out on an innocent woman? The fact that someone got the best of you that day of the escape is the only reason you've arrested my daughter, isn't it? You have to have a scapegoat. You're makin' her one."

"That redhaired vixen daughter of yours ain't as innocent as you want to believe she is," Sheriff Nolan said, rising slowly from his chair. He made a wide turn around the desk and stood eye to eye with Earl. "She was used as a diversion to what was ready to happen. She flirted with me and once she had me, hook, line, and sinker, I was hit from behind."

Sheriff Nolan slipped a hand inside his right pocket and took a ring of keys from it. He jangled the keys in front of Earl's eyes. "There ain't no rule sayin' you can't visit your daughter," he said tauntingly as he held the keys closer to Earl. "Go on. She's in the first cell. She's a lucky one. She has the cell all to herself. Most other prisoners are cooped up together. But none complain. They like it that way when the night gives them the privacy to do what they damn well please with one another."

Anxiety almost making him dizzy, Earl snatched the keys from the sheriff, then headed toward the door that led to the back room. He flinched when the sheriff stepped in front of him, and opened the door.

"You didn't think I'd let you go visit your daughter alone, now did you?" Sheriff Nolan said, chuckling. He nodded toward the interior. "Go on. Get in the cell with her. But don't forget, I'll be watchin' your every move."

Earl set his jaw, then walked past the sheriff. When he caught sight of Elizabeth standing in a far corner of a cell, his gut twisted and tears splashed from his eyes. "Elizabeth," he whispered. Just saying her name seemed to tear his heart to shreds.

He went to the cell. Elizabeth gasped when she saw him there. His fingers fumbled with the keys, trying to find the one that fit the lock.

She ran to the front of the cell. She clasped the bars. "Father, you've come," she cried.

She then stared icily at the sheriff who was mightily amused watching her father try to find the right key.

Finally a key turned in the lock. Earl slammed the door open and rushed inside the cell, embracing Elizabeth. "Are you all right?" he asked.

"No one has harmed me," Elizabeth said, giving the sheriff another cold glare. Then she pleaded, "Get me out of here, Father. I don't want to spend another night in this . . . in this hellhole. It's even worse than Maysie described. At night . . . at night—"

She stopped and turned her eyes away from him, haunted by the sounds that she had heard the night before. There were moans of pain, and many more of lusty pleasure. As the moonlight had filtered through the narrow windows, she had seen many varieties of sexual activity acted out before her. What she had seen had not only startled her, but sickened her as well.

Earl had seen and heard enough. He turned and faced the sheriff. "I demand you release her immediately," he said, his voice growing louder with each word. "She's no criminal and you know it. Set her free or I'll—"

"If you so much as even look like you're going to threaten me I'll lock you up with your daughter and throw away the key," Sheriff Nolan spit out between clenched teeth. He nodded at Earl. "Forget this foolishness of takin' your daughter with you tonight *or* tomorrow. When the judge arrives from San Francisco, she'll get her day in court. But until then, she's mine. Do you hear? Mine."

Earl's jaw went slack and his heart fell to his feet. He realized that no matter what he said to the sheriff, Elizabeth was to remain in jail.

He turned slowly to Elizabeth and drew her gently into his arms. "I've got to go," he whispered. "But I'll manage to get you out of here. Somehow."

"Please do," Elizabeth whispered back, feeling safe and loved because he had come.

But then Earl whispered something else to her, something that proved that he had little trust in her. That he might even believe that she was guilty of helping in the escape.

"Elizabeth, whose hide are you protecting?" Earl whispered, not allowing her to jerk free when she tried. "Where've you been? With Indians? I saw the Indian saddle. Everett told me that you wore an Indian dress the day you returned home. Tell me, Elizabeth, why?"

Elizabeth pressed her lips together, refusing to respond. She was glad when the sheriff's voice boomed from behind her father, making him release her from his tight grip.

"Come on, you've been in there long enough," Nolan barked.

Her father stepped away from her and gazed into her eyes. She turned her back on him, dying a slow death inside over the way he was looking at her—as if *he* were the judge and jury, handing down a death sentence. Without her having even told him about Strong Heart, he seemed to already know her secret—the secret that she had thought to have locked safely within her heart.

Now what would he do? she thought despairingly to herself.

Earl stared at Elizabeth a moment longer, then stormed from the prison. He lifted himself into his saddle. He was filled with anguish and doubt over Elizabeth's part in the Indian's escape. Her silence was troubling.

But how, he wondered? When would she have met an Indian? It made no sense, no sense at all. Then he recalled how she had somehow managed to get herself involved with that young girl, Maysie.

He now had to believe that she had gone against his orders more than once. She had wandered wherever she pleased when he was not there to stop her.

The thought angered him. Yet, no matter what she had done, no matter how defiant she had become, he would do everything to free his daughter from prison. Only then could he force the answers from her. And this he must do. He hoped that what he would find out would be less awful than it now appeared to be.

He sent his horse into a gallop away from the prison, already devising a plan in his mind as to how Elizabeth might be set free. Morris Murdoch. Morris must have connections—he would surely know who to cut deals with in Seattle to get Elizabeth out of the prison.

"Yes, that's what I'll do," Earl said to himself as he guided his horse through the town. "I'll ask for Murdoch's help. I'm going to ask him to use whatever influence he has to get Elizabeth back home with me."

He gave the prison a look over his right shoulder, then rode onward.

* * *

Elizabeth moved halfheartedly to the bunk in her cell and sat down on its edge, peering at the darkened sky through the window.

Another night.

Another hell.

When would it end? If ever?

20

I think and speak of other things,
To keep my mind at rest.

—John Clare

Discouraged over not finding the raiders after having scoured the countryside looking for them, Strong Heart sat beside a blazing fire in the newly constructed council house. Many braves around him were discussing the matters of their village, especially their plans for the upcoming salmon harvest.

Strong Heart was not only displeased about his unsuccessful search, but also worried about his father. He had not joined the council today. When he had gone to his father's longhouse early this morning, his mother had greeted Strong Heart at the door and dissuaded him from waking his father. His leg wound had kept the old chief awake most of the night.

Guilt filled Strong Heart. Twice now he had let his father down—the day of the raid Strong Heart had not been there to fight for his people, and now he had not found those responsible for his father's injury.

He had let his mother down, as well, by not being able to find her father.

At least there was one thing that could bring some sunshine into his heart as he sat listening to the other braves debating. His *la-daila*. His Elizabeth with the luminous green eyes and hair the color of flame.

Soon she would join him again and then his burden would be lightened. She had a way of making his losses bearable, giving him the strength to forge ahead to the future.

Something one of the braves was saying brought him back to the present.

He listened intently, realizing that while he had been thinking he had missed something important.

"As we have discussed before, again I say that we should forget the salmon harvest this year," the brave was saying, shocking Strong Heart clear to his core. That any brave would ever think such a thing, much less speak it aloud!

Strong Heart leaned forward, his hands resting on his knees. The same brave quickly explained his reasons.

"I say let us catch the salmon for the white men and take the money they have offered instead of keeping the salmon for ourselves." The brave looked nervously over at Strong Heart, whose expression was stern and forbidding.

"I . . . I . . . would even accept their offer to work in their fishery," the brave continued warily. "Why should others have the money, when it could be ours?"

"This that I am hearing, from a brave who has always prided himself on living away from the ways of the white people, basking in the pride of being Suquamish, living only for the honor of being Suquamish, makes Strong Heart ashamed," Strong Heart scolded. His gaze roamed the circle of braves. "Are there others who feel the same? Would you rather work for the white men than your very own people? How could any of you forget the importance of the salmon to the Suquamish? It is what sustains us through the long, harsh winters. Without the salmon, many would go hungry!"

His eyes bored into the one brave that had spoken so favorably of working for the white people, becoming their slave as had so many of their forefathers so long ago.

"This that you bring before our braves today—this talk of working for white men," Strong Heart said, his voice flat, "why do you?"

"Two white men came to our village while you were gone to set Four Winds free from the white man's prison," the brave said, his face flushing under Strong Heart's stare. "They sat in council with your father and made offers that sounded foolish until . . . until . . . after the raid, and I saw how quickly things could change for our people. In one instant, the salmon that we would harvest could be taken from us by fires, set by evil raiders. Now I see the importance of learning ways to feed our people other than the salmon run each autumn."

Strong Heart rose slowly to his feet, towering over the braves in council. With his fists on his hips and his legs spread, he glared from man to man. "Who were these white men intruders?" he asked, his voice filled with wrath. "A name. Do you have names?"

"Morris Murdoch was the only name that stays in my mind," another brave said, looking sternly up at Strong Heart. "The other name has flown."

A smooth and clear voice suddenly spoke from behind Strong Heart, who turned in surprise. His father was limping into the council house with the aid of a staff. Strong Heart started to go to him and was stopped by what his father was saying.

"I, too, have forgotten the white man's name due to all that has happened since their visit," Chief Moon Elk said. "But, my son, while you were gone on your search for the raiders, I sent out scouts to see where the white men were building their fishery that they spoke so openly of—where they wish to enslave our people for what they call wages. This building in which salmon will be processed to sell to other white men sits on the shores of the Sound, close to the hallowed grounds of our people. The white man's house that also sits on our hallowed grounds is lived in by one of the men who came to us with cheap offers of the heart."

Strong Heart's heart constricted and his throat went dry, stunned by what his father had said. In his mind, he saw that day when he had stood on the butte, studying the men working on the shore, erecting a building. He had wondered what it was for.

The realization of who the man was whom Chief Moon Elk was speaking of sent a wave of despair through Strong Heart, making him weave with the pain that the knowledge brought him.

The man was Elizabeth's father! It had to be.

His heart now beat rapidly with anger, as he recalled her explanation for her father's decision to move to the Pacific

Northwest. She had spoken very skillfully around the truth—not actually lying to him, yet not being altogether truthful.

It sickened him to know that all along she had known of her father's schemes to entice the Suquamish into leaving their way of life to take up the white man's culture!

She had surely known, also, that her father had chosen *his* village to work his schemes on. And yet she had not admitted it to Strong Heart.

The thought that she could betray him in the slightest way tore at his very soul, making her betrayal lie heavy on his heart. He fell speechless in front of his father.

Chief Moon Elk went to the circle of men and sat down among them. Strong Heart silently followed and sat down beside his father.

Elizabeth! he despaired to himself. His *la-daila*!

Strong Heart would not allow himself to believe that she would betray him. Knowing her as well as he did, he had to believe that her purpose for lying to him had a good reason.

Ah-hah, he silently decided—yes, he would believe that his woman had lied for a good reason.

As his father conversed with the other braves, convincing them to stay with their people and participate in the salmon harvest only for their people, Strong Heart's thoughts turned elsewhere.

He began thinking about the timing of the white men's visit to his village with offers that they had, in turn, refused, and the massacre that had occurred shortly after.

He could not help but suspect that Elizabeth's father had led the raid in retaliation for the Indians' turning him down.

Would her father have planned the raid in order to frighten the Suquamish into bowing down to his wishes when he came back?

Strong Heart momentarily held his face within his hands, slowly shaking his head.

No! he cried silently to himself. It could not be. Elizabeth was too sweet—too wholesome—to have a totally monstrous father who would kill and maim innocent people.

His father's voice brought Strong Heart out of his turmoil.

He turned to his father and listened to him be the leader who Strong Heart could remember from childhood. As Strong Heart looked slowly around him, he could see that what his father was saying was reaching the braves, persuading them to agree with his every word and command.

"I will listen to no more talk about assisting the white men," Chief Moon Elk said firmly. "Our people will fish the salmon as we always have. It is time to concentrate only on the welfare of our people. We must begin the preparations for the march to the canyon where we have always harvested the salmon in the autumn of the year."

Chief Moon Elk shifted his eyes to Strong Heart. "My son, do you have anything to add?" he said, placing a hand on Strong Heart's shoulder.

Strong Heart felt proud of his father at that moment, and was relieved that his father was able to ignore the pain of his leg, and lead his people again.

The raiders at least had not robbed him of his strength of spirit.

"You have said it all quite eloquently, my father," Strong Heart said, placing a hand on his father's that rested on his shoulder. "There is nothing more that I can add."

When his father leaned over and drew him into a fond embrace, Strong Heart closed his eyes, reveling in this closeness between himself and his father. Strong Heart's place was here, at his father's side. He tried to force Elizabeth from his mind, yet she always seemed to return, haunting his every thought.

He knew that no matter how hard he tried to convince himself that he could do it, he would not be able to forget her all that easily.

* * *

The mountains were a hazy purple against the darkening sky. A deer roasted on a spit over a campfire, sizzling in its own juices.

Four Winds sat quietly in the growing shadows away from the other desperadoes and renegades, listening to Morris Murdoch tell the men about Elizabeth's imprisonment, and that her father wanted her set free.

Four Winds ran one hand along the cold steel barrel of a pistol lying in his lap. He had just cleaned its chambers and reloaded it with soft-tipped bullets. He wondered what he should do about this latest piece of news that could eventually involve his friend, Strong Heart. When had Strong Heart set the woman free? He had seemed determined to keep her as his captive.

No matter, though, Four Winds thought to himself, how she happened to leave Strong Heart. It was the fact that she was jailed in that miserable prison that bothered him.

Not because he was concerned about *her*. Strong Heart was his only concern. If the authorities managed to get information from Elizabeth concerning Strong Heart and Four Winds, they might join Elizabeth in jail and be hanged as criminals.

On the other hand, if the desperadoes went to the prison and broke her out, what then? If they let her return home, the sheriff would only arrest her again.

But if they did not return her home, where would they take her?

If she was not in the custody of Strong Heart, Strong Heart was in danger. It was Four Winds's duty to warn him, for Four Winds owed him a favor for having released him from prison.

Ah-hah, he had to warn Strong Heart of the danger that this woman posed for him—even though revealing this to Strong Heart, would also be revealing that he was not the innocent man that Strong Heart had thought. His best friend would know that Four Winds *was* a renegade, who had joined up with his old friends again. The excitement that riding with outlaws offered had become too thick in his blood to leave.

Four Winds rose quietly to his feet, making sure not to draw undue attention to himself. He continued to listen to Morris Murdoch, who was the leader of the gang.

"Men, let's go and get Earl's daughter out of prison," Murdoch urged. "What can it hurt? You need some excitement in your life now, don't you, since you've been forced to lie low in the hills. Staying away from raidin' until things cooled off a mite. Set his daughter free and we'll hide her someplace where the sheriff can't find her. Earl will have to accept that as a condition of her being rescued. And he will. The fool. He doesn't know that he doesn't have much time left to enjoy her. After everything is set with the Suquamish, I plan to kill Earl and take complete control of the fishery."

Morris laughed throatily. "But all in due time," he said, sipping from a cup of coffee. "Everything good comes to those who wait."

As the men put their heads together and began making plans on how to break Elizabeth out of the prison, Four Winds slipped away unnoticed.

When he got to the horses, he went to his and very easily untethered it and launched himself into the saddle.

Knowing how to be as quiet as a panther in the night, he urged his horse in a soft lope away from the campsite.

Yet again he worried about telling Strong Heart that he was at heart a renegade—an outlaw. But his loyalty to his friend was much stronger than his fear of being condemned in Strong Heart's eyes.

When he was far enough away from the campsite, Four Winds bent low over his horse and sent it into a hard gallop across the land, hoping that he could get to Strong Heart's village in time. Strong Heart would have to make his own decision about what should happen to the woman.

21

A burden still of chilling fear
I find in every place.
—JOHN CLARE

Elizabeth's cell was dark, with only thin beams of moonlight sifting through the bars above her bunk, where she lay in a fetal position. She clutched her arms around herself, shivering not so much from the chill of the night—but from the horror of everything that went on in the jail after the cloak of night had fallen. The moon had given off enough light for her to see bodies scrambling together, fulfilling their lusts once again, tonight.

And now everyone but her seemed to be asleep. Snores, groans, and women sobbing in their sleep reached Elizabeth's ears. Maysie had been right to have pitied the women in this godforsaken place. In the larger cells women and men alike were housed. Elizabeth had seen too many of the women bent to the wills of the men.

No matter what their crime might have been, only stealing a piece of bread to keep from starving to death, most of the women in this prison were treated like animals. Elizabeth wished that she could do something to help them, yet she could not even help herself!

Tears splashed from her eyes as she thought of Strong Heart. She could not expect Strong Heart to help her, for he did not even know that she was in the prison.

But her father! Why hadn't he gotten her out of this hell-hole? He had money, plenty of money. Surely he could have found a way to pay for her release!

The sound of the sheriff's office door opening startled Elizabeth. With trembling fingers she reached beneath the mattress and found the fork that she had hidden there after her evening meal. She didn't trust the sheriff, or his deputy. She had never forgotten how the sheriff had tried to rape her on her first visit to the prison on the day of Four Winds's escape.

To protect herself, she had managed to steal a fork from her dinner tray. She wasn't sure how much damage a mere fork could do, but at least it would give her a slim chance of protecting herself.

Her eyes wide, she watched a form moving in the dark toward her cell. She slid the fork beneath a fold of her dress, clutching desperately to the handle.

Her heart pounded as she saw the man take a ring of keys from his back pocket and sort through them, until he found the one that fit the lock of Elizabeth's cell.

The door creaked slowly open and she was finally able to see who it was now standing over her, slipping the ring of keys back into his pocket, his free hand at the fly of his breeches, eagerly undoing its buttons.

"Deputy Bradley," Elizabeth gasped, inching her way from the edge of the bunk, then hugging the wall with her back when she could go no further.

She still held the fork in her hand. Her throat was dry and fear gripped her hard in the pit of her stomach.

"Don't say a word, slut," Deputy Bradley said through yellow teeth, his coppery mustache twitching as he spoke. "Just keep still or I'll do worse than rape you. I'll save the judge a day in court. If you're dead, he won't have to bother with rulin' you innocent or guilty."

His words made Elizabeth feel as though ice water had been poured into her veins. She was shocked that this man could be this devious—this heartless. Until now, of the two men who controlled the jail, Elizabeth had thought that she could trust Deputy Bradley more. He appeared young and not yet as hardened as Sheriff Nolan.

When Deputy Bradley dropped his pants Elizabeth thought this might be her best opportunity to make her attack. But as she took the fork out from beneath her dress, the moonlight flashed on it, revealing it to Deputy Bradley. He jerked it from her hand before she could even plunge it into his face.

Deputy Bradley tossed the fork aside and quickly straddled Elizabeth. "Bitch," he said, holding her wrists to the bunk, one of his knees shoving her dress upward. "You think you can stop me? It's been too long since I've had me a woman like you to let anything stop me from gettin' what I'm after."

His lips crushed Elizabeth's with a wet, slobbering kiss as he started lowering his manhood toward her. Panic rushed in her like wild fires spreading through dry brush. Elizabeth raised one knee and hit him hard in the groin with it. He leaped away from her with a yowl and clutched himself where she had caused the damage.

Elizabeth jumped from the bunk and grabbed the fork from the floor and held it threateningly before her, her eyes flashing. "Get out of here and leave me be," she said breathlessly. She was stunned to see that he seemed unable to move as he still held himself, moaning and groaning.

Suddenly she was aware of something else. The commotion had awakened all of the prisoners. They were shouting and jeering and mimicking the deputy. The place was in an uproar.

Deputy Bradley glared at Elizabeth as he slowly leaned over to pick up his pants. Not bothering to put them on, he inched around her and left the cell. He stopped long enough to fish his keys out of his pocket, then locked the cell behind him.

Elizabeth breathed hard as she watched him limp away, tossing curses over his shoulder as the prisoners continued to jeer and mock him.

Then Elizabeth sank back down onto the bunk, fearing the rest of the days and nights of her incarceration, for surely the deputy would find a way to make her pay.

* * *

A movement in his longhouse awakened Strong Heart. He groped around until he found the knife that he always kept close beside his bed, and then bolted from his sleeping platform, the knife poised for its death plunge.

When Four Winds came out of the shadows and stood over

the dying embers of the firepit, Strong Heart sighed and lowered the knife to his side.

"It is unwise, *me-sah-chie,* bad, to enter a dwelling unannounced, whether it is night or day," Strong Heart said, bending to place the knife back on the floor.

He then gestured with a hand toward Four Winds. "*Mitlite,* sit down, my friend," he said softly. "Tell me why you have come in the middle of the night to awaken Strong Heart. What news do you bring me?"

Strong Heart watched Four Winds carefully as he sat down, his dark brown hair held into place by a colorfully beaded headband. Strong Heart remembered his father suspecting Four Winds of being among their village's attackers. Strong Heart still could not believe his friend capable of such a fiendish act.

"There is not much time for talk," Four Winds said, his expression troubled.

"There is not time for you to tell me if you have rejoined your people?" Strong Heart asked, raising an eyebrow. "There is not enough time for me to ask of your people's welfare?"

"No," Four Winds said, placing his hands on his knees, leaning on them as he locked his eyes with Strong Heart's. "There is no time for idle talk of family. I have come with news of something other than my people, or yours."

Strong Heart's spine stiffened and his jaw tightened. "What news then is it that you bring me, that you find it important enough to awake me from my sleep?" he asked. "Tell me now, Four Winds. What is it?"

"It is because of the woman with the hair of flame that I come to you tonight," Four Winds said, seeing alarm enter his friend's eyes. "Strong Heart, she has been arrested. She is in Copper Hill Prison. She is accused of being a partner with the one who set me free which, of course, is you, my friend."

Strong Heart's mouth gaped and his heart seemed to stop beating, the shock was so quick and overwhelming.

Then he bolted to his feet and began scrambling around the longhouse, slipping into his buckskins and moccasins. With a growl, he grabbed his rifle and held it up in the air. "They shall die for doing this to my *la-daila,*" he cried, forgetting all of his doubts about Elizabeth. At this moment, there was no doubt exactly what she meant to him, and always would. He must save her.

He turned to Four Winds as he rose to his feet. "You will ride with me?" he said, his eyes dark with emotion. "My friend, you will help me set her free?"

"This I would do gladly, except . . ." Four Winds said, lowering his eyes, for now was a time of truth between friends—a truth that might turn them into enemies.

"Except what?" Strong Heart dared to ask, seeing now that something was very wrong in Four Winds's demeanor. Instead of being proud for having brought such news to a friend, Four Winds was acting as one who had something to be ashamed about.

Strong Heart's pulse raced as he waited for Four Winds's explanation. They did not have much time to waste, when his beloved was at the mercy of too many whose hearts were black. He must *hy-ak,* hurry, and get to her before she was harmed by the *cultus,* worthless man, the sheriff.

Yet, because of friendship, he must wait for Four Winds to say his piece.

Four Winds looked slowly up at Strong Heart. "You did not ask me how I knew about the white woman being in the prison," he said, his voice quiet.

"I saw no need," Strong Heart said, his puzzlement deepening. "If Elizabeth is jailed, surely those in the city know, and such news spreads quickly."

Then Strong Heart was shaken by a thought. "But you, my friend, should not be near the city, or with those who would hear such news," he said slowly. "You should be with your people, or still be hiding in the hills."

Strong Heart walked around the fire and came eye to eye with Four Winds. "Tell me, my friend, how do you know about Elizabeth?"

Four Winds lifted his chin and folded his arms across his chest. "The news traveled to the band of outlaws of which I am a part," he said, holding his voice steady, although his heart was pounding like distant thunder within his chest. "Now you know that the law was not wrong about me. I *am* a criminal who enjoys raiding the white settlers. Elizabeth's father is friends with the leader of the gang. The father asked his help in setting Elizabeth free from prison. They are on their way even now, Strong Heart. We will not be able to reach Elizabeth before the gang gets to her. It is dangerous for you, Strong Heart, either way—whether she is in prison, or freed by the outlaws. If she is able to point an accusing finger at you for setting me free, *you* could be the one that will use the hangman's noose that has been readied for me."

Strong Heart was silent and numb from Four Winds's confession. He recalled his ravaged village the day after the fatal attack on his people, and his father's thoughts about Four Winds's part in it.

He reached a hand to Four Winds's throat and sank his fingers in it. "I do not know if I should call you *pelton,* foolish, or brave, for coming to my village tonight with the pretense of being my friend," he said, his eyes filled with fire.

Four Winds paled and his eyes widened. "What do you mean?" he gasped. "What are you saying? I have done nothing to cause you to turn on me, my friend. I have come to you tonight, for payment in part for what you did for me. But, most of all, I have come because of our lifelong friendship. Why do you doubt me? Why do you treat me harshly, instead of as a friend?"

"By the cover of night you did not notice that my village is being rebuilt, and that some of the totem poles stand half burned by such raiders that you profess to being part of?" Strong Heart hissed. "Can you say that you do not know of the plight of my people? That you did not ride with your friends against my people? Against me?"

Four Winds tried to shake his head, the effort only causing Strong Heart's fingers to dig more deeply into his flesh. "Believe me when I say that I know nothing of such a raid," he rasped out. "And since my return to my comrades, there have been no raids, not even on the settlers. They are lying low, waiting for things to settle down since my arrest. They . . . they . . . are taking a chance riding into town to help the white woman escape.

They do this because the man who is their leader asked them to, and owe him much. He keeps them in food and clothes in harder times. They did not notice when I slipped away to warn you."

The thought again of Elizabeth in the prison caused Strong Heart to wince and his heart to cry out in pain. He dropped his hand away from Four Winds. "We will talk later of these things that are new between us," he said thickly. "For now, Four Winds, my heart and mind is full only of Elizabeth. Let us ride together as friends. Let us take this woman from the prison. Then, as friends, we will talk. You can explain to me why you have chosen the life of crime over the congenial life of the Suquamish."

Four Winds nodded and they left the longhouse in a rush. He waited for Strong Heart to go to his parents to explain why he would be gone, and for Strong Heart to get his horse.

Soon they were riding hard beneath the moonlight, Four Winds giving Strong Heart questioning glances. "This woman!" he finally shouted. "She means much to you? You find her special?"

Strong Heart turned flashing eyes on Four Winds. "She is my life!" he confessed loudly, his words echoing far across the land, through the forest, and to the sky.

22

Whatever on my heart may fall,
Remember, I would risk it all!

—ADELAIDE ANNE PROCTER

It had been a day's ride for Strong Heart and Four Winds—a ride against time. Finally, at midnight the next night, they arrived on the butte that overlooked Copper Hill Prison.

Strong Heart glared down at the prison, seeing no activity, or light glowing from any of the barred windows. The only light that was evident was in the sheriff's office, and even that was only a dim golden glow as it shone through the glass panes.

Strong Heart gave Four Winds a quick glance. "You know the dangers and yet you still come with me to the prison?" he asked, his hand resting on the stock of his rifle that hung from the side of his saddle. "We could be hanging side by side on the platform tomorrow if we do not succeed in releasing my *ladaila* from prison. You would risk that for my woman?"

"No," Four Winds said flatly, giving Strong Heart a steely gaze. "I do it for *you,* my friend."

This proved many things to Strong Heart—the most important being that Four Winds could not have participated in the raid against Strong Heart's people. It would not make sense to go against Strong Heart one minute, then ally himself the next.

He reached over and placed a firm hand on Four Winds's shoulder. "Friends forever?" he asked, his face questioning.

Four Winds placed a hand on Strong Heart's. "Forever," he said vehemently. "Now, and always!"

Strong Heart nodded, then dropped his hand back to his rifle, and quietly studied the prison again. He nodded once more toward Four Winds, then slapped his horse and began edging his way down the side of the butte. Four Winds followed him into the forest that bordered the prison.

When the prison was in sight through a break in the trees, Strong Heart felt a fever of anticipation building within him as he slipped easily out of the saddle.

Four Winds dismounted and soon they were moving stealthily through the forest. Their hands clutched their rifles, and their eyes darted about them, watching for any sudden movement.

"I fear that this is too easy," Strong Heart whispered to Four Winds, stopping at the edge of the forest, to stare at the door that led into the prison. "I see no activity—no people. Is everyone asleep?"

"It may appear so but I was housed in the prison long enough to know the nighttime activities there," Four Winds whispered back. "They are unpleasant, yet the sheriff and his deputies have a hands-off policy. Whatever happens in the shadows behind the bars in the business of the prisoners—and their victims. But *ah-hah,* this time of night the sheriff or whoever is in charge, sleeps. We shall enter the prison unnoticed. We shall leave just as easily."

What Four Winds had said about the activity in the cells after dark made Strong Heart feel ill. Who was to say what may have happened to Elizabeth?

His jaw tightened. If Elizabeth had been defiled or even so much as touched by any man in that prison, the man responsible would not live to see the next sunrise! Strong Heart would take much pleasure in plunging a knife into the man's dark heart!

Not letting his imagination distract him from his purpose, Strong Heart began running softly toward the door of the prison. His moccasined feet were as quiet as the pads of a cat. He glanced over at Four Winds, glad to be with his friend again on an adventure. As children, they had sought out the dangers of the forest beyond, enjoying the challenge of the bear, the panther, and the wolf.

Yet this that they were doing tonight was even more challenging than anything else they had done in the past. For Strong

Heart's reward would be to hold Elizabeth in his arms again, to become her protector for all their tomorrows.

Looking warily from side to side, seeing no sign of anyone, Strong Heart and Four Winds stopped long enough to lean their backs against the prison wall, to get their breaths.

Strong Heart cocked his rifle and Four Winds cocked his.

They stared into each other's eyes, then nodded in unison, and crept to the door.

Strong Heart nodded at Four Winds, then nodded toward the door latch. He then stood aside with his rifle ready to fire as Four Winds followed his silent bidding and slowly opened the door.

Strong Heart looked inside the sheriff's office, and he could see that a deputy was there instead of the sheriff. The deputy was fast asleep at the desk.

Gripping his rifle, Strong Heart moved stealthily and quickly into the room, Four Winds behind him. Strong Heart rendered the deputy unconscious with a blow to his head from the butt of his rifle. The man never knew what hit him.

"The keys," Strong Heart said, standing guard beside the door that led to the cells. "Four Winds, get the keys."

Glancing over his shoulder at the deputy, Four Winds went to the pegs on the wall and slipped a ring of keys from them. Standing his rifle against the wall, he sorted through them. Soon he and Strong Heart were standing in the shadows of the back room, the moonlight sifting through the small windows of each of the cells the only light.

Everything was quiet, except for snores from the cells on either side. This made Strong Heart breathe easier, knowing that while everyone slept, his woman was safe from abuse.

Peering through the darkness, Strong Heart checked the cells, determining who was housed in them. His pulse raced.

The moon was shining on long and drifting red hair that hung over the side of the bunk in the first cell. Strong Heart recognized the exquisite creamy skin of Elizabeth's face as she lay asleep on her side, her dark brush of lashes on her cheeks.

Strong Heart was for the moment too overcome to move.

Such a sight as this sent his heart into a tailspin of love for his *la-daila*. How could he ever live without her?

His gaze lingered on her lips, remembering how passionately moist they could become as he kissed her.

Then he lowered his gaze to where the tantalizing cleavage of her breasts could be seen where her dress dipped low. Her translucent body seemed to gleam in the moonlight.

He wanted to take her in his arms and press her against him and challenge anyone who might try to separate them.

Four Winds had stopped beside Strong Heart. He saw Elizabeth in the cell, then turned his eyes back to Strong Heart. He placed a hand on Strong Heart's shoulder. "We must *hy-ak,* hurry," he whispered. "The sheriff might come and check on things."

"Ah-hah," Strong Heart whispered back, shaken from his reverie. He realized how foolish it had been to allow his thoughts to interfere with his need to move quickly to get Elizabeth safely from this prison.

Four Winds went to the cell and slipped the key into the lock. The click of the tumblers echoed all around them, awakening not only Elizabeth, but some others.

Elizabeth sat up with a start, her eyes wide. She gazed in terror toward the open cell door. Then she gasped with surprise as she saw Strong Heart rush into the cell toward her.

"Strong Heart?" she said, tears spilling from her eyes as he gathered her into his arms and began carrying her from the cell. She looped an arm around his neck and clung to him. "I should've known that you would find out and would come for me."

When Four Winds moved past her and Strong Heart, toward the door that led to the office, her eyes widened. "And Four Winds is here also?" she asked, looking questioningly into Strong Heart's eyes. They stepped into the office, the shouts and cries of the other prisoners a loud rumble behind them.

She then paled as she looked down at the deputy with blood streaming from a gash at the back of his head. Strong Heart hurried toward the door that led outside. "Is he dead?" she asked, her voice hushed. "Did you have to kill him to set me free?"

"He is only slightly injured," Strong Heart said, heading outside toward the cover of the forest.

Elizabeth held on to Strong Heart as he carried her away from the awful prison. She pressed her cheek against his chest, then looked quickly over his shoulder. The wails of the women who had been left behind sent shivers up her spine.

"Those poor women," she cried, reaching a hand out toward the prison. "We must go back. We must set them free! You don't know how so many of them are forced to live! I was left alone. I was one of the lucky ones!"

"There is no time," Strong Heart said, running up to his horse and quickly placing her in the saddle.

He jumped before her into the saddle, then looked over at Four Winds who was astride his horse. "Four Winds, would you say that the town is deserted enough for us to make our escape through it?" Strong Heart asked, his horse pawing at the ground nervously. "Climbing the steep butte will slow our escape. I feel that it would be much faster to ride through the city and lose ourselves in that stretch of forest that is not so hilly."

"*Ah-hah,* I feel that you are right," Four Winds said. "And for the comfort of the woman, I think that escape is best."

Strong Heart nodded, then flicked his rawhide reins and sank his moccasined heels into the flanks of the roan, sending it out into the open, and down the steep grade of street beside Four Winds's horse.

When they reached First Avenue, they slowed their pace, not wanting to draw undue attention from those who still lingered along the boardwalks and those who swayed drunkenly outside the saloons.

Elizabeth clung to Strong Heart's waist, fearing capture. Then her attention was drawn to someone besides the loitering drunks. She drew in a breath when she recognized a young lady walking out of a saloon, steering a man who teetered alongside her.

"Maysie!" Elizabeth gasped, stunned to see how gaudily

Maysie was dressed, and how thickly painted her cheeks were with rouge. The bright red dress that Maysie was wearing was cut short above her knees, with layers upon layers of lacy petticoats beneath it that bounced as she walked. The bodice was cut low, revealing all but the nipples of her breasts. Her hair was tied up in a loose chignon, with a few curls of hair that coiled down on each side above her ears.

Elizabeth's heart sank at the sight. It saddened her to see that Maysie had gone back to whoring. Yet she was at least relieved to know that Maysie was alive, if one could call that sort of life *living*.

Then Elizabeth's attention was caught when she heard Four Winds gasp as he saw Maysie being escorted from the saloon. She could hear him utter something under his breath as his eyes became filled with hurt, and she had to wonder what Maysie was to him.

Had they met in the brothel? Had he bought time with Maysie, and then fallen in love with her?

She dispelled these thoughts as she remembered the urgent matter of their escape. Strong Heart headed toward the forest, away from the direction of her house.

"You aren't returning me home to my father?" she asked, then realized how foolish the question was before he even answered her. If she returned home, the sheriff would come and get her again as soon as he knew about the escape. She had to hide from the sheriff. She was now a fugitive, along with Strong Heart and Four Winds.

She knew that a speedy escape now was of the essence, not only for herself, but for the man that she loved. He had risked his life again for her.

Oh, but how could she ever truly repay him? How?

Strong Heart looked over his shoulder at her. "You are going to my village again, and this time not as my prisoner, but as my beloved! I was foolish to leave you behind. This I will never allow again! You will be at my side at all times—even during those times I am called away to serve as speaker for my people. My *la-daila*, you will never be in danger again. Never!"

Tears streamed down Elizabeth's face and her eyes gratefully shone at Strong Heart.

Then as Strong Heart turned away from her, she hugged her arms more tightly around his waist, locking her to him. She pressed her cheek against his back, knowing that words were easy—but not always so easily kept.

Although Strong Heart was with her, that did not mean that she was safe. Should the sheriff form another posse and set out on a search for them, could they escape forever?

She closed her eyes tightly, trying to block out such fears.

At this moment she *was* safe, and she would revel in it. And she was with her beloved again!

23

Ah! What is love?
It is a pretty thing.
—Robert Greene

The sun was just rising in a great splash of orange. The birds were waking in the trees overhead. Fish were fastened in strips to willow poles stuck in the ground near the campfire. The delicious aroma of the juices as they dripped into the flames, tantalized her as it filled the air. A spring, its bubbly water sweet and pure, flowed nearby.

Elizabeth was weary from the long ride from Seattle, and was feeling as if history was repeating itself as she sat beside the campfire, listening to Strong Heart and Four Winds discussing Four Winds's association with the outlaws.

When the words got heated, she looked guardedly from one to the other.

"Four Winds, when I set you free from prison, it was my sincere belief that you were not linked with the outlaws in any way," Strong Heart said, his jaw tight. "And now I discover that you are. Do you not see how foolish this makes me appear?"

Four Winds glowered at Strong Heart. "Had you known I was guilty of choosing my own way of life—the life of a renegade—you would have let me, your childhood companion, hang," he said dryly. "You would condemn me to death?"

"In my heart I would not want to," Strong Heart grumbled. "But, *ah-hah,* yes, I would have no choice but to allow the noose to be slipped over your head. What you stand for does not show a Suquamish brave well in the eyes of all who see you. As a renegade, you do not set a good example, Four

Winds, for the children of your village or mine. Tell me, Four Winds, why did you choose this road that you have followed?"

Four Winds hesitated. He took a willow pole with its skewered meat from the ground and handed it to Elizabeth. He did the same for Strong Heart, then took some for himself. Yet he only stared at it, instead of eating.

"At first I thought what I was doing was best for our people as a whole," he mumbled. He looked slowly up at Strong Heart, who also was not eating. "I saw the onslaught of white settlers as a threat to our existence. I rode with the desperadoes only to frighten the whites from our land." He lowered his eyes again, then said softly, "After a while what I was doing was more for excitement than for our people. In a sense, I was free again, with no white authority dictating to me how I should live."

His jaw tightened. "It is good to be free," he said forcefully.

"Do you not see that Strong Heart is even more free than you?" Strong Heart said, placing a hand on Four Winds's shoulder. "You became the hunted the moment you raided and killed that first white settler."

"You are now the hunted, also, my friend," Four Winds said, swallowing hard. He clapped his free hand onto Strong Heart's shoulder. "And it is because of me that you are. It would have been best had you allowed me to die, Strong Heart. It would have been best for all concerned."

Strong Heart turned his eyes to Elizabeth and gave her a lingering look. He knew that she would have been better off had she not become involved in these escapes, yet if she had not, they would have never known the wonders of the love they felt for each other.

And theirs was a special love—enduring to the end of time! For this, he turned grateful eyes to Four Winds and could not find it within his heart to totally condemn him.

"It is never too late for you to turn your back on this wrong life that you have chosen," Strong Heart said, dropping his hand from Four Winds's shoulder. Four Winds lifted his away.

"That is not what I wish to do," Four Winds said, his eyes

holding steady with Strong Heart's. "It is still the life that I want. Do not fight me over it. I have my life. You have yours."

There was a strained silence between them. Four Winds turned his eyes away and began pulling meat from his stick with his teeth, slowly chewing it as he stared into the flames of the fire.

Elizabeth waited breathlessly for Strong Heart's next move, then relaxed when he also began to eat. Not taking her eyes off the two Suquamish braves, she also began eating, hardly tasting the food. The tension between Four Winds and Strong Heart seemed wound so tight it might snap at any moment.

Then Strong Heart spoke abruptly, breaking the silence with his forceful voice.

"Four Winds, I urge you to reconsider this choice that you have made," he said, laying his stick and half-eaten food aside. "It is time for you to choose sides—to live still as a renegade, or the life of a Suquamish brave who shares each and every breath and deed with his people."

"You ask the impossible of Four Winds," Four Winds grumbled. "I cannot do this thing you ask. I have already deceived my friends last night. I cannot do anything else against them."

Elizabeth's mind was spinning with questions about many things. How had Four Winds known about her? Why had he cared? Why would he help release her if he was aligned with outlaws?

He had been motivated by friendship—friendship with Strong Heart.

But this was not answer enough for her. She would ply Strong Heart with many questions once they were alone.

"You are too hasty in your response tonight," Strong Heart said. "Because of what we were to each other as children, I will wait for you to think this through, this that I ask of you. Such a friendship as yours and mine cannot so quickly be cast aside, like something trivial and worthless. *Ah-hah,* I will await your response another day."

"*Kloshe,* good," Four Winds said, nodding, relief showing in his face. "*Ah-hah,* that is good."

"Four Winds, you said that you had nothing to do with the raid on my people, and I believe you. But I must ask you again if you think those of your outlaw band are responsible?" Strong Heart said, lifting up his stick and biting pieces of fish from it.

Four Winds took a bite of his own fish, then laid it aside as he looked at Strong Heart. "If I knew the answer, I would tell you," he said. "As I have told you, I did not return to my outlaw friends immediately after my departure from you the night of the escape. I went to the hills for two nights and two days. When I returned, they were also in hiding, and nothing at all was said about any raid on your people."

Strong Heart frowned as he thrust his stick into the flames of the fire and watched it catch fire and burn. "Of course, they would not mention it in front of you," he said in a low grumble. "You are Suquamish. They would expect you to still have some loyalty to our tribe. They would not want to give you cause to go against them, especially after hearing that it was your Suquamish friend who set you free."

"Perhaps so," Four Winds said, nodding. "But as far as I know, my friends are innocent of the crime."

Strong Heart turned his gaze to Elizabeth, now recalling that Four Winds had told him that her father was a friend to Morris Murdoch, the leader of the outlaw gang. His eyes narrowed, thinking about the two white men who had come to his village with proposals.

One was Elizabeth's father. The other was Morris Murdoch.

And now that he knew that Morris Murdoch was the leader, he suspected even more strongly that Elizabeth's father and this Morris Murdoch had played a role in the raid on his village. Either Four Winds was lying, or was innocent of knowledge.

But he would not mention this to Elizabeth just yet. She had been through enough without having to worry about her father's association with outlaws.

Ah-hah, yes, for now all that was truly important to him was that his woman was with him again and his people were readying themselves for the salmon run. Everything else would come later.

And it would come. Everything had an end—even the lives of those who were responsible for the massacre in his village.

"It is time that I part from you again, my friend," Four Winds said, pushing himself up from the ground. "Let nothing cause our friendship to end. To me, it is most valuable."

Strong Heart rose to his feet and went with Four Winds to the grazing horses. When Four Winds turned to him, Strong Heart hesitated, then flung his arms around Four Winds and gave him a tight hug.

"I will await word of your choice in life," Strong Heart said huskily. Then he stepped away from Four Winds and watched him climb into his saddle and ride away.

Strong Heart returned to the campsite and sat down beside Elizabeth. For a moment he stared gloomily into the fire, so many things troubling him.

Then he turned to Elizabeth and took her face in his hands, and gently drew her nearer.

"I can depend on you to always remain true to my heart?" he asked softly, his eyes searching hers for the answer that he sought.

"Ah-hah," Elizabeth said. Her using the Suquamish word pleased Strong Heart. His smile broadened, causing Elizabeth's insides to begin a slow, sensual melting.

"Forever and always," she added softly, fastening her arms around his neck, urging his lips to hers.

As he kissed her, his fingers crushed her hair and his body pressed hers to the ground.

The kiss continued and his hands busied themselves with undressing her. Then he drew apart from her long enough to remove his own clothes. He knelt over her, the golden flames of the fire reflected on his body giving it a coppery sheen.

Elizabeth caught her breath when Strong Heart stretched out above her, bracing himself with his arms, his hands laced with hers, and holding them slightly above her.

With a knee he parted her legs and soon she felt the wonders of his manhood pressing gently into her soft folds.

Elizabeth wrapped her legs around him, her hips responding to his touch as she raised her pelvis toward him.

She drew in a breath of wild happiness as he entered her in one deep thrust.

Elizabeth moved her body sinuously against his and drew him more deeply into the warmth of her body, only half aware of her whimpers.

Then a rush of pure bliss flooded her senses and his body jerked and spasmed into hers. She again knew the true meaning of his wild embrace.

* * *

Sheriff Nolan walked listlessly into his office, his jaw puffed out with a fresh wad of tobacco. Then he almost choked on it when he discovered Deputy Bradley dead on the floor, a knife protruding from his back. Then his own body jumped when someone stepped up from behind him and knocked him unconscious with the butt of a pistol.

A bandanna hiding his face, Morris Murdoch slipped his heavy pistol back inside its holster and hurried to the door and looked toward the forest. He motioned with a wave of his hand for the other outlaws to make a rush on the prison. He grabbed the keys and went to the back room to set Elizabeth free. Then he stopped in surprise. She wasn't there.

He stormed down the long corridor of cells. "Where is she?" he shouted, looking from prisoner to prisoner. "Who took her?"

"Let us out of this hellhole!" was the response from several prisoners who spoke almost in unison. "Who cares what happened to that woman? Set *us* free, damn it!"

Morris looked nervously from cell to cell. He stopped a few times to stare at women who appealed to him with their tearful eyes, their hands reaching through the bars toward him.

Then he went to one cell in particular, glaring at the man who stood close to the bars. He reached inside and grabbed him by the collar. "I've come for only one lady and by God, if you value your life, you'll tell me who took her away," he said angrily.

The man made a strangling noise as Morris's fingers twisted the collar. "It . . . was . . . dark," the man said, gasping. "No one could see who took her. But . . . it . . . was a man. He carried her away. That's . . . all any of us know."

Wondering who could have gotten there before him and his men, Morris mouthed an obscenity as he released the man.

Several of the outlaws rushed into the back room, then stopped and gawked.

Joe Feather went to Morris. "You'd best get her and let's get out of here," he said, his voice low. "It's almost daylight. Someone's bound to come and catch us here."

"She's not here," Morris grumbled, his brows meeting in a frown. "Goddamn it all to hell, she's not here."

"Where is she?" Joe asked, tipping his hat back with his forefinger.

"Who's to say?" Morris said, shrugging. He stroked his chin, looking at the prisoners.

"I'd say that's good," Joe said, patting his holstered pistol. "I didn't take much to this escape, anyhow. What were we going to do with her once we got her? She'd just draw the law to us, that's all."

"If we don't do something about these prisoners, the law'll get drawn to us now, no matter how you look at it," Morris said, pushing aside Joe and stomping back to the sheriff's office. He gestured. "Come with me. We've things to do."

Joe Feather scampered after him. They joined those who were inside the office, their firearms drawn.

"Let's get a fire goin'," Morris said, his eyes gleaming as he went to the desk and grabbed up several yellowed papers and began scattering them around the room. "Frank? You go start setting the prisoners free. Panama? You stand guard outside and see to it that no one sees what we're doin'. If someone comes even near the prison, shoot 'em. We've got to make a clean sweep of this mess we've made today. And we don't need no witnesses."

Frank went to Morris, his pockmarked face wary. "The

prisoners?" he asked in a monotone. "Don't you think they'll be witnesses if any of them gets caught?"

"As I see it the community is going to be too busy fighting the fire to worry about catchin' escaped convicts. And these people aren't going to stay in these parts any longer than they can help it. They've already got a taste of what it's like to be here at Copper Hill Prison. They won't allow it to happen again. I'm sure they'd kill themselves before coming back. Why would they tattle on those who've been kind enough to set them free?"

"I guess you're right," Frank said, taking the keys Morris handed to him. He left, and soon there was a stampede from the back room as men and women ran from their cells, breathlessly free.

"Clear out of here!" Morris shouted to his men. "I'm going to set everything on fire!"

Soon flames were flickering from the barred windows and the panes of the front windows exploded, spewing glass everywhere.

"Get back to our hideout, quick!" Morris shouted as he ran toward the forest for his horse. "I'll meet you there later. I've things to do here in town."

By the time Morris was riding nonchalantly down First Avenue, the fire wagons were already clanging and rushing up the steep hill toward the prison. Black smoke billowed up into the sky, darkening the heavens as if it were midnight, instead of early morning.

Morris rode onward, ignoring the clamor of people who were riding their horses toward the prison. He knew what they would eventually find—two bodies, not a hundred. And it would be hard for them to identify whether they were the sheriff and the deputy.

No one would ever know how it had happened, or who had caused it.

Or who had taken Elizabeth away? And why? Had they known about his plans? Or had it just been coincidence that someone had gotten there before him?

In this life, there seemed to be nobody who could be trusted. No one!

He rode on to Earl's house and found him already at the fishery, getting an early start on the day. After securing his horse's reins to the hitching rail, Morris went inside the fishery and stood over the desk, where Earl was entering some figures into a ledger.

Earl looked up at Morris, his eyes eager. "Well?" he said quickly. "Did you find a way to free Elizabeth?"

"I didn't have to, it seems," Morris said, trying to fake concern. "When I got up this morning, I saw the flames shooting up into the sky from the prison. Earl, the fire wagons could do no good. By the time they got to it, it was gone."

Earl's knees weakened and his heart leapt into his throat. He started to rise from his chair, but he was too weak to stand. "Tell me," he said, his voice rasping. "What-what about Elizabeth? Did-did someone get her out before the prison burned?"

"Someone came and told me that everyone in the prison had been set free before the fire started, even Elizabeth," Morris said, seeing the relief in Earl's eyes. "As best they can tell, the sheriff and deputy perished in the fire."

"But Elizabeth?" Earl stammered. "What of my Elizabeth? Where is she? Who is she with? It's like before. She's been abducted! But by who?"

"Better she's been abducted, than dead," Morris said, shrugging. "And one thing for sure, Earl, there is something positive about this happening. Your daughter's name is now free and clear of any guilt. The sheriff and deputy are dead. They were the two who was responsible for her being there. And all of the records that could show her as having been there, and why, have been destroyed in the fire."

Earl nodded. Then he felt despair over losing his daughter again. He was beginning to think that he would never, ever, see her again, and felt that it was his punishment for having neglected her all of those years when he had been fortunate enough to have and love her.

He silently vowed to himself that if he ever had the opportunity to be her father again, he would make everything up to her. He would show her what a father's true devotion was all about.

24

All night upon mine heart I felt her warm heart beat,
Night long within my arms in love and sleep she lay.
—Ernest Dowson

Mount Rainier was rising through morning fog as Strong Heart's village came into sight. Elizabeth clung to Strong Heart's waist as his horse cantered slowly across the land, her gaze drawn to the activity of some Suquamish women on the sandy bank of the river.

Using wooden sticks bound loosely with a twist of cedar bark, a young woman carefully extracted a hot rock from a bed of coals. With the sizzling rock securely clamped in the tongs, the woman ran a few steps across the beach to some women who were working around a big, square wooden box filled with steaming water.

Quickly the girl dipped the hot rock in a small container of water to rinse off the ash from the fire, then dropped it into the box.

"What are those women doing?" Elizabeth asked, her curiosity aroused. She was glad to have something to say to break the silence that had fallen between her and Strong Heart the closer they had come to his village.

It puzzled her how his mood had changed from being caring and loving the previous evening, to someone distant now, as if he was carrying the burden of the world on his shoulders.

She had to believe it was because many duties awaited him helping his father prepare for the salmon run.

Elizabeth prayed that his moody silence had nothing to do with her. Yet, she could not see any reason why it should. Nothing had changed between them that she was aware of.

Strong Heart was silent for a moment longer, then heaved

a sigh and answered her. It seemed to her a halfhearted explanation, as though it was bothersome to him to answer. Again she was puzzled. Usually he was anxious to explain the ways of his people to her.

Why would it be different now? she wondered, feeling unnerved by his attitude.

"The women are boiling whale blubber to extract oil from it," Strong Heart said, gazing over at the activity. "My braves must have found a whale washed up on the beach at the mouth of the river, where the river and sea join. You see, Elizabeth, my tribe does not hunt whales, but we have learned to take advantage of stray carcasses. This whale will provide our people with much blubber, which can be used in many ways. Our braves are always on the lookout for such a catch as this."

"And soon you will participate in the salmon run," Elizabeth said. The thought of the salmon brought her father to her mind. Again she had given him cause to worry, perhaps enough to even forget about his fishery.

But she doubted that anything could cause him to lose interest in his business. Not even her disappearance. His work was his life—not her. He would probably mourn her loss for a brief moment, then move ahead with his plans.

And if he had loved her as a devoted father should, he would have found a way to get her out of that dreadful prison.

As it was, only Strong Heart seemed to truly care enough, and now even he was acting strangely.

She was disturbed by how he had called her by her name a moment ago, instead of his *la-daila*.

Confusion flooded in, in greater intensity. She searched through the past few hours, to remember if she had said or done anything that might have angered him, yet was unable to find anything that was less than beautiful: The way he had held her. The way he had kissed her. The way he had made love to her.

It was all too perfect for him to be behaving so oddly now.

Strong Heart's jaw tightened at her mention of the salmon run, for it brought him back to why he was in such a sullen mood today. He had decided to confront her about her father as soon as they got settled at his longhouse. He would question her as to why she had found the need to lie to him about her father, instead of being honest with him.

Trust was needed in a relationship, and now it was evident that it was lacking between them.

Ah-hah, he had laid his anger aside long enough to rescue her from the prison, and even through the night as he held her in his arms, for it had been such relief to know that she was safe. During those special moments with her, when he was thankful she was alive, he had forgotten why he should be angry.

But now, it was different. He had to know the truth. For every time he held her in his arms, he did not want to think that he was holding someone who could be less than truthful with him.

He expected that the woman who was soon to be his wife should have no reason to feel that she had to lie to him.

He did not want to tell her that they could not be married—that she wasn't worthy of a man who would one day be a powerful chief.

Ah-hah, he would soon have this much needed talk with his woman.

Anger flared in Elizabeth when Strong Heart ignored her mention of the salmon run.

Well, she quickly decided, she had taken all that she could of his silent moodiness!

"Let me off the horse," she said, her eyes flashing into Strong Heart's as he turned his head quickly to look at her. "It is apparent that my mere presence is a bother to you, so stop your horse so that I can walk the rest of the way."

She glared at him defiantly. "Better yet, perhaps I should just turn around and start walking back toward Seattle," she stormed. "I don't want to be anywhere I'm not wanted, or be with someone who treats me as though I am nonexistent."

Strong Heart stared at her, stunned by her sudden rush of temper. Then, remembering his own reason for being angry with her, he turned his eyes ahead. He kept his horse going in a steady lope, refusing to allow Elizabeth to do as she wanted.

At this moment, he was determined to have his way. She would not get away from his questions that easily!

He smiled to himself, though, thinking that perhaps she was even more beautiful angry—with her green eyes flashing, and her cheeks rosy with rage. It would be so easy to forget his suspicions and return to the way it had been between them before he had discovered that she had not been totally truthful with him. Instead of questioning her and finding out something that might cause a total estrangement between them, ignorance might be best.

But he was a man of truth. So his wife must be a woman of truth.

"Stop!" Elizabeth shouted, pummeling his back with her fists. "Let me down. If you don't, I'll jump."

Strong Heart wheeled his horse to a quick stop, then turned to Elizabeth and jerked her around, so that she was on his lap. He held her in place with his strong arm, and proceeded on toward his village.

"*Nah,* look here," he grumbled. "We are almost at my village, and then we will go to my longhouse and talk. But until then, sit quietly and do not make a spectacle of yourself."

"Why are you doing this to me?" Elizabeth asked, angry tears spilling from her eyes. "Last night, everything was so perfect between us. Today? You act as if you don't love me. Why did you set me free from the prison if . . . if . . . you don't even care for me anymore?"

"I will care for you until the end of time," Strong Heart said, his voice solemn as his eyes looked into hers. "But there is something left unspoken between us. Today, before the sun dies in the sky, I will have the answers that I am seeking."

"Answers?" Elizabeth said, sniffling and wiping tears from her eyes with the back of her hand. "Answers about what? You seemed content enough last night. Why now, Strong Heart? Why?"

"Last night was last night," Strong Heart grumbled. "This is now. *Now* is when I want the answers. Perhaps I should have questioned you last night, but I didn't. So be it, Elizabeth. Just be patient with me. I have been, with you."

Elizabeth shook her head slowly, her mind seething with frustration. "Sometimes you talk and act in riddles," she murmured, turning her eyes from him. Her shoulders slumped dispiritedly. She knew she would feel better if she allowed herself to have a good cry.

But she did not have time to think further on it, for Strong Heart's horse had reached the outer fringes of the village and children were running toward them already, shouting Strong Heart's name, their dogs yapping at their heels.

Strong Heart smiled at them and kept riding on past the newly erected totem poles and into the village. Women sat outside their lodges, spinning the underside of the cedar bark which looked like flax, with distaffs and spindles. Others wove it with strips of sea otter skin on looms which were placed against the sides of their houses.

When Strong Heart started riding past his parents' large lodge, Elizabeth saw his mother step outside. A smile of relief was on her tiny face as she gazed adoringly up at her son, a fist clutched over her heart as she bid a silent welcome to Strong Heart. He returned the welcome, in kind, and rode on, drawing rein before his longhouse.

Strong Heart eased Elizabeth from his lap until her feet were placed firmly on the ground, then slid from the saddle himself. Elizabeth stood with her arms folded stubbornly across her chest as he secured his reins to a post. She jerked away from him when he reached for her elbow to escort her into the house.

"Don't worry," she said, her voice low, yet angry. "I shall go into the longhouse without assistance." She turned and stood on tiptoe, lifting her face to his. "And I shall not make a scene. I'm just as anxious to get this over with as you."

Then, her lips quivering, she reproached him. "I hope to understand soon why you are behaving so . . . so . . . cold to me. It wasn't my fault that I was taken to the prison and jailed there."

She raised her eyes to his. "I didn't ask you to come and get me either," she said, her voice breaking. "You could have left me there just like my father. Why *did* you come for me, if all that you had planned was to chastise me for . . . for . . . only God knows what? In truth, I am now no better than when I was in prison."

Strong Heart's eyes wavered and a slow pain circled his heart to see his woman tortured by what he was forced to do.

He gestured with his hand. "Go inside," he said softly. He followed her, then he pointed toward a soft buckskin cushion filled with cottonwood floss. "*Mit-lite,* sit down beside the firepit."

Disconsolately, Elizabeth sat down on the cushion and crossed her legs beneath her skirt. She was suddenly mortified by the appearance of her dress. During their journey, she had not thought to be concerned about how disheveled she was after being imprisoned for so many days. Each evening she had been given a basin of water, with which she kept herself clean, but her clothes not only smelled of the jail cell, but now also of horse sweat.

As Strong Heart sat down beside her, and began building the fire in the firepit, Elizabeth watched him, her heart pounding. She was glad when the flames were curling around the logs, so that Strong Heart could say what he wanted to say to her.

When he turned her way and began talking, she turned pale and gasped. His question was proof of why he had been treating her as if she were no more important to him than a stranger.

"Elizabeth, it is *me-sah-chie,* bad, to tell lies, especially to tell a lie to the man you have professed to love," Strong Heart began solemnly, his gaze steady on her. "Why did you lie to me about why your father is in the Pacific Northwest?"

"How do you know about that?" she murmured, nervously brushing a strand of hair back from her eyes.

"Your father, along with another white man who is known by the name Morris Murdoch, came to my village just prior to the raid on my people," he answered. "I was not here. I had left to free Four Winds from prison. But my father and the other braves have told me why your father and Morris Murdoch were here—to trick my people with their white man promises to catch the salmon for them instead of for our people. And they urged our people to work in the fishery that they have built on the beach close to the hallowed land of the Suquamish. Why did you not tell me that your father was building a fishery, and for what purpose? Why did you not tell me that your father planned to come to my village and speak in council about the salmon? Why, my *la-daila*? Why?"

Elizabeth's mouth gaped, stunned by what Strong Heart had said. Her father had been trying to push his ideas on Strong Heart's people? She had not known exactly which Indians he had visited, and did not know why she had not considered this possibility before now.

But that Strong Heart saw her as a liar hurt more than anything had hurt her in her life, for she was not a liar. She had only told him a half-truth, hoping that she would never have to tell him the whole truth about her father. She had hoped that her father would make his contract with another village, leaving Strong Heart and his people in peace.

Elizabeth went to Strong Heart, bending on her knees before him. She held his face between her hands, feeling him grow tense at her mere touch. "Darling, I told you a nontruth only . . . only to protect you," she pleaded. "I didn't want my father and the man I loved to clash over differing ideals. Both of you have wills of steel. I . . . I . . . felt that if you fought with my father, *you* would be the eventual loser, and the hanging platform still haunts me. And, Strong Heart, I didn't know that my father was coming to *your* village. Please believe me. I didn't know."

Strong Heart searched her eyes, and when he saw the apology and the hurt in their depths, he placed his hands at her wrists and drew her to him, holding her against him. He gazed down at her. "I believe you did this from your heart," he said. "I believe you did this for the man you love. I *do* understand your motive, but never lie to me again. I value honesty in everyone, especially the woman I love."

He was very close to telling her the other thing about her father, but something stopped him—perhaps feeling that enough conflict and doubt had been between them for today. Or perhaps he did not want to discover that her father was guilty of killing his people. This man that he doubted, would soon be his father-in-law, a man he wished to have peace with. For this man would one day be his children's grandfather, and it would not be good to have a grandfather who was despised by their father.

"Please never treat me so terribly again," Elizabeth mumbled, near tears. She flung her arms around his neck and drew his lips close to hers. "I love you so, Strong Heart. I would never do anything to hurt you. Surely you know that. I only want what is best for you—*and* your people."

"*Ah-hah,* yes, I believe that is so," he whispered, brushing his mouth across her lips, his hands eagerly undressing her. "But for now, my *la-daila,* do only what is best for me."

"You call me *la-daila* again instead of Elizabeth," she sighed, so glad to have the wrinkled dress off, and to feel the wonder of the warmth of the fire against her flesh. She giggled. "That proves that you are no longer unhappy with me."

Strong Heart pulled away from her and began to undress. "That is so," he said, laughing softly.

When he was naked, he reached for a basin of water fresh from the river. He took the basin over to Elizabeth and handed it to her. "Cleanse me. Then I will cleanse you," he said throatily.

Elizabeth picked up a buckskin washcloth, and then a piece of soap that Many Stars had placed there. It was quite a sacrifice on her part, for the chances of getting perfumed soap here in the wilderness were slim.

Meditatively, Elizabeth began to bathe Strong Heart, drawing a moan of pleasure from deep within him when she reached that part of his anatomy that was swollen and throbbing in her hand. She dutifully caressed it with fingers that were slippery with soap suds.

She continued caressing Strong Heart, watching his eyes become glassy with passion. He clutched his hands in her hair and he urged her lips where her fingers had just been. She scarcely breathed and her eyes widened, not sure of what he was asking of her.

But further urgings made her understand. Her pulse raced and her knees grew weak as she tasted him for the first time.

The pleasure that she was giving was intense, for his body had stiffened and his eyes were closed, while soft moans rose from deep within him.

She pleasured him in this unusual way for a while longer. Then he placed his fingers to her shoulders and urged her down on her back on the soft cushioned floor. She became the recipient of the same sort of caresses as he took the soaped cloth and began stroking her all over as he washed her.

He knelt down over her, parting her legs, and he touched that most sensitive part of her with soapy fingers, where her heart now seemed to be centered. She closed her eyes, wishing that the pleasure would never end.

Then it seemed to intensify as she felt something even more wonderful caressing her swollen bud. Her whole body throbbed with pleasure. When she opened her eyes and gazed down at him, she was surprised to see that his mouth was the source of her pleasure, his tongue feverishly moving over her.

When she could not take much more without going over the edge into total bliss, Elizabeth took his face with her hands and urged him to move up. Soon his manhood was in rhythmic strokes within her, his lips on her breasts, moving from one to the other, setting her aflame with desire.

Moments later they reached that peak of passion they had been seeking, taking from one another all that they could give. Then they lay together, their breaths mingling as they looked with rapture into each other's eyes.

"I could never have sent you back to your world, no matter if you had not had a good reason for lying to me," Strong Heart confessed. "My love is too strong for you to lose you."

"I would have never gone, had you even ordered me to," Elizabeth whispered back, leaning to flick her tongue into his mouth.

* * *

Earl lifted his saddle onto his horse, then gave Morris a frown. "I've lost the battle with my daughter," he said sadly. "But I won't allow it to happen between me and the Suquamish.

By damn, I will have their support. I must. So, Morris, I'll be a few days tryin' again. You stay put and see to everything here at the fishery. Perhaps one man alone can do what two men together couldn't at the Indian village."

Morris smiled crookedly and gave Earl a mock salute as he launched himself into the saddle. "Good luck," he said, smiling smugly to himself. He had done his part by ordering the raid on the Suquamish. Now it was Earl's and Morris's time to reap the harvest of that raid.

25

When the praise thou meetest
To thine ear is sweetest,
O then remember me!
—Thomas Moore

Dressed in a soft buckskin dress, and having joined Strong Heart's parents for breakfast the next day, Elizabeth sat beside Strong Heart in Chief Moon Elk's longhouse sipping deer-bone soup from a wooden bowl. She watched Strong Heart and Chief Moon Elk, who were also eating breakfast. Pretty Nose was close to the fire, already preparing frybread for lunch.

"You say that Four Winds is a renegade?" Chief Moon Elk said, pushing his empty bowl aside. "My son, did I not tell you that his blood is bad? Much more pointed to his guilt than to his innocence."

"*Ah-hah,* yes, sad though it makes me to say it, I now realize that, in part, you were right about Four Winds," Strong Heart said, his face solemn.

"Four Winds is small in his shame," Chief Moon Elk said, his eyes angry. He sat back against a willow backrest. "He is a man who is hard to know, for his blood is quick to turn bad. Why does he carry such a bad heart for us, my son?"

Strong Heart placed his spoon into his empty bowl. He gazed intently at his father. "Father, one thing that I still see as a truth is that Four Winds had nothing to do with the raid on our people," he said. "His heart is *good* toward our people. It can never be any other way."

Strong Heart gave Elizabeth an uneasy glance, still having not told her all that he knew about her father and his possible role in the raid. Each time, just as he would start to tell her, she would either hug him, or give him a sweet look that always held such tenderness for him.

He had not wanted to tell her anything that might cause her pain, or that might cause a strain between them.

She was home now, where she belonged—with *him,* and *his* people. She would soon forget her uncaring father.

And so would Strong Heart, for there was no actual proof that her father had had anything to do with the raid.

Pity the man, though, should Strong Heart ever learn the opposite. Strong Heart would stop at nothing less than squeezing the life from him with his bare hands. . . .

Before Chief Moon Elk responded to Strong Heart, a commotion outside the longhouse drew his eyes to the door. He then looked over at Strong Heart. "My leg still pains me too much to go and see what is causing the stir among our people," he said. "My son, go and see who it is."

Elizabeth rose to her feet and went to the door with Strong Heart. As he opened the door, she stopped. "My father," she said, as she watched Earl approach on his horse, with many Suquamish braves walking on either side of him. Their rifles were aimed at Earl.

Her anxiety was not caused as much by the sight of the weapons aimed at her father, but by the danger of him finding her there. Her presence would prove Strong Heart's guilt in helping her escape from the prison.

She would not allow any harm to come to him, even if she had to sacrifice telling her father that she was alive and well.

"Strong Heart, I must hide," she said, stepping back from the door. "That's my father. He must not be allowed to see me." She looked frantically around her. "Strong Heart, where can I hide? Where?"

Strong Heart was stunned to realize that the man approaching was her father. That he had the nerve to come to the village so soon after the raid was astounding.

Yet was that perhaps a part of his plan from the beginning? To come back to a weakened people who might then be willing to do anything to help put their lives back together again?

And then there was Elizabeth. *Ah-hah,* he knew, also, that it was best that her father did not see her there.

But now she might find out the ugly truth about her father,

for Strong Heart was not going to spare questions once the man was sitting in council with him and Chief Moon Elk.

Strong Heart grabbed Elizabeth by the arm and quickly ushered her away from the door. Chief Moon Elk and Pretty Nose were watching with keen puzzlement in their eyes. He took Elizabeth behind a skin curtain that hung to the floor. Behind it were hidden the treasures of his father and mother in pits under wooden platforms.

"You stay here until he is gone," Strong Heart said, his eyes on hers. "My *la-daila,* soon you will hear things spoken to your father that may confuse or even hurt you. But these things must be said to him. Strong Heart needs answers about many things. I believe it is your father who can give these answers to me."

"Answers about what?" Elizabeth said, her pulse racing. "I . . . I . . . explained about the fishery. What else is there, Strong Heart? Tell me. I have the right to know."

"*Ah-hah,* and so you do," Strong Heart said, smoothing a lock of hair back from her brow. "And I should have told you sooner, rather than have you hear it now, in this way."

"Then tell me," Elizabeth said, tensing when she saw the stubborn set to his jaw. "Please, tell me."

"There is not time," Strong Heart said. Then he turned and left her with her eyes wide in confusion.

Strong Heart stepped outside just as Earl was dismounting. Strong Heart folded his arms across his chest, torn by feelings about this man that soon would be his father-in-law. He hoped with all of his heart that he was wrong about this man.

But so much pointed to Elizabeth's father's guilt, Strong Heart could not help but find himself already hating him.

Earl turned slowly around and faced Strong Heart, wondering who he was, and why he was standing at the door of the chief's house, as if guarding it. He swallowed hard, then extended a hand to Strong Heart.

"I'm Earl Easton," Earl said, his voice unsteady, as he felt the heat from the gray eyes that were boring into him. "I don't believe I had the pleasure of meeting you when I was here before?"

Strong Heart ignored the handshake and did not answer him for a moment. He was still studying this white man, trying to see if he carried innocence or guilt in the depths of his eyes. His eyes were the same color as Elizabeth's, which made him most definitely Elizabeth's father—and a man that Strong Heart did not want to hate.

When he saw that this brave was not going to take his hand, Earl slowly lowered it to his side. He cleared his throat nervously, glancing questioningly at the totem poles that were partially burned and then at the ones that seemed to have been newly erected and painted.

He then looked slowly around him, puzzled by the newness of many of the longhouses. What had happened here since the time he had come to talk business with the chief? It appeared as if some great fire had ravaged the village. Yet beyond, where the forest stood mighty and green, there was no sign of fire.

It made him uneasy, yet he again turned and faced Strong Heart. Nothing would dissuade Earl from his purpose for being here.

"I have returned to speak business with Chief Moon Elk again," Earl said, clasping his hands nervously behind him. "Would you please take me to him?"

Strong Heart stood there silently for a moment longer, then nodded toward the door. "Come with me," he said, turning and walking back inside the longhouse.

Earl followed him inside and stopped at Strong Heart's side. Earl's eyes widened as he stared down at Chief Moon Elk, whose one leg was stretched out before him, evidently wounded. Earl wondered how he had been wounded, and by whom.

Strong Heart gestured toward his father and his mother.

"My father, Chief Moon Elk, and my mother, Pretty Nose," Strong Heart said. "My father will speak to you again. I will listen, then speak to you myself as soon as my father is finished with you."

Earl paled and grew unsteady on his legs as he looked in surprise at Strong Heart. "You are Chief Moon Elk's son?" he said softly. "I did not know. You did not sit in council with your father and me before."

"That is so," Strong Heart said, glancing toward the curtain, knowing that this white man would be quite surprised to know that at the time of his last visit, Strong Heart had been with his daughter. This man would be even more surprised if he knew that his daughter was there even now, hiding from him in the Suquamish chief's longhouse.

It gave Strong Heart a smug feeling to keep these secrets from the scheming white man.

Elizabeth chewed nervously on her lower lip when she heard how wary her father's voice sounded. She was guilt-stricken over deceiving him. But the fact that he was there, instead of elsewhere with a posse searching for her, gave her cause to again doubt his love for her.

Tears flooded her eyes. She now understood why her mother had disappeared all those years ago more than ever before.

Wiping the tears from her eyes, she leaned nearer to the curtain and listened closely as Chief Moon Elk began to talk in a monotone to her father.

"*Mit-lite,* sit down," Chief Moon Elk said, gesturing toward a cushion on the floor opposite the fire from him. "You did not hear me well the other time you were speaking of fisheries and salmon to me. Did I not tell you that my people caught only for our village? Why do you waste your time coming again?" He looked past Earl, at the door. "And where is the man who goes by the name Morris Murdoch? He did not accompany you this time to hear a more determined no from my lips?"

"No, he did not come this time," Earl said, resting his hands on his knees as he crossed his legs. "He came the last time mainly to direct me to your village. I knew the way this time. He stayed behind and is tending to our business. I am the spokesman for the two of us now. I hope that you will give me another chance to explain the benefits to your people of working under my employ. Perhaps you have had time to think about it? To see the worth of my plan, as I see it?"

Earl glanced down at Chief Moon Elk's festering wound again. "You have had a mishap since I was last here?" he said, raising an eyebrow. He looked slowly up at the chief again. "How unfortunate. I'm sorry."

Strong Heart went and knelt beside his father, gently touching his father's leg, and glaring at Earl. "*Ah-hah,* my father is ailing," he said, glad that his father was giving him the opportunity to speak as he sat in stone-faced silence. "Can you truthfully say that you do not know the cause? Did you not see the burned totem poles as you entered our village? Did you not see the many new longhouses in my village? Of course you could not see the ashes of many of our people that have been spread across our land, and across the waters of the river. This has all happened since your last council with my father. Can you tell me that you do not know why this has all happened in our village? Can you?"

Elizabeth blanched and she placed her hands to her cheeks, her eyes widening in stunned surprise at what Strong Heart was saying without actually accusing her father. She shook her head, her thoughts flying, putting ghastly things together that she did not want to believe or accept. She would not believe that her father was driven by so much greed that he would have had a part in the attack on this village!

Yet, she knew that was what Strong Heart was leading up to. And surely her father had guessed as much, as well.

Her heart pounding, Elizabeth leaned her ear even closer to the curtain, growing cold as she continued to listen.

"What are you suggesting?" Earl gasped, looking quickly from father to son. "What do you think I am guilty of? Or should I even ask?"

"Your council with my father came suspiciously close to the raid on my people," Strong Heart hissed. "Can you deny that after my father turned your proposal down, you returned to our village and wreaked havoc on our people? To frighten us into doing as you ask, or to weaken us so that we would see no other way of survival except to take money earned from you? Do you think that we do not see right through such a scheme as this?"

Elizabeth quickly clasped her hand over her mouth and gasped. She swayed with a sudden light-headedness, to know that she had guessed right at what Strong Heart was thinking.

No! She would not allow herself to believe her father was guilty of such a heinous crime. He had never stooped to such tactics to get his way.

And why should he now? He was a rich man who did not need to go to such extremes as this to make more money for himself.

No. She could not, *would* not believe this of her father, no matter how greedy or ambitious he was.

Earl rose shakily to his feet, his knees weak with fright. "I am innocent of this that you are accusing me of," he said with a slight gasp. "I am not the sort to kill for my own gain. Please believe me. I did not even know of the tragedy, or I would have never come here. Especially alone. Doesn't that prove that I am innocent? I am not a foolish man. If I had any inkling of your having just suffered a raid, I wouldn't have set foot in your village, for fear that I would be accused of it. I value my life more than that. I am not the sort to take chances with it."

Earl's mind was calculating things, and his thoughts led him to what Morris Murdoch had said about having taken care of things. Could Morris have somehow attacked the village?

The thought sickened him, and now he wished that he had investigated his partner's credentials more than he had. In truth, he did not know much about him, except that he had had the money to back up his desire to be Earl's partner in the fishery venture.

Strong Heart rose to his full height and began walking slowly around the fire toward Earl. "You must show me proof that you had no part in the raid," he said, his voice cold. "Your partner, Morris Murdoch? Did you not know that he is the leader of an outlaw gang? Do you deny aligning yourself with such desperadoes? Do you deny that you did not ride with them that day, side-by-side with your partner, purposely murdering my people?"

Earl took a shaky step backward, his heart thumping, his eyes wide. "Morris . . . is . . . the leader of a gang of outlaws?"

he said, his voice thin. "God. God in heaven. No! I did not know. Tell me it isn't true. Tell me it is a ploy you are using to trick me."

An involuntary shiver coursed through Elizabeth, after learning the news about Morris Murdoch. But she wasn't truly surprised, when she recalled his eyes—how cold and empty they appeared.

And she could not help but feel sorry for her father, his voice revealing to her that he had not known this about Morris, and that he was most definitely innocent of everything.

Seeing that her father was concerned, she did not want the confrontation to continue. She feared what would happen to Strong Heart if her father ended up dead and the authorities were brought into the matter. Elizabeth saw no other recourse than to stop what had begun.

Elizabeth stepped hurriedly from behind the curtain and rushed toward her father.

Earl was shocked by her appearing from nowhere.

"Elizabeth?" he gasped. He placed his hands on her shoulders and held her at arm's length as he looked her up and down. "Good Lord, Elizabeth. What are you doing here? And why are you dressed in such . . . such garb as that?"

Then in a flash he remembered the Indian saddle that he had found hidden in the stable and the horse that had not been theirs. He recalled Everett telling him about Elizabeth wearing an Indian dress, and began putting two and two together.

"I'm safe, Father," Elizabeth said, her voice trembling. "That should be all that matters. Not how I happen to be here, or why I am dressed in such a way." She swallowed hard. "But that you are here, and that you are being accused of what I know you are innocent of is why I revealed myself to you. Otherwise, Father, I would have stayed hidden behind that curtain. It was my intention never to return home again."

Earl turned pale. "Never?" he gasped. "Elizabeth, why? Never is a long, long time. Have I been this unbearable to you? Did my neglect turn you totally against me?"

"It was not your neglect that made me fall in love with

Strong Heart," Elizabeth said. "That alone is the reason I have decided to stay with Strong Heart—to be his wife."

Earl gasped and slowly shook his head. "No," he said thickly. "You can't be serious."

"Very," Elizabeth said, then turned her eyes to Strong Heart. "Darling, I grant you that my father is capable of many things, but he could never kill anyone. My father wouldn't come to your village, killing and maiming. Please believe me. Please don't harm my father." She swallowed hard again. "I know that he didn't know about Morris Murdoch. I could tell how shocked he was when you revealed this to him. He had no idea he had aligned himself with such a man as that. Please let my father leave the village unharmed. For me, Strong Heart? For me?"

Strong Heart and Chief Moon Elk exchanged troubled glances, then Chief Moon Elk broke the silence. "White man, you can go, but leave my people in peace," he said with a grumble. "Do not bring your words to us again. This is our life. We want to live it without your interference."

"I understand," Earl said, then reached for Elizabeth's hand. "Come home with me, baby. It's safe to now. The sheriff and deputy are both dead, and all of the records were burned in the fire that ravaged the prison. Come home with me, Elizabeth. Let me make all of this up to you. Take some more time to . . . to consider these plans to marry someone of such different customs. Please? For me? Give me another chance?"

"The prison caught fire?" Elizabeth asked, her eyes wide. "What of all those people who were imprisoned there?"

"It seems whoever set the fire also set everyone free," he said, then paled again as he realized that whoever had set Elizabeth free, had most probably set the fire. Yet she seemed genuinely surprised to know that the prison had burned.

"Thank goodness for that," Elizabeth said, sighing. "Those poor women."

"Come home with me, baby," Earl persisted.

Elizabeth was suddenly torn, fearing that rejecting her father might make him become bitter toward Strong Heart, making him do something foolish—like turn Strong Heart in to the authorities.

For this alone she knew what her decision must be.

She went to Strong Heart and took both of his hands in hers. "Darling, trust me when I say that I must return with my father for a while," she said softly.

She stood on tiptoe and leaned up near his ear, whispering, "After I am assured that I have made all the wrongs right between me and my father, I will return to you. We shall be married then. Trust me, darling. This is best for all concerned."

Strong Heart glowered down at her, silence like a wall between them as Elizabeth awaited his answer.

"I feel that what you are doing is wrong," he finally said. "But I will not stop you from going. Soon I will come for you, after the salmon harvest."

Tears welled up in Elizabeth's eyes. She flung herself into his arms and hugged him tightly, dreading leaving him, yet knowing that she must.

Always and forever she would do anything and everything to protect him.

26

> Go from me, yet I feel that I shall stand
> Henceforward in thy shadow.
> —Elizabeth Barrett Browning

It had been a long journey, where feelings had been revealed between Elizabeth and her father that had never been aired before. She now knew that he sincerely loved her, and he knew the depth of her love for Strong Heart.

Sitting beside a campfire the night of their journey home, she had explained everything to her father—about the first time she and Strong Heart had met, and about the times he had saved her life.

Her father now knew that her time with him would be short, for she was going to return to Strong Heart soon. And her father had promised not to interfere.

Riding side by side toward the huge gate that led into their estate grounds, Elizabeth glanced toward the Sound, and then at the fishery. "Father, what are you going to do about Morris Murdoch now that you know of his involvement with outlaws?" she asked, shifting her gaze to her father. "Surely you will separate yourself from him. You don't actually need him. You have always done quite well for yourself without the aid of a partner. It should be no different now."

Earl gave Elizabeth an unsteady glance. Although she had been truthful with him about everything between herself and the Indian, he still did not feel that this was the time to reveal his financial status to her. He had hoped to turn everything around to his favor, before telling her about his bankruptcy in San Francisco.

And now, even though he had not yet found any Indians who would work for him, he still saw his fishery as something that could succeed. He had many men under his employ. Certainly they could catch enough salmon to turn over a substantial profit for him.

He decided he would wait and reveal his money problems to Elizabeth *after* he had solved them.

As for Morris Murdoch—the son of a bitch, he thought bitterly—he was still needed, no matter how he had accumulated his riches. Earl was depending on Morris's money for his survival until his fishery showed a profit.

"I don't want to rush into anything with Morris," he finally said, guiding his horse through the wide gate, Elizabeth's horse keeping stride with his. "If he's a criminal, I don't want to do anything that might get him riled up against us. Who knows what he's capable of? I think I'll feel him out—see if I can ease him out of the business, slowlike, so's not to have someone like him out for revenge later."

"Perhaps you're right," Elizabeth said softly, then her eyebrows lifted when she saw a fancy horse and carriage parked in front of the house. A footman waited beside the carriage.

"Whose carriage is that?" Earl said, studying it. "I don't recognize it. And who would come calling, anyhow?"

He paused, then looked over at Elizabeth. "Besides Maysie and Strong Heart, have you made an acquaintance you haven't told me about?" he asked.

"Father, I believe I've told you everything on the way back from Strong Heart's village," Elizabeth said, laughing softly. "There's nothing else to say, or anyone else to explain. I have no idea whose carriage that might be."

Her eyes lit up with a thought. "Except for Maysie," she said. "Could it be Maysie?"

Then she frowned, recalling the last time she had seen Maysie—how she was dressed and whom she had been with.

"No. I'm sure it's not her," she quickly added. "I doubt we shall ever see her again."

"I'm sorry about Maysie," Earl said, giving Elizabeth a heartfelt, apologetic look. "Sorry as hell."

He then slapped his reins and urged his horse into a gallop toward the house, Elizabeth following his lead.

When they reached the house, both dismounted and secured their reins to the hitching post, then took the stairs together up to the porch.

Before they had a chance to open the door, it burst open and Elizabeth found herself suddenly engulfed in a woman's embrace. Her father gaped openly at the affectionate scene.

Elizabeth stood, shocked to her core, stiff and silent. It was her mother! Her mother smelled sweetly of French perfume, and wore a soft mink wrap around her shoulders.

"Marilyn?" Earl finally stammered out, his surprise and shock immense. "My God, Marilyn!"

"Mama?" Elizabeth said, all of her resentment of her mother's abandonment overwhelming her.

Marilyn stroked her daughter's back through the buckskin fabric of her dress. "I'm here now, darling," she whispered. "Oh, Lord, Elizabeth, I'm so sorry for what I did. So very sorry."

Elizabeth's mind cleared and she recalled her mother's reasons for having disappeared in the first place. A warmth of love and understanding flooded Elizabeth.

With tears streaming from her eyes, she returned her mother's hug. "Mama," she cried. "Oh, Mama. I've missed you so much!"

Earl cleared his throat and stepped up to Marilyn and tapped her lightly on the shoulder. "If I may interrupt this tender scene, I would like to know where you have been, and why you have chosen to return now," he said hoarsely.

Her brilliant red hair swirled into a chignon atop her head, her vivaciously clear, green eyes sparkling, Marilyn swung away from Elizabeth and smiled up at Earl. "Hello, Earl," she said, extending a gloved hand. "It's been a long time."

Earl gazed down at the extended hand for a moment, then lifted his hand and clasped his fingers around hers. "A damn sight longer than is decent," he said in a growl. Then he did something that made Elizabeth gasp. He gathered Marilyn into his arms and held her in a tight embrace. "Damn it, Marilyn, why'd you have to disappear on us? Did I make life that unbearable for you? If so, I'm sorry. Damn sorry."

Elizabeth placed a hand over her mouth, to try and stifle her sobs as tears washed across her face. For so long she had wanted her parents to reunite, but had never counted on it. Especially after they had moved from San Francisco. That Marilyn was now here stunned her. But the fact that both her mother and father seemed genuinely happy to see each other again seemed to make all the wrongs right.

Marilyn eased from Earl's embrace. She was still a beautiful woman. Her magnificent breasts strained against the silk fabric of her pale green dress, and the gathered full skirt emphasized her tiny waist. "There's so much to say," Marilyn said with a soft purr. "Let's go inside. Frannie has prepared tea."

Marilyn turned back to Elizabeth and placed her hands to her cheeks. "Darling, when I heard that you and your father had moved just outside of Seattle, and that you had been abducted, I just had to come and see your father about it," she said. "A team of wild horses couldn't keep me away."

Again she hugged Elizabeth. "But you're all right," she whispered. "My baby is all right."

She stepped back and looked Elizabeth slowly up and down, puzzlement in her eyes. "A buckskin dress?" she asked. "Isn't that what Indians wear?" Her eyes focused on Elizabeth. "Have you been with Indians, Elizabeth?"

"Yes, ma'am, I have," Elizabeth said, lifting her chin proudly. "And, Mama, I'm soon to marry one."

"What?" Marilyn gasped, placing a hand to her throat. "An Indian? You are *marrying* an Indian?"

"Don't make it sound like I'm about to commit a crime, Mama," Elizabeth said, her eyes flashing. "If you want to talk about crimes, what you did—"

A sudden presence at the door stopped Elizabeth's outburst. She caught sight of Maysie, then rushed to her and hugged her. "Maysie," she said, clinging tightly to her. "It's so good to see you."

"Your mother asked me to direct her to your house," Maysie said softly, smiling as Elizabeth stepped back and clasped one of Maysie's hands.

"Mama?" Elizabeth asked, giving her mother a quick

glance, then looking again at Maysie and seeing the modesty of her attire. It was not anything like the skimpy dress that Maysie had been wearing the last time Elizabeth had seen her. Today she wore a pretty cotton dress trimmed with eyelet lace. "How do you know my mother?"

"I work for her," Maysie said matter-of-factly, smiling at Marilyn. "She's given me a home, food, clothes, and a reason to continue living."

Earl went to Marilyn and tilted her chin up with a forefinger. "What does she mean?" he said ominously. "Where do you live? And what sort of establishment do you run?"

Marilyn's smile faded along with her courage. "Please let us go inside," she murmured. "I . . . I . . . shall explain everything then."

Earl nodded, and placed a hand at Marilyn's elbow, ushering her past Maysie and Elizabeth, and on inside. Elizabeth and Maysie followed. They were soon sitting comfortably before a roaring fire in the fireplace, and sipping tea. Frannie stood by the door, marveling over Elizabeth being home again.

"Start from the beginning, Marilyn," Earl said, lighting a cigar, flicking the match into the curling flames of the hearth. "For years now my imagination has conjured up many things that may have happened to you. But never did I envision you living in Seattle. It's just recently become somewhat more civilized. Before, it was just men and whores in this town."

The cigar almost popped from between his lips as he spoke the word "whores." He blanched at the thought of what Marilyn might tell him.

He looked at her, marking that she had not aged hardly a year since he had last seen her. He remembered her in bed—how she had seemed to have had experience way beyond what he had taught her—his virginal wife—on their wedding night. She had seemed to know skills of lovemaking that would make a church mouse blush.

He had to wonder if she had since improved her skills.

Now, after seeing her again, he knew that he still loved and adored her with all of his being, and he would have her back in a minute, should she offer herself to him.

Elizabeth sat with her back straight on the sofa, Maysie beside her, both listening intently as Marilyn started to speak. Elizabeth's heart cried out to her mother the more her mother tried desperately to explain.

"Earl, you know how it hurt me every time you left to travel to the Orient, and other strange places, leaving me behind to sleep alone at night," she began, giving Elizabeth an uneasy glance.

She cleared her throat nervously, then looked at Earl again. "Earl, you seemed to have forgotten that you had a wife," she said, near tears. "I couldn't bear those lonely nights any longer. I . . . saw . . . no choice but to leave. I came to Seattle to seek a new way of life and earned top dollar in a brothel. I saved my money to buy my own place. Earl, I am now madam of the classiest brothel in Seattle. Maysie works for me there."

There was a sudden silence in the room. Then Earl rose from the chair and went to the fireplace and placed his arm on the mantel, leaning his brow against it.

Wide-eyed, and choked up, Elizabeth watched as her mother went to her father and gently placed a hand on his shoulder. "Earl, it's not that bad," she said softly. "Please. It's not that bad. I am respected. Truly I am."

Earl turned slowly to face her, then ran a finger down the perfect outline of her face. "I'm sure you are," he said, his voice shaking. "And I am sure many have asked you to give up that sort of life, to become their wife. Did you tell them that you already had a husband? Or did I not exist for you anymore?"

"I have never forgotten you," Marilyn said, tears falling from her eyes. "It's just that I wanted what you did not give me. But I have never considered marrying anyone else. In my heart, I had . . . I had hoped that somehow you and I could eventually work things out. It's just that when I got involved in my business, making a success of it, the years seemed to slip by so quickly. And here we are now, much older, and hopefully wiser. I still love you, Earl. Truly I do."

She turned her weeping eyes to Elizabeth. "And look at our daughter," she said, a sob lodging in her throat. "She's all grown up and so, so beautiful." She turned to Earl again. "Thank you, darling, for taking such good care of her."

Earl and Elizabeth exchanged quick glances, both recalling their conversations around the campfire. Then Earl turned his eyes back to Marilyn. "I did the best that I could under the circumstances," he said, drawing Marilyn into his arms. "It's so good to hold you again, Marilyn. There's been no other woman for me since you left."

Elizabeth could not hold back a sob of joy when her mother and father suddenly kissed. Her whole world had suddenly turned right side up again!

Yet she was afraid to hope, to truly hope that just one kiss and a few words of apology could truly right things all that quickly.

She looked over at Maysie, and took her hands in hers. "Tell me all about things," she murmured. "Tell me how you met my mother, and then began working for her."

Maysie explained about having contemplated suicide again, and how Marilyn had stopped her. She described Marilyn's house to Elizabeth, and how she happened to become a prostitute again.

"But I'm trying to change," Maysie quickly defended herself. "Honest, I am, Elizabeth. In fact, I've fallen in love. Like you, I love an Indian. His name is Four Winds. He came one night with some white men for our services. Four Winds chose me. There has been only one time since then that I've slept with another man, and that was the night the prison burned. There was this fellow that I had been with before, who was down on his luck. I felt sorry for him. I went with him only to cheer him up. Since then, there has only been Four Winds. He sneaks into town as often as he can to be with me."

"Four Winds?" Elizabeth gasped. She doubted his worth, yet knowing how special the love of an Indian could be, did not share her doubts with Maysie. "How nice, Maysie. I hope you'll be happy."

"I hope to marry him one day," Maysie said, her eyes shining. Marilyn suddenly came over to them.

"Maysie and I really must go," Marilyn said softly. She

bent over Elizabeth and placed a hand to her cheek. "I'll be back, if you wish me to."

Elizabeth nodded as she looked wistfully up at her mother. "Please do," she murmured.

Maysie gave Elizabeth a hug. "I'll come also," she whispered. "That is, if you aren't too upset with me now that you know that I . . . that I have returned to prostituting."

Elizabeth returned the hug. "I'm just glad that you are all right," she assured her, stroking Maysie's long, black hair. She leaned back, her eyes stern on Maysie's. "But be sure about Four Winds before marrying him. He seems to be a complicated man."

"I think I know him better than anyone," Maysie said, smiling sweetly as they rose from the sofa.

Earl walked Marilyn to the door and stepped out into the shadows on the porch. He drew Marilyn into his embrace again. "I should hate you for whoring around," he said, gazing down at her with watery eyes. "But somehow that doesn't seem to matter. Come back soon, do you hear? Let's talk some more."

"I'd love to," Marilyn said, her green eyes flashing up at him.

Earl lowered his lips to her mouth. She circled her arms around his neck and returned the kiss. Then she broke quickly away from him and descended the steps as Elizabeth stepped outside on the porch.

Soon Marilyn and Maysie were in the carriage riding away, both waving out the windows.

Tears flooded Elizabeth's eyes, happiness warming her heart. She had seen her parents kissing. She saw the possibility of her childhood dream coming true—that her parents could be together again. They did seem to still be in love, no matter that her mother had lived the life of a whore.

Elizabeth knew that she was going to have to accept that, the same as her father. Perhaps her mother might not need to have a business much longer, if her mother decided to return to her father.

Dusk had fallen and the moon replaced the sun in the sky,

casting long shadows in the forest beyond. Just as Elizabeth started to turn, to go inside the house, she stopped in surprise.

"Strong Heart's grandfather!" she said, in hardly more than a whisper. She had seen a fleeting movement within the forest. It was the old man with his staff. "My Lord, that has to be Strong Heart's grandfather."

Earl stepped to her side, following her gaze. "What is that you said about Strong Heart's grandfather?" he asked, glancing at Elizabeth.

"I know that I saw him," Elizabeth said, rushing down the steps toward the forest. "The old man with the staff? That's Strong Heart's grandfather."

"Elizabeth!" Earl shouted, racing after her, stunned to hear that she thought some old man she had seen lurking in the forest was related to Strong Heart.

Then he was taken by a quick thought. If this elderly Indian was Strong Heart's grandfather, and if he could help find him for Strong Heart, couldn't that work to his advantage? He could return Strong Heart's grandfather to the village and surely Chief Moon Elk would offer a reward.

The reward that Earl would ask for was what he had already asked for—cooperation with the salmon run, and his fishery!

"Stop, Elizabeth!" he shouted. "Wait up."

Breathless, Elizabeth stopped. When her father caught up with her, she continued running with him until she was through the wide gate and into the outer fringes of the forest.

She and her father searched for a while. When the moon was covered by dark clouds, and lightning began flashing overhead, they returned to the house, and went to their separate rooms.

Elizabeth was glad to find Frannie preparing a warm bath. As she undressed, she had to listen to Frannie's scolding about not letting Frannie know that she was all right.

Elizabeth sank into the bath, enjoying its warmth. Frannie quit her fuming and tenderly washed Elizabeth's hair. After Elizabeth ate supper she went to bed.

* * *

In the night, she was awakened by a frightful dream. Sweat pearling her brow, Elizabeth bolted to a sitting position. Her eyes wild, she remembered.

She had dreamed the house was on fire. She had dreamed that she had been trapped. She could even now feel the smoke stinging her throat and eyes, and her fingers felt raw from clawing at the door, trying to get it open.

"I'm afraid to go back to sleep," she whispered. She stepped from the bed into her soft slippers.

She pulled a robe around her shoulders and went to the window, peering through the sheets of rain that splashed against the pane.

She hugged herself, her mind whirling with many thoughts. She missed Strong Heart so much that her insides ached from longing for him.

Then the dream returned to her.

The fire! It had seemed so real.

Even Strong Heart could not have saved her, had he even been there.

Shivering, she turned and stared at the bed, then reluctantly went back and lay down. She willed her eyes to close, then found herself in another sort of dream—one which warmed her through and through, as Strong Heart held her close, telling her over and over again how much he loved her.

And then Strong Heart's face turned into the face of the older Indian, causing her to awaken again with a start, her eyes staring.

27

My face in thine eye, thine in mine appear.
—Donne

Last night's nightmares were still haunting Elizabeth, even though it was midmorning of a bright and clear day, and the house was warmed by the sunlight streaming through the windows. Delightful odors were wafting from the kitchen, tempting her, but Elizabeth grabbed a shawl from a peg on the foyer wall and went outside and stood on the porch, to breathe the fresh air.

As she peered into the forest, she tried to think about her times with Strong Heart. Then the memory of the elderly Indian with the staff intruded, bringing back the nightmares again. The fire in her dream had surely been set by the elderly Indian. She recalled with a shudder how Strong Heart's face had turned into the old man's.

Needing to find something that would get her mind off her unpleasant and puzzling thoughts, Elizabeth lifted the skirt of her cotton dress and descended the steps. She gazed down the steep hill to the beach, where there was not much activity, with the fishery having been completed and ready for the salmon run.

"The salmon run," she whispered to herself, wondering if her father or Morris Murdoch would be visiting Indian villages, seeking their assistance in catching the salmon.

She heaved a deep sigh. At least Strong Heart's village was no longer the target for salmon discussions. After their talk, her father had promised he would keep his hands off.

She went through the wide gate and followed the steep path

that led to the beach. Another unpleasant thought chased away the clinging memories of her nightmares: Morris Murdoch.

If her father had to explain to Morris why they were not going to pester Strong Heart's people again, it would lead to further conversation in which Earl might state exactly why he had chosen to leave them alone. Then Morris Murdoch might elicit more answers out of her father which could not only place her in danger, but also Strong Heart and his people.

She had to hope that her father's word was solid, and that his feelings for her would keep all conversations with Morris directed away from Strong Heart and her.

When she reached the beach, she walked past the pier. It was difficult to walk across the rocks on this stretch of beach. She slipped and slid, and was glad when she found more solid footing as she hurried on toward the huge fishery that loomed up from the land. Built of wood, with a shake roof, it was not an unsightly building, but she saw it as something ugly. Because of it and what it represented, many Suquamish had died.

She needed to see her father today, to ensure that things were still wonderful between them, so that she could make her plans to return to Strong Heart. Elizabeth quickened her pace. When she walked past an open window she heard her father and Morris Murdoch in a conversation that made her heart turn quickly cold. She stopped and moved closer to the window, hugging the wall with her back so that her presence would not be discovered. She leaned her ear closer to the window and discovered to her chagrin that her father *did* have a devious side.

Inside, she saw nets being woven. Earl and Morris discussed spreading these large nets across the shallow parts of the river to catch the salmon before they had a chance to get upriver to the canyon, where the Suquamish were known to fish.

Her heart pounded hard as she listened to her father and Murdoch laughing together and boasting about showing the Suquamish a thing or two. She listened to them as they planned to place the nets in the water before night fell.

This angered Elizabeth. She was hurt that her father was

not even considering her feelings in his plans. He knew that she was going to return to Strong Heart, to marry him—to *live* with him, and that the salmon harvest was a large part of his people's survival—which, in turn, also meant hers.

Her mind spun with confusion as to what she could do about it. She was only one person. There was no way she could destroy the nets once they were placed in the water. And she could definitely not destroy them beforehand, for her father and Morris Murdoch would not give her the chance.

"What can I do?" she whispered to herself, feverishly racking her brain. She felt bitter knowing that her own father had lied to her and Strong Heart. She could not help but believe that her father had planned the raid on the village with Morris. She could not allow their scheme against the Suquamish to succeed.

She had to warn Strong Heart. But how? she despaired to herself. Although she had become familiar with the forest, and the way to Strong Heart's village, it was dangerous for her to travel alone through it.

She had to seek help from someone. But who?

Then the answer came to her. "Four Winds," she whispered. "Yes, Four Winds!"

Maysie had said that Four Winds came often to see her now. If Elizabeth went to her mother's brothel, she could wait until Four Winds arrived, tell him about the nets that would ruin the Suquamish salmon harvest, and see if he would take her to Strong Heart, and together they could warn him. Then Strong Heart could do what he must to save the harvest.

And this would be a way for Four Winds to prove once and for all whether or not he was a true friend of Strong Heart.

Her pulse racing, her knees weak from fear of being discovered before she reached the stables, she crept away from the fishery and made a turn which would take her out of view from the fishery.

She ran up the path, and once on level ground again, ran breathlessly to the stables.

Elizabeth was soon riding hard on the road toward Seattle, her red hair blowing loosely in the wind. Her shawl was tied securely around her shoulders, but gave her scant protection from the cool autumn air.

But she did not seem to feel the cold. Her thoughts were on her mother and where Elizabeth would have to go to see her again.

An involuntary shiver coursed through her at the thought of meeting her mother in the brothel. Her memories of her childhood, when her mother had been "Mama," made it hard to accept the kind of life that her mother now led.

In her house there were certainly no storybooks read to small children before bedtime.

Although it seemed to take forever, Elizabeth finally reached the city. The hardest part now lay before her—finding her mother's house.

Her horse walked in a slow gait down First Avenue. The skirt of her dress whipped above her knees as the breeze blew in from the Sound. Elizabeth blushed and smoothed her dress back in place when the men loitering along the thoroughfare began teasing and flirting with her.

Normally, she would ride on past, ignoring their taunts, but today she had to find answers that could help keep Strong Heart and his people fed for the long winter ahead.

And who but these brash, insulting men would know where the most lavish of whorehouses was located?

Although hating what she had to do, Elizabeth wheeled her horse around and headed toward a group of men. When she drew rein beside them, her face still hot from blushing, she summoned up the courage to talk to them. One man in particular stood out from the rest, his blue eyes as cold as winter as he ogled her.

She realized that these men must think that she was a loose woman, looking for a man who would pay her to lift her skirt for him.

The thought not only embarrassed her, but appalled her.

And the questions that she was finding hard to ask, the question alone would confirm what they thought of her—that she was, indeed, a prostitute.

"Might one of you gentlemen tell me where I can find the

place run by Marilyn Easton?" she said. Those words were like stab wounds to her heart—words which joined her mother's name to a whorehouse. Elizabeth did not know if she could ever accept what her mother had become.

She stiffened, and she tightened her fingers around the horse's reins as the men did just as she had expected, treating her as if she were a whore. They said things to her that sent chills up her spine.

She bore all of their abuse and jokes until she got the directions to her mother's house.

She turned her horse around again, leaving behind the men, who still shouted filthy things after her. She was glad when a turn up another street took her away from them.

Soon she found herself staring at a large white house that looked innocent of its true nature. It was two storied with black shutters and flower boxes at the windows and a white picket fence surrounding a yard that displayed varieties of roses in full bloom. A swing hung from a porch that reached around three sides of the house.

It looked like the house of a happy family—not the home of women who sold their bodies. It looked like the house where Elizabeth had been raised as a child, before her mother had fled.

Feeling suddenly dispirited, the past rushing in on her in waves, she drew rein outside the fence and slid from the saddle.

Staring up at the house again, she tied her horse next to other drowsing horses at a hitching rail, then took a deep breath and went on through the gate and up to the porch. With a trembling hand, she raised the large brass knocker and knocked.

Her heart pounded as she waited for the door to open. When it did, she found her mother standing there, ravishingly beautiful in a sleek, black satin dress with a low bustline which revealed the upper curves of her breasts. A diamond necklace sparkled against her lily-white throat, and her red hair was curled in a tight chignon atop her head. Elizabeth found herself at a loss for words.

Marilyn gasped, then took Elizabeth by the hand and ushered her into the house. "My dear, I did not expect you to come so soon to see your mother," she said. She drew Elizabeth into her arms. "Darling, thank you for coming. I . . . I . . . didn't sleep at all last night, for fear that you would not accept me as I am now. Your being here tells me that at least you are trying to understand."

Elizabeth wanted to shout at her mother, ask her why she was so concerned now over how her daughter would feel, when all those years she had not shown any caring—had not even let Elizabeth know where she was. Even on her birthdays, Elizabeth had not received a word from her mother.

But Elizabeth held her tongue, and checked her emotions. She must force herself not to allow any of the things that had lain heavy on her heart through all those long years, to ruin what might happen now. Her mother and father might become reunited.

Yet, she wondered, should she even wish for such a reconciliation? Her father had just proved to her that he did not deserve anything but loathing.

And Elizabeth had come to her mother's house today with other things than family on her mind.

Strong Heart. She had to help Strong Heart!

Elizabeth broke from her mother's arms and started to ask for Maysie but stopped when her eyes were drawn to the rich furnishings of her mother's house. Women lounged on the plush, bright red velveteen chairs and sofas, clothed in undergarments and their faces painted. She was aware of a man and a woman coming down the spiral staircase, arm in arm. The woman was giggling and the man seeming quite pleased not only with her, but also himself. He strutted down the steps in expensive clothes, sporting a sparkling diamond in the folds of his cravat.

Then Maysie came into view, thankfully alone. Today she was dressed in a simple cotton dress with a high neckline, her face bare of any paint.

When Maysie saw Elizabeth standing there, she lifted the skirt of her dress and ran to her, flinging herself into Elizabeth's arms.

"I'm so glad you came," Maysie murmured, clinging to Elizabeth. "I thought you might hate me after seeing that I had returned to the life that you tried to help me escape from. I'm so glad that you don't hate me. Oh, Elizabeth, I'm so very happy."

Elizabeth hugged her for a moment, then stepped back. "I could never hate you," she said gently, touching Maysie's cheek. "But I did not come to tell you that. I've come for something else. Maysie, I need to see Four Winds. Will you be seeing him soon? I very desperately need his help."

"What sort of help?" Maysie asked, clasping her hands behind her.

"Strong Heart," Elizabeth said, trying to ignore the boisterous goings on in the room as other men arrived to seek the pleasures of the women. "I've got to get to Strong Heart. It's very important. And I don't want to travel through the forest alone. I thought that Four Winds might go with me."

Marilyn paled and went to Elizabeth. "Darling, you can't be serious," she said softly. "You could be harmed going to see this Indian. Let him come to you."

"I can't wait," Elizabeth said with a sigh. "What I need to tell him can't wait." She was afraid to say anything else, for fear that her mother might not be quiet about it.

"And, Mother, please don't say anything to anyone about this," Elizabeth blurted out. "Even after Father finds me gone, and should he come to you, don't tell him where I've gone. It's of vital importance that he does not know."

"Elizabeth, it isn't right to keep secrets from your father," Marilyn said, then held her breath when she saw accusal flash in her daughter's eyes. Marilyn realized that she did not have the right to tell Elizabeth not to keep secrets, after she had kept so many for so long.

"Mother, you must promise me," Elizabeth said firmly.

"I won't say anything," Marilyn promised.

Maysie took both of Elizabeth's hands. "You're in luck," she said, smiling into Elizabeth's eyes. "I was just on my way to see Four Winds. I meet him from time to time, now that he no longer rides with the outlaws."

"He's no longer with the outlaws?" Elizabeth said, raising an eyebrow.

"For me, he has decided not to ride with them any longer," Maysie said, sighing happily at the thought. "But he's laying low for now so the outlaws won't find him and kill him for turning on them. I know where his hideout is. Come on. I'll take you to him."

Elizabeth hugged Maysie gratefully. "Thank you," she said, a sob lodging in her throat.

"And he'll do whatever he can to help Strong Heart with whatever problem he has," Maysie said, stepping away from Elizabeth. "He's talked to me at length about his feelings for Strong Heart. He said that he was willing to do anything for his friend."

Elizabeth felt as if the weight of the world had been lifted from her shoulders. She was so relieved that she knew that she *could* count on Four Winds. She gave her mother a quick hug and kiss, then left with Maysie.

* * *

Soon they were riding through the forest, their horses lathered with sweat as they were pushed to go quickly. The women reached a meadow of blowing grass and wild flowers. Elizabeth's red hair was like flickering flame as the wind whipped it around her face; Maysie's was like trembling black satin as it blew and shimmered in the sun.

Elizabeth glanced at Maysie and felt warm inside, for she had never seen Maysie so alive and vital as now, and Elizabeth was proud to think that she was partially responsible for that.

Yet there was Four Winds. Elizabeth knew the power of an Indian's love. That it was special, and oh, so wonderful. Maysie was inspired now by such a love, which would lead her into a different life—a life of total caring and commitment, instead of one of degradation.

"Up ahead yonder," Maysie informed Elizabeth. "Four Winds is hiding in an abandoned mine shaft."

They rode onward, then dismounted when they reached the

mine shaft. After securing her horse's reins, Elizabeth went with Maysie into the dark shaft, then stopped with a start when Four Winds stepped suddenly out of the shadows, blocking their way, a rifle aimed directly at Elizabeth.

28

Joy so seldom weaves a chain
Like this tonight, that O! 'tis pain
To break its links so soon.
—THOMAS MOORE

Terrified, Elizabeth stood in the mine shaft, staring at the rifle, and at Four Winds's face that was distorted with hate. She grabbed Maysie by the hand and attempted to run away with her, but her feet seemed frozen to the ground, unable to move as Four Winds began pulling the trigger. . . .

Elizabeth awakened with a start, and looked anxiously around her, then sighed with relief when she realized that she had had another nightmare. Her dream was far from the truth of what had really happened. When she and Maysie had gone to Four Winds, he had quickly offered to take Elizabeth to Strong Heart. He urged Maysie to return to Seattle, promising that he would return for her later.

Elizabeth and Four Winds had ridden hard to reach Strong Heart's village, and as quickly as Strong Heart had been able to round up many braves, they had left by canoe on the river. Going by canoe would make it easier to remove the nets.

Elizabeth had fallen asleep on soft pelts on the floor of Strong Heart's massive canoe, snuggled beneath a warm bearskin. She lifted the bearskin aside, and rose to sit on the seat just behind Strong Heart. She felt his eyes on her as he turned to check on her welfare. She smiled at him, so glad that he had allowed her to come on this mission so she could settle the score with her father, herself. He was a man that she no longer knew—a man guided by treachery and greed.

It tore at her heart to know this side of her father, and she doubted that she could ever forgive him.

When Strong Heart turned his gaze back to stare down the

avenue of the river, Elizabeth reached for the bearskin and wrapped it around her shoulders, content at least for the moment. For she had proven where her loyalties lay by having brought Strong Heart the news of the nets.

Four Winds had also proven his loyalty to Strong Heart, and now rode in a canoe that was moving beside Strong Heart's.

Driven by the sinewy arms of the oarsmen, the many intricately designed canoes pushed their way down the cold river that wound through the black forest and beneath the majestic bluffs, the long oars rising and falling in regular strokes.

The moon shone brightly onto the water, turning the tossing waves into flashing jewels. The wind soughed, and somewhere in the distance an owl hooted.

Elizabeth gazed at Four Winds's canoe. The moonlight revealed its decorations of sea otter teeth and the prow handsomely carved in the design of a whale. As were all of the canoes traveling the rushing waters tonight, the canoe that Four Winds commanded had been hollowed by fire and adz and was very sleek, designed for fast, silent travel.

Elizabeth looked down at herself. Many Stars had urged her to change her clothes before setting out on this journey. Elizabeth had had just enough time to change from her cotton dress into a fine, white buckskin dress, and comfortably soft moccasins. Many Stars had plaited Elizabeth's hair, so that it now hung in two braids down her back.

Elizabeth ran her fingers over the soft fabric of her buckskin dress, gazing at Strong Heart. His back was to her, she admired the definition of his muscles beneath the fabric of his own buckskin shirt. The fringes of the sleeves and his long brown hair lifted and waved in the breeze.

She looked down at the muscles of his arms, as they flexed and unflexed as he drew his single oar rhythmically through the water. She knew the strength of those arms, and desired to be held within his powerful embrace.

Then she stiffened and she grabbed ahold of the side of the canoe, for up ahead was a sudden cottony layer of fog which would hinder the view of the braves as they looked for the nets.

It seemed as though her father had planned it this way—that he had the power of even changing the mood of the weather to suit his purpose.

But the steady movement of the oars did not slacken. They slid into the fog and as if guided by some unseen force, they did not crash into any floating debris, or the banks of the river.

The canoes kept a steady pace, the sound of the oars making contact with the water now almost eerie in the dim haze.

Elizabeth now felt strangely alone, for she could not even see Strong Heart through the denseness of the fog. It was as if she was the only person in the world.

Then the canoes slid from the screen of fog, and once more followed the moonlit path on the water until Strong Heart raised a fist in the air in a silent command for his braves to stop. As his canoe came to a halt in the water, so did those that followed.

Elizabeth's breath quickened as Strong Heart, along with the other braves, turned the direction of their canoes and paddled slowly toward shore.

Once there, they pulled their canoes ashore on a spit of sand. Elizabeth nodded a silent thank you to Strong Heart as he helped her from the boat.

It was then that she got her first look at the nets that stretched across this narrow span of the river, as if a monstrous spider had spun a web.

A tremor coursed through Elizabeth, seeing how completely the waters were covered by the vast nets. There were nets crisscrossing the water, her father and Morris having evidently not taken any chance that should one net fail to stop the salmon, the others wouldn't.

Knives flashed in the moonlight as the braves left their canoes and ran toward the nets. Elizabeth followed Strong Heart, slipping her own knife from a sheath that she had tied on her leg beneath the skirt of her dress—a knife that Many Stars had lent her.

With eager fingers and a building rage against her father, Elizabeth waded into knee-high water, and stood at Strong Heart's side as they quickly began cutting the nets to shreds.

She was so determined to make things right for Strong Heart and his people, she didn't even notice how numbing cold the water was. The only thing that was important to her now was to help Strong Heart destroy the nets. Any day now the salmon would be appearing in hordes in these very waters.

They must become the harvest of the Suquamish, not her father and Morris Murdoch!

Just as the dark began to dispel with the sun's rising, the last net was cut loose. And with the same silence that had brought them there, the Suquamish braves entered their canoes and shoved off into the water. Only when they got several miles up the river did they let out shouts and whoops of victory, Strong Heart and Four Winds's the loudest of them all.

When Strong Heart turned to Elizabeth and motioned with a hand for her to come and sit beside him, she moved quickly to his side and snuggled against him.

"This thing that you have done for my people will never be forgotten," he said feelingly. "And that you brought Four Winds, so that he could prove his worth again to the Suquamish, and his devotion as a friend to me, warms my heart, my *la-daila*."

"I'm so happy that everything turned out all right," Elizabeth said, her eyes shining at his. "I even feel important now. Even your braves look at me with a different look in their eyes, as though . . . as though I now belong."

"You do, and you always have," Strong Heart said, never missing a stroke with his oar. "Have you returned to stay with me now, to be my wife?"

"Ah-hah," Elizabeth murmured. "My life with my father as I have known it is now a thing of the past. I could not bear to even face him now, knowing what he is capable of."

"My *la-daila,* forget your bad feelings," Strong Heart softly encouraged. "Let us live for tomorrow. Today and forever throw all bad thoughts away!"

"I shall try," Elizabeth said, badly wanting to, but knowing that it would not be as easy practiced as spoken.

* * *

The sky was dark again when Elizabeth woke up beside Strong Heart in his longhouse. She had drifted asleep in his canoe again, and had not even been aware of when they had arrived at his village, nor of being carried to shore to his longhouse.

Now, as she awakened she felt a warm body lying behind hers. Strong Heart's nakedness against her own made a thrill shoot through her, for it seemed so long since they had been together intimately.

Elizabeth drew in a breath of joy and closed her eyes when she felt Strong Heart's hands moving over her back, down to cup her buttocks. Then they moved lower still, around to caress her at the juncture of her thighs where her heart seemed centered in its wild beatings. As one of his hands caressed her there, the other moved onto one of her breasts, pinching the nipple to a tight peak. Elizabeth's breath became short and raspy. Then his powerful hands were at her waist, turning her around to face him.

The fire's glow revealed that his eyes were heavy with passion. He reached for her hair and began slowly unbraiding it. She took this opportunity to run her own hands down the magnificence of his body—long, lithe, and aroused.

Her hair, now free of its plaits, drifted across the sleeping platform. Strong Heart moved to his knees and straddled her. She gazed up at his lean, bronze face and touched one of his cheeks almost meditatively as she felt the strength of his manhood probing where she so unmercifully throbbed.

Filled with an overwhelming longing and need that felt like exquisite pain, she opened herself up to him and locked her legs around his waist and drew him deeply into her.

With a groan, Strong Heart pressed deeper. He circled his arms around her and lifted her closer to him, his mouth lowering toward her lips, kissing her urgently, eagerly, drugging her. Her own kisses were desperate and hungry.

His tongue sought through her lips until he touched her tongue. His hands were on her breasts, feverishly fondling her, as she wriggled her body against his in response to his wonderful ways of pleasuring her.

Again they kissed. Strong Heart's desire was a sharp, hot pain in his loins, surges of heat welling up in him, filling him, threatening to spill over.

His hips moved masterfully, faster and deeper. Feeling release so near, and wanting to postpone it because that would bring their lovemaking too quickly to a close, Elizabeth caught her breath, not daring to breathe, or to feel.

But the attempt to not give in to the ecstasy was in vain, because one more deep thrust within her, and one more flick of his tongue through her lips, and she was gone. Surges of euphoria flooded her through and through, making her feel as if for a moment she was spinning, deliciously spinning.

She clung tightly to Strong Heart as his body momentarily stiffened, and then he plunged one last time into her. Then he held her tightly to him as his body quivered and jolted against hers, his moans of pleasure mingling with her own as their lips slowly drifted apart.

Afterward, Strong Heart rolled away, and lay on his side, facing her. "Have I told you before that you are more beautiful than all the skies?" he said softly, placing a gentle hand to her cheek. "After the salmon harvest, we will be two hearts becoming one life, one flow. Ours will be a love everlasting."

Elizabeth nestled closer to him, as he moved his hands around to her back, caressing her. "Each moment with you is sweeter than the last," she whispered, sighing when his hand went to the most delicately tender spot at the meeting of her thighs, smoothing his fingers slowly back and forth, arousing passion inside her again.

"Perhaps Four Winds and this white woman named Maysie can find the same peace? The same paradise as we?" Strong Heart said, drawing his hands back up her body, now pressing her breasts. "This woman. She is surely the cause of Four Winds rethinking his future, and the direction that he was taking with his life. If she is at all like you, he is blessed—*doubly* blessed."

Elizabeth did not want to disappoint him by revealing to him that this woman was the woman he had dragged half drowned from the Sound. That Maysie had lived the life of a prostitute until lately, when she gave herself solely to Four Winds.

No. It was best not to reveal that Maysie had, in a sense, taken a similar road in her life as Four Winds—the *wrong* road. These two unfortunate people were finding salvation in each other's company, pulling themselves out of degradation into something that could be ideal, if they would only accept it.

The sound of people talking and moving anxiously outside the longhouse drew Elizabeth's attention toward the door. "Tomorrow we leave for the canyon?" she asked, raising up on an elbow. "I am so happy to be able to partake in the salmon harvest with you. It will be such an adventure."

"It won't begin the moment we arrive," Strong Heart said, rising from the platform and slipping into his fringed breeches. "After we reach the canyon, there could be several days of waiting for the right moment to start our harvest. And even then, we may have to wait awhile longer."

Elizabeth rose, stretched, then drew her buckskin dress over her head. "Why is that?" she asked, pulling the dress down her slender body, enjoying Strong Heart's look of admiration as he gazed at her.

Strong Heart admired her a moment longer, feeling the flicker of heat in his loins that Elizabeth's loveliness always sparked. Then he looked away from her and knelt on one knee beside the glowing embers of the coals in his firepit. "The salmon chief, Smiling Wolf, is the one who gives the signal for the beginning of fishing each season. No one dares approach the river to fish, unless he has given them permission."

He took a short stick and stirred the coals among the ashes. He scattered some wood shavings into the small, glowing embers. As they burst into flames, he placed more twigs on until the fire had grown enough for a larger piece of wood, which he quickly laid across it.

Elizabeth picked up her hairbrush and began brushing her hair in long, even strokes. "I have never heard of a salmon chief before," she murmured.

"The Suquamish salmon chief is a leader separate from the tribal chief," Strong Heart said, going to the door when he heard a faint knock. He said thank you to Many Stars when she handed him a huge, steaming pot of clam soup, then took it and hung it over the fire.

He turned to Elizabeth as she sat down beside him, handing him a wooden bowl and spoon, keeping one for herself. "Smiling Wolf is a shaman, a religious man," he explained further. "He is believed to have 'salmon power,' the ability to make the salmon reappear on schedule each year."

Elizabeth dipped soup into both of their bowls. She was always glad to learn more of his customs, knowing that was her true way of being totally accepted in his community.

Strong Heart gazed warmly at Elizabeth as she began sipping soup from her spoon. "*Ah-hah,* soon the gifts of the sea will bring prosperity to the tribe for one more long winter of cold moons," he said, then began eating too, thinking that finally everything was as it should be in his life, and especially his *la-daila*'s!

He would not allow himself to think of all of the ways that this could change, just in the blink of an eye. This was now, and in his heart, now was *forever*.

* * *

Later, when Elizabeth was comfortably asleep on the sleeping platform, a rug drawn snugly to her chin, Strong Heart placed a cloak around his shoulders. Lifting a heavy buckskin bag and slinging it across his shoulder, he took a long, lingering look at Elizabeth, then turned and left the longhouse.

The moon was only occasionally visible through the foliage overhead. Strong Heart ran through the forest, knowing where he must go to assure a bountiful harvest of salmon. This year it was more important than any other, because his people had already lost too much.

He would go to the medicine rock and honor it with tokens of worship. The medicine rock had the power to grant a wish to those who visited it. With their wishes they sought to bring back their health, or to heal a broken heart. Strong Heart sought to quicken the run of the salmon.

When Strong Heart reached farther along the banks of the Duwamish River, far from where his village slept silently during this midnight hour, he proceeded carefully up a steep embankment above the river. His gaze locked on the face of a brown, curving rock, and a tree that grew straight out of the rock. He could already see that others had come to honor the rock's powers, because many gifts hung from the bare limbs of the tree, like offerings placed upon the altar of a church.

Strong Heart moved carefully onward. The rock was exceedingly hard to reach. This was deliberate because a white man had destroyed one of the earlier altars of his people, and had taken the wampum and beadwork for himself. This special location of the rock was to discourage those who would easily avail themselves of the offerings of the people of his tribe.

After finally reaching the rock, he gazed in wonder at the preponderance of gifts. Hardly a space remained for Strong Heart's own offering. A broad smile touched his lips and he now knew that all would be blessed this season of the salmon run. It seemed that every able person of his village had come to the rock with their wishes.

Strong Heart knelt and placed the bag on the rock at the base of the tree and smiled heavenward.

29

When did morning ever break
And find such beaming eyes awake
As those that sparkle here!

—Thomas Moore

The drums had throbbed and the chants had echoed to the heavens all night. It was now dawn on the river and the drums and chants had ceased. Elizabeth sat before the campfire, warming her hands as the sun rose slowly in the sky. She gazed around her at the faces of the Suquamish people as the women cooked over the hot coals of the fires, the braves scurried about preparing their methods of catching the salmon, and the children romped and played, their excitement evident in their eyes.

Two days ago they had arrived where the big river roared and foamed as it squeezed through the nearby canyon. They now waited for the Suquamish's most important event of the year, the time when salmon fought their way upstream through the canyon to reach their spawning riffles.

The sun now deliciously warming the air, Elizabeth turned from the fire and gazed at Strong Heart as he joined the others. He was sharpening the tip of a light-weight, short harpoon for throwing at the salmon.

Her gaze shifted, seeing others making nets of bark, and holding spears with various types of points. Some were preparing dip nets—bags of netting attached to a wooden frame on a handle.

Others were preparing a fence weir, to throw across the river later to block the salmon from traveling upstream after many had been allowed to pass by so they could spawn. From a platform on the weir, the Indians could easily catch the salmon with their dip nets and gaff hooks. Strong Heart had told her that these fence weirs were called fish-herding fences.

Elizabeth noticed that today, even though it was late autumn, Strong Heart and his braves wore only breechcloths and sported arm and leg bands twisted and woven of shredded bark.

Elizabeth's eyes were drawn elsewhere, as a heron with slow, flapping wings rose from one place along the shadowy banks of the river, skimming a few yards to settle again.

Farther up the river, a family of three black bears on a fishing expedition paused to look at the Suquamish intruders. They then ambled farther up the river, stopping again to wade into the water that was already teeming with hordes of silvery salmon. Soon they were feasting on their prime catches.

A movement overhead made Elizabeth look up. A red-tailed hawk soared, then landed on an old snag and surveyed his hunting territory, alert for a midmorning snack. Blue jays scolded from the riverbank trees. A kingfisher was a flashing arrow as he hustled upstream on some busy errand.

The hubbub around Elizabeth stilled. She turned wondering eyes to see why. She was filled with awe as the salmon chief made an appearance, walking slowly toward the riverbank. His long robe flowed around his legs, his gray hair dragged the ground behind him. The many winters of his age had bent him like an old tree.

Strong Heart's father followed, limping as Pretty Nose supported him by holding on to his elbow. Strong Heart joined them, their eyes on the salmon chief.

Elizabeth rose slowly to her feet and stood with the other women, behind the men and Pretty Nose. Many Stars moved silently to stand beside Elizabeth. They exchanged quick smiles, then Elizabeth became absorbed in the same ritual that she had now seen twice since their arrival at the swift waters of the canyon. Each day, she and the Suquamish had watched the salmon chief as he walked down to his special vantage point above the river. He had spent the other days motionless, staring at the fish passing upstream. Each time he had announced that the salmon were moving in the river, crowding into the quiet waters. He had said that more and more fish were passing upstream, and soon the harvest would begin.

Today Elizabeth felt the building anticipation of the Suquamish, hoping that today would be *the* day. Even now she could see the splashes of hundreds of salmon fins.

Many Stars clasped one of Elizabeth's hands and squeezed it affectionately as they awaited a response from the salmon chief.

Strong Heart had explained much of this ritual to her on their way to the canyon. He had said that his people assumed that as the salmon chief stood peering down into the river, the old man was talking to the fish, wishing them a safe journey, and thanking them for appearing in the river again. The people believed that he possessed salmon power, a special relationship with the fish.

Hadn't the salmon chief, as a young man, been selected by the salmon themselves?

Hadn't he, like his predecessors, struck a bargain with the salmon that they would crowd into the river at this time of the year?

And, at this special place, they would show themselves so that the people could harvest them.

The people knew that part of the bargain between the salmon and the old chief was that the fish would not be disturbed until many had swum on to the upper river, to provide food for other tribes at less favorable fishing stations.

This was true, but the old chief also knew—perhaps the salmon had told him—that fish must be allowed to escape farther upstream to spawn, to ensure that the runs would continue in future years.

Finally, after days of watching the river and meditating, Chief Smiling Wolf turned to face his people, to make the eagerly awaited announcement. "My people, the first salmon can be taken today!" he shouted, his old eyes gleaming.

There was an uproar of celebration reaching to the sky. Then there was silence again as Smiling Wolf turned to face the river, and in a low monotone, thanked the salmon for appearing again and allowing themselves to be taken, so that the Suquamish could live.

Then Chief Smiling Wolf moved aside, mingling with the watchers as everyone pushed forward to stand at the riverbank.

Elizabeth and Many Stars rushed to find an open space among those who were crowding together, their eager eyes watching something. After squeezing into the crowd, Elizabeth gasped with fear as she watched Strong Heart, one of the tribe's better fishermen, descend a wet, slippery cliff to a niche in the rock just above where the water cascaded through a chute in the canyon. She watched as one other brave followed, handing Strong Heart a spear. A line attached to the spear was piled neatly in front of Strong Heart's feet, where it could run out rapidly. The other end was tied to a stake that the brave drove into a crack in the rock.

Elizabeth placed a hand over her mouth to stifle another gasp. She had not known that Strong Heart was going to be doing this, or how dangerous and difficult spearing fish in the torrent was. Should he slip and fall into the churning waters or against the rocks below, he would not have hardly any chance of surviving. She now understood why he had not shared this part of the ceremony with her.

She breathed much easier when another brave handed a rope to the one who was standing just behind Strong Heart. She thought that this rope was to be tied around Strong Heart, in case he did lose his balance.

But, no! she groaned to herself. Strong Heart shook his head, refusing to use the lifeline. He was the chosen spearsman today. He stood intently watching the movement of the fish below him, his arm cocked.

Elizabeth took some relief that the brave who stood close behind him kept a watchful eye on Strong Heart, ready to use the safety rope in case he fell into the torrent.

Elizabeth glanced down at Many Stars as she edged closer.

"Strong Heart does not wear the safety rope on this special occasion today because he fears that the salmon might be offended if he appears too cautious," Many Stars whispered, smiling up at Elizabeth. "And do not fear. Strong Heart has been the lead fisherman for many years. He has not yet fallen into the waters."

Elizabeth weakly returned her smile, trying to take some reassurance from what she had told her.

Then she turned her eyes back to Strong Heart, and her heart did a great leap when suddenly his arm sprang forward, the spear flying to a fish struggling at the base of the canyon.

Everyone cheered when the spear went through the thick body of the salmon, just in back of the head. And as it flipped and flopped in the water, Strong Heart grabbed the line and quickly brought it in—the first catch of the salmon harvest.

One quick thump with a wooden club and the fish lay still on the rocks. Strong Heart removed the spear, and climbing away from the river, went to Smiling Wolf and lay the salmon at the feet of the chief.

The old man knelt on one knee and meditated a moment over the fish, then with a gesture signaled a woman to come to him.

Elizabeth watched as the woman picked up the fish and carried it to a place of scoured rock beside the river. The rock was pitted with kettle-sized depressions, a result of glaciers and floods in the distant past.

The woman proceeded to clean the fish with the traditional tools—short bone shafts edged with razor-sharp rock chips set in slots. As each one dulled, they were discarded and other blades were fitted in the slots.

"This form of tool that Brown Susan is using is as old as the beginnings of our people," Many Stars whispered, leaning closer to Elizabeth. "Our ancestors thousands of years before brought similar tools to the New World across a land bridge over the great sea."

Elizabeth smiled at Many Stars, glad that she was able to participate in the rituals of the Suquamish.

For a moment her thoughts drifted to her father, wondering how he had reacted when he found the nets destroyed. She could not help but smile smugly at the thought. Yet she was sad at the same time, for her father was now lost to her forever.

And she would never experience the wonderful joy of seeing her mother and father reunited. It most surely would not happen now.

She belonged to Strong Heart now—not her troubled parents.

Pulling herself out of her sad thoughts, she looked toward several women who had been tending a fire while waiting for Strong Heart to spear the first salmon. The women began using sticks to pick up hot rocks from the fire and took them to one of the depressions in the rock, which had been filled with water, and threw the rocks into it.

Elizabeth saw that the rock kettle was about four feet wide and fairly deep. And when the water in it began to boil, the women put the salmon in it. After it was cooked, they removed it and began cutting it in small pieces, and distributed it, until everyone had had a taste of the first salmon.

Then the true harvest began.

Elizabeth was relieved when Strong Heart came down from the high rock. She smiled sheepishly at him as he turned her way, his eyes dancing, his face split with a wide grin.

Then she stood back with the other women as all of the men and boys joined in the harvest.

When the red rim of the sun slipped over the western horizon, and the shimmering afterglow faded into night's darkness, the extent of the day's catch was counted. Chief Smiling Wolf began supervising the distribution of the fish to the women, the shares based on family size. Elizabeth had been told earlier that on an average day, twelve hundred fish, averaging sixteen pounds each, were caught.

Strong Heart came to Elizabeth, pride shining in his eyes. "Was it not a good day?" he boasted, slipping an elk-skin robe around his shoulders as the deep purple shadows of night brought with them the cooler temperatures of late autumn.

"A very good day," Elizabeth murmured. "And so interesting. I loved every minute of it, Strong Heart. Thank you for allowing me to be a part of it."

"Many moons ago, when the world was new, my ancestors discovered this fish which crowded into the rivers at the same time each year," he said, wrapping an elk-skin robe around Elizabeth's shoulders. "They discovered that salmon was an abundant, reliable, nutritious food, and that it could be stored for the winter when other food was scarce. After my people found the salmon, and knew how to process it for storage, we were freed from the necessity of following game. Permanent villages became possible."

He swung an arm around Elizabeth's waist and began walking her toward the river, where he soon found a quiet place for them to sit in privacy. He drew her lips close to his, their eyes twinkling into each other's. "A reliable food supply always makes possible more children," he said thickly. "My *la-daila,* soon we must discuss how large a family we will add to our people's population."

She thrilled at the thought of bearing his children, and at the thought of their sons being the mirror image of their father.

She twined her arms around his neck and accepted his gentle, sweet kiss. Afterward, she was not surprised when he stretched out beside her and lay his head in her lap and fell asleep, exhausted from the long day of fishing.

As he lay there, sleeping soundly, Elizabeth contentedly stroked his dark hair, the pool of water before her blooming with stars.

30

How delicious is the winning of a kiss!

—Thomas Campbell

Several days later the Suquamish were back at their village. This salmon harvest had been one of the largest in the history of Strong Heart's people. The salmon had been dried in the sun on huge racks, then smoked, and much of the dried salmon had been stored in baskets or wrapped in mats in food storage pits. The pits were six feet across and roofed with sticks and mats and then covered with rocks to protect them from animals.

Besides that which had been stored, baskets were filled with dried salmon stacked in and around the village. There were more than one hundred stacks. Each stack contained ten thousand pounds of dried fish. Some Indians from the foothills of the Rocky Mountains had arrived with horses and buffalo skins to trade for the preserved salmon.

With Strong Heart on one side of her, and Four Winds on the other, Elizabeth sat spellbound as she watched the male dancers. They celebrated the success of their salmon harvest, and welcomed the visitors who had come from far away to trade.

She had always loved the Fourth of July celebrations in San Francisco, with the fireworks bursting forth in the sky in various, blinding colors and shapes.

But tonight, as the moonlight flowed down from the sky with a white satiny sheen, she was more in awe of the dancers as they jumped and bounced in fast movements around the outdoor fire in time to the steady beats of the drums. They were only in breechcloths, their mantles trimmed with small bells, and they carried huge, beautifully flaked blades of red obsidian—a form of wealth to the Suquamish.

One by one, the braves leaped around the circle of fire, chanting their songs, their bare feet thumping, raising dust from the ground, their copper bodies gleaming in the light of the fire.

The rich smells of fish cooking drew her attention. There were large cooking kettles set over fires behind her, and fish were being broiled over the open fire and on beds of coals.

She smiled at Many Stars as she stood with the other women as food was steamed in large, shallow pits filled with hot stones. Elizabeth had helped place the food on the stones earlier in the evening. The whole affair had then been covered with leaves and mats, with hot water poured through to the stones. Soon after that, the wonderful fragrances had wafted upward, proving to Elizabeth that this strange method of cooking proved most effective.

She turned her eyes around quickly as the dancers stepped aside and one of them stepped close to the fire. When he poured large amounts of olachen oil on the fire, it blazed up fiercely, drawing sighs from the crowd who watched, their eyes wide.

And the dancers continued to dance, this time more wildly, more athletically, as their bodies turned and twisted, and their heads bobbed.

Elizabeth smiled to herself, deciding that, yes, tonight was a feast of sights, sounds, and smells—a night that she would never forget. Earlier, before the sun had set, there had been many contests—wrestling, shooting arrows and throwing lances at marks, foot and canoe races, and tugs-of-war. Strong Heart and Four Winds had participated in them all, the competition growing fierce between them. But in the end, they had fallen to the ground laughing, more amused than angered by whoever had won the most matches.

Elizabeth now turned her eyes to Strong Heart as he sat so proudly beside her. Like his father, who sat on a high platform with his wife presiding over the celebration, Strong Heart wore a headdress bearing carved figures, painted and inlaid with iridescent shells, spiked with sea lion whiskers, and hung with ermine tails.

His cloak was of costly sea otter fur and flakes of mica had been dusted on his face, glittering in the soft light of the fire.

To Elizabeth, he looked like some mythical god, so breathtakingly noble in appearance, a man of inscrutable self-poise and dignity. It was at this moment hard to believe that she had ever had the opportunity to meet him, let alone be *loved* by him.

And to think that soon she would become his wife was even more unbelievable, for he was not an ordinary man, by any means.

He was special. So very, very special.

Strong Heart felt Elizabeth's eyes on him. He reached over and took her hand in his, squeezing it lovingly. "My *la-daila*, you look beautiful tonight," he whispered, his eyes admiring her. Many Stars had made the dress specially for Elizabeth out of white doeskin, fringed at the hem and at the ends of the long sleeves. Colorful beads and porcupine quills had been embroidered in intricate designs onto it.

His gaze moved to Elizabeth's hair, admiring the wreath of roses that Many Stars had also made for her, another token of her undying friendship for this woman whom Strong Heart had chosen to be his wife.

Elizabeth lowered her eyes, blushing as she felt herself being scrutinized with such admiration by the man she loved. She never wanted to disappoint him, and did not feel as if she had tonight. She felt especially lovely wearing the gifts made by Many Stars's delicate fingers. In time, when she learned the art of making these beautifully designed clothes, she would pay her friend back in kind.

Many Stars was suddenly before her, offering her a large, elaborately carved dish, decorated with the crest of Strong Heart's family, piled high with fish and cooked salmon on skewers.

Elizabeth accepted the offering of food, as other maidens offered the same to Strong Heart and Four Winds.

Long feast mats were unrolled before them to serve as a tablecloth, and for napkins, bundles of softly shredded cedar bark were distributed.

Having not eaten since breakfast, Elizabeth joined Strong Heart and Four Winds as they enjoyed the feast, washing down the assortment of fish with clam juice.

There was more dancing and merriment until the ghostly hour of midnight, delighting those who sat there. Then an elder of the village stepped forth, and began entertaining them with long, often humorous tales of the adventures or misadventures of such picturesque characters as the raven and mink, and of his own childhood, when he had been young, agile, and mischievous.

When he was done, everyone walked to him and gave him warm hugs, then went their separate ways to their longhouses.

Four Winds reached out and clapped a hand onto Strong Heart's shoulder. "It is time for my return to Seattle," he said. "My woman awaits me."

At this mention of Maysie, Elizabeth lowered her eyes, and thought of her mother. She would never understand how her mother could have chosen to be a prostitute. Yet who was Elizabeth to cast blame on anyone?

Everyone was driven by something—and her mother had been forced to find a way to survive away from a man she had grown to loathe.

"And so you plan to marry her soon?" Strong Heart said, rising with Four Winds. Elizabeth rose slowly to stand beside Strong Heart, locking an arm through his, as a way of proving to herself that she had gained more in life than she had lost when she had fallen in love with Strong Heart.

"This is my intention, *ah-hah*," Four Winds said, nodding. He glanced over at Elizabeth and smiled, then looked into Strong Heart's eyes again. "And you? You will soon marry this woman whose hair is the color of flames?"

Strong Heart turned his eyes to Elizabeth. He smiled warmly at her. "*Ah-hah*, soon," he said, nodding. "Now that the salmon harvest is behind us, and my people are content with what life offers them, *ah-hah*, soon we will be celebrating a *potlatch* in our village. You will join the celebration? You will bring your woman so that she will celebrate, also, with us?"

"*Mah-sie*, thank you for the invitation, but I do not think so," Four Winds said, his face turning solemn. "You see, I must return to my people. I must prove to them that I am worthy of being called Suquamish again. They will sit in council and decide my fate, whether I live it as Suquamish among them, or whether I am destined to live as a white man, yet hidden away from the gang that I no longer belong to."

Strong Heart placed his hands on Four Winds's shoulders. "My friend, should you be turned away by those in your village, come to mine," he said passionately. "You will be welcome." He dropped a hand from Four Winds's shoulder and clenched it into a fist, placing it over his heart. "My *tum-tum*, heart, is warm toward you, forever."

Four Winds glanced over at Strong Heart's father, whose eyes seemed to be boring holes through him, then looked uncomfortably back at Strong Heart. "I do not believe your father shares the same sentiments as you about Four Winds," he said, his voice breaking. "Four Winds has made his past, so Four Winds will make his future. But, again thank you, my friend, for your offering to Four Winds. Never will your kindness be forgotten."

"That is good," Strong Heart said, nodding. "That is how it should be."

Four Winds hugged Strong Heart tightly. Then he stepped away from him to hug Elizabeth. Then he walked away, his chin lifted with dignity and pride.

"There goes a good man," Strong Heart said softly. As the drums drifted into silence in the distance, Strong Heart playfully lifted Elizabeth up into his arms and began carrying her toward his longhouse.

"The true celebration begins now," he said huskily, molding one of Elizabeth's breasts with his palm. "You are not too tired, my *la-daila*, to partake in our private celebration of life and love?"

Elizabeth lay her cheek against his chest. "I will never be too tired for you, my love," she murmured, knowing that was true. From the depths of her being, that was true.

* * *

As Four Winds made his way toward his horse that was waiting with the others in the corral beneath the stars, his steps were light, his heart filled with thanks, and much love toward his friend, Strong Heart. Never could any man find such devotion in a friend—such unwavering loyalty. And Four Winds knew that even if he tried until the day he died, he could never find enough ways to repay Strong Heart for his kindness to him.

Four Winds's footsteps suddenly faltered and his breath quickened when he heard muffled voices coming from somewhere close by. Since everyone had retired to their dwellings, this made him suspicious of anyone who might be outside.

He moved stealthily toward the sound of the voices, staying hidden behind trees until he found a group of braves huddled behind a boulder, the moon's glow not yet reaching them.

But Four Winds did not need the moon to identify the men. He knew their voices, each and every one of them.

He pressed his back against a towering elm tree, and leaned his head closer to the speakers, growing cold inside over what these men were plotting without the consent of their chief or his son.

It could bring the total wrath of the white community down on the Suquamish village.

He did not intervene, knowing they would not listen to him. He learned that the braves wanted to travel to Seattle, and once and for all burn the old house that sat on the hallowed ground of their ancestors. They were also going to rid the land of the fishery that was a threat to their future, and the white man who had brought so much sorrow into their lives.

* * *

Silkenly nude, Elizabeth reached her arms out for Strong Heart as he washed the last of the glittering mica from his face. "Come to me, my love," she said, her voice foreign to her in her need to touch his sleek body. His arousal was quite evident as his manhood stood erect, like a gleaming, velvet rod.

Strong Heart tossed the cloth aside, his heart pounding hard within his chest at the mere sight of Elizabeth. Her opened arms beckoning to him promised much that made his heart sing. Strong Heart paused a moment longer to take in the loveliness of her.

His gaze burned upon her bare skin as he looked at her perfect breasts with their taut nipples and tantalizing cleavage, her slim and exquisite waist, and her hips so invitingly rounded.

His eyes stopped and rested on her central tuft of hair at the seam of her thighs. His hand circled his throbbing shaft as he moved to his knees and straddled her.

"Place your hands where mine is," he said huskily, sucking in a breath of pleasure as she did as he asked. He withdrew his own hand and threw his head back and groaned as her fingers moved up and down, making him feel as though he might explode within her fingers, the longing was so powerful.

And when he felt her mouth on him, her tongue sensually stroking him, he stiffened and had to place his hands to her shoulders to urge her away from him, for another moment of such wonderful kisses and he would no longer be able to hold himself back.

Strong Heart settled himself over her, his tongue brushing her lips lightly. He then pressed his lips softly against hers as he entered her in one thrust. His lean, sinewy buttocks moved, her hips lifted to welcome their even strokes. His hands went to her breasts, stroking and kneading them, as his mouth seized hers, darting his moist tongue between her lips.

And then his mouth moved from her lips to her breasts, as he kissed first one nipple, and then the other. Then he sucked the nipples hungrily.

Overcome by passion, Elizabeth gave a little cry. Again his lips were on hers, silencing her with a fiery kiss, his thrusts becoming more heated, driving harder inside her.

She clung to him, this raging hunger that always came from being with him being wonderfully fed. She knew that his hunger was as great as hers, in the hard, seeking pressure of his lips as he continued kissing her, his steel arms enfolding her.

An incredible sweetness swept through her then, and her body exploded in spasms of desire just as his own body quaked against hers.

After the tempest had subsided, they lay in each other's arms, their passion having given way to peace. Elizabeth scooted closer to him and kissed his brow. "After we are married, will you still find such bliss within my arms?" she whispered. "Can a love like ours last forever, Strong Heart? Can it?"

He caressed her skin lightly with his fingertips. "Even after thirty-seven winters I shall still desire you," he whispered huskily. "So shall you, Strong Heart."

"Even after we are grandparents of perhaps even a thirty-year-old grandson?" she said, giggling at the thought, hard to envision herself that old, and finding it even harder to envision Strong Heart as anything but young and virile. Even his father was still a handsome man in that he did not seem to be in his fifty-sixth winter of age.

Her man would remain ageless, especially within the deepest recesses of her heart.

"Even after we are grandparents of many grandchildren," Strong Heart said, drawing a blanket over them as the wind whipped suddenly down the smoke hole.

Elizabeth snuggled against him. "I had such a good time tonight," she said drowsily.

"That is good," Strong Heart said, smiling into the darkness as the fire had now burned down to low embers. "It is good, also, to know that our people will not lack for nourishment this long winter ahead."

He leaned up on an elbow, smiling down at Elizabeth. "But one must never forget that the wind, rain, and sun also nourishes the bodies of the Suquamish braves," he murmured. "There are many things that help sustain the body—food, pure air, water, and sun are our medicine."

A sound outside the longhouse, where the village now lay in a long past midnight slumber, made Strong Heart bolt to a sitting position. By instinct, he reached for the rifle that he kept on the floor beside the sleeping platform, then crept from his bed and moved stealthily toward the door.

"Strong Heart?"

The voice of Four Winds broke the silence, drawing Strong

Heart's eyebrows up. "It is you, Four Winds?" Strong Heart said, jerking the door open. "I would have thought you would be many miles away by now. Why are you here?"

Elizabeth drew a blanket around her as she rose from the sleeping platform to stand beside Strong Heart as Four Winds entered. Something about his attitude and the worried expression on his face made her grow cold inside, and her pulse begin to race.

31

My lips are always touching thine,
At morning, noon and night.

—John Clare

"Tell me, my friend, what brings you back to Strong Heart's dwelling?" Strong Heart asked, frowning as he gazed into Four Winds's troubled eyes. "What keeps you from traveling on to Seattle, where your woman awaits your return?"

"What I have seen and heard delayed my journey," Four Winds said, his jaw tight.

"What did you see?" Strong Heart asked.

"I have uncovered a plan that includes some of your village's most devoted braves," Four Winds said, glancing over at Elizabeth. "These braves were in a secret council at the edge of the village, beside the corral. They have left to burn down the old house that sits on Suquamish hallowed ground and the fishery that has been built close to it. It is their plan to once and for all rid the Suquamish ancestral burial grounds of the evil white man who they feel is responsible for the raid on your village, along with the business that threatens to ruin the Suquamish's future salmon harvests."

Elizabeth gasped and paled. Four Winds had just described her father, his house, and fishery. Although she no longer loved her father as a daughter should, she did not want to see him murdered.

And what of Frannie? Sweet Frannie! She could be burned alive in the fire, or shot as she was trying to flee.

No!

It couldn't be allowed to happen!

She turned to Strong Heart and grabbed him by the arm.

"Strong Heart, you've got to stop them," she said, her voice quavering. "Please go and stop the braves."

"It is probably too late," Four Winds said solemnly. "I came as soon as they left on their horses, but they have got such a head start, I doubt anyone could catch up with them."

Elizabeth lifted her chin stubbornly. "Strong Heart, I will go alone if you will not accompany me," she said firmly.

When Strong Heart did not answer her, Elizabeth leaned up into his face. "I shall, Strong Heart," she cried. "Although my father may be guilty of many evil things, I can't allow him to be murdered. At least I shall try my damnedest to stop it from happening."

Having never heard Elizabeth speak a curse word before, Strong Heart realized just how determined she was to go to her father's rescue. And he was glad to see such a dedication to her parent, even though Earl did not deserve such loyalty. It was proof that her heart was not easily swayed. And that was good.

He gazed down at his woman for a moment longer, then turned to Four Winds. "I shall go and do what I can," he said grimly. "You will ride with me again, Four Winds? It will be like many moons ago, when you and I rode side by side on all sorts of adventures."

Elizabeth heaved a sigh of relief, and even before Four Winds had agreed to accompany Strong Heart on the journey, she had rushed to the curtain at the far end of the longhouse and lowered it. Standing behind it, she began dressing. She was going. No one could keep her from it. Not unless Strong Heart tied her to the sleeping platform.

"*Ah-hah,* my friend," Four Winds said, nodding. "Four Winds will ride with you. While you are getting dressed, do you wish that I go and awaken other braves to accompany us? Do you wish to travel by canoe or by horse? I shall ready whichever mode of travel you prefer."

"It is best to go by horseback," Strong Heart said, walking briskly away from Four Winds. He flung the blanket from around his shoulders. He yanked on his breeches, and slipped his shirt over his head. "If we traveled by canoe, and the authorities began hunting for us, we would be too easily spied on the river. On horseback, we can be more elusive."

He sat down and pulled on his moccasins. "And no other braves," he said flatly. "The journey will go more quickly with less."

He rose to his feet, grabbing a headband, and placing it around his head. "Ready two horses," he said flatly. "Yours and mine. I will be at the corral soon, Four Winds. We will ride hard, hopefully to soon overtake those braves who have decided to do that which should have been debated in council."

Fully clothed, Elizabeth stepped from behind the curtain. "Four Winds, prepare *three* horses for travel," she said, her hands on her hips. "I am also going."

Strong Heart turned and faced her. He knew her stubborn nature, and her determination to stop the attack on her father, but he had not expected her to want to go.

And although she thought that what he was readying to do was solely for her benefit, it was not. His motive in this was a selfish one—to protect his *people.* He knew that if the Suquamish braves succeeded, the repercussions against their people would not be worth the victory. The white authorities would come to his village and take away those who were responsible for the fire and perhaps the murders of some white people. They would be hanged. And then the people of his village would be forced to move to a reservation, where they would lose all of their freedoms—all of their joys.

He did not want Elizabeth to slow him down. Already they had taken too much time in talking.

He went to her and gently took her face into his hands. "It is best that you do not go," he said, his voice slow and measured. "The journey will be done at a hard gallop so that we will be able to get there in time. My *la-daila,* it is late. Go to bed. This time tomorrow night I will be warming the blankets with you again."

Elizabeth stuck to her guns. "No matter what you say, I am going," she said. She stepped away from Strong Heart and glared at Four Winds. "Go and prepare *three* horses. If you don't, then your journey will be slowed by having to wait for me to get my horse ready, myself, for I am going!"

Strong Heart gave Elizabeth a long, frustrated stare, then turned and nodded to Four Winds. "Prepare three horses," he murmured. "We shall be there shortly."

Four Winds looked from Elizabeth to Strong Heart, then nodded and left with hurried steps.

Elizabeth turned to Strong Heart and flung herself into his arms. "Thank you," she cried. "Thank you for not ordering me to stay behind. If you had, I'm not sure what I would have done. I would not have wanted to embarrass you in front of Four Winds. Thank you for not giving me cause to."

Strong Heart stroked her long and flowing hair. "I do not embarrass all that easily," he said, chuckling. "But it is best that a woman does not show defiance to her man in front of friends. Tonight it came close to that, but I closed my eyes to it. Your reason for behaving this way was understandable. No matter how evil your father is, within your heart there will always be a corner reserved for the man who helped give you breath and life."

Tears streamed from Elizabeth's eyes. She was so grateful to this man whose compassion ran so deep.

"But I do worry about how you can stay in the saddle through the long night when you have yet to have any sleep," Strong Heart said, easing her from his embrace, and holding her at arm's length.

"Do you not recall the nap you and I took early this afternoon, anticipating the late hours of the celebration?" Elizabeth asked, wiping tears from her eyes. "I rested well then, Strong Heart. I am fine for the whole night of travel. Honest, I am."

"Ah-hah," he said, smiling down at her. "I believe you are." He walked away from her and grabbed his rifle, then nodded toward her. "Let us leave now. Let us hope that when we return it will be with a light heart."

"Yes, let's," Elizabeth vowed, rushing from the longhouse with him.

Four Winds had brought the saddled horses to the house. As Strong Heart and Four Winds swung themselves into their saddles, Elizabeth leaped into her own, her heart pounding. She feared that they would be too late.

As they rode from the village, she tried to keep her spirits high. Courage was now needed as never before.

* * *

Elizabeth had known the ride would be excruciatingly hard, for she had been on this same journey enough times now to know how tiring it was to stay in the saddle for so long. She had managed to keep up with Strong Heart and Four Winds the long night through and soon they would be arriving at her father's place. To her chagrin, they had not caught up with the Suquamish who had left before them.

The sky was just lightening along the horizon when Elizabeth's gaze was jerked upward. She was quickly overcome by a horror when she saw the flames of a great fire in the sky.

"No!" she cried. "We're too late!"

She broke away from Strong Heart and Four Winds and urged her horse into a hard gallop toward the dire signs in the heavens. The nightmares that had troubled her now rushed back into her consciousness. She recalled the fire, and how she had been trapped in it.

Surely the nightmare had been an omen. Yet those trapped within the flames were her father, and sweet, innocent Frannie, and all of the other servants. They must have been asleep when the fire had been set. Surely they had had no chance of getting out alive.

Guilt ate away at her for how she had turned her back on her father, even though he had deserved it.

Now she would never have a chance to tell him that, no matter what he did, she loved him.

And neither would he have a chance to redeem himself of his crimes.

When she reached the outskirts of her father's estate, she could see the flames engulfing both the house and the fishery. She almost fainted from the sight. Nobody could have survived the fire. And even though she had Strong Heart's devoted love, this was the worst moment in her life.

She quickly dismounted, and had to force herself not to go farther, but to stay hidden in the shadows of the forest. She couldn't allow anyone to see her or Strong Heart. She did not want Strong Heart to be blamed for the fire.

Elizabeth gnawed on her lower lip as she frantically looked for her father and Frannie among the spectators watching the fire. When she saw them both, as well as the other servants, clustered together outside the tall, old gate, she cried with relief.

Elizabeth then searched around her for those who had set the fire. When she found no sign of Strong Heart's braves anywhere, she realized that they had left the minute they had seen that their fires had caught hold.

Breathlessly, Strong Heart and Four Winds dismounted close to Elizabeth, their eyes on the fire.

Strong Heart went to Elizabeth and swept an arm around her waist. Together they witnessed Morris Murdoch ride up, and dismount close to Earl.

* * *

Morris squinted his eyes as he gazed at the roaring flames and the falling walls of the house as it swayed in the brisk wind that blew across the Sound.

"I saw the smoke in the sky from my home," Morris said thickly. "Somehow I knew it was your house—and our fishery. I notified the firehouse. The fire wagon should be arriving soon." He turned wondering eyes to Earl. "Earl, what happened?"

"All I know is that the screams and shouts of my servants awakened me and then I smelled the smoke and saw flames leaping up to the second floor of the house," Earl said, nervously raking his hands through his hair. "I barely got out alive. If not for the rope bolted to the floor in my room, to be used as a fire escape, I . . . I . . . wouldn't be here to tell about it."

"You didn't see anybody?" Morris prodded. "You don't know how it got started?"

"The house is old," Earl said, his voice thin. "We've had a few problems with our fireplaces. Faulty flues. I guess that's how it started." He gazed down at the flaming fishery, his heart sinking as he watched the building collapse into a pile of burning rubble. His whole world was falling apart before his very eyes. "I . . . I . . . guess the wind carried sparks from the house to the fishery. It's gone, as well."

* * *

Elizabeth's head jerked as she saw a movement in the forest behind her out of the corner of her eye. She turned and grabbed Strong Heart's arm. "Darling, I just saw the elderly Indian again," she said in a rush of words. "Your grandfather. I saw him over there."

Her words trailed off when the old Indian stepped into full view, leaning on his staff, his faded old eyes gleaming happily as he watched the flames eating away at the house. At close range, Elizabeth saw that the man was short, thin, and bowlegged. His gray, unbraided hair was worn to his shoulders, and he had a benevolent face. He looked like an aging philosopher whose strength had waned, yet whose mind was still active.

Stunned by the sight of his grandfather, Strong Heart stared at him for a moment. But when Proud Beaver's eyes turned to him in recognition, the spell was broken and Strong Heart could not get to his grandfather quickly enough. He went to him and embraced him.

"My grandson, my deed is done," Proud Beaver said in a gravelly voice. "Please take me home—take me back to our people."

Strong Heart parted from his grandfather, an eyebrow lifted. "Deed?" he said, his eyes locked with his grandfather's. "What deed, Grandfather?"

As his grandfather's gaze shifted and stopped again on the raging flames that lit the night like daylight, he smiled triumphantly. Strong Heart followed his stare, and without being told, understood that it had not been the braves who had set the fire.

"The fire," Proud Beaver said, nodding. "It is my doing, not our braves who came shortly after I had set it, bearing their own lit torches. When they saw the burning house, they fled quickly. I did not allow them to see me. I did not yet want to leave. It pleasured me too much to see that which desecrated our hallowed ground for so long finally destroyed."

He smiled at Strong Heart. "I also destroyed the fishery," he said happily. "It was easy. The fires burned swiftly. My heart sang while watching it."

Fearing for his grandfather's life, Strong Heart whisked him away into the shelter of the forest. Elizabeth and Four Winds followed, leading the horses behind them.

Strong Heart turned his grandfather to face him again. He placed a gentle hand on his frail shoulder. "Grandfather, I have been searching for you for so long," he said. "Only recently did my search become a desperate one." Strong Heart lowered his eyes, hating to be the bearer of sad tidings.

But knowing that he had to do it, he began speaking again, but this time in a low, almost apologetic tone.

"Grandfather, in your absence there has been a raid causing much bloodshed and devastation at our village. But your daughter and Chief Moon Elk lived through the raid. I was not there at the time of the attack because I was searching for you. I then returned to find you and to take you back so that you could mourn the deaths of those you loved. Again, I did not find you. Yet here you are. How is it that you were so elusive, and now you are here, allowing yourself to be seen?"

"There is a cave that tunnels down through the earth, and stops at the far end beneath the house that I have set fire to tonight," Proud Beaver said softly. "I have been living there, finding the relics of the Suquamish dead, and burying them where they belong, in the earth of our people. Now our ancestors can finally rest in peace."

"*Ah-hah*, that is so," Strong Heart said, drawing his grandfather into his arms, hugging him tightly.

Feeling the tears welling against her lower lids, Elizabeth

placed a hand to her mouth, and stifled a sob that this tender scene between grandfather and grandson had evoked.

She then looked through a break in the trees at her father, glad that he was at least alive. She wondered what he was going to do now, now that his dream had died in flames.

But she didn't have much more time to think about it. Strong Heart was lifting his grandfather into his saddle. Then he helped her into her saddle and swung himself in front of her.

Strong Heart reached a hand out for Four Winds, their hands clasped tightly. "My friend, come soon to our village," Strong Heart invited. "Come and join the *potlatch* that precedes my marriage to my *la-daila*. Bring your woman. Let us be married together!"

Four Winds smiled over at Strong Heart. Elizabeth thought it a bashful sort of smile. Then Four Winds rode away toward Seattle without a word.

Elizabeth clung to Strong Heart's waist as he nudged his heels into the flanks of his horse, and they were quickly riding through the forest.

* * *

The firewagon made its arrival. But it was too late. And even though Morris suspected that Indians had set the fire, he didn't tell anyone. He had his own plans of revenge. He had found the destroyed nets in the river and he knew who was responsible.

He rode away without saying anything about it to Earl.

* * *

Downtrodden, with Frannie trailing behind him, her face sad and covered with ashes, Earl went to his ship, the only thing that he had left in the world. He had lost his daughter, his home, and business. He had lost his wife a second time, it seemed, for she had not made any more overtures toward him. And, except for faithful Frannie, he had dismissed his other servants.

He leaned against the ship's rail, staring up at the smoky remains of his house, and at what remained of his fishery. He had no reason to live now. His thoughts strayed to the small derringer that he kept hidden beneath his bunk in the master cabin.

That could end it for him, quickly.

Fearing his mood, Frannie hurried behind Earl as he entered his cabin. He was too quiet—his eyes seemed like a man's who no longer had hope. She didn't know what he might do in this state of mind, and hoped that she could stop it.

She almost ran into him when he stopped abruptly.

Earl was shocked by who he found standing in the shadows, a lantern giving off only a faint light to see by.

"Marilyn?" he gasped. "What are you doing here?"

Frannie said nothing, only stood by in surprised silence. She had never forgiven Marilyn for leaving Elizabeth, but now she hoped that Marilyn could be her master's salvation tonight—a night when she had seen him lose everything. The only other time, when they had met recently, Frannie had divined something in Marilyn's eyes and voice that proved that she still loved Earl.

"I saw the fire in the sky and since it seemed to be coming from here, I couldn't help but come to see for sure," Marilyn said, moving closer to Earl. She was lovely tonight in a flame-red velveteen dress with black lace at its high throat, and at the end of the long sleeves.

Her hair was hanging long and free down her back, seemingly an extension of the dress, with its brilliant red coloring.

"When I saw the house on fire, I realized just how much I still wanted you—how much I still love you," Marilyn continued softly. "Earl, if you can find a way to forgive me for what I have done since having left you, I promise that I will start all over again with you. The life that I have been leading is not at all what I want. I . . . want to be with you. Under any circumstances, I want to be with you."

"But I have nothing now," Earl said, his voice breaking. "Nothing at all to offer you. All of my money, except for what I can get from the sale of this ship, was tied up in the fishery.

And it is gone. I'm broke, Marilyn. Virtually broke. I have nothing left to offer. Nothing."

"You have yourself," Marilyn said, placing a gentle hand to his ash-begrimed face. "Darling, I will discharge all of my girls. The house can be a real home, where you and I can live as man and wife and grow old together."

Feeling as if God had seen his remorse and, knowing that he was contemplating suicide, He had sent Marilyn to him for his salvation, Earl tearfully drew her into his arms.

Their tears mingled, they were so glad to have found each other again.

Frannie turned her own eyes away, hope now rising inside her for her own future. Without Master Easton, she had no future. She sure enough wasn't prepared to go and live with Elizabeth and her Indians. She feared Indians more than she feared living alone.

* * *

Daybreak came with a glorious sunrise, and also with the thundering of many hooves as the Suquamish braves' horses fell into stride on both sides of Strong Heart's and Proud Beaver's. They had obviously seen Strong Heart arrive to observe the fire, and had hidden in the forest, waiting for him to turn back toward the village, before joining him.

Strong Heart glared from man to man, silently condemning them for having gone behind their chief's back to do as they pleased, even though it was for the best of reasons.

But he was glad that they were blameless for the fire. Now there was only one man to blame, and no one would ever think he was the arsonist.

That made it easier to forgive the braves, and ride with them on toward their village.

"I'm so tired," Elizabeth said, laying her cheek on Strong Heart's back. "Strong Heart, I know that I said that I could withstand this long ride, but now I'm not sure if I can. Another half day on the horse will be too much for me. Please let's stop, Strong Heart. Please let me rest awhile."

Realizing that if Elizabeth complained, she was actually deadly tired, and he could not see himself forcing anything on her. He glanced up at his grandfather who rode proud and sure in his saddle, and then over at all of his braves. If they all stopped, the chances were that someone might come along and put two and two together, thinking they were all responsible for the fire.

But if only he and Elizabeth stopped, it would look less conspicuous; it would look innocent enough.

He raised a fist in the air and shouted to the braves to stop. And after explaining that the braves should go on, and accompany Proud Beaver back to their village, Elizabeth and Strong Heart were alone. A campfire was soon going by a meandering stream, and Elizabeth slept in Strong Heart's arms.

Strong Heart drifted off too and was not aware of a lone horseman riding his horse in a soft trot beside the campsite. The horseman's eyebrows raised as he saw Strong Heart and the white woman lying at his side—this was a strange sight, indeed.

He rode onward, his eyes gleaming. He had found something to laugh about when he reached Seattle and visited his favorite saloon.

32

> If ever two were one, surely we,
> If ever man were lov'd by wife, then thee.
>
> —Anne Bradstreet

The afternoon was fading, the distant hills shaded in purple and gray when Elizabeth awakened. At first she was startled, wondering where she was, and then it came to her—she and Strong Heart had broken away from the others to rest.

The fire, she thought brooding to herself. It had taken away her father's dreams, but surely for only a while. As determined as he was, he would rebuild and then Strong Heart's grandfather would have placed himself in jeopardy for naught.

Then what? Would Proud Beaver return, to wreak destruction on her father again?

This time, would her father die?

The thought sent an involuntary shiver down her spine.

She forced herself to think of better things—of her future with Strong Heart, of being his wife, and the mother of his children. Soon that dream would become a reality, and she would let nothing or nobody stand in the way of the happiness that she had found with this wonderful man.

"My Suquamish *husband*," she whispered to herself, testing the words on her lips, loving them.

Rising up on one elbow, she gazed at Strong Heart. She smiled and reached a hand out toward him, yet did not touch him for fear of waking him. She had sorely needed sleep, but it appeared that Strong Heart had needed it worse than she. He still slept soundly, his breathing even, the artery at his throat pulsing with a steady beat.

Her mouth felt as if it was filled with cotton. Elizabeth turned and looked at the stream that caught the last flickering rays of the lowering sun in its rippling water. Careful not to disturb Strong Heart, she rose quietly to her feet and went to the stream and knelt beside it.

After taking several gulps from her cupped hands, she refreshed herself by splashing water onto her face. She rose slowly again, her stomach growling with hunger.

She turned and glanced at Strong Heart. He was still asleep.

She then spied a bush which displayed an array of bright red berries beside the stream, but it was quite a distance from the campsite.

Her hunger overpowering her caution, Elizabeth started walking toward the bush. When she nearly reached it, she stopped when she heard the sound of an approaching horseman.

Fear grabbed at her heart, for she had wandered too far from Strong Heart to get back to him quickly enough. She looked anxiously around her, searching for something large enough to hide behind.

But she found only a copse of birch trees with narrow trunks. She had no choice but to remain in the open, at the mercy of whoever was coming her way. Her only hope was that the horse's hoofbeats had awakened Strong Heart and he had found her gone. And he would come looking for her with the protection of his rifle.

Elizabeth's eyes widened when the horseman came into full view, quickly recognizing Four Winds. He had seen her just at the same moment she had seen him, it seemed, for he was now raising a hand in the air in silent greeting.

Elizabeth sighed with relief. Then her relief was replaced with apprehension. Four Winds had said that he was going to see Maysie, so why would he be this far from Seattle? Four Winds drew his horse to a skittering halt.

Elizabeth ran to him as Four Winds slid easily out of the saddle, facing her with a frown. "Four Winds, what is it?" she asked, her voice anxious. "What are you doing here? And where is Maysie?"

"I shall go for Maysie later," Four Winds said in a grumble.

"Strong Heart's and your welfare came first." He looked past Elizabeth's shoulder, seeing Strong Heart asleep in the distance.

He then placed a hand on Elizabeth's shoulder. "I must go and warn Strong Heart," he said solemnly. "There is not that much time."

Elizabeth paled. "Warn him?" she murmured. "Warn him about what? And what do you mean by saying there is not that much time? Tell me, Four Winds. Tell me now."

"On my way to get Maysie, I saw a posse leaving Seattle," Four Winds explained. "I searched for my informant friend who knows everything about everyone to ask where the posse was going. He told me that a rider had come into town, and had been bragging and laughing during a poker game about seeing an Indian and a white woman asleep together in the forest. The new sheriff in town picked up on it and recalled the talk about a woman having escaped prison on the night of the prison's burning. He figured that this could be the one. He said that she fit the description of the missing woman." Four Winds paused for a second, and then continued. "The sheriff said that any woman who was sleeping with a low-down Indian would be the sort that would be an escaped fugitive," he hissed out. "The sheriff also said that the Indian was more than likely the one who had set the fire, and helped her escape. The sheriff gathered together a posse and rode out of town, heading in this direction. Knowing the paths of the forest so well, I took a shortcut, hoping to reach you before those who would like to hang you and Strong Heart."

Elizabeth's head was spinning. What should she do? She turned and gazed at Strong Heart, a sob lodging in her throat at the thought of this wonderful man possibly being arrested. The thought of the hanging platform haunted her. She had to do something to protect Strong Heart from having to face such a ghastly end as that. His people depended on him. He was the future for his people. And although he was also her future, her *life*, she suddenly knew what she must do to save him.

She turned to Four Winds and grabbed him by the arm, her eyes pleading. "Don't go to Strong Heart with this news. I have a plan that will spare him the humiliation of being arrested. Please cooperate with me, Four Winds. Will you?"

"What plan?" Four Winds asked, raising an eyebrow. "What do you have in mind?"

"I will leave Strong Heart while he sleeps, ride on and meet the posse, and draw them away from Strong Heart," Elizabeth said hurriedly. "Four Winds, don't you see? It is the only way! It is best for Strong Heart. It is best for his people. Please trust me. Don't awaken Strong Heart. Let me go alone."

Four Winds was torn, yet saw the logic in her plan. And even though he knew that Strong Heart might hate him for it, he decided that, *ah-hah*, he would do as the white woman asked.

"Take my horse," Four Winds said, handing the reins over to Elizabeth. "It would wake Strong Heart if you went for his."

Weak with fear, yet digging deep within herself to find the courage to make this sacrifice for her beloved, Elizabeth nodded and lifted herself into the saddle. "Thank you," she said, gazing down at Four Winds. "Thank you for understanding. You see, Four Winds, I love your friend more than life itself. I only hope that this plan works."

Four Winds gave her the direction that she should take in order to run head-on with the posse. Then he stepped back and allowed her to leave, although he knew that the dangers were many in agreeing to the schemes of a woman. But for Strong Heart, he would do anything.

Turning slowly, he looked toward his sleeping friend, wondering how he would tell him. He knew that Strong Heart would become crazed with anger. Then, after he calmed down, hopefully he would understand both his woman's and his best friend's motives—which were for the benefit of the Suquamish.

It felt good to Four Winds to be doing something that was no longer selfish.

He waited for some time, to give Elizabeth a good start, then went to Strong Heart and knelt beside him. "Strong Heart, wake up," he said, touching his arm, and gently shaking it. "It is I, Four Winds. Wake up."

Strong Heart blinked his eyes as he stared blankly up at

Four Winds. "Four Winds?" he said, rising to a sitting position. "What are you doing here?"

Then Strong Heart's eyebrows lifted when he looked at Elizabeth's empty blankets. He bolted to his feet and looked anxiously around him, then faced Four Winds as he rose to stand before him.

"Where is Elizabeth?" Strong Heart demanded, glaring at Four Winds. "She is not here and you *are*. Why is that, Four Winds? What have you done with my woman? When we last parted it was as friends—as trusting friends. And now I find my woman gone. Where is she, Four Winds?"

Four Winds placed both of his hands onto Strong Heart's shoulders. "My friend . . ." he said, and went on to explain what he had heard, and what Elizabeth had decided to do.

Strong Heart was breathless with a building rage that Four Winds had allowed Elizabeth to do something as foolish as this.

"If my woman suffers at the hands of the white authorities, you will pay the price," Strong Heart said, jerking free of Four Winds's grip. "I must go and find her. If I am too late—"

Four Winds interrupted Strong Heart. "I pray that you listen to reason," he said, his voice low. "Ride on to your village. Consider the welfare of your people!"

"Do you not see that I am considering the welfare of my people by *not* going to my village without Elizabeth?" Strong Heart said between gritted teeth. "*Ah-hah*, it is true that I will one day be chief of my people. But do you not understand that a chief whose life is empty from the loss of his woman is no chief at all? And that my people would suffer because of it? I must go for Elizabeth. It is my duty to protect her—the woman who will one day be a Suquamish princess!"

"I beg of you to reconsider," Four Winds persisted. "Should the white woman be arrested, she would not be jailed for long. Her father would find a way to get her freed!"

"That is not so," Strong Heart grumbled. "Her father is a worthless man who thinks only of himself!"

He suddenly realized that they had only one horse between them, and he set his jaw as he glared at Four Winds. Strong Heart would not be the one who would be forced to walk. Four

Winds had been foolish enough to give his horse to Elizabeth, so Four Winds would have to pay the price by going on by foot!

But even as Strong Heart was angrily thinking this, he knew that Four Winds would not suffer at all without a horse. The village was near, and Four Winds was known for his ability to beat anyone who challenged him in footraces. Tonight, Four Winds would use his skills well, it seemed.

"Which way do I go to find my *la-daila*?" Strong Heart said, scowling into Four Winds's face. When Four Winds did not respond and instead stubbornly set his jaw, Strong Heart placed his hand at Four Winds's throat and began softly squeezing. "Tell me, or . . . you . . . shall die!"

Knowing that Strong Heart was angry enough to do as he threatened, Four Winds gasped out the answer.

Strong Heart released his hold on Four Winds, and then without another word, not even a farewell, Strong Heart ran to his horse and was soon riding away through the darkness.

He prayed to the Great Spirit that he would not be too late.

* * *

Starlight, pale and cold, filled the black, velvety sky. The moon lit the meadow that stretched out before Elizabeth like lamplight, enough for her to see the men approaching her on horseback in the distance. Panic swept through her. For an instant she wanted to turn her horse around and retreat into the forest that she had just left.

But the haunting memory of the hanging platform coming quickly to her mind kept her urging Four Winds's horse into a steady gallop toward the posse, her chin held high. She would not let Strong Heart down, now or ever.

And this was the only way.

Elizabeth drew her rawhide reins tightly and waited. She was soon surrounded by the men, with their firearms drawn and aimed at her. Her gaze stayed on the man in the lead, his sheriff's badge reflecting the moon's glow back into her eyes.

Sheriff Ethan Dobbs tipped his wide-brimmed Stetson hat

at her. "Sheriff Dobbs at your service, ma'am," he said in a Texan drawl. "Will you pleasure us men with your company into Seattle? Of course, you know we cain't take no for an answer."

Deputy Franks, a youngish man with a spray of golden hair escaping the brim of his hat, edged his horse closer to the sheriff's. "Sheriff, where's the Injun?" he said, his dark eyes raking over Elizabeth, grinning at her from ear to ear.

"Ask the woman," Sheriff Dobbs said, nodding toward Elizabeth, who had not yet spoken a word for she was terrorized by the number of men and their weapons.

"Ma'am," Deputy Franks asked, now moving his horse closer to her. "There was an Injun with you. Where is he now?"

"I don't know what you're talking about," Elizabeth finally said, hating it when her voice broke from fear. "And may I ask why you have stopped me? I am on my way to Seattle. My father is waiting for me. Please allow me to pass."

She knew that she had never been good at lying, but she was giving it her best. Yet she feared that no matter what she said, she was going to be arrested. Hopefully, she could talk them out of searching further for Strong Heart. If not, she had failed him miserably.

"It's too bad such a looker as you has to also be a cheat and a liar," Sheriff Dobbs said, nodding for Deputy Franks to rejoin the others. "Come along peaceful-like, miss. Don't force me to put handcuffs on those pretty wrists of yours."

Her hopes rising that they were more interested in her than Strong Heart at least for now, Elizabeth nodded. "All right," she agreed. "I'll cooperate. Just please don't handcuff me."

"I said I wouldn't if you came along peacefully," Sheriff Dobbs growled, nodding an order for the men to holster their firearms.

But before they had a chance to, Strong Heart could be seen riding across the meadow in a fast gallop toward them.

Elizabeth turned with a start and felt faint when she saw that it was him, but understood why he had come. For the same reason as hers, he was ready to face the white authorities—to protect his love.

"It's the Injun!" Deputy Franks shouted, then rode on and met Strong Heart's approach. He soon returned with Strong Heart's weapons laid across his lap, and Strong Heart at his side. "By damn, Sheriff, he's come to give hisself up. Ain't that a hoot?"

Sheriff Dobbs rode up beside Strong Heart, slowly looking him up and down. "Do you have a name?" he asked, spitting over his shoulder.

"*Ah-hah,*" Strong Heart said stiffly, as he gazed lovingly at Elizabeth.

"And what the hell does that mumbo jumbo mean?" Sheriff Dobbs said in a feral snarl. "Speak English when you're speaking to me. Do you hear me, damn it? I ain't no heathen with a heathen's education."

Elizabeth paled as she saw the fire leap into Strong Heart's eyes as he turned them on the sheriff. And she blamed herself. If she had awakened Strong Heart and fled with him into the hills, instead of trying to take everything into her own hands, perhaps her beloved could have been spared this humiliation.

But, in time, they would have been found, and then how much worse would it have been for him? No matter what she would have done, it would have been wrong.

"Strong Heart," Strong Heart finally said, then turned his gaze back to Elizabeth. "The woman. Release her. She is innocent. I shall take her place in the jail cell."

"Hah, ain't that a laugh?" Sheriff Dobbs taunted. "Injun, you are both under arrest." He leaned his face into Strong Heart's. "But don't get any crazy ideas that you two'll share the same cell. We won't have no Injun fraternizing with any white woman, even if she is the criminal kind, herself."

Tears flooded Elizabeth's eyes and she had to look away from Strong Heart. Her heart was heavy from having failed the man she loved. She flinched when she heard the snap of handcuffs and knew that Strong Heart was not being treated as gently as she. In the heart of white men who did not understand the honor of an Indian, the Indian always posed a threat to them.

Hanging her head, Elizabeth rode off with the posse, Strong Heart somewhere behind her. She did not have to see him to know that he was even now a noble presence as he rode with his shoulders squared, and his head lifted high.

33

Thy love is such I can no way repay.

—Anne Bradstreet

The next day was gray, a light drizzle misting the air. Maysie drew back a sheer curtain and peered up the long avenue, disheartened. Four Winds had not come for her as promised. She nervously wrung her hands, fearing that the reason for his absence might be that he had been gunned down by the outlaws that he had abandoned.

Or perhaps the new sheriff had caught up with him and had thrown him back in jail.

She would not allow herself to believe that he had second thoughts about taking her away to be his wife. He had spoken with such sincerity when he had talked about taking her to his village, so that they could both begin a new life there.

He had talked about how one day he would be chief, if his father had not yet chosen someone else to take his place.

"My dear, hasn't he arrived yet?" Marilyn said, moving to Maysie's side. She took Maysie's hand. "Please quit worrying. He'll be here. I saw how he looked at you, my dear. No man looks at a woman like that unless he loves her."

"Oh?" Earl said, entering the parlor. "Does that apply to me? Do you see me look at you in a special way, darling?"

As Marilyn made her way toward him, her blue silk dress and the many ruffled petticoats beneath it rustled voluptuously. Earl gazed at her, then looked around the room. Its decor had changed to something more modest. The red velveteen chairs, lounges, and drapes had been discarded. In their place was more simple furniture—that which matched Marilyn and Earl's finances.

Although Marilyn had had a roaring business during her reign as the renowned madam of Seattle, the man in charge of her ledgers *and* her money had fled, taking with him a good portion of what she had earned.

But there was enough money to last for many more years if they spent wisely, not wasting a cent of it.

Earl's heart warmed and his eyes twinkled as Marilyn locked her arm through his, gazing up at him as if she had never loathed or deserted him.

"My darling Earl, although it is dreary and gray outside, inside, where you are here with me, I see only sunshine," Marilyn murmured, rising on tiptoe to give him a soft kiss on his lips. "And don't you smell the delicious dinner Frannie is cooking for us? Your favorite, Earl—beef pot roast and for dessert, a mouthwatering rhubarb pie."

"You'd better keep an eye on that Frannie," Earl teased. "She's a woman after my heart."

Maysie was enjoying this scene of love and devotion between Marilyn and Earl. She smiled as Earl looked over Marilyn's shoulder and winked at her.

Then she turned her eyes back to the road. As a horseman turned into the lane that led to the house, she stepped closer to the window and placed her hands on the sill, her heart skipping a beat. Then it slowed to its regular pace when she saw that it was not Four Winds.

Earl heard the horse drawing close outside, and he bristled, thinking that perhaps it was a gentleman who did not yet know that this house was no longer a bordello. He eased away from Marilyn, ran a nervous finger around the white, tight collar at his throat, and walked toward the foyer.

With blinking eyes, Marilyn went after him. "Please don't think that every time a man arrives here, it's for the wrong reason," she pleaded, catching up with him as he reached the front door. "There are legitimate reasons why I have callers. And Earl, I have a friend who is looking for Thomas, my accountant. It might be Sam, Earl. He may have found Thomas."

Earl sucked in an uneasy breath and raked his fingers

through his hair. Then he turned to the door and stared at it as the knocker sounded three knocks.

Stiff-legged, Earl jerked it open, Marilyn at his side. Both stared at a youthful, pockmarked face, and long, stringy hair hanging from beneath a sweat-stained Stetson. The boy's clothes were wet from the misty rain. Earl recognized him as one of the workers that he had hired for the fishery—now unemployed, thanks to the damnable fire.

"Well, hello, Brad," Earl said, extending a hand toward the lad. "What brings you here this time of day, and in the rain?"

"Mr. Easton, it's something I heard," Brad said, removing his hat, holding on to the brim and slowly turning it between his fingers. "I thought you should know. Or has someone else come and told you?"

"Told me what?" Earl said, raising an eyebrow.

Brad looked from Earl to Marilyn, and then back at Earl. "It's your daughter," he said, his voice weak. "She's-she's in jail. And so is that Indian that she ran off with."

Marilyn placed a hand over her heart.

Earl had to grab hold of the doorjamb, to steady himself in his alarm over what he had just heard. "Elizabeth?" he said, almost choking on the word. "My Elizabeth? She's in jail? Again?"

"The posse brought her in just a while ago," Brad said, swallowing hard. "And they brought in the Indian, too. There's a rumor that there might be a hangin'. Maybe *two*."

"My Lord," Marilyn gasped, swaying as a nausea swept through her. Then she crumpled to the floor in a dead faint.

Earl was in a state of shock, but when Marilyn fainted, he came to life. "Marilyn!" he shouted, falling to a knee beside her.

He swept her into his arms and carried her to the parlor, stretching her out on the sofa. "Maysie, get some smelling salts," he shouted.

Wide-eyed, and numb from the news of Elizabeth's capture, Maysie hurried and got the smelling salts.

She went back to Marilyn and knelt beside her, waving the salts beneath her nose. Marilyn began coughing and rolling her head from side to side. Her eyes flew open and she sat up on the couch.

"Are you going to be all right?" Earl asked, placing a hand to Marilyn's cheek. "I must go to Elizabeth. I've got to find a way to get her out of that place."

"But, how, Earl?" Marilyn cried, sniffling into a lacy handkerchief that she had taken from the pocket of her dress. "That requires money, Earl. We do not have that kind of money."

Earl began pacing back and forth across the carpeted floor in a frenzied manner. "There must be a way," he said, his throat tight.

Brad, forgotten in the doorway, overheard their dilemma. He took it upon himself to enter the parlor. "Sir, might I make a suggestion?" he asked, clasping his hands behind him.

Earl stopped. "Eh, what is that you said, lad?" he asked, staring at Brad.

"I know someone that's interested in purchasing your ship," Brad said. "This man came into town yesterday on a clipper ship. He's spread the word that he's prepared to buy anyone's ship, should they have any for sale. Seems he hit it rich panning for gold in San Francisco. He says he wants the ship to travel the high seas, more for pleasure than for business."

Earl listened with a quickly beating heart, his eyes anxious. "His name," he said, going to Brad. "Lad, give me his name. I think he may have found a buyer."

"He's stayin' at the Gooseneck Inn on Third Street," Brad said, placing his hat on his head as Earl took him by an elbow and began pulling him toward the door. "Should I go and fetch him for you, sir? I could have him back here to talk business with you quicker than you can wink your eye."

"That won't be necessary," Earl said, ushering Brad on outside. "I'll tend to it myself. Thanks, lad. Thanks a million."

"My pleasure," Brad said, tipping his hat and going to his horse.

Earl went to the hat rack and got his top hat, and gathered his white gloves from a table in the foyer. Then he turned and met Marilyn's approach. He embraced her. "I shouldn't be long," he tried to reassure her. "And when I return, by damn, Elizabeth will be with me."

Marilyn gazed up at him. "What about Strong Heart?" she asked softly. "You know how Elizabeth feels about him."

"Let Strong Heart take care of himself," Earl muttered, still resenting how the Suquamish had turned his offer down. He could not help but feel that if that deal had gone through, things would somehow be different.

Deep inside himself, where he weighed matters to find answers to whatever happened to him, he knew that somehow the fire had not started from a faulty flue.

A fire that fierce, one that had spread and burned that quickly, had surely been set.

But there was no proof, and his life was now changed because of it. He had to make the best of what he had left—and a big part of that was Elizabeth.

Marilyn watched Earl as he rushed out the door. Maysie came to her and slipped an arm around her waist, and they listened to Earl riding away on his horse.

Then Marilyn broke away from Maysie. Numbly, she closed the door and went back to the parlor and sat down, staring into space, feeling nothing but dread and impending doom.

* * *

Elizabeth shoved her breakfast tray aside, her appetite gone as she surveyed her surroundings. The cells were overcrowded with prisoners—men and women.

Although this was a new jail, smelling of fresh wood and plaster, it could not take away the feeling of terror that gripped her at the thought of what lay ahead. She had heard the sheriff and deputy laughing and talking about hangings—hers and Strong Heart's.

Yet she knew that they did not have the power to sentence anyone. A judge would be coming from a neighboring city to make that decision.

Hers and Strong Heart's futures were in the hands of that judge.

There may never be a marriage. There may never be children. There may never be a Chief Strong Heart.

Elizabeth's gaze shifted, and her heart ached when she saw Strong Heart sitting cross-legged on the floor of his cell across the way from hers. His hands rested on his knees, his eyes unwavering as he stared straight ahead. She had heard him chanting quietly only moments ago, and realized that he had been trying to reach his Great Spirit. Just as she had been trying to reach her own God with soft prayers to be set free from this place of degradation.

A commotion in the outer office took Elizabeth's breath away as she recognized her father's voice. Then there was only a hushed murmur of conversation between the sheriff and her father.

She waited eagerly. Soon they were coming toward her, a key in the sheriff's hand.

Elizabeth's eyes met her father's, seeing a twinkling in them and a smile that told her that somehow he had managed to get her free.

She could not believe it, even when the door creaked open and the sheriff gestured for her to step outside the cell.

"Elizabeth," Earl said, drawing her quickly into his arms, hugging her tightly. "I've come to take you home. Baby, I've come to take you home."

At this moment, Elizabeth cast aside all resentment toward her father. The fact that he had managed to get her free was all that mattered.

Then she blanched and looked over at Strong Heart, who was now standing in his cell, his hands gripping the bars. As their eyes locked, she felt torn with grief, knowing that whatever bargain her father struck, it did not include her beloved Suquamish brave.

"I can't," she said, moving quickly back inside the cell. She even closed the door. "If Strong Heart isn't going to be released, *I* shall not leave."

Earl frowned. He yanked the door open and placed a hand

on Elizabeth's arm. "You're not going to stay here another minute," he said, his voice flat. "Elizabeth, damn it, let's get out of here while the getting is good." He leaned close to her ear. "I paid the sheriff under the table. If anyone figures it out, we'll both be locked up. Come on. We'll see to Strong Heart's release later."

Elizabeth's eyes wavered as she gazed with longing at Strong Heart. But the thought came to her that there might be some benefit in her not being in jail. Strong Heart could be better served if she was free. Even though her father had said that he would see to Strong Heart's release later, she knew enough about the way things were between the Indians and the whites to realize that no matter how much her father paid, Strong Heart would not be set free without a trial.

And she doubted her father had any intention of getting Strong Heart out of there. It was all up to her, and she had a plan. She would speak up for Strong Heart at his trial. She would make sure that he was set free, for she already knew what she was going to say to ensure it.

"All right, I shall go with you," Elizabeth consented. Then she went to Strong Heart's cell and placed her fingers over his. "Darling, do not think that I am deserting you. I have a plan that will set both of us free. Please have faith in me. Soon, my darling. Soon we shall be married. Soon we shall see small footprints in the snows of winter—our children's footprints, my love. Our children's."

With many eyes on her, Elizabeth stood on tiptoe and kissed Strong Heart. Then, with tears burning at the corners of her eyes, she fled the jail with her father. She was numb as she rode the streets on horseback with him. She expected to be taken to his ship, where she supposed was his home until he could rebuild his fishery.

But her mouth dropped open and she emitted a low gasp of wonder when her father took her to her mother's stately house. She was speechless, until she was inside and she saw the changes—not only in the decor of the house, but also the sincere warmth between her mother and father.

"Elizabeth," Marilyn said, rushing to her after giving Earl

a deep kiss. She touched Elizabeth's face, then seemed to be feeling for broken bones as she touched her all over, tears rushing down her cheeks.

"Oh, sweetheart, you *are* all right, *aren't* you?" Marilyn said, flinging herself into her daughter's arms.

"I'm fine," Elizabeth said, smiling at Maysie as she stepped into view. Then her smile faded when she realized that Maysie's exit from Seattle with Four Winds had been delayed because of his loyalty to Strong Heart.

She eased away from her mother and everything about her father and mother's reunion was explained to her, even the revelation of her father's bankruptcy in San Francisco, and his subsequent money problems.

Elizabeth suspected that her father had probably gone back to his wife only for the security that she offered him.

That suspicion was squelched when her mother explained her own money problems, and how Earl had managed to get enough money to set Elizabeth free.

"You sold your ship?" Elizabeth asked, astonished. "Father, that ship meant the world to you."

Earl went to Elizabeth and took her hands in his. "My daughter means even more than that to me," he said thickly.

Elizabeth's feelings were beginning to soften toward her father. Yet nothing could excuse the fact that he had plotted against Strong Heart's people.

No. She doubted if she could ever truly forgive him.

34

The heavens reward thee manifold I pray.
—Anne Bradstreet

The courtroom was packed with people who were curious to see an Indian put on trial. A strained hush came over the crowd as Strong Heart was escorted into the room and led to a chair at the front.

Elizabeth sat between her mother and father, looking sedate and prim in a plain cotton dress devoid of frilly trim, and wearing a matching bonnet. Her hair streamed long and free from beneath it across her shoulders and down her back. Frannie sat beside Marilyn.

Maysie sat on Earl's other side, wearing a dress as colorless as Elizabeth's, and sporting a bonnet where, beneath it, she had woven her hair into a tight bun. Her face was pale and lined with sadness. Maysie's gaze moved slowly around the room as she looked for Four Winds, even though she knew that he would not be there. He was still wanted and he could not take his place alongside Strong Heart. He had already had a trial, one which had condemned him to *death*.

At times, Maysie had grieved over Four Winds, thinking that he had forgotten her. She knew that she should hate him for his deception, but her very soul cried out to be with him again, and would not lose hope. It was this trial, which had brought lawmen from all corners of the Pacific Northwest, that had frightened Four Winds away.

Elizabeth strained her neck to see over the shoulder of a man in front of her. But she still could not see Strong Heart easily. There were people blocking her view.

Nervously chewing on her lower lip, she settled back in her

chair. Then she sat more erect and felt an anxious blush rise heatedly to her cheeks as the judge came into the room and took his place on the bench. He reached for his gavel and slammed it hard against the top of his desk.

"Let's have silence in the room and get on with this," Judge Cline said, looking soberly at Strong Heart, pausing as he studied him. Obviously he was assessing this man whom he would either set free or condemn to death.

Elizabeth watched the judge, seeing so much about him that hinted that his reputation for being a kind and considerate man could be true. Behind gold-rimmed glasses were dark eyes that looked gentle and caring. Although his thinning hair and bent shoulders indicated that he was perhaps in his early seventies, there were not many lines on his face. This man had smile wrinkles at the corners of his eyes and mouth. His color was good. His voice was pleasant when he talked to the two attorneys who sat on opposite sides of the room from each other. No jurors had been chosen for this particular trial. The judge would be judge *and* jury today.

"I have read the record of the accused," Judge Cline said, his voice smooth and even. "I see that he is accused of helping more than one person escape from Copper Hill Prison." He studied the papers that he was now laying out on the desk. "I see here that he is also blamed for the deaths of the sheriff and his deputy, and for setting fire to the prison."

He removed his glasses and sucked on one of the stems, again looking at Strong Heart intently. "That's an awful lot of meanness for one man to get into, wouldn't you say, young man?" he asked, laying his glasses aside, leaning forward, his eyes locked with Strong Heart's. "What do you have to say for yourself?"

Strong Heart rose to his feet and squared his shoulders. "Strong Heart is guilty for only two things of which he is accused," he said plainly, glancing over at Elizabeth. "My friend Four Winds had an unfair trial. Nothing was proven that should have condemned him to the hangman's noose. I saw no other choice but to set him free. Elizabeth Easton was unjustly arrested by the corrupt sheriff and was treated disrespectfully by the deputy. She did not deserve to be housed with criminals, under a sheriff and deputy whose respect for law and order was a mockery to the white community as well as the red. For this, I became her judge and jury. I set her free. These things I confess to, and it seems everything else which followed was by chance."

Judge Cline raised a shaggy, gray eyebrow, his gaze moving slowly to Elizabeth, whose testimony was to be heard today. He thought of her as nothing less than beautiful, and he could understand why any man would be pulled under her spell. Even an Indian.

Looking closer, he saw how frightened she was, and understood. Her testimony today was the only one, besides Strong Heart's, that he would listen to.

Judge Cline looked at Strong Heart again. "You may be seated," he said. "And thank you for your honesty. An honest man is hard to find these days. It is refreshing when I come across one." He smiled warmly at Strong Heart as he slowly sat down. "Lad, this trial won't take long, I can promise you that."

Hearing Judge Cline speak so kindly to Strong Heart gave Elizabeth cause to hope. The judge narrowed his eyes as he stared at her, again.

Then Judge Cline gently spoke her name, and gestured for her to come to the podium to take a seat. Her legs trembled as she rose from her chair. The whole courtroom had fallen into a hushed silence, everyone shocked that she, a white woman, would testify on an Indian's behalf.

And she alone knew that they had not seen or heard anything yet. Before God and the town, she was going to openly defy all the unspoken laws that had been set down between the whites and Indians.

And she was going to do more than that.

She was going to reveal things to these gawking, high and mighty people that would set their tongues to wagging into the night and many days to follow.

When Maysie reached a comforting hand to her, Elizabeth took it and clung to it for a moment, then went to the podium.

She sat down gingerly on the padded seat after swearing to tell the truth, and nothing but the truth.

"We won't bother with cross-examinations nor such bunk as that today," Judge Cline said, causing a stir in the courtroom which the judge ignored. He leaned to one side, eye to eye with Elizabeth as she turned to him. "Young lady, just tell me everything you know about what has brought Strong Heart to this courtroom. You are speaking on his behalf. I, as well as everyone else in this room, am prepared to listen. Begin speaking and you won't be interrupted until you are finished."

Elizabeth was amazed at the generosity of this judge, having feared the day that she would have to face him. The authorities whom she had already had dealings with in Seattle had neither been respectable nor honest.

But again, this man made her feel as if there was some hope—some reason to believe that justice would be served, and her love would be set free so that they could resume their lives together.

"Your Honor, I have never met a kinder or gentler man than Strong Heart," she began softly, fighting back tears as Strong Heart gazed devotedly up at her. She wiped her hands on her skirt and continued. "This man has saved my life not once, but many times. He did this at the risk of losing his own life. But do not get me wrong, I do not sit here testifying in his behalf because I feel as if I owe him for his kindness. It runs deeper than that. I testify for him because I know him to be innocent, and very wronged by the white community. This man, who will one day be a great chief, has been humiliated before the whole town, and made to sit in jail beside the most degenerate of criminals." She cleared her throat, then looked over at the judge. "Your Honor, I was also wrongly jailed and placed with hardened criminals. The sheriff and deputy treated me as less than a lady by . . . by . . . trying to rape me," she said, her voice growing in strength as she spoke. She aimed her speech solely at the judge. "Strong Heart knew that I was innocent. He released me. It was after we fled Seattle that someone else went to the prison and set it on fire. The deputy and sheriff both died in the fire. So as you see, he is innocent of that crime."

The judge found her story plausible. For years, he had known Sheriff Nolan's wicked reputation. He was surprised no one had torched the prison before.

Elizabeth looked over at Strong Heart. "He released Four Winds from the prison because of loyalty to a friend he did not believe was guilty of any crime. This man, whom some would relish seeing hanging from a noose, has a big, kind heart. There is surely no one else quite like him on the face of the earth. Because of his beliefs and loyalties, he has risked his life over and over again these past weeks."

Again, she looked at the judge. "And for this he might be condemned to die," she said, her voice breaking. "And, Judge Cline, if you need proof of his whereabouts on the night of the fire and deaths of the sheriff and deputy, I can vouch for him. After he released me from the prison, we traveled quickly into the forest where we camped, so that we might rest before traveling on to his village. And by a campfire I made love with this man who will soon be my husband."

The shock of this statement registered and the whole room seemed to reverberate with the gasps and exclamations of dismay.

Judge Cline's eyebrows shot up in amazement at Elizabeth. Then he picked up his gavel and slammed it against the desk. "Order in the court!" he shouted above the clamor. "We . . . shall . . . have order in this court!"

Everything became quiet, except for a few whisperings. The women's eyes rested accusingly on Elizabeth, apparently appalled by the thought of a white woman stepping forward and brazenly admitting to having slept with an Indian.

Yet she held her chin high, her eyes unwavering as the judge looked at her again.

"Continue," Judge Cline said, a quiet smile pulling at his lips.

"Judge Cline, I believe I have said my piece," Elizabeth murmured, smiling back at him.

"A testimony like I have never heard before, and perhaps

won't hear again," Judge Cline announced, laying the gavel aside. He sat back in his chair, rocking slowly back and forth as he placed his fingertips together before him.

Then he leaned forward, his elbows on the desk, and began to speak again. "Never have I seen such courage as you have portrayed today, young lady," he said. "I'm inclined to believe you, for you knew the repercussions before speaking up—the way people would react to such a statement as this. That you could be shunned by the white community. Yes, young lady, it must be true, or you wouldn't have taken the chance of harming your reputation by telling a story like this—"

A sudden commotion at the back of the room made Judge Cline lose his train of thought. He stared at an Indian who was making his way down the aisle. A ripple of excitement flowed through the crowd at his presence.

Judge Cline slammed his gavel down, causing a quick silence to ensue. He glared down at Four Winds as he came to stand before the bench, his jaw set with determination.

"What is the meaning of this?" Judge Cline asked, leaning forward. "Do you not understand that you have just interrupted a court of law?"

"*Ah-hah*, yes, I understand," Four Winds said, folding his arms across his chest. "And that is why I am here—to speak for my friend, Strong Heart."

Four Winds glanced over at Strong Heart, relieved that he had not come too late. Then he smiled at Elizabeth.

He turned and found Maysie in the crowd, the hurt in the depths of her eyes making his heart ache. The knowledge of what he had to do to guarantee his friend's freedom had kept him away from Maysie.

She had to learn to live without him, for he would not be free to love her. His announcement today would condemn him in the eyes of the white community, and even his own people's eyes, forever. There would be no future for him.

"Well?" Judge Cline said, a touch of impatience in his voice. "Speak up and say what is on your mind so that we can get on with the proceedings at hand."

"I have come to tell the truth about everything," Four

Winds said. "Strong Heart is innocent of all crimes. It is I who am responsible for everything that has happened—even my own escape from the prison."

He held his gaze steady with the judge's, hoping that his lies would be convincing enough, for this was the last thing that he could do for his friend.

Tomorrow, they both would probably be swaying back and forth on the gallows for all to see.

"Continue," Judge Cline said, finding this hearing very interesting.

"When Strong Heart came to visit me in prison, I grabbed Strong Heart's pistol and forced him to get the keys to set me free," Four Winds said, knowing that his story would stand up because those who could refute it were dead. "I abducted Strong Heart and Elizabeth that day. Hang me, not Strong Heart."

Judge Cline leaned back in his chair, his eyes twinkling with amusement, for he could tell a lie when he heard it, and he knew damn well that Four Winds was lying to protect his friend.

Yet, that didn't matter. He had made his mind up already.

"Are you finished?" Judge Cline asked Four Winds.

"Ah-hah," Four Winds said, nodding. "That is all I have to say."

Judge Cline leaned back in his chair for a moment, looking from Four Winds to Elizabeth, and then to Strong Heart. He smiled warmly at each of them. "You are all free to go," he said finally. "I have witnessed something here today that is rare. Loyalty. An intense loyalty between friends, and loved ones. Although the law has been broken by first one, and then another of you, the reasons for these actions have not been selfish ones. It was always because each of you saw a wrong that was being done to the other."

Judge Cline rose from his chair and stood tall behind the bench. "And," he said, his gaze moving about the room, silencing the commotion his verdict had stirred, "prejudices are more to blame for what has happened here than anything. Because of my decision, perhaps prejudice can be lightened in this city."

He grabbed up his gavel and pounded it one last time. "Court is adjourned," he shouted. "Clear the room. And good day."

He picked up the stack of papers from the desk and paused to wink good-naturedly at Elizabeth. Then with long strides, he left the room.

No one left the courtroom. Everyone was shocked by the judge's decision. After a moment, the spectators stirred and began to leave. Some of them smiled and nodded at Elizabeth and Strong Heart, seeming more touched than disapproving of their love.

Elizabeth ran to Strong Heart, flinging herself into his arms. "Darling, we're free," she cried. "Free! Our dreams are going to come true after all!"

"Because of you," Strong Heart said, framing her face between his hands. Then he looked at Four Winds. "And because of Four Winds. How will I ever be able to repay him?"

"No payment is needed, I am sure," Elizabeth said, turning just as Maysie stepped before Four Winds, gazing up at him with tear-filled eyes. Tears flowed from her own eyes when Four Winds suddenly grabbed Maysie into his arms and fled the courtroom with her.

"It seems all is forgiven between them, also," Elizabeth said, laughing softly. She wiped her face as her parents and Frannie approached her and Strong Heart.

"I . . . I . . . hope I didn't embarrass you too much today, by being so open," Elizabeth said, lowering her eyes.

"We're very proud of you, darling," Marilyn said, pulling Elizabeth into her embrace, and then giving Elizabeth up to Earl as he also hugged her.

For the moment Elizabeth relaxed in her father's arms, then broke away from him. She looked from her mother to her father, knowing they had their own guilty secrets—especially her father. She felt lucky that Strong Heart would even accept her as his wife, with such a father as hers.

She then gave Frannie an affectionate hug. "Thank you for so much," she whispered, swallowing back a sob of happiness. "Had it not been for you, Frannie, I'm not sure what would have happened to me. You were all that kept me safe in my childhood. Thank you from the bottom of my heart."

Tears fell from Frannie's eyes. "Honey chil', you were my baby for so long, how can I say good-bye?" she said, clutching Elizabeth. "But you go on with that man of yours and Frannie understands. Be happy, Elizabeth. You deserves all the happiness in this world."

Elizabeth gave Frannie a kiss on her soft, round cheek, then stepped back and looked adoringly up at Strong Heart. "We really must go," she announced. She kissed her parents, then left the courtroom with Strong Heart at her side.

Once out on the wooden sidewalk, she laughed joyously as Four Winds rode past with Maysie sitting before him on the saddle. Two horses followed them. She waved at them. "Wait up!" she cried. "Wait up!"

"Four Winds works miracles, it seems," Strong Heart said, laughing. "He has brought my horse for me, and has also found one for you. Let us ride, my *la-daila*. We are free—free as the wind!"

Feeling giddy with happiness, Elizabeth and Strong Heart mounted up and rode away with Four Winds and Maysie.

They rode for a while, then wheeled their horses to a halt. "Four Winds, you are coming to my village?" Strong Heart asked, looking at Four Winds with the eyes of a boy, feeling humbled in his friend's presence. "You can share in the wedding and *potlatch*. Friends should share everything." He laughed softly as he glanced over at Elizabeth. "Except, of course, wives."

Four Winds burst into laughter, then stopped. "No, I have thought it over and it is best that I go to my village and make things right with my people," he said seriously. "But I will ride with you as far as your village, then we shall say our farewells there."

Strong Heart nodded. "That is good enough," he said. He

turned to Elizabeth. "Come, my love. There will be no more looking over your shoulder. We ride on open land in peace!"

Elizabeth inhaled a deep breath, loving the sound of those words, and how wonderful they made her feel inside.

35

> While we live, in love let's so persevere,
> That when we live no more, we may live ever.
> —ANNE BRADSTREET

The sun was setting in the west behind the distant mountains, sending off streaks in the sky that resembled streamers of orange satin.

A damp chill suffused the air as the three horses rode from an open meadow into the forest where autumn blazed. Yellowed sycamore leaves dropped into streams and sailed away. Elizabeth smiled and gazed over at Strong Heart and Four Winds as they rode side by side. Maysie was now behind Four Winds, holding his waist.

Strong Heart and Four Winds were lost to the world as they talked about their past—where they had gone on their childhood adventures, or had challenged each other in all kinds of games.

It touched Elizabeth deeply to see them goodheartedly joking between themselves. Strong Heart seemed to have forgotten that Four Winds had for a while ridden with outlaws. Four Winds had redeemed himself totally by helping Strong Heart become a free man again.

Elizabeth felt such tenderness toward Four Winds, for if not for him, there would have been no future for her and Strong Heart. To her it had looked bleak these past few days!

But now, she sighed to herself, everything was all right and would soon be perfect, when she and Strong Heart joined their hands and hearts in marriage.

She shifted her eyes to Maysie, glad that for her, life was finally going to be good. There was a look of peace and contentment in Maysie's eyes as she sat in the saddle behind Four Winds, her lustrous long hair flowing in the wind.

Elizabeth shook her own hair so that it fell away from her face and shoulders. She had thrown her own bonnet into the wind shortly after their departure from Seattle. She lifted her eyes to the heavens where stars were just emerging in the twilight and the moon had risen over the mountain peaks to replace the sun. She closed her eyes, reveling in this new freedom which would last forever.

Her peace was shattered when horses suddenly appeared from behind the trees a short distance ahead, plunging toward them. For a moment she was too stunned to think, for she had not expected anybody to try and stop their journey to Strong Heart's village. He had been exonerated of all charges. She had thought they were free to ride without fear, or of having to defend themselves against—

Elizabeth's thoughts stopped still when she quickly recognized Morris Murdoch among those approaching.

Four Winds, too, recognized the members of the outlaw gang that he had been part of.

They saw that these men were not innocent passersby, but were intent on attack as they jerked their weapons from their holsters and opened fire.

"Find cover quickly!" Strong Heart shouted, edging his horse back beside Elizabeth's. He snatched her reins and led her horse with his into a thicket of trees. Four Winds followed and he and Maysie slid quickly from the saddle.

Four Winds grabbed his rifle from its holster and tossed it toward Maysie. "I hope you know how to use this," he shouted.

Maysie caught the rifle, paling as she stared down at it. Then she positioned herself beside Four Winds as he started firing with a pistol at the attackers.

Elizabeth stood bravely beside Strong Heart, firing a pistol he had given her, while he used his repeating rifle. The outlaws sought cover. The shooting did not slow as gunblasts erupted from both sides.

Then there were the sounds of other horses coming, making

Elizabeth and Strong Heart exchange worried glances. Elizabeth feared that this was the end, for surely those arriving were more outlaws. The attack made no sense to Elizabeth, unless it was revenge for Morris Murdoch on the Suquamish for thwarting his business plans. Or the attack could be for another reason—against Four Winds, for turning his back on the outlaws to live the life of an Indian brave again.

But then the outlaws ceased firing and mounted their horses, fleeing in the opposite direction of the arriving horses. Elizabeth knew that whoever was approaching was not coming to help the outlaws.

Lowering her pistol to her side, Elizabeth stepped out into the open with Strong Heart, Four Winds, and Maysie. They watched as several horsemen, the sheriff and her own father in the lead, rode on past. They heard gunfire erupt between the fleeing outlaws and the posse.

"My father?" Elizabeth whispered. "Fighting alongside the law?" She shook her head, having never been as confused as she was now.

She ran with Strong Heart toward the confrontation a short distance away. She paused to catch her breath, then saw the bodies that lay strewn along the ground, the stench of gunpowder lying heavy in the air—the fight was over.

Jerkily, and with an anxious heartbeat, Elizabeth's eyes moved from man to man on the ground, praying that her father was not among them.

But before she could find out, there was a noise in the trees behind her. As she turned, she cried out a warning to Strong Heart. Morris Murdoch, on his horse, his eyes crazed, was trying to run Strong Heart down.

Strong Heart heeded her warning. He turned on a moccasined heel and leveled his rifle at Morris and fired. His aim was accurate as Morris's body lurched with the sudden impact of the bullet in his chest. His horse reared and threw him to the ground, where he lay, blood pouring from his wound.

Elizabeth could not stop the tears of relief when she saw her father step into sight from some bushes. Yet she did not go to him. Even now she still could not go to him and throw herself into his arms, declaring how happy she was that he was all right—and to thank him for having come when he did.

No.

A part of her held back, while another part of her fought the stubbornness that held her there.

Earl walked slowly toward Morris Murdoch, his pistol aimed at him, not trusting that even though he looked injured, he might not be.

Earl glanced over at Elizabeth, so glad that she was unhurt. Yet he ached inside when she did not come to him and welcome him. He had to correct that. Now!

Earl was going to see to it that Morris Murdoch cleared his name, or else. He saw that Morris was not mortally wounded, and that he would stand trial.

That is, if Earl did not kill him first.

Morris's chances were better in court than with Earl, and Morris surely knew that, for there was dread in the depths of his eyes as Earl knelt beside him. The fingers of Earl's free hand grabbed hold of Morris's hair, lifting his head up to look eye to eye with Earl.

"You son of a bitch, you tell my daughter the truth about everything, or so help me, Morris, I will take you and make you die a slow, torturous death," Earl said between gritted teeth. "And don't think the law won't allow it. I'd be saving them money by not having to pay a judge to hand down your sentence."

Morris coughed and clutched at his chest wound, blood seeping and through his fingers. "You damn bastard," he said, his eyes hazy with pain. "You damn bastard. I should've known you'd be bad luck. You brought your bad luck with you from San Francisco. You threw it my way. Damn it, I should've known that you were a worthless dumb ass, unable to make things work right."

"My daughter," Earl said, yanking harder on Morris's hair. "Damn it, Morris, tell my daughter the truth. Tell her that I had nothing to do with the attack on the village. Tell her that the only thing I did that was underhanded was place the nets in the river." He leaned closer to Morris's face. "Tell her now, or be sorry."

"How'd you know about this ambush?" Morris breathed out between gasps of pain. He closed his eyes wearily. "Who doublecrossed me? Who?"

"You aren't as smart as you think you are," Earl said, laughing sarcastically. "There are several among your gang who have turned informants to bargain for their freedom. They were smart enough to know that the end was near for your bastard gang of outlaws."

"The dumb asses," Morris said, his eyes flashing with anger. "How could they?"

"Enough of this," Earl said with a snarl. "I'm waiting for you to tell the truth so that not only my daughter will know it, but also so that Strong Heart can hear you."

When Morris stubbornly clamped his lips together, Strong Heart stepped forward and knelt on the other side of him. Elizabeth moved closer, her pulse racing.

Strong Heart yanked his knife from its sheath at his waist, and placed the sharp blade against Morris's throat. "You speak the truth now," he said, his eyes lit with fire. "Do it for my woman. She deserves all truths. She has earned them."

Fear creeped into Morris's eyes. He gulped hard and stared up at Strong Heart. "Her father is innocent of everything, except for putting the nets in the river," he cried out. "Please. Please . . . move that knife away. I . . . I . . . don't want to die."

Tears streamed from Elizabeth's eyes. She reproached herself for believing all of those ugly things about her father, when all along he was mostly innocent.

Innocent!

Now it was *his* turn to forgive, it seemed, for she had treated him callously instead of trusting him. In truth, her father had been as wronged as the Suquamish. He had been used by Morris Murdoch in the worst way.

Earl rose slowly to his feet. He flipped his pistol into its holster and turned to Elizabeth. His eyelids heavy, he beckoned for her with his arms to come to him.

"Baby, I'm sorry for all of this," he said thickly. "My choice of partners was bad, don't you agree?"

Elizabeth brushed tears from her cheeks and she swallowed back a sob as she broke into a run and flung herself into his arms. "I'm the one who is sorry," she sobbed, clinging to him. "Will you ever, ever be able to forgive me?"

"How can you ask that?" Earl said, holding her away from him, so that their eyes could meet. "Baby, you have done nothing to be forgiven for. It was your father who is to blame for everything. I'm sorry that I gave you cause to mistrust me. And I shan't ever cause you another moment's stress or worry. Your mother and I are going to start a new life together. My life will be centered around family, not business. Will you be a part of our new life, Elizabeth? It would make everything complete for me and your mother."

"Are . . . are . . . you asking me not to marry Strong Heart?" she asked, her voice wary.

"Not at all," Earl said, smiling down at her. "Your mother and I want to wish you much happiness with Strong Heart. And we would like to be invited to your wedding. Do you think that can be arranged?"

Fresh tears rose in Elizabeth's eyes—joyful tears. She again flung herself into her father's arms. "Yes, yes," she cried. "It can be arranged."

Strong Heart looked on, his heart warm, his eyes smiling.

36

If ever wife was happy in a man,
Compare with me, ye women, if you can.
—Anne Bradstreet

On their wedding day, Elizabeth sat in the council house on a high platform piled comfortably with soft furs, overlooking their guests: Suquamish from this village and from the reservation. She watched wide-eyed as Strong Heart participated in what was known as a *potlatch*. She would have felt awkward except that she was not alone on the platform. Her parents sat on one side of her and Strong Heart's parents on the other side.

Even sweet Frannie had overcome her fear of Indians and had been persuaded to attend. She sat quietly beside Elizabeth's mother, casting Elizabeth occasional weak smiles.

Several Braves circled outside of the onlookers, dancing to the sound of drumming on a hollow box. Many of their steps consisted of springing into the air from squatting positions, or turning fast on their heels in a narrow circle. Their headdresses were wide bands of deerskin to which were attached the scarlet-feathered scalps of the pileated woodpeckers and they carried the skins of albino deer, their heads stuffed and also adorned with bright red woodpecker scalps.

There was choral singing in the background accompanying the drumming and dancing.

As Elizabeth watched, Strong Heart handed out gifts to guests who sat around the fire in the firepit. Her hands stroked her cloak of softly woven wool, trimmed with sea otter fur.

Beneath her cloak she wore a dress of doeskin, whitened with clay, and trimmed with the milk teeth of elks, and with tips of turkey feathers and porcupine quills. On her feet were knee-high moccasins, adorned with brightly painted beads.

She felt lovely, and Strong Heart was so handsome, in his own cloak of sea otter fur, the festive occasion marked by his wearing red cedar-bark head rings filled with loose white down, and a stiff, tire-like bark collar.

As they had dressed for today, she had watched him pull on leggings and a breechcloth painted with various colors in bright designs beneath his cloak.

She had then seen him as he added the sparkling flakes of mica to his face, which even now glittered under the fire's glow.

She knew that she had to grow used to these new customs, yet this *potlatch* did not seem appropriate for the occasion. In her culture, presents were given *to* the bride and groom—not to those who attended.

But Strong Heart had explained to her that sharing one's wealth was an honor. The more a person gave to others, the more important he was in their society. The *potlatch*, meaning 'gift giving,' was a way of celebrating important events—today a marriage of a most important man to the woman of his choice.

Strong Heart had warned her not to be alarmed by the amount of gifts that he would give away at the *potlatch*. He told her that in the coming years, there would be more such celebrations, to impress upon others the wealth that proved his worthiness of the title of chief. They were necessary, these times of spreading his wealth among those who were less fortunate than he or Elizabeth.

Elizabeth had not told him of her uneasiness about this, because she had no right to. She had chosen to live the life of the Suquamish. So she would have to accept all the ways *of* the Suquamish. And she would. In time, she would know as much as the other women.

Forcing herself not to think about how strange this gift giving was, Elizabeth watched and nodded her approval at Strong Heart each time he held up an object for her to see before he gave it away. Once this exhibition of wealth was over, they would finally join hands in marriage.

She still could not believe that all of the obstacles had been removed and that their lives were going to become normal, with the insanity of the past behind them.

And it had been the same for Four Winds and Maysie. A runner from his village had come to Strong Heart with the news that Four Winds had been accepted into his community, and that he and Maysie had shared their vows as man and wife already.

Elizabeth and Strong Heart had delayed their wedding day, giving Elizabeth's parents time to get there to be witnesses to their joyful marriage.

Still she sat patiently as she waited for Strong Heart to bring his gift giving to a close.

But he kept moving around the crowd, his generosity great today. Elizabeth could not help but covet the trade blanket that he was handing to one woman. It was beautiful—dark blue with a red border, embellished with heraldic beasts outlined in pearl buttons.

She also silently admired the baskets, beautifully carved boxes, and decorated hides that he gave away.

And then, surprising Elizabeth, Strong Heart stopped before her parents. "Come with me," he said, gesturing toward her father specifically. "Your gift awaits you at the river."

Earl's mouth opened in wonder. Then he left the platform as Strong Heart continued waving for him to follow.

The drumming, singing, and dancing ceased. Elizabeth and everyone else followed Strong Heart and her father outside, where the western mountains were flushed a red gold, and down to the river.

Strong Heart went to the sandy beach and walked toward a lone, intricately carved canoe. He went to it and laid a hand on the prow, turning and smiling at Earl. "This is my gift to you," he said. "This will make it easier for you and your wife to come and see your daughter from time to time. The rivers are more gentle than a horse to a woman's behind."

Strong Heart glanced over at Elizabeth, his eyes dancing. He hoped that she was remembering their many adventures on horseback. He had silently marveled at her tenacity to keep up with him. He had also seen her grimace while rubbing her sore behind. How her muscles must have ached when they had not been able to stop and rest as often as she would have wished.

Ah-hah, a canoe would be better for her mother, whose age matched Strong Heart's own mother's. His mother would rather do anything than climb on a horse.

Elizabeth was touched by Strong Heart's thoughtfulness. She went to him and linked an arm through his, as she watched her father look over the canoe, obviously moved by it.

"This is so kind of you," Earl finally said, looking up at Strong Heart with grateful eyes. "I never expected a gift—especially one of this magnitude. I accept it heartily. Thank you." He gestured toward his wife. "Marilyn, darlin', come and see this. The designs carved on this canoe are magnificent. So detailed." He then noticed something else. Many pelts were spread across the seats. "We shall return to Seattle in this canoe, and leave the horse and buggy in exchange."

Earl shifted his gaze to Strong Heart. "That is, if you don't mind taking the horse and buggy off our hands," he said, knowing that this was the only way Strong Heart would accept anything in return for the generous gift.

"That will be acceptable," Strong Heart said, smiling back at Earl, realizing exactly what Elizabeth's father was up to and understanding.

Then Strong Heart clapped a hand to Earl's shoulder. "Now, I would share my life with your daughter," he said.

"I give her to you with my blessing," Earl said, his voice soft, emotion running through him that showed in his eyes as they were suddenly filled with tears.

Strong Heart nodded. "She will fill my days and nights with much gladness," he said.

Strong Heart dropped his hand from Earl and turned to Elizabeth. "My *la-daila*, it is time now for us to return to the council house and join our hands in marriage," he said, his eyes shining into hers.

He then leaned his lips close to her ear as he drew her into his arms. "And then, my darling, we shall celebrate in private," he said huskily. "Does that sound acceptable to you?"

"Yes, quite," Elizabeth whispered back, thrilled clear to the core with an intense joy.

* * *

Strong Heart knelt over Elizabeth beside the low, flickering flames of the fire in their longhouse. Her back was pressed into the soft pelts beneath her. She reached her hands to him and sought out the feel of his sleek body. His eyes swept over her with a silent, urgent message that she understood.

As if cast under some sensual spell, Elizabeth moved her hand to his pulsating hardness that he pressed toward her in an open invitation to caress it. Her fingers stroked him there. His breath came in short rasps, his eyes closed, as he began moving himself boldly within her fingers.

Feeling the heat of his manhood, and seeing the pleasure she was giving him, she raised up on an elbow and moved her lips to him, remembering the other times she had done this for him.

But this time, Strong Heart placed his fingers gently on her shoulders and urged her away from him, easing her back down onto the pelts. "My *la-daila*, your skill at giving me pleasure is almost more than I can bear," he said softly. "The art of restraint that I learned as a child almost becomes lost to me when your hands and lips are on me in such a way. If I were a selfish man, I would allow such caresses until my passion was fully spent. But because I love you so much, and want you to share the total ecstasy of our moments together, I cannot go further with this lovemaking until it is shared equally by the both of us."

"But I wanted to give you that sort of pleasure," Elizabeth said, reaching a hand to his face, softly touching it. "Don't you understand that giving you pleasure, pleasures me?"

"Pleasure?" Strong Heart said, a mischievous gleam in his eyes. "Let Strong Heart show you what true pleasure is, and then see if we either one has cause for complaint."

"All right," Elizabeth said, giggling as he leaned over her

and his hot breath raced across her creamy skin. "Whatever you say. You are my husband. Do as you please with me."

Her soft laughter faded into moans when Strong Heart's hands and his tongue skillfully searched over her for her pleasure points, his engorged manhood pressing against her thigh, pulsing in its building need to find a home inside her, where she also so unmercifully throbbed.

When Strong Heart's mouth covered Elizabeth's with a fevered kiss, she ran her fingers along his satiny hardness, then spread her legs apart and placed the tip of his manhood where she was open and ready for him. She caught her breath and a lethargic feeling of floating claimed her when he thrust deeply inside her and began slowly stroking her, then moving faster in quick, sure movements.

As he held her in a torrid embrace, his mouth demanding and hungry, yet sweet, she writhed in response as his lean, sinewy buttocks moved. She began to move against him, her breasts now rising beneath his fingers, his tongue brushing her lips lightly.

He then buried his face next to her neck, breathing in the sweet smell of her, and cradling her in his arms, his passion cresting as she clung and rocked with him. His body turned to liquid fire as her fingers made a slow, sensuous descent along his spine, then splayed against his buttocks. Her fingernails sank into his flesh, urging him more deeply inside her.

His movements became maddeningly fast, sweat lacing his brow and back as he placed his hands on her buttocks, holding her in place as they continued to give and take pleasure from each other.

And then he drew away from her.

Elizabeth questioned him with her eyes, and when he drew her up on her hands and knees, she puzzled over what he might do next, yet was not afraid. This wonderful feeling that had risen inside her, had blotted out all other sensation, other than desire for more and more. Her thirst for her beloved was never quenched.

Strong Heart positioned himself behind her, parting her thighs, then pressed his pulsating hardness deeply within her again. As he held on to her waist, he drew her back to meet his thrusts, glad that she understood and began moving against him, moaning.

His hands crept around and found her heavy breasts, and cupped them with his warm fingers. With quick thrusts of his pelvis, he could feel his passion peaking.

Elizabeth felt a tremor begin deep within her, and then it exploded in spasms of delight, matching his own release as he clung to her, his body trembling against hers.

Afterward, a great calm filled Elizabeth, but this was not long lived. Strong Heart placed his hands at her waist and lowered her onto her back on the furs, his lips roving over her again, her every secret place opening to his tongue.

Shaken anew with the intensity of her desire, Elizabeth welcomed him atop her, taking his mouth savagely with hers as he plunged deeply within her.

She began to move against him, her hands clinging to his sinewy shoulders, until once again they found that precious moment of bliss, which passed much too quickly, but was never, never forgotten.

Strong Heart rolled away from Elizabeth. Then he drew a blanket over her up to her neck. He lay down beside her, sharing the blanket. "Tomorrow we travel to Seattle," he said, causing Elizabeth's eyebrows to lift.

She raised up on an elbow, staring disbelievingly at him. "I would think that would be the last place you would want to be," she said. "Let us not tempt fate, darling. We have finally found peace. I don't trust leaving your village so soon after what happened in Seattle."

She leaned closer to him. "And why on earth are we going?" she asked, seeing an amused glint come into his eyes.

"You will see," he said, with a low chuckle. "You will see."

"Does that mean that you aren't going to tell me?" Elizabeth said, annoyed by his laughter.

"That is so," Strong Heart said, turning so that their bodies met beneath the blankets. He combed his fingers through her hair. "*Ah-hah*, my *la-daila*, that is so."

"Just tell me whether or not it is something that will add

to our happiness, not take away from it," Elizabeth said, pouting.

"It is something wonderful," Strong Heart said, piquing her curiosity even more.

But her frustration did not last long, because his lips and body were sending her into another world of joyful bliss.

Tomorrow?

Who cares, she thought to herself? Right now was all that mattered. Tomorrow? Surely nothing could be as wonderful as *tonight.*

37

I love thee with the breath,
Smiles, tears, of all my life!
—ELIZABETH BARRETT BROWNING

It was not as amazing to Elizabeth that she would be nearing the outskirts of Seattle with Strong Heart, but that many of his people had accompanied them in their large, beautiful canoes up the serene river with the trees bent above it like lovers. And still Strong Heart would not tell her why they were making the journey.

It seemed everyone knew, but her.

But she had quit asking and watched as Strong Heart, sitting before her in their canoe, drew his oar through the water with his muscular arms, an elk skin coat snug against his lithe body. He made the chore of manning the canoe look effortless, as did the other braves accompanying him in his great vessel, each man's oar moving in cadence with the other.

Elizabeth turned and looked at the other canoes following Strong Heart's down the long avenue of river. She saw Many Stars, Strong Heart's grandfather, Proud Beaver, and Strong Heart's parents. His father's leg had healed. Many braves had been left behind to guard the village, but many were here today on this puzzling venture to Seattle.

When Many Stars saw Elizabeth looking her way, she waved, her bearskin pelt drawn snugly around her own shoulders.

Elizabeth returned the wave, then turned her eyes ahead, forcing herself not to become impatient. Soon they would arrive, and then she would know. She hoped that Strong Heart would understand when she asked to go and see her parents. It was wonderful to have a true family again, even though she was no longer a part of their world. She had prayed since their separation that they would come together again and make up for the long years lost to them and her.

And God had heard her prayers.

Oh, so often he had heard her prayers, and she was thankful!

The air, rich with the scent of cedar, had turned colder and brisker halfway from the Suquamish village. The wind whisked the leaves overhead, their rustlings similar to the sound of softly falling rain. A deer drinking thirstily at the riverbank, where the shallower water bubbled over white pebbles, was startled by the appearance of the canoes and darted to safety in the cedar's gloom. A woodpecker lightly beat a tattoo on a hollow tree.

Huddled beneath a warm bear pelt, the fur turned inside to give her more warmth, Elizabeth gazed up at the leaves of the trees, drinking in the beauty as if she were partaking of a vintage wine. She had never witnessed such breathtaking colors before as were displayed on these trees of late autumn.

There were orange-hued leaves, and purple and red. The most magnificent of all were the birches with their golden leaves clinging to the snow-white bark of the trees. The water was golden with the reflection of the trees.

A wind brought down a flotilla of leaves and they sailed off downstream in disarray, like a convoy without a commander.

It was so beautiful, Elizabeth almost forgot why she was there. Watching the seasons parade past filled her with peace.

She drew the fur more closely around her shoulders, lifting her nose to inhale the sweet, fresh fragrance of the air. Then she grew tense when she saw what appeared to be a snowflake fluttering slowly from the sky, sparkling like a miniature diamond against the gray gloomy clouds that were battling the sun for space, soon erasing it from the sky.

She looked anxiously at Strong Heart, wondering if he had noticed the snowflake. She also wondered what the chances were that a snowstorm might come from those clouds overhead. Mount Rainier already had a coat of snow enwrapping its great peak. This was her first winter in the Pacific Northwest. She had cause to fear the fierceness of the winds, the dangers of the snows, and the long days and nights of isolation when she would be confined to the longhouse.

But that latter thought made her relax from her worries. Not only would she be isolated in the longhouse, so would her husband. They knew ways to pass the long hours. It gave her a thrill even now to think about how those hours would be spent.

Then her thoughts returned to their journey and where Strong Heart was guiding his canoe. Her heart seemed to leap into her throat and her eyes grew wide as she watched the canoe sliding through the water in the shadow of a sheer cliff, gnarled cedars clinging to its sides, close to the land that was owned by her father. The reason she had not recognized it earlier was because the house was no longer there.

When they passed the high hill that had once been dominated by the old mansion, Strong Heart began drawing his canoe even more closely to the shore. She quickly saw the pier where her father had moored his ship, and on that pier stood her parents.

"Mama?" Elizabeth gasped, sitting forward on the seat. "Papa?"

She could not hold back her questions any longer. She tossed aside the bearskin on her lap, and in her long robe of rabbit fur went and squeezed herself between Strong Heart and the brave sitting next to him, and sat down. "Why are my parents there on the pier as if waiting for us?" she asked, her words tumbling out in a rush. "Strong Heart, please tell me what is happening. It isn't fair that I am the only one who does not know!"

"*Ah-hah*, it *is* time that you should be told," Strong Heart said, turning a smiling face toward her. He paused from his paddling. The others rowed the canoe to shore.

"My *la-daila*, soon the hallowed ground of my people will be returned to us," he said feelingly. "Your father has given it back to us. After today, the ancestral burial grounds will not be disturbed by the presence of white men any longer."

He frowned at the towering, grotesque fence. "My people

have come to witness the removal of the fence that glares like an enemy, standing for everything bad to the Suquamish." He looked over his shoulder at the canoes following close behind his. "In its place will be erected a massive totem pole, which will stand guard over the land that houses many Suquamish spirits!"

Elizabeth's lips parted with a slight gasp, everything he said flowing like a stream of sunlight into her, warming her through and through. "My father is doing this thing for you?" she finally said.

She turned her eyes to her father who was wrapped in a long robe of elk skin, beside her mother who was as warm in her own white rabbit fur coat.

Elizabeth cast Strong Heart another quick glance, knowing that the robes her parents wore had to be gifts from him, for they were identical to those that Strong Heart and Elizabeth wore. It was a wonderful thing—this amity that had grown between her husband and her parents. It could have been just the opposite—unbearable—and something that would have strained her marriage to Strong Heart.

But now everything was perfect. She prayed that it would continue to be this way.

She decided to accept things as they were now and count herself blessed.

After the canoe was moored and Strong Heart helped Elizabeth from it, she ran to her mother and embraced her, then turned to her father.

Her eyes filmed with tears as she hugged him. "Papa, thank you for what you are doing today," she said. She stepped away, yet held his gloved hands within hers. "Surely no one has ever been so generous. Especially now that you are poor. You could have sold the land for a profit. Instead, you are giving it to the Suquamish. Thank you. Oh, thank you."

"Yes, it seems that when I was searching to find a way to gather up enough money to pay your way out of the prison I forgot about what I could have got from the land, and only sold my ship," he said, chuckling. "It is good that I had that lapse of memory, baby, for it's doing your father's old heart good to see the beaming faces of these people whom you have joined." He cleared his throat nervously. "I . . . I . . . only wish that I had never gone to their village in the first place. If I hadn't, Morris Murdoch would have seen no need to do what he did, to cause Strong Heart's people such pain."

Marilyn stepped close to Earl. She placed her arm around his waist. "Darling Earl, that's in the past," she said softly. "Let us look now to the future. It will be as if our past never was. We are blessed, Earl, to be given this second chance. Let's not have any regrets, and spoil what should be a joyful day for everyone."

Earl dropped Elizabeth's hands and turned to his wife, giving her a soft kiss on the lips. Elizabeth watched them, glorying in the moment, then turned and watched the Suquamish make their way up the steep path, the braves carrying thick, heavy ropes. Others were toting a large totem pole, the designs carved into it bright and threatening. She had not noticed this pole earlier, for the canoe carrying it had stayed far behind the others.

Chief Moon Elk and Pretty Nose came to Elizabeth and her parents. After embracing one another, they all began ascending the steep path. Proud Beaver was assisted by two braves, his staff held proudly in one hand.

After they all reached the summit, they stood back in silence as the ropes were placed around the sharp pikes of the fence, and in one yank, the fence was toppled to the ground with a loud crash.

Many shouts and cheers rose into the air. The upturned faces were touched by the snowflakes that were falling thickly from the gray sky overhead. Elizabeth no longer feared the snow, for she saw that it had a purpose today. It was beautifying this land that had been dirtied so long ago by the first white man who had walked on the soil of the Suquamish ancestral burial grounds. It was covering the black ash remains of the house, and the destroyed fishery below.

Yes, it did seem a new beginning for these people, and Elizabeth was glad that she was able to be a part of it. What tales she and Strong Heart could tell their children!

Suddenly she felt nausea rising through her, threatening to spoil everything. She placed her hands over her stomach to steady it and smiled. She had been experiencing these feelings the past several days, and she understood why. She most definitely understood what missing a monthly flow meant. And she had missed hers! If everything stayed as sweet as now, she would be giving birth to Strong Heart's child before their next autumn salmon run.

"And what do you think of my surprise?" Strong Heart said, coming to Elizabeth with a broad smile.

She smiled impishly up at him, wondering what he would think about hers?

When Proud Beaver stepped into view, held on both sides by braves to steady him, Elizabeth forgot her surprise. It was so touching to see the elderly Indian watch the raising of the totem pole. He had achieved his goal, and even more, it seemed. His noble old face held great dignity, and his fading eyes were now able to watch for the last flickering of life's sunset in peace.

"I'm very pleased," she finally said, gulping back a sob. "So very pleased, Strong Heart."

"I knew that you would be," Strong Heart said, squaring his shoulders proudly. He circled an arm around her waist and drew her close beside him. Then he smiled a silent thank you to Earl as Earl turned his gaze his way.

Earl returned the smile.

38

> Love is a circle that doth restless move
> In the same sweet eternity of love.
>
> —Herrick

It was another autumn. Oaks that had glowed like hot coals only two weeks before, now delivered up brown leaves to a chill wind. Sycamores already raised bare, white arms in surrender to winter's advance. The geese had flown toward warmer climes, the frogs had buried themselves two feet in mud, and the animals of the forest had thicker fur.

The sun hung coldly in a western sky that was streaked with long, uncertain bands of red, and the dry, rich scent of the fallen leaves was almost painful in its sweetness. Lakes gleamed like hand mirrors, reflecting the gold of drooping willows.

Her three-month-old son in his little *guyou*, or cradle basket, on the ground beside her, Elizabeth was on a food-gathering trip. Wrapped in a warm fur coat, she was digging roots and acorns in the oak groves. When she returned home, she would soak and hull the acorns, and grind them to meal in a shallow stone mortar, leaching the bitter tannin out of the meal. Then she would cook it into a nourishing gruel.

The Suquamish's main food was fish. And while it was the men's duty to catch the salmon and bottom fish, it was the duty of the women to dig clams and collect shellfish from the beach.

Elizabeth had already gone by swift canoe to the inlets and bays of the Sound, gathering enough shellfish for winter. Sticks of hardwood had been used to dig up the mollusks. The shells provided useful material for tools or utensils. Large mussel shells were ground sharp to form a woman's knife. Deep clamshells made convenient spoons for sipping broth.

On another journey, she had gone with other women to the

prairies and mountain slopes and picked berries while their men had hunted.

Today her mind was not on her digging, or on the long winter ahead. It was on Maysie. A runner had carried the news to her and Strong Heart that Maysie was having trouble with the birthing of her first child, and may even lose it. It had been almost a week now since Elizabeth had heard anything else, and she was tempted to beg Strong Heart to take her north to see to Maysie herself.

For the sake of her own child, she set this thought aside. She had to think of her son's welfare first and foremost. She had been lucky with her own birthing. Her son had even come a month early, and was no less strong because of it.

"My woman works too hard today," Strong Heart suddenly said from behind her. He came to her and placed a hand at her elbow, urging her to her feet. "Come. Let us return home. Let us sit and watch our son as he grows."

Elizabeth laughed softly, loving how Strong Heart was so proud of his son. "*Ah-hah*, yes, let's go and watch our son grow," she said, lifting the heavy basket of roots up from the ground, proud of her work today.

She waited as Strong Heart went and picked up the *guyoo*. It had been brightly painted by him before the child's birth. When he very gently drew back a corner of the blanket, to peer down into his son's face, Elizabeth saw the pride in his eyes, and her thoughts went back to the day that their son had been born to them.

Elizabeth had been lying there for hours, struggling with her labor. Just before the final shove that had brought their son into the world, a red-tailed hawk had somehow managed to get into their longhouse, squawking desperately and flapping its great wings.

Strong Heart had managed to catch the hawk within the folds of a blanket and carry it outside to freedom.

Moments later their child's first cries filled the air, and their son was quickly given the name Red Hawk, for the bird that had come into their house as an omen.

"He is quite beautiful, isn't he?" Elizabeth asked, falling

into step beside Strong Heart as they walked through the forest toward the village.

"A man or a boy is not beautiful," Strong Heart said, yet smiling at Elizabeth. "He is *handsome*. Is he not?"

"*Ah-hah*, handsome," Elizabeth said, humoring him. "Of course he would be, for you are his father."

Strong Heart did not have a chance to reply. In the distance a horseman was fast approaching them. Strong Heart quickly handed the *guyoo* to Elizabeth and reached for the knife at his waist. Then he relaxed his fingers and dropped his hand away from the weapon as he recognized the brave on the horse. It was Pale Squirrel, the cryer coming from Four Winds's village again.

Elizabeth grabbed Strong Heart's arm. "I hope the news is good," she murmured.

Pale Squirrel halted before them and raised a hand in greeting, his face wide with a grin. "A child was born to Four Winds and Maysie five sleeps ago," he proudly announced.

Elizabeth and Strong Heart felt a great relief flow through them, and then they asked whether the child was a son or a daughter.

"A son was born to them, his chosen name—Strong Winds—a name that is taken from the special friendship between Four Winds and Strong Heart," Pale Squirrel said, his eyes shining as he looked at Strong Heart. "Do you approve, Strong Heart?"

"You take word back to Four Winds that Strong Heart accepts this honor with a warm and thankful heart," Strong Heart said feelingly.

"*Ah-hah,*" Pale Squirrel said, nodding.

"Before you leave on the long journey north again, come to our house and celebrate the birth of our friends' son with us," Elizabeth said, smiling up at Pale Squirrel.

"Your invitation is a gracious one, but Pale Squirrel cannot accept," he said softly. "I am eager to return to my people. They are celebrating now, but it will continue for many days, for I have another announcement for Strong Heart and his woman. Four Winds's father has given Four Winds the title of chief, himself worn and weary with an ailment that takes away his strength. Four Winds has accepted, and reigns even now as chief!"

At first, Strong Heart was stunned by the news—that Four Winds was chief. Then he felt a great happiness. If Four Winds had the duties of chief, husband, and father to attend to, he would not have the opportunity to return to an outlaw's life. *Ah-hah*, this news filled Strong Heart's heart with much gladness!

"How wonderful for Four Winds and Maysie," Elizabeth said, then lifted a hand to Pale Squirrel when he seemed anxious to leave. "Thank you for coming with the news. That was so kind of you."

Pale Squirrel accepted her hand, then accepted Strong Heart's hand, clasping it tightly. "Come soon and sit in council with my people," Pale Squirrel offered. "Send a runner to announce your arrival and we will feast and sing in your honor."

"The snows are near, but when spring arrives with its new grasses and warm winds, we will come north. The sons of Four Winds and Strong Heart will become friends, as their fathers have been for many, many moons," Strong Heart said, squeezing Pale Squirrel's hand.

"*Kla-how-ya*, good-bye, my friends," Pale Squirrel said, then wheeled his horse around and rode away.

Strong Heart turned to Elizabeth. He brushed a red lock of hair back inside her hood. "My *la-daila*, my heart sings with happiness," he said softly. "And so much is because of you. *Mah-sie*, thank you."

"You are my happiness," Elizabeth whispered, leaning into the palm of his hand as he rested it against her cheek. "You and our son, Strong Heart. *Mah-sie*, thank *you* for making it all possible. Had you not been there so often, I would not be alive. I don't feel as if I can ever find ways to truly repay you for risking your life to save mine."

"You have already given me all that I ever want as payment," Strong Heart said, drawing her near to him as they walked on toward the village. "I have you—and I have a son. Who could ever want for more than that?"

She stopped and turned to face him, smiling mischievously. "Are you saying that you do not want a daughter?" she teased.

Strong Heart's eyes lit up. "Are you saying?" he gasped out, almost speechless.

"*Ah-hah*, I do believe that I carry another child within my womb, my darling," Elizabeth said, nodding up at him. "And I am almost certain it will be a girl, for I will wish upon stars every night to make it so."

Strong Heart placed a fist over his heart. "My *tum-tum*, heart, is filled with the joy of the moment," he said. Then, as Red Hawk began to cry, Strong Heart began rocking him in his arms as they went on to their longhouse.

After the baby had been fed and was soundly asleep in his crib, and they lay beneath warm furs beside the fire, Elizabeth moved easily into Strong Heart's arms and welcomed his wild embrace as they made love more passionately than ever before.

Life was finally so *tsee*, sweet, for them, so very, very *tsee*.